MW01672367

MISSION OCTAGON

MISSION OCTAGON

A NOVEL

KEN SMITH

Brown Books Publishing Group
Dallas, Texas

Mission Octagon

© 2005 Ken Smith

All rights reserved. No part of this publication may be reproduced, stored in any retrieval system, or transmitted in any form or by any means, mechanical, photocopying, recording, or otherwise, without permission in writing from the publisher, except by a reviewer, who may quote brief passages in a review to be printed in a magazine or newspaper.

Manufactured in the United States of America.

For information, please contact:
Brown Books Publishing Group
16200 North Dallas Parkway, Suite 170
Dallas, Texas 75248
www.brownbooks.com
972-381-0009

ISBN 0-9753907-6-7
LCCN 2004116008
2 3 4 5 6 7 8 9 10

DEDICATION

To my father, Senior Master Sergeant George Thomas Smith, who instilled in me his personal beliefs . . . mainly that there is no shame in hard work.

ACKNOWLEDGMENTS

Writing this novel has been an adventure, one that would never have happened without the support of my family and friends.

I wish to thank my father and mother for their undying love, sacrifice, and support. I wish to also thank my brother Tom for always being there for me.

Since my parents died fairly young, I would like to thank my surrogate family:

My dad's brother Jerry, and my Aunt Dot, who insist on calling me their adopted son. My mother's sister Ida Mae and my Uncle Robert, whose door was and is always open.

My best friend Ron Fraga's parents Roland and Peggy, who consider me a third son. And, Ray "Red" Ryder, my dad's friend from youth and a quiet listener when I need it.

I wish to also thank the following for their love and support:

Joanne Smith because she has always been there and always will be.

Herschel Justus for allowing me to be a friend when he really needed one.

Brian Alcock, my best mate of twenty years and my copilot on numerous auto jumble sorties.

Sam Louder, who remained my friend when "the family" didn't want him to.

Boyd Jenkins, who defined what friendship should be.

Glenn Guild for his unwavering friendship.

Barry Farmer, a man of uncanny common sense and a loyal friend.

Denise Kingsley, a quiet lady of dignity and the role model for overcoming adversity.

I wish to acknowledge my publisher Milli Brown and the staff at Brown Books for their belief in my book and for their help in taking my "words on paper" and making my idea of becoming a published author a reality.

To Clyde Hall, past President of Savannah State College, thank you for your stewardship and vision.

Also thanks to John Demel, my college advisor, who became a good friend.

And last, to Sister Julie, my college English teacher, who planted the seed of an idea of writing a novel into the head of an obnoxious engineering student.

PROLOGUE

Today had been the hottest in a series of unbearable days. Temperature in the nineties, humidity somewhere around 200 percent, sweltering and steamy, predictably sunny, and generally speaking, just plain damn uncomfortable. A typical June day in Savannah.

For the locals, it's uncomfortable. For the visitors, or in Smitty's own particular case, revisitors, it's intolerable. As he headed west on I-16 with the afternoon sun in his eyes, he realized how exhausted he was, and how little he was looking forward to what lay ahead.

As his customized Hurst/Olds settled in around sixty, he switched on the cruise control, switched off his brain, and settled back for a few minutes to collect his thoughts and relax before the last stop. The earlier calls to friends and acquaintances were merely the preliminaries. His friends were still here, but changed, the city still here, but different. This was the main event, the important one . . . the real reason he came at all.

No, there was nothing for Smitty here now except memories neatly catalogued and filed away like keepsakes in Granny's hope chest—all but one. He was on his way to face this last unfiled memory in the only way possible—head on! Whether the resulting impact would be as gentle as a newlywed's first kiss or as violent as a midair collision, he had no way of knowing. He only knew that it had to be faced. Eighteen months had passed since his last duty-forced visit. And so he was returning. Maybe to atone for the past, maybe to learn to live with the present, or maybe . . . just maybe . . . to justify his future . . . and his very existence.

That last thought stayed with Smitty as he guided the car off the interstate and onto Denner Road. Eighteen months ago, the guilt had been extreme. Death follows life as surely as spring does winter, but in this case, it was different. He knew! And for the false echoes of dignity and honor, he'd kept silent, and as a result, a man had died. His wandering thoughts almost made him miss the turn for Forest Hills. Smitty pulled in, parked, got out, locked the Hurst-mobile and began to walk up the long, narrow pathway toward his destination.

As he approached the veterans' section, he watched as a middle-aged couple shuffled along. They stopped and the woman gently placed flowers on a well-manicured grave and wiped away a tear as she stared in stony silence at the marker that read Beloved Son. And underneath, some dates. Dates that revealed that the young man had been barely old enough to vote . . . and far too young to die. The last word on the marker explained more than a thousand-word essay: Vietnam.

This simple scene touched something deep inside of Smitty. Old soldiers may fade away, but young soldiers leave empty holes in loved ones' lives—holes that will never be filled by flag-draped coffins, gun salutes at dawn, or occasional visits to cemeteries.

An involuntary shiver raced through him. There's a strange fascination in cemeteries—looking at the markers, and the few sketchy details available, trying to imagine what this person was like when he was part of the living.

Smitty came here much better prepared: to his left, friends; to his right, friends of friends; and straight ahead, someone who was oh-so-much more. The marker said First Sergeant. The marker said World War II, the marker said Korea, the marker said Vietnam. The marker said dates; Smitty's heart said more. The Ol' Sarge was his mentor and his taskmaster, but most of all, the Ol' Sarge was Smitty's friend. Unfortunately, he was also the ghost of Christmas past. But he's a ghost Smitty was proud of.

He died at fifty-four, but lived more in one lifetime than most people do in ten. The Ol' Sarge had fought and adventured over half the world for three decades. The memories of the short time they'd had together would have to be enough. Enough to balance Smitty's guilt at having contributed to his death.

"There's nothing you could have done." As this thought occurred to him, Smitty realized that the words had been spoken—but not by him! Smitty whirled around, instinctively assuming his most menacing stance, to find an air force general, a genuine four-star general, standing behind him with his arms folded, shaking his head with understanding.

"Who the hell are you?" Smitty snapped. The remark, like the stance, had been instinctive also—the general had damn near scared him out of his skin.

"Now just take it easy, son," he said.

"Take it easy, my ass! You damn near got your head knocked off."

"As I said," he interrupted, "take it easy. You've never learned to control that temper, have you? Letting your instincts take over has gotten you in trouble in the past. And I imagine that it hasn't exactly endeared you to the civilian personnel you associate with.

"Oh, I know quite a bit about you," the general continued, reading Smitty's exact thoughts. "Except for one person, I probably know more about you than anyone else in the world."

"The Sarge." Smitty shrugged without expression.

He nodded his head in agreement. It was not a statement that called for an answer.

"You sent for me."

"Yes, indeed." The general smiled again, with a pleasant but irritating Cheshire cat smile that gave away nothing, but implied everything.

"How do I know that?"

"Fair request." He measured the look on Smitty's face. "You're here because of a communiqué, which reads precisely as follows: 'Meet me tomorrow at 1600 hours at the permanent residence of the most important man in your life.'

"Like all young men who have been trained in the science of survival until instincts become reactions, you showed up,"—he glanced at his watch—"at 1510 hours to survey the perimeter, and to establish possible defensive positions and escape corridors, in order to gain an offensive edge by watching your adversary approach. Nicely done, m'boy, nicely done indeed. It's a pleasure to see that the government's money wasn't wasted. You've learned your lessons well. So did I . . . I showed up at 1430 hours . . . I taught the class.

"Now that we've established my bona fides, verify your own."

Without a word, Smitty pulled from his pocket a crumpled piece of notebook paper. The paper had the soiled, well-used look of a sawbuck that had been in circulation for years. In the last twenty-four hours, Smitty'd read and reread the note enough times to commit the contents to memory. The general had quoted it exactly. Smitty passed it across.

The general examined the note and gave Smitty an unblinking stare.

"Anything else?" the general asked in the tone of a judge who's just about to sentence a convicted child molester.

"Not unless you want my identifying birthmarks."

"Cute." He nodded, turned away, and paced slowly to the shade of a nearby tree.

The general crooked a finger in Smitty's direction. As Smitty approached, he put his arm around Smitty's shoulders and maneuvered him into a position with his back firmly braced against the oak. Motioning Smitty to stay put, he continued to examine the note, meticulously straightening folded corners and creases in silence, staring intently as if expecting a mysterious invisible message to suddenly leap off the page.

Translation—he was thinking. So was Smitty. Thinking about the relationship between grizzly old first sergeants and Academy-type four-star generals that would send that general all this way to talk privately with Smitty, a year and a half after a death. Whatever the general had planned, he'd planned it well. Smitty knew it was far too early in this cat-and-mouse game for panicky lunges. The next move was the general's.

Finally, the older man nodded, folded the paper, stuffed it in his pocket, and turned.

"Okay," he said. "Let's begin."

As they stood there eyeing each other, Smitty's first thought was that it was about time. This thought, and all others, washed away as quickly as a beachfront condo in the path of a sixty-foot tidal wave as pain and nausea blurred his vision, buckled his knees, and doubled him over in agony. The son of a bitch had kneed Smitty in the balls.

The general drove his forearm under Smitty's chin and lifted upward, slammed his head into the tree, and compressed his windpipe, which made breathing a most difficult task indeed. It was as complete a job of incapacitation as had been done on Smitty in some time.

"I'm only going to say this twice—a first time and a last time. If you ever pop off to me again in the manner you used when I first approached, you'll spend so much time recuperating that, in all probability, they'll name a hospital wing after you. Is that perfectly, unmistakably, absolutely CLEAR?"

"Yes, sir," Smitty said. He meant to make his reply sound crisp. What actually came out sounded more like off-key high notes from the soprano soloist for the Vienna Boys' Choir.

The general released Smitty and backed away in measured steps. He stood waiting, while Smitty's breathing and heartbeat returned to something near normal. As the stars in his head cleared, Smitty trudged over to where the general was standing. Then mechanically, like a zombie in a late-night horror movie, Smitty extended his right hand and said in a slurred voice, "We understand each other."

The general nodded and clasped the proffered right palm. Shaking off the wooziness, Smitty jerked the man forward with his right hand, reached back to his heels, and followed through with all his strength with his left. Fueled by embarrassment, adrenaline, and anger, the resulting connection was every heavyweight's dream. A dull, flat thud was followed by a backward head snap and rolling of the eyes. The general staggered backward, taking three drunken steps before losing his battle for balance, and with a final, futile, arm-waving stumble, landed flat on his back. Muhammad Ali couldn't have done it better.

But Smitty wasn't Ali or the iron hero of a Western movie. His left arm was numb clean up to the shoulder, with the aftershock seeming to paralyze his whole body. He felt like he'd just hit a wall.

As the general lay there, shaking his head back and forth, trying to clear the cobwebs, Smitty had his first real chance to look him over. For a man who had to be near sixty, he was in pretty good shape. His six-foot-two frame was lean and trim in the uniform ornamented with twelve rows of combat ribbons, the hair was salt-and-pepper gray, the face craggy and seasoned. Whoever this old ringknocker was, he'd definitely been around where things were noisy.

But by far the most dominating feature was the eyes: cat eyes that could hold you, precision eyes that could bore right through you, military eyes that commanded with a stare. As the general pushed himself to one knee, Smitty stood transfixed, like a possum caught in a car's headlights. The glare from those eyes stayed unblinkingly on Smitty as the general shakily regained his feet and approached.

At a distance of three feet, the general stopped, stuck out his right hand, and said, "We understand each other."

Smitty cautiously reached out to take his hand. Their hands touched once, then again, before they hesitantly, but firmly, shook hands.

"You pack quite a wallop, son," the general said. "I've been hit with rifle butts that didn't hurt as much," he finished as he patted what was in the formative stages of becoming a fairly good-sized mouse under his right eye.

"So do you, General. I don't think I'll be able to even think about any sort of carnal contact for a couple of weeks."

"From what I hear about your personal life, that shouldn't cause any problems at all," the general said.

Smitty chuckled, and as another humorous thought struck him, he began to laugh.

"Would you mind telling me what's so goddamn funny?" the general asked.

"Well, General," Smitty began, as he wiped at teary eyes. "I don't think I've ever hit anybody so hard who I know so little, but instinctively like so much. Especially," he paused to fight off another laughter attack, "considering I don't even know your fucking name."

"Damned if that's not true," the general snorted. "Damned if it's not," he repeated, as a smile spread across his face.

"Tell me," he continued, grimacing as he touched his right cheekbone a little too firmly. "Do you always go around introducing yourself in such a high-handed fashion? I don't think I've ever seen that particular style listed in any of the etiquette books I've read."

"You just don't read the right books, General. That's SOP for four stars."

"If that's the case, I suddenly find myself hoping that I never run into you if I ever earn my fifth star. Your SOP for that must come with a murder warrant."

The last comment sent both of them into more outbursts of laughter, which would have made them look, to a casual passerby, more like a couple of drunks in church than two people who had traveled many miles to a covert meeting. With the passage of a minute or so, the laughter began to subside. The brief respite was only that. The general was back on the beam, and back in control.

"Son, it looks like both of us took off on the wrong runway. So, suppose we hit the restart button on this aircraft and try another takeoff," he said.

"Well, we piled the first one up; we could only do better. Let's go for it."

"Barney Thompson," the general said, as he extended his hand.

This time, Smitty didn't hesitate. Behind all this light-hearted banter, he sensed he'd just shaken hands with someone who was the Sarge's lifelong friend and with someone who would become one of his. He also thought he'd just passed another test in the continuing rodent-and-feline contest. No question but that the game was continuing. Barney's warm handshake implied that the qualification match for establishing his trust and respect had been successfully completed. The main event was about to start—like everything in this clandestine rendezvous, Smitty surmised—when the general was damn good and ready.

"Son?"

"Sir?"

"Gotta smoke?"

"Only cigars."

"Outstanding!" he boomed. "Of all my bad habits, cigars are my favorite."

Smitty produced his cigar case and lighter, handed Barney one, and took one for himself. As Smitty lit first Barney's and then his own, Barney nodded his thanks, but stopped Smitty as he made to return the lighter to his pocket.

"Never yet seen one of those Zippos that didn't have some interesting bit of philosophy on it. Pass it across," he said in a voice that had the unmistakable ring of an order in it.

"When I die, I know I'll go to heaven, because I've already been to hell," Barney read aloud. "I certainly can't disagree. About the only thing we accomplished over there was the rape and pillaging of a generation of people," he nodded, as he flipped the lighter back. "From a military standpoint," he admitted, "the war was a complete waste."

"From every standpoint," Smitty corrected.

Without a word, Barney turned and walked a few steps away, puffing his cigar and gazing at the surroundings. "Nice place for a cemetery, isn't it? Nice and quiet." At that moment, almost as if cued, out on Denner Road a car with a sky-high rear end, big fat tires, and tomato cans for mufflers went roaring by. "Well, sometimes."

Abruptly, Barney switched subjects. "Say, m'boy, you don't mind if I call you that, do you? Good," he continued without waiting for an answer. "You knew a great deal about my friend, didn't you?" He nodded in the direction of the grave.

"Yeah, a fair amount, I guess."

"Quantify a fair amount."

"Well, I think he talked more to me than anyone else,"

"Why do you think he talked to you?" Barney asked.

"Oh, probably because I'm a good listener, and first sergeants are good talkers,"

"One more time with truth, my friend," Barney snapped.

"That was his way of showing you how much he cared," Smitty confessed.

"That's more like it, m'boy," Barney said. "I think you knew more than a fair amount."

"General, what's the point of—?"

"Ah, ah, ah," Barney interrupted. "All in good time m'boy. I've got a question for you. It's something that I've never known the answer to and thought you just might."

"Shoot."

"I crossed paths with the Sarge in the spring of '59, just before I got my first star. I distinctly remember him saying he was getting out at twenty because something that happened in World War II had ruined his chances for making chief master sergeant. But he stayed on for thirty—thirty-two years, as a matter of fact. Got any idea what changed his mind?"

Smitty thought the question sounded so innocent and open that it could be just what it appeared to be: an honest, sincere request for information. *And then again,* he thought, *maybe it wasn't.* Smitty shot a sharp glance at Barney, looking for an indicator, but could find no help there. Barney was busy examining a part of the oak tree that didn't seem important enough to rate such scrutiny, and was wearing a give-away-nothing poker face.

Smitty continued his intensive visual examination, looking for any weakness, any chink in the general's armor that would betray him. Of course, it would probably be as easy as trying to get him to be totally open with the Senate Armed Services Committee, but there had to be a way of reading that granite face, and Smitty was determined to find it.

Then Smitty had it. Of all things, it was the eyes. An ever-so-slight dilation of retina, causing a minuscule enlargement of the pupil, and he had him.

Smitty also now had, or at least thought he now had, some idea of what this bizarre tryst was all about. Simply put, it was about information. Somewhere in this, the general was looking for confirmation that Smitty had specific information, which quite obviously must be related to the Sarge, or his life, or to Smitty, or maybe to the World War II mission that had ruined the Sarge's career. It only remained for Smitty to try to figure out just what it was in particular he was after, why he wanted it, and probably most important of all, what he intended to do with it once he got it.

Having established this monumental advantage, now what? Smitty felt like a Chihuahua that just caught a Greyhound bus and comes to the shocking realization that the damn thing is so big that he can't even pee on the tires. Barney had thus far demonstrated an uncanny ability to use silence to his advantage. The only thought that occurred to him was to do the same thing in return—to wait him out, and by doing absolutely nothing, to force the general to show his hand. Smitty wouldn't have long to wait. A slight rise in the shoulders indicated that Barney was about to speak.

"Did you understand what I said, son?"

"Yes, I did, General. I was just pausing to reflect on why that question is important enough for you to haul me out here for a clandestine meeting on the hottest day of the year," Smitty said. "If that's all you wanted to know, you could've let your fingers do the walking."

"Son, that was just something I've always wanted to know the answer to. If you don't know, then maybe you are not as well-informed as I thought; in which case, you're absolutely correct, we may as well adjourn."

Well, so much for the plan, Smitty thought. The old fart had him and he knew it. Smitty couldn't hide the fact that he wanted to know what this was about more than Barney wanted to tell. The way the question was asked, Barney was looking for an update. It was June of '76; '59 was a while back, damn near a generation. A lot had changed, a lot had happened, and more importantly, a lot hadn't.

A disillusioning thought occurred to Smitty: this, in fact, was a game. But you had to look past the Webster's definition to the seamier synonyms, such as scheme, profession, or hunting for fun. To find out what this scenario was all about Smitty was going to have to give Barney what he wanted, which would include as much detail as he could remember, and as much as he could probably imagine. Then, and only then, would Smitty be in a position to demand an explanation in return.

"Barney," he said, without expression, "I know the answer to why the Sarge reenlisted. What happened afterward is kind of long and hard to explain."

The general walked to the shade of the oak tree and sat down against it, stretched out his legs, crossed his feet, clasped his hands behind his head, and grinned at Smitty from around the cigar clenched in his teeth.

"Son, this cigar has put me in a relaxed listening mood. Tell me what you do know." Barney gestured to a spot next to him. "Come on, m'boy, don't looked so surprised. Even generals sit down on the grass and relax once in a while. Join me!" The statement was an order, not a suggestion.

As Smitty sat down beside the older man, not fifteen feet from where the Ol' Sarge was buried, Smitty's mind was racing—racing back in time. Back to memories rusty from disuse. Back to all the stories he'd been told, and all that he'd heard. Back to an April day and a freak accident, when a man's judgment would be proved wrong, and a son's honor would be vindicated.

Back to a time when a war hero was president, and another soon would be. Back to a time of innocence and cars with fins, when one man's decision, made in the wake of a rebuffed sexual advance, would alter the course of destiny for his family, and all who came in contact with him . . . forever.

"It was April, Barney . . . April of '59 . . . in a typical '50s middle-class Savannah neighborhood . . . a nine-year-old boy entered his house to the sound of his mother's screaming voice . . ."

CHAPTER ONE

"I don't care! I told you that if you reenlisted and accepted this overseas assignment that we're through, and that's final."

"Just who the hell do you think you are, Queen Elizabeth?" Dad roared back. "Well, I've got news for you, your highness! I have reenlisted, and am leaving for England on May 15. You can stay here, go to your mother's, or go to hell, for all I care, but you'll be going there alone. The boys are going to England with me."

"Like hell they will, they'll—"

"Shut up!" Dad interrupted. "I haven't finished yet. For months now I've been arguing with you and it hasn't changed a goddamn thing. I've tried reasoning with you, but you just won't listen, and last night, when you refused to make love, that was the last straw—"

There were no signs of dinner being prepared that Kevin could see as he entered the kitchen. One of Dad's standing rules was that supper be ready when he got home from work at five-thirty. The only exceptions were Dad's alerts at the base, birthdays, Mom and Dad's anniversary, or other special occasions. Dad particularly looked forward to those "special occasions" when Mom would, in Dad's words, "get herself all dolled up."

A beauty in her youth, she was easing gracefully into middle age; her five-foot-five frame was highlighted by flaming red hair, high cheekbones, and a clear complexion. Added to that was a slim waist that hardly showed any effects of childbearing, and a chest that attracted more than its fair share of attention in a sweater. The combination caused her to, at times, be vain, and sometimes teasingly seductive. An attitude that had been misinterpreted on occasion by other NCOs in the outfit at company gatherings—a misrepresentation that, more than once, Dad had dealt with swiftly with the time-honored military accident known as "slipping on a bar of soap in the shower."

Kevin went from the kitchen into the living room and turned on the TV set. He sat down on the sofa, but the sound of something thumping against the wall between the living room and his parents' bedroom made Kevin jump. Mom was a thrower when angry; fortunately, her aim was terrible.

When Dad had pulled into the driveway fifteen minutes ago, he had been wearing his winter dress blue uniform—the one he wore only for formal occasions—with nine rows of service decorations on it that showed off Dad's five-foot-ten-inch squatty frame in the best light, and overawed the hell out of more senior officers with less chest confetti. With thinning gray hair and a rugged face, seasoned by almost twenty years of military service in two wars, he cut quite a figure while inspecting the troops or disciplining young airmen. He also did a pretty good job of intimidating nine-year-old boys.

"Now, I'm gonna try and explain one last time why I reupped," Dad continued in a lowered voice, but Kevin was still able to hear both of his parents as clearly as if they were sitting right across from him. "Let's review our situation from the beginning."

Mom's in for it now, Kevin thought to himself. Dad had begun speaking to her in that cold, hard, authoritative tone of voice that only a career of meting out disciplinary actions as a first sergeant could develop. He would start out lecturing you, and in fifteen minutes, could make you feel so guilty and small that you could leave the room by walking under the closed door . . . with plenty of headroom to spare.

"You're awful positive that I shouldn't have reenlisted. But what else am I going to do, huh? Answer me that. I mean, I think I've done pretty well, when you take everything into consideration."

"I left my dad's farm in '39 in the tenth grade because I had no intention of spending the rest of my life with my ass behind an ass. Then the war started. We met, then broke up when I found out the truth about you before I was sent overseas. But you kept writing, and we started again when I came home. Remember, despite what had happened, I forgave you, and we married just before D-day."

The authoritative edge was gone from Dad's voice now. He wasn't arguing anymore, he was pleading—pleading for his wife, and his very existence.

"Thank you for constantly bringing up the past and holding it over my head. It really endears you to me," Mom said.

"Well, what about after the war?" Dad asked, ignoring her snipe. "If you recall, I did get out of the service in '47, went home to Pennsylvania, and got a job in the steel mill. But, after two weeks, when I decided that I didn't want to spend the rest of my life working in that goddamn mill, you didn't object too strenuously about me going back in the service, now did you?"

"We could have gone to my home in Atlanta. My dad could have gotten you a job with the railroad," Mom interjected.

"As what? Your dad was a conductor, not a vice president," Dad snapped. "Anyway," Dad said, easing into a more even and reflective tone. "The last fifteen years haven't been so bad; I'm not saying it was easy, but we made it, didn't we? God, remember the monsoon in Okinawa in the late '40s?

"You were pregnant, and I didn't know it, when I left you behind in Kansas. Major Martin and I had gone to Japan in anticipation of the North Korean buildup. You were two months' pregnant again when I was sent back to Korea after being wounded. Kevin was three when I came home from Korea and we bought this house.

"The last six years here in Savannah haven't been so bad, have they? The kids have grown, we've got a house full of furniture, a car we own free and clear, and along the way I was even able to build myself a workshop, and acquire a few power tools."

"And that's just why I don't want to leave," Mom said. "I've made friends here. I've settled here. Things are different now. It's not just you and me, pack our bags, and move. We've got two kids, and this house. Moving is not a simple thing. It means uprooting everything we've worked for the past six years."

"What about the next fifteen years?"

"What do you mean?"

"I'm talking about the rest of our life. Look, I reenlisted because I like this kind of life and it's the only thing I know. But also, if I retired now, I'd have to go out and get another job anyway, because I'd only get half salary. But if I stay in for thirty, I'll get three-quarters of my base pay, and we should be all right.

"When I ran into Lieutenant Colonel Martin at the Pentagon last year, he told me that there are some big pay raises coming for service people in the next few years, and I want to stick around to cash in on them."

"What is it with you and the colonel?" Mom asked, her voice rising. "Can't you think for yourself?"

"Honey, I've known him since the war. The colonel has been awful good to me. If it wasn't for his protection, I'd have been kicked out of the service a long time ago," Dad answered. "And by the time I get out, Billy will be twenty-two, going on twenty-three, and through college."

"What about Kevin?" Mom interjected sharply.

"What about him?"

"You're always talking about college for Billy, but you never mention Kevin."

"Ah, honey, you gotta understand. I like Kevin just as much as Billy, but I just don't think he's smart enough for college. I mean, he's always doing dumb things and telling lies. If he doesn't change I'll be surprised if he's not in some kind of serious trouble by then."

The statement made Kevin shiver out on the couch. Yeah, he'd lied to Dad once, six months ago, about taking the change off the top of the milk bottles, because he was afraid of Dad's fierce temper. But when he told him the truth, which was that he was put up to it by his older brother, Billy, Dad didn't believe him. Dad blatantly favored his firstborn, *but no matter what happens,* Kevin vowed to himself, *I'll make positively sure that Dad's statement never comes true.*

"Now, take Billy on the other hand," Dad went on. "He's a son a man can be proud of. He's never in any trouble in school and gets excellent marks on his report card. Kevin is always in trouble. How many times have you had to go to school because he was throwing temper tantrums? And on his last report card he got a couple of F's in reading and math."

"But honey, he's just a little slow, that's all," Mom said. "Give him a little time, and he'll learn."

"Yes, but that's exactly my point," Dad said. "If he's slow now, what's he gonna be like by the time he's old enough for college? By then, he'll have failed a grade or two, and will probably get drafted by the army anyway. If that's the case, the best thing he could do is to enlist in the air force and put in twenty years or so."

"Like you?" Mom asked, the edge back in her voice.

"And just what do you mean by that crack?"

"Just what I said," Mom said. When it came to arguments about her kids, Mom's red hair was more than a match for Dad's Irish temper. "There's more than one way to make a living besides the service. He can be a carpenter, a plumber, an auto mechanic, or a lot of things."

"But, you've got to plan ahead. The future will be here before you know it."

"We'll worry about the future later. Let's settle the present first," Mom insisted. "Although I don't like it, I'll go with you to England. But let me warn you, that's not the end of this. When we return from this tour, we're going to sit down and have a long talk about the future, which, from where I stand right now, doesn't include spending the next ten years moving from place to place. And one more thing: You've got to promise to take me on a tour of Europe while we're there."

"Aw, honey, you know those things cost a lot of money, and—"

"I don't care," Mom interrupted. "I'm not going all the way to England for three years and not be able to come back and tell my friends that I went to Paris, Rome, Vienna, and—"

"Okay, okay, you win," Dad said. "But it's sure going to cost a lot of money."

"Take it out of the money you're saving for Billy's college," Mom said. "And another thing, while we're on the subject of the kids, you'd better start to make Billy mind. You're spoiling that boy."

"I am not," Dad said, becoming defensive. "Besides, every father spoils his firstborn and namesake a little."

"Well," Mom said, "you'd better start to discipline both boys the same. Billy is starting to get a pretty smart mouth on him."

"If he is, it's only because Kevin puts him up to it."

"Okay, don't listen to me. But don't complain to me in ten years when you can't make Billy mind," Mom said.

"Don't worry," Dad snapped. "It's the other one I'm worried about."

Kevin tried his best to look nonchalant as his parents emerged from the bedroom and walked into the living room. He managed to pull it off with his mom, who, with a cheery grin, said, "Hi, son. You better wash up. We'll be eating in a few minutes." She continued on to the kitchen to begin preparing a late supper.

Dad stopped in the front of Kevin and fixed on him with a severe look. "Have you been eavesdropping on your mother's and my conversation? Huh?"

Kevin was caught. On one hand, he was deathly afraid of Dad's temper; on the other, he was even more afraid of lying to him because Dad always found out. "Yes, sir," Kevin finally murmured. He might be afraid, but he wasn't going to run, no matter what the possible consequences.

"You little—," Dad said, as he raised his hand to strike. "I oughta slap your teeth down your throat."

"Smitty!" Mom said from the kitchen doorway. "He couldn't have helped overhearing the way we were yelling at each other. Leave him alone."

"All right," Dad growled. "But don't ever let me catch you doing that again or I'll blister your little butt."

Dad walked into the kitchen and muttered to Mom, "See what I mean? And you want to send him to college."

Kevin sat on the sofa and silent tears ran down his cheeks. Mom's concern was nice, but Dad was the one whose opinion counted. And no matter what he did, Kevin knew it was impossible to change Dad's mind. Dad prided himself on being an expert in the handling of men, and he was; it's just that he wasn't an expert at handling little boys. He was used to the discipline of the service, where he need only give an order to be instantly obeyed. He just couldn't, or wouldn't, learn that kids needed explanations, not discipline, and understanding, not lectures.

Kevin's private reverie was interrupted suddenly as Billy came bursting through the front door.

"What's the matter with the little baaaby? Is the little baaaby crying, huh?" Billy tickled Kevin patronizingly under the chin.

"Is it gonna wet its little pants, um?"

As his brother leaned forward to tickle him again, Kevin reared up from his crouched position on the sofa, balled up his fist, and hit his brother in the mouth with all his strength.

Billy was two and a half years older than Kevin, a foot taller, and a good twenty pounds heavier. Whenever he fought with his brother, the result was always the same. Billy would goad Kevin into a fight and then beat him up.

When Kevin appealed to Dad for help, Dad would always say, "A man has to be able to take care of himself in this world. If you don't want Billy to keep beating you up, pick up something and even the odds." Then he would turn to Billy and say, "Billy, one of these days, you're gonna hit that boy one time too often, and he's gonna come off the floor and beat the crap out of you. And when that happens, don't expect any help from me, just like I don't give Kevin any help now."

To which Billy would always brag: "I ain't worried. I'll always be able to handle the little squirt."

And that's just what was happening now. Billy was handling Kevin, or maybe manhandling was a better word. Kevin had gotten in a solid first punch, which rocked and staggered Billy backwards a step, and started a pretty good flow of blood from his nose, but that was all. Billy, seething with rage at the sight of his own blood, had waded into Kevin with a vengeance. He was being badly beaten by the time Dad heard the commotion and ran into the living room to break them apart.

"I'll kill the little twerp," Billy shrieked, bouncing on his toes trying hard to get around Dad's restraining arm.

"Billy, break it up. You proved your point," Dad said.

"Well, he started it. He hit me first."

"Is that true, Kevin?"

"Yes, sir," Kevin got out through his tears.

"Go to your room," Dad commanded.

"But Daaaaad?"

"I said go to your room!" Dad roared. "You hit your brother and then want me to stop it when you lose. Well, from now on, you start something like this, and I'll let your brother beat you senseless. Now, go to your room. You can come out when you think you can act like a man."

Kevin went to his room and began to cry again. It was always the same. Dad would take Billy's word for things without giving Kevin a chance to explain.

Two nights earlier, Billy had been throwing a rubber ball against their bedroom wall after they had gone to bed. Billy heard Dad coming before Kevin realized what was going on. He threw the ball quickly onto Kevin's bed, rolled over, and pretended he was asleep.

When Dad came in, Kevin tried to tell him what had really happened. Dad had looked quickly at his brother, saw he was asleep, and Kevin had gotten a spanking. "Not," his dad had said angrily, "for bouncing the ball, but for lying to me. If you do something, be man enough to own up to it."

As soon as Dad left, Billy sat up in the next bed, laughed, and taunted him. Kevin lay in his own bed crying. But the tears of pain slowly turned to tears of rage. Someday, he'd show 'em all. His brother Billy—who knew he could get away with anything and set Kevin up to take the blame—but especially his dad, who wouldn't trust him. Someday, he'd show 'em. Someday, if it was the last thing he ever did.

Kevin lay in bed thinking. The last six months had not been easy on him, but he was learning some very hard, very useful, and long-lasting lessons. He'd been yelled at, more often than not, undeservedly, but the effect had been the opposite of what was intended. Instead of feeling sorry, Kevin felt mad and frustrated. Anger, when measured and controlled, can be a great motivator. It had been for Kevin. And frustration? Frustration turned outward was rage; frustration turned inward was motivation.

The more he was blamed for things, the more enraged he got. And the more determined to prove his dad was wrong about him. *Now,* he thought to himself, *what can I do for Dad that will make him happy?* After several minutes, the answer came to him. But to do it, Kevin would have to have the house to himself. Since Mom and Dad were going to a picnic tomorrow, they'd be out of the house, and Kevin knew just the right way to get rid of his brother.

With this thought lodged firmly in his mind, Kevin drifted off to sleep, excitedly anticipating the Sunday to come.

"Keeeevin? Rise and shiiine," Mom called, as she knocked lightly on the door and walked into Kevin's bedroom.

"Oh, you're up," Mom said, surprised. "Come on to breakfast, son. You don't want to be late for Sunday school."

Kevin wouldn't be late. The excitement of the night before had carried over 'til morning. Usually he had to be blasted out of bed in time for Sunday school, but today he was up and almost dressed when Mom came in.

"You were up early today, that's good. You're finally beginning to get with the program," Dad nodded as Kevin sat down at the breakfast table. Kevin's anger and resentment began to rise. He'd never, never, be part of the program.

"Yes, sir," Kevin answered quietly.

"Now, Mrs. Brown is going to drive you and Billy to Sunday school since your mother and I are going to a picnic out at the base. Kevin, you mind Billy. And Billy, don't you go off and play baseball and leave Kevin alone, understand?"

"Yes, sir," Billy answered with confidence.

"Yes, sir," Kevin answered.

Kevin's quick response caused Dad to give him a long, thoughtful stare. After several seconds, which to Kevin seemed like hours, Dad finally nodded and without further comment, left the table.

The deceptive cooperation and the bright replies didn't bother Kevin at all. He'd often heard Dad say, "The end justifies the means."

On the way home from Sunday school, in the car, Kevin started to put his plan into effect. He yawned and stretched several times before announcing his intention to Mrs. Brown, and more importantly to his brother, to take a nap when they got home.

Kevin watched from cracked eyelids as Billy collected his bat and glove and went off to play baseball with his friends as soon as he thought Kevin was asleep. He had overheard his brother say, "Come on, the little twerp won't wake up for hours. No reason for me to sit around babysitting."

Kevin's plan was off to a good start. Getting rid of his brother had been predictably easy.

A cynical smile formed slowly on Kevin's face as he watched the disappearing figures of Billy and his friends from the living room window. With a final nod, Kevin turned and skipped out the back door to Dad's workshop.

Kevin's plan was to clean up Dad's shop for him. But he hadn't realized what a big job it was going to be.

The six-foot workbench was cluttered with hand tools, drills, and miscellaneous odds and ends from past and present projects. The table saw was on wheels, though right now, it was hard to tell since the sawdust was piled almost all the way up to the top of the stand. Everywhere Kevin looked, pieces of wood and scraps of steel were leaning against walls and piled deep in corners. And if that wasn't enough, all the porch end tables had not yet been stored away in the upstairs attic.

Well, Kevin had often heard Dad say that the best way to do an impossible job was to pick a starting spot and dive right in. "Because," he had said, "the longer you sit and do nothing, the harder the job seems to become until it becomes almost impossible to start at all."

After one more brief glance around the workshop, Kevin decided that before he could clean up, he'd have to put away the tools and clear the workbench and surrounding area so that the attic steps could come down. His plan was under way.

"Oooooooh, Kevin! Is your daddy ever gonna be surprised!" Kevin looked up from sweeping the floor to see Sara Lee Young, the next-door neighbor and his mom's best friend, standing in the doorway of the workshop. She was in her late forties, gray-haired, with grown and married children of her own. She was also Kevin and Billy's babysitter when they were younger. Kevin called her "Aunt Grandma," because she truly was like a second grandma. She seemed to be smiling and laughing all the time. Her deep country drawl made even serious things seem funny.

"What're you doin', boy? Tryin' to get on yer daddy's good side?" she asked, cackling.

"Yes, ma'am."

"Okay, I jus' came over to check on what yer up to. Your daddy asked me to keep an eye on you boys while they's away. If you need help, jus' you holler over the fence and I'll have Buddy come on over."

"Yes, ma'am, I'll do that."

Kevin watched Mrs. Young walk back across the yard and climb over the ranch style fence into her yard. *Mom would never be caught climbing over the fence,* he thought to himself. She said it was unladylike.

It had taken all afternoon, but Kevin was nearing the end of his cleanup project. All he had left to do was store the end tables in the attic and he'd be done. *A good thing,* Kevin thought to himself. Dad was due back soon and he wanted to be done and back in the house when they came home.

With that thought, Kevin went down the attic steps, dragged the first end table over, and started up the steps, bumping it along behind him, one step at a time, because of its bulk and weight. Kevin would pull the end table up one step with his hand, balance it, and step up and grab the next step with his other hand.

Using this step-and-fetch routine, he worked the table up the ten steps until he was just below the attic floor ledge. Because the distance from the last step to the ledge was a little higher, Kevin had to reach up and at the same time balance the table. As Kevin's hand grabbed the top ledge, he suddenly found, to his horror, that there was no place to grab onto. The attic floor was completely smooth right to the edge.

In a desperate attempt to avoid falling, Kevin let go of the end table, which tumbled noisily down the steps. But, that only served to unbalance him even more. Kevin swayed back and forth on the step, like a tightrope walker who had just stumbled and was trying desperately to recover before losing the fight to maintain his balance. He fell down the steps, landing squarely on the overturned end table, before rolling off and hitting his head on the concrete floor.

Kevin knew he was badly hurt. His head ached fiercely, his chest hurt, his eyes were suddenly misty, and blood was dripping freely from a nasty cut on his chin. No matter how he tried, he couldn't seem to get up.

From his position on the floor, Kevin could see out the door of the workshop. He saw Mrs. Young cross her yard at a dead run, vault cleanly over the fence, and continue running toward him. It was the last thing he saw before losing consciousness.

Kevin had vague memories of being put in a car and driven somewhere very fast. Other, even blurrier memories of being poked, prodded, and having lights shined in his eyes before being undressed by someone with very soft hands, and drifting off to a disturbed, pain-filled sleep. Sometime after—Kevin had no idea of how long—a voice had started to talk to him. And, from what Kevin could determine, had talked continuously ever since. "Don't worry, son, you're going to be just fine."

Someone was alternately stroking his forehead and kissing him gently on the cheek. Kevin responded to this with an involuntary shiver and noticed an immediate change in the tone of the voice. It had suddenly taken on feeling, cooing expressively into his ear in a low tone that seemed to be choked with emotion.

Kevin awoke to see his mom's tear-stained face staring lovingly at him. "Oh, son, you're awake. I've been so worried about you," she said, patting his cheek affectionately. "You've had a bad fall, but you're going to be just fine now, son, just fine."

"That's right, son, you're going to be okay."

Kevin turned his head in response to see Dad smiling down at him from the other side of the bed. Kevin was somewhat bewildered by all of this kind attention. He wondered what had happened that would make both of his parents be nice to him at the same time, especially Dad.

"Where am I?" Kevin asked, his confusion making him hesitant.

"You're in the base hospital at Hunter," Dad said. "You were transferred here three days ago from the city hospital that Mrs. Young brought you to initially. You fell from the top of the attic steps in the garage and landed on the end tables, before rolling off and hitting your head on the concrete floor."

Kevin's bewildered look quickly turned to a grin when he saw Dad smiling at him. "Don't worry about the rest of this, troop, you're gonna make it."

"What's the rest of it?" Kevin asked.

For just a brief instant, the smiles vanished from both Mom and Dad's faces as they shot a sharp glance at each other before Dad continued in the same measured tone as before.

"Well, you've sustained some broken ribs as a result of landing on that table, and some internal bleeding and external bruising to go with it. But that appears for the most part to be under control. It took about twenty-five stitches to close that cut on your chin, and you've dislocated your jaw. When you hit the floor, you jarred your head real good. The doctor says you'll probably have a few headaches for about the next three weeks. So, you'll be staying here until the worst of this is passed."

"Am I in trouble?"

"Of course you're not in trouble, honey," Mom said soothingly. "This wasn't your fault. It's just one of those things that happen. It was a freak accident."

"Now, if you'd cracked that concrete floor with that hard head of yours, we'd probably look on this whole matter differently," Dad said with a laugh.

"Oh, Smitty, stop it!" Mom protested. "You'll scare him half to death."

"He knows I'm just joshing him, don't you, boy?"

"Yes, sir," Kevin answered, still unsure of how to respond to his dad's sudden attitude change.

"It's a good thing Mrs. Young was in her backyard and saw you through the shop window as you fell. She got you into her car immediately and on to the hospital.

"Billy was telling me that this happened just after you and he finished cleaning up the shop and he went off to play baseball with his friends. You know, next time it might be a good idea to follow Billy's advice. He told me that you two had agreed to wait until I got home to put those end tables in the attic," Dad finished in a voice tinged with reprimand.

Kevin glanced at Dad. He couldn't believe what he had just heard. What did Billy have to do with this? How did he manage to convince Dad that he was involved with this? It didn't make any sense, but it probably wouldn't do any good to tell the truth because he wouldn't be believed anyway.

"Yes, sir," Kevin muttered.

"What's wrong, son? Something seems to have upset you. Are you hurting? Do you need something?" Dad asked, misreading Kevin's look of astonishment for pain.

"No, sir."

"Okay, son, you just let the nurse know if you need anything, and they'll bring it right to you.

"Well, look, I got to go back to work. I just came down on my lunch break to check up on you and see if you or Mom needed anything. I'll stop by on my way home and we'll talk then," Dad said, patting Kevin on the arm before heading out the door.

Kevin rolled away from his dad as he left, and in so doing, completely forgot about Mom, who was now staring straight at him and could not fail to see what Kevin had been trying so hard to hide—the tears that were flowing freely down the sides of his face.

"What's the matter, son?" Mom asked, as she gently stroked his head.

"Nothing," Kevin managed through his tears.

"Well, something your dad said has upset you terribly. I can't fix it if you don't tell me what it is. Won't you please tell me?"

"It won't do any good. No one will believe me anyway."

"Try me."

"Well," Kevin began, "I wanted to do something special for Dad to make him like me, so I thought up the idea of cleaning up his shop to get on his good side. But now it appears that it didn't do any good."

"But that's not true, son. Your dad was telling me how impressed he was that you and Billy took it on yourself to do that for him. He was really pleased. Honestly."

"But that's just the point," Kevin said, sniffling.

"What's just the point, son?"

"Aw, forget it. It doesn't matter anyway." Kevin suddenly found himself tongue-tied when it came to confessing the whole truth. Even though his brother deserved it, something inside him just wouldn't allow him to do to Billy what Billy almost certainly would do to him if the circumstances were reversed.

Mom was quiet for a moment. "Are you trying to tell me, without telling me, that you cleaned up the shop and that your brother had nothing to do with it?"

"Let's just forget it. It doesn't matter now anyway. Besides, I'm tired and want to take a nap," Kevin said, rolling away from Mom and pretending to be falling asleep.

"Your brother wasn't even home, was he?" Mom asked, walking around the bed and leaning down directly into Kevin's face. "You know, when Billy was telling your dad about this, I sensed something was wrong, but I just couldn't put my finger on it until now. I'm betting that not only was he not there, but, crafty little devil that you are, you probably figured out an intentional way to get him out of the house."

Mom tickled Kevin until he began to giggle. "Well, one thing's certain: you've got that same stubborn streak in you that your father has, so you'll never tell me what really happened. Men." She sighed.

"Don't worry, son, you just take a nap for real, and leave this to me. I know just how to get this across to your father." Mom kissed Kevin lightly on the cheek and left.

Kevin drifted off to sleep to diminishing sounds of Mom's high heels as they clicked purposefully away and thought how funny it was that without intending to, he had apparently accomplished more than he'd ever expected. He supposed that what Dad always said was true: "If you always tell the truth, sooner or later someone will stumble across it and, if for no other reason than ignorance, believe it."

With each day that passed, Kevin was recovering with the speed of healthy youth. He was moved from intensive care to a private room in the pediatric ward, complete with a fifteen-year-old girl across the hall, recovering from an appendectomy. She was blonde, cute, friendly, and very well-developed for her age, and they took to each other immediately. Together, they passed the hours watching TV, playing games, or just talking.

Since Kevin was now ambulatory and being held mostly for observation, he quickly got the layout of the hospital down, and then took Claire-Beth, his new friend, on a personally guided tour via wheelchair. These activities served both as a pleasant contrast to his recent painful injuries and as a distraction from worrying about the results of the meeting between Mom and Dad.

Kevin knew that a meeting, or more likely knowing Mom, a confrontation with Dad had occurred. Although Mom had been to see him daily and talked to Kevin three or four times a day by phone, Dad had not returned that evening as promised, nor had he called. Whatever the result, it must have been a doozy. His father had not been to see him in person in three days.

As he gazed absently at the setting sun outside his hospital window, he suddenly sat straight up in the bed. A staccato, hollow, clicking sound, followed closely by a more solid, sturdy, thudding noise could be clearly heard on the linoleum floor, increasing in volume as it came down the ward toward Kevin's room. Kevin's quandary would soon be at an end. His parents were here.

Kevin could feel the tension between them as they entered the room. Mom's smile was hollow, not quite reaching the corners of her mouth, as she kissed Kevin lightly on the forehead and murmured about how well he looked and how fast he was recovering. Maybe the greeting was sincere. Kevin had failed to notice. His total energy, his total focus, was on Dad. He stared unblinking, totally concentrating on his father, who seemed to feel the effect of Kevin's intense gaze, and, uncharacteristically, fidgeted uncomfortably beside the bed searching for the right way to begin.

"How have you been, son?" Dad began.

"Okay."

"Just okay? You seem a whole lot better than that. The doctor tells me that you'll be ready to go home in a few days. And I understand that you've become quite a lady-killer." Kevin shot a sharp glance across the hall, grateful and relieved to find that Claire-Beth was not there at the moment. "And bon vivant around the hospital."

Knowing instinctively that Dad was uncomfortable and unsure, Kevin shrugged without expression.

"Look, son, I apologize for not coming to see you the last few days, but I've had an

ORI—Operational Readiness Inspection—at the base, and you know how those things are."

Kevin glanced at Mom, who smiled back nervously, before turning back and nodding at Dad.

Kevin watched in amused silence as Dad glanced at Mom, saw her icy stare, and returned his eyes to him.

"Ah, son," Dad tried. "Concerning the incident in the garage, your mother explained to me what really happened. And well, I'd, ah, like to, ah, say I'm sorry for getting the facts wrong. I'm even sorrier that you almost killed yourself trying to prove something to me that I should've seen all along. I guess I've been wrong for some time about a lot of things concerning you and Billy.

"Your mother and I have been discussing this at some length." The emphasis on length was unmistakable. "We have come to some agreements on how to fairly handle the two of you from now on."

"Such as?"

"Well, ah, we decided that from now on, both of you boys should be disciplined the same."

"Big wow. Billy gets believed, I get the blame. That what you call fair?" Kevin's mouth twisted with contempt.

"I guess I can understand how you feel, son, all things considered. In the past couple of days, your mother has forced me come to terms with the fact that I've been treating you unfairly. But I promise you that things are going to be different. When I said disciplined the same, I meant it. From now on, whenever there's a disagreement between the two of you, you both will be punished evenly. Both your mother and I feel that this is the only fair way to assure that each one of you is treated equally by us. We figured that as soon as you both recognize this, it will cut down considerably on the number of disagreements you both have. The same fair treatment will extend across the board to your future education, outside activities, or anything else."

Kevin was stunned by Dad's open confession. He was not sure what he had expected, but this was not it at all. Instinctively, he glanced at Mom, and felt instantly reassured as she smiled warmly, first at Kevin then at Dad.

As Kevin focused again on Dad, he saw, for the first time, that there was another person under the rough exterior. A person with feelings, a person who could hurt, and perhaps most importantly, a person who could love.

"I didn't know you cared," Kevin shocked himself by saying.

Dad broke into an unexpected laugh. "Yes, son, now that you mention it, I guess I do. I've always had a tough time verbalizing what I've felt. Might still have if it hadn't been for you and your mother." Dad glanced at Mom who gave him her very best up-from-under look. "You're so very much like me that maybe we can learn from each other."

Kevin saw Claire-Beth enter her room across the hall with a friendly wave in his direction. A sudden thought struck him. "Dad, Claire-Beth's father is a colonel. Do you know him?"

Kevin's question seemed to affect Dad in some indefinable way.

"We've traveled some together," he said, ruffling Kevin's hair. And with a quick, "See you later, son," he turned and abruptly strode out of the room. Kevin was not sure but thought he'd seen a tear forming in the corner of Dad's eye as he walked away.

Kevin looked at Mom, who said, "You know, I think you've developed beyond your years, sport. In all the time we've been married, I've never seen your father show as much feeling as he just showed with you. I don't know how you did it, but you touched something deep inside and brought to the surface emotions I've not seen in a long time." Mom paused for a moment then repeated in slow recognition, almost as if in a trance, "A long time."

Mom brightened and announced, "I think I'd better go after him and see if I can help. You going to be all right now?"

"Yes, I'll be fine," Kevin replied.

"Okay, then," Mom said, kissing him on the cheek. "See you later, honey."

"Yeah, see you later. And Mom?" Kevin said, as she was just about through the door "Thanks."

Mom paused in the doorway and smiled at Kevin. "No, son. It's I who should be thanking you."

The sound of Mom's heels could still be heard clicking down the hall when Claire-Beth came into the room and noticed Kevin staring out the window. She sat down on the end of his bed, followed the direction of his stare and was still trying to figure out what had Kevin so preoccupied when Kevin saw his mom run out of the hospital doorway and bound into Dad's arms.

Kevin and Claire-Beth watched from the window as his parents hugged and kissed each other on the front lawn and snuggled close on the front seat of the car as they drove away.

"Parents!" Claire-Beth said. "Yours are as weird as mine!"

After almost three weeks in the hospital, and one week after the emotionally charged meeting with his parents, Kevin was released. He said quick good-byes to the doctors and nurses, with whom he had become something of a favorite. And to Claire-Beth, who unexpectedly kissed him on the lips and hugged him so tightly against her firmly developing chest that Kevin was afraid his mending ribs had just suffered a serious setback.

In truth, Kevin had a huge crush on Claire-Beth and suspected that maybe she had a little bit of a crush on him, but he knew that once they left the neutral ground of the hospital there would be no further contact. The reason was in no way related to the five-year age difference between them; Claire-Beth's dad was the wing commander and a chicken colonel, whereas his dad was just a sergeant.

There was an unwritten but rigidly enforced rule that officers and noncoms didn't fraternize, and this seemed to be doubly true where their offspring were concerned. It was a perverse kind of prejudice, buoyed by pride, each insisting that his kids were too good to be seen with the other. Kevin did not really understand, or for that matter agree with this, but he knew it was hopeless to try to change it.

On the ride home, Kevin sat between his parents in the front seat and listened politely as they chatted gaily about what had been happening since he'd been in the hospital. Kevin heard little of what they said. From his position in the middle of the seat he had only to tilt his head upward a bit to clearly see in the rearview mirror, the obviously brooding face of Billy, who returned his quick glances with a Boy,-what-I'm-going-to-do-to-you-when-I-get-you-alone stare.

Kevin was going to enjoy this newfound sense of power he suddenly had in the family. It was ever so satisfying to know that his brother, for the first time, could do absolutely nothing about it.

But in the days that followed, Kevin found his new sense of power short-lived. Kevin at first had thought that with the passage of a few days things would get better, but such was not the case. It had been almost six weeks since Kevin's fall, and things had slowly but continuously deteriorated.

To say that the family routine was abnormal would be as acute an understatement as referring to Ted Williams as a fairly decent ballplayer. Mom was pleasant with Kevin, friendly with Billy, and tense with Dad. Dad's manner with Kevin was formal, obviously that of a man trying hard to keep his temper in check, and he was closely watched by Mom. His contact with Billy was another matter altogether.

Billy was bearing the full brunt of Dad's embarrassment at not discovering the truth about the garage incident and at having been duped by Billy for an uncertain amount of time before that. As a result, Billy was uniformly spiteful to Kevin, making hateful remarks that Kevin knew instinctively were directed only at him because Billy would never dare say them to Dad.

Almost before Kevin knew it, May 15 arrived. Packing, farewell parties, and good-bye hugs and kisses were exchanged in kaleidoscope fashion as the family prepared to uproot for the journey to England. The cherished '53 Plymouth was sold for three hundred dollars, the house was rented, and all the shop tools were crated and trailered to Grandma's in Atlanta to be stored under her house until the family's return. Because of the weight restriction, most of the heavy furniture was put in storage, with only the kitchen utensils and linens being taken along. Most of Billy and Kevin's toys suffered the Plymouth's fate. They were able to take only one footlocker of personal possessions apiece.

Except for a permanent two-inch scar on his chin, most of Kevin's physical damage from the fall had healed. What had not healed either in Kevin or in the rest of the family was the emotional impact of recent events. As they boarded the plane for the flight to England, the family was truly in a state of turmoil.

CHAPTER TWO

The fourteen-hour airplane trip had been taxing. Mid-Atlantic turbulence had caused the aging DC-3 to be pitched and tossed like an amateur rodeo rider on a killer bull. Most of the passengers made frequent use of the paper bags provided. Mom and Billy had been violently ill at least twice during the flight; Kevin hadn't thrown up or even been bothered by the foul odor which seemed to be everywhere. In fact, during the height of the turbulence, Kevin had volunteered to go aft and retrieve additional bags for Mom, Billy, and neighboring passengers.

The bad weather had followed them right through to landing. A steady rain was falling at Lakenheath Air Force Base and had not slowed noticeably in the last two hours as they rode the bus northward to their final destination.

England in '59 was considered to be excellent duty for a serviceman. The cost of living was low, and by comparison, service pay high. It was a country filled with charm, adventure, and memories from past days of glory.

Kevin wasn't the only one experiencing altered emotions. Memories not yet a decade and a half distant were silently being relived as Dad stared intently at seemingly empty roadways and deserted buildings. In his memory, he saw airfields filled with bombers, adventurous nights paid proper respect only by the young, and the faces of men who now soldiered with the angels.

The rain, like the family mood, remained heavy as the bus pulled into the town of Dearfield and deposited them unceremoniously in front of the Tell Hotel, the only hotel in town, before driving on to other air force bases farther to the north. With twenty-four straight hours of traveling behind him, Kevin was asleep almost before his head hit the pillow.

"Keeevin, Biiilly, rise and shine!" Mom knocked lightly on their hotel room door and walked in. "Hurry up and get dressed, boys. The car from the base will be here in one hour, so we'll just have time for breakfast before we go.

"Oh," Mom paused as she was leaving, "be sure and dress warmly; it's pretty cold out there."

"It's more than pretty cold out here; it's freezing. This place is going to be the pits," Billy complained, as he opened the window and stuck his head out into the fog-laden air. "It must be forty degrees out there. I wonder when it starts to get warm."

"That depends on what you mean, lad," the hotel owner's wife said, entering with the morning tea and towels. "Aye, it's a bit nippy in the early morning, but the sun will be up shortly, and it'll warm up right proper in the afternoon. 'Course it'll probably not be as warm as you're used to, but you lads'll learn to adapt to it. Ever since the war, Yanks have been coming here and complaining about the weather. Others before you have adapted; I'm sure you chaps will too.

"To help you get started, I brought you a nice hot cup o' tea. You drink this straight away and it'll warm you up right as rain. I brought towels also; the facilities are at the end of the hall. Be sure to knock, as someone's probably using them, it bein' the time of the morning it is and all. Now, hurry along. I heard your mum say you got to leave in an hour. Cheerio."

"Talks kinda' strange, don't she?" Billy asked.

"Yeah," Kevin agreed. "Wonder if all English people talk that way?"

"Don't know; they probably do. You know this place has got to be weird. I mean, can you imagine? The bathroom at the end of the hall?" Billy said contemptuously.

After a breakfast of scrambled eggs, extremely salty bacon that resembled pork rind, warm milk, toast made from very thick, hard bread, and jam with seeds in it, the car arrived and they were off to the base. The car proceeded straight down the main street, the only major street from what Kevin could tell, passing an array of shops that seemed to be a beehive of activity.

When Billy asked why things were so busy at this time of the morning, the driver, an airman who looked to be about twenty-five, answered, "People here have no refrigerators, so they can't store food and they must go to the market daily to shop."

To Mom's uncomprehending stare, he remarked, "Don't worry, ma'am, you'll get used to it. We have."

At the end of the main street, the road curved sharply around to the right, passed the train station on the left, and continued out of town past rows of neat houses with immaculately landscaped yards. Almost before Kevin knew it, the houses abruptly ended, and the car passed on through the middle of fields of young wheat for no more than three miles before coming to the first of a row of buildings that was the beginning of RAF Dearfield Air Station. The base on the right was offset on the left by woods, and the enlisted and officers' quarters were separated by a field.

The car passed inside the main gate and circled the roundabout before heading down a main street and stopping at a brick building that looked more like a fortress than U.S. Air Force headquarters on the base. The building was surrounded on all entrances by concrete walls that appeared to be at least three feet thick. To the sides and back were peculiarly shaped, grass-covered mounds that were at least twenty feet high, and at the moment, they were being mowed by English soldiers who were using a power mower with a rope to pull it up and down from the top.

As Kevin pointed at this and touched Billy on the arm, the driver nodded in the direction of the mounds and said by way of explanation, "Bomb shelters. Left over from the war. My kids just love to go exploring around here. This was one of the bases that was bombed during World War II. You'll find those things out in the middle of nowhere. From what I understand, the whole damn island was one big military complex."

"It was!" Dad said suddenly, to no one in particular.

"You were here during the war, Sarge?" The driver asked conversationally as they passed inside.

"Here and there," Dad answered, evading the question.

"Gee, it must have been really something. My dad never left the States during the whole war; enlisted right after Pearl Harbor, too."

"Tough break, kid," Dad grunted, cutting off the conversation as quickly as a snuffed candle. Whatever memories were hidden away, it was evident that Dad wished them to remain so.

"Smitty! Damn glad to see you," a voice boomed from down the hall. "Been waiting for weeks for you to show up. In fact, once I found out you were up for overseas assignment, I requested you personally," an air force full colonel said enthusiastically as he bounded down the corridor. He grabbed Dad's right hand, almost before it could be offered, and shook it repeatedly like a pump handle, while thumping Dad warmly on the back with his left.

"And how are you, Mrs. Smith? You're looking as lovely as ever. I think you're even prettier than the last time I saw you; Kansas in '47 or '48 or thereabouts, wasn't it?"

"Yes, it was, Colonel Martin," Mom answered in a subdued voice, averting her eyes. Obviously, she held the colonel in somewhat lower regard than Dad.

"Oh, call me Chuck, kiddo," the colonel interrupted. "Smitty and I go back too far to stand on formality. Hell, I was just a green first louie when we started hanging around together during the war. Taught me most of everything I know. A damn good man, your bunkmate.

"And these must be your kids. The taller one looks like you, ma'am; the shorter one is the spittin' image of you, Smitty. What are your names, boys?" the colonel asked, clasping both of their hands, but without causing any serious limb damage.

"Billy, sir."

"Kevin, sir."

"Say, Smitty, that younger one there, he's a lot like you, I can tell. You just grow up to be half the man your daddy is, son," the colonel said as he patted Kevin on the head and nodded to his father, "and you'll have it made."

"Yes, sir," Kevin responded in admiration. He had never really understood what his dad did, but it was clear that the colonel did.

"Well, I'll leave you folks to get settled. I'll see you in my office tomorrow at 0800 hours, Smitty. We've got a big job ahead of us, and I'm damn glad you're here. I need your, ah, special talents in the worst way. See ya," the colonel said ambling back down the hall in a fashion that more closely resembled a man out for his Sunday constitutional than a person picked to command an obviously important American military station.

"Who was that?" Billy asked in a low voice.

"The base commander of the American contingent," Dad answered formally.

"Golly, Sarge, you and the colonel must go back a long way," the driver said, wide-eyed.

"We've traveled some together," Dad admitted. Then, he added as an afterthought, in an almost prayerful tone, "Yeah, we definitely did do that."

The rest of the introductions were not as exuberant as the initial meeting with the colonel. The day seemed to drag by for Kevin and Billy as their parents met with one person after another, signed papers, asked questions, and went through the rigors of establishing a new residence.

They were to be billeted in the noncommissioned officers' quarters across the road, which they could occupy immediately after the inventory was completed—the house being furnished right down to silverware in the drawers. Billy and Kevin would be attending the school in the village and would be enrolled for the balance of the spring term tomorrow. By prior arrangement, Dad had purchased a car, a brand new car at that, from a dealership about thirty miles away. Kevin was somewhat perplexed by the kind of car they had bought: a 1959 Hillman Minx Estate wagon, whatever that was.

On the way back to the hotel, they were taken to their new residence for a walk-through. Compared with their previous house, this was a shed at the county dump.

Downstairs heating was via a coke stove, fueled by a carbon form of coal, almost like charcoal, in the kitchen, and a coal fireplace in the living room. Bins for both were strategically located just outside the kitchen door, next to the tool shed. The range was electric, extremely greasy, and ancient. There was no refrigerator or washing machine. There was a cold box cabinet in the corner of the kitchen with vent holes to the outside. There was also a scrubbing board, which Kevin guessed passed for the English version of a Maytag washer.

Upstairs, there were wall-mounted space heaters in two of the bedrooms, the master bedroom, and the one next to it, which Billy quickly took dibs on once he realized the third bedroom over the stairwell was smaller and without heat or closet space.

The house itself was a duplex with a postage stamp front lawn and an average size backyard that opened onto a central field with all the other houses around the block. The only saving grace was that it was on a corner lot.

As Kevin stared absently out of the car window on the return drive to the hotel, he had a feeling of foreboding. Since his accident, and the vast amount of idle recovery time that surrounded it, Kevin's perceptions had sharpened. All his instincts told him that this tour would be the period of truth in their interfamily relationships.

"Good show, lad, jolly good show!" Mr. Barnes yelled. "You Yanks are really beginning to understand sums. Here's a pence for crackers and one for your friend also," he said, as he flipped the coins to them.

As Kevin bought his crackers and ambled through the schoolyard at recess, he felt deservedly self-satisfied with Mr. Barnes's praise, especially in light of recent problems between the Americans and the school. Kevin, as well as all the other Yanks, was having a spot of bother adapting to the English curriculum and to the school itself.

There had been several meetings between the teachers and the American parents to discuss these problems, but the faculty had steadfastly, almost it seemed with malice aforethought, refused to alter or make any concessions at all. After all, the principal had stated tersely, "You Americans wouldn't make any adjustments for one of our students who was enrolled in an American institution, so why should we make any for you?"

The problems within the school continued out to the courtyard at recess. Simply put, the English students hated the sudden influx of Americans, probably because of the stories their parents had told them about Yanks and their obnoxious conduct during the war. The cultural differences created an atmosphere of taunting, mistrust, and bloody confrontations.

After one such donnybrook, which looked more like a Harlem street gang confrontation than schoolyard fisticuffs, American tensions heightened considerably when the principal blamed the Americans for provoking the entire incident, suspended fourteen of them, Kevin included, for a week, and took no action at all toward their British counterparts.

Billy had complained to Mom of the unfair treatment in the school, in what was from Kevin's point of view, an emotion-filled argument that focused more on winning support than on truthfulness, especially when you considered that Billy was one of the main taunters. Mom had been compassionate and comforting to Billy, but when she had discussed this with Dad, she had not found the same sympathy.

Dad believed that life was like a poker game; you played the hand you had to the best of your ability. It was pointless to waste time on the one you wished you had. Dad had taken the position that the kids would just have to adjust to their surroundings, the same as anyone else, and had lectured Billy and Kevin to that end. This had a dual effect. Mom became the organizer for other American families with similar concerns, and Billy became further alienated from Dad and aligned with Mom.

Kevin had accepted Dad's advice, seeing it as common sense. This had, in turn, alienated Kevin from Billy even more and caused friction between Kevin and Mom, which she, in turn, took out on Dad.

In the six months since they had arrived in England, this vicious circle had been repeated many times within the family. To the outside world, his parents looked like the all-American couple; but Kevin knew better. He'd overheard the bedroom arguments.

"Hey, Yank. I want a word with you!" The voice that interrupted Kevin's musings belonged to Woody Sherman, a British classmate with curly hair and rosy cheeks who was, like Kevin, one of the bigger kids in his respective group. In the past year, Kevin had gone through a growth spurt, gaining thirty pounds and seven inches. Kevin was stockier now, bigger than Billy, and towered over him by four inches. But he'd also grown up emotionally, developing a keen sense of right and wrong and the intestinal fortitude to do something about it.

"What's on your mind, ol' chap?" Kevin asked sarcastically.

Breathing deeply, in a visible effort of restraint, Woody continued. "Look, mate, I know that relations haven't been the best between us, but this is something that's more important than our personal disagreements."

"And just what could that be, mate?" Kevin answered in the same snotty tone as before.

"Ah, come on, Woody, the bleeder ain't gonna listen. This was a stupid idea in the first place." The scathing remark came from a muscular, craggy-faced kid named Paul, who was standing immediately beside Woody. "Stupid blighter probably won't be good enough anyway. Just look at 'em; thinks he's too good for us, he does," Paul continued.

"Now just hold on, mate. We don't know what he'll say until we ask him," Woody said.

"Well, I've been against this from the start, and so have most of the rest of us. Bleedin' Yanks have caused nothing but trouble from the moment they came here," Paul continued.

Nods and murmurs of assent were echoed by the rest of the group, which Kevin quickly counted to be eight. He looked around for support from other Americans in the yard, and to his horror, realized that he was alone.

"Ask me what?" Kevin asked, trying desperately to hang on to his composure.

"Yeah, ask the beggar. Get it over with," said an unseen voice from behind.

"All right, all right. Just cork up, so's I can," Woody commanded.

"Look, Yank. You know we're playing Devon next week in a football match for the conference championship."

"Yeah, so?"

"Well, Evert, our regular goalie, got kicked in the shin in our last match and broke a bone in his leg. Mr. Barden, the PE instructor, said that he'd been watching you and that you handle the goal right well. We was jus' wonderin' if you'd consider taking his place?"

Kevin's first instinct was to laugh right in Woody's face and tell him to kiss off. This was the same person who'd repeatedly shown himself to be one of the more ardent antagonists of the Americans; and a person to whom Kevin personally owed a broken nose, courtesy of one of Woody's well-landed right hooks in one of their three fistfights to date. But, Woody's vulnerable face forestalled his sneering response. This was a serious offer.

"When's the game?" Kevin asked, his straightforward tone matching Woody's.

"A week from Thursday at Devon."

"When do you need a definite answer?"

"As soon as you can, mate. What with practice and all, we'll need as much time as possible for gettin' ready."

Kevin was silent for a moment, then asked, "Why me?"

"Because you're the best we could find," Woody answered candidly. "Besides, the other 420 students turned us down. You're the only Yank we know with even a trace of skill for our game. You're our last hope, mate."

"Well, circumstances being what they've been," knowing smiles and accompanying laughter echoed Kevin's feelings, "I think I better ask my parents for permission."

"And if their permission was not an issue, what would your answer be?" Paul interrupted harshly, grabbing Kevin roughly by the arm in a viselike grip.

"Then I'd probably say yes," Kevin retorted, shaking himself free from Paul's grasp, then brushing past Paul and striding away with a sigh of relief.

Kevin was certainly in the middle of it now. Word of Woody's offer and Kevin's reply had spread quickly through the school. To Kevin's American friends, he'd sold out; to the English, it was an insult to think a Yank could possibly play football as well as a native Englishman. Kevin could see Mom waiting for him as he got off the city bus that he took home from school every day. Unfortunately for Kevin, by the look on her face, it was obvious that she'd heard too.

"I want to talk to you, young man," Mom began. "Billy tells me that you've agreed to play on some English soccer team at school. Is that right? 'Cause if it is, you can just march your little butt to school tomorrow and tell them no. Is that clear?"

"Well, no, as a matter of fact, that isn't real clear at all."

Mom's hand stung as it made contact with Kevin's face. The accompanying words, something about being a smart ass and sassing back, were lost on Kevin, who was concentrating with all his strength on not crying.

"I've been working like a dog these past months, organizing the other American mothers to put these people in their place, and just when I'm on the verge of getting a lawyer of importance to listen to our complaints, you go and pull an incredibly stupid stunt like that. Now, you go straight upstairs to your room, and don't you dare come out until your father comes home."

At the top of the stairs stood Billy, wearing his very best are-you-going-to-get-it-when-Dad-comes-home smirk.

"What a dumb ass," Billy said.

"Better than being an asshole," Kevin shot back as he pushed past Billy and slammed the bedroom door behind him.

"Hi, son. Your mother tells me you've been stirring up some trouble at school today. You wanna tell me about it?" Dad asked, walking through Kevin's bedroom door.

"Do you mind if I ask you something, Dad?"

"Fire away, troop."

"I don't understand what all the fuss is about. I mean, it's only a soccer game. What's the big deal?"

"Well, son, I think the problem is not so much you as the ballpark you're playing in." Acknowledging Kevin's confusion with a half wave, Dad continued.

"You see, we Americans are guests in this country, in much the same manner as a visiting baseball team, and as such we should be respectful of their customs. The problem is that Americans by nature are very self-confident. We have a well-founded confidence based on our own short, but very successful, history and rapid rise to world prominence. This self-confidence is often misconstrued by others as arrogance. The typical reaction to this is jealousy, which comes back in the form of hostility toward us. During the war, these differences were so acute that the English had a saying about Americans: 'Overpaid, oversexed, and over here.'

"So you can see that a lot of the tensions that you and Billy are experiencing at school are perfectly normal, given the circumstances. You brash young fellows arrive from America, and to the English girls, you seen very worldly and exciting compared to the local young lads. They see this, know that they cannot compete with this 'grass is greener' mystique, and hard feelings are the direct result."

Kevin's eyebrows wrinkled as his perplexed look showed his confusion. "I understand what you've said, but how does that relate to the kids at school, and how does that explain Mom's reaction?"

"I was just coming to that," Dad said.

"You see, once people have taken a position on an issue, they often find it very hard to back down from the stand they have taken. This is due to something called ego, that certain something inside you that gives you the courage of your convictions. In much the same manner as you were hesitant to say yes to your friend, that same inner feeling makes the other person reluctant to change also.

"You know, son, I want you to remember something. The hardest thing is to do what's right; the easiest is to do the right thing. Doing what's right means standing up for a principle or a friend, no matter what the consequences. Doing the right thing means going with the flow and never taking a risk.

"What you and your friend did today was to put aside your emotional differences and concentrate on the problem. Once you did that, the problem, like most problems, was solvable. Your friend made an honest, sincere, and open request for assistance. Sensing his honesty, you responded to it in kind. That was very mature of you.

"To people on the outside who are clinging to their emotions in lieu of facts, you appear to have sold out or betrayed your own kind. To be perfectly honest with you, your mother is caught up in the same whirlwind. She is being driven by her emotions based on her own personally held sense of perceptions, and as such, since the assumptions were not based on hard facts, all assumptions from that point onward are also in error.

"But, let me make this very clear to you: That is my problem to solve, not yours. Your mother is a good woman and my wife; any problems relating to her are my concern in total. Do you understand?"

"Yes, sir," Kevin answered. "So what do you think I should do about the soccer match at school?"

"What do you want to do?"

"I want to play," Kevin said firmly.

"Then that's what you ought to do. A man who wants to do the right thing and has the courage of his convictions can be beaten, but he'll never lose."

"Good save, Yank!" Woody whooped gleefully as the penalty free shot, that had been headed directly for a corner of the net, was deflected over the top of the goal by Kevin's outstretched fingertips. The sound of the whistle meant that they'd won. It was a sweet victory over interconference rival Devon, a larger school from a higher class area, whose dominance was long established.

"You did it, mate. What a bleedin' save that was!" Paul yelled as he jumped into Kevin's arms.

Other team members crowded around, expressing similar sentiments, which Kevin returned with equal enthusiasm. The game-saving block had been the height of a last-period comeback that had erased a three-goal deficit, due mostly to an emotionally stirring speech by Mr. Barden, spectacular play by Woody and Paul, and countless saves on goal by Kevin.

"You know, Yank," Paul said, "I had my doubts about you when this thing started, what with the trouble we been havin' and all, but you sure earned my respect today."

"Mine too!" Woody echoed. "Look, Yank, you played a great game today, and well, we all just thought that you deserve the game ball. Here," Woody said unceremoniously as he shoved the ball hard into Kevin's stomach, causing him to let out an involuntary grunt.

"Tell you what you do, mate," someone echoed from behind. "Catch us in a good mood, when we're not hating Yanks, and we may even sign it." As Kevin returned his laughter and extended congratulations to his teammates, he couldn't help thinking that his dad had been right again.

Even though Kevin had received his dad's permission to play on the team, he still worried about reactions on the part of the other Americans, the English, and to be perfectly honest, his mom. But, Dad had told him that things are never as bad as they seem, and that with the passage of time, emotions subside and life goes on.

And that's just what had happened. There had been some initial hard feelings, but, as the day of the match drew near, these feelings had diminished, to be replaced by passionate school spirit, surprising even the school faculty and the American Coalition for American Student Betterment, headed by Kevin's mom. The hard feelings of before seemed to have vanished so completely that it was almost as they had not existed at all. Nobody talked about the problems, just the game. Miraculously, almost as if they were interconnected, the American students seemed to be making it in the classroom also.

"Hey, Kevin!" Kevin's American friend Sammy called out as they ran off the field. "That was some game today. You really showed them guys that a Yank can play on an English team."

"After we teach you blighters cricket, you'll think that your baseball's a ruddy cake-walk in the park," Paul shot back as they continued off the field to a well-earned shower. But, not before Kevin caught a glimpse of his dad standing discreetly at the back of the crowd, in his very best tweed English outfit, complete with dapper English hat, puffing his pipe with what could only be described as a satisfied smile.

"Smitty, I think you have a damn good idea, a damn good idea." Chuck pointed his cigar for emphasis. "We've got to do something about all our guys, and I think you've hit the nail smack dab on the head."

"Thank you, Colonel," Dad said.

"You know the rules; it's Chuck when we're alone."

"Thank you for that too, sir. I know your rules. I just have never gotten comfortable being on a first-name basis with a senior officer."

"Well, get comfortable," Chuck said impatiently. "I'm the same guy you contemptuously called Butterballs in the war and later referred to as Major Marvel in Korea."

"Colonel, I'm a career man; and I'd never refer to a senior officer in such an unprofessional manner," Dad interrupted stiffly.

Chuck made no effort to conceal his frustration. "The hell you wouldn't. You been breathing turbo-prop fumes or something? Your opinion of most officers is well-known, and frankly, well-founded. So cut the crap.

"Besides, you and I survived the Octagon Mission. You earned the right to call me anything you damn well please. Are we clear, First Sergeant?"

"Yes, sir, Colonel, uh, that is to say, yes, Chuck," Dad answered, discomfort evident in his voice.

"Good," Chuck said with a dismissive nod. "Now, back to business. You know as well as I do that this assignment has to succeed. With what those crazy Russians are cooking up, we could be in a shooting war any day. That makes the timely and successful installation of those Titans very, very important. And since our express purpose for being over here is to supervise the installation for all the missiles in the northern sector, the one thing I don't need is our boys going off base, getting liquored up, and spilling their guts about what they do for a living. I think the locals would react rather strongly to the fact that they're living right next door to a primary target in the event of a nuclear war.

"Now, light up that pipe, and tell me about this idea you've been working on to address our morale problem."

Kevin had not intended to eavesdrop. It had been purely accidental . . . well, almost.

He'd been dispatched on his bicycle by Mom to bring Dad his dinner. Although it was seemingly an easy enough task, it was a good deal more difficult in reality. It was wintertime in northern England, February to be exact, and bitter cold. The temperature hadn't been within waving distance of zero in over three weeks. The roads were icy and treacherous. Kevin had left his bike at home, choosing instead to hike the two miles to the American headquarters. By the time he arrived, ears, nose, and toes were frozen, and, finding the orderly room where Dad's desk was deserted, he'd huddled next to the coke stove until his frostbitten extremities had returned to a temperature approaching normal.

With warmth returned, Kevin had shucked off his heavy wool winter coat and, checking the hallway, had tiptoed back into the orderly room and positioned himself in Dad's chair, fantasizing himself in a similar position of authority when he grew up.

It was during one of these daydreams that he had heard voices from the colonel's office next door. There was a pass-through in the adjoining wall for Dad and the colonel to exchange documents; it was only partially closed. Instinctively, Kevin was out of the chair and had dropped below the window to avoid detection, intending to crawl around the desk and back to the front of the orderly room. But, like the proverbial cat, his curiosity had gotten the better of him and he'd crouched very still, turned his listening gear up to high, peeked over the sill, and tuned in for the show.

"Look, Chuck, the biggest problem with the troops is that they miss their way of life. They're lonesome. So, this is what I've got in mind to deal with this."

WHAM! The sliding window had slid shut with a heart-stopping crash. Kevin remained frozen in his position just below the window, certain that he'd been discovered and expecting Dad and the colonel to come charging in and snatch him from his listening post. Ten seconds passed, and then his worst fears were confirmed.

Dad, followed by the colonel, entered the orderly room and walked directly toward him.

"Son, don't you know it's impolite to eavesdrop on a private conversation?" Dad said angrily as he stopped in front of him.

"I didn't mean to," Kevin said. "It just sorta happened when I sat down at your desk."

Glancing at the colonel, Dad turned, crouched down on one knee until he was eye to eye with Kevin, and said firmly, "Son, you are never, I repeat, never, to discuss what you overheard with anyone. Do you understand?"

"Yes, sir," Kevin answered, his voice trembling.

"Okay then, go on down to the day room and wait for me there. As soon as the colonel and I are through, I'll take you home," Dad said more calmly.

"Yes, sir," Kevin said. He brushed past Dad, tiptoed past the colonel as soundlessly as if the linoleum floor were made of lamb's wool, and ran down the hall toward the day room as fast as his feet would allow. If his retreat had been photographed, it would have made a handy training film for prospective second-story men making a hasty getaway after the alarm had sounded.

"How much do you think he heard?" Kevin overheard the colonel say from behind.

"I don't know," Dad answered seriously.

"Well, one thing's certain, he'd better damn well keep his little lip zipped about the Octagon Mission, or it's your ass, Smitty. And his, too, if he ever talks about it to anyone. Is that clear!"

"I don't think that will be a problem, Colonel," Kevin heard Dad answer, their voices fading as he entered the day room and dove headfirst onto the couch. "For me or my son either."

"You'd better make damn sure!"

What Kevin had overheard had scared him very badly. Kevin's secret fear was war . . . and what it would feel like to die in one . . . whatever the reason. This Octagon Mission that the colonel had referred to so threateningly must have occurred during the war and been very important, important enough to intimidate a ten-year-old boy into silence.

"Hand me that wrench, son."

"Yes, sir." Kevin quickly retrieved the tool, climbed the stepladder, and handed over the wrench.

Dad was the chief foreman of a remodeling project in the back of the headquarters building, a large, hangarlike room that had served as a ready room for pilots during the war. The central room walls had been paneled, with arched doorways on both sides leading to a company workshop on the right and game rooms on the left. Currently the ceiling was being lowered from its current fourteen-foot level to eight feet through the use of extensive amounts of angle iron, all cut by hand, to create a supporting framework. Just to the left of the door, a bar, complete with sink and cold storage, had recently been completed. Kevin had wangled himself a job after school as bar stocker and all-around helper.

As Kevin became an established fixture during the construction, Dad, as well as other sergeants in the company, had begun to teach him elementary tool use and had trained him to operate some of the simpler shop tools. At Dad's request, Kevin had been cutting one-and-a-half-inch strips on the band saw to be used as spacers for attaching the dropped ceiling panels.

"Can I help with anything else?"

"Yeah, you're a short guy and can stand up in this framework, so how about coming up here and holding the wrench on these bolts so Red can tighten them," Dad said.

"You hold them with the wrench, and I'll tighten them from the other side, okay?"

"Yes, sir."

The person on the other side was a young staff sergeant named Red Benson. One quick glance and it was not hard to tell why his nickname was Red.

Red was an Indiana farm boy who'd joined the air force in 1950, rather than get drafted by the army. Red joined thinking he'd miss Korea. As usual, the plan backfired.

Having grown up on a farm, where a person was required to develop many kinds of skills, Red was a pretty fair carpenter. He and Dad had been the mainstays in the building of the barroom, working tirelessly late into the night for months on end.

It was past twelve when Kevin and Red finished the night's tasks. Their well-earned drink at the bar, a 3.2 beer for Red, a coke for Kevin, was suddenly interrupted by a scream from the shop. Both Red and Kevin were met at the doorway by Dad, holding his right hand around the index finger and thumb of his left hand. Kevin's focus went immediately to the peculiar way Dad was holding his left hand. The blood was squirting freely from the index finger joint and the last two inches were no longer there.

"Kevin," Red said urgently. "I'll get your dad into the car. You go into the shop and find that finger and wrap it in a cloth and get out to the car as fast as you can, you hear?"

"Yes, sir," Kevin made no attempt to move.

"Kevin!" Red roared. "Get moving! This is no time to be squeamish or get sick on me. They'll be plenty of time for that later. Now move!"

Red's authoritarian tone galvanized Kevin into action. As he entered, Kevin quickly surveyed the shop and located the finger wedged between the table saw and the cover plate. Seizing a screwdriver off of the workbench, he levered up the plate, removed the bloody piece of finger, and grabbed a cloth on his way out the door.

Kevin raced up the hallway and rounded the corner without slowing down. Careening off the walls like a banked billiard ball to the front of the building, he dived in the open backdoor of the Hillman, and with Red revving the four-banger to previously untried rpm's, they went racing into the night.

"How are you, Kevin?" Dad asked. "Been taking care of everything, school and so forth?"

"Yes, sir. How are you?"

"I'll tell you honestly, I'll be a lot better off when I get out of here. The food's awful. I miss your mother's cooking. Not to mention her cold feet at night."

"Oh, Smitty, stop!" Mom sighed. "You'll give these boys terrible ideas about hospitals."

"I wasn't talking about the hospitals, kiddo." Dad grinned mischievously.

"Well, you'll give them bad ideas about that too," Mom shot back stiffly, with a wounded look that didn't quite come off.

"How's the hand, Dad?" Billy asked.

"Okay, son. And how've you been?"

"I'm okay. I've been taking care of things while you're in here."

"Well, that's good to hear, son."

"Yeah, don't worry about a thing, Dad. You can always count on me."

Dad nodded. "I know I can, son."

"Well, I hope you are out of here real soon. I'll come to see you whenever I can," Billy said. He started for the door, turned around, and seeing that Mom wasn't following, walked back to her, and began to tug on her arm.

"C'mon Mom, we'll be late," Billy said, pulling Mom toward the door.

"Just a minute, Billy," Mom said, resisting. "I'd like to stay and visit with your father a little longer."

"But, Mom," Billy whined. "We'll be late, and I promised Jennifer I'd get to the dance early."

"You'd better go, before Number One Son has a heat rash," Dad snorted.

"Well, if you think that's best," Mom agreed, apparently relieved that someone else had made the decision.

"Kevin. Here's a shilling for the bus ride home. Be home at six, and don't be late. My bridge party starts at seven, so I'll have little enough time to get you boys fed and over to Mrs. Hill's for the evening." Mom pecked Dad on the cheek, patted Kevin on the chin, and breezed out the door after Billy. "Bye, dear. See you tomorrow."

With Billy and Mom no longer there, it seemed uncomfortably quiet in the room. It had been three and a half weeks since the late-night race to the hospital, which had been, for the most part, in vain. The doctor had been unable to reattach the finger, although, with a clever surgical procedure, he had been able to stitch up the thumb, just behind the nail. It looked funny to see the nail without the pad behind it, but the prognosis was for complete recovery and use of the thumb.

How the accident occurred, no one was sure, not even Dad. One minute he was cutting a board, then apparently, a piece of sawdust got in his eye. He'd turned his head for just a fraction of a second, and when he'd turned back, the finger was gone.

"This is the first time I've had a chance to talk to you alone since the accident. That was a very brave thing you did, son," Dad said. "Red tells me you handled yourself real well."

"Thank you," Kevin responded in a low voice. "But, I just did what Sergeant Benson ordered me to do."

"Having any nightmares about it?" Dad asked.

"How did you know?" Kevin looked up.

"Oh, your ol' man is pretty perceptive when he wants to be. There's nothing like having to deal with life's harsh realities to change a man. You've grown up a lot in the past year. Had to. You had that painful fall, had to adjust to different customs here in England, and now have to see your dad get a finger hacked off. I'll tell you, to retrieve that finger took a lot of guts. Don't know if I'd have been able to do it," Dad shivered distastefully. "One, or all of those things, would have been enough to give me sleepless nights."

"Dad, you mean it's all right to be afraid?"

"All right? Hell, in certain circumstances it's down right unnatural not to be."

"But you don't ever seem to be afraid of anything," Kevin objected.

Dad was quiet for a moment, then patted the bed. "Sit down on the bed, partner. I want to explain something to you."

Kevin sat down and Dad continued. "Son, there's nothing wrong with being afraid. It's what you do when you're afraid that counts. Fear is the kind of thing that, left unchecked, magnifies itself in your mind until it can quite literally paralyze your thoughts and actions. So, when you feel uneasy about a situation, the smartest thing to do is to acknowledge to yourself that you are afraid—an admitted problem is half-solved—and say to yourself, 'Okay, given the situation, what do I have to do to resolve it?' If you follow that approach, you'll always be able to think yourself out of a tight spot."

"But, what do you do if there is no way out?"

"That in itself is a form of a solution. Not the ideal one but a solution just the same."

"I don't understand."

"Well, let me see if I can explain it a little better.

"If you find yourself in a no-win position, facing certain death in a downed aircraft, for example, and you have made up your mind that there is no way out, you've examined the facts and come to the solution that there isn't one. "So now, you have to do the next best thing, like we were talking about before, or, do the right thing. Make peace with God. If it's a war, take some of the bastards with you, things like that. And by doing that, a lot of times you'll come up with a solution that you didn't think of before. The point is, as long as you keep thinking and reasoning, there's always a chance. When you stop, there's none."

"Oh, I get it," Kevin said, nodding slowly. "If I find solutions for the things that I'm afraid of, then they're no longer fears. Is that right?"

"You're dead center on the bull's-eye, troop.

"So, you see, if you're having nightmares about something, and you wake up in a cold sweat, figure out a solution to the nightmare and the problem is solved. As a matter of fact, I do the same thing for everyday-type problems that occur to others. I see the problem and rehearse in my mind what I'd do in similar circumstances. Then, when a related type of problem happens, my instincts kick in before fear even comes to bat."

Dad gave Kevin an affectionate pat, brightened, and announced, "Enough of this kind of talk. I'm sure you've got better things to do than sit around here all afternoon. Besides, I'm tired and want to take a nap. You run along."

Kevin was halfway out the door when Dad's soft call of, "And, son," caused him to turn.

"If it helps you any, I've always found that the fear is magnified when you try to do the right thing rather than do what's right."

"Why is that?" Kevin said in a puzzled voice.

"Because, like I told you when we talked about this a couple of months back during that soccer ruckus, when you do the right thing, you always have to worry about what other people think. When you do what's right, you're only answerable for your actions to God."

Kevin nodded in understanding, and as he walked from the hospital he had a feeling he would remember his father's sage advice for a long, long time . . . probably a lifetime.

The summer had passed for the Smith family without serious incident. Its high point had been a camping trip across the European continent, visiting eight countries in forty-five days. Included in that were two- and three-day stays in Vienna, Venice, Rome, and Paris. There were a curiously long four days spent driving around the German countryside with Dad looking intently at various locations, which on the surface seemed to have no attraction whatsoever.

For the most part, Mom was tolerant of this "vacation detour." Kevin understood, and Billy was downright crabby. Those attitudes pretty much summed up the whole vacation in Kevin's mind. Dad went to appease Mom and relive his memories. Mom went so she could go home and tell everyone about the "glorious trip to Europe" she'd taken. Billy and Kevin did not get a vote.

Even though they went more or less under duress, having lost an appeal to be allowed to remain with the neighbors, they went with decidedly different attitudes. Billy complained from the moment the vacation started until it ended. If it wasn't the camping out and having to pitch the tent every night, it was the food, or the endless hours in the Volkswagen bus they'd borrowed from a major in dad's outfit. As they moved from one place to the next in almost forced march-type fashion, Kevin wasn't any happier about it than Billy, but he'd decided to make the best of it. Surprisingly, he'd secretly enjoyed himself. Kevin wondered silently to himself how many other ten-year-old American boys had been to the Vatican and seen the pope celebrate a mass. Not many, he suspected.

Their travels continued in the fall. Dad had more free time and weekend trips were common until the weather turned bad in early November. But, this slack time in Dad's schedule had been invaluable. If there was a tourist attraction on the British isles—from

Shakespeare's shack, to smooching the ol' Blarney Stone—they'd been there, rolling up mile after mile on the trusty little Hillman.

It had been eight months since Dad's accident, and close to ten months since Kevin had listened in on Dad's game plan for improving morale with the colonel, a well-founded strategy that could only be termed a complete success.

The bar, appropriately named "Smitty's Smoker," had officially opened in May with a party and drinking binge that left anyone entering the building for the next two days instantly intoxicated from the fumes. Buildings had been appropriated from the RAF to create a service club complete with a ballroom and a two-lane bowling alley, which was opened in June. A post exchange was operational by July. The Labor Day dance featured an American band and singer. A Halloween dance and trick or treat for the soldiers' children was held at the service club in late October; and in a similar fashion, a sit-down Thanksgiving dinner was prepared and served at the service club by the new mess hall.

The direct result of this "home away from home" strategy was a significant drop in incidents with the local constables concerning the young airmen in the squadron. And, the drastic reduction of discontent resulted in a previously unheard of reenlistment rate of 100 percent. The colonel pointed to this as one of the major reasons why his group was the only one in England currently on schedule with regard to operational targets.

To that end, a lion's share of the credit went to his "first shirt," whom the colonel had nominated for senior master sergeant and NCO of the year, both of which Dad was awarded going away.

Despite all these positive signs of successful adjustment by the American contingent, Kevin still felt very strongly about his earlier perceptions concerning his parents. Even though they had not had a serious argument in months, things just didn't feel right at home. They were too polite with each other, almost formal at times, like two neighborhood dogs circling each other warily trying to decide when and where to bite next.

Kevin had tried to discuss his feelings with Billy but had gotten nowhere. Kevin was quickly coming to the conclusion that Billy was just like Mom. He saw only the obvious and didn't have, or didn't care, to think about anything that didn't affect him personally or that required the capacity to think beyond the present.

A week before Christmas, a storm dumped three feet of snow on Dearfield, then, uncharacteristically, remained stationary over the area. By Christmas Eve, the base was virtually at a standstill, buried under mounds of snow, with drifts over twelve feet high a common sight. The snow grounded all incoming and outgoing flights except, miraculously, the incoming flight from the States with the Christmas presents that American families ordered months ago from the Sears catalog.

"I told you it was a mistake to come to this godforsaken place. Just look at the mess; it'll take hours to clean up and get everything ready for the boys' Christmas."

"Now, just simmer down, honey. I admit it'll take a couple of hours, but we'll get it," Dad answered soothingly.

"Don't you 'just simmer down' me! I've told you and told you, I'm tired of this place—and tired of this kind of life—and I want to go home."

"You're just tired. How's about you go on to bed and I'll finish up."

"Stop patronizing me, goddammit! You haven't been listening to a thing I've said!"

"I have been listening," Dad began, making no attempt to conceal his own rising anger. "But this discussion, frankly, is beginning to get a little old. Our tour here is half over, and all you've done is complain. Nothing I've done seems to please you. The new car didn't, the trip to Europe didn't, and the weekend outings didn't. What is it you want from me?"

Mom was silent for a moment. "I don't know . . . but I'm beginning to honestly feel that there's one thing I don't want."

"What's that?" Dad asked in a weary tone.

"You!" Mom answered bluntly.

"Are you sure?" When Mom didn't answer, Dad continued. "Maybe you need some time to think it over. I know you've been under a lot of pressure lately, and I got a very special Christmas present for you."

"What's that?" Mom's scowl relaxed.

"A trip home to visit your mother. Here's the ticket. You leave January 4."

"Are the boys going along?"

"No, you've never been separated from them since they were born. They're old enough now to get by without you for a while. And I've already arranged for Mrs. Hall to take care of everything while you're gone."

The sound of running footsteps was followed by Mom and Dad hugging and kissing as she jumped into his arms. "Oh, honey, thank you, thank you. This was the perfect gift. I'm sorry for the things I said earlier. I guess I'm just tense," Mom apologized.

"That's all right, dear, I understand," Dad acknowledged softly.

"C'mon hon', let's hurry up and get everything set up for the boys. Then you can take me upstairs to the bedroom and thank me properly," Dad said.

"You dirty old man," Mom said. "How come I can never stay mad at you?"

"It's probably directly related to the size of my weewee," Dad replied with a smug expression.

Suddenly serious, Mom said, "One of these days, you're not going to be able to come up with the right thing to say at the right time. Then what are you going to do?"

"I guess we'll cross that bridge when we come to it," Dad said quietly, then murmured under his breath. "And given the stormy nature of our relationship, we probably will."

One of the improvements recently completed to their living quarters was the installation of an oil-fired heating system. The ductwork was also a perfect listening post from which Kevin had overheard last night's conversation between his parents. Dad's last thoughts stayed with Kevin as he watched the Christmas morning mayhem.

Mom was all aflutter over her impending trip home, Billy was excited about his new bicycle, Santa had brought Dad a set of spotlights for his movie camera, and Kevin's gifts had added additional cars and accessories to his already rather large Matchbox car collection.

During Christmas week, there were numerous parties at the service club and at the homes of other friends and neighbors. Although Kevin wasn't there, he heard reports of an altercation at the New Year's party. The details never came out, but there must have been some truth to it, as one of the officers was shipped stateside inside of twenty-four hours. The fact that there were no going-away parties, gifts, or anything else lent credence to the rumors. He was hustled out of there before the ink had dried on the orders.

Kevin went to bed early on January 3. At 0500 hours, they were driving Mom down to London to catch her flight for home. Although only slightly more than 220 miles, the trip took well over five hours on the rutty and winding roads. The return trip in the dark, with the roads icy, would be even longer. Tomorrow would be a long day.

"Bye, dear. Have a good flight, and I'll see you in two weeks," Dad smiled as he hugged and kissed Mom good-bye at Heathrow Airport.

"I will, honey. Now take care of the boys." Turning to Billy and Kevin, she said, "Now you boys mind your father. I'll miss you both. Come and give me a hug."

"Ah, Mom, I'm too old for that kind of stuff," Billy complained as he reluctantly allowed himself to be hugged, leaning away quickly when Mom went to kiss him.

Kevin hugged Mom enthusiastically. Her kiss left a perfect set of lip impressions on his cheek. "I'm sorry, dear," Mom said gaily as she pulled a tissue from her purse, dabbed it with spit, and wiped his face.

"Got your tickets?" Dad asked.

"Right here in my purse," Mom patted it. "London to New York to Washington. Then an overnight layover, and on to Atlanta."

Dad looked thoughtful, then said, "Where did the side trip to Washington come in? I thought I booked it direct from New York to Atlanta, on the same day."

"Ah, yes, that's right, you did. But since I'm going right by there, I thought I'd stop and visit an old girlfriend I haven't seen since the war, stay overnight, then go on to Atlanta the next day," Mom answered quickly.

"Sort of forgot to tell me you changed your itinerary, didn't you?"

"Well, uh, yes, I guess I did," Mom said uncomfortably. "But look, honey, it was just the excitement of the trip and all."

"I see."

The PA system announced the last call. "Well, I've got to go, dear, before they close the doors. Now, you be good." She hugged Dad again quickly, and with a wave to Billy and Kevin, turned and walked hurriedly toward the door that led to her plane.

"See you soon," Dad called after her with a half-wave.

"Of course, dear," Mom said, running quickly up the steps and through the airplane door without looking back.

"I don't understand what she meant by that," Kevin said, as they turned to walk back to the parking lot.

"I do," Dad said heavily.

Hours later, in the car, as the boys were returning to Dearfield, Dad's reply still bothered Kevin. Checking the backseat first to assure that Billy was still asleep, Kevin asked, "Dad, what did you mean when you said you understood what Mom meant?"

Dad blew out a big cloud of smoke from his pipe before answering and said solemnly, "Your mom is a little upset with me right at the moment."

"What about?"

"At the New Year's party, the officer that she'd been working with on that student betterment thing—the one you knocked the wind out of by crossing the picket lines to play on the soccer team—got a little out of hand with your mom and I had to help him see the error of his ways."

"What do you mean, the error of his ways?"

Dad tapped the ashes from his pipe into the cutoff beer can he'd specially designed for the purpose, and said, "Doesn't matter now. The problem corrected itself rather quickly. The colonel had him shipped stateside."

"Where to?" Kevin asked.

Dad inspected the depths of his empty pipe. "To the Pentagon in Washington."

"The same place Mom is going?"

"Yup."

Kevin wanted to say something, but was not sure what. By the tone of Dad's voice, it was obvious that there was a lot more to the story than Dad was willing to tell, and perhaps more than Kevin wanted to know.

"That doesn't matter, does it? Mom's going there to visit her girlfriend."

"No, son, it doesn't matter," Dad said dryly.

Kevin was silent for a moment as he tried to digest what he'd been told. He squirmed uncomfortably in the car seat. "It's just a coincidence, isn't it?"

"I dunno; your guess is as good as mine," Dad answered in a faraway voice.

Kevin shook his head. "I don't understand."

"It would seem pretty logical to me that if you were going to stop and visit someone you had not seen in almost twenty years, that you'd confirm the arrangements in advance. Right?"

"Yeah, right, so?"

"So, I made a call. The friend your mother is going to see died in a car accident six years ago," Dad said.

Dad seemed on the verge of saying something else, then hesitated, deep in thought as he refilled his pipe. Kevin waited in expectation.

Suddenly Kevin asked without thinking, "Do you think it's connected to this guy who got sent home?"

Dad answered tersely, "Look, I don't know where this line of questioning is leading, but I want you to drop it right now, is that clear?"

"Yes, sir," Kevin answered, painfully aware that he was probably on the right track.

Dad stared unblinkingly out of the windscreen at the blowing snow that appeared to be dancing in the car's headlights. Exhaling deeply, he said in a softer tone, "Son, the firmest foundation for any relationship, whether it's husband to wife, or friend to friend, is mutual trust. Even though I'm uncomfortable with her little side trip, I trust her, and therefore am assuming that she'll make the reason known to me when she's ready."

"Now," Dad said, abruptly changing the subject. "When we get home, I got a list of chores for you and Billy that I promised your mother I'd have done before she got back. At the top of your list is to clear out the tool shed. Then I want you to help me down at the shop on a couple of improvements for the Smoker."

After a few more comments and nods of assent from Kevin, the conversation dried up. The monotonous trip began to wear on Kevin, and as he became drowsy, he wondered how his earlier thoughts could have been so far off the mark. Dad was making plans for when Mom returned; everything was perfectly normal.

CHAPTER THREE

"There's no friggin' way I'll ever agree to that, Smitty; no way at all. You must be out of your fuckin' mind for even suggesting it." A chorus of noise arose immediately as members of the NonComs street gang argued among themselves the controversial proposal to admit blacks to the gang.

"Keith, you've got your head up your ass; we need these guys. The Cuban gangs are getting better and better. We're fightin' a war on two fronts. If we make a peace pact with the black gang then we'll have the goddamn bastards outnumbered."

"I'm with Keith," interrupted a tall, muscular kid named Glen. "I don't want no niggers in this here gang," he drawled. "Besides, how you expect us to trust 'em? Most of these jungle bunnies don't even know who their daddy is. They all inbreed; makes 'em unstable and untrustworthy as hell."

Fighting back an urge to grab Glen, who was Keith's henchman and designated lackey, and shake him severely by the throat, Smitty continued. "We've already lost three guys when they got caught outnumbered; the last one got a knife stuck right between his ribs while at least five black gang members stood and watched. What do you prejudiced bastards have to say about that?"

"Smitty, this is a pointless discussion. You've been arguing this for the last hour and it's going nowhere. I'm the leader, and what I say goes, and I say no," Keith finished emphatically.

Smitty did a slow 360 of their meeting spot in a deserted warehouse barely two miles from downtown Miami, to get his emotions under control and think. He'd known that it would come down to an ultimatum from Keith, but the idea had to be brought up. Keith was the leader because he was the oldest, the biggest, and the meanest kid in their gang, not the smartest; he wasn't the world's most benign despot. Parliamentary debates and points of order were not his strong suit. Keith's rule remained: "If I don't understand it, we don't discuss it."

"I don't think we're quite through with this subject yet," said a voice with a French accent.

"We formed this merry little band for our own mutual protection," the speaker continued as he walked into the light, puffing on a cigarette that dangled rakishly from the corner of his mouth.

"This is not a black-white thing, gentlemen; it's a survival thing. Wars make strange bedfellows. Since we're in one and outnumbered, I don't think we can afford to be that choosy about screening our prospective allies. Smitty here has gone and made all the initial contacts, worked out agreements, and taken all the risks while we sit here on our fat asses and bitch. I think we should put it to a vote; my vote is in favor of the proposal. What about the rest of you guys?"

"Frenchy, we're not voting on anything," Keith said angrily. "I'm the leader, and I've already made my decision."

"Maybe it's time for a new leader, mon ami," Frenchy answered right back. "One, who, as Smitty so eloquently put it, and I quote: 'hasn't got his head up his ass,' end quote."

Frenchy was not as big as Keith, but though small framed, he was lightning quick and amazingly strong. The result of a wartime marriage between a French dancer and a New Orleans hustler temporarily turned soldier, Frenchy was a perfect union of the two. His mother's good looks and his father's smoothness had made him very popular with the young ladies and very unpopular with their fathers. One father in particular had had plans for Frenchy's future that had driven the boy to the streets of Miami.

He and Smitty had taken to each other immediately. It was Smitty who had lobbied for a change in the gang's membership rules to allow Frenchy's admission.

A feather landing on a Persian carpet would have sounded like a boilermakers' convention compared to the absolute quiet that followed Frenchy's challenge. Nobody moved, nobody talked, nobody breathed. Keith's reaction was predictable; the switchblade gleamed evilly, reflecting off the glazed, dingy windows of the skylights.

"Frenchy, you're a dead man," Keith hissed through clenched teeth. "You and Smitty have been causing trouble and questioning my authority since you joined, and now you're gonna pay. I hope you don't have any plans for the rest of your life, you mother-fuckers, 'cause you're gonna be dead in exactly one minute." Keith stalked toward them, waving the blade menacingly.

Frenchy had anticipated Keith's move. He'd pulled his belt, took two turns around the adjustment end, and was circling the buckle like diminutive David with his slingshot as he got set to take on mighty Goliath.

The fight was over almost before it began. Keith made a sweeping, off-balance thrust which Frenchy easily sidestepped, bringing the buckle across Keith's wrist with a deadly combination of strength and fear-induced adrenaline. The sound of wrist bones fracturing shattered the silence. Keith cried out in pain as he grabbed his useless right hand, dropping the knife in the process. Frenchy followed up the belt with a well-aimed kick to Keith's testicles and a solid punch that left little doubt that a visit to the dentist would definitely be in order.

The gang members, staring in stunned silence and disbelief, had not fully recovered from the main event when the sound of boxes being crushed and empty fifty-gallon drums being turned over announced that another bout was under way. Glen, who had planned to brain Frenchy with a length of pipe, had been interrupted by a flying kick from Smitty.

"Next!" Smitty shouted savagely to no one in particular as he and Frenchy assumed back-to-back positions, clearing their own blades in the process.

A minute passed, then another. They circled, still back-to-back, warily examining each gang member eye to eye until satisfied that the fight was truly over. With the passage of another minute, Smitty and Frenchy began to believe it.

The silence was broken by Jimmy, a tall, skinny kid with the biggest zit on his forehead that Smitty had ever seen and a set of buck teeth that made Bugs Bunny's seem like a minor overbite.

"Well, I guess we're desegregated," he said conversationally. "What orders, leader?" Leaving the question undirected, Smitty suspected, to see who would answer.

"Better ask Smitty," Frenchy said firmly. "He's running the show from now on."

"Why not you? You beat Keith," Jimmy asked.

"I might have beat Keith, but look who was paying attention to everything else while the fight was going on. We need somebody who's thinking all the time. I might be the brawn, but Smitty's the brains."

"What orders, leader?" The question was directed at Smitty from Tom, a short, compact kid with red hair and freckles.

"Break up and drift out of here a couple at a time so as not to upset the local heat. I'm going over to see LZ and tell him the outcome of our, um, meeting. Meet back here tomorrow at sundown, so we can get organized on how to jointly manage our territory."

"What about Keith and Glen?" Charlie, a gangly kid with horn-rimmed glasses and a four-inch knife scar on his jaw, nodded at the unconscious form of the former leader and the groggy form of his henchman.

Smitty was quiet for a moment, then answered. "Leave 'em; Glen can get whatever help Keith needs. If he can't, tough shit."

"As you say, leader," said an unrecognizable, fading voice. "As you say . . ."

"Thanks, Frenchy," Smitty said, as they walked alone back toward the housing development.

"Think nothing of it, mon ami." Frenchy waved a hand dismissively.

"Of course, I probably should brain you for sticking me with this goddamn mess," Smitty added irritably.

Frenchy shot a shrewd sideways glance at his friend, and answered earnestly. "I don't see what you're so pissed about. You're a better man for this job than that Neanderthal Keith and you know it. I've been in the gangs in Orleans; this is a different kind of war. We're not really fighting the Cubans, we're not fighting the blacks, we're fighting our own government and that stupid Cuban Subsidy Act."

"I have to admit you have a point."

"Of course I have a point, you asshole!" Frenchy boomed cheerfully, giving him a playful head slap.

"You understand the whole thing so well, you lead it," Smitty said.

Frenchy suddenly grabbed Smitty by the arm and spun him around until they were eye to eye—the fact that they were standing right in the middle of a busy street did not seem to faze Frenchy in the least.

"Now you listen to me, mon ami; we'll not speak of this again. If this was just a gang war, then you're right, I would lead it, but it's much more than that. This is going to be settled by negotiation, not by force. You're always thinking ahead; you rehearse situations in your mind and then react instinctively when the need arises. That's what we need now: forethought, planning, and careful negotiation. Charging around like a stampede of wild horses will only lead to further useless injuries and death. Your challenge is to straighten this mess out, not inflame it. To negotiate a peace, not arm for war. To show these guys how to live, not teach them how to die."

Smitty was silent for a long time, he'd no idea how long. Truth, honest truth, is such a rare commodity that when it's heard, the time to digest and understand it becomes an insignificant entity. Smitty nodded slowly to himself—not only in understanding, but in acceptance—and without a word, turned toward the black district with a purposeful step.

"Smitty?" Frenchy called after him solemnly. "I just hope you're up to it, man."

"So do I," Smitty murmured to himself without turning around. "So do I."

Smitty smiled in sudden reflection as memories of a happier time invaded his thoughts unexpectedly. The happier time that had sneaked up from the darkest recesses of his mind had been Christmas 1960. They were a family of four then; now they were only three—and in those days, before his similarities to his father began to be increasingly obvious—he was still known as Kevin.

Mom had left England on January 4, 1961, to visit her family in the States for two weeks as planned. From there, life became a series of unattached coincidences.

First, Mom's father had become ill and she had decided to remain stateside for another month until he recovered from a bout with pneumonia. A month quickly spread to two, then three, as complications set in.

Mom was not halfway through her problems when Dad and other selected NCOs and officers from all over England were suddenly pulled out of their current duty station on forty-eight hours' notice and reassigned to Rhein Main Air Force Base in West Germany.

The next three months contained a series of alerts, war games, and nuclear simulations that basically amounted to nothing more than diplomatic chess between the Soviet Union and the United States regarding the current state of affairs in Berlin. Unfortunately, the military served as the pawns, and even worse, uncharacteristically, the families were brought along and billeted in temporary quarters at leased hotels. Time hung heavy on their hands as the cold war heated up over the Bay of Pigs and yet more tensions in Berlin. Three months became five.

As five months became six, the events, and the reasons behind them, became clear. Dad was the NCO in charge of assuring that the expedited schedule for getting all Titans operational in West Germany was achieved. Dad and the other NCOs were rarely seen at home. So little in fact, that the standing joke was that any wife who became pregnant during this time must be having an affair; the husbands had not been "in residence" enough to "take care of their homework."

Dad had a hotel suite, with both sons bunked across the hall in a room. Since Dad was rarely there, care and feeding was assumed jointly by all of the wives of other NCOs. When school began, buses were provided to take the dependent children to the local school at the base. Playmates were each other or the local kids who lived around the hotel. Social activities were confined to within the hotel itself or occasional bus outings to the base, always with the caveat that the air force NCO at the desk know where they were going, who they were going with, and when they would be back. The net effect was that the families lived day to day in a constant state of tension, never knowing what would happen next.

Next, in this instance, became a ten-month stop back in England—first at Lakenheath Air Force Base for six months for something called European Operational Simulation—followed by a return to Dearfield for four months to complete the tour in May of '62.

Dad was given an all-day sendoff by the American command. Chuck Martin, the former commanding officer and present base commander of Lakenheath, flew up for the going-away party. In Dad's honor, he brought along a group of his former flying buddies who put on a precision air show that dazzled the onlookers.

A country fair jet jockey in his own right, Chuck did not fly with them. He was now a brigadier general and had told everyone within hearing distance that it was time he started to act like an officer and a gentleman. Chuck obviously was extremely selective in what constituted the definition of proper behavior; at the party that night, resplendent in grass skirt, he had been declared the winner of the hula contest.

Although Dad had smiled and been pleasant throughout the entire time, he'd never fully relaxed and enjoyed himself. Mom had not come back to join them when they returned from Germany. Although Dad put on his best face in describing the decision as a joint agreement, there was no way to hide the disappointment in his face. Dad would not talk about the subject at all. When pressed, he always said that she was stateside taking care of her ailing father. "And besides," he'd add in a mischievous voice that didn't quite come off, "us guys enjoy batching it." Nothing could have been further from the truth.

This sobering reality set in when they were packing to return to the United States. Dad's next assignment was to be Homestead Air Force Base south of Miami, Florida. Several of the key NCOs, technicians, and officers from Dearfield were also headed to the same south Florida installation.

On the surface, they were simply a group of veteran servicemen, who, it was assumed, knew how to finagle the system and move together from one base to the next. The fact that their special skills in missile technology might be useful in light of goings-on in Castro's Cuba was not being admitted to by anyone, least of all Dad.

Curiously, General Martin was not joining them. When his assignment in Great Britain was completed, he was to be posted to the Pentagon, responsible for assessing combat readiness and operational morale for the entire southern United States.

Dad always said that the military was the "world's biggest family," in that you might soldier with someone in one location, then run into him again ten years later at another post and pick up right where you left off. Kevin had a feeling that they'd cross paths with the general again.

But, more importantly, what Kevin and Billy had long suspected was now a reality: Mom was not coming back. When packing for the trip home, Dad had separated Mom's personal effects and had them shipped to her parents' house in Atlanta, while the balance of their possessions was sent directly to Florida.

Nothing was said about divorce because evidently there was not to be one. When questioned, Dad replied simply that they were living apart.

"That's far enough, honky," the unseen voice commanded, snapping Smitty back to reality. "State your business."

"I want to see LZ," Smitty stated flatly.

"Well, he don't want to see you, or any other honky muthafucka'; now clear out and don't come back."

"Listen, stupid, you're just the night watchman. If I had the time or energy, I'd dig you out of your hidey-hole, slap the living shit out of you, carve you up with my blade, then toss your remains in Biscayne Bay. Now why don't you be a good little boy, and run along and tell your 'brutha' that Smitty wants to see his black ass," Smitty snarled.

Footsteps echoed hollowly down the alley to the right as the unseen guard trotted away, presumably to get his leader. Five minutes passed before the footsteps could be heard again, only this time it was not the soloist of before; it sounded like an entire orchestra.

"This better be worthwhile, honky."

"You must be LZ," Smitty ventured. "I'm Smitty, the leader of the NonComs; we need to talk."

"I thought Keith was the leader," LZ said curtly.

"He was."

"Well, what happened?"

"Slipped on a bar of soap in the shower," Smitty said with a smile.

"Lot of that going around just now." There was no mistaking the malevolent smile and the deadly intent behind it. "You said we need to talk; about what?"

"About getting together."

"Getting what together?" LZ asked with suspicion.

Smitty rubbed his chin thoughtfully. "Getting our gangs together; joining forces, if you will."

LZ snorted contemptuously. "You must be out of your fucking mind, man!"

"It must be the way I put this suggestion across that upsets people so much," Smitty observed sadly, shaking his head in dismay. "Keith's reaction was about the same as yours."

"You don't expect me to believe you're serious about this fucking idea, do you?"

"What other reason would I have for coming here?" Smitty asked.

"What reason indeed? I'll give you credit, white boy, you've got a lotta guts for even coming here. The last white meat that wandered onto our territory wound up sliced like a Thanksgiving turkey." He gave Smitty an appraising stare. "There must have been some small amount of discussion with the rest of the NonComs before you strolled over to offer this little treaty."

"Yeah, little bit," Smitty conceded. "Little bit."

"How in the hell did you ever get them to agree with this?"

Usually, curiosity killed the cat, but in this case, it might save this little pussy's ass. If Smitty could get him talking, and then thinking, there might be a chance. "Well, not to put too fine a point on this, but, I, um, sort of gave them the idea that the deal was already made."

"You what!" LZ interrupted incredulously.

"Now hold on! Hold on!" Smitty raised his hands. "Let me explain."

"Explain nothing, you motherfucker," LZ shouted. "I'll kill you myself."

Before Smitty could even think about reacting, the knife cleared LZ's pocket and in the same motion made a sweeping pass at Smitty's head. He tilted his head sideways and back in a desperate attempt at avoiding having his throat cut. He just about made it; the very end of the switchblade caught him just below the right jaw, slashing an incision about two inches in length and at least a eighth of an inch deep.

By Smitty's rough calculations, he was encircled by at least thirty dudes, all of whom were preparing to play follow their leader. If Smitty were forced to bet on the chances of surviving the next two minutes on himself or a milk cow caught in the middle of a school of piranha, he'd take every last cent he could beg, borrow, or steal and put it squarely on Bessy's nose.

A voice from the not-so-distant past was making itself heard in his mind. Thoughts about how to handle fear, what to do when you're afraid, and that sometimes when there is no solution, that in itself, is a solution. He'd a plan; it was not, he had to admit, much of a plan, but since there was no other solution, and he was going to die, he figured insanity was as good a defense as any.

"Well, gentleman," Smitty said cheerfully, "Looks like I'm going to die here, so how about I invite a few of you along for the ride?"

"This dumb son of a bitch is nuts," a kid standing to LZ's right said. "Let's kill the crazy bastard."

"Yeah, let's kill the crazy bastard!" Smitty repeated. Screwing up his face in what he hoped would pass for a wild and psychotic expression as he produced his own weapon, he brought the four-inch blade into view with a press of the thumb switch.

"And by the time you're done killing me, I'll have killed a couple of you, and that will just solve everything won't it? Then," he continued, waving his switchblade wildly with a crazed expression, "my guys will come over here, kill a couple more of you, you'll kill a couple of them, and then for good measure, the Cubans will pick off half a dozen of us both.

"While we're busy killing off each other, what happens to our dollies who depend on us for protection from the common enemy?" Smitty asked, surveying the group, looking for any sign, no matter how small, that his words were having an effect. "And what happens to our territories while we fight it out?

"Less than an hour ago, Frenchy and I gave our reasons to the NonComs and the same ones apply to you: This is not a black-white thing, gentlemen, it's a survival thing. Wars make strange bedfellows. Since we're in one and outnumbered, I don't think we can afford to be that choosy about screening our prospective allies. If you dumb asses can't see that, then stick it right here." Smitty ripped open his T-shirt and pointed to his heart, daring any one of them to step up and be the first.

LZ approached, and slowly brought his switchblade up in the direction of Smitty's heart. Smitty flinched instinctively in anticipation of being mortally wounded. Instants passed like hours before he realized that the sudden jerk he'd felt was not a thrusting incision; it was LZ cutting a rather generous length off of what had been his shirt, folding it into a crude bandage, and applying it with surprising tenderness to the knife wound that was bleeding profusely, changing most of what was left of his white T-shirt to red.

"You're not only the ballsiest son of a bitch I've ever met, you're also the craziest bastard in Dade County," LZ said. "There's only two things that stop me from killing you now: one, what you said might be, I repeat—might be—true, and second," he paused for effect, and smiled acidly, "you'd probably come back to haunt me, just for the fun of it.

"Take off. We'll discuss your idea amongst ourselves. I'll meet you tomorrow at your expressway underpass at 6:00 PM and tell you what we decide. You'll guarantee safe passage into your territory and back out again."

"You have my word," Smitty replied solemnly.

"I believe you. You'll be safe leaving here, too." As they shook hands and he was escorted away, Smitty overheard LZ muttering to himself in wonderment. "Do you believe that crazy son of a bitch? Went to his own gang and announced a treaty between us, and didn't even bother to tell us first. He's either the stupidest or the smartest idiot I ever seen; I wonder which."

Smitty walked away, wondering when his luck would run out.

"Daaaaad!" Billy screamed as he ran into his dad's bedroom. "Come take a look at Kevin; he's bleeding."

The bedsprings creaked as Dad bounced off and came running into the living room.

"Let me take a look at that, son," Dad said, as he tilted Kevin's head to examine the wound.

"I think we'd better get you on down to the hospital; that gash looks as though it'll take a couple of dozen stitches to close." Dad went about the apartment gathering up shirt and shoes and collecting his wallet and keys. If he was excited, no trace of it was evident.

"What happened to my little baby brother? Not so tough after all?" Billy asked spitefully. "If all those gangs you hang out with are made up of pussies like you, no wonder you got knifed. You probably think you're a tough little shit, but I can still take you with one hand."

"Why don't you go fuck yourself," Kevin hissed in a low voice so that only Billy would hear.

"I'll tell you how it happened," Billy continued in a voice loud enough for Dad to hear. "He was hanging around with those hood friends of his, and he probably smarted off to one of them and got stuck. Serves him right."

"Billy, shut up," Dad said sharply. "How it happened is not important right now. There'll be plenty of time for that later. What's important at the moment is to get your brother to a hospital."

"Sure," Billy said. "You always stick up for Kevin, no matter what he does. But if I so much as look at you sideways, you slap the crap out of me. Well, I'm tired of this and want to go and live with Mom in Georgia."

"Son," Dad replied wearily, "we'll discuss this some other time. Right now, I want you to go across the hall and stay with Mrs. Langston until I get back, understand?"

"Yes, sir."

"I meant what I said, Billy; we'll discuss this when I get back," Dad said, patting Billy on the arm and motioning him to leave.

"I'm looking forward to it," Billy said, storming out of the apartment ahead of Dad and Kevin.

The neighborhood being what it was, before Kevin climbed into the Hillman, he surveyed the surrounding parking lot with practiced eye, searching for any signs of unfriendly activity; his surveillance ended at their dingy two-bedroom apartment on the southwest side of Miami. There were more than two hundred apartments in the complex, all uniformly awful, but with widely diverse inhabitants.

The predominant ethnic group was Cuban, outnumbering the blacks by a two to one margin; whites were a distant third. Most of the Cubans were refugees; either before Castro or after, it didn't appear to make much difference. The common bond was poverty and survival, both of which were root causes of tensions on the street, and they had the lowest spot on that food chain locked up. Far from home, isolated and alone, in a world of unfamiliar customs and language, the Cubans had long ago forsaken basic human dignity in an all-out effort to survive.

Recognizing their economic and social disadvantages, the U.S. government had passed the Cuban Subsidy Act with great fanfare and the best of intentions. It was supposed to help the Cuban people get on their feet economically, by matching, with federal funds, the salary of newly employed Cuban nationals for the first six months from their date of hire. There was, however, a major flaw in the thought process: The lawmakers, in their infinite wisdom, forgot to take into account the unspoken law of American capitalism—greed.

Because of language and other barriers, the only jobs that the majority of the Cubans were qualified to do were low-paying, nonskilled manual labor; these were the self-same jobs that were the backbone of the American teenager's cash flow. In record time, the local businessmen realized that they could hire the Cubans for about half what their American counterparts would cost. This set in motion an escalating series of events that had now become uncontrollable.

It started slowly. Teen bewilderment at the sudden lack of jobs turned to frustrated anger as the reason for it became clear. Appeals to local businessmen were unsuccessful because, as they said, "You can't blame us; we're businessmen, and if we can reduce costs by hiring cheaper help, we're gonna do it. Besides, these Cubans want to work, not like most of you spoiled Americans who show up late and lazy."

The frustration led to taunting, which inevitably turned to violence. Scattered incidents of shoving and pushing were followed closely by bouts of fisticuffs. Events escalated alarmingly when one of these bouts of fisticuffs ended in a death—the result of one badly outnumbered and frightened Cuban teen who, fearing for the life of his date, had pulled a knife, and in the process of waving it menacingly, accidentally slashed the throat of a white American counterpart.

In the telling and retelling of the incident, the accidental slashing became a brutal stabbing. Resentment and anger on both sides grew, as did the number of violent confrontations.

Inevitably, gangs and territories formed, ostensibly for protection. Since "The Fucking Act" as it came to be called had been passed two years earlier, there had been half a dozen white deaths, as many again black, and at least twice that for the Cubans, the majority in the last six months. The fuse was already lit and sizzling toward the dynamite at record pace; one more incident, and it would blow.

"Dad, where are you taking me?" Smitty asked.

"To the hospital at the base."

"Won't they ask a lot of questions about this?"

"Probably will, I expect."

"What are you going to tell them?"

"The question is not what I'm going to tell them, but rather, what you're going to tell them."

"Yeah," Smitty nodded wearily. "Been thinkin' about that myself."

"I bet you have, son. Anything you'd like to rehearse on me first?"

"Nothing that you'd believe."

"Oh, I don't know about that," Dad said easily. "Pretty smart you know; been around a long time; long enough to recognize a knife wound. In fact, I'll bet if you tell me the truth, I might be able to help you come up with a good alibi."

"But you just said that I got this from a knife, and that is the truth," Smitty replied in a puzzled voice.

"That's not the truth I'm after, Smitty, and you know it," Dad said firmly.

"Why did you call me Smitty?"

"Unless my sources are incorrect, that's now how you're addressed. Any of your buddies in the NonComs know you as Kevin?" To Kevin's incredulous stare, Dad admonished with a smile, "As I said, son, pretty smart, you know."

"But if you know what I'm doing, then you know the truth."

"I know the whats from the police and the neighborhood scuttlebutt; what I'd like to hear from you is the whys."

"You seem to be pretty well-informed already," Smitty conceded.

"Intelligence is the first arm of warfare."

"You know the Cuban Subsidy Act—" Smitty began.

"You mean 'The Fucking Act'?"

"Yeah, that's the one. That's what started all the trouble. Now it's gotten out of control. The whites are fighting the blacks, and both are fighting the Cubans."

"So which one of them gave you that little souvenir? And more importantly, why?" Dad nodded at the makeshift patch on his chin.

"One of the black guys," Smitty said morosely, then added cynically as an afterthought. "I was trying to do the right thing and propose a peace treaty with him."

"Why a peace treaty?"

"It's the only solution that I can think of to try to stop the violence. If we can't change the act, at least we can try to live with it. If we make peace with the blacks, then neither one of us will be fighting on two fronts. Maybe we can protect each other's rears."

"That's pretty smart for a fifteen-year-old. You've thought it out well. Don't be too surprised, though, if events don't go as you planned," Dad said thoughtfully.

"Why?"

"Son, I've been involved in countless missions in World War II and Korea, and I can tell you from experience that things seldom happen as you plan. The smart man hedges his bets. After the first shot is fired, success is often the result of a set of options well thought out in advance, with survival the reward for that particular brand of initiative."

"Are you telling me, without telling me, that you approve of what I'm doing?" Smitty asked.

"No, indeed. What I'd like to see is for you to concentrate on your studies at Bayside High, take a serious interest in your trumpet like your brother has his saxophone, and have other normal teenage experiences. But a man can run away from everyone and everything except the face he shaves in the mirror every morning—in your case, peach fuzz with a wet towel." Dad chuckled lightly and brushed Kevin's chin affectionately.

"As you yourself just said, you've chosen to fight for what you think is right. As long as your motive is to stop and prevent, and you're aware of the personal risks involved when you buck the system, no matter how much it hurts me personally, I can find no valid reason to intervene."

"What do you mean by buck the system?" Smitty asked.

"When you have evaluated the facts and come to a different conclusion than the consensus, and continue to support those beliefs in the face of pressure to give in, then that's bucking the system.

"In your case, most people—your brother, the police, the neighbors—consider you a hoodlum. As I said, if you are aware of their feelings and are strong enough to stand tall for what you believe, and your aims are pure, it's not my place to stop you.

"Now," Dad said, abruptly changing the subject as they drove through the Homestead Main entrance and turned in to the hospital. "What are you going to tell the doctor about that gash on your chin?"

"Oh, I guess I'm going to tell them that I—"

"Slipped on a bar of soap in the shower," Dad growled resignedly, shaking his head in dismay, as he harmonized with his son. "You know, in my twenty-five-plus years in the service, I came up with a name for characters like you."

"What's that?"

"Incorrigible."

"Guess I'm just a chip off the ol' block," Smitty grinned.

"You're all of that," Dad said, as they got out of the car. "Maybe even a little bit more." He put his arm around his son and hugged him in an uncharacteristic display of public affection as they walked toward the hospital.

"I came to talk, white man," LZ said, as he and Smitty shook hands perfunctorily. "Before we can agree on a peace pact, my guys have several, um, suggestions that they'd like to see added to whatever set of rules you honkies have in place."

"Such as?" Smitty asked suspiciously, as similar murmurs of mistrust rippled through the white gang.

"Well, the first thing is a common name; you're the NonComs and we're the Black Knights. We need a new name that works for both of us."

"Got anything in mind?"

"Hey, man, that's your department; you white guys are supposed to have the big brains. Us black guys only got the big balls." LZ said, grabbing his crotch and grinning smugly.

"This might be the shortest fucking union in history, asshole!" Smitty snarled.

"You might be right, white man!" LZ said curtly, as the blade cleared his pocket, opened, and arched in Smitty's direction.

Smitty had seen that move before—less than twenty-four hours ago—and had a twenty-eight-stitch incision to prove it. The knife passed cleanly overhead as Smitty dropped to one knee and then drove his right fist squarely underneath LZ's rib cage, causing him to gasp involuntarily as the force of the blow dislodged the air from his lungs faster than a pinpricked balloon.

They came expecting to finalize the loose ends of a peace pact. This unplanned turn of events had caught both groups so completely by surprise that no one reacted at all; they stood dead still and waited expectantly to see what the two leaders would do next.

The force of the blow dropped LZ to one knee as he labored to breathe. But Smitty suspected that LZ was faking. The rasping was forced and sounded unnatural.

Smitty's premonitions were well-founded. Microseconds later, LZ exploded from his crouched position, driving murderously upward with the knife.

Using speed he'd never known he had, Smitty sidestepped the thrust, allowed the knife to pass cleanly under his right arm, then trapped LZ's wrist between his arm and side. Since step one was a success, Smitty immediately applied step two: he hit LZ behind the right elbow with all the strength he could muster with a left uppercut, momentarily paralyzing LZ's entire right hand, and causing him to drop the knife.

Smitty released LZ, backed away, and said, "Look partner, don't you think this has gone far enough?"

"Not yet, you motherfucking son of a bitch!" LZ shouted. He suddenly spun around, tugged a gun from inside the coat of one his lieutenants, arced it over the top, cocked it, and lowered it slowly and deliberately. Smitty's heart stopped; his breath caught in his throat as he watched the .38 complete its final sighting: Smitty's head.

It never made it. A short, muscular arm intercepted the weapon before it could lock in on its target, pushed LZ's arm straight up, and slid a finger underneath the trigger, rendering the firing mechanism unworkable. A voice said conversationally, "Commissioned Knights."

"What did you say?" LZ and Smitty demanded in unison as they involuntarily snapped their heads in the direction of the voice.

"Commissioned Knights, mes amis," Frenchy said through gritted teeth, struggling to hold his leverage against LZ. "That's the name for our new gang. It has a part of both of our gangs and, if you think about it, represents just what we're trying to do."

"What the fuck are you talking about, man?" LZ yelled as he snatched the gun out of Frenchy's grasp and held it aloft in firing position.

"You explain it to him, Smitty. Maybe the stupid idiot will listen to you," Frenchy said.

"He's right, man; don't you get it?" Seeing LZ's confusion, Smitty continued. "Look, protecting our territory is what we're both after, right?"

"Yeah, right; so?"

"So, didn't you ever read books? Protection is for our mutual safety against a common enemy; our aim is defensive protection, sorta like them knights at King Arthur's court. And since we're taking on the additional job of protecting our families and friends we've 'commissioned' ourselves for the job."

"Commissioned Knights," LZ nodded in understanding. "You're right, it's perfect." He handed the gun back to its original carrier.

Smitty decided he'd never met anyone like LZ. His rage seemed to be a volcano that he could turn on and off at will.

"You're pretty quick for a white man," LZ said, rubbing his right arm to restore circulation.

"Must be all them big brains," Smitty said acidly.

The body went rigid and the stare turned cold for an instant, before LZ grinned cheerfully. "No, in your case, I think it's them big balls. You sure there ain't some black blood in your family somewhere?" Members of both gangs laughed, and LZ said, "You know Smitty, I think this can work out after all."

"Depends on what other suggestions you've got."

LZ huddled with his gang for several moments then turned back to Smitty. "You and I plan everything together?"

"Yep."

"I run my guys; you run yours?"

Smitty nodded.

"One of my guys in trouble, your guys come to help?"

"And vice versa," Frenchy added.

LZ nodded in return and asked, "Your terms?"

"Everything you said, plus one," Smitty responded flatly. "You, representing your gang, have to pass our initiation test; which is to steal a car."

"If you lard-ass white guys could do it, I can, too. You got a deal, white man." He and Smitty shook hands to the chorus of cheers from members of both gangs.

"Just as long as you guys don't try to use our bathrooms," said the tall, skinny black kid with the gun.

"Shit, man! That all you want? When you said initiation, I thought you had something tough in mind; but if all you want is for me to steal a car, no sweat," LZ said, after the laughter died down.

"Oh yeah, asshole. If you think it's so easy, maybe we should make the requirements a little tougher," Jimmy said.

"Makes no never mind to me; anything you can come up with, I can handle."

Jimmy wasn't quick on the uptake. He was unprepared for debate with people he'd been raised to believe were socially and intellectually inferior.

Smitty started to intervene, thought better of it, and decided to watch and see what would happen. If the blacks were to become an integral part of the gang, instead of mere window dressing, the rest of the group was going to have to accept them as equals first.

"Well, um, I, ah—"

"Oh lawdy mercy sir, yo' sho' has got a hat full of ideas," LZ mimicked, in his best Uncle Remus voice. "Why, I's just a poor ol' black boy, but I's can sholy see when I's in the company of a much smarter person dan myself."

"You going to let him talk to me like that?" Jimmy turned to Smitty for support.

"You started it; you finish it."

"Keith would have stuck a knife up his ass for talking to a white man like that," Jimmy grumbled.

"If you think that's the appropriate course of action, be my guest," Smitty said easily as he flipped open his knife and held it out by the blade end in Jimmy's direction.

"Tell you what Jimbo," LZ said, breaking the uncomfortable silence—and more importantly, taking Jimmy off the spot. "You pick out the kind of car you like best, and that's the one I'll steal."

"A Corvette," Jimmy said defiantly. At least that was his intent. LZ was reputed to be the fastest man on the west side with a blade; Jimmy's eyes betrayed his relief at having avoided a confrontation with him.

"Any particular color?"

"I always wanted a red one."

"Consider it done, man," LZ said confidently as he patted Jimmy on the shoulder, getting a nod and a nervous smile in response.

As the meeting broke up, people began to drift away in groups of three or four until only Smitty and Frenchy were left. "You know, Frenchy," Smitty said thoughtfully, "that gun introduces a whole new element to this."

"I was just thinking the same thing myself," Frenchy admitted. "Knives and clubs are one thing, but guns are an altogether different matter. We must be cautious."

"We must indeed," Smitty agreed. But he suspected in his heart that the fuse in the automatic detonation sequence had already been lit and that events would propel towards the inevitable explosion. As with most explosions, there would be no winners. Just those left alive and those who were dead.

The phone rang at 7:30 PM in Smitty's apartment. Billy answered, listened, and turned and tossed the receiver to Smitty with a sour comment of, "There's some nigger on the phone for you. It's not bad enough that you got to hang out with those 'friends' of yours, now you're not only hanging out with the spooks, but you're letting them call just like they belong here."

"What's the matter, brother? 'Fraid my hanging around with them might cause you to lose your social standing at the yacht club?" Smitty shot back as he put the phone to his ear and dismissed his brother by turning away.

"Your brother sounds like a real asshole, man," LZ said.

"Certified."

"Would you like me to have him meet some of the brothers up close and personal?"

"Naw, that won't be necessary. Some people are born to be assholes; others grow up to be one." Smitty smiled a knowing smile at his uncomprehending brother, who'd no way of knowing how close he'd come to getting the shit kicked out of him, and would never have believed that Smitty had actively averted it. "What's up?"

"Can you be at the bowl at 8:00 PM?"

"What for?"

"Hey, man, you're the one who thought up this crazy entry requirement. I'm gonna take down the 'Vette and figured that a couple of you guys ought to be present to learn how it's done."

"Cocky son of a bitch, aren't you?"

"Guilty on both counts, man."

"Okay, we'll be there." Smitty hung up, grabbed his coat, and was halfway out of the apartment when Billy called him back.

"Better watch your ass, little brother," Billy began as he walked over and stood directly in front of him. "I overheard some of the guys at school talking. That guy you got into it with a couple of days back is planning revenge."

"You mean Keith?" Smitty asked sharply.

"I didn't catch the name, but I think that's the one. He's heard about the thing with the blacks and is stirring up all the other kids, and spreading stories about you that even I can't believe are true. I asked Dad about this; he said he'd rather not discuss it, because he knew you were headed for trouble, but he didn't know how to stop it. He said you were like a plane that flames out fifty feet off the runway. A crash is a forgone conclusion; all that can be done at this point is to try to survive the impact."

"Thanks for the warning, brother," Smitty said sarcastically.

"If that's the thanks I get, that's the last time I'll try to help you, shit head."

"If you really want to help, come with me now," Smitty said.

"Why? So I can waste my time, get all busted up, and maybe lose my life championing a lost cause? I'd rather go surfing."

"And you probably always will," Smitty said sadly, making no effort to conceal his anger and disgust as he brushed his brother aside and slammed the door. There was something not right about his brother. Smitty could feel it. He just couldn't put his finger on it . . . yet.

"Where the hell is he? It's 8:15!"

"Easy partner, he'll be along," Frenchy said patiently.

"This guy is wacko. Hell, man, the deal is to steal a ride, not take some bigwig's prized sports car," Smitty said.

The red convertible glistened in the streetlights of the deserted parking lot. The damn thing was visible for 150 yards in all directions. If LZ was fixing to borrow this beauty, he had his work cut out for him.

"Look," Frenchy said, pointing across the lot at a figure emerging from the shadows. "I don't fucking believe it."

Neither Smitty nor Frenchy were sure who it was at first and, when they did recognize him, they weren't sure that they wanted to.

LZ wasn't walking in the direction of his target; he was strutting, with one of those new transistor radios glued to his ear, and he was dressed more like a south side pimp than a car thief.

He sashayed up to the car, produced a coat hanger, slid it through the weather-stripping, and was inside in three seconds flat. Just as quickly, he popped the hood, produced from his pocket a three-foot length of wire with the insulation stripped back an inch, wrapped it around the terminal of the coil, and was in the process of connecting it to the solenoid screw on the starter when a police cruiser rounded the corner and pulled up alongside.

"What are you doing, boy?" the officer asked, stepping out of the car and shining his footlong flashlight directly in LZ's eyes.

"Shit man! Get that fuckin' light outta' my face," LZ said indignantly. "It's bad enough that I go and shell out all my girls' hard-earned cash for a honkymobile so's I can keep up my image, but then to have a damn starter problem on my brand new ride and have to hot-wire it," LZ continued shaking his head in disgust, "and then to get rousted by a badge with an attitude problem for us brothers. I tell ya, man."

"Uh huh, just show me your license and registration so I can make sure you own this car, and I'll be on my way."

"Here, man," LZ said, passing across his license with his registration paper clipped to it. "What do you think I'm trying to do, steal my own ride? Besides man, I bet you wouldn't hassle a white dude like you hassling me."

"Take it easy, kid. I'm not trying to hassle you, just doing my job." The officer looked at his registration, made a note in his notebook, and passed it back, his last traces of suspicion vanishing.

"Okay, man. It's cool," LZ conceded. "Now, since we're blood brothers and shit like that, why don't you let me borrow that flash, so I can see how to connect this wire to the starter and jump this dude off."

LZ took the light, produced his blade, and used it to jump across the starter to solenoid terminals. As the car turned over, LZ quickly closed the hood and his knife, returning the light to the cop as he slid behind the wheel.

"That's some knife you carry, son; borders on being illegal."

"You know how it is in my line of work, man. Gotta protect my girls from the competition."

"Keep it between the white lines," the officer said, patting the car door. He got into his patrol vehicle and drove away.

"Man, that was unreal!" Smitty said, running up to the car. "How the hell did you get a driver's license and papers so fast?"

"Ain't no big thing, white boy," LZ said with a superior smile. "Didn't nobody ever tell you honkies about the old man over on 64th?"

"I've seen some nervy people in my day, but I have to admit, that was the smoothest move I've ever seen," Frenchy echoed when he joined them seconds later, after pausing at the building long enough to be sure the police had truly gone.

"Ain't you ever heard of 'The Purloined Letter'? The best way to hide something—or steal it—is do it right up front."

Smitty and Frenchy gaped at LZ, who said acidly: "Hey man, don't you white guys ever read books, poems, and shit like that? C'mon, climb in, and let's take this sucker out to the Rickenbacker Causeway and see what she'll do."

As they drove away, LZ asked, "How come you two were the only ones to come witness my grand act of larceny?"

"Nobody else wanted to come," Smitty answered truthfully.

"Glad you guys came," LZ said seriously. "Glad you cared enough; never had friends like that; think maybe I do now."

As the car accelerated onto the causeway, Smitty felt a closeness to his friends that owed nothing to cramped quarters. Frenchy must have been on the same wavelength. "Except for Smitty, neither have I."

Smitty felt that his two compadres were waiting for him to say something also. He quickly discarded his first thought as corny; then suddenly, Dad's thoughts about bucking the system and believing in something came back to him. On reflection, his original thought didn't sound too bad at that.

"You know," he said thoughtfully, "I've got a feeling that the three of us are going to be friends for a long time."

"Yeah, man," LZ quipped. "Like the married couples say; 'til death do us part."

"We could always get divorced," Frenchy said.

"No way, man," LZ said solemnly. "It would have to be death."

Smitty had an uneasy feeling that LZ was right.

Death it was. But it didn't happen to LZ or Frenchy, it happened all around them. Billy had been right about Dad's premonition, Smitty about his earlier feelings. The burning fuse had reached the dynamite; the resulting explosion spared no one on the west side from the concussion or aftershock.

Strangely enough, Armageddon occurred while LZ, Frenchy, and Smitty were joyriding in their "loaned car," which they conveniently left where it could be easily discovered—in the mayor's parking spot at city hall. After a quick stroll along the hotel shores, they were returning to the neighborhood when the lights and sounds of a police crime scene a block away lured them.

"Well, if it isn't the west side's answer to Attila the Hun," Detective Wallace said cynically in greeting to Smitty as they approached. "Since when did you gentleman of the white persuasion take to running with your darker counterparts?"

The detective, who with elevator shoes could just manage the five-foot-eight-inch height he claimed, was in his twenties; he was lean, average looking, and had brown kinky hair and a permanent sneer on his face. He looked too young to have a gold shield, especially considering his cynical, disrespectful attitude toward older superiors, and it was said he was not well-liked or trusted by other members of the force who disagreed with his intolerant stance on the youth gangs.

"It's the environment we live in, sir," Frenchy said in his most dignified and formal manner. "We run together because we're afraid of muggers, or cops who don't know the difference between the law and the truth. As for our darker friend here, it was the lesser of two evils."

"What are you talking about, asshole?"

"Smitty here gave me a choice," Frenchy continued in his most eloquent style. "Said I could either allow my sister to date a police detective or make friends with the blacks." Frenchy put his arm around LZ, grinned evilly, and said, "It wasn't even close."

"Why you little bastard," the detective said, reaching out to grab Frenchy, who slapped his arm away like it was a pesky fly.

"That'll do, Detective," a voice commanded from behind.

"Evening, boys," the voice belonged to the chief of homicide detectives, Stanley Baker, a dumpy twenty-something-year veteran of the force with a kind face, a balding forehead, a belly that was losing its battle not to sag over his belt buckle, and an easygoing demeanor that was surprisingly effective. Rumor had it that his laid-back approach to his job was due to losing it on one too many missions during the war. Stan the Man, as he was called after the St. Louis baseball great, was well-liked and highly respected—on the force and on the street. He was a tough man, but one known to be a straight shooter.

"It's convenient that you're here; I was just going to have you, um, picked up and escorted over here. Come with me, please. Detective," Baker nodded in dismissal at the detective who walked quietly away, but not before giving LZ, Frenchy, and Smitty a glacial look.

"I don't think he likes me very much," Smitty said sadly.

"I don't think he likes anyone very much," Stanley responded cynically. And almost as an afterthought, "Especially you, kid!" He pointed his finger at Smitty.

Baker led them around to the alley behind the abandoned building and announced to the miscellaneous cast of policemen, "Clear the crime scene out. I want to talk to these guys alone."

As the policemen were moving away about thirty yards outside the cordons, Smitty surveyed the area. There were two lumps on the ground covered by tarps. One appeared to be a body; the other looked more like a tent with a singular pole in the middle.

"I thought you gentleman might save me a lot of time in identification," he said, yanking the tarp off the first lump.

He no longer needed a tube of Clearasil for his acne or a dentist for his buckteeth because most of his face was gone. But, there was enough for Smitty to see a big zit on the forehead and know that Jimmy would never own that red Corvette.

Jimmy had died in agony. He'd been systematically beaten to death with a two-pound sledgehammer—the steel end of which was directly where the jawbone should have been; the handle, however, was curiously missing. Smitty had never in his life seen a body so horribly disfigured. It wasn't a body at all, just a mass of twisted bones and flesh thrown haphazardly in a bloody pile.

"Know him?" Baker asked heavily.

"Yeah," Smitty replied woodenly, fighting back the urge to throw up. "It's Jimmy, one of the kids from our building."

"You mean your gang," Baker corrected , dropping the tarp back in place and proceeding to the next one.

Smitty glanced quickly at his friends and could see clearly that he was not the only one who was nauseated. Both LZ and Frenchy looked as bad as he felt right now, and as the captain started to lift the next tarp, Smitty knew the worst was yet to come.

His instincts were on target, so was his inquisitiveness. The second body was not so disfigured, but she too had died violently.

Facedown, bent over a small round barrel, lay the naked body of Gena, Jimmy's girlfriend. Just visible between her spread legs was the protruding end of the hammer handle; it didn't require an awful lot of imagination to conclude where the other end was. A four foot, one-inch diameter steel rod had been inserted in her rectum, driven completely through her body, and embedded in the filling cap hole in the center of the barrel, impaling her in this ghastly position. A small pennant was attached to the rod. A slight gust of wind caused it to flap open; in the semidarkness of the alley, Smitty recognized the single star of the Cuban national flag.

"I suppose you're going to tell us this girl was a candy striper on her way home from visiting the elderly and that your dead friend over there heroically gave his life by trying to save her," Detective Wallace said, walking up silently in defiance of the captain's orders. He aimed a wad of spit in the direction of the flag. It missed completely and landed directly on Gena's right buttock. "Bull's-eye," he crowed.

Something popped inside Smitty's head. He turned on the detective and hit him with more force than he'd ever hit anyone in his life. The detective's head snapped back so fast that he looked like he'd been clotheslined. The detective hit the ground and backflipped before coming to rest facedown in a puddle of Jimmy's blood.

"Bull's-eye!" Frenchy echoed, raising circled finger and thumb in the universally understood gesture.

"Hold it!" Baker shouted sharply, as a uniformed officer ran toward them, starting to draw his service revolver; the urgency in his voice froze the young man in his tracks. "Put that thing away right now! We already have two dead in this alley tonight, there's no need to add to that total."

The officer glowered at Smitty, Frenchy, and LZ as he slowly released his grip, allowing the sidearm to slide back into its holster.

"Whether you know it or not, rookie," Baker said. "I just saved your life. Look!" He nodded in their direction. "Look at their hands, idiot!" Frenchy and LZ had their knives drawn and at the ready. "Before you even got that cannon clear of the holster, you'd have been dead where you stand.

"That black boy over there would've carved you up like a butcher's steak before you even got off the first round. Then I'd have had to kill him, with the odds-on favorite bet that the muscular white chap would've got me in the process. And for what? To satisfy the ego of a horse's ass," Baker said bitterly.

"But, sir? That thug hit a policeman," the officer protested.

"If he hadn't, I would have. Son, violence only leads to violence. Don't you think that there's been enough here, huh?"

"Yes, sir."

"If you think so, don't you think the detective should have, also?"

With agonizing slowness, the rookie nodded his head.

"Boys, I know this has been a shock to you, but I'm afraid it's not over yet," Baker said bluntly.

"What do you want now?" Smitty asked in a tired voice.

"I want you three to come down to the station and answer some questions. Specifically on your whereabouts earlier tonight."

"What happened?" Frenchy asked.

"Three hours earlier, at about nine o'clock, two Cuban couples were murdered in the same grisly fashion," Baker said, escorting them to a waiting police cruiser.

Somewhere a church bell chimed twelve times, announcing the start of a new day and the end of the old. There'd be neither for Jimmy and Gena. They'd not lived to the end, nor seen the beginning. Smitty had a feeling that they were the first of many.

Smitty was wrong. Jimmy and Gena were not the first of many; they were the last of a few. There were no more murders on the west side. This was in no way due to any lessening of tensions between the gangs, which had, if anything, been heightened, but rather to the mayor—and one thousand national guardsmen who were now conducting around-the-clock patrols of every street, every alley, and every deserted building where trouble had been known to occur. This was not the proverbial ounce of prevention; it was more like a couple of tons. The proverbial pound of cure was yet to come.

"We're wasting our time, Captain. We know he did it or at the very least ordered it done," the detective said angrily. "We've been at it for over six hours, and the son of a bitch won't crack. Captain, why don't you take a little walk, and I'll discuss it with him in private?

"Besides," Wallace massaged the two-inch adhesive bandage that had been placed across the bridge of his recently broken nose. "I owe this little shit and would dearly love a chance to see how good this tough guy is when he takes on someone who's ready for him."

"I think perhaps it's you who should take a break, Sergeant, and let me talk to him," Captain Baker said without expression.

"But, Captain—"

"Now."

He waited until the detective and his partner, Detective Something-or-Other, had left the room and closed the door behind them, then turned back to Smitty and said wearily, "Okay, kiddo, let's go through it one more time."

Smitty rubbed the sleep from his eyes and yawned loudly. "I've already told you what happened. Fifteen times we been through it, and the story hasn't changed from what you have on that paper; I got nothing more to say."

"Listen to me you idiot," the captain said exasperatedly as he grabbed Smitty by the shoulders and shook him hard enough to loosen a couple of fillings. "We have witnesses who are ready to testify that they overheard you planning the execution of those Cubans as a way of warning them to stay off your territory. For most of the night you've been jerking me around and I'm tired of it.

"Now, boy, so help me, you're going to tell me the truth or I swear to God I'll let the sergeant tear you limb from limb."

"Who are your seeing-eye dogs?" Smitty asked, his voice rising to match the captain's. "Besides, I've already told you I had nothing to do with those murders."

"Where were you at the time?" the captain snarled back, ignoring Smitty's question altogether.

"Like I've told you, and told you, and told you, I was taking a walk along the beach trying to work things out with LZ and Frenchy. We were on our way back to the west side when we walked up to the crime scene where Jimmy and Gena were murdered."

"And like I told you, and told you, and told you," the captain said irritably, "we already have a positive ID from the officer on LZ, placing him at the Orange Bowl at 8:45 PM in a red Corvette. Another officer reported seeing a car matching that description on the Rickenbacker Causeway with three people inside who bear an amazing similarity to you three gentlemen. The description of the car matches the one found abandoned in the city parking lot by a guard on a sweep at 9:20, which is approximately the time of the murders. That car was literally covered with the fingerprints of you three stooges. We have motive, we have two witnesses, and we have you placed at the crime at the time it was committed. How in God's name can you continue to stand there and deny the truth?"

"Look man, I've already explained all that—"

"Yeah, yeah, I know, I know, some bullshit about an initiation," the captain said.

"It's the truth!"

"Well, I don't believe you!"

"Then go fuck yourself, 'cause that's all I got to say!"

The captain shook his head in finality and got up and left the room. Wallace and the other detective soon returned.

"Now then," the detective grinned wolfishly, slamming a blackjack across the edge of the table, "since you refuse to confess voluntarily, we're just going to have to beat it out of you. I'm gonna enjoy this. Stand up, fuckface."

When Smitty made no attempt to move, the sergeant reached down, grabbed him by the shirt, and jerked him upward. Smitty had anticipated this and didn't resist; in fact, he gave the detective more assistance than he bargained for. Using his legs like a springboard, he thrust forward, driving his forehead directly into the broken nose of the detective, who screamed in agony as he fell backward against the wall, bounced off it like a caromed billiard shot, and collapsed in a heap on the floor.

Smitty wasted neither time nor feeling on the moaning figure on the floor. Using the chair as a step, he leaped onto the table and launched himself at his other adversary. The force of the impact as Smitty's feet connected with the unsuspecting detective's chest knocked the wind out of him as he toppled over like a fresh-cut fir.

More by sheer luck than anything else, Smitty had managed to land on his feet. He had just resumed his seat and finished working out a cigarette from the pack on the table—a difficult task since his hands were cuffed behind him—and gotten it in his mouth when the door burst open, hitting the recumbent detective squarely in the beak again, bringing renewed, louder moans.

"You guys must be the role models for the Keystone Kops," Smitty said smugly around his cigarette. "Light?"

There was something familiar about the sound the Zippo made as it clicked open and lit Smitty's cigarette. An arm had reached round the captain and offered the fire, a blue-sleeved arm. The sleeve was attached to a blue jacket, an air force senior master sergeant's jacket with ten rows of combat ribbons. Smitty peered around the captain and felt both instant relief and absolute horror at what he saw; Dad was the keeper of the flame.

"You want to tell me what happened here, boy?" The captain motioned for two nearby officers to remove the two detectives.

"Slipped on a bar of soap in the shower," Smitty said. "Next time you send a couple of your henchmen in to help me recall the events as you want them to be, you might at least send someone who's not so klutzy."

"What the hell are you talking about?" the captain responded stiffly, as other uniformed officers appeared in the doorway and carried the two injured figures from the room.

"Now it's my turn not to believe you," Smitty said, as he stared at the captain's bewildered face before motioning toward the recumbent detective. As he was rolled over, first the leather strap around his wrist and then the blackjack itself came into view.

"You think I sent them. Honestly, son, I'm as surprised to see them in here as you are. I told them to keep an eye on you—from the hallway—until I came back; I went downstairs to get your father. Since I've been unsuccessful, I thought he might be able to help you understand the seriousness of your situation."

"He'll tell the truth," Dad said flatly, fixing Smitty with his first sergeant's stare. "Young man, I understand you've been giving everyone a rough time around here for the last six or seven hours. Before the next hour has come and gone, I'm going to have the truth from you. If I don't, you won't be a bother to anyone anymore, because you'll be on the wrong side of the ground before the breakfast bell sounds."

Smitty knew from experience that this was no idle threat. His swagger had gone; Dad had just passed sentence . . . in advance of hearing the evidence.

Smitty told Dad and Captain Baker everything that had happened from the day the argument took place in the warehouse with Keith and Glen right up to the scene in the alley. He held nothing back, but not because he was afraid of the legal repercussions. Those were mouse farts compared to the repercussions of lying to his father.

"Well, that certainly explains a few things," Captain Baker said.

"Such as?" Dad barked. It came out as a command, not a question.

"Would you care to guess who the two eyewitnesses are?" the captain asked evenly.

"Keith and Glen," Smitty said.

"On the nose, kiddo."

"What are you going to do now?" Dad asked.

The captain rubbed his day-old stubble thoughtfully. "I dunno. There's some very heavy political pressure coming down from the mayor's office to solve this gang problem once and for all. Seems your activities are dominating the papers and screwing up the tourist trade."

The captain surveyed the depths of his coffee cup as if the answer were floating there in plain sight. He sighed and smiled tiredly. "Listen, kid. I want to thank you for telling me the truth, because it did one very important thing. The mayor would shit a brick if he heard me say this, but it definitely convinced me that you're one of the good guys."

"Thanks, Captain," Smitty said, and meant it.

"C'mon, Sarge, let's go see what kind of bargain we can cook up with the DA to keep this little asshole from ending up bent over a bed frame with his cheeks spread for some big hairy guy in the funhouse."

As Smitty was led to a holding cell across from the interrogation room, Dad and the captain stood talking in the hall. Curiously, Dad was doing most of the talking. The conversation lasted ten minutes and finished with Captain Baker nodding his head and smiling in agreement as they shook hands.

"Mr. Smith, after extensive discussion with Captain Baker and the juvenile authorities, I've decided that the correct sentence in this case will be in two parts. First, effective forty-eight hours from now, you are to be out of the territorial limits of the state of Florida, to which you are not to return, to any county, for any reason, for a period of five years. Second, I am placing you on a strict noncombative restraining order. This order prohibits you from engaging in any form of altercation, shoving match, fistfight, or any other form of hostility or even an argument that can lead to hostility for that same five-year time frame.

"You are a very violent person. You have a deep-seated hatred burning inside you that must be cured if you are to function as a productive and useful member of society. I don't mind telling you that if it was not for the intervention of Captain Baker, who assures me that this sickness inside you can be cured—a fact that I personally find very hard to believe—you would be on your way to juvenile detention until your eighteenth birthday and then would have spent the balance of the five years in the state penitentiary.

"Hear me, and hear me good. Any violation of the above provisions for any reason at all during this five-year time frame, I repeat, any reason at all, and you will be returned here to serve the entire five-year sentence in a state institution.

"It is my sincere hope that if you are forced to live like the weak you so blatantly persecute, then you may learn to appreciate the fact that they have a right to exist also.

"Remember, the Bible says the meek shall inherit the earth—"

"But only after the strong have tamed it," Smitty interrupted, setting off a buzz of conversation in the courtroom. The lawyer Dad had hired elbowed his ribs hard.

"Young man, one more such outburst, and I'll hold you in contempt of this court," the judge said harshly.

"No problem, Ace; I have nothing but contempt for this court," Smitty said.

"Bailiff, remove this piece of scum from my courtroom, now." The judge slammed his gavel with his right hand and waved Smitty away with his left.

"I just hope you don't lose your life the next time you get mugged, and someone who wants to help can't because of some asshole judge's nonviolent restraining order," Smitty yelled back, as two court attendants and Dad hustled him out of the courtroom.

"Well, you certainly did yourself proud in there," Dad said when they were finally alone in the hallway outside the court. "What in God's name got into you? What are you using your brains for, huh? The captain went out on a limb to make a deal to keep you out of jail, and what do you do? You damn near blow it by throwing a temper tantrum right in front of the goddamn judge."

"That's no deal, and you know it. What do you use your brains for? It's a cover-up, and you know that, too. Getting rid of me and the other, quote, troublemakers is fixing the symptom and not the problem; but you know that too, don't you?

"You've always told me to do what was right and fight for what I believed in. What happened to all those pretty speeches? When I really needed your help, did you stick your neck out and help? No, you just stood by and let them hang some bullshit rap on me for grand theft auto, assaulting a police officer, resisting arrest, and any other trumped-up charge they could think of, up to and including raping the Mother Superior of the Little Sisters of the Poor.

"You talk about duty, honor, loyalty, and all that crap, but I think you're a paper tiger," Smitty said.

His face stung as Dad backhanded him.

"Now you listen to me, boy," Dad said savagely, pointing his finger almost in Smitty's eye. "You can't solve the problems of the whole world; it's just too big. This is only the first time in your life that things didn't go as you planned. That's part of growing up. And if you can't accept that, then you have got a problem, and neither I nor anyone else can help you. You got screwed; big deal. It ain't the first time, and it sure as hell won't be the last. The real question is what are you going to do about it? Are you going to prove them right by going back to your old ways, or wrong by sucking it in and beating them at their own game?"

Dad wasn't going to run from this one; that much was certain. He was waiting for an answer, an answer he'd get before they'd leave this room. Smitty studied Dad's face during his lecture. He was right, damn it, but it just didn't seem fair.

"All right, Dad," Smitty finally answered in a hesitant voice. "We'll try it your way."

Dad reached out, put his arm around him and looked Smitty in the eye. "C'mon son, let's go."

"Hi there, kiddo; how's my girl?" Dad spoke into the phone. As he listened to the response, his smug expression changed to a frown. "Now, hold on a second, honey. I called you for a reason." He listened again, then replied, "And that's why I'm calling you. There is a problem with one of the kids, and I need your help." To the response, he answered, "No, he's not sick; in fact both of the boys are in perfect health."

The answer was longer this time before Dad interrupted tersely, "Look, we can argue about who was right and who was wrong five years back some other time. Are you going to help me or not?" To the obvious question, Dad responded, "I just need to bring Kevin up to stay with you until I can get my transfer processed. He got in a little trouble down here, and part of the agreement is that I get him out of the state in forty-eight hours." Dad's face flushed with anger at Mom's response. "No, he hasn't followed in his father's footsteps and beaten someone half to death in a drunken rage.

"He just had a little problem with the cops, juvenile delinquency stuff. They felt that maybe a change in the environment would help. So all I need is for you to look after Kevin and Billy until my change of duty station request is processed. I called Chuck at the Pentagon, and he's having the orders expedited for my twenty-six terminal, which means I get to pick my last duty station. If you could just look after them for about a month, I can be on station at Hunter in plenty of time for the kids to get enrolled in school."

Mom's reply was longer this time. So long, in fact, that at one point Dad held his hand over the phone and said, "Your mom's a little pissed with me. Seems she has a 'friend' down here who's been keeping her right up-to-date on current events. Blames me personally for the whole mess; been talking to a lawyer about getting custody of you two. Curious," Dad said.

Dad returned the phone to his ear, and abruptly cut Mom off. "Look, I refused to send the kids home from England in '61 when you wouldn't come back, and that is not a discussion I wish to pursue at this time, either.

"Yes or no, will you take the boys? If not, say so, and I'll call up my brothers and have one of them do it.

"That I'll agree to," Dad nodded into the phone. "When I get settled in Savannah, you bring the kids down, and I'll sit down and discuss with you calmly and rationally what is best for both of them.

"Now, I'll be leaving about four in the morning, and if everything goes all right, I should roll into Atlanta about eight tomorrow night." Dad exhaled heavily and continued in a more neutral tone. "I'll tell ya, you won't hardly recognize these two."

This time, it was Mom who cut Dad off. He listened, tensed, and with a curt, "See ya tomorrow night," slammed down the phone and walked away into the bedroom, muttering.

Kevin had neither time nor opportunity to make contact with LZ or Frenchy; even if he had, he wasn't at all sure they'd have connected anyway.

The deaths of Jimmy, Gena, and the four Cubans had been the last straw for the mayor. Heeding the advice of the city prosecutor's office, the mayor had authorized the immediate arrest of all known gang members on the west side. The resulting blacklist contained 150 names of known or suspected gang members.

The huge list was compiled by one of the city's district attorneys with the aid of a certain homicide sergeant, who, it was indisputably felt, would be a much better choice for assuring that a complete and comprehensive list was assembled than that "bleeding heart captain." The final list was comprehensive enough to include many youths who had done nothing more than stay out late.

American jurisprudence and legalities took a backseat to expeditiousness. Smitty was lucky. His "case" was heard and tried in all of twenty minutes; most didn't get even that. The parents or legal guardians were brought in and told point-blank to get their troublesome offspring out of town. No hearing, no trial, no defense. Smitty's nemesis Keith, and his sidekick Glen, were missing from the rogue's gallery.

The roundup of the infested herd had begun with Smitty, LZ, and Frenchy being taken into custody. Inside of twenty-four hours, the stream of cars heading north on U.S.-1 looked strangely like a hurricane evacuation. Frenchy was already gone, flown home to New Orleans on a prepaid fare by his father to face the problems of his pecker. (One father in particular, due to his daughter's unplanned pregnancy, had matrimony plans for Frenchy's future, which drove Frenchy to the streets of Miami.) LZ was probably halfway to Orlando by now on his way to stay with an aunt in Chicago; he'd honked as his car went past the apartment. Smitty, Billy, and Dad had finished packing the car and were now eight hours behind LZ, headed toward Atlanta, to Mom, to Grandma, and ultimately, to a new home in Georgia.

They'd dealt with the symptom, but not the problem. As the sounds of WQAM faded from the car radio, Smitty knew that this was just a remission . . . the cancer would strike again.

CHAPTER FOUR

Mom, I'm so glad to see you!" Billy yelled, bounding from the car almost before it had rolled to a stop in Grandma's driveway in the Atlanta suburb. "I missed you so much, and I'm sure that now that I'm going to be living with you, things will be much better."

Kevin's and Dad's exits from the car were a bit more subdued.

The Hillman's generator had stopped charging just as they crossed over the state line into Georgia, and together they had worried the car on into Atlanta. After turning the car off, they had immediately raised the hood, located the generator, and were in the process of estimating the time required to remove and repair the defective part—a prodigious process that involved removal of the battery and battery box just to get to the dynamo in the tightly packed engine compartment—when Mom approached with Billy glued to her side.

"My, Kevin," Mom said, looking astonished, "how you've grown. Come over and give your old mother a hug and a kiss."

Kevin obligingly did. Five years before, he had had to stand on his tiptoes to hug his mom; now it was the other way around. After giving him a kiss on the cheek, a kiss that, Kevin noted, still left impressions from too much lipstick, Mom stood Kevin and Billy back to back, and was genuinely surprised to find that Kevin towered over Billy by at least six inches.

"Smitty, I wouldn't have believed they could have grown this much, especially Kevin. You must have been feeding them pretty well," Mom said.

"Too bad you weren't around for the day-to-day version," Dad said coldly.

"Now Smitty, I know you're upset with me for not coming back to England, and then for not rejoining you in Florida, but for the sake of the kids, can't we put that behind us? After all, I did agree to take care of the boys until you can get your transfer processed. As a matter of fact, I've been talking with Mama, and we both wouldn't mind if they just stayed on right here with us."

With a sigh, Dad said, "One, they're not kids anymore; they're young men. Billy is almost eighteen, will be a senior in high school, has a driver's license, and drinks beer. Kevin is fifteen, will be a junior, is learning to drive, and as you can see, is man-sized right now.

"Two, and let's make no mistake about this, the proposition of these young men living with you is not open for discussion now or any time in the future. You didn't want them five years ago, even though you tell everybody that will listen that you did, and they're past the point where they need a mother."

"I think we should put that to a vote," Billy interrupted suddenly, "and I vote to stay with Mom. At least then maybe I'll get a fair shake." Turning to Mom, Billy said, "You don't know what it's like living with Dad. He favors Kevin over me constantly. He orders us around, makes us do chores, and makes us get after-school jobs instead of giving us an allowance like the rest of the guys. When I got a driver's license, he didn't even buy a second car, so I'd have something to drive."

Mom looked at Dad, then at Kevin, and was just about to answer, when Dad interrupted tersely, "Young man, when you turn eighteen, and are of legal age, you can go and live with whoever you damn well please. Come to that, I'll be very glad to assist you by throwing your spoiled, snotty ass out. Until then, I'm your legal guardian, and you'll live where I say, and do what I tell you, exactly when I tell you to do it; do you understand me, buster?"

Dad's glare encompassed both Billy and Mom.

"Now, since we're done exchanging greetings, Billy, I want you to get the suitcases out of the car. Kevin, you fetch the tool bag from the spare tire compartment under the back floor, remove the generator, open it up, and tell me what parts you need to repair it."

"Why can't Kevin help me with the suitcases first?" Billy complained.

"Because he's going to be working on repairing the car—unless you want to get your hands dirty fumbling around under the hood?" Billy glared, but made no response.

"Let's get going, gentlemen. Your assignments are to be completed before you come in to eat. Kevin, call me when you get that generator apart. I'm going inside and have a private talk with your mother."

Taking Mom by the arm, Dad started to walk up the driveway to the front porch.

Kevin was just removing the tool bag from the car when he overheard Mom ask Dad, "Can Kevin really fix the car by himself? I mean, he's only fifteen years old and doesn't even know how to drive yet!"

Dad answered, "Hell, not only can he fix the Hillman, but leave him alone with your car for five minutes, and he'll strip it."

"You drive carefully, now, and come to see us whenever you can," Mama said. "Pappy and I enjoyed having you boys here for the month, and we'll miss you, ain't that right, Pappy?"

"Yeah, that's right," Pappy agreed, although with not nearly the enthusiasm of Mama.

"I should be back tomorrow, Mama. It takes about six hours to drive to Savannah, so I'll plan on staying overnight with Sara Lee and driving back in the evening," Mom said.

"Too bad you don't plan on staying permanently with your husband," Pappy grumbled.

"Pappy, you hush up," Mama scolded. "She's our daughter, and if she wants to stay with us until she gets her problems worked out, then we should let her."

"Working out your problems should take a week or two. She's been here five years. World wars don't last as long as her problems," Pappy retorted.

Mama opened her mouth to answer, saw the look on Pappy's face, thought better of it, and turned to her daughter. "Don't you pay that old man no never mind. You're welcome here for as long as you want."

"That's right, dear," Pappy agreed. "Any chance you could make it one week a year?"

Ignoring her father, Mom leaned out the passenger-side window to give her mother a quick kiss, and turned to Billy, who was driving. "Let's go, son." Billy pulled out of the driveway, and they were on their way to Savannah to meet Dad. For Kevin, it wasn't a moment too soon.

Dad had advised him to make the best of it until he could get all the arrangements made. He'd promised he'd be in Georgia in time to enroll them in school in September, but the month in between had been pure hell.

Although he dearly loved being around his grandparents, especially Pappy, who had a part-time job in an automotive parts store and took Kevin with him to work, he missed his friends terribly. After the initial change of scenery had worn off—which took about a week—Kevin found life here incredibly boring.

He'd rooted around under the house to inventory and pack all of Dad's tools that had been there since they went to England in '59, did several other little jobs that he'd been requested to do, and fixed a couple of things that were wrong with Mama's '49 Ford, but by the end of the second week, he was out of an occupation.

His feelings of loneliness were compounded by Mom, who insisted on parading both him and Billy around to all her relatives and friends, most of whom Kevin did not know well enough to feel comfortable with. The discomfort was compounded by the still-fresh physical and emotional scars from the last six months. Unaccustomed to and unskilled in social repartee, Kevin came across to people as sullen, withdrawn, and deeply troubled.

Billy, on the other hand, basked in the spotlight of Mom's affections. He was exuberant to all of Mom's relations, flamboyant with social contacts, and flattering and attentive to Mom. Everyone commented on how lucky Mom was to have a son who was so polite and thoughtful.

Kevin wasn't alone in his adjustment period. He'd talked to both LZ and Frenchy by pay phone on three different occasions: same circus, different cast of clowns.

LZ hated living with his well-heeled aunt in the Chicago suburbs. She made him attend a primarily white school where he obviously didn't fit in. Ditto Frenchy with his parents, who were still trying to force him, for the sake of family honor, to marry the rich bitch and settle down.

Since all three were under the same nonviolent restraining order, they all had to be extremely cautious in how they acted and what they said, lest they unknowingly provoke an incident.

"Penny for your thoughts," Mom said, leaning over the backseat and touching Kevin on the arm lightly.

"What?"

"Are you all right, son?" Mom asked. "You look a little pale."

"Yes, I'm okay," Kevin answered.

"He's probably just lonesome for those thugs he used to hang out with, Mom," Billy said. "If Dad didn't fill you in, I'll be more than glad to tell you the whole story."

"Your father and I discussed this with Kevin in some detail, son."

"Yeah, but I'll bet he didn't tell you everything," Billy answered back.

"Your brother has been through a rough time. How he is dealt with will be a subject that will be mutually agreed to by your father and myself and is absolutely no concern of yours. Do I make myself clear?"

"Yes, ma'am," Billy answered.

"And another thing," Mom continued. "Your father and I agree that if Kevin's to have any chance at all of succeeding in his new environment, the book on the past has to be closed. Your father is going to mention this to you also, but I wanted to be sure I covered it so you would know that we're in agreement. You are not to disclose, or even hint, at the trouble your brother had in Florida. We feel this is the only way that he has a chance to change his life and recover from what has happened to him. Do you understand?"

"Yeah, I understand," Billy said, unable to hide his dejection.

Mom glanced back at Kevin, gave him an encouraging smile, then continued. "Your father and I are going out to dinner tonight and discuss some form of mutual custody so that you two will be spending time with both of us. This will give you exposure to two different points of view and will allow me to help you learn some of the niceties of society that only a mother can bring."

Kevin admitted silently to himself that the plan his parents had agreed to seemed just and fair. From the scowl on Billy's face in the rearview mirror, it was obvious that he didn't think so, but so what? Billy's protesting comments were lost on Kevin, who drifted off to sleep and did not awaken until they arrived in Savannah.

"Kevin, we're here, son," Mom said softly, shaking him by the arm. Kevin yawned, sat up, and stretched to find himself right back in the same driveway that had been his marble arena just six years before. The house seemed smaller, the pine trees bigger, and the neighborhood in general a little more run-down.

The house had been rented when they left Georgia in '59 to go to England. As each successive tenant came and went, the house had fallen little by little into disrepair, until now. It was in such a state as to be almost uninhabitable.

It was badly in need of paint, and water spots on the ceiling betrayed a leaking roof. A catholic assortment of old furniture, clothes, and debris was strewn haphazardly around, adding to the overall impression that the house was the victim of an inside tornado.

The yard was in no better shape. Dad's prized lawn was now crabgrass and weeds, with large, bare, brown spots in between. The shrubbery was overgrown, dead, or badly in need of pruning and replanting. Rotting plywood, old pieces of steel, and miscellaneous car body parts littered the backyard.

The workshop was an even bigger disaster. There were no doors or windows left in working condition. Shelves and brackets were nailed up on the walls haphazardly. The attic steps, the scene of Kevin's Waterloo, were gone, with nothing but an empty ceiling hole to mark their passing. From what could be seen through the hole, the attic was full of useless junk.

Kevin was just returning from his personal reconnoiter when Dad pulled up in the front yard.

"Hi, son. You're earlier than I expected," Dad said with a cheerful smile as he walked up and shook hands. "I'm glad you arrived safely. Where's your mom and Billy?"

"They've gone next door to Mrs. Young's."

"See the house?"

To Kevin's eye-rolling grimace, Dad responded heavily, "Yeah, really something, ain't it? Gonna take a lot of work to get this billet in order, but I don't think it's beyond repair for a couple of fairly decent carpenters such as you and me, do you?"

"As Tonto said to the Lone Ranger, 'What do you mean, you and me, white man?'"

"Hey partner, I'm getting too old for this kind of stuff; that's why I went and had me a couple of strapping youngsters, so I'd have some help."

"Slave labor is what you mean," Kevin retorted.

"A rose by any other name," Dad boomed right back.

"You know, son," Dad said, in a serious tone, "I can't tell you how much I missed having your ugly puss around for the last month, and Billy's too. And I'm certain, now that you're away from that environment, that things will be much better for you personally."

"To be perfectly honest, I miss it; I miss it terribly," Kevin said.

"At this stage, son, that's perfectly understandable. A month after I came home from both World War II and Korea, I was depressed and missed the comradeship of the guys. As you develop new interests and meet new friends, that'll pass. Hang in there, troop; it'll fetch you 'round, I promise."

"Thanks, Pop," Kevin said, as he reached out to hug his dad, who returned the hug with equal emotion. "I just feel so alone."

"All true warriors will always miss the war," Dad explained. "It's the place where they feel the most used and the most important. The trick in peacetime is to find an alternative interest to channel your energies. Got it?"

"Got it." Kevin nodded.

"Now, how about let's put on a happy face. Here comes your mother and brother, and you don't want them to see a tough guy like you with tears in your eyes, do you?"

Kevin brightened, forced a smile, and said, "How is it you always seem to know just what a person's feeling and just the right thing to say?"

"Oh, probably because I'm one fart smeller; I mean one smart feller," Dad grinned mischievously as he patted Kevin on the back. Kevin smiled in return.

"You be good and mind Mrs. Young. Your father and I should be home around eleven," Mom said gaily as she kissed Kevin lightly on the forehead and started for the door.

"Oh, and another thing—"

"Will you just git on." Mrs. Young scolded. "They's big young 'uns now and can take care of themselves. If anything comes up, me and Clark can handle it."

Mom, obviously embarrassed at having been reprimanded in front of her offspring, turned slowly back to the door, and without another word, left to join Dad in the car.

"She's a worrier, that's for sure," Clark, Sara Lee's husband, said, as he watched from the window as Mom and Dad drove away.

"Yer mom's nervous about that there dinner with your father," Sara Lee said. "Been hopin' for some time that he'd chase her; looks like he finally made the first move."

"I don't understand," Kevin said, perplexed.

"Your mommy's a proud woman," Clark said. "All she ever talked about the last five years she'd come to visit was your pop and how she didn't know how good it was until it was gone. But for all that, she'd never call him, no matter how hurt she was. Said some darn fool thing about it bein' a matter of pride."

"Yes, sir, that woman's got strange notions when it comes to men," Sara Lee agreed. "Hell, it were her fault in the first place."

"I'm sorry, I'm afraid I'm totally confused," Kevin said.

"Well, boy, it's as simple as this," Clark said. "Your daddy caught some guy making a pass at your mom. I don't know the details exactly, but I do know that he beat the poor bastard within an inch of his life."

"Yer mom said yer daddy were a barbarian, and said she weren't a-gonna live with him no more unless he changed his ways," Sara Lee said, picking up from Clark.

"Her attitude didn't make no sense to your daddy, and when he told her so, she said that he acted like he thought she'd caused the whole thing and didn't trust her. Said until he apologized, both to her and to that there fella he beat up, he could just live on his own."

"Always thought there was more to that story than she'd told," Clark said thoughtfully, rubbing a bristly chin of four-day-old white beard.

"Well, you just keep them thoughts to yourself, old man," Sara Lee said pointedly. "What they's a' doin' ain't our concern, so just you hush up about it and let's change the subject."

"Please don't feel bad on my account," Kevin said. "I pretty much knew all of that before, except for the part about the reason for Mom not returning. And I have to say I've wondered about the circumstances myself."

"Well, now you know," Sara Lee answered dismally. Then she brightened. How come you didn't go to the drive-in with Buddy and Billy?"

"They didn't invite me," Kevin said. "And besides, I'm kind of tired anyway and thought I might just go to bed early."

Just as he was about to switch on the bedroom light, he saw the light turn on briefly next door. His parents led each other toward the bed, then the light clicked out.

Kevin sat on the bed for a long time and looked out the open window across the twelve-foot space that separated this bedroom from the one his parents had used when they had lived there before. He wasn't tired; far from it. Kevin thought how ironic it was going to be for Billy when he found out that things were, in fact, going to be much better. His feelings kept him wide awake for hours. Kevin stared out the window of the darkened bedroom and searched without answer for a solution to the rage he felt burning inside.

"Billy, Kevin, your father and I have some wonderful news for you. We've decided to live together again. Won't that be wonderful, to be a family again?" Mom asked, as they sat in the booth at the local restaurant where Dad had taken them for breakfast.

Kevin, though hardly surprised, was genuinely pleased for Dad, and showed his support by reaching over and hugging Mom, and saying, "Congratulations, and good luck."

"Thank you, Kevin," Mom said in return, surprised and pleased by Kevin's uncharacteristic display of affection. "Same to you, Dad." Dad responded with a half-nod and a rakish wink.

"Billy," Mom began in the same happy tone as before. "What's your opinion?"

"Oh, I think it's great, too," Billy said lifelessly. "It just sort of caught me by surprise, that's all. I think it's fantastic, I really do."

"How did you convince Mom to stay?" Billy continued in the same dead tone.

"Oh, I've got some hidden qualities that just ain't evident on the surface." Dad grinned roguishly, pointing at his crotch.

"Smitty!" Mom's cheeks reddened. "You're terrible; you really are."

Kevin, recalling the events of last night, was just about to laugh, but thought better of it, though he couldn't suppress a smile.

"And just what are you grinning at, young man?" Mom asked.

"Me?" Kevin asked with exaggerated innocence.

"Yes, you."

Kevin threw up his hands and said, "Ah, nothing . . . nothing at all."

Mom fixed Dad with a glacial stare, and finding no one home there, turned to Billy unexpectedly and asked, "What are these two up to?"

"I honestly don't know," Billy said, looking to Kevin for explanation.

Kevin dropped his hands into his lap, out of Mom's sight, made a circle of his left index finger and thumb, and see-sawed the second finger of his right hand back and forth through the circle.

Billy looked momentarily perplexed, then grinned slyly.

Mom turned to Dad and said, "Do something!"

"Well, just what do you want me to do, honey? They're about grown and are pretty well-versed on what married couples do after the lights go out," Dad answered.

Mom, realizing that she was outnumbered, said, "The first thing we're going to get is a big lock for our bedroom door."

Kevin started to laugh.

"All right, mister smarty pants," Mom said. "Out with it."

"I was just thinking," Kevin said, "The second thing ought to be soundproofing."

The eruption of laughter from Dad and Billy was spontaneous and loud, causing other diners to stare at them out of curiosity. Kevin joined in and, despite her best efforts at maintaining her dignity, Mom did also.

"Very funny!" Mom said, trying hard to sound angry. "Well, one thing's for sure, living with you three lechers will never be boring."

"Just you hang in there, kiddo," Dad said cheerfully, patting Mom on the thigh. "It'll fetch you around."

On the return drive to their house, everyone seemed to be in a genuinely good mood. Kevin hoped it would last, but he was still tormented by demons from the past. Demons that he hoped would not rear up to shred the happiness of the present.

The first months back in the old homestead passed quickly. Dad and Kevin, with reluctant help from Billy, worked long hours in the evenings to fix up the house. Within two weeks, the outside was scraped and painted. Two more, and a new roof was in place. Another month, and the inside was painted, hardwood floors revarnished, carpet installed in the living room, and all of the debris hauled away.

By the fourth month, the yard had been reseeded, the trees trimmed, and new trees planted as required. With the worst of the work behind them, Dad was now down to doing special renovation projects—his shop being the first one—while Mom focused on refurbishing the house with new furniture for the living room and master bedroom.

Their family life was running along pretty well, too. At work, Dad was busy with his new assignment. Mom had reestablished her friends and social contacts, and Billy had blended well into the new high school. Kevin had begun to settle down a little but was still tense and aloof and seemed to have problems making friends.

Kevin still thought of LZ and Frenchy, but the phone calls had dropped from three a month to about one, the nightmares still occurring at about the same proportion. Things were going well for the Smith family as 1965 drifted lazily to a close. Kevin hoped it was not the quiet before the storm.

The year 1966 was not yet a month old when Kevin's earlier fears came true. But the storm, when it broke, was none of his doing.

Kevin, Mom, and Dad had gone to a drive-in movie, and returned to the house around midnight. A note from Benny, the next-door neighbor and a Savannah police officer, was pinned to the mailbox. The note said that Billy was under arrest and was being held in the Savannah Beach jail for driving under the influence. That part was bad. The next was worse. Benny went on to say that Billy would probably be held without bail on a drug distribution charge.

Mom stared at the note in shocked disbelief, Dad in anger. Kevin found it of particular interest that Mom immediately blamed Dad for this "latest chapter in the Sergeant Smith Military Handbook for Child Rearing." It seemed premature.

Dad reacted differently. Even though Kevin could see the anger in his eyes, he took Mom's abusive comments with cool detachment, said nothing in return, went to the phone, called the police sergeant, thanked him earnestly for the tip, and agreed wholeheartedly when the officer suggested that he accompany Dad on the drive down to the beach together to find out what the facts of the matter were.

Inside of five minutes, while Mom sat crying and cursing her own personal misfortune, Dad was out the door with a nod for Kevin to follow.

"Your mother doesn't handle things like this very well, so keep an eye on her, okay?" Dad instructed, as he started up the Hillman.

"Well . . . okay," Kevin answered noncommittally.

Picking up on Kevin's disapproval, Dad said, "Little disappointed in her aren't you?"

"Yes, as a matter of fact, I am."

"Don't be; two things to remember. One, your mother has been exposed to life's harsh realities only once—and then it wasn't her fault—for the most part because I've shielded her. Two, that's the main reason I married her. She was the only thing I ever had in my adult life that wasn't corrupt and vile; remember that."

"Yes, sir," Kevin answered.

"Now go on back inside. You're in for an interesting night. Ignore most of what you hear; it's emotion talking. From time to time answer affirmatively, let her talk out her frustration until it winds down, and then try to get her to bed. I'll be back as soon as I can."

"Can do."

"You've got the duty, troop; carry on."

"Well, what did your father have to say? Bet he said I was just acting like a hysterical female, like all of them, didn't he?" Mom asked bitterly.

Trying his best to seem nonchalant, Kevin answered, "Not at all. Dad just said he was very concerned about you and wanted me to keep an eye on you until he got back."

"Are you sure that's all he said?" Mom squinted her eyes at Kevin.

"Scout's honor." Kevin grinned, holding up the appropriate three fingers.

"You were never a Boy Scout and couldn't be one if you wanted to. Based on what I heard about Miami, there's not a single commandment that you didn't break," Mom said with a half-smile.

"Oh, I don't know. I don't think I ever got around to coveting my neighbor's wife."

Mom laughed in spite of herself, and said, "You're silly; that's one of the Bible commandments, not the Boy Scouts."

"Depends on which troop you were in, Red."

"Oh, you're as crazy as your father." Mom ran to Kevin for a comforting hug.

"That's me," Kevin responded. "Son o' Crazy."

"That's Crazy Horse," Mom corrected.

"Dad always said the nag came with the marriage," Kevin said.

"You're impossible," Mom said, pulling apart to arm's length.

"You know, Dad says I'm incorrigible. That's a pretty heavy burden you two are giving me; it could lead to complexes and all sorts of things. I mean, how would you like to have to go around introducing yourself as the son of Mr. and Mrs. Smith, the union of incorrigible and impossible. Real strong argument for birth control . . . "

"Oh, stop it!" Mom said, laughing. Abruptly, she became sober and stared Kevin straight in the eye. "I love you, son."

"And I love you, too. Now why don't you go fix your ugly face, and I'll get us a couple of beers. That way when Dad gets back you'll be nice and relaxed—and drunk."

"That's all right, son. I think I'll just go to my room and rest until your father gets back." Mom turned to leave and was just about through the doorway into the hall when she called back, "Oh, and son, thanks."

"Yeah, remember the next time I get into one of these things, you owe me one."

"Count on it," Mom said, disappearing into her bedroom and shutting the door.

Dad returned with Billy around 5:00 AM. Kevin had gone to bed around 3:00 AM, but the sound of Dad's screaming from the living room brought him fully awake in an instant.

"Boy, we've been discussing this all the way back from the beach, and no matter how many times you tell it, this cock-and-bull story just doesn't hold water," Dad said.

"But Dad, if you'd just listen to me. It wasn't my fault. Sure, we had a little too much to drink, but I swear to you that I didn't know one of the guys had grass and the needle until we were stopped by the police and searched," Billy said defensively.

"Bullshit!"

"It's not bullshit. I swear it's the truth."

"How doesn't matter; you're the one who got caught. Besides, you're almost eighteen years old; you should have known better," Dad said.

"But, Dad—" Billy whined.

"But, Dad, nothing," Dad interrupted. "As of right now, you are on my permanent shit list. And you know what that means: no privileges, no dates, no car. When you're not in school, you're to be in this house until further notice. Got it?"

"If it was Kevin you'd listen," Billy muttered, walking out of the living room. A door slammed.

Dad followed quickly and banged loudly on the bathroom door. "You get your ass out of that shitter, boy; we're not through discussing this yet."

"I'm taking a crap and tired of taking yours; go away and leave me alone," Billy said through the locked door.

This last statement seemed to send Dad over the edge. He rocked back on his left foot and kicked the door open with such ferocity that when it burst open, it drove the handle through the adjoining bathroom drywall.

"You little son of a bitch. If you think you're man enough to talk to me like that, then you'd better be man enough to back it up!" Dad roared.

Kevin had been listening and watching from his bedroom. The solid, hollow sound that followed, Kevin knew all too well. Dad had just belted Billy in the mouth with a clinched fist. This was followed by tumbling sounds, which indicated that the blow had knocked Billy into the bathtub.

Kevin ran to the bathroom entrance. Dad had plucked Billy from the bathtub like a feather and was preparing to hit him again.

Kevin grabbed the wrist at its fully cocked position, pulled sharply backward and, with a fair amount of difficulty, dragged Dad out into the hall. Billy collapsed on the floor like a crumpled bath towel.

Dad, rabid with anger, lunged blindly at Kevin, screaming incoherently. The gleam of Kevin's open switchblade stopped him in midstep as suddenly as if he'd just run into an invisible wall.

Before Kevin could say anything, Mom yanked open the bedroom door, instantly sized up the situation, and screamed "Smitty!" at the top of her lungs.

Dad stood rigidly still, glaring first at Kevin, then at Mom, then back at Kevin, before dropping his shoulders in resignation. The outburst was over—at least for the moment.

"Mom," Kevin said. "You see to him; I'll see to Billy." Never taking his eyes off Dad, Kevin slowly closed and pocketed his knife. Stepping past Dad into the bathroom, he picked up a washcloth, rinsed it in cold water, and began wiping the blood from his semiconscious brother's face.

"C'mon, honey," Mom said, taking Dad by the arm and escorting him into the bedroom, forcing him to lie down on the bed before turning around and closing the door. The Yale lock made what seemed an extraordinarily loud noise as it clicked into the locked position.

Kevin spent close to ten minutes ministering to his brother before finally getting him groggily to his feet and half-carrying him to bed.

Billy tried to speak, but his bruised and swollen face would not allow the words to come out. Kevin smiled at his brother, patted him understandingly on the arm, and said, "Get some sleep, slugger," closing the bedroom door quietly as he left.

As he crossed the hall to his own room, Kevin paused at the sound of crying coming from his parents' bedroom.

Dad was crying quietly and muttering over and over, "I just don't understand where I failed . . . I just don't understand where I failed . . ." Mom shushed him to silence saying, "It's okay, honey; you're tired. Go to sleep and we'll talk about this in the morning."

Kevin lay down on the bed, sighed deeply, and closed his eyes. Recalling thoughts from years earlier, he wondered why Ricky Nelson never seemed to have to deal with these kinds of real-life problems. Ozzie and Harriet would have been understanding and comforted young Dave. It was his last conscious thought.

Surprisingly, the Saturday night blowup was not brought up the following day. The incident was totally ignored. Dad avoided both him and Billy, Kevin suspected due to embarrassment. Mom was tentative in her dealings with Dad, sympathetic with Billy and Kevin.

Tensions began to lessen with the return to normal activities during the week, with the only visible evidence being Billy's black eye and swollen face. Eventually, at Mom's insistence, Dad accepted Billy's version of what happened, used his connections downtown to make a deal with the police to have the drug charge dropped and the DUI reduced to reckless driving and paid the fine, and the whole incident faded into memory.

Near the end of January, the week Kevin was to take his driving test, two seemingly unrelated events happened: the house was burglarized and Dad was assigned TDY to Germany for three months.

It was a strange break-in. The thieves took only a couple of pellet rifles, a camera, and the cash that Mom kept in a fake box of frozen corn in the freezer. The police wrote the whole thing off as kids, but this didn't seem likely to Kevin, even though Dad appeared to accept their logic. It just seemed strange that they would know exactly where to look for the cash.

When Kevin raised this point to the police, they dismissed his concern and assured him that, based on their experience, this was the first place the robbers would look. Kevin still didn't buy it. It was too neat, too clean.

When Dad left for Germany, he left the Hillman, which, with the purchase of a '58 Chrysler New Yorker for Mom, had been relegated to the role of second car, in the care of Billy. Within one month, the car was inoperable, largely because of shabby treatment on the part of its operator.

The old Hillman had pretty close to a 150 thousand miles on it when Dad left. When Billy beached it, it had 151. Dad was not two days gone when Billy strapped on roof racks for surfboards, folded the rear seat down, threw some mildewed carpet in the cargo area, and hung stringy looking curtains around all the back windows.

Calling it his surf wagon, he missed no opportunity to spin doughnuts, fishtail, shift at high rpm, and subject the car to any other abuse he could think of. Incredibly, he had no fewer than four fender benders within a week, transforming what had been a nice little car easing gracefully into its last years into a dilapidated pile of junk.

His crowning achievement occurred when the heater shorted out. Since Billy had no automotive knowledge and certainly wasn't going to drive a car with no heater all the way back from the beach in the dead of winter, he wrapped a piece of tin foil around the blown fuse and came home. He had just made the subdivision when the car died.

When Kevin looked under the hood, every wire in the harness was either burned in two or fused together in a charred, blackened mess. Billy blamed the whole thing on the fact that the car was old and unreliable; besides, he told Mom, if Dad truly loved him, he'd have bought him a good car, not left him this old piece of shit.

Kevin found it hard to feel any sympathy for Billy; he'd his own fish to fry. Since the move, Kevin had been unable to escape from his feelings of isolation and anger. Having transferred at the start of his junior year, he'd had trouble blending in and making real friends; acquaintances, yes, friends, no.

These feelings contributed to aggressive behavior that had led to several run-ins with the local school bullies. Run-ins that, because of his restraining order, he'd had to walk meekly away from, accepting the brand of coward, when he could've easily won. He desperately needed an outlet for his frustrations. Inadvertently, Billy's troubles with the Hillman provided the answer to Kevin's own problems, and ultimately, the emotional salvation for which he'd been so desperately searching.

The prospect of trying to restore the car to working order intrigued Kevin. He'd fooled around with cars but done nothing of this magnitude. With the help of the mechanic at the service station where he'd gotten a part-time job as an attendant, Kevin was able to hot-wire the car and get it started, only to discover an additional major problem: the engine had a rod knock and would have to be rebuilt.

Fortunately, a kid at school had a Hillman, and more importantly, a 1960 convertible for spare parts. Having just sold his driver, he let Kevin have the parts car for twenty-five dollars. Although some of the trim, grill, and superficial items were missing, the power train and wiring harness were completely intact. It took him six weeks, working strictly by the workshop manual and the mechanic's advice, but he was nearing the end of the repair process when Billy walked into the shop.

"Hey, little brother, you've been in here tinkering with my car for a month and a half. Dad's due back Friday afternoon, so you'd better get it fixed, or I'll tell Dad that you broke it," Billy said snottily.

"You ought to give up on being a surfer, partner, and become a porn star, 'cause you certainly got the balls for it," Kevin replied.

"Maybe Mom's fooled by your line of technical bullshit; but it don't fool me. There wasn't that much wrong with this thing to start with. You just wanted an excuse to show everybody how smart you are, at my expense, and I'm serving notice that I'm not going to let you get away with it. Understand?" Billy said.

"Yeah, sure," Kevin said.

"Now that you know who's boss, I want that car back together and operational before we leave to pick up Dad at the base; I have a date and Mom has a bridge party, so I can't use her car. Are we clear on that, little brother?"

"No problem. You'll have your wheels."

"Good." Billy turned on his heel and exited the garage, not seeing Kevin's smile or hearing him mutter, "Only when the Red Sea parts again . . . big brother."

"Dad! I'm glad to see you. Welcome home," Billy said, running forward to be the first to greet Dad as he stepped off the plane at the Hunter Field flight line.

"Good to see you, son," Dad said, shaking hands with Billy.

"Dad, I've got bad news about the car—"

"Tell me about it later, son," Dad interrupted, as Mom, unable to wait for Dad to walk to her, ran the last ten steps between them and literally jumped into his arms.

"Welcome home, honey. I missed you terribly," Mom said, hugging then kissing him passionately.

"I missed you too, kiddo. Especially the parts that are normally covered by clothes," Dad said, putting his arm around her as they walked to the car, patting the side of her right breast to emphasize his point.

"Smitty!" Mom said. "Stop that; what'll the boys think?"

"Kevin, what's prevention selling for in the PX these days?"

"Six cents a pack."

"Any questions?" Dad said with a smirk, as he patted her on the rear end.

"I assume that Billy and I are bunking at Mrs. Young's tonight?" Kevin inquired politely.

"Bet on it, troop," Dad said.

"C'mon, Billy. Let's leave these two lovebirds alone while we go get Dad's trunk and B4 bag."

In the car on the way home, Billy again brought up the subject of the Hillman's condition and was just starting to inform on Kevin, when Dad cut him off and said tersely, "We'll discuss it tomorrow."

As the car headed down Raines Avenue, Kevin could see Billy's miffed expression in the streetlights. Nothing worse than a stool pigeon with no shoulder to shit on.

Kevin had gotten up early Saturday morning and had just finished cleaning up the garage around noon when Dad walked in carrying a six-pack of 3.2 beer.

"Hi, son," Dad said. "How's my boy?"

"I'm fine. You, however, look all in; tough night?" Kevin asked.

"I'll tell ya' partner. Sex is the greatest, goddamndest, most wonderful thing in the world," Dad said, as he handed Kevin a cold one. "You ought to try it sometime."

"It is, and I will. Just as soon as I find a willing partner."

"With all those battle scars, an ugly buzzard like you better start with a blind one," Dad said.

"Speaking from experience, no doubt," Kevin shot back.

"Don't worry about it, son. It'll happen; just be patient," Dad said. He turned and surveyed the forlorn-looking Hillman. "What's the verdict on the car; got it running yet?"

"Sure do," Kevin said proudly.

"Billy said it wouldn't start when he tried to use it yesterday; so how come it runs today?" Dad asked, raising his eyebrows.

"'Cause I put the rotor button back in the distributor this morning," Kevin said with a grin.

"The hell you did," Dad said, and snorted.

"The hell I did," Kevin said.

Dad opened the hood and said, "Fire her over."

The engine caught at the first turn and, after initial choking, settled down to purr like a well-oiled sewing machine.

"Runs good." Dad nodded approvingly as he looked closely at the spotlessly clean engine compartment.

Glancing up, he caught sight of the Hillman carcass, and walked out of the garage to give it the once over. His examination did not fail to notice that the area under the hood usually taken up by the engine and transmission was empty, and that the wiring harness was missing. After a few other cursory inspections he returned to the garage and said with a satisfied nod, "You did a good job with the changeover, son. But one thing puzzles me, why'd did you change the wiring harness?"

Kevin nodded to the corner of the garage where the old engine and transmission were sitting with the fused wiring harness on top.

Dad whistled as he inspected the harness. "Pretty bad. This was no engine fire; it's the result of a short. How'd it happen?"

"You called it; a short," Kevin said.

Dad gave Kevin an icy stare, turned and looked at the dinged body, the surf racks, and the tires worn on the outside. "Billy."

"The how's don't really matter, do they?" Kevin asked without expression. One informer in the family was more than enough.

Dad surveyed the car sadly and agreed, "No, son, I guess they don't." He brightened and said, "You're a pretty broad-minded young lad, I'll concede that."

"What do you mean by that?"

"Well if it was me, I'd be a trifle bit upset if somebody did this kind of damage to my car."

"But it's your car," Kevin said, puzzled.

"Not anymore."

Kevin was quiet for a moment, had a sudden insight, smiled, and pointed to his own chest.

Dad nodded slowly. "As an old expression says, you save a life; you own a life. You revived it; you own it."

"But what are you going to drive?" Kevin asked. "And what about Billy?"

"I have a line on the old Ford Wagon that's been passed around the company for me. As for Billy, it'll be interesting to see what form of transportation he comes up with. When I informed him of my decision this morning, he was quite upset; more to the point, he was downright pissed."

"When you informed him this morning?"

"I thought I'd trained you better," Dad said. "Son, your old dad's been around the block a time or two, and worked on enough cars to know when one's been misused, and more importantly, smart enough to figure out who doesn't have the skill to fix it."

"What was Mom's reaction?"

"'Bout what you might expect. Said I'm favoring you over Billy, that kind of thing. Don't worry about it; I can handle it," Dad finished in a voice that betrayed him.

"Obviously you told her this morning, not last night," Kevin concluded.

"One of the service axioms is to first complete your assigned mission, then explain your reasons. If you do it the other way around, you'll be dead, and only you'll know why."

"When did you first have an insight on Billy?" Kevin asked suddenly.

"End of January."

"But that was before you left for Germany."

"It was also when the so-called break-in occurred."

"I've always suspected that something was wrong with that caper," Kevin agreed. "What really happened?"

"By now that should be obvious." Dad reached on top of a cabinet, pulled down the two supposedly missing pellet rifles, and tossed the lighter of the two to Kevin.

"Where'd you get these?" Kevin said, as he pulled back the bolt, suspecting he already knew the answer.

"Where do you think?"

"I think you bought them back from whoever Billy sold them to," Kevin said.

"Dead center of the bull's-eye, troop. Finish it," Dad said.

"Well, it's obvious, the break-in was a setup. Who else would know the exact location of the cold cash?"

"Correct; go on," Dad said, handing Kevin a fresh brew.

"The key question is, why?" Kevin said, thinking out loud. "Could be to cover an outside expense; like maybe a drug expense?"

"Also obvious," Dad said impatiently. "But what's behind it; what's the root cause?"

Kevin took a couple of long pulls on the beer can and suddenly he had it. "Actually, it's pretty complex."

"Simplify it," Dad said.

"You're a man in the middle, serving too many masters."

"Go on." Dad nodded.

"The root cause is Mom. You said it yourself, she's the only thing in your life that wasn't vile and corrupt. Therefore, it follows that your renewed living arrangement had something to do with a deal concerning Billy, not me.

"Billy's got a pretty severe case of insecurity. No doubt Mom is using this little fact to her advantage, and more importantly, your disadvantage."

"How?" Dad asked.

"I was just coming to that," Kevin said. "Billy's a pretty nervous person. He's not only superficial, but at times can be downright devious, the result, no doubt, of being spoiled at an early age. Now that he's older, he thinks that anything he does is all right, and that the more he does wrong, like calling attention to himself through running with the surf crowd or whatever, the more you'll help by fixing or dismissing things as you did when he was younger.

"The problem is, you've recognized your mistake, and so has Mom. She's using Billy as a club against you; she's blaming you for the things he does as a result of the way the two of you brought him up. She's probably tying me in as failure number two, and insists that you should have listened to her in the first place. You want to do the right thing, but you're powerless. If you do it, Mom will probably leave.

"As you often say, more wars have been started down through history by that little thing women sit on between their legs than by all other causes. The handle of the club is her living with you.

"Now I know why you blew up when Billy got busted for drugs. You already knew he was using them, and when he told you off, you belted him out of frustration. You made a deal with the devil and now you're being gored by the horns."

Dad exhaled deeply, fired the ever-present pipe and blew a cloud of smoke from the side of his mouth. "You're absolutely correct. I did make a bargain, and I don't like it. It goes against my every instinct. Sooner or later, no matter what the reason, a man has to be responsible for his own actions. I've done more things against my judgment since we moved back to Savannah than I've ever done in my life. And to tell you the truth, it's eating my guts out."

"That was pretty much evident when you didn't punch my lights out when I tried to stop you that night in the bathroom."

"I couldn't have if I'd wanted to. You were my conscience talking."

"So what are you going to do now?"

"To be honest with you, I just don't know. I thought your mom was what I wanted, but sometimes wanting in your mind pales in the harshness of reality," Dad said.

"I got only one request," Kevin said.

"What's that?"

"Don't use me as a bargaining chip against Mom with Billy."

"I don't understand."

"Then I'll make it clear. As long as your problems are with Billy and Mom, I'm sticking—no matter what you decide to do. But the first time you use me or something I own to keep your account square with Mom, I'm outta' here faster than the man of steel can change in a phone booth. Deal?" Kevin held out his hand.

"Deal," Dad said, as they shook hands firmly. "I think I'm gonna need you, just as a sanity check, before this is all over."

"Now," Dad said, turning toward the car. "How about you let your old man give you a few tips in body work so that we can make this old clunker a respectable set of wheels for a high school kid to drive to school."

But Kevin wasn't listening, he was thinking. Thinking that his father was right about the deal they'd just made, but that he was going to be right also.

Kevin was, in military terms, moving out smartly. His established curfew was 11:00 PM, it was ten of, he'd eight miles to go, and the Hillman was floored at eighty-two miles per hour in an all-out attempt to make it in before the deadline. Normally, he headed for home with the idea of arriving about ten of, but he'd blown a front tire, changed it at record speed, and that fifteen-minute delay had made the difference.

It was October, a school night, and Kevin was pulling out all the stops in a desperate attempt to make it. He came to a sliding stop in the front yard at three minutes after, ran across the yard, bounded up the steps, and burst into the family room to find Dad sitting contentedly, puffing his pipe.

"You're late," Dad said to Kevin without bothering to look up from the magazine he was reading.

"Yeah, I know; but I would've been on time if—"

Dad stopped him in mid-sentence by holding up his hand under his throat and giving it the military cut engines motion.

He held up his open-handed palm and said, "I don't want to hear it; you know the rules. Your curfew is 11:00 PM. Not one after, or five after, or even two after. If I let you get by with being three minutes late now, then pretty soon it'll be 11:15, then 11:30, and so on. Then six months from now, we'll be arguing over why you're two hours late. Rules are rules, I don't have many, but they're absolute. Gimme."

Reluctantly, Kevin peeled the car key off his key ring and dropped it in Dad's hand.

"You get it back in a week. Until then, the car stays put, right?"

"Right," Kevin said, flopping down on the sofa and giving his father his most wounded look. "Crap. I had a date for this Friday, too."

"You don't anymore; at least not if you have to drive," Dad said unsympathetically. Seeing Kevin's disgusted look, Dad asked, "So, what happened?"

"Had a flat; if it hadn't been for that, I'd have made it in plenty of time," Kevin responded.

"If you thought you were going to have a flat tire on the way home, you should have left in plenty of time to change it and still get in before curfew."

"That's not fair," Kevin complained.

"Life's not fair, sport, and it only gets tougher as you go along. Part of growing up is making commitments and being the kind of person that can be counted on. How long do you think you'd have that job as a mechanic if you didn't show up on time? Not long, I'd bet. You, yourself, have told me how frustrating it is when your replacement doesn't show up on time at work. Doesn't the same principle apply here?"

"Yeah, I guess it does."

"Then you've sentenced yourself. All I did was carry out the verdict," Dad explained patiently.

"You know," Kevin said, getting up from the couch and heading toward the door to the kitchen. "You're a pretty tough nut to crack."

"Hey, partner, if you get by me, the rest of your life will be a downhill slide."

With a nod, Kevin turned and went to bed.

As it turned out, Kevin did in fact have a date after all the following Friday. Kevin's previous summer job, until he'd been canned for talking back to the manager, was ticket taker at the Raines Street drive-in. He'd formed a friendship with the cashier, an older girl of about twenty-one named Glenda.

Glenda was what could best be described as full-figured. An ash blonde, she was built along the same lines as Sophia Loren, plus about twenty pounds around the hips. The guys in the concession stand referred to her as the Duchess and said she was stuck up. To most people, she seemed sullen and withdrawn.

Kevin had a different view. There was a deep sadness in her eyes that stayed with her even when she smiled, which was not often. After they got to know each other better, Kevin learned why.

The mechanical unreliability of the Hillman and the threat of missed curfews frequently caused Kevin to end up relying on his thumb to get back and forth to work.

When Kevin had mentioned this to Glenda, she'd volunteered to give him a ride home at quitting time, which was usually about a half-hour after intermission. They'd fallen into the habit of sitting in the car, watching part of the replay of the first feature or just talking. This had led to casual outings to indoor movies or the local hamburger drive-in.

Through time, they'd confided in each other. It was during one of these car-talk sessions, that she'd disclosed to him that she had married a Parris Island marine at seventeen and been widowed at eighteen when he'd stepped on a land mine in Vietnam.

Even after Kevin had been fired from the drive-in, his and Glenda's friendship had continued. Glenda was a frequent visitor to the service station where he worked, and Kevin would regularly show up at the drive-in on Friday after his shift ended. Glenda would wave him on through, explaining to the ticket taker that he was her brother.

Although they held hands when they walked together in and out of movie theaters or restaurants, and cuddled in the car for mutual comfort when they talked, they had not so much as even kissed. Glenda definitely aroused deep feelings in Kevin—to say nothing of the arousal of his manhood when he got a glimpse of her bountiful cleavage. But Kevin had no previous experience with sex and sensed that it would be wrong for him to make the first move. If the relationship was to become intimate, then Glenda would have to take the first step.

Glenda had stopped by the station and asked Kevin to make arrangements to get off work on Friday, as she wanted to do something special that night. When Kevin told her of his grounding, Glenda said she would be by his house to pick him up at 5:30.

"Glenda!" Kevin said, jumping into the front seat of her '66 Impala. "You look stunning. What's the occasion?"

"Thank you, kind sir. The occasion is a special secret that I'll tell you about later. I've prepared a snack for us to eat on the way to a place I want you to go with me. It's about an hour away, so just sit back and enjoy the ride—and the view." She finished with a seductive wink that would have given a dead man a woody.

As the car sped along, Kevin found it hard to look at Glenda indifferently. Normally very plainly dressed, she looked altogether different tonight.

Her hair was freshly permed, her makeup careful. She had on a fresh white vee-necked blouse, which revealed a generous amount of cleavage and did nothing to hide the lacy, all-but-translucent bra underneath. A hip-hugging slit black silk skirt, black hose, and three-inch black high heels completed her transformation from dowdy cashier to voluptuous, and very desirable, beautiful woman.

"Caught you," Glenda said, as she caught him giving her the once-over, twice. "You like?"

Kevin nodded. "My husband always liked this outfit; said it made me look like a cross between a movie star and a hundred-dollar hooker, especially when I wore these." Kevin's eyes followed Glenda's hand as she pulled her skirt up far enough for Kevin to see the stockings held tightly in place by a matching black garter belt with chrome clasps.

"There's also a matching set of lacy black bikini panties. I'll be glad to show you those when we stop, if you want?" Glenda asked mischievously, her eyes twinkling.

"I'll, uh, take your word for it," Kevin said.

Glenda laughed easily and said, "Suit yourself."

South Carolina was their apparent destination since they had quickly crossed the Talmadge Bridge and had turned off of U.S.-17 North and were now headed towards Beaufort.

She'd made small talk about one thing and then another, to which Kevin had mostly nodded in reply. He was curious about their endpoint, and nervous about what Glenda had in mind. This was a Glenda that Kevin had never seen before: confident, poised, and strikingly beautiful.

The lights of Parris Island Marine Base were in sight when they pulled off on a side road and stopped in front of an expensively maintained private cemetery.

"C'mon," Glenda said, taking his hand and leading him through and around the graves with a practiced skill that implied that she'd been here before. She stopped suddenly in front of a plain grave with a simple marker with a Marine Corps emblem on the headstone.

"Your husband."

"Larry, meet Kevin; Kevin, meet Larry," Glenda said, switching on the flashlight she'd removed from her purse.

"Larry, you'd like Kevin, he's younger than you in years, but every bit your equal in maturity. He's the first man I've met, since you, who makes me feel good about being alive. After you, I thought there'd never be others; now I know that there will. They'll possess your best qualities: your independence, your sincerity, and your strength. I'll try to instill in them the lust for life you instilled in me. I'll become their teacher and confidante, but most of all, I'll become their friend.

"Kevin," Glenda said, as she took Kevin by the arm. "You'd have liked Larry. He was the same age I am now when we met.

"I was a runaway from a broken home, working at a drive-in. He married me, even though he didn't love me, and in spite of the fact that he knew I was pregnant by the manager where I was working, to assure my baby would have a name and a father. He stayed with me after the miscarriage because he fell in love with me, and I with him. He made me feel special.

"He believed fiercely in his cause, the way you do yours. He had the same lust for life as you, and like you, could change things by his mere presence. He was my first love; and he'll always be special."

The hand holding the flashlight shifted suddenly, illuminating the lower part of the gravestone. Kevin could feel the sweat forming in the small of his back as he matched Glenda shiver for shiver: the date was today, just three years ago exactly.

"It's the anniversary of his death; that's the special occasion," Kevin said solemnly.

"It is, yes, but that's not the special occasion," Glenda said. "That comes later. Come on."

Glenda put her arm around Kevin, who reciprocated as they returned to the car. As Kevin held the door for Glenda, she did not sit, put her legs together, then swing them in a ladylike fashion into the car, but chose instead to step in. The slit skirt flared open. Kevin saw that Glenda did indeed have on black lacy bikini panties, a perfect match for the garter belt.

"Where to now, mystery woman?" Kevin said, as they regained the main road toward Hilton Head.

At Glenda's insistence, Kevin was now driving, with Glenda snuggled in the middle with her hand resting on his thigh. When Kevin had made no move to reciprocate, Glenda had raised her skirt until a generous length of garter strap was visible over the top of the stocking, taken his right hand, and lodged it securely under the stocking top, giving Kevin a raging hard-on that he was sure Glenda could plainly see.

"You just do the driving, honey; I'll do the navigating," Glenda said suggestively, reaching up and unbuttoning another button of her blouse.

Like a robot, Kevin responded to Glenda's commands until he found himself in the parking lot of a one of the swankiest hotels in Hilton Head.

"I booked a suite for the weekend. Grab the basket out of the trunk," she said.

The suite was like nothing Kevin had ever seen before. It seemed half as big as Dad's house and probably twice as expensive. The bed was one of those huge round affairs with satin sheets, and the bathroom had a tub big enough to swim in. It looked like something out of a James Bond movie.

"It's the honeymoon suite. Give you any ideas, baby?" Glenda cooed.

"Oh, a couple," Kevin said, unable to hide the nervousness in his voice.

"This is the special occasion. I've decide to celebrate my return to living by teaching my special friend about life," Glenda said, pushing Kevin down on the satin sheet. She stood in front of him and unbuttoned the last three buttons on her blouse, seductively pulled it out of the waistband of her skirt and slid it slowly off her shoulders, letting it fall to the floor. Next, Glenda slithered out of her skirt, and fell on top of Kevin so that her breasts were inches from his face.

"The clasp is in the front, baby," Glenda said, rubbing her exposed cleavage on his chin.

As Kevin started to slide his hands to the front of the bra, Glenda suddenly rolled off the bed, and said impishly, "Not so fast, stud. A woman likes to be wined and dined before she's bedded.

"Besides, before I get down to ripping your clothes off, I suggest you call your dad and tell him his little boy ain't coming home. And after tonight," Glenda said, sensuously caressing her breasts and running her hands down to her panties, pulling them tightly, exposing generous tufts of hair in the process, "he may find that no little boy lives there anymore."

When Kevin made no move to comply with her request, Glenda picked up the phone, dialed his home number and, on hearing a hello in the receiver, thrust the phone at Kevin and flopped over next to him on the bed to listen in.

"Uh, hi, Dad, this is Kevin. I, uh, called to tell you I don't think I'll be able to make it home tonight. And I didn't want you to worry."

"Well, tell me where you are son, and I'll come and pick you up," Dad said in a concerned voice.

"Well, you see, I don't think that will be possible. I'm over in Hilton Head and in no condition to drive home." The last statement was completely true. In his constant state of erection, it was impossible to stand up straight.

"Do you have a place to sleep?"

Glenda suddenly reached over him, grabbed the phone and answered, "He sure does."

"Oh, I see," Dad chuckled. "Got your protection with you?"

"He sure does," Glenda repeated quickly, and then added as an afterthought, "and I brought spares."

"Hope you know Braille," Dad said, as he hung up.

"What did he mean by that?"

"Private joke."

"Well, banter with these," Glenda said, unsnapping her bra and placing his hands on her breasts, in the process giving him a tongue-lashing kiss that made his heart leap in his chest.

"I see, said the blind man," Kevin said, as he came up for air.

"Baby," Glenda said, rocking back on her knees. She unsnapped the crotch of her panties, unzipped his pants, and removed both pants and underwear in one motion. "After this weekend, your vision is going to be so good that science will demand your eyes as live telescopes."

"What a way to go," Kevin agreed. Glenda slid on the protection, and her naked body fell on his, causing his hardness to slide easily into her well-lubricated channel.

"Oh, baby," Glenda moaned. "It's been so long, and I need it so bad."

As Kevin's first orgasm erupted deep inside Glenda, Kevin had to agree that Dad had been right; it was the greatest, most goddamndest feeling in the world.

"Well, well, well. Look what the cat dragged in. You look all in; tough weekend pass?" Dad said, as Kevin walked into the workshop Sunday morning, looking to all the world like someone who had just spent the past week astride a horse.

"I was just thinking of sending a posse out for you. This woman must be really something," Dad said.

"She is," Kevin admitted, then added with bravado, "and was, twelve times."

"Horny little bastard, aren't you?"

"Just a chip off the ol' block," Kevin said with a grin.

"You know, son. There are only two kinds of women in the world: ladies and otherwise. So far, I ain't never met no otherwise. Point made?" Dad said.

"Point made," Kevin agreed.

"Now, if you think you can keep the tiger in the cage, I've been waiting for you to get back. We've got a mission to prepare for," Dad said, his voice suddenly serious.

"What's up?" Kevin said, his tone changing to match Dad's.

"Notice anything different around here?"

"Yes, as a matter of fact I do. Billy's old Falcon wagon is sitting out front, and my Hillman is curiously missing," Kevin said.

"Give the troop a cigar. Care to guess why?"

To Kevin's silent shrug, Dad continued. "Your brother blew the motor in his wagon. He made it to the house last night when I wasn't home and conned your mom out of your car. He called a couple of hours ago and said he was broke down and needed us to come and get him."

"Where is he?"

"Jacksonville," Dad said.

"Jacksonville?" Kevin repeated in amazement. "What the hell's he doing in Jacksonville?"

"Apparently, running away from home," Dad said. "That is, of course, until he ran into trouble."

"Rescue mission?" Kevin inquired with a lifted eyebrow.

"Leaving within the hour," Dad said.

"Shotgun?" Kevin asked.

"You know the rules; you aren't allowed across the state line for any reason."

"Shotgun," Kevin repeated.

Dad thought for a moment, then smiled and said, "Yes, son, I think I would very much like to have you along."

Ignoring Mom's protests, they loaded the trunk with tools and a tow bar that Dad had made especially to fit the Hillman's bumper bolt holes, and were off within the projected hour. They had cleared the city limits, and were about an hour and a half down South 17 when Dad began to vent his frustrations.

"You know, son. I just don't know what to do about your brother. I thought allowing him to live away from home in his first year of college at Barnstein might help give him some sense of responsibility, but I guess I was wrong. He's living in that damn rundown house with two surfing buddies at the beach and failing in school. And the damnedest part is that, like an idiot, I'm paying the tab.

"This is the last straw. I'm going to have it out with your mother when we get back. Her plan of appeasement isn't working worth a damn. It's not fair to Billy, it's not fair to you, and most of all, it's killing me."

"Sure you've thought this whole thing through?" Kevin asked. "Couldn't the same case be made concerning me?"

"I have, and it doesn't," Dad said equably. "Your case was entirely different. You were a victim of circumstance; it often happens that way. You weren't lying, cheating, or stealing for your own personal selfishness. Your intentions were good; the politicians just got in the way, that's all." Dad lit his pipe and blew out a big cloud of smoke. "Your brother is an entirely different matter. He runs from responsibility; you covet it. The only possible cure is a good stiff dose of reality."

"Your mind's made up?"

Dad started to answer, then nodded silently at the state of Florida sign as it slid swiftly past them. "Welcome to the Sunshine State, outlaw."

"I won't tell if you don't," Kevin said.

"Mum's the—"

Dad's reply went uncompleted; the car was the culprit. It sounded like an elf had suddenly appeared with a five-pound sledge and was practicing for the finals of the jingle bell ringing competition. The clanging of metal on metal was teeth-grating. The engine died instantly, killing the power steering and power brakes in the process, but despite that Dad successfully manhandled the big New Yorker off to the side of the road.

Kevin saw the problem as soon as he raised the hood. The belts were a twisted mess, and the bolts that had held the crankshaft pulley to the damper had sheared off. After bouncing off the underside of the hood and denting it, the pulley had come to rest on the intake manifold. Fortunately, other than cutting the upper radiator hose, the pulley had miraculously managed to miss the water pump and radiator itself.

"What's the verdict, son?" Dad said, joining Kevin at the front of the car with a flashlight retrieved from the glove compartment.

"The patient's wounded but, with three or four hours' effort, should be well again."

"Quarter to eight," Dad said, glancing at his wristwatch. "I'll see if I can flag down a car to get us in to a service station for a tow truck." Dad nodded as he confirmed Kevin's assessment.

Curiously, Dad didn't have to flag down a car. One stopped.

"Have a breakdown, pops?" A husky young male voice said sarcastically as he walked into the glare of the flashlight.

"No thanks, we've already had one," Dad shot back.

Kevin heard a second door slam and the sound of other footsteps in the semi-darkness. He glanced quickly at Dad, caught his subtle nod, and slowly reached his hand onto the engine and grasped the pulley and surreptitiously slid it behind his back.

"Aw, now that ain't very social of you, pops. Especially since me and my buddies stopped out of the goodness of our hearts to help a stranded motorist."

In the glare of the flash, Kevin could see the youth's smirking expression.

There were five of them, each with the same eager smirk. They stood in a semi-circle around Kevin and Dad. Three were closer to Dad than Kevin. They obviously considered him a bigger threat.

That was fine with Kevin. The two assigned to him looked to be the easiest to take out, and take out it would have to be.

"Okay, grandpa, we can make this as easy or painful as you want. You give me your wallet and your watch and we'll get out of here, and you and your grandson can get on with your roadside repair."

"Two things, dickface," Dad said. "First, don't call me pops or grandpa or any other fucking name you come up with."

"Why, I'm very sorry, sir. We're just trying to earn a dishonest living and wouldn't think of offending you. Right, boys?"

"Second," Dad continued sternly, ignoring the interruption, "I think you'd better get back in your car and get the hell out of here before I get mad."

"Oooohhh!" the leader responded. "Please don't hurt me, mister barroom brawl—"

Dad and Kevin went into action simultaneously. Kevin kicked the nearest thug squarely in the balls and used the pulley to shatter his collarbone. He dispatched the second in the same quick and efficient manner and turned, intent on helping Dad.

Dad didn't need any help; he was doing just fine. He'd purposely lined the leader up for a backhanded judo smash and had executed it perfectly.

The fourth figure was quick. He pulled a hunting knife from the back of his belt, but Dad was quicker still. He snapped off the car antenna, and literally whipped him into submission until he dropped the knife, covered his face, and cowered. A well-placed kick to the head put him into sleepy time.

The fifth backed away, threw up his hands, and pleaded, "Please, sir, I've had enough. Besides, this wasn't my idea. I didn't want any part of it, but the others forced me into it."

"Quiet, shit-for-brains," Dad said, grabbing him none too gently with his left hand, rearing back with his right, and following through with a beautifully thrown right uppercut. As Dad made contact with his right, he released his grip with his left, and the unconscious figure fell like a redwood. He looked at Kevin and said conversationally, "I see you've been in on these sparring sessions before."

"Yeah. It's kind of amazing. People generally assume that when they're talking to you, or taunting you, as the case may be, that you'll do them the courtesy of listening. Nice to know that an old grandpa like you hasn't lost his touch." Kevin grinned cheekily.

"Guess I'm the one who's a chip of the ol' block now," Dad conceded with a nod.

A second car had stopped and a solitary figure was now walking toward them in the darkness. Both Kevin and Dad were instantly alarmed. The figure was carrying a military issue .45.

"Evening, gentlemen," the voice said. "Don't think I'll need this now," he said, as he stuck the pistol in his belt. "Thought you might be in a spot of bother, but I can see that assessment was premature. You guys did right well, better than some of my boys did last month when they went on liberty, broke down, and got rolled by these assholes."

"Got a name, friend?" Dad asked politely.

"Chief Petty Officer Dalworthy, Jax Naval Station; Jim to you guys. I called for help on my radio; the cops ought to be here shortly. Excuse me."

One of the hoods that Dad had taken care of was starting to get shakily to his feet. Jim helped him up, inquired if he was all right, and on receiving an affirmative nod, reared back, and hit him squarely on the jaw with a clenched fist that effectively turned out his lights once again.

"These bastards have been preying on my boys and stranded motorists for months. The local cops seem to be conveniently busy when these things happen and have been 'unable to apprehend them' despite several eyewitness descriptions."

"But if what you say is true, then the local cops won't bother to show, will they?" Kevin asked, trying hard to hide the panic that was settling over him. Local cops asked questions, questions Kevin couldn't afford to answer.

With a tolerant smile, Jim answered. "An absolutely correct assumption, young man. That's why I called the state boys, to assure that this incident is investigated thoroughly."

A wailing siren confirmed Jim's words. Within moments, the deserted stretch of South 17 was transformed into a maze of flashing lights. Ambulances arrived and carried off the injured combatants.

A quick call on the police radio produced a local tow truck to haul the big Chrysler to a local gas station. The state boys had been there approximately half an hour, and were just completing taking statements, when the local chief of police arrived at the scene.

"Evening, Officer. I heard what happened over the radio. Sorry we couldn't get here sooner, but one thing and another kept us. Know what I mean?" He looked just the way Smitty imagined every redneck Southern law officer did. Forties, short, portly, and almost comical in his Smoky the Bear hat.

"Oh, I know just what you mean, Chief," said the state trooper, a sergeant.

"Well, I appreciate your help, but me and my deputies can handle this thing from here on in. I heard you identify those boys. They're just local kids full of piss and vinegar."

"Is that a fact?"

"Yeah, so if you just leave everything to me, I'll see that they're properly punished."

"I'm afraid I can't do that, Chief."

"Why not?"

"Well," the trooper paused to motion to several fellow patrolmen, who surrounded the chief. "According to one of those boys, you were getting 20 percent of their take to assure that they were never caught."

"That's a lie. No matter which one of them said it," the chief responded indignantly. But the sweat was flowing freely down his face.

"Maybe, but we'll let the courts decide that." Turning to his officers, and making no attempt to hide his disgust, he ordered, "Take this scum over to the patrol vehicle, cuff him with wrist and ankle bracelets, and take him directly to the barracks. Get in touch with the governor's office, ask them to obtain search and seizure warrants for his office and personal residence, then report back to me personally with your findings."

As the chief was led away, alternately protesting his innocence and threatening retaliation for this humiliation, the sergeant turned back to Jim, Dad, and Kevin and said, "Gentleman, the state of Florida is in your debt. The only way the state, and the South in general, is ever going to shake off its speed trap reputation is to clean out these pockets of local dishonesty.

"Thanks again for your assistance. I'll be in touch with you if I need further clarification of your statements. Goodnight." He gave them an informal salute and walked toward his vehicle.

"Chief Petty Officer Dalworthy," Dad said, "I don't know about you, but I could sure use a beer. It's been a helluva night."

"On me, men," Jim said crisply. "C'mon, I'll give you a ride in."

As Kevin slid into the backseat of Jim's car, he had to agree. All in all, it had been a helluva night; come to that, it had been a helluva weekend.

Was the weekend just the preamble to events to follow? Smitty suspected it would be more the hard knocks of the latter . . . rather than the ecstasy of the former . . . .

CHAPTER FIVE

Okay, Kevin, you've paid your debt to society. You may take the book home," Miss Simpson said.

"Thank you," Kevin replied, glancing toward the door.

"What are you so nervous about, young man?" Miss Simpson asked suspiciously.

"Ah, nothing," Kevin said.

"Afraid someone will see you in here kissing up to your English teacher?"

Kevin blushed a deep crimson and blustered, "Of course not."

"Aaah," she nodded, paused, and grinned impishly. "Then you're just shy because you don't want anyone to know that you have a huge crush on me."

"Um, yes, ma'am, that's it," Kevin said, hurriedly exiting the classroom, his neck burning as he felt the amused stare of Miss Simpson on his back. Kevin did have a special feeling for her, but it had nothing to do with amore.

Their regular English teacher, a single and desperate blonde named Miss Walker, was replaced in mid-October, when she began to obviously show signs of eating for two. After much hemming and hawing, the school board decided that to allow her to continue to teach would set a bad moral example for the students and effectively condone promiscuity.

There would be no such problem with her replacement. The board persuaded Miss Simpson out of retirement to take over the class on an interim basis. Given the teacher shortage, interim became permanent in short order.

She was on the dark side of sixty, with a face like a deformed prune. With snow white hair pulled tightly back in a bun, rimless glasses, shoes that looked like army boots, and sack dresses that implied that her breasts and navel were now in the same general latitude, the prospect of her developing the same problem as her predecessor was remote.

But what she lacked in physical allure she made up for in character. She was one, and she had it by the carload lot, as Kevin soon learned.

Kevin studied just enough to pass in school. It wasn't that he was particularly lazy or hated school; mainly, he found it boring. Kevin had concluded that to most teachers, their work was a job, not a calling. Since they approached education indifferently, so did he. Miss Simpson made an immediate impression on him that forced him to reevaluate his earlier conclusions.

On Miss Simpson's first day, Kevin decided that she was a senile old biddy, though he had to grant that she was enthusiastic. As she spoke of the lasting pleasures of learning, he opted for the temporary pleasure of sleep.

He woke with a start. Miss Simpson slammed a wooden ruler across his desk with as much force as her bony little five-foot-nothing frame could muster.

"There'll be no sleeping in my class, young man." Kevin snatched the ruler from her hand, snapped it in half, and threw it out the window.

The next thing she did came as a complete surprise to Kevin, as well as everyone else in the room. She turned on her heel, clomped to the front of the room, and calmly wrote Kevin's name on the top right-hand corner of the blackboard. Next to that, she wrote 65¢, turned, and announced to Kevin that until he paid his debt to society, he'd not be allowed to participate in any of the classroom's activities.

Kevin had replied that this would be just fine with him because he didn't care about any of this school crap anyway.

With a challenging twinkle in her eye, Miss Simpson had replied with equal coolness, "You will."

Much to the amazement of Kevin himself, Miss Simpson's prophecy came true.

As the weeks rolled by, her enthusiasm and bubbling personality had won over most of the class. Kevin continued to resist, the bill growing to four dollars and change as Kevin turned more rulers into kindling.

But she wouldn't let him sleep and wouldn't let him participate in class until the debt was paid. She did, however, give him a book to read, with the strict understanding that it was not to be taken from the room. When Kevin got interested in the book and requested permission to take it home, she quietly pointed to the corner of the blackboard, smiled, and held out her hand, palm up. Kevin had slammed the book down and stormed out of the room.

The final capitulation had come today when the principal dropped by the classroom, "Just to see how you're getting along."

Seeing Kevin's name, and the dollar amount, he immediately asked in a suspicious tone what it was for. Miss Simpson replied, in a voice cool as a frosted beer glass, that the amount was the total collected to date for a Christmas party—and that Kevin was the treasurer. Her tone and manner were so convincing that the principal believed it wholeheartedly, and so did Kevin, until he remembered who the major—the only—contributor was.

After his last class, he'd sneaked back to her classroom and paid the bill. He was granted permission to take the book home for the weekend.

"What are you doing, troop? Improving your mind?" Dad asked. It was three in the morning.

"Just a book," Kevin answered.

"A book?" Dad reached out and took the novel from Kevin's hands. He examined it briefly and passed it back. "That's kind of a switch for you; your usual bill of fare is war comics, isn't it?"

"Still is," Kevin replied. "This is just a temporary side trip. What gets you up at this time of the morning? Don't try to tell me it's just Mother Nature calling."

"It's this whole damn mess," Dad said, flopping down in Kevin's desk chair. "Ever since we brought your brother home from Florida two months ago, things just haven't been going right, and given the current state of affairs, it's only likely to get worse."

"Your restriction plan for Billy isn't working out?"

"Hell, no, it's not working!" Dad shot back. "And it's not because I haven't tried. It's your mother; she literally has me by the balls. She claims that Billy would have never have tried to run away if I'd not given you preferential treatment."

Seeing Kevin's shoulders arch forward—a preparatory movement to an emotional protest—Dad waved him to silence then continued. "You don't have to tell me; I know. For some reason that makes no sense to me, she thinks I give you everything and your brother nothing."

"Doesn't she understand that I work and pay for everything, from the parts for my cars to my own underwear?"

"I've told her that, but she says that I favored you when you two were living with me by teaching you how to do things and take care of yourself."

"Well, as I recall, you did try to teach both of us. Billy was bored stiff and you finally gave up. In fact, I seem to recall Billy saying that he didn't need to learn this 'lower life-form stuff' since he was going to be a professional surfer and would use the money from contests and endorsements to buy a new car and pay someone to keep it serviced," Kevin said irritably.

"You remember that line too, huh?" Dad smiled wryly.

"And isn't this the same dude who, in front of Mom, called you a 'money-grubbing capitalist' when you tried to make him pay the expenses for that little jaunt to Florida two months back? What does Mom say to that?"

"She says he was just upset and didn't mean it."

"What does she say about the car engine for the Falcon that you rebuilt and paid for, after Billy left the dipstick out and drove it all the way from the beach with no oil? An engine, that I might add, you put the squeeze on me to help you change."

"Trots out that same old excuse about favoritism and such."

"Sounds like you're damned if you do and damned if you don't."

"I'm fucked," Dad said bitterly, as he rose to go. "But not for long." He smiled.

"What have you got up your sleeve?" Kevin asked.

"Oh, I think we'll see some of these things clear up shortly before Christmas."

Kevin rubbed his chin thoughtfully; it was mid-November. "What's so special about then?"

"Nothing much," Dad said, "except that's when Billy's college grades come out."

"Anticipating the worst, you've got a plan."

"Bet on it, troop."

Dad was just about out the door when a sudden premonition stuck Kevin, and he called after him softly, "Dad."

"Yes."

"Remember our deal."

"I'll try," Dad said, closing the door behind him.

You'll do better than try, Kevin thought to himself. *At least if you still want your number-two son around for cheap child labor.*

"Who was that guy I pointed out to you who asked me to dance tonight, baby?" Glenda asked, as Kevin slid into the driver's seat.

"Oh, uh, that's John. He's the starting quarterback on the football team."

"He seemed dumbfounded when I turned him down when he asked me for a dance."

"Probably was a first. All the little high school cuties fall all over themselves every time he says hello," Kevin explained. "Funny thing is, get John alone, and he's a nice guy; get him in front of a crowd, and he turns into a real asshole."

"You know, it's funny you should say that," Glenda said. "Even when he was coming on to me with his macho approach, there was something in his voice that left me with the same impression."

"Where was I when all of this happened?"

"You'd gone to the bathroom. As soon as you left, I noticed him staring at me. You weren't even across the room when he swaggered over and said, 'Hey baby, what say you dump the boy and dance with a man?"

"Ooooh, what'd you say back to him?"

"I prefer quiet, thoughtful boys, to loud boorish men—anytime."

"Thanks," Kevin said, patting Glenda's leg.

"You're welcome, baby," Glenda cooed back, nuzzling his ear. "My mom's out of town. Why don't we go to my apartment?" she asked suggestively, unzipping Kevin's pants, reaching in, and stroking him to an instant erection.

"Are you trying to take advantage of a minor?"

"Every chance I get," Glenda said, shifting in the seat and bowing her head. She made loud slurping sounds as she successfully inhibited Kevin's abilities to drive.

"You'd better cut that out, or we'll never make it to your apartment," Kevin said, breathing heavily. "Besides, my ol' man will kill me if I bring his new Plymouth home with stains on the seat."

Glenda sat up suddenly and said, "Okay, baby, I'll be a good little girl." She packed him away and zipped up his pants. "But only if you fondle me until we get there."

"The things we do for love," Kevin said, as he dutifully inserted his hand under her dress and into her panties.

"Um," Glenda said, sighing with pleasure. "Now I'm the one who's gonna stain the seats."

"Then I better quit," Kevin said, breaking off contact as suddenly as Glenda had.

"Bastard," Glenda said, in mock protest. "Come to that, how'd you happen to get your dad's brand-new car anyway?"

"Indentured servitude."

"I don't understand."

"All I had to do was change the oil, give it a tune-up, rotate the tires, and give it a good wash and wax."

"I see what you mean." Glenda nodded. "You did all that for me?"

"You bet. Don't think I want you showing up at the school Christmas dance in my old Hillman station wagon, do you?"

"Was I all right?"

"You were more than all right. You were the hit of the dance. Most of the guys there showed up with awkward teenagers in their first formal dress. I was with a woman. Every guy that passed within three feet of you tried to look down the front of your dress." He snapped her garter.

"You'll pay for that," Glenda said, grabbing him and squeezing his crotch very hard.

"So will you, kiddo," Kevin said, skidding the car to a stop in the apartment parking lot. He grabbed at her rear end as he chased her into the apartment and slammed the door.

Kevin awoke with a start. His lungs felt like a basketball that had just been slammed down on the floor with such force that all the air had rushed out at once. The hardwood floor was living up to its reputation; so was something else—Dad's fist.

Kevin tried to get up, and was quickly knocked back to the floor by a backhanded clenched left fist. A second attempt served only to convince Kevin that Dad was ambidextrous—he got the same shot, only with the right. Kevin sure didn't know what the hell was going on, but until Dad calmed down, he was not going to even attempt to get an answer.

Kevin retreated under the bed, sliding all the way to the opposite side, out of Dad's reach.

"Come out from under there, you little son of a bitch!" Dad roared.

When Kevin didn't move, Dad seized a baseball bat, got down on his hands and knees and began poking Kevin with it, trying to flush his quarry.

"What's got into you?" Kevin demanded.

"If you aren't out of there in exactly ten seconds, so help me, I'll rip the bed apart and drag your goddamn ass out of there. Do you understand?" Dad continued in a voice that could probably be heard all the way to the base flight line.

"Smitty!" Mom shrieked from the doorway to Kevin's bedroom. "Have you lost your mind?"

"Stay out of this; this is between me and my son," Dad snarled.

Tugging firmly on Dad's arm, Mom managed to pull him to his feet and restrain him in the far corner of the bedroom. "Come on out, son," Mom said.

Kevin cautiously extricated himself and got to his feet, a prudent distance away from Dad.

"Now," Mom said, tying in the bathrobe she'd thrown on hurriedly as she ran from the shower, "you want to tell me what's going on here?"

"I'll tell you what's going on here," Dad began, his rage so all-consuming that it came out as a sputter.

"Smitty. Calm down, get yourself under control, and just tell me what this is all about," Mom said.

"I'll tell you what this is all about," Dad said through gritted teeth. "I loan your son our new car, our brand new car, and how do I get it back?"

As Dad continued to glare unblinkingly at Kevin, Mom turned and stared also. Kevin held his hands up, totally bewildered. Dad stepped forward and said savagely, "Wipe that stupid, innocent-looking smirk off your face, or I'll knock it off."

Exasperated, Kevin responded, "I think you've lost your goddamn mind."

Dad was fast; but Kevin was faster—the message had been telegraphed by Dad's eyes.

Kevin's left hand shot out, grabbing Dad's right arm at the wrist, stopping it in midflight. Finally, and with a great deal of difficulty, Kevin slowly pushed the arm away, and down to Dad's side.

Neither spoke, nor moved, nor blinked. Mom seemed quite content to stand silently to the side and await the outcome.

"I'll kill you!" Dad bellowed.

"Well, before the sentence is carried out, your honor, how's about a last wish." It was a statement, not a question.

"What?"

"Tell me what in the hell this is all about."

Dad exhaled deeply as Mom said, "Yes, tell us what this is all about."

Dad glared at her sharply and said, "I made a deal with your son. I would loan him the Plymouth for his Christmas dance. In return, he would return it to me in the condition in which I loaned it to him."

"Yes, so?" Mom asked.

"So, I go out to inspect the car, the first thing this morning, and find that he's used it for a bedroom on wheels."

Mom looked at Kevin, who was totally confused and made no attempt to hide it, then at Dad for a further explanation.

"You're going to force me to produce the evidence in front of your mother?" Dad asked.

"Yes," Kevin said. "I think I am."

Dad left the room and went into his bedroom. Kevin heard the sound of a dresser drawer being opened and closed then the sound of Dad's footsteps as he marched back into Kevin's bedroom.

As Dad rounded the doorway, he brought his right arm around from behind his back, and flipped a folded white spandex garment that unfurled as Kevin caught it with both hands.

"I found this in the glove compartment; a women's girdle," Dad said triumphantly, snatching the girdle back and holding it up in front of Mom's face.

"So?" Kevin asked. He'd no idea where it came from. And he could personally testify to the fact that Glenda wasn't wearing one last night.

"That's my girdle," Mom said quickly.

"What?" Dad's head snapped around faster than Jack could pop out of his box.

"That's my girdle," Mom repeated irritably, stepping forward and taking the garment from Dad's unresisting hand. "You remember we went to the drive-in the other night. I got uncomfortable and went into the bathroom and took it off and put it in the glove compartment. I must have forgotten to take it out."

"Don't you lie for—"

"I'm not lying," Mom interrupted with a stare at Dad that would have melted ice. "How dare you even suggest such a thing?"

Kevin had just begun to crack the first trace of a smile, when a glare from Dad wiped it clean as quickly as an eraser does chalk. Dad definitely looked like he had tight shorts now, with jock itch for good measure. Dad's face was blushing a deep crimson. He was embarrassed and clearly at a loss for words.

"Well? Isn't there something you want to say to your son?"

Dad shifted uncomfortably from one foot to the other, clasped and unclasped his hands together in embarrassment, marched up to Kevin, jabbed his finger at his nose from a distance of three inches, and snapped, "Well, it should have been his!" Without further comment, he walked rigidly out of the bedroom.

"That man is—!" Mom said, stamping her foot in frustration.

An insight gripped Kevin, and he suddenly burst out laughing, and said, "Yeah, and he probably always will be."

"I want you in by 1:00 AM, troop," Dad said, as Kevin started for the door. "And you know what happens if you're late."

"1:00 AM." Kevin winced. "Everyone else is staying all night. Why can't I?" Kevin already knew the answer even before he asked the question. But he would always test the limits—even though the chances of Dad changing his mind were remote.

"Two reasons," Dad said. "First, you know the rules of your probation; you're supposed to be home by midnight, and I'm stretching it by an hour as it is. Second, I've got a lot of experience at these kind of parties; seen 'em all the time in the service. Things have a way of getting out of control. And you know damn well as I do, that you can't afford to be anywhere near one of these affairs when the shit hits the fan.

"One o'clock," Kevin nodded, "and not two past one or three past one. Or pretty soon it'll be 1:15—" then scurried out the door well in advance of the paperback Dad had thrown at him, in pretended anger, from his chair.

After grounding him for missing curfew the last time, Dad had told Kevin when he handed him back his car key that in the future the punishment would be exponential. When Kevin asked what he meant by that, Dad explained that the penalty for missing curfew the next time would be two weeks, then four weeks the next time, then sixteen weeks if there was a time after that.

As with all the other of Dad's rules, this one would be rigidly enforced, and Kevin was secretly glad. He'd seen the results of other permissive parents who were lax or wavered in their disciplinary approaches.

Although there had been a few uncomfortable moments at the breakfast table the morning after the girdle incident and Kevin had to put up with some pretty heavy badgering from Mom and Billy—both of whom could not seem to understand Kevin's refusal to be angry over Dad's actions—the previous week's outburst was all but forgotten by Kevin. Dad was a man of strict principles, and more importantly, he stuck to them when things got rough. He'd never let Dad know this, but Kevin secretly admired him for his actions. You could question his methods, but Dad was a man who faced things head on, and when he did, he left the weak and the undecided in the dust.

Just as important, he respected the warrior who fought the good fight, who refused to let petty ego and jealousy cloud future interactions. Tonight had been a classic example. He'd been sound and logical in his reasons for enforcing his curfew. His comments had served as a warning, a warning that Kevin took to heart as he stopped to pick up an underclassman who did not yet have a driver's license.

"Hi, Kevin, thanks for giving me a ride," Ted said. He was a short, stocky Jewish kid whose widowed mom watched over him so closely that it seemed as if she were an attached appendage. Kevin was surprised she'd even let him go to the party.

"No problem," Kevin responded. "Used to be in the same situation myself a couple of years back."

"Where's that luscious girlfriend of yours tonight?" Ted asked.

"Had to work," Kevin said.

"You are balling her, aren't you? She's just too fine not to enjoy," Ted said, as he licked his lips.

"Sorry, I don't give references," Kevin said.

"Ah," Ted said wistfully, "I bet she's a good fuck."

"Listen, asshole," Kevin said, reaching out and grabbing Ted by the jacket. "Don't you ever refer to Glenda like that again. What goes on between the two of us is none of your business. I repeat—none of your business. One of these days you and all these other bunch of idiots are going to grow up and understand that there are only two kinds of women in the world, ladies and otherwise.

"And so far, I ain't never met no otherwise," Kevin finished, releasing Ted with a slight push that bounced him off the passenger door.

"Okay, man; I'm sorry," Ted replied, wounded, as he readjusted his clothes. "I didn't know you were so damn touchy."

"That's not the point, Ted," Kevin said, beginning to calm down. "You've got to decide whether you're going to be part of the crowd or stand up for yourself. The crowd will encourage you to think as they think, act as they act, just so they can feel secure. If you stand up for yourself, it's a lonelier road but a lot more satisfying."

"Speaking from experience?" Ted asked.

"What do you mean?"

"There are a lot of stories circulating around school about you. The hottest one says that you're hiding out from some trouble somewhere else, reason being that you killed a dude in a fight. The same fight that got you that scar on your chin. They say that's why you walk away from fights: because you're afraid if you start, you'll lose control and kill someone."

"Whoever's spreading that drivel is barking up the wrong tree," Kevin said, while inside he was sweating at how close Ted had unknowingly come to the truth.

"There must be some truth there somewhere. When I was working in the principal's office the other day, I overheard him ask that your file be pulled. When the secretary asked why, he said he wanted to personally investigate some irregularities in your transcript that had been reported to him. So watch your ass, pal."

"Don't worry, there's nothing to it," Kevin said with confidence he didn't feel.

"Look," Kevin said, quickly changing the subject. "Do you want me to give you a ride home, when I leave at twelve?"

"Won't be necessary, I'm staying all night; Mom gave me permission."

"Okay, but be careful drinking, huh," Kevin said.

"Yes, Daddy," Ted said cheerfully.

"Hey," Kevin said with a shrug as they got out of the car at Larry's house. "I'm just trying to keep you from looking like a dumb-ass underclassman around all the seniors."

Kevin had found several things unsettling when he'd entered Larry's house. First, his parents were not home, and there were no other adults there to act as chaperones to assure that things did not get out of hand. Second, this was supposed to be a party, but it was a drinking binge. Except for one guy, no one showed up with a date. Third, the guy who did bring a date—looked as if she'd got in line twice when they were passing out the bodies—had said, when she was out of earshot, that he had brought her solely for the purpose of getting her drunk and fucking her brains out. Fourth, and finally, Larry's house was about twenty miles from town in an isolated wooded area where acres separated neighbors should trouble start. All of these things convinced Kevin to refrain from drinking and keep a close eye on the people and events.

Getting bombed and making an ass out of yourself seemed to be some kind of idiotic teenage rite of passage. But for the life of him, he just didn't see the big deal about getting drunk.

Kevin's dad had offered him his first 3.2 beer at thirteen sitting in the kitchen of their home. After that, if Kevin wanted a beer, it was readily available in the kitchen fridge for the taking. The result of which was that drinking, or getting shitfaced as his peers called it, was not that big a deal to him. There was just one caveat. Under no circumstances was Kevin permitted to drive if he'd been drinking.

Like all of Dad's rules, it had a zero tolerance and immediate consequences that were well-discussed in advance. Dad referred to this as a death penalty because of its degree of harshness. And, like his rigid enforcement of the curfew, this one had an even tougher penalty should he violate it.

If Kevin was picked up for a DUI, brought home by the police, or if Dad so much as smelled alcohol on his breath or clothes, his car would be sold and he would never again drive a car registered in Dad's name. Which was another was of saying that he would not be able to drive again until he could buy a car in his own name at twenty-one.

Right now Kevin had a feeling he was going to wish other parents were as resolute.

Three hours later, Kevin could see that his warning to Ted had been timely; too bad he'd not taken it to heart. Ted obviously had little experience in drinking. He, along with just about every other guy at the party, was acting loud and obnoxious and alternating trips into the surrounding shrubbery to P&P—puke and piss.

Kevin had broken up three fights, stopped two others before fists started to fly, and, generally speaking, had been busier than a one-armed paperhanger at a wallpaper hanging convention trying to keep order.

Things seemed to be quieting down, and Kevin had just sat down to take a well-deserved break, when a scream from down the hall launched him out of his chair. He ran quickly down the hall, scattering revelers like tenpins, as he pushed his way in the directions of the screams, which seemed to be coming from Larry's parents' bedroom.

Kevin broke open the bedroom door with a well-placed shoulder and burst into the bedroom. He focused immediately on the bed, where Kristie—the only female at the party—was being held down by three guys, naked, as a fourth lewdly chewed on her nipples and fondled the fur between her spread legs. Ricky, her date, was also naked and rolling on the floor in a drunken haze.

"Hold her steady," the one on top said sadistically as he unzipped his pants. "This bitch has been asking for it all night, poking those big tits in everyone's face, and now she's going to get it."

Kevin's reaction was immediate. As the would-be rapist reared up on his knees to position himself for entry, Kevin grabbed him by the hair with his right hand, pulled him over backward, and as he descended, hit him very hard with an open left-handed judo smash. His nose made an eerie snap as it broke cleanly as he fell off the end of the bed, hitting the floor headfirst and rolling into a disheveled heap.

Kevin dispatched the second youth in similar fashion. Since he was using both hands to hold Kristie by the left arm and left leg, Kevin hit him with a backhanded judo smash that bounced him off the wall like a flippered pinball. He stumbled over the prone figure of Ricky, hitting his forehead on the nightstand before landing solidly on the concrete floor.

The blind fury and rage that Kevin had kept bottled up inside for so long came bursting to the surface like an exploding volcano. He leaped onto the bed, used it as a springboard, and kicked the third youth, the one holding down Kristie's right arm and right leg, in the balls. He fell to the ground in agony immediately.

It had taken perhaps five seconds to handle the first three. In that time, the fourth ceased trying to stop Kristie from screaming; one of his fingers had gotten a little too close to her teeth, and she'd damn near bitten it in two.

Seeing his three friends dispatched quickly and the odds no longer in his favor, he sprinted for the door, holding his digit in pain, intent, it seemed, on running down the hall for what Kevin presumed were reinforcements.

He never made it. Kevin kicked the open door shut with his right foot. As the would-be rapist ran by him, Kevin grabbed him by the hair with his left hand and forced his head into the door with such force that his teeth left imprints. He spiraled slowly downward with a stupefied gaze.

"Oh, thank God!" Kristie said, sobbing uncontrollably as she flung her arms around him. "They burst in here suddenly, punched Ricky, and were going to rape me."

What a news flash. Kristie had come to the dance in a summer dress that showed too much cleavage. She'd flirted with every guy there, never missing an opportunity to bend and give them an eyeful. Alcohol and teenage hormones make for a lethal combination.

Earlier, Kevin had suggested to both Ricky and Kristie that things could get out of control and that they should leave, but both had ignored his warnings. Nothing justified rape, but they hadn't been smart.

With a great deal of difficulty, Kevin pried open her viselike bear hug, held her at arm's length, shook her firmly and said, "Kristie, you've got to get yourself under control quickly."

"But you don't understand. They—"

She never finished her sentence. Kevin's hand stung as he slapped her with a good deal of force across the face and said bluntly, "Now, you listen to me, sweetheart. In about thirty seconds they're going to come riding in here with more reinforcements than I can handle. There'll be time for crying and explanations later. Right now, the key thing is for us to get out of here." Kevin paused, surveyed the bedroom, then quickly seized a corner chair and hooked it under the knob.

"That ought to hold them for a minute or two," Kevin said. He jerked open the closet door, located a robe, threw it at Kristie, and said, "Put this on, slip on your shoes, and gather up your and Ricky's clothes. Quick."

Kevin admired the way she was responding, upset or not, without any of that silly schoolgirl modesty about her state of undress. Kristie had obviously decided there were more important matters to deal with than whether or not Kevin got an eyeful of her as she stooped to rake together their clothes.

There were two chairs in the bedroom. Kevin picked up the second and, using it like a fireman's ax, quickly dispatched the bedroom window and inner frame, giving them an escape path and turning the chair into kindling in the process.

Kevin snatched Ricky off the floor and tossed him over his shoulder like a sack of flour, stepped up and over the sill, turned and helped Kristie through, steadying her by holding her hand, and had silently led her around the back of the house toward his car.

The dense shrubbery was his ally now. Using it as cover, he successfully steered Kristie to his car, and got her and Ricky safely stowed aboard on the floor of the backseat. Kevin put the Hillman in neutral, turned the wheel, and quietly turned it around and pushed it down the dirt driveway toward the road.

Kevin had accomplished this so stealthily that no one in the front yard twenty yards away had even noticed his departure. He pushed the car about fifty yards, then jumped in, pulled the choke, turned the key to ignition, pressed the clutch down, put it in gear, and popped the clutch. The trusty little four-banger caught at the first turn. The music from the house was so loud that Kevin was sure that no one heard his car start. With a quick glance back to confirm this, he turned onto the road and accelerated quickly away.

"Okay, you can start breathing again," Kevin told Kristie as the car hit cruising speed and he turned on the lights.

"Are you sure?" Kristie asked nervously, slowly rising from her hiding spot.

"Yes, I'm sure," Kevin said. "Look, why don't you dress yourself and then Ricky, and then we'll decide what to do."

The road that time of night was deserted. Kevin had the Hillman floored, intent on putting as much distance as possible between himself and the party-hardies. His reactions to Kristie's call for help had been instinctive. He drove on in silence, listening to the rustle of clothing as she dressed and thinking of the possible ramifications of his earlier actions.

So deep in thought was Kevin that he jumped like someone who'd just stuck his finger in a light socket when Kristie leaned forward suddenly and kissed him on the neck. "Sorry, Kevin," Kristie said, climbing over the bench seat and settling in beside him. "I didn't mean to startle you. I just wanted to express my gratitude for what you did for me."

"You go through life saying thanks like that, and you'll never want for friends,"

Kevin said.

"What's wrong? You seem upset about something," Kristie asked.

"Oh, uh, I was just thinking. From the brief glimpse I got of those guys, I didn't recognize any of them as our classmates," Kevin said.

"No, they weren't; I'm sure of that. And I'll tell you how I know," Kristie said, anticipating Kevin's question. "They all had beards; that would make them older, probably in their twenties. When they were holding me down, I got a good look at them, especially the bastard that was on top."

"So, what do you want to do?" Kevin asked. The one thing Kevin didn't want was the police. If the police were to be involved, Kevin was not going to be the one to suggest it.

"Well, I'm not going to tell my mother or the police, that's for sure."

"Would you mind telling me why?" Kevin asked, trying hard to control his own inner elation.

"There are three very good reasons," Kristie said. "First, have you ever taken a good look at me and listened to half the stories the guys tell about me? I have no intention of allowing myself to be publicly humiliated and giving all the lying assholes the satisfaction of thinking that they're right."

Kristie was right; Kevin had heard the stories. According to the rumors, she had zippers on the crotch of her underwear for convenience. He lifted an eyebrow in disbelief.

"You don't believe me," she said.

To Kevin's silence, Kristie commanded, "Pull over."

Kevin slowed and pulled the car to the side of the road. While he was doing this, Kristie braced her back against the seat and rocked up on her feet. She pulled up her dress, pulled down her underwear and turning it inside out, pointed to a gauzelike red stained substance inside.

"When you get home to your mommy, ask her why a girl on her period would use a Kotex, if she's not a virgin," Kristie said.

One look in her eyes and Kevin knew that he'd not have to get a second opinion. "I believe you," Kevin said, as he regained the road.

"It's important to me that you do."

"You said there were three reasons," Kevin said uncomfortably, changing the subject.

"Second," Kristie said, "my mother would first kill me then demand that they be arrested and castrated. And to be honest with you, I think I'm partly to blame for what happened. The police would probably agree. I've been out of my training bra a long time, and I let Ricky take me to the party, get me drunk, and undress me. The only reason he didn't succeed in screwing me was that he got turned off by my period.

"Third." Kristie sighed deeply. "I don't want you to get into trouble."

"What?" Kevin asked breathlessly, as the light socket zapped him again.

"I don't want you to get into trouble," Kristie repeated.

"I don't understand," Kevin said, puzzled.

"I think you do; and so does my mother.

"It's simple. My mother says that when she's seen you, you're just like my father, who was killed in Korea. You have the smile that never quite touches the eyes and the heavy expression of someone who's seen harsher times. That's what's got you so upset. You reacted instinctively, laid out four assholes, and now you're worried about the consequences."

"You're pretty smart for a dumb-ass underclassman," Kevin said.

"You'll find other things to like about me," Kristie said. "And now that I think on it, there's a fourth point."

"What's that?"

"I think you gave those guys much more punishment than the law ever would. My hero," Kristie said, pecking him on the cheek again.

Kevin had to admit as he pulled up in front of Kristie's house, there was more to this girl than the eye could see. Maybe she acted like a bimbo in public because that was what people expected of someone who looked the way she did. Maybe Kevin had seen the real person underneath. He hoped so—from the brief glance he'd had, Kevin certainly liked what he'd seen.

"Aren't you going to kiss me good night?" Kristie asked expectantly.

"Yeah, sure," Kevin said. He was not expecting what happened next. Kristie put a lip lock on him that alternately curled his toes and stirred his loins. The kiss was long, deep, and passionate. Kristie took his left hand and placed it on her right breast. As Kevin began to instinctively fondle her, he felt the nipple grow until it poked through the bra and dress like an acorn jutting from an oak branch. Kevin had a sudden flash of Glenda and broke the kiss off suddenly and looked away.

"If you're worried about Ricky, don't be," Kristie said, misinterpreting his thoughts. "We're really just friends. And I've got a feeling," Kristie said, as she jumped out of the car, "that you and I are going to be much, much more. Bye, babe."

Kevin was halfway to Ricky's house when he came to. He was badly hung over and didn't say ten words all the way home, seeming to accept, without comment, the explanation that he'd gotten drunk, passed out, and was being driven home by Kevin, after dropping Kristie off.

Kevin judiciously left out the fight and his involvement, telling Ricky that he'd rolled off the bed and passed out. Kevin reinforced this by asking Ricky if he'd porked Kristie. He replied in a slurred cocky voice, "Hasn't everybody?"

Despite the side trips, Kevin still rolled in ten minutes ahead of curfew and went straight to bed with one thought lodged firmly in his mind. He had a feeling that he'd not heard the last of either the fight or Kristie.

From the opening school bell, the hallways were teeming with stories of the week-end beer blast. Typically, each time the story was retold, the facts became dimmer, while the juiciest parts about the so-called gang bang and resulting fight grew with each telling.

By the time Kevin walked into his last period band class, the party had become a Roman orgy and/or a Watts riot, depending on your point of view. An eerie silence fell over the band room as Kevin entered. Heads turned and Kevin could feel their eyes follow him as he took his seat in the first trumpet section next to Ricky, who was the first chair.

"Kevin, I want to talk to you outside," Mr. Wilkins, the band teacher, said tersely. Kevin followed him outside, to a chorus of murmuring, with Kristie's sympathetic smile, the only friendly expression in a sea of scowls.

"Tell me about it," Mr. Wilkins said.

"Tell you about what?" Kevin asked, concentrating very hard on trying to make his answer sound normal.

Mr. Wilkins exhaled. "Okay, Mr. Smart Ass, we'll play it your way.

"I want you to tell me from the beginning about the party at Larry's Saturday night. I want to know about your participation in the gang-rape of one of my band members, how much alcohol you supplied, and finally, I want the names of the members of your gang who brutally beat up and hospitalized three college students, one of whom was a congressman's son, not to mention doing over $4000 worth of damage to Larry's parents' house."

"From the way you're telling the story, sounds to me like you've already got the facts, leastwise, the ones you wanna believe," Kevin said contemptuously.

"Now you listen to me, you smart-ass son of a bitch," a voice said, as it approached. "We do have the facts; and we know all about it," Mr. Lazenby, the principal, said. "And we know all about you, too. This," he paused to wave a sheet of paper at Kevin menacingly, "is a transcript of your high school grades and more importantly, a copy of a confidential police report from Miami, Florida; ever heard of the place, punk?"

"Yes, as a matter of fact, I have," Kevin responded. "Place where hypocritical, limp-dick high school principals with homely fat wives go to stare at the bikini babes, wet dream, and jerk off."

"Mr. Wilkins, take Mr. Smith down to my office and wait there." The emphasis on Mr. was unmistakable. I want to get a firsthand report from this boy Larry. I understand he was most cooperative in giving us all the details of this sordid business."

"Hey, Mr. Lazenby," Kevin called out, as he was led away. "People who live in glass houses . . . " The principal stared at Kevin. "If you want to know what it means, just ask your preggo daughter, the college cheerleader. Word is she does a superb job of lifting spirits—of her entire college football team."

"Get that bastard out of here or I swear I'll personally beat the crap out of him myself," the principal screamed.

"Mr. Smith, I'm . . ."

"Excuse me," Dad said, cutting him off in mid-sentence with his first sergeant's glare. "I earned these stripes on my sleeve and this confetti on my chest. I am a senior master first sergeant in the United States Air Force. Civilians usually address me as sergeant, or Sergeant Smith if you must be formal."

"Uh, very well then, Sergeant Smith. I'm sorry to have to ask you to come here on such short notice."

"Excuse me, Principal Lazenby. Do you happen to know how to spell point?" Dad asked.

"Yes, I—" Mr. Lazenby's face flushed as he stopped, realizing that the trap had been sprung.

"Very well," he continued, his jaw tightening, and his eyes narrowing in anger. "As a result of eyewitness testimony, we have no choice but to suspend your son from school indefinitely for inappropriate conduct. Whether or not criminal charges are brought is a matter for the parents to pursue; frankly, I expect you'll be hearing from the police shortly."

"Is that a fact?" Dad asked, as he spent what seemed like an inordinate amount of time studying and fiddling with the flame in his freshly lit pipe. "And just what do you mean by inappropriate conduct?"

Mr. Lazenby glanced at Mr. Wilkins, who shrugged his shoulders, and continued, "A party was held Saturday night at which alcoholic beverages were served to minors. Fueled by this, a young student was raped. When a group of college students tried to stop this savage act, others, acting under your son's direction, attacked and severely beat up three of these boys.

"This became the impetus to ransack the house where the party was being held. According to our eyewitness account, your son was behind the planning of this party and participated in the assault and resultant hostilities.

"I have here a report from the Miami Beach Police Department. It states that your son was head of the NonComs street gang when he was arrested on suspicion of murder of four Cuban teenagers. Apparently, a plea bargain of some sort was arranged by which the case would not be brought to trial if you agreed to remove your son from the state for a period of five years.

"Frankly, as a school principal charged with assuring the safety of the students that attend here, I'm personally shocked that a person of this caliber is allowed to walk freely among decent people."

The principal didn't know it, but he was in for it now.

Dad always said that the best lawyers usually won because they knew their side of the argument, the opposition's side of the argument, and why their side was better. Dad now knew the opposition's side; Kevin had told Dad every single fact of the events of Saturday night over breakfast Sunday morning, in as much detail as he could remember. The cross-examination was about to begin.

"Who's your eyewitness?" Dad asked.

"We have a sworn statement from Larry, the boy at whose house the party was held."

"What about the young lady involved?" Dad continued. "What's her version?"

"Well, naturally, we're not going to embarrass her by putting her through the torment of have to relive this hideous experience. There's no need; we have an eyewitness account, and her mother refuses to allow it anyway."

"I see," Dad said.

"I'm so glad that you do," the principal said, misinterpreting Dad's response. "Now, if you'll just be so good as to take your son out of here quietly, I'm sure that we can come to some amicable arrangement and avoid further embarrassment for everyone."

"Like what, for instance?"

"Well, I really hadn't given the matter much thought. Better to leave that sort of thing to the school board to decide."

"Just how did you get involved in all of this?" Dad asked.

"The mother of one of the boys at the party called my home at 3:00 AM. Seems her son had been picked up by your boy and taken to the party at Larry's house. He was supposed to have been home at midnight. I called the police and asked them to ride by and check the house. When the first officers arrived, a fight was in progress on the front lawn, they called for backup, and before everything was under control, it required ten officers and three ambulances to restore order and take care of the injured. The owners, Larry's parents, are just heartsick over the damage to their property."

"Well, if that happened at my house," Dad began slowly, "I expect I would have been, too."

"I must say, Sergeant Smith, I'm most impressed with your attitude in this manner. But then again, I suppose when you have a son who is constantly in trouble, you must get used to it."

"Oh, I do. It's part of my job to discipline young people when warranted. By the same token, it's also part of my job to objectively investigate to assure that all the facts come out," Dad said firmly.

"But there are just one or two things that don't seem to fit together here that perhaps you could enlighten me on before I have this kid shot at sunrise tomorrow."

"Such as?" the principal asked.

"Well, for one thing, I don't quite see how my son could have been involved in the attempted rape. If he was, it'll probably go down as the first time in history when someone participates in a rape, beats up the four attackers, and then drives the victim and her date home because the young man had gotten himself too inebriated to drive.

"Second, I don't see how my son could have been involved in the fighting and ransacking of the house, when by your own testimony right here in this office, you admitted that these activities took place between 3:00 and 4:00 AM. Time is a key issue, when you figure that Kevin took the young lady home first, doubled back to Pennington Park and dropped off her date, and still walked through the front door of my house at 12:51 AM."

A mime would have sounded like a brass band compared to the absolute stillness in the office. The principal and the band teacher were motionless.

Grasping for any response, the principal stammered, "Uh, Mr. Smith, that is to say, Sergeant Smith, I respect your attempts to protect your son by lying for him—"

"Listen to me, Principal," Dad hissed, leaping across the room, grabbing him by the tie, and in the same motion slamming him against the wall with a force sufficient to skew the president's picture hanging on the wall.

"I make my living by bringing facts to light, not by covering them up," Dad said, emphasizing his point by shaking Lazenby by his tie knot and speaking from a distance of three inches.

"At breakfast Sunday morning, Kevin told me every single detail of the incidents that took place at the house, from the moment he arrived, until the moment he walked through my front door, and frankly, his version is quite a bit different from yours, to say nothing of being much more believable.

"After your call, I phoned a desk sergeant downtown. He provided me with some interesting details on you. The most significant of which concerns your daughter, who got pregnant by some lowlife, and then lit out for parts unknown." Dad had moderated his tone to that cool, detached voice that had the unmistakable ring of sincerity.

"The record shows you fought in Europe during the war, so down deep, you must be a pretty good man. Are you going to allow the hatred in your own heart to ruin a young man's reputation and maybe his last chance to get an education and make a clean break from the past?"

Dad released the principal, crossed the room, sat down in a chair, gave the bewildered band teacher a cursory smile, lit up the ever-present pipe, and waited.

The principal slowly crossed to his desk and sat down, never for a moment taking his gaze away from Dad. Slowly, he reached for a pack of cigarettes on his desk, nodded his thanks thoughtfully as Dad leaned forward and proffered a light, rocked back in his chair, put his feet up, and continued to stare silently at his adversary.

A minute passed, then another; each man puffed in silence, choosing to keep whatever thoughts they were generating to themselves.

The silence was finally broken by Mr. Wilkins.

"Mr. Lazenby, you're not going to fall for this scam, are you?" he asked.

"No, I don't think I am," he said, buzzing his intercom.

"Yes, sir," the box crackled in response.

"Helen, I want you personally to walk down to the band room and wait there until the end of the period. When Miss Kristine Peterson comes out, escort her back to my office."

Looking Dad straight in the eye, he continued. "Before this day is done, we're going to separate the innuendo from the facts and objectively get to the bottom of this matter."

"Well," Dad said. "I've got to be getting back to work. So I'll be running along."

"Leaving?" the principal asked, astonished. "I thought you'd want to stay until this matter was cleared up."

"No need," Dad said. "I have a hunch you'll get the straight of it now. If you listen to my son's version, I think you'll find that it corresponds pretty closely to the truth; I did."

All the facts did come out; and Kevin's version became the accepted truth. But that was by no means the end of it. Fueled by jealousy, hatred, and insecurity, the talk refused to die. And Kevin's past now seemed to be common knowledge.

Kevin would walk into rooms and the conversation would drop to a murmur followed by whispers and nods, all of which, from what Kevin could overhear, got more outlandish with each retelling.

His fellow classmates, including many of his so-called friends, refused to look him in the eye. Mr. Wilkins, to cover his own embarrassment at having been duped, had suddenly dropped Kevin and Ricky down to fourth and fifth position in the trumpet section and, when they had objected, had volunteered to give them passing grades if they chose to quit the band for a study hall period until graduation.

Curiously, no punitive action was taken against Larry, who had fabricated the cover-up to try to obscure his own complicity. Kevin suspected that this was because his father was a county commissioner and his mother a well-known socialite.

School was not the end of the hostility zone, merely the beginning. You didn't have to be a rocket scientist or genius to see that Mom was making Dad's life pure, living hell.

Mom was most distressed over the fact that this "sordid affair" had caused her to lose the presidency of the Savannah Garden Club, a position that she'd apparently sought for years.

The fallout didn't end there; it had spread to Billy also. He'd been dating a girl from a very well-to-do family. Her parents, already dismayed that the courtship had gotten far more serious than they'd preferred, had reacted immediately to Kevin's troubles by forbidding their daughter to ever see Billy again. Billy whined incessantly about this to Mom, who in turn used it against Dad, and the whole vicious cycle continued.

"Kevin! How could you?" Mom sputtered. "As if we haven't suffered enough embarrassment, now I understand you're leading some kind of student protest in the band?"

Before Kevin could begin to answer, Mom continued harshly. "Just you wait 'til your father gets home, young man; I know he spoiled you and favored you over Billy, but this is the last straw. This time I'll see to it personally that you're punished for your actions."

Kevin could hear the staccato clicking of her high heels on the sidewalk as she stalked back to the house. The sound irritated Kevin almost as much as Billy's snickering holier-than-thou expression as he entered through the open garage door.

"Your ass is in for it now, little brother. You heard what she said, dude; you're history. And from what I hear from the ol' alma mater, you're history there, too," Billy said triumphantly.

"One more smart-ass crack, dipshit, and you'll be history here and now," Kevin shot back.

"Big talk, little brother. I'm shaking all over," Billy retorted, but Kevin could see the nervous twitch in his eyes.

Kevin should have let it pass. He knew Billy was scared and was just putting on an act for the benefit of two scraggy-looking surfing buddies who were standing on the driveway just outside. But he'd backed water so much lately that he was up against the falls. He had to go forward; backward was no longer an acceptable alternative.

He turned, strode directly over to Billy, shoved him roughly against the garage wall, and asked, "Care for a little action, big brother?"

Billy lunged at Kevin, his face contorting in rage as he swung blindly with his right fist.

Kevin leaned away, easily avoiding the intended blow, stepped forward and made a solid connection of his own right fist with Billy's jaw.

Billy staggered backward against Kevin's current project, a Hillman convertible, slid off the fender, and landed solidly on the garage floor, his face masked in pure hatred as he glared, unable to rise.

"Asshole in the corner pocket!" Kevin said, nodding smugly. Turning to the driveway, he hollered, "Next!" Billy's two cohorts appeared to be fair-weather friends. Even before Kevin's challenge, they bounded for their car, started it, and, with a spraying of sand and gravel, were gone.

Kevin turned back to Billy, leaned over, grabbed him by the shirt, and was just about to hit him again when a noise from behind caused him to hesitate.

"Teeenhut!" Dad barked, bursting through the same door recently exited by Mom. "You snap to, buster, and I mean now!

"Boy!" Dad hissed, stepping directly in front of Kevin, "You are within an eyelash of getting your butt kicked, but good."

"But Dad, you don't understand—"

"Shut your face, boy!" Dad bellowed. "The only sounds I expect to hear from you are farts escaping from that narrow ass of yours, as you jump like the famous nursery rhyme cow in an undying effort that might cause me to alter my present intended action of beating you into a pile of cowshit and using your remains to fertilize the rose bushes.

"It's you who doesn't understand; you only think you do. I've put my job, my marriage, and everything I own and believe in on the line for you, and how have you repaid me? You're constantly in one scrape after another, and the story is always the same: you're misunderstood or a victim of circumstance. If I was to stretch all your coincidences back to back, they'd reach the next fuckin' galaxy."

Dad turned and walked over to where Billy was slowly regaining his feet and began to help him up. Sensing a golden opportunity, Billy came to life at once.

"Did you see how he brutally attacked me?" he yelled. "Not only did he attack me for no reason at all, then he went after my two friends. I tell ya, Dad, I agree wholeheartedly with Mom, he is mentally ill. He should be committed."

"Billy," Dad said, "first, let me tell you that I overheard the entire conversation between you and Kevin, and frankly, if I'd have been in Kevin's position, I would have hit you more than once. In fact, if it wasn't for the fact that I'd have to answer to your mother, I probably would have just walked away and let him beat the living shit out of you.

"God forgive me for speaking the truth, but frankly, young man, you're about the most miserable excuse for a human being I've ever seen. You're sneaky, conniving, and will lie, cheat, and even steal from your own family to get your own way."

Billy turned and ran toward the open garage door. His reactions were slow, however, and Dad grabbed him from behind and, with a powerful flip, spun him around like a top, holding him firmly in place with a viselike grip on his arm. "As long as I'm clearing the air here, you may as well hear it all.

"For a long time now, I've known about every deceitful and spiteful thing you've done. But for the sake of what I thought was love, and was in reality only a contemptible attempt by me to avoid loneliness, I've looked the other way as you used and manipulated people for no better purpose than to make yourself feel important.

"Well, that's all over now, buster." Dad reached in his back pocket, pulled out a folded paper, and stuffed it emphatically in Billy's shirt pocket. "Your college grades: four

F's and an incomplete. Along with it is a letter informing me that you've been a disruptive influence in class and as a result have been expelled.

"For a long time now, there's something that I've wanted to say to you, something that needs to be said, and now I finally can. Number One, you're done."

Dad released Billy and backed away. "Now, you talk if you wanna. 'Cause I'm done, done with your incessant lying and whining, done supporting you, and most of all, done with you in my house."

"It's your fault that I'm the way I am," Billy said bitterly. "You made me this way."

Dad was thoughtful for a moment then answered sadly. "Yes, son, I suppose it is. But sooner or later, a man has got to start to take responsibility for his own actions, no matter what the source. For a long time now, you've stood on the sidelines and neither fished nor cut bait. Now you have no choice. I've given you the rod and the worms. Whether or not you starve is up to you."

Wordlessly, Billy left the garage. Dad watched him leave. He suddenly looked as if a huge weight had been lifted from his shoulders. Kevin thought back to their middle of the night conversation a couple of weeks back. Dad did indeed have a plan. He obviously knew well in advance that Billy was in trouble in school. But he'd kept silent and sprung his trap at the right moment, one when Mom would be powerless to stop him.

"Now as for you, Number Two," Dad said, "I don't deny Billy deserved a good ass-kicking, but I thought you were more of a man than to be coerced into fisticuffs by a semistoned surfer.

"What I just said about Billy goes double for you. From now on, you're gonna be so clean, you're gonna squeak like a new combat boot. I don't know what this latest round of trouble you've gotten yourself into is all about, and I don't care. You fix it today, boy, or don't come home tonight."

"I might just take you up on that, Pops," Kevin said. "After all the speeches and all the lectures you made to me about fighting for what's right and standing up for others and all that other horseshit you've been spewing, it's pretty disgusting to find that, in the end, you're nothing but a pussy-whipped old windbag. You may have fucked up Number One, but you ain't gonna fuck up Number Two."

Kevin knew what Dad's response would be but didn't care. His right fist made solid contact with Kevin's jaw as it rocked him backwards. Hatred burned inside of him with such intensity that Kevin hardly felt the blow. He stared unflinchingly back at Dad, never showing a trace of pain.

"Is that the best you've got, mister big, tough first sergeant?" Kevin snarled through clenched teeth. "If it is, you better find a different line of work before those kids in your outfit find out what a pantywaist you really are."

"Get out!" Dad screamed. "Get out of here before you make me do something I might regret."

Kevin turned and was halfway out the door when Dad called after him.

"Kevin?" Dad walked over and wrapped both of his hands around Kevin's forearms. "Don't you understand, son, that at your age, I can't afford to let you win?"

With a contemptuous grunt, Kevin shook off Dad's hold and said coldly, "At my age, you can't afford to let me lose."

Kevin brushed past him and walked up the driveway to his car. As he rounded the corner of the house, he saw Billy sobbing in Mom's arms.

"Perfect," Kevin said, making no effort to conceal his sarcastic expression. Mom looked solemnly at Kevin. Kevin sighed, got in his car, and drove off.

"Come in, Kevin. Kristie will be ready in a few minutes. I thought in the interim, ah, perhaps you and I could sit down, and I could get to know you a little better."

"I'm sorry," Kevin looked at Kristie's father without expression. "Mr., uh—"

"Oh, yes, of course, how stupid of me. My name is Bernard Bernstein," he said formally, using English pronunciation for his first name. "Kristie's mother and I are going to be married next month; I'm going to be Kristie's new stepfather."

Kevin knew immediately that he wasn't going to be given a chance to get acquainted. He was going to be given the bum's rush.

Pity. He'd been looking forward to taking Kristie out, and now he'd never get the chance. But as LZ always said, "If you know they wanna buttfuck ya, don't make it any easier by bending over." Kevin would see to that himself. He sat down and waited for the game to begin.

"Well, what is it you'd like to know?" Kevin asked.

"Oh, I don't know," Bernie said. "I guess I should start by thanking you. I understand from Kristie's mother that you saved her from a most embarrassing moment!"

Kevin burst out laughing. "A most embarrassing moment? That's what you call attempted gang rape? What do you call what happened to your people during World War II? A preplanned population reduction?"

"I see you're living up to your much-publicized reputation," Bernie said stiffly.

"Give me plain truth over phony repartee anytime."

"Well, I couldn't agree with you more. So let me speak a little at you," Bernie paused, exhaled heavily, and continued. "I don't think you're the kind of young man I want my stepdaughter to associate with any more than I'd want my own daughter to."

"Well, at least we agree on one thing, Bernie. I have no desire to be seen with Miss Training Bra, either. So, what's the criteria for the stepdaughter, Bernieo?"

Ignoring Kevin's slap at Miss Stuck-Up 32A Cup, Bernie said tightly, "For the short term, we want our daughters to complete their high school education and then get a college degree. With these lofty goals, we feel they would be much more compatible dating individuals who share those same ideals. Frankly, young man, if one-tenth of the stories I've heard about you are true, you just don't seem to fit that description at all."

"Well, sir, not that it matters at this point, but we're closer than you might think," Kevin said, getting up and starting for the door. As he grabbed the handle, he turned back and said with a sudden conviction that surprised even him, "I'll go to college. Now given the fact that I don't have all the financial advantages that you can provide for your family, I might have to take a few work detours along the way to build up some cash reserves. But make no mistake about it: I'll go. I'll major in engineering . . . and I'll graduate and become one of those Joe College types, too."

Kevin paused as Kristie entered the room. In her tight-fitting summer dress with a neckline that showed just the beginnings of what Kevin knew was beautiful cleavage, he had to admit to himself that she looked gorgeous.

As hard as it was, Kevin dragged his eyes off Kristie, back to Bernard, and continued. "The only thing we differ on is the short term. You want to get Kristie through college; I just want to get Kristie." With a rakish wink and a roguish guttural growl, Kevin left, but not before catching Bernard's outraged look and Kristie's seductive wink.

Well, as usual, you fucked that up royally, Kevin thought to himself as he regained the main road from the exclusive subdivision. *But the superior son of a bitch pissed me off.* Too bad, a hot date with Kristie would have swung the pendulum back to positive for the day's roller-coaster events.

First there'd been the fight at home, which Kevin rated a draw. Then there was the band thing, which was a win-the-battle/lose-the-war proposition, in that, when Kevin and Ricky refused to play, Mr. Lazenby successfully changed Wilkins's mind and they were restored to their rightful places. But the football team got trounced in the regional playoff tonight.

The after-game date with Kristie had been a spur-of-the-moment request from her. Glenda had to work, and Kevin had agreed to pick Kristie up at home after she changed and to take her to the traditional hamburger drive-in, after-game gathering.

Since it was only 9:45 PM, Kevin thought about going over to visit Glenda at work and waiting for her when she got off at ten, but decided to just pack it in and go on home. Two blocks from the house, his radar went on; all the house floodlights were on.

As Kevin pulled up in front of the house, the first thing he noticed was that the rear ambulance style door on his Hillman Husky—the car he'd bought for twenty dollars, not running, and had rebuilt—was open and was half full of boxes. He was at the base of the steps when the door burst open, and Billy exited carrying what, from the brief glimpse Kevin got as he raced by, looked to be a box of towels and bed linens. The kitchen was a beehive of activity as Mom bustled around the kitchen, excitedly filling boxes with her spare utensils.

"Oh, Kevin, isn't it thrilling?" Mom paused momentarily, kissing Kevin on the cheek.

"What's all the fuss about?" Kevin asked.

"Oh, I can't stop to tell you now, I'm far too busy." Kevin was far too tired to even care what this was all about. Apparently, it didn't affect him, and for once, Kevin didn't seem to be the cause. Wordlessly, Kevin stretched, yawning loudly, and grabbed a Coke out of the fridge. He had started for his room when Mom called after him.

"Um, son, your father wants to talk to you," Mom said, carefully averting her eyes. "He's waiting for you in the garage."

Taking his cue from Mom's reactions, Kevin entered the garage with trepidation. There must be a new star in the East. That's the first thought that struck him as he entered. There, in work clothes, was Dad, working on Kevin's current project, the Hillman convertible.

"You need the practice?" Kevin asked.

"Not really," Dad said without looking up. "I just got tired of sitting in front of the tube and know that you've been working a lot of hours and haven't had a chance to work on this heap." Kevin's radar clanged like a World War II submarine Claxton.

"You mean to tell me, in the midst of that ransacking going on inside, you just suddenly decided to come out here and give me a hand?"

When Dad continued to work with no response, Kevin said, "Look, Dad, you and I have had our disagreements, but they were always honest, not underhanded. Mom is brushing me off like a cheap pass, and you're acting like a rookie doctor that's having trouble telling the patient he's terminal."

Dad's head popped out from under the hood. His angry expression softened immediately when he saw Kevin's wounded expression. "You're right, son. It's not my style, so here it is straight from the hip," Dad said, laying down the wrench and facing Kevin. "Your brother and Leslie snuck across the border into South Carolina tonight and got married."

"I more or less figured that by the way Mom was acting," Kevin said bluntly. What's the rest of—?" Kevin broke off suddenly as a thought flashed. Then another, and another, until his eyes became narrowed cat slits.

"Now wait a minute, son," Dad said. "There are reasons for this that you couldn't begin to understand."

"Oh, I understand," Kevin said. "I've been sold out by a supposed man of principle, to a woman who has few, for a brother who has none."

"Son," Dad said. "I know right now this seems terribly unfair, but when you get a little older, I'm sure you'll begin to see things my way."

"Don't hold your fucking breath waiting for that one."

"Look partner, that herd of cars you have are all in my name. So if I choose to give one of them to your brother as a wedding present, there isn't a damn thing you can legally do about it. Besides, you still got three left, so what are you complaining about?" Dad retorted defensively.

"And I suppose it doesn't make any difference to you that I bought the parts for every single one of them with my own money. I put that Husky together to use as a driver until I got this convertible completed. Then I was going to sell it and use the money to turn the stock engine in my 'Vette into a real asskicker," Kevin said, exhaling deeply to bring his emotions under control. "And remember, Daddy-O, who repaired your Hillman wagon after Wax Breath there fucked it up, and then gave it back to you when you needed a car because you'd taken your car and Mom's car and traded them in on the new Plymouth. Like you always say, fuck me once, shame on you; fuck me twice, shame on me.

"Hope you enjoyed it, cause you'll never get another chance," Kevin said, walking out of the garage and slamming the door in sheer disgust.

Kevin was halfway back to the house when the sound of the garage door slamming again caused him to turn around.

"Let's get one thing straight right here and now," Dad said, walking toward Kevin. He jabbed his finger repeatedly into Kevin's chest to emphasize each word. "Whether you agree with my decision or not, make no mistake about it: as long as you live under my roof, you'll live by my rules. Is that clear?"

Kevin snapped to rigid attention, cracked off a razor-sharp salute. "Yes, sir, First Sergeant, sir. I understand your directive and will obey it explicitly."

With a military about-face, Kevin marched off around the house, making sure to keep his back ramrod straight until he was well out of sight.

"Baby, this is a mistake. You, better than anyone else, should know that you can't run away from your past. It'll catch up with you; it always does," Glenda said, turning away to stare silently out the window as they drove on in silence.

After leaving Dad standing in the walkway, Kevin walked straight to his car, ignoring a smiling Leslie on the way. He had the key in the ignition when Dad's directive hit him. *Knowing that creepy bastard, he'd probably have me arrested for car theft. Well, fuck him.* Kevin knew how to beat him at his own game.

He jumped out of his car, ran around to his bedroom window, climbed in, and taking only the clothes—right down to socks and underwear—that he'd purchased with his own money, stuffed them into an old army duffel bag that a friend had given him, and exited the same way, less than two minutes later.

Kevin walked the half-mile up the street to the end of the subdivision, then two blocks right to a phone booth and made two phone calls. Exactly fifteen minutes later, Glenda skidded to a stop, responding to the first call. As long again, and Kevin was holding his last paycheck from the service station where he worked as a mechanic as a result of the second call.

They'd driven to Glenda's apartment, where'd she'd spent the first two hours trying to calm him down and the next two trying to talk him out of it, once he'd told her what he had in mind. For the first time, they'd argued openly, as dawn arrived and they began their journey. Glenda's last outburst had left an eerie silence between them, a silence that would be broken soon: the Florida border was only fifteen miles ahead.

"Glenda," Kevin said softly, "I know you don't believe this, but I'm not running away from my problems, I'm running to them—to solve them. Then I can start over."

"We've been over this a hundred times," Glenda said. "If you truly wanted to start over, we'd be headed north to my grandma's house in Carolina, not south to Florida."

"Glenda, I can't even support myself, let alone you," Kevin said. "Christ, my brother just pulled that same Casey at the Bat routine."

"But, baby, we'd be different from them," Glenda said. "You could get a job as a mechanic anywhere, and I could easily get my old job back as a bookkeeper at my grandfather's furniture business. We could stay with my grandparents; they'd love to have us."

Glenda slid across the seat and put her arm around Kevin. "I would think about you all day, make love to you all night, and be your total and exclusive full-time woman," she cooed in his ear.

"Honey, I wish I could say that I was tempted by your offer," Kevin said. "But don't you see that if I did that, then I would be running away? I would have fixed the symptom, but not the problem. To have any sort of future, I've got to cure this cancer at its root cause. And that root cause exists in a police file in Miami. It's followed me around for two years, rearing its ugly head every time I have a chance to be a normal person.

"When I clear this up, I'll be back." Then he added as an afterthought, "And if you still want to, maybe we'll give Carolina a try."

"I still wish you'd change your mind," Glenda said, sensing that the die was cast.

When Kevin gave her a very hard stare but made no response, Glenda brightened and said, "Okay, baby. If we can't be together in Carolina, I guess I could get used to Florida."

To Kevin's disapproving grimace, Glenda asked, "Why not?"

"You know very well why not," Kevin said abruptly. "I'm wanted in Florida. The minute you cross the state line with me, it's a felony."

"I don't care," Glenda said.

"Well, I do," Kevin said. "If I could, I would; but I can't. It's tough enough to hide out on your own. Never mind trying to do it with a voluptuous dolly like you to attract attention."

The last statement had a finality that made Glenda lapse into silence. They drove the final miles to the border, lost in their own thoughts. Kevin pulled over fifty yards short of the state line billboard, grabbed his bag, then the two of them walked hand in hand right to the edge of orange juice land.

Kevin turned to Glenda to speak, but was silenced by her finger on his lips, followed by a deep and passionate kiss.

"Come back to me, baby," Glenda said, as tears began to trickle down her cheeks.

Kevin nodded his head slowly, wiped away one of her tears, and said, "I will. Bet on it, troop."

Kevin shouldered his duffel, and began to walk backward to the oncoming traffic with his thumb out, never for an instant taking his eyes off Glenda. He'd covered only thirty yards when an eighteen-wheeler pulled over. As he climbed up in the cab, Kevin glanced back at Glenda. She held her face in her hands and was now sobbing uncontrollably. With a half wave that she either didn't see or couldn't acknowledge, Kevin climbed inside.

"Where you headed, buddy?" the truck driver asked.

"Miami."

"You're in luck; me too. Gotta drive straight through to meet my deadline. So you can keep me company and help me stay awake."

"My pleasure," Kevin said. It suddenly struck him how ironic a twist of fate it was that found him trying to do the right thing, in the wrong place, at the right time, that had served as the impetus that had toppled them from the laboriously balanced beam that they called a family. Kevin may have been the cause, but Dad was the effect.

Thoughts of pure hatred of his father clouded out all of his other conscious senses, except sight. His eyes were on the truck mirror, and a girl he'd left crying in the chilly Georgia morning mist.

CHAPTER SIX

"Man, whoever said that home ain't like you left it sure did know what the haps' were," LZ said.

"I concur, mon ami," Frenchy agreed. "I think it's time to blow this nowhere scene."

"What have you guys got in mind?" Smitty asked.

"What say we lift a ride and split for the coast?" LZ said. Smitty and Frenchy stared disapprovingly. "Hey, man it was just a joke; can't you honkies take a little humor?"

"Yeah, make some," Frenchy shot back. LZ gave him the finger.

Frenchy and LZ continued baiting each other, but Smitty wasn't listening. He'd tuned them out and was stuck on LZ's opening point.

Whoever made that rather astute comment about home was certainly right on as far as Smitty was concerned. He'd arrived here seven days before Christmas. Miami was definitely not like he'd left it; it seemed incomprehensible that it was only two short years ago.

The old neighborhood was effectively gone, split right down the middle by a new expressway that separated his old stomping grounds as effectively as the Berlin Wall. Gone too, were most of the people the three of them had known. To build the latest imitation autobahn had required the complete destruction of an area about two city blocks wide, and the displaced had scattered to the wind. A passing hurricane had dealt a crushing blow to the remaining forty-year-old structures. All that was left were rows of sparsely populated buildings with boarded-up windows and curbs lined with the rusting carcasses of stripped cars.

Smitty had discovered LZ by surprise, when he found him sacked out in the same warehouse that Smitty had planned on using for a hideout. After swapping updates, Smitty found that LZ's story was much the same as his.

Home cooking with Auntie in Chi-town was about as unappetizing as Smitty's own dinner entrée. LZ had come back to Miami only two weeks before Smitty and was just as disillusioned about the prospects for the immediate future.

Just for old times' sake, they had placed a call to Frenchy, and after several phone calls—Uncle Wealthy had tossed him out—were able to locate him working as a janitor in a bar in New Orleans. It took no convincing at all for Frenchy to chuck his job and grab the next bus south.

In the last three weeks that lapped over into 1967, they'd discussed many options, some far-fetched, some with merit. But Smitty had no multiple choices; this was a true-or-false test. The answer had to be the truth. He'd already lived all the lies he could stand.

"Hey bro'," LZ said, thumping Smitty on the arm to bring him back to reality. "Did you hear what Frenchy said, man?"

Catching Smitty's bewildered stare, Frenchy piped in, "I'm serious, man, we should join up."

Pausing for effect, and shooting Smitty a wink that LZ didn't see, he continued, "Besides, it's a great place for juvenile delinquents like us to find ourselves, learn a trade, become useful productive citizens, shit like that."

"I think I'm gonna throw up," LZ said. "Besides," he paused, "I don't want to hit this one too hard, but there are a couple of points that seem to have escaped you. Like the fact that we're all still seventeen and would need our parents' permission. And even if we got it, enlisting here in Florida would land us in the slammer. I seem to recall we've all had some minor brushes with the law, and we aren't even supposed to be here. Or have you fine gentleman forgotten these minor points?"

"Well," Frenchy said, "it was just a thought, my friends. What else are we going to do?"

"It might not be such a bad thought at that," Smitty said. "And there may be ways around these fine points that LZ brought up."

"Like for instance?" LZ asked.

"For starters, LZ, how's about you drop over to 64th Street and look up a mutual acquaintance by the name of Old Louie." Smitty was just about to explain why when he caught LZ's nod.

"I'm on it brother. But I'll need some green."

Wordlessly, Smitty fished in his pocket and peeled off three crisp hundred-dollar bills and slapped them into LZ's hand. "Work on him, man. We'll need everything we've got for traveling cash."

"Frenchy, how much you got?"

"'Bout three hundred."

"Give it to me," Smitty said, holding his hand and waiting until Frenchy passed over his bankroll.

"What's your birth date, Frenchy?" LZ asked.

"January twenty-fifth."

"That's right. I'm the twenty-first, and Smitty here's the baby since he was born on the twenty-ninth." More than once, they had marveled at the fact that they all were born in the same year, in the same month, and only eight days apart. "How should we fill in the rest of it, Smitty?"

"Would you tell me just what you two are up to?" Frenchy said.

Ignoring Frenchy completely, Smitty continued. "Back up the birth date one year, so we'll all be eighteen now. Make everything else the truth except parents. List them as deceased. To avoid tracing, we've got to come up with something simple but good enough to throw any bicycle seat sniffers off the track."

"How about sticking to the truth, but just add a little on, and provide a false scent?" Frenchy asked.

It was Smitty and LZ's turn to look bewildered now.

Frenchy gave both of them his very best look-who's-in-the-dark-now grin. "When you go over to see Old Louie, the forger, have him throw in three copies of the Dade County order remanding us to the custody of the U.S. Army due to violation of stipulations of parole. At the same time, we set up our cozy little retreat here with unmistakable clues pointing to the fact that we've split for the West Coast to seek fame and fortune. Arrange to tip off the cops, and there we have it."

"It's perfect, man," LZ said excitedly. "We've chilled the cops and everyone else at the same time. They'll be searching the entire West Coast high and low looking for us. In the meantime, we go play army for a couple of years until this entire thing blows over. Our sentence is up in three years anyway, so by then, everything will be cool."

"Sounds like a plan, guys," Smitty said. "LZ, can Old Louie handle all the paper?"

"No sweat, man," LZ answered. "Might take a couple of days and a little extra green, but he'll handle it."

Smitty nodded and he turned to Frenchy. "It was your plan, dude. You got the job of baiting the trap."

Frenchy acknowledged him with a crisp thumbs-up. "Done, mon ami. Since LZ and I are doing all the grunt work, what's your part?"

"I'm gonna spring the trap, and I know just how to do it."

Frenchy held up a finger. "Time frame?"

"Let's make it the end of next week," Smitty said.

"That's your birthday, man," LZ said.

"If this works like we plan, maybe we'll head out to Disneyland to celebrate," Smitty said. "And a few old debts are gonna get paid in the process." *And maybe a few things credited to new accounts . . .* he added silently to himself.

Smitty used half of Frenchy's contribution on one purchase. A hundred and a half was expensive, but as he held the object in his hand, a feeling of power he had not had for a long time was reborn.

Smitty thought Frenchy's idea about joining up was a masterstroke, especially since he'd originally suggested it. But Smitty was going to alter the agreed-to plan by just a tad. He smiled to himself in self-satisfaction, held up his recent acquisition, and said to it harshly, "Between you and me, baby, we're gonna settle a few old scores, and maybe just get us a little truth in the process." The nickel-plated Smith and Wesson .357 Magnum gleamed silently.

"Hey, Copper! Gotta match?"

The instincts were good, the reactions even better. He whirled around and, in the same fluid motion that showed he'd done this more than once before, began to slide his service revolver from inside his jacket.

Smitty was faster. He stepped forward, jamming the reaching hand farther into the coat and shoving the S&W right up against his nose.

"Evening, Captain. Not going to look very good for the chief of homicide to go and get himself mugged in his very own driveway."

The eyes widened, first in fear, then wider in recognition. "Little off your range, aren't you, boy?" Captain Baker said calmly. "Figured you'd be talking with a twang by now."

"Very funny," Smitty said, brushing aside the captain's hand and relieving him of his service revolver. "You guys only carry these pissant .38s. How the hell . . . ?"

The front porch light had suddenly come on, and the door was being opened. Smitty cursed silently to himself and instinctively pointed his weapon in that direction.

"Hello dear, I thought I heard someone—"

An attractive woman in her early forties stopped in midsentence as she saw the gun sighted in her direction. She looked first at her husband, then back at Smitty, and pulled a small boy to her waist as he started to run past her, intent on jumping into his father's arms.

"It's all right, dear," the captain said easily. "Just a rookie undercover with a little nervousness problem." He reached out slowly and, meeting only token resistance from Smitty, pushed his arm down so the weapon was pointing at the ground.

"Take Stan Junior, and go on back inside. This young man is one of our people from the west side, and as I said, he's into something a little bigger than he is, that's all."

As she started to turn away, Baker called after her, "Oh, and Betty, set an extra place at the dinner table. I think a good, hot meal is just what this jumpy young chap needs."

All pretense of pleasantness vanished as the door closed. The captain spun around, his face contorted with rage. "And now, shit-for-brains, suppose you tell me just what the hell this is all about, and it better be good!"

"I came for information," Smitty responded weakly, caught off guard by the captain's forceful approach.

"Information about what?" he spat back.

"I want to know who was responsible for the frame on Frenchy, LZ, and me."

"I don't know what you're talking about," he said stiffly.

"The hell you don't," Smitty shot back, feeling his anger and determination return. "Ever since that night at the police station when I saw you and Dad shake hands in the corridor, I've known something was rotten in that deal. Now you're going to tell me what, or—"

"Or you'll what?" the captain said with a snort. "You'll shoot me?" He paused, shook his head sadly, then said, "Go ahead. Pull the trigger. Then you can really be a murderer, not just framed as one."

Smitty brought the gun up to the captain's face and pulled back the hammer. "Don't go betting that I won't."

"Son, I have no doubt that you'd kill a man for any number of reasons, but this isn't one of them. You must believe me, we, your father and I, did what we thought was best for you and all the rest of those young men."

"You knew my father before we moved to Florida, didn't you?"

Stan reached in and slowly removed a pack of cigarettes from his pocket. He offered one to Smitty, which he took with his free right hand. Stan cautiously lit first his then Smitty's. "We've traveled some together.

"Look, sport, there was some very heavy pressure being brought to bear by the mayor's office to solve this gang problem once and for all. I'll admit, in retrospect, that a lot of that pressure seemed to center on you and whoever else was part of your sphere of influence. You know, young fella, now that I think on it, not only did the mayor's office seem to have you targeted, but the district attorney's office seemed to be taking an extraordinary interest in you, also."

"Why?"

"Don't know exactly, but it's too late to ask now," Stan said. "The peckerhead that seemed to be leading the charge moved on to some other job in Washington 'bout nine months ago."

He said abruptly, "Your being here means everything obviously didn't go as planned. But I can assure you we were not motivated by any malice towards you or any of the other young men."

Smitty stood and eyed the captain through the sight of his newly acquired cannon. If the captain was afraid, no trace of it showed in his face. His words raced though Smitty's head over and over in an endlessly repeating cycle. Slowly, the words became thoughts; the thoughts became sentences. The sentences led to conclusions, conclusions that convinced him that the captain was right. He lowered the gun.

Effortlessly, the captain took both Smitty's weapon and his own from Smitty's yielding hands. He returned his own weapon to his shoulder holster, then put his arm around Smitty and led him over to the front porch. As they sat down together on the second step, the captain said, "Now, partner, you want to tell me what this is all about?"

And tell him he did. Feelings kept bottled up inside for over two years gushed up like Old Faithful. He couldn't explain it, but Smitty felt inexplicably drawn to the captain. For over an hour, Smitty sifted through the ashes of the fire that burned inside of him, slowly, ramblingly, bringing Baker up-to-date since his sudden deportation from the state. Judiciously, he omitted his involvement in the incident in Hillsdale and their immediate plans for the future.

The captain listened silently, interrupting him with a light touch on the arm only when his wife brought out dinner on paper plates, and then wordlessly motioning him to continue when she had gone back inside. When Smitty had finally talked himself into silence, the captain offered cigarettes, which they smoked in quiet, deep thought.

Smitty was unsure of his next step. Did it include arrest, conviction, and jail, as the sentencing judge had solemnly promised? Or even if he believed his story of being here to clear the record, would he be willing to listen to Smitty's plan to help clear his name, the names of the rest also? Threats had failed; facts were the only option left.

The captain thumped his cigarette butt halfway out onto the St. Augustine lawn, blew out a last cloud of smoke, rubbed his stubbled chin thoughtfully, and said, "Son, I'm afraid that I'm the root of your problems. And unfortunately, I'm also the one who's going to have to tell you the truth. Namely, that you're beating a dead horse. What happened two years ago is ancient history; the best that you can do now is put it past you and go on with your life."

"Captain, I can't do that!"

"Would you mind giving me one good reason why?"

"I'll give you two good reasons," Smitty said. "Gena and Jimmy."

The captain was silent for a moment. "I'm afraid I don't understand. All the evidence we had linked those two killings to the Cuban gang revenge."

"That's only a plausible story if you believe the Cuban couples were killed by the American gangs. And to what end, Stanley?" The use of his first name caused the captain to look at him with a raised eyebrow. "What good could it possibly serve?"

"Are you defending the Cubans for their actions?"

"Good God, no," Smitty said. "But just for a minute, forget that you're a police officer, and think with your heart, not your crime-numbed brain.

"We, at least I, knew that the city was just looking for any excuse to bust our butts. And even with the black guys coming in on our side, we were still outnumbered. Why would I go and inflame an already tense situation? It would be like pulling the pin on a grenade padlocked to my balls."

"I must say, young man," the captain said thoughtfully, "that you make some interesting points."

"I've had a lot of time to think about this, and I've come to the conclusion that this whole thing is just like a visit to the wharf in San Francisco."

To the captain's uncomprehending stare, Smitty answered. "Everywhere you turn, there's a whiff of fish."

"Obviously, you didn't come waltzing all the way down here hell-bent on clearing things up without a fairly good idea in that flat head of yours on how to do it." The captain turned to face Smitty. "And perhaps, just perhaps, the outcome might be a better version of the truth you so highly prize."

So Smitty gave it to him. It wasn't the master strategy for the D-day invasion, but Smitty thought it had a chance to succeed. The key was the captain himself. When Smitty began to explain his plan, the captain looked uncomfortable; when he'd heard it all, he looked downright stunned.

"Son, you're out of your goddamn mind," Stan said.

"Well, Stanley," Smitty said in exasperation, "you got any better ideas?"

"Didn't that father of yours ever bother to teach you any manners? The name's Captain Baker, or Captain, boy."

"Yes, sir, Captain Baker, sir," Smitty said crisply, with a formal salute and an informal wink.

The captain shrugged his head in defeat. "Son, that plan of yours is the most harebrained, half-assed scheme I've ever heard of. At the very least, it'll probably screw up my career royally. We'll probably all get killed." He shook his head sadly. "And me just ten years from retirement."

"Well, look at the bright side; if I'm right, you'll probably be the next chief of police," Smitty said.

"And if you're wrong?"

"Then in all probability, your wife is going to make one hell of an attractive widow," Smitty finished, getting up from the porch and walking across the lawn.

"Hey?" The captain called after him. "Give me one good reason why I should trust you."

"I'll give you two reasons," Smitty said, as a wry smile spread slowly across his face. "One, because I'm a chip of the old block, sir. And two, because you know my ol' man, and like you said, you've traveled some together."

The captain nodded in acceptance—a nod Smitty acknowledged with a half-salute.

With a returned salute, Captain Baker nonchalantly flipped Smitty's new possession back to him. "You better keep this handy. I have a feeling you're gonna need it."

The captain turned and went inside his house. Through the open curtains, Smitty saw the captain's wife hug him with a worried look. A hug he returned with the same expression.

"LZ," Smitty said, rubbing his forehead in a vain attempt to chase away a pounding headache. "What's the story on paper?"

With a self-satisfied grin, LZ laid three envelopes in front of Smitty. "Check these out, man."

Smitty loosened the metal clasp on the envelope and carefully removed the contents. There were five articles in the envelope: a driver's license, a social security card, a birth certificate, a copy of his high school transcripts from Savannah, Georgia, and a truly official looking document—complete with the signature of the judge who had sentenced him—remanding him to the custody of the U.S. Army.

Smitty read this document most carefully, because his future—and quite possibly his survival—depended on it. It was full of legalistic ten-dollar language that basically stated that Smitty had been arrested after a high-speed chase in Miami and had agreed, in lieu of sentencing on past convictions as well as pending violations, to enlist in the U.S. Army for three years.

The document stipulated that presentation of an honorable discharge would constitute grounds for successful completion of the agreement and all pending charges would be dropped. It also stated that all past convictions would be subject to review based on meritorious service. All in all, it was quite believable, an excellent piece of work, and a first-class forgery.

"This is really quite something," Smitty said, whistling appreciatively. "Old Louie did a first-rate job. Are yours and Frenchy's papers the same?"

"Man, they're so alike, if people just glance at that stuff, they'll think we're identical triplets," LZ said.

Frenchy opened his envelope and read the same letter with the same impressed whistle. "Two questions," Frenchy said. "One, how did you get my high school transcript to match, and two, why do the other documents, especially the driver's license, look so worn?"

"In answer to both, Ol' Louie deserves all the credit," LZ responded. "Seems he's very fond of you, Smitty, and remembered what you were trying to do here on the west side. He came up with the idea of phoning back to your and Frenchy's high schools, and telling them that he was juvenile court officer so-and-so, and that you had been arrested and were going to have to finish your high school courtesy of the state, and would they very much mind sending your transcripts and what courses you had planned to take to completion, so that the state could establish a plan for helping you."

LZ grinned. "The lady at your school was especially cooperative, Smitty; she even volunteered her views on you personally. Seems she was not at all surprised to hear of your latest, quote, "escapade with the law." Threw in a few slurs at the state of Florida for allowing such hooligans to be shipped to Georgia to become a burden on the decent and god-fearing Savannians, and shit like that."

"Well," Smitty said in his best John Wayne accent. "Sometimes a man's gotta do what a man's gotta do, Pilgrim."

"Hey, man. I didn't know you did impressions," LZ said. "That's a great Ethel Merman."

"Asshole," Smitty shot back.

"You know, that's how Ol' Louie came up with the idea of making all the rest of the stuff well-worn," LZ said.

"I'm afraid you lost me," Frenchy said.

"I just told him to make it look like Smitty's ass."

Smitty started to reply, remembered his own advice in similar circumstances, and said nothing.

"How did he know what Smitty's ass looked like?" Frenchy asked.

"I told him his head and ass were interchangeable parts."

"Okay, man," Smitty said. "The paper's solid. Now shut your ugly black ass up, and let the Froggy talk."

Frenchy gave his very best imitation of a croaking frog. "Have you noticed, my friend, that since old Smitty went off and spent a couple of years with those ax-handle-wielding grits"—this in reference to a rather obscure Atlanta restaurant owner who vaulted to national prominence and eventually to Georgia governor by passing out ax handles to his employees to prevent black people from entering rather than desegregate his establishment—"He's become rather obvious in pointing out ethnic backgrounds."

"Yes, I've noticed that," LZ said, nodding. "Better check his bag; he's probably got one of them wood-chopper limbs in there, man."

"You know," Smitty said, "I gotta get me one of those. Then when I go back to Georgia, I could get myself a great job."

"As what?" LZ snorted.

"Lieutenant governor, man," Smitty shot back.

Both LZ and Frenchy looked at him like he'd lost his mind. Trying hard to hold back laughter, Frenchy said, "And just what makes you so eminently qualified for the position, Mr. Lieutenant Governor, sir?"

"Well, my fellow Americans, if the upstanding citizens of the Peach State are willing to elect that ax-handle-wielding fucking idiot governor, the very least he could do is to go and get himself an assistant who knows how to actually use one of those things. 'Course, now I've a feeling that my candidacy would be short-lived in that my campaign promise would be to use the goddamn thing on the very asshole himself."

LZ nodded at Smitty. "I think you would, too."

"Bet on it, mon ami," Frenchy added. "If Smitty didn't, it'd only be 'cause I beat him to it first."

LZ stared at his friends. "I got your message, bros. You two are really different from all the other white guys I know."

"That's because you're really different from all the other black guys we know," Smitty said.

The ensuing silence lasted a long time. As Smitty looked into the faces of his friends, he knew that he'd have others, but like a first love, these two would always be special.

"And now that we've got the mutual admiration society over with, can we get back to business here?" Smitty said, toughening his voice. "LZ, the paper will pass muster. What'd it set us back?"

"That's the funny part, Smitty," LZ said softly. "Ol' Louie wouldn't take a dime. Said to tell you that you owe him one. Said you'd know how to make payment in full."

"And I do, too," Smitty said. "And I will," he finished with sudden conviction, as a faraway look came over him.

"You all right, man?" Frenchy said, reaching out and touching him lightly on the arm.

"Huh? Ah, yeah, I'm fine," Smitty said, flushing with embarrassment of having been caught with his psyche hanging out.

"Ah, Frenchy, what's your plan to bait the trap?"

"Ah, my friends, we're all set," Frenchy said. "Now, this is how we proceed, gentlemen . . ."

Smitty listened to the plan with only passing interest; he'd already heard the basics from Frenchy before, and like everything else Frenchy did, his plan was thorough and complete. Smitty wondered idly to himself if Frenchy would be as euphoric twenty-four hours from now when he found out about the new ending Smitty had written to his carefully conceived script.

He glanced at his watch. It was two minutes after twelve. Frenchy was still answering questions from LZ as Smitty lay back on an old pile of packing material to sleep. Smitty had come to depend heavily on his premonitions, and if what he was feeling now came to be . . . he was in for one hell of a seventeenth birthday.

"Smitty, look!" Frenchy whispered, grabbing his arm and pointing to the entrance to the warehouse. "What the hell is that bastard doing here?" he added.

That "bastard," in this case, was none other than Smitty's old nemesis Keith, their ex-gang leader, followed closely by Glen, his muscular henchman.

"Smitty?" Keith called out. "It's showdown time, asshole. Come out, come out, wherever you are." Glen added chicken-pecking calls that sent goose bumps running up and down Smitty's flesh as they reverberated off the steel-plated walls.

From their perch up in the catwalk in the rafters of the warehouse were Smitty, LZ, and Frenchy, watching.

"Man, we've got to get that motherfucker outta here," LZ said. "He's gonna throw off our timetable. The cops are due in twenty minutes."

"Maybe, we oughta just drop on down there and have a talk with them," Smitty said. He pulled out his .357, flipped open the chamber, slid in a sixth round, and flipped the chamber shut.

Frenchy and LZ stared open-mouthed at the weapon. "Where did you get that?" Frenchy asked.

"You son of a bitch!" Frenchy said through clenched teeth. "You knew they were coming; you planned this. What are you up to?"

"Oh, let's just say that between now and when the cops show up, me and my lethal friend here are going to inject our friends down there with a little truth serum."

"What's the plan, man?" LZ said, suddenly supportive.

"LZ, left flank; Frenchy, right flank. But be careful, these guys are carrying, and there's got to be more than just those two scumbags."

"How much time you gonna need, mon ami?" Frenchy asked.

Smitty touched him lightly on the arm. "Ten minutes."

"Cutting it pretty close, aren't you?" LZ asked.

"As long as we cut it," Smitty said, as they moved off silently down the warehouse catwalks.

"Where is that fuckhead, man?" Glen said, unable to hide his nervousness.

"Relax, man," Keith answered. "That chicken-shit is here; I can smell him."

"You know profanity is the language of the ignorant," Smitty said nonchalantly, in a voice that belied the butterflies he was feeling inside as he stepped suddenly into clear view from behind a stack of crates. "It's something the insecure and uneducated use to cover up their own feelings of inadequacy. As long as you're in my home, you really should use better manners."

"You ain't got that big, stupid-looking Frenchman with you now. You made a mistake coming back to Florida; you're gonna die this time," Keith said.

"Don't you have enough blood on your hands already?"

"I don't know what you're talking about," Keith answered quickly. Too quickly.

"I'm talking about what happened two years ago. And the pain and the suffering you caused to hundreds for no more reason than to prop up your wounded little ego."

"Fuck you, man," Glen said.

"Well," Smitty said, "this is indeed a special day. Your gerbil actually spoke up on his own. Did you feel a chill as the air rustled past your balls from where his nose has been shoved up your ass?"

Smitty moved, but Keith moved faster. "Do it, please do it," Keith yelled, taking what looked like a .38 from his jacket pocket. Smitty silently released his grip on his own unopened switchblade. It slid from his hands and clattered noisily on the concrete floor.

"Any last requests?" Keith asked with a smile.

"Man, you're fucking nuts," Smitty exclaimed. Keith had produced a gun, but Smitty had a feeling that somewhere more artillery was close at hand.

"Oh, I'm nuts, am I? I'm not the one who's wanted by the police and fixing to spend the next three years in the funhouse. Or at least, you would have. You're not going to have to worry about that, though, 'cause you're gonna be dead in one minute."

"Before you waste me, answer me just one question." Smitty prayed silently that Frenchy, LZ, and his invited mystery guest were ready to enter and sign in, please.

"One question, scumbag; then you die."

"Why?"

"I'd have thought you'd have it figured out by now; you're the smart one," Keith smiled evilly. "You and your Boy Scout friends were standing in the way of the American free enterprise system. The one thing my friends and I didn't count on was you making peace between the gangs. You got in the way of a thriving business. We were making a bundle selling weapons, alcohol, and drugs to both sides. And then the really bitching part was while you idiots were fighting for your territorial rights, we were ripping off the local merchants right and left and making sure the gangs got the blame. Brilliant, right?"

"Oh, yes, brilliant," Smitty said. "You're a nuclear fuckin' physicist; takes a real bright boy to be some big-time operator's lackey. Bet you never did any of the dirty work yourself, did you?"

"That's where you're wrong, man," Glen screamed suddenly, pushing past Keith, his switchblade waving wildly. "I'm gonna cut you man. I'm gonna cut you like we cut them Cubans and them—"

"Shut up, man," Keith ordered. "Just shut up. Don't you tell this motherfucker anything, you hear me? Nothing. All our troubles will be over once we waste this fuck."

Smitty glanced quickly at his watch: eight minutes. Two minutes to go. But it might as well be two hundred. It seemed impossible that he could keep them talking for two more minutes before Glen made good on his promise to cut his head off, but he had to try.

An old counsel's wise words came rushing to the surface; crystal clear, Smitty could hear Dad's voice: "Sometimes when there is no solution, that in and of itself is a solution. As long as a man keeps thinking, there's always a chance." The sarge's words gave Smitty new breath.

"Hey, needledick," Smitty said. "Too bad you didn't sample some of Gena before you killed her; she was a great fuck. But then again, you couldn't, could you? Word on the street is that you and your eunuch boyfriend there are boyfriends in the truest sense of the word. Probably the only hard-on you got that night was from Jimmy. Did you give him a little fondle before you killed him, huh, sweetie?" Smitty made three smooching sounds.

Smitty had gone too far. He could see it in Keith's eyes. Keith was going to kill him now. Kill him just like he'd promised. And the ironic part was that Smitty might just have to stand there and let him. He'd promises to keep, and he'd keep them, even if it cost him his own life.

Keith approached slowly, savoring his moment of victory. "You know, I was going to kill you quickly, then find that fuckin' Frog, and that nigger friend of yours and take them out, too. But now, I think I'll make you pay for those insults. You're gonna die slowly, just like Jimmy.

"We're gonna stake you out, and then take you apart slow, just like we did Gena. And, you know what, since you're so keen on it, I'm sure Glen would be happy to butt-fuck you the same way he did Gena, with a rod clear through your ass."

Something snapped inside Smitty then. He was going to terminate, with extreme prejudice, the inhuman piece of filth before him.

He never got the chance. The warehouse suddenly lit up like a Hurricanes night game at the Orange Bowl. Before he could settle his personal score with Keith, who'd prudently dived behind a stack of crating material, Smitty would have to deal first with the six "friends" Keith had brought along for protection.

Smitty pulled his weapon as he dove for his own cover but was not quick enough for the one on the right. He had his weapon lined up on Smitty and was sighting to fire when a shot rang out, pitching him backward from the force of the shell.

The one next to him fired off two rounds in the direction of the shot. Smitty watched in horror as Captain Baker pitched backward on the catwalk above him, bouncing off the handrail, before collapsing face down, apparently dead.

Smitty's first shot found its mark. The one who'd shot the captain died instantly as the .357 shell shattered his breastbone and exploded his heart.

The third was as good as dead. He'd only started to raise his weapon when LZ's accurately thrown knife landed in his chest. The one on the far right died simultaneously as Frenchy stepped from the shadows, wrapped his massive arms around his neck, and snapped it like a dead twig.

Frenchy notched number five by relieving number one of his now-useless weapon and firing it at point-blank range three times.

LZ struck again with his deadly throwing arm, and the last of the support team fell silently to the ground. That left only Keith and Glen, and there'd be no escape for them this night. Smitty would see to that personally.

The deafening gunfire had barely ceased when another shot sounded from above. Glen tottered for a moment, back and forth on a stack of crates, before dropping the sawed-off shotgun he'd been aiming at Smitty, and toppled slowly to the floor below. Smitty gave the captain a half-salute, which he returned and motioned to the far end of the warehouse before collapsing into unconsciousness.

"LZ, Frenchy, secure the area, and take care of the captain. I'm going after Keith," Smitty barked, breaking into a run in the direction the captain had motioned.

Smitty checked his watch. God, it had taken less than thirty seconds for seven people to die. Time was not his friend, either. The cops must have heard the shooting, and might jump the gun and show up early. They were due in nine minutes. Smitty figured that he had six minutes. Six minutes to flush the rabbit. A rabbit that was armed, a rabbit that was expecting him, and perhaps most importantly, a rabbit that knew that in order to go on living, his stalker must die.

"Take him down, man!" LZ called after him. "Take him down!"

Knowing that Keith had a fifty-yard head start, Smitty took a desperate gamble in an attempt to cut him off. Holstering his weapon in the rear belt clip, he vaulted cleanly onto a four-foot stack of crates, climbed into the rafters, and worked his way to the ventilation windows leading to the tin roof. He stepped out into the cool Miami night to await his quarry. Keith had to come this way; it was the only exit from the offices above the warehouse floor. Smitty had seen him run up the steps and go inside. He knew that Keith would wait, then come out the rear window, and cross the roof this way. It was a well-worn path; Keith and Glen had used it the night they killed those Cubans. It was the only way they could have gotten away unseen.

There was a night chill in the air, but Smitty was sweating like someone who'd just spent an hour in a sauna. He hoped the captain was still alive. Stan the Man was definitely on the side of the angels; be a real pity if he didn't stick around to cash in for taking all the risks.

Keith was coming. Smitty heard the squeak of a window being opened slowly by someone who was obviously trying hard to avoid just such a noise. Silently, he readied his weapon. This book was past due; Smitty was going to cancel his library card—permanently.

Slowly, like a figure advancing out of the fog in a late-night horror movie, Keith's hulking frame emerged from the shadows. As always, the first thing Smitty noticed was the eyes. Keith was scared. Even in the half-light and shadows, he could see the nervous twitching of the eyes as Keith glanced constantly over his shoulder, expecting his adversary to attack from behind.

"Evening," Smitty said. Keith froze. "Turn around slowly. I want you to see the face of the chicken-shit scumbag who's going to blow your head off."

"Look, Smitty," Keith said, his voice breaking up from fear. "This has all been a big mistake, just like you said. I'm just the lackey; I just did what they paid me to do. You've got to believe me; if I had known that things would get out of hand the way they did, I'd have walked away. Honest."

"Yeah, right," Smitty said. "And the next pope is going to be a black Southern Baptist from Georgia."

"Oh, Jesus, I swear it's the truth," Keith pleaded.

"You wouldn't know the truth if it was tattooed on your ass."

Keith opened his mouth to respond but, seeing the determined look in Smitty's eyes, shrugged his shoulders in resignation. "So, what's next?" Keith asked.

"It's over. It ends, here and now."

"You'd kill me in cold blood?"

"Yes, I will, but not for myself, and whether you believe this or not, not even to avenge the murders of Jimmy and Gena and those Cubans," Smitty said quietly.

"Then why?"

"Your death will serve one purpose. It will sure as hell prevent you from inflicting further pain on others."

Keith, sensing the end was at hand, made a last desperate attempt for survival by tugging his handgun from his pocket. This time, it wasn't even a contest. Smitty fired three times. The first shell struck Keith squarely in the forehead, snapping his head back. The second struck him in the chest, driving him backward toward the warehouse windows. The third drove him through them. The gunshots were still reverberating in Smitty's ears when Keith's lifeless form disappeared toward the floor below.

Smitty walked to the window and glanced down through the jagged frame at Keith. The eyes were still open. He stared in silence at his late adversary. My God, forgive me, he thought to himself, but he could feel no sense of remorse at Keith's death. He was a fiend—grade-A number one. Keith had sentenced himself; Smitty was just the executioner.

Smitty's glance turned to the catwalk and Stan. LZ and Frenchy had turned him over and made him as comfortable as possible. When Stan saw Smitty starring down at him, he said something in a low voice to Frenchy that prompted the Frog to motion urgently for Smitty to come down.

Anticipating the worst, Smitty bounded down toward the catwalk.

"I see you got your truth," Stan said weakly. "Was it worth the price?" he rasped, coughing up blood from the effort.

Smitty glanced down at the warehouse floor; bodies littered the ground like hurricane refuse. Then he looked at Stan. He'd taken the first round through the chest, the rasping breathing evidence that the lung was collapsing already. The second had just about torn his right shoulder off. His nice clean detective's suit was wrinkled and bloody.
Looking Stan straight in the eye, Smitty nodded sadly. "Yeah, Stan; it was worth it."

"I think so, too," Stan rasped. Despite Frenchy's best efforts, the captain was losing a lot of blood, too much blood. The captain opened his mouth to speak again and touched Smitty lightly on the arm. "Listen," he said in a voice that was almost a whisper.

Smitty didn't hear it at first; then, he nodded his head. A police siren sounded in the distance. Before Smitty could determine its range, he heard a second, then a third. The message was clear: Reinforcements were on the way.

Wordlessly, Smitty looked at Stan, who grunted in return. "Get the fuck out of here, and let me die in peace."

Smitty fought back tears. "I promise you, captain, I'll get the other two."

"What other two?" LZ asked.

"There's two men left to get: the man who gave the orders to Keith and the man who told them where to look."

"C'mon, mon ami," Frenchy said, tugging at Smitty's arm. "We've got to split. The heat is just blocks away."

"Captain . . . "

"Don't," he rasped again, nearly losing consciousness for his effort. "Where?" he managed through more coughed-up blood.

"The army," Smitty said. He softly wiped away the blood dripping from the corner of Stan's mouth and chin. The captain wrinkled his brow and tried to speak, but he'd not sufficient strength, his facial expression a clear enough indication of disbelief.

"Okay, okay," Smitty said. "The truth is, we all thought that we'd about worn out our welcome in the southeast, so we thought we'd drift on out to the West Coast and soak up some California sun."

"Good idea," the captain answered, in a voice just above a whisper.

Frenchy tugged silently on his arm again, and Smitty rose to his feet to go. He was halfway through the warehouse window when he stopped, hesitated for a moment, then turned, went back and knelt by the captain, took his hand, looked him straight in the eye, and said, "And I promise you that the three of us are through with brushes with the law. We're going to stay out of trouble for the next three years, until our probation is up."

"Bullshit," Stan said with sudden forcefulness.

"Well, at least we're going to try." Smitty pulled out his .357, wiped it clean of fingerprints on Stan's coat, and gently placed it in the captain's hand. "Good-bye, Stan . . . and thanks . . . thanks for believing in us . . . thanks for believing in me."

Smitty could feel Stan's eyes burning a hole in his back as he turned and stepped through the window just moments before the first of many police cruisers skidded to a stop. A part of him still wanted to go back. Stan was a friend; he didn't feel right leaving him like that. But there was nothing he could do.

Nothing more he could do here at this particular moment. But as the late Keith had confirmed, a lot more was at stake here than just simple territorial infighting. Whoever had told Keith what to do had a boss, and that boss must have a boss also, and if Keith's deathbed confession were true, then that big boss was making a bundle off everyone's misery.

It dawned on Smitty that this person could be the one who conveniently kept the locals in Savannah so well-informed and up-to-date on his history. But again, the question was why. Had he inadvertently stumbled onto something? Was it just coincidence, or was he being led? Was he that big a thorn in their side, or just a gnat to be indifferently swatted away?

Smitty sensed it must be the former. Why else would they have tracked him to Georgia and continued to ensure that he was on everyone's shitlist? Smitty had to honestly admit that he hadn't a fucking clue.

He'd come back to Miami, naively it now seemed, assuming that the source of the cancer was in a police file in the care of Stan the Man. He was leaving now believing that the disease had spread and was much bigger, much harder to identify and control. The symptom was Miami, but the source was somewhere else unknown. But Smitty knew one absolute truth: whether it was real or not, he'd damned well better act like it was if he wanted to continue to live.

Besides, as Stan had just confirmed, if he stayed, he'd not be free to continue the fight—a fight that he had a feeling would take him through a lot of detours and a lot of places.

"Well, Smitty, I have to admit, that's a unique way of celebrating a birthday," LZ said when they were a safe distance away. "You honkies sure do go out of your way to show a fella a bang-up good time."

"Yes, my friend, it was," Frenchy chimed in. "What do you have planned for your next birthday, a border war?"

"By my next birthday, we may all be in a real war, wishing we were back inside these borders."

It was not a statement that called for an answer. They watched in silence from their safe haven as the police and the ambulances swarmed in and out of the warehouse, each boy knowing in his heart that if Smitty's prediction came true, the chances of any of them seeing his twenty-first birthday were slim indeed.

CHAPTER SEVEN

All right, you shit heads, back on the bus. It's still eight hours to your basic training base at Fort Jackson, South Carolina; you're on the army's time now. That means you, boy!" The MP growled, shoving LZ none too gently in the direction of the door. LZ glowered at him and made no move to proceed until Frenchy and Smitty each took an arm and dragged him back on board.

"Hey, man, cool it," Frenchy whispered, as they walked him to the back of the bus. "Remember we said we could do this army thing standing on our heads, right? So don't let some dumb-ass army idiot get you, my friend. He's probably only the first of many."

"That's right, brother," Smitty said. "Not everybody's able to put up with an ugly fucker like you the way we are. He probably just thinks he was doing his part for old Lady Bird's beautification project,"

LZ laughed in spite of himself. "If that's the reason, he should be in Washington trying to give the first lady's two raving beauties nose jobs."

When the three of them were seated again on the back row of the bus and the bus was under way, Smitty unfolded the paper he had bought at the rest stop just outside Daytona Beach and began to read aloud in a low voice to Frenchy and LZ an update on the hottest news story in Florida since Hurricane Betsy.

MANHUNT FOR MURDER SUSPECTS NOW FOCUSED IN WEST

Police today said that they are concentrating their search in the western states for the three convicted teen gang leaders suspected in the deaths of eight members of rival gangs on Miami's west side on January 29, 1967. The three, all convicted felons banished from the state in the infamous blacklisting of over 150 teen gang members two years ago, are the prime suspects, based on evidence found at the scene.

"In the loft area of the warehouse, hidden under a stack of crates, we found their driver's licenses, wallets, and a stash of money that was obviously meant to be traveling cash, as well as maps, brochures, and old copies of the Sunday LA Times *with want ads circled," Police Deputy Commissioner Gordon said. "Their names are being withheld from the public to aid the police in their capture. If we identify them, every long-haired freak will help hide them. We don't want to turn them into folk heroes like Bonnie and Clyde," the deputy commissioner added.*

Also found at the scene were scraps of paper with mathematical calculations on them, which police later determined to be the exact price of three bus tickets to Los Angeles, California. Police have alerted all law enforcement agencies from Florida to the West Coast along all prospective routes of travel.

Chief of homicide detectives, Stanley Baker, wounded in the gun battle, remains in critical condition at a Miami hospital today. Doctors successfully removed two bullets from the shoulder and lung in a six-hour operation Tuesday. One bullet struck the lung, ricocheted off a rib, and lodged against the left ventricle of the heart. The chief has been unconscious since and has been unable to shed any light on this grisly event or what the circumstances were that led him to be in the warehouse that night.

Deputy Commissioner Gordon declined to speculate at a morning news briefing. "Until we catch those three and can question them, we don't have a clue as to what actually happened." He further declined to comment on the involvement of Captain Baker, stating that the captain's presence was probably a result of acting on a tip.

"Well, boys, looks like we pulled it off," LZ said. "That idea you had, Frenchy, about leaving our old driver's licenses in wallets was a stroke of pure genius."

"Should keep the cops busy for a while," Frenchy said, nodding. "At least until the whole story blows over."

"Couple of things still bugging the shit out of me, Smitty," Frenchy said. "How in the hell did you arrange to get the late, lamented Keith there, and how did you get Captain Baker to help?"

"Yeah, man. You set us up; I'm still pissed about that, too," LZ said.

Frenchy and LZ had a right to be pissed. Smitty had never bothered to ask for their opinion or even their help; he just assumed they would be there. From the looks on their faces, maybe he was mistaken.

Exhaling heavily, Smitty said, "I knew that sooner or later, I was going to have to face the music with you two clowns, so here goes.

"There was just something that didn't figure about this whole business two years back, right from the start; it was too neat, too well tied together. The more I thought about it, the more convinced I was that this whole thing had to be a frame. The confirmation of this was when I got into trouble in Savannah after that party. My records, and yours too, were supposed to be sealed, with the information not to be disclosed without a court order.

"But, surprise, surprise, not only does everyone down to the janitor know about my past, they even have copies of the court records from down in Dade County. That could mean only one thing: someone on the inside of the Miami Police Department or the city government was watching very closely to ensure that harm continued to come to me on just the slightest provocation."

"Hey, mon ami," Frenchy interjected suddenly, "the same thing must have happened to me. It seemed that everyone in New Orleans knew everything about me, too."

Smitty and Frenchy looked at LZ, who thought for a moment, then nodded his head slowly in agreement.

"Once I was convinced that it was a frame, my first thought was that it was Captain Baker who was behind the whole thing. That's what originally brought me back to Miami—the hope of getting him to tell me why and clear our names. I thought Baker was involved because the night we were brought in, I saw the captain and my old man talking out in the hall, before shaking hands on something.

"When I went to see the captain at home last week, I asked him what they said that night. He told me that they were not striking a deal; in fact, it was just the opposite. Dad was defending me, cursing Stan out for hauling us in on trumped up charges, and threatening to break his fucking neck unless we were released immediately. Stan said he didn't believe it himself, but that it was out of his hands. He further explained that the word had gone out that as soon as possible we were all going to be prosecuted and sent to state institutions.

"As Stan explained to Dad what he did know, Dad calmed down and then suggested that Stan use his influence to arrange to have us removed from town and dispersed out of the state of Florida—save the taxpayers millions, that kind of thing. Stan said that he thought this was a great idea, and to cement his support, they shook hands."

"Well, if not the captain, then who?" LZ asked.

"Who comes in three parts," Smitty answered evenly. "The person who did the dirty work, the person who told him to do it, and person who told them where to look.

"The person who did the dirty work was the most obvious. And if you think about it for a minute, you'll get the connection, too. Who would have known enough about us to personally arrange those murders, then to make sure we got the blame?"

"Keith," Frenchy and LZ answered in unison.

"Right on, brothers; collect your sixty-four dollars," Smitty said. "When I went to see the captain, I told him all of my suspicions just as I have with you. I agreed to tell him where, when, and exactly what time we were going to spring the trap, so he could tell the police. When we agreed on 9:00 PM for the police to arrive in the warehouse; Stan agreed to be there at 8:00 PM.

"Then Stan called Keith, disguised his voice, and said that 'the man' wanted to meet him at the warehouse at 8:30 PM sharp. He told Keith that I was back in town and that, to kill me, he would be paid twice what he got paid for doing those Cubans and a bonus for killing you two. When Keith showed up at the warehouse, Stan had the proof that someone inside the precinct or the city government was the tip-off man."

"So that's how Keith knew we were there," LZ nodded, understanding. "But why didn't you tell us?"

"I didn't know myself until they actually showed up," Smitty continued. "The killings weren't part of the original plan. I'd hoped to be able to keep Keith talking until the cops arrived in response to Frenchy's plan, but we sorta had to improvise."

"Boy, is that an understatement," LZ whistled softly to himself.

"Anyway, Stan figured that once he picked up those assholes, he'd get one of them to talk. Then he'd have the inside contact and maybe a lead to the head honcho himself. I didn't in my wildest dreams ever figure that we'd end up with an updated version of the Saint Valentine's Day Massacre."

"Now I understand why you asked me to bring up the army thing, my friend." Frenchy said. "It didn't have shit to do with LZ taking the idea better from me than from you, did it?"

When Smitty failed to answer, Frenchy grabbed him none too gently by the shirt, yanked him forward until they were eye to eye. "Did it?"

"No, Frenchy." Smitty shook his head. "It didn't. But it was the only thing I could think of that would allow us to right a horrible wrong without becoming one ourselves."

"Fuck, man," LZ said. "You're one devious son of a bitch. I'm probably gonna wind up getting my ass shot off in Vietnam. And for what? A fuckin' principle."

Not since their initial meeting had Smitty seen LZ glare at him so hatefully. A quick glance at Frenchy confirmed that if Smitty were running for mayor, he'd not get that vote, either. He really couldn't blame them, but he was a little disappointed.

He'd known this was coming, and now that it was here he had two clear choices. He could fold his hand by getting up and taking another seat in the bus, a move that would be tantamount to ending their friendship. Or he could take them on, endure their anger, and maybe save their friendship in the process. The latter choice won in a landslide; besides, Smitty had a feeling that they were going to need each other to survive what lay ahead. The stakes were too high to check: he had to raise.

"All right you fucking crybabies, I think I've had just about enough of the wimpy guilt trip you candyasses are trying to lay on me," Smitty began. "If you two idiots would stop and think of all the consequences for a minute, then you'd realize that in the process of getting at the truth about the others, I also got us off the hook."

"Yeah, man, I guess they just forgot to print in the article what time the ceremony is for us to receive the key to the city," LZ shot back.

"And then they'll naturally want to give us a ticker-tape parade for such outstanding community service," Frenchy said.

"Will you two let me finish?" Smitty said. "I'd give you guys anything I own; can't you give me a little trust in return?" Their eyes were still hard but less so. They'd hear him out now, but heaven help him if it wasn't good.

"First off, in one sense, you've a right to be pissed, but in another, you shouldn't. I didn't ask for your help; I counted on it. I counted on it for the same reason we always count on each other: friendship.

"True friendship doesn't ask questions or expect explanations; it's just there. I can't speak for you guys, but from my standpoint, it always will be. I'm sure before I cash in this life for the next, I'll have others, but none will be as special as ours," Smitty said, as he met them stare for stare.

LZ opened his mouth to reply but was interrupted before the first words could escape.

"All right, what the hell's going on back here?" the MP said, marching down the aisle toward Smitty and his two friends. "You maggots better pipe down and get some shut-eye while you can, 'cause you sure ain't gonna get any rest in the army."

"Well, if it isn't Sergeant Fuckin' York," Smitty said, as the MP came to a stop in front of them.

"What did you say, soldier?" the MP asked sharply.

"Which part didn't you understand?"

"You better watch your mouth, soldier, or I'll knock that sneering grin into the middle of next week."

Recalling a line from one of his favorite movies, Smitty smiled wryly and said, "I tremble at the thought of such violence."

"You just better watch it, or I'll report you."

"Now, that was original," LZ said. "To graduate from MP school do they teach you any other tricks like sit up, roll over, beg, shit like that?" LZ continued to the accompaniment of several quiet laughs from the troops in the seats near the back row.

"You're now on my personal shit list, too, boy." The emphasis on *boy* was unmistakable.

LZ started to rise, but a quick hand from Smitty stilled his forward progress.

Not to be left out, Frenchy added his croaking frog sound, producing open laughter from a now fully awakened bus.

"You got a name, soldier?" the MP asked, raising his clipboard.

"Puddin' tane," Smitty said, enunciating each syllable with exaggerated slowness.

"Very funny," the MP said, trying to cover his embarrassment at having written down the first three letters of the childhood rhyme.

"And you, mister sound effects?"

"French Puddin'," Frenchy said crisply.

"I see," he responded tersely. "Then you must of course be . . ."

"That's right, brother," LZ said, a wolfish grin spreading slowly across his face. "The one, the only, Chocolate Puddin'."

Smitty thought that LZ had missed his calling; he should've been a comedian. The last remark was delivered with perfect timing, throwing the entire bus into an uproar of sidesplitting laughter.

Realizing he was losing control, the MP jerked his nightstick from the belt and pushed it forcefully under LZ's chin. "Now this is the last time I'm going to ask you nicely. What's your name, boy?" Again, the unmistakable emphasis. Smitty wondered if this young man had any plans for the rest of his life, which was going to be about thirty seconds, if Smitty didn't put a stop to this.

"Lucius . . . Zachariah . . . McCord, Junior," LZ answered through clenched teeth, fire in his eyes.

"No shit, man!" Frenchy said in genuine surprise. "I never thought LZ stood for anything."

Reveling in his newfound control, the MP repeated the stick-wielding procedure on Frenchy. "And you?"

"Johnsele . . . Napoleon . . . Douchet," Frenchy said, exaggerating his French accent.

"And you, funny man?" the MP continued, pointing the stick at Smitty.

"Englemeyer . . . J. . . . Futchitwanger," Smitty said slowly and evenly. "Esquire."

From the look on his face, it was obvious the MP did not believe any of them. As more of a delaying tactic than anything else, he asked, "What's the J stand for?"

"Jesus," Smitty answered.

"You fucking smart ass," the MP said, raising his stick and bringing it forward in the general direction of Smitty's collarbone.

Smitty's left arm shot out and stopped the weapon. At the same time, Smitty produced his switchblade and placed it firmly against Armband's throat.

"The army supposedly teaches you to kill people. Well, not to put too fine a point on it, asshole, but my associates and I have a fair amount of firsthand practical knowledge in that area. If I were you, Mr. MP, which I assume stands for Masturbating Pudfucker, I'd just wander on back to the front of the bus and leave me and my two friends alone. In fact, since the main reason we're here is for wasting Neanderthals like you, one more won't matter one fucking bit."

Smitty pushed the MP away roughly. He slowly closed his knife and sat back down between his two friends. The MP glared at him and turned on his heel. He marched away to the front of the bus—to the accompaniment of catcalls and scattered applause.

"Now then, gentlemen," Smitty said. "What were we discussing, before we were so rudely interrupted?"

"I'm tired and want to take a nap. Tell us later, brother," LZ responded.

"Yes, mon ami," Frenchy said, nodding. "Whatever the reasons, I'm sure you had good intent."

Their friendship was back on an even keel. But Smitty wondered if LZ and Frenchy would be as trusting if they knew there was much more to the story than this briefest of explanations.

"Now, then. Why don't you amuse me for a few moments, Private, by telling me your side of the incident that occurred on the bus," the captain began coldly. "And I might add that unless you want to spend every waking moment of your indoctrination process grinning at yourself through a latrine mirror, it had better be good!"

Smitty stared blankly back at the captain, then over to his newfound "best friend," and was on the verge of giving an explanation when a comical thought struck him. As a result, he could not suppress a smile that spread slowly across his face. A smile that drew an immediate reaction from his self-described mother, father, and main man to Uncle Sam, his drill instructor: Sergeant Sean Brown.

"Private Smith! You wipe that smile off your face, and I mean now!" he bellowed, jumping right in front of Smitty until their noses almost touched. In Sean's own words, from their initial orientation that morning, he was "five-feet-five and pound-for-pound the meanest Mick around."

"As you say, Sergeant Brown," Smitty said.

"When I or any other person of superior rank speaks to you, Private, you will respond in only two ways: yes, sir, or no, sir. Is that absolutely clear, Private?" he roared.

"Uh, well, now that you mention it, Sergeant, that's not quite clear at all," Smitty said.

"Which part didn't your minuscule brain understand?"

"Well, seems I read somewhere that persons of lesser rank address NCOs by their insignia of rank. While the proper procedure for addressing commissioned officers is by their rank followed by sir. Or have I been misinformed?"

Smitty could remember seeing tomatoes that weren't as red as the main-man's face at this moment. Smitty'd failed to fall for the old gambit of responding to the sergeant's outburst with a crisp, "Yes, sir," which would have given the sergeant an additional chance to publicly berate him and further establish his intimidation pattern.

"Why, you smart-ass son of a bitch!" the sergeant began, grabbing Smitty and shoving him against the wall with such force that the president's picture bounced off the wall like a hotly returned handball.

"Boy, you just made the mistake of a lifetime. Nobody fucks with me and gets away with it, nobody. You're gonna become my personal pet project. When you speak, I'll hear. When you move, I'll see. When you fuck up, I'll catch you.

"Ever' bunch of recruits has one fuckin' smart ass in it, and I make it my personal business to run that little bastard clean outta this man's army. You got me, boy! Your fuckin' ass is mine today, but it'll belong to Leavenworth before I'm through. We'll see just how smart you are then," Sergeant Brown screamed.

"Take your best shot, dog-shit breath," Smitty said.

"Why you cocksucking little faggot."

"That will do, Sergeant," the captain said. In addition to being Mother Nature's answer to a full-face wart, the sergeant was obviously hard of hearing too, since the captain's statement had not altered his actions in the least. "I said," reaching out and managing to pry the sergeant's knuckles from Smitty's arm, "that will do."

They stood glaring at each other, each hoping the other would flinch first in their silent tug-of-war. Smitty had a feeling, from the way both parties were responding, that this was not the first disagreement they'd had.

Never altering his glare, the sergeant said, "Yes, sir," and backed silently away.

"You get this, Private. The sergeant is here to train you to survive in combat. And if you listen to him rrrrreal carefully, you just might live long enough to legally vote. Now you get your ass out of here while I'm still in a good mood. Dismissed!"

Smitty cracked off a crisp salute, executed a perfect military about-face, and marched out of the room with his back ramrod straight.

As the sergeant opened the door for Smitty, he smiled triumphantly. A smile that Smitty returned with a silent "fuck you" that the captain didn't see. Sergeant Brown's smile vanished. He was halfway around the door when the captain's commanding voice brought him to a halt.

"Close the door, Sergeant; I want a word with you."

Smitty had a passing thought about listening against the door, but the first sergeant seated immediately outside appeared to be purposefully placed there to thwart any such thoughts.

"Move out, Private. Double-time your ass back to the barracks, and get your shit squared away," he said.

Smitty exhaled deeply as he dog-trotted down the corridor, out of the command center, and across the compound back to the barracks. He'd a passing thought at slowing to a walk, but figured that the first sergeant might be standing at the window watching. A quick backward glance proved him right.

He winced at the wall of noise that enveloped him as he jerked open the door to the barracks and passed inside. The place was absolute pandemonium as new recruits scurried back and forth across and between bunks, talking excitedly among themselves.

He managed to make it all the way to the other end of the barracks without injury, to where Frenchy and LZ waited expectantly. "So, how'd it go?" LZ asked.

"Oh, not so bad," Smitty said, vaulting cleanly up on the top bunk next to Frenchy and LZ, who'd staked out the top and bottom bunk against the wall. "A little yelling, a few threats, but no permanent damage."

"What about the sergeant? He looks like trouble," Frenchy said.

"Ah, he's what my ol' man used to call a regular army clown," Smitty replied airily. "If he wasn't in the service, he'd probably starve."

"Yoooou g-guys had b-better be c-careful," a stuttering voice said from directly below him. "T-that sergeant is a t-tough dude." The owner of the voice rolled out of the bunk and stood up.

Smitty thought he'd just jumped into the Jack-and-the-beanstalk yarn at just about the part where the beans get planted, and then shoot skyward like a hot rocket. There just seemed to be no end to this lad: six-foot-eight at least, with massive shoulders, and arms that made Frenchy look like a midget.

Walter was a gentle giant. A little slow on the uptake, he wore extremely thick glasses and had a laugh that was a high-pitched hiss. His stuttering was obviously related to a nervous condition, but Smitty'd a feeling that if the big man ever got mad, he'd probably make Attila the Hun look like a choirboy.

"In-n-n-n the last g-gr-roup, he b-br-roke a recruit's n-nose and jaw," Walter said with a trace of fear in his voice.

Smitty looked at LZ, then back at Frenchy, both of whom were giving him a what-the-hell-have-we-got-ourselves-into look.

Smitty cleared his throat. "Thanks for the information, Walt; I'll keep your advice in mind." Smitty reached out and shook Walt's hand.

Walt beamed back at Smitty like a newborn that had just gotten a fresh diaper. Smitty'd a feeling that because of his rather awkward, gangly, almost comical looks, no one before had ever taken him seriously, preferring instead to write him off as a buffoon or a moron.

At that moment, the pandemonium changed to out and out hysteria as the barracks doors were kicked open with such force that the doorknobs made impressions in the adjoining wall. Two shiny new forty-gallon galvanized garbage cans were airmailed in with sufficient velocity that they landed a good thirty feet inside. The lids separated on impact, rolling around the linoleum floor, careening off metal bunks like orphaned hubcaps on a metal bridge. The lights were turned on and off four times in rapid succession, further adding to the chaos.

"All right, you maggots, haul your asses outta them bunks and snap to," Sergeant Brown bellowed, striding confidently into the room and roughly shoving into formation recruits who came within his grasp. He was followed by an equally impressive-looking corporal who passed as the assistant drill instructor.

"When I say attention, I want you so fucking rigid that I hear your eyeballs click as I walk by." His voice could have won him the hog-calling contest at the county fair, hands down.

As he passed each recruit, he seemed to know just which buttons to push, delivering scathing remarks that had each one wincing in fear. Even though the sergeant tried to hide it, he grimaced involuntarily as he reached the end of the barracks and caught sight of Walt.

"What's your fucking story, four eyes?" Sergeant Brown spat, glaring directly at Walter.

"J-j-j-just w-hat do y-you mean, S-sergeant?" Walt answered.

"What's your fucking name?" he said.

"W-w-w-w-walter We-e-ellmen," he stuttered, his face bathed in sweat.

"W-w-w-w-well, W-w-w-w-w-walter, just how did a disgusting piece of shit like you ever get in this man's army?" the sergeant mimicked. "Who the hell would let something like you enlist? Your parents must have paid off the local draft board. That how it is? You from a rich family, boy? Huh? Answer me!"

"N-n-n-noooo, S-s-s-sergeant, I ain't f-f-f-from no rich family and—"

"Then you must be a big faggot since you bunk directly under this idiot," the sergeant said, gesturing at Smitty.

"I ain't no faggot," Walter said.

"Then—"

"I think the only faggot here is the one who keeps calling people that, looking for new friends in the shower," Smitty interrupted, making smooching sounds and tossing the sergeant a kiss.

"You motherfucking son of a bitch." The sergeant screamed as he leapt from Walt to Smitty.

What happened next did not catch Smitty completely by surprise. He could have stopped it, but didn't; should have stopped it, but couldn't move out of the way in time.

His face stung, and he felt the well-known taste of blood in his mouth in response to the sergeant's slap. But there was more. Smitty suddenly felt as if his face were on fire. He could feel the wetness as blood began to run down his cheek. The sergeant was wearing a peculiarly pointed ring on his right hand—to his horror he saw that the ring had the pointed side down. Intentionally. It had left a two-inch gash on Smitty's left cheek.

Unfortunately, the worst was not over yet. The sergeant had reached the end of his swing, and, like a golfer starting his follow-through, was beginning to bring his arm around, intent on delivering a second blow with the back of his hand. But not, Smitty noticed, before he rotated the ring so that the point was now outward.

LZ's left arm shot out, stopping him in his tracks. Almost as if by magic, his switchblade appeared at the sergeant's throat, instantly halting him as if he had turned to stone.

The corporal ran forward to assist but had his progress seriously impeded by a well-placed foot from Walt, who tripped him as he went by, sending him sprawling across the highly polished floor like a car skidding out of control on an icy road.

Realizing no help was coming, the sergeant tensed his shoulders, a move Smitty knew was preparatory to making a defensive strike. He had only begun to bring his left arm around to grab the knife when he began to slowly sink toward the floor.

The reason for this seemingly unexplainable loss of muscular control was Frenchy. Or perhaps it would be more accurate to say that it was Frenchy's brand new army issue combat boot, which he had used to kick the sergeant squarely behind the knee, with a great deal more force than had recently been used by the sergeant on the barracks door. As he spiraled slowly to the floor like the melting Wicked Witch from Oz, the entire barracks let out a collective gasp.

They stood in shocked silence as fifteen seconds passed, then another fifteen, before the sergeant could move.

Not without a great deal of difficulty, and certainly not on his first attempt, the sergeant awkwardly lurched painfully back to his feet with the help of the corporal. He shook him off angrily and, limping noticeably but with absolute hatred burning deeply in his eyes, advanced on Smitty and his friends, balling up his fist as he came.

"Tenhut! A voice shouted from behind, instantly halting the sergeant's forward progress and causing his head to snap around in that direction.

The captain marched across the room directly to the sergeant as though he were a combat objective that must be taken. At a distance of two feet, he stopped, did a quick 360 degree turn, not failing to notice the blood running freely down Smitty's cheek, or the obviously out-of-formation positions of LZ and Frenchy, and the wrinkled and disheveled appearance of the corporal. But he failed to see LZ's blade; it had vanished as quickly as it had appeared.

"You seem to be having some problem standing at the military attention position. Are you injured?" the captain asked.

"No, sir," he answered. "It's just an old injury acting up a bit."

"I see." Although it was plainly evident he did not. He looked over at Smitty. "What happened to your face, private?"

"Slipped on a bar of soap in the shower, sir."

"Uh, huh."

"And you?" The captain nodded at the corporal, who glanced at the sergeant for direction, and finding none forthcoming, merely shrugged his shoulders in silence.

The captain rubbed his chin thoughtfully. "Sergeant, I want you, and you,"—he pointed to the corporal—"and you,"—he pointed at Smitty—"and you,"—he pointed at LZ—"and you,"—he pointed at Frenchy—"to join me for a private conference in the latrine right now!"

The captain followed them down the barracks to the latrine and closed the door as he passed inside. Taking their cue from the captain's mood, they all fell in at attention, the sergeant and the corporal on one side, with Smitty, LZ, and Frenchy facing them at a distance of six feet.

"Gentlemen," the captain began. "I want it clearly understood—by all of you—that I will tolerate no more of this kind of behavior. The next occurrence, no matter how small, no matter who starts it, no matter whether it occurs on post or off, and I will personally see to it that all of you spend a major portion of your adult life breaking rocks at Leavenworth. Do I make myself CLEAR?"

"Yes, sir!" all five answered in unison.

"Sergeant," the captain said, stopping directly in front of Brown. "That cut on the private's cheek looks suspiciously similar to one on the face of another young man from the last group through here. You assured me that it was the result of an injury sustained in training. Well, training has not even started yet for this group, and all of a sudden, there's another. Frankly, I'm finding your previous statement a little hard to believe."

Turning from the sergeant to Smitty, the captain continued, "And you are just as much to blame. I have not the slightest doubt that you provoked whatever happened tonight in a manner similar to whatever happened on the bus this morning.

"You gentlemen don't have to love each other, but you have to get along. Therefore, effective immediately, the following is now in place: You, Sergeant, will be held personally accountable for the successful graduation from basic training of these three young men. If they don't finish, you're finished as a drill instructor. Their failure will be your failure; a failure that, if it's within my power, will most certainly cost you a stripe. And if I find out that you've been striking these men, your career in this man's army will be over—I'll see to that. Is that clear?"

"Yes, sir."

"One more thing, Sergeant. While it's true that these young men have been in a fair amount of trouble in the civilian world, they were also leaders of youth gangs—an experience that, if they're properly trained and motivated, might make them pretty good NCOs. I will expect you to keep that in mind during the course of training."

"Yes, sir."

"Now, as for you three," the captain said, as he turned to face them. "That sergeant over there is one of our most experienced NCOs. He fought in Africa, was wounded in Sicily, and was in the first wave at Omaha Beach. He was wounded again in Korea and has just finished his second tour in Vietnam. He's tough, tough as nails, but he has a wealth of actual combat knowledge. If you close your smart-ass little mouths and listen, he just might impart a sufficient amount of that knowledge to get you home from Vietnam standing upright."

"Yes, sir," Smitty, LZ, and Frenchy answered in unison.

"Very well. I don't expect to have this kind on discussion with anyone involved here again. If I do, you'd better put your head between your legs and kiss your asses goodbye because I'll most certainly make you regret the day of your conception.

"Good evening, gentlemen."

"All right, privates," the sergeant hollered past Smitty. "You better hit them bunks; 0500 comes mighty early." He paused, looked at Smitty and his two friends, and said in a voice oozing sweetness more artificial than saccharin, "And if it's not too much trouble, would you three gentlemen be so kind as to comply?"

After lights out, Smitty lay awake and thought about the sergeant's parting comments. Leopards didn't change their spots, and neither would the sergeant. His finishing remarks were about as subtle as the Hatfields inviting the McCoys for a light repast, with just as deadly a result. Smitty was certain that this was just the end of round one in what would surely be a long series of bloody skirmishes.

Six weeks into basic, things had begun to seem normal. The captain's warning on that first evening had been taken to heart by Smitty and his two friends and apparently by the sergeant also. Sergeant Brown carried out his training program within the army guidelines. Initially, he avoided direct contact with Smitty, LZ, and Frenchy, preferring to leave that task to the corporal. But as the weeks passed, they seemed to have won him over to the point that he now treated them just like any other recruits, mostly because of Smitty's plan.

After thinking for most of the night about the scuffle, Smitty had awoken LZ and

Frenchy at 0300 hours, and the three of them had talked in the latrine and put the plan to work at 0445 hours

When Sergeant Brown roused everyone at 0500 hours, he gave the entire barracks two minutes to get into fatigues, get the bunks made, get their shit squared away, and fall in at attention in front of their racks for inspection. Prior to starting, the captain joined him in the barracks . . . "just to see the nature of the recruits that we're receiving these days," he had said noncommittally.

Since no one had, as yet, received formal training in doing things "the army way," the results were predictably disastrous. That was, until he got to the bunks of Smitty, LZ, Frenchy, and Walt. Not only were the bunks made in correct military fashion, the footlockers and the clothing racks were perfect also. The sergeant was stunned and, try as he might, could find nothing wrong with their appearance, their racks, or their clothes.

He bounced a coin on all four beds, to see if they were tightly made; he pulled the trays out of all four footlockers looking for the slightest imperfection; and he removed the hanging uniforms looking for improper placement of insignia. The captain was quick to compliment the four of them on their area, and the sergeant had to grudgingly agree, especially when the captain went so far as to have everyone else parade by for a view.

As they were double-timing back from breakfast that morning, Smitty sent a silent telepathic thanks to his dad, who'd forced Billy and him to pass the same kind of "barracks inspection" every Saturday morning before receiving their allowance, and for having taken him along, literally hundreds of times, when he did barracks inspections of his own outfits. The procedures were second nature now.

So Smitty, LZ, Frenchy, and their newest fourth for bridge, Walt, were driving the main man for Uncle Sam fucking nuts. Using Smitty's memory and their own experiences as guides, they were living, breathing examples of the perfect army soldier. Having survived on the streets, they were in much better shape than the average recruit and easily kept up with the sergeant on exercises, hikes, and the much-vaunted infiltration course. Smitty, LZ, and Frenchy finished first, second, or third in all the events, and they studied their manuals ahead—with a flashlight in bed after lights-out—so that when the sergeant asked a question, they were ready with the answer.

Wherever possible, they protected Walt, urging him on in physical activities and taking turns tutoring him on army procedures. But despite their best efforts, the sergeant was merciless in his attacks on the big fellow. He'd taken to calling him "Waaalter" in a high-pitched, nasal voice. The sergeant seemed to be taking out on Walt what he really wanted to inflict on Smitty and his friends.

The conscientious efforts of Smitty and his friends had not escaped the attentions of the captain, who complimented the sergeant frequently on the progress he was making with them. By the end of the third week, all three had been made squad leaders and were the recognized leaders of the group.

The last day of the sixth week found Sergeant Brown not in a good mood. When he flashed the lights, the recruits were not fast enough, so they had to climb back in their racks, lie at military attention, and on his signal, scramble back into formation again. In the sergeant's opinion, the second time was no better than the first, nor was the third, fourth, or fifth. On the sixth try, he appeared to be satisfied, and the day's activities began for everyone except Smitty.

Smitty'd been fighting a cold for ten days, a cold that had turned to the flu three days earlier. When he went on sick call, the doctor put him on two days' bed rest. Today had been the second of the prescribed two-day period. Smitty, still feeling weak from the flu, had slept most of the day and did not awaken until the rest of the company had returned from dinner.

"Good evening, gentlemen. Did you enjoy serving your country today?" Smitty said, yawning.

LZ looked up and gave Smitty the finger.

"Tsk, tsk, tsk," Smitty admonished. "Guess you pansies can't cut it without your old buddy Smitty around."

"When I haul your honky ass out of that rack and put a hurtin' upside your head, we'll see who can cut it," LZ shot back.

"Ooooh, you get racial when you get mad, don't you, big fella?"

Before anyone could respond, an orderly appeared and handed a note to Smitty.

"What's it say, man?" LZ asked, his irritation replaced by concern.

"It says I'm to report for kitchen duty tonight at 0015 hours," Smitty said.

"Must be some mistake, man," LZ said to the orderly. "Smitty here is on two days' bed rest because of flu."

"There is no mistake," the orderly said. "Sergeant Brown was quite specific."

"Oh, Sergeant Brown," Smitty nodded. "Here's my order signed by Captain Billingsly, the doctor, excusing me from duty for forty-eight hours. So why don't you just go on back and acquaint Sergeant Brown with these facts," Smitty said, as he passed over the copy.

"I will, but I don't think he'll like it. He was quite specific in his request."

"Well, so is the doctor," Smitty responded.

"Sounds pretty suspicious, man," LZ said, after the orderly had left.

"Does at that," Smitty nodded thoughtfully. "Wonder what the old moose fart has up his sleeve?"

"I dunno, but I think LZ and I had better hang around the barracks tonight rather that go on weekend pass," Frenchy said.

"Naw, you guys go on. If I get to feeling better, maybe I'll join you tomorrow."

"Y-y-y-y-you s-s-s-sure?" Walt asked with obvious concern.

"Go on, have a good time. And take this big lad with you," Smitty said, giving Walt a good-natured thump on the back.

With final waves, the three of them left to catch the bus to town.

Smitty rolled over to go back to sleep. For the first time in months, he was beginning to feel really good about things in general. This army thing wasn't so bad; he was secretly beginning to like it. And he'd a feeling that the same was true for LZ and Frenchy. Maybe the reason was that, for the first time since he'd been railroaded out of Florida, he felt that he belonged to something, or was at least doing something that mattered.

Who are you kidding, shit head? Smitty said to himself in disgust. *The real reason was that you never had much of a home, and what you had sucked, and the envy was eating your guts out.*

The one time Smitty'd been on pass, he remembered walking around the town, just observing people. He watched with jealous envy families picnicking in the park, mothers preparing the meal from picnic baskets, and fathers playing catch with their sons. In the privacy of his rack, his thoughts turned to Glenda, and he felt a familiar stirring in his loins. God, he missed her, and not only sexually. From Glenda, his thoughts wandered to Stan the Man—out of a coma now, he'd heard.

As he felt drowsiness overtaking him, he reflected that the army had definitely been good for him. He had thought he was in pretty good shape before, but he recognized that he truly was in good shape now, both physically and mentally. He was a squad leader, and the captain had said that if he kept up his current level of achievement, he'd make a recommendation for PFC at basic graduation. This thought stayed with him as he drifted off to sleep. After years of turmoil, it was nice to finally be in a tranquil mood.

Tranquility was short-lived. It ended with a thud as he hit the floor. His first thought was that he'd simply rolled out of his bunk. He was just chiding himself for being so stupid when he felt the toe of a combat boot as it kicked him in the ribs.

Not yet fully awake, but conscious enough to take instinctive evasive measures, he rolled under the bunk next to him and tipped it back at the unseen aggressor. As the top bunk tipped and separated from the lower, Smitty removed the bunk spacer, a two-foot piece of steel that weighed about five pounds.

Sensing the unseen aggressor near, he swung blindly, and was rewarded with a bone crunching sound, that, Smitty knew from experience, would leave someone with an arm in a sling for the next six weeks.

Fully awake now, Smitty could see an MP holding his left arm with his right, whimpering in pain. He had two friends, who backed away. Behind them was Sergeant Brown.

"Your ass is mine now, boy," Sergeant Brown said. "Assaulting an MP will get a fucking delinquent like you an all-expenses-paid pass to the stockade, a quick courts', and an extended stay in Leavenworth.

"Knowing that you weren't feeling good, I stopped by to check on you. And knowing your history of violence, I brought along three MPs for backup. When I tried to wake you up, you opened your eyes and told me to fuck off, then rolled over.

"Now, I cannot tolerate such abuse. I nudged you a little harder, and when you shook me off again and attempted to roll away, you rolled off the bed. When I reached down to help you up, fearing you might have injured yourself, you told me that you were going to kill me, at which point I took defensive measures by delivering a judo kick to the ribs and calling for the MPs to subdue you, with, I'm not at all surprised to see, the expected results.

"Now, son, you're already up on charges of assault and threatening the life of a superior. Don't make it worse by doing anything else."

Smitty waved the pipe menacingly as he backed slowly away toward the end of the barracks. He needed time to think. He didn't recall saying any of those things to the sergeant but couldn't be sure. He thought it was a frame, but the sergeant was holding all the cards, and more violence now would only make matters worse. He flipped the bunk spacer onto a nearby mattress.

"Take him, boys," the sergeant shouted.

The two remaining MPs rushed forward, grabbed him, and threw him against the wall, spinning him so that his face hit, starting a nosebleed. Then they hustled him off to a waiting Jeep and on to the stockade.

Telling every comrade they ran across of the fate suffered by their colleague as a result of Smitty's "brutal assault" didn't earn him the fragile package treatment. By the time they had him processed and jailed, Smitty had quite a few bruises to show for his "voluntary surrender." He sat in the cell in thoughtful silence, knowing that, given the weight of the evidence against him, a lot of things could come of this, all of them bad.

"Wake up, you son of a bitch," the stockade sergeant said. "The army says we got to feed you bastards, but they don't say how, so here." The sergeant threw lukewarm oatmeal through the bars of his cell.

Smitty was just wiping the porridge out of his eyes when the sergeant said, "Coffee."

Smitty looked up at the sergeant defiantly and said, "Seconds?"

"Why you cock-sucking maggot. Brownee told me you'd be trouble." He reached through the bars, intent on grabbing Smitty by the throat and yanking him against the bars. Smitty was prepared and slid adroitly out of his reach. The sergeant banged his elbow on the bars and cursed.

"Gimme the keys to this maggot's cell," the sergeant screamed.

"No, Sarge, don't do it," a younger MP pleaded, jerking the keys out of his reach. "We gotta save enough of him for them to court-martial."

"Get this, boy. After the trial, and while they're waiting to ship you to Leavenworth, you and me are gonna find a nice, quiet, dark cell with no witnesses around, then see how many times we can get you to slip on a bar of soap. That's what happens in here to soldiers who bust up my MPs; you're gonna pay," the sergeant promised as he stalked away.

"Here's a towel to wipe that slop off," said the young MP. "How's the face?"

"Thanks, it hurts like hell," Smitty answered, taking the towel and making running repairs as best he could.

"Yeah, I bet it does. What the hell did you do, man? Get caught screwing your DI's daughter in his bed?"

"I don't think you'd believe me if I told you."

"Try me," he said.

Smitty stood sizing him up thoughtfully. He was young, but not that young. Smitty put him at mid- to late-twenties, and the hash on his sleeve verified that he'd reupped. He looked too bright to be a two-stripe MP, almost like a college whiz kid or something. But still Smitty needed to talk to somebody, if for no other reason than to see if he could make some sense of this mess.

"Unlock the door and come inside."

When the MP hesitated, Smitty said, "Come on. I haven't hit an MP in at least eight hours or so. I think the craziness has worn off by now."

The MP laughed and said, "Okay, partner, you don't look as violent as most of the loony tunes we get through here. Step back."

Smitty tried to piece together the events of the previous night. The MP's look of disbelief began to fade as he filled in the background.

He spent two hours telling and retelling his version, with the MP interrupting him often to clarify points that were muddled. "Well, I think I've got a clear picture from your point of view," he finally said.

"The basic points are, there's been bad blood between you and your DI, noted by your captain, and that you suspect this whole thing was a setup designed by him to get even. That about it."

"Yeah, that's it. Thanks anyway for listening," Smitty said, offering his hand.

"Yeah, I just wish I could be more help," the MP said, as he shook hands then left the cell. "But sometimes," he said, pausing at the corridor doorway, "help isn't as far away as it seems. See ya."

Smitty lay down on his bunk and thought about the MP's last remark. Help seemed about as close as Antares.

Nothing more happened that day, mostly because the MP who'd listened so attentively never let Smitty out of his sight. The next day was Sunday, and the only news was from the friendly MP, whose name turned out to be Jim.

As he passed over three packs of cigarettes and some candy from LZ, he said he'd overheard Sergeant Brown and the stockade sergeant talking, and that Smitty was scheduled for a hearing with a three-officer review board first thing Monday morning. When Smitty pressed for more details, the young MP became suddenly vague and silent.

At 0700 hours, Smitty was unceremoniously rousted by having his rack overturned and dumped on the floor. He was provided with a fresh uniform and told to be cleaned up and ready to go in ten minutes. When Smitty innocently asked where, his minder told him that he was going to get fucked: officially by the army today and by him personally tonight. He shivered.

Smitty tried hard not to show how queasy he felt when he entered the hearing room. The three-man board consisted of a regular army full colonel, a Green Beret lieutenant colonel, and a major who apparently was a lawyer. All three looked solemn and, judging from their faces, had been through this unpleasant duty before. They didn't like it but wouldn't shirk it.

Also present were Smitty's company captain, Sergeant Brown, four MPs, and the stockade sergeant, who was present as a material witness for Sergeant Brown.

"Captain," the colonel began mildly. "I don't think the defendant needs to be manacled in that fashion, do you?"

The captain looked at Sergeant Brown without expression and said, "No, sir."

"Begging the colonel's pardon," the stockade sergeant said, standing up, "the prisoner has already seriously injured one of my men and has required restraining actions while in the stockade this weekend. May I respectfully suggest to the colonel that we leave the bracelets on."

The colonel made no effort to conceal his displeasure. "First off, this man is not a prisoner; he's a defendant. Second, this is a hearing, not a torture session; physical restraint is not required. Third, judging from the bruises and the discolored skin on this young man's face, I'd say offhand some of your 'restraining methods' are in need of review."

The stockade sergeant opened his mouth to speak, thought better of it, and nodded to an MP, who dourly stepped forward to remove the handcuffs and the ankle restraints.

The colonel rubbed his chin thoughtfully. "As a matter of fact, Sergeant, I think we can take this procedure a step further."

"Yes, sir," the sergeant said.

"You and your MPs can wait outside—"

"I can't do that, sir," the stockade sergeant interrupted. "The Uniform Code of Military Justice specifically states that—"

"Sergeant, I said you're dismissed."

"Yes, sir. But of course, sir, since there is a clear violation of procedure here, I have to phone the provost marshal and report that you ordered me to leave a prisoner without official supervision."

"The Uniform Code also states that this man is entitled to legal counsel, Sergeant, who I'm certain will want to ask a few pointed questions about those bruises on this young man's face."

The colonel pointed his finger at the stockade sergeant. "If you're still standing here in ten seconds, you're going to start receiving the same treatment from me, personally. Dis-missed!"

The four MPs were scurrying for the door even before the colonel finished. The sergeant, for all his earlier defiance, was headed for the door at a forced march pace also.

"Now then, is this man's counsel present?"

"Here, sir," a familiar voice said from a side door. In the last couple of days, Smitty had come to know its owner's face well. Only the last time he'd seen it, it had been atop a corporal's uniform with an MP's armband.

"I apologize for being late, sir, but I was tied up finishing another case. We're spread kind of thin." He smiled and gave a barely perceptible nod to Smitty.

"I can imagine." The colonel turned and said, "Private Smith, you are charged with assaulting a superior, assault with intent to maim and injure, assault with a deadly weapon, resisting arrest, and disorderly and disruptive conduct while under incarceration. How do you plead?"

The MP/corporal/captain/Jim whispered quickly in Smitty's ear, then Smitty said, "Not guilty, sir."

"Let the record show that the defendant has entered a not guilty plea," the colonel said. "Also let the record show that, after reading the preliminary paperwork on the charges filed by this man's drill instructor and the sergeant of the stockade, that, in the interest of expediency, I am making a recommendation that we drop the minor charges and deal strictly with the two major charges, namely, assaulting a superior and assault with a deadly weapon. Do you concur, Captain?"

"Yes, sir," Jim responded.

"Good. Now then, to come directly to the point, this is a hearing to determine if a formal court-martial is warranted. As such, it will be as informal as possible. The two main charges were filed by the defendant's drill instructor. Sergeant Brown, come forward and be sworn."

After the sergeant was sworn, the colonel said, "Be seated, and tell this review board, in your own words, the circumstances surrounding the filing of these charges."

"Well, sir, let me first say that it was with a real heavy heart that I was forced to take this action against one of my own recruits," Sergeant Brown said. "When one of my boys fails, I feel like I've failed, too . . . "

"So do I, Sergeant," the colonel said. "Let's dispense with the artificial concern and stick to the facts. If you truly felt that way, this review board would not be in session right now."

A profound silence fell. Finally, Brown broke it.

"Very well, sir," he said. "At 2100 hours the previous Friday . . ."

Smitty temporarily tuned Sergeant Brown out. He'd heard this version before, and it didn't sound any more plausible the second time around. Smitty was scared, but he meant to think his way out if he could.

He assembled the facts, shuffled them like a cards, and prepared to deal his hand. He whispered quickly to the captain, who shushed him to silence. And not a moment too soon; Sergeant Brown had just finished his version of what had happened.

Remember the puzzle, Smitty prayed silently to himself. Get all the pieces sorted out, Jimbo, before you start to put it together.

"Sir," Jim began respectfully, "may I ask questions based on the statements made under oath?"

"Yes."

"Sir, just one other question, before we begin. The sergeant has referenced facts from the sergeant of the stockade. Can I also reference facts from people who are not present now, with the understanding that those statements can be taken down and documented later?"

"In a formal trial, that would be hearsay evidence and, therefore, inadmissible. But since this is a hearing to determine if a general court-martial is warranted, I am going to allow you some latitude as long as the facts are reference only."

"Thank you, sir."

"Then you may proceed."

"Sergeant Brown, how long have you been in the army and, of that time, how long have you been a drill instructor?"

"I have been in the service twenty-seven years and am on my fourth two-year assignment as a drill instructor. I enlisted the day—"

"Excuse me, Sergeant. Colonel, would you please ask the sergeant to answer just the questions that were asked and skip the elaborations?"

"The witness will answer just the question asked."

"Thank you.

"And are you a good drill instructor, Sergeant?" Jim asked.

"Best damn DI in the army."

Smitty caught Jim's almost imperceptible nod and interjected, "Colonel, I must concur. I grew up under a career first sergeant, and next to my father, Sergeant Brown is the most competent drill instructor I've ever seen."

"Sergeant Brown, who is currently rated the top recruit in your class?" Jim continued, changing tracks.

"He is," the sergeant mumbled, pointing at Smitty.

"I'm sorry, Sergeant, I'm afraid I didn't hear you. Would you please speak up?"

"He is," he repeated.

"Is it not true that the purpose of basic training is to instill discipline?" Jim asked.

"Yes, it is."

"And isn't the end goal of that discipline to train soldiers in fundamental fighting methods until reactions become instinctive?"

"Yes, it is."

"Now, as to the assault charge, dismissing the circumstances that provoked it for just a moment, and based on the testimony you just gave, isn't it possible—no, make that expected—that when your best recruit, trained by the best DI in the army, is assaulted from a deep sleep, that he would instinctively lash out in self-defense?"

The sergeant opened his mouth to speak, but the captain cut him off.

"Before you answer that question, Sergeant, let me remind you that if that statement is not true, then you must be guilty of perjury. I mean, if you're truly the best DI, and Private Smith is truly the best recruit, then he is a reflection of your excellent teachings. Therefore, if all of the above is true, and he's guilty of assault, then you are, also. Since, by your own admission, you taught him everything he knows."

Both the lieutenant colonel and the major on the review board were holding their faces with their hands to keep from laughing. The colonel was snickering quietly to himself, while Jim was looking at Sergeant Brown with the innocence of a newborn. The sergeant looked totally confused.

"Yeah, but it's the reasons that are important here," the sergeant said. "This little bastard disobeying an order provoked this whole incident."

"Sergeant, did you bother to read the pass signed by the doctor?"

"No, sir."

"It states," Jim removed a copy from a folder he had brought with him, "that prior to returning to duty, Private Smith is to be reexamined to assure that he is completely recovered.

In point of fact, Private Smith was obeying his orders; it was you who were not."

The colonel looked at the lieutenant colonel and the major on both sides, and on receiving their affirmative nods, looked up at Smitty and said bluntly, "Case dismissed."

Jim turned and shook hands with Smitty, and said, "Looks like you beat the rap, killer." Then he whispered, "Obstacle course, 2200 hours. Bring the other three musketeers." He was gone before the stockade sergeant reentered the room.

"Shall I return the prisoner to the stockade, sir?"

"That won't be necessary, Sergeant. With the help of his legal beagle, the little desperado beat the rap," the colonel said, still barely able to contain his laughter.

The stockade sergeant looked sharply at Sergeant Brown, who shrugged his shoulders helplessly in return.

Smitty suddenly realized that he'd gained more than a dismissal; he'd probably gained his life. The stockade sergeant had been cheated out of the plans he'd made for a murder.

"Where is he, man?" LZ said. "It's ten after."

"Relax, mon ami," Frenchy said. "Smitty said he'd be here; he's just running a little late, that's all."

"I-i-i agree w-w-w-with L-l-l-Z," Walt added. "T-t-this could b-b-b-be-e-e another t-trap."

"Hey, this guy saved my bacon. He'll show," Smitty said. "Be patient."

They didn't have long to wait. They all heard the footsteps and silently spread out. Whoever this guy was, he wasn't much of a soldier. In the still night air, his footsteps sounded like an advancing tank as they crunched the branches and leaves.

"Private Smith? Private Smith?"

As he stepped past the climbing wall, Smitty grabbed him from behind, covering his mouth with his right hand, used his left to twist his arm around his back, and led him out of sight behind a hedge.

"There's no need—"

"Shhh!" Smitty cut him off, whispering urgently, "Be quiet! You're being followed."

Even in the darkness of the South Carolina night, Smitty could see his eyes widen with fear. When he heard other footsteps, they got wider.

"Don't talk, don't move, if you want to live!"

They stood silently as two men approached.

Smitty recognized one of them, the wakeup caller. But the jungle fatigues were a 180-degree turn from his natty MP's uniform of this morning, to say nothing of the distinctly non-army-issue pistol with a silencer he carried in a hand the size of a shovel. His partner was likewise attired and armed.

Smitty and Jim watched as the two advanced silently past them. They'd continued only twenty feet more when their progress, as well as their health, was seriously impaired.

Frenchy stepped from behind a tree and delivered a perfect home-run swing with a bunk spacer to the head of the MP closest to him. Walt showed no such finesse. A towering right seemed to physically move the wakeup specialist four feet sideways before he hit the ground. One quick glance, and Smitty knew he'd not be rousing anymore unfortunates, unless it was in hell.

Everyone remained absolutely still, waiting to see if they'd been heard or if more reinforcements were on the way. A minute passed, then two. Smitty was waiting for LZ's all clear.

"It's cool, man, no one else is following," LZ said, appearing beside Smitty out of nowhere.

"Jesus Christ, man. You scared the shit out of me," Smitty said.

"Sorry. We'd better do this fast. That asshole is gonna be looking for these two to report in."

"Walt, climb that tree over there and keep a sharp lookout," Smitty said. He turned to Jim. "Okay, partner, which is it, MP asshole or ambulance chaser?"

"Little of both," Jim responded. "I am a lawyer, but I'm also on an undercover assignment as an MP. I think you know why, right?"

"To catch that bastard sergeant and put him in his own stockade," Smitty responded. "And I take it," he rubbed the back of his neck, "that I just happened to blunder along as bait."

"Not happened, sport; planned."

"Come again!" Smitty said.

"That stockade sergeant's had you zeroed in from the first day you arrived, almost as if he'd been expecting you," Jim said.

"I think maybe he was," Smitty mused. He changed the subject. "So, what's the purpose of the late-night rendezvous? You and your boss, the colonel, got some other little chore that needs attending to?"

"How did you know that?" Jim was dumbfounded. "Actually, it's the Green Beret lieutenant colonel."

"It figured." Smitty held up his hands and began to tick off the points. "The other three musketeers were there in the barracks when that phony CQ showed up. My money is on his being another one of the stockade sergeant's henchmen." Smitty looked up at Jim, who nodded his head in agreement.

"I win my bet," Smitty said. "Sergeant Brown was faked out, too. After the goon left, LZ, Frenchy, and Walt left the barracks, ostensibly to catch the bus to town. But they knew something was wrong, so they doubled back and hid near the barracks and waited.

"They overheard Lard Butt tell Sergeant Brown that he'd tried to have an orderly wake me up for an emergency call but that I told him to fuck off. He then told Sergeant Brown that he'd sent a separate message ordering me to report to the provost marshal, which I had refused.

"Sergeant Brown being Sergeant Brown, he swallowed that yarn hook, line, and sinker, and said he'd get that little bastard up. And as he started inside, the stockade sergeant said, 'You'd better take my three MPs with you as witnesses, in case he causes trouble.' Naturally, Sergeant Brown bit on that one, too." Smitty lit a cigarette and blew out a cloud of smoke. "And the rest, as they say, is history."

"Whew!" Jim said. "I'm impressed. But how did you manage to get all this information if you never made contact with your friends?"

"When they hauled me out to the Jeep, I saw LZ crouched in the shadows. He pointed at me, then flipped me the bird, which could only mean that I'd been fucked. Then you delivered the mail yourself on Sunday, when you gave me those three packs of cigarettes and the candy. LZ had written the details down and slid them into one of the packs.

"Weren't you afraid that they might search them?"

"Chance they had to take, man," Smitty said.

Both stood silently in the crisp night air, thinking. Smitty used to think he was jinxed; now he was sure of it. Trouble followed him everywhere. The question was why.

It wasn't too hard to guess what Jim was thinking: how to get Smitty to volunteer for the plan to catch that fat-assed sergeant red-handed. If he didn't want to stand here and freeze his butt off, Smitty thought he'd better suggest something.

"Look, Captain, if what you want to do is trap that bastard, then I think my friends and I might be able to help you. We've got a fair amount of experience at that sort of thing."

"What?"

Smitty held up a finger and said, "Don't ask. What you don't know, you can't tell." Smitty walked about four steps before he turned around.

"And don't worry, Jim. I want that bastard just as much as you do, maybe even more. See ya."

Smitty motioned to his three friends, who dropped into step beside him. "Got some unfinished business guys; it concerns that sergeant."

"Gonna give him the Keith treatment, huh?" LZ asked.

"I'm beginning to think we should all be bankers," Frenchy said.

"W-w-w-why's t-t-that-t?" Walt asked.

"Because we're so damn good at account balancing."

"Well, if the plan I've got in mind works, then we should all be opening our own branches," Smitty said. *And if it doesn't,* he thought to himself, *then the stockade sergeant will finally get his wish . . . the murder will yet be committed.*

The news of Smitty's exoneration had barely made the latrine-o-gram when it faded faster than a retracted headline. The hot story the next morning was about the two MPs found dead in jungle fatigues with silenced pistols on the obstacle course the night before. For the next twenty-four hours, one hot rumor had been supplanted by another, each a little more bizarre than the last. The one that seemed to be sticking was that it was some kind of feud and that they had been the victims left behind. The stockade sergeant was tight-lipped and silent, refusing to even speculate on the cause. His only comment being that it had been a 'tragic accident' and was being investigated.

The week passed quickly. Sergeant Brown kept a respectful distance from Smitty, as did Smitty from the sergeant. It was the end of the seventh week, and Smitty had to admit that the sergeant's methods were starting to work. Even the gangly were starting to shape up and walk with a proud gait. Reactions were becoming instincts. They no longer thought as many; they acted as one.

They passed the Friday inspection and for the first time found the quarter Sergeant Brown always said he hid in the barracks to see if they'd cleaned everywhere. So confident had they now become that they didn't just take the quarter, they left him fifteen cents change.

Surprisingly, instead of being angry, Sergeant Brown beamed with pride. He winked at the captain, who nodded his head in satisfaction. No company demerits meant that, for the first time, the entire unit got a weekend pass. Smitty and his friends stayed together and went light on the Friday-night drinking; they were going to need all their wits for what lay twenty-four hours ahead.

"E-e-e-excuse me, Captain, m-m-may I h-have a w-w-word with you, sir?" Walt asked, as the company captain came down the steps from his office quarters.

"Make it quick, Private," the captain said, glancing at his watch. "I have to pick up my wife at the airport, and I'm late now."

"S-s-sir, I ain't n-no s-squealer, but there's gonna be trouble in town tonight," Walt continued, shifting his weight back and forth from one foot to the other nervously.

"Have you discussed this with your drill sergeant?" the captain said testily, clearly indicating his irritation at the breach of military protocol.

"No, sir," Walter said, as he began to sweat profusely.

"Why not?"

"B-b-because the sergeant is t-the one who's going to s-start it."

"Explain."

"I-i-i overheard him t-t-telling another sergeant that t-t-tonight was the night that they were finally going to get that b-b-b-bastard."

"That bastard being Private Smith, I take it?"

"Y-yes, Sir."

I want to thank you for telling me this, Private. I assure you that I will take the proper action. Good night." The captain started to go back inside, then stopped and turned. "Oh, and Private, let's keep this between you and me."

"Yes, sir."

After the captain was out of sight, Walt broke into a dead run. His pace never slowed until he reached the phone outside the PX. He dialed a number from memory and said, "Hey, bro, Daddy just found out ten minutes ago about you knocking up his little girl." And without another word, hung up with a satisfied smile.

The phone's ringing snapped the provost marshal's desk sergeant out of his day-dream. He listened respectfully, and said, "Yes, sir," before hanging up the phone. He pivoted around in his chair and punched a switch on a second phone. "Sergeant Brown's captain just called. There's going to be trouble between him and that private in town tonight."

"Perfect," he responded. "Then that little bastard will be mine." The phone went dead in the sergeant's hand. He hung up quickly; too quickly to hear the second click of another phone disconnecting.

"Sergeant Brown, Sergeant Brown," LZ said, catching up to him on his way back to the barracks from the NCO club. "I've got to talk to you."

"What is it, son?"

"It's Smitty, uh, that is Private Smith. He's in big trouble, at least he will be, if you don't help."

"What the hell is this all about, soldier?" Sergeant Brown said.

"I don't exactly know myself, Sergeant. It's just that I overheard a group of MPs talking about some sort of trap that stockade sergeant set to catch Smitty."

"Christ, that little fucker's always in trouble. What's he got himself into now?"

"I don't know Sergeant, but you'd better get downtown quickly, or it'll be too late."

"Wait here." He ran back in the NCO club and was back outside in less than two minutes, along with three other DI's, all of whom looked as though they enjoyed fighting more than fucking. "You stay here, Private. Let's not make this any worse than it already is. Let's go, boys."

LZ watched them as they sprinted to the sergeant's car, leaped in, and drove away in a tire-squealing hurry. He stepped into a phone booth and said to the voice that answered. "Hey, hey, hey; four irate fathers on the way." Even before the last words were out, he was talking to dead air.

Smitty waited ten minutes from the phone call before leaving the rented hotel room himself. If everything worked, then an hour from now Smitty would have fucked up an asshole permanently. If it didn't, then in all probability, his ass would be the one getting fucked . . . permanently.

The main strip was bustling with the normal Saturday night crowd. As far as the eye could see, the street was an endless collection of sleazy bars, cheap motels, and strip joints. It was the underbelly typical of any service town.

The locals cursed it; the city government deplored it. But past paying lip service, no one seemed to want to really do anything about it. It brought in money no one wanted to do without.

Smitty stood on the corner next to the sign for the Sleep Cheap Motel and waited. With a wry smile, he noticed that it flashed in one-second intervals the news that rooms were available by the hour. He now understood the perplexed look the clerk had given him when he asked for the room for the entire night—probably thought he was going to have an orgy.

In the best military tradition, Smitty and his friends had contingency plans for whoever showed up first. Ideally, it would be that fat-assed stockade sergeant, followed quickly, Smitty hoped, by Sergeant Brown and his three cohorts. Further reinforcements were on the way in the guise of LZ and Big Walt, with Frenchy and his bulging biceps never far out of sight.

This was a risky plan, far more so than with Keith, mainly because the stockade sergeant and his reactions were less familiar. The whole plan depended on their collective assessment of him as a bully. If their calculated risk worked, they'd be brilliant strategists; if it didn't, they'd be fuckups. Dead ones, probably.

"Head's up, Sonny, them's military cops comin'." A grizzled old wino with a stringy beard touched Smitty lightly on the arm, accepted a dollar from him, and shuffled toward a military police Jeep that had just skidded to a stop thirty yards away.

Smitty slid back into the shadows, out of sight, with a silent prayer for the wino, who was now approaching the MPs looking for his next handout.

Smitty watched as the stockade sergeant got out of a Jeep with three other MPs. Two other Jeeps, also with four occupants each, pulled up at the same moment. He'd figured on four to six, tops. Twelve against three would not have had a bookmaker doing cartwheels.

"Hey man, gimme a dollar?" the wino asked loudly, stumbling up to the stockade sergeant. Waiting until passersby began to look in his direction, he grabbed the stockade sergeant's arm. "Come on, man, you can spare a dollar."

The stockade sergeant shoved him away roughly. "Get the fuck away from me, you useless piece of shit."

The wino went down like a Polooka who'd been paid to take a dive on cue. With his face wincing in pain, he grabbed the stockade sergeant's leg. "You ought not to be a treating me like that, Sergeant; I didn't never drink at all until I was wounded at the Canal."

The stockade sergeant shook off the wino's hands with a half kick that struck him in the ribs. It seemed to physically lift the old sot clear of the ground and punt him three feet before he landed heavily in a disheveled heap. He lay motionless, clutching his midsection in pain and sobbing loudly. The crowd, which had gasped at the stockade sergeant's first shove, now reacted to his kicking of the feeble old man with angry threats and taunts.

Smitty had certainly seen enough. He ran from the shadows to the old man and knelt down beside him. "Easy partner; just take it easy." Smitty rolled him over gently. He reached in his pocket, pulled out a wad of bills, and pressed them into the man's hand. "Here you go. Go get yourself a room for the night in that motel."

The old man smiled through tears of gratitude. "Thanks, son. It's good to know we're not forgotten by everyone."

Smitty had started to help the old man to his feet, when several members of the crowd came forward to assist. Together, they got him standing upright, dusted him off as best they could, handed him his hat, and sent him on his way.

Smitty turned to the stockade sergeant. "Little hard on the old man, weren't you?"

"Why don't you mind your own fucking business?"

The crowd responded to this with more angry taunts.

"Sorry, I just couldn't. Try as I might, I just can't ignore my daddy's advice," Smitty said.

"Yeah, what's that?"

"My ol' dad always said that it's one of God's little jests that there are more horses' rectums in the world than horses." The crowd responded with laughter and scattered applause. "And it's my civic duty as a patriotic American citizen to be on constant guard to try and right this terrible imbalance."

"Are you calling me a horse's ass?"

"Oh, no, Sergeant. But if the shoe fits . . . "

Smitty's response brought widespread laughter and thunderous applause from the assembled crowd. A crowd that, Smitty was happy to see, was supplemented in the background by Sergeant Brown, his three fellow noncoms, and just to the right of them and behind, LZ and Big Walt—the betting was even money now.

Clearly embarrassed and, in an obvious attempt to regain control, the stockade sergeant barked, "All right you name-calling smart ass, you're under arrest. Take him, boys."

As the two MPs raised their nightsticks and stepped forward intent on bashing Smitty's head in, they were restrained and hit from behind in the kidneys by Sergeant Brown and one of the other noncoms.

"Get the fuck out of here, Smitty," Sergeant Brown screamed over the shrieking of the crowd.

Smitty ducked a swinging nightstick, hit the unseen culprit in the throat with a judo smash, pivoted, and with a quick dart broke away from what was now spreading into a full-sized street fight. The twelve MPs, outnumbered now four to one as the partisan crowd joined in, were in the process of getting back in spades what they handed out in clubs.

Smitty wasn't of a mind to run from a fight but obviously someone else was. After throwing one of his men at Smitty, the stockade sergeant had bullied his way through the crowd, kicking two drunken bystanders in the process, and was now sprinting down the alley beside the motel, with Smitty in hot pursuit.

The fat bastard had a twenty-yard head start. At the back of the motel, the alley gave onto a back street that was used for deliveries. It had no streetlights, only what light escaped from windows above. The sergeant had vanished. The alley was filled with dark shadows and a dozen doorways, dumpsters, and other places of concealment.

Smitty did a mental coin flip and veered right down the alley away from the motel. He slowed to a walk, straddling the imagined centerline, and crept slowly and carefully along.

Smitty heard a slight noise to his right. A swiping knife slashed his sleeve and shaved off the hair on his arm, but failed to cut him.

"You're gonna die, fuck head," the sergeant said, panting. "Nobody crosses me and lives."

"Yeah, I know. That also applies to people who don't cross you, too."

"Fuck you," the sergeant grunted.

"Bet you'd like to do that, wouldn't you? That's what this whole thing is about anyway, isn't it? You and that cast of Neanderthal faggots haul in recruits on some trumped-up charge, and then your henchmen tell them that they can get 'special' treatment if they give you 'special' treatment in return.

"But something went wrong in the last recruiting class, didn't it? One of the sheep refused to be slaughtered and fought back. You and your guys beat him senseless, then tied him face down, bent him over a table, then literally fucked him to death. You ruptured his intestines when you forced that nightstick all the way up his ass. He bled to death in agony; you watched and laughed."

"You can't prove a thing," the sergeant said shakily.

"I don't have to prove it; the army already has. They're just waiting for an excuse to pull you in, and now they've got it. You're finished."

Smitty suddenly had a startling revelation, a feeling that he'd been in this movie before, with Jimmy and Gena. The methods were the same. It couldn't be related . . . or could it?

"I may be finished, but I'll take you with me," the sergeant said, bringing Smitty back to reality.

In the half-light of the dim back street, Smitty felt his blood turn cold. Knives were one thing, but silenced pistols were quite another. The hand was steady, the face firm. In almost grotesque slow motion, Smitty watched the hammer being pulled back slowly. He tensed himself for the blast and prepared to die.

A shot rang out. The sergeant was flung backward and landed facedown in an oily puddle.

From behind, the unseen shooter stepped past Smitty, rolled the sergeant over with his foot, and verified that his shot had found its mark. Dropping the shotgun into the crook of his arm, he fished out a pack of cigarettes, offered one to Smitty, and took one for himself.

Smitty nodded his thanks and said, "Nice shot."

"You're welcome," Jim replied.

"Thought you were just an imitation MP," Smitty said.

"Daddy is a hunter," Jim said. "Taught me."

"What's the score back on the street?"

"Let's go find out."

They turned and had taken only two steps when the street filled with reinforcements from the alley. Leading the pack was Sergeant Brown, followed by the other noncoms, LZ, and Big Walt. Frenchy, not there at the start, had appeared, seemingly from nowhere.

"Are you all right?" Sergeant Brown asked, his concern genuine.

"Yeah, I'm fine," Smitty said.

"What about our burly friend?"

"Slipped on a bar of soap," Jim said, patting his weapon. He put his arm around Smitty and escorted him from the alley.

They were halfway through the parted crowd when Smitty heard Sergeant Brown's gravelly voice say, "Well, one thing's for certain. The son of a bitch sure as hell won't be slipping on any more."

The last weeks of basic passed quickly. The eighth week was filled with stories of "the rumble downtown with Sergeant Brown." The local papers played it up, and the mayor and other self-important dignitaries deplored and ranted about the army to any group of reporters who would listen. But by the end of the week, the stockade sergeant had been quietly flown home to Texas for private burial, and the twelve MPs were treated and released at the base hospital and, along with a dozen others, were quietly removed from the post and transferred to Fort Lawrence, Kansas, to await the military courts.

The ninth week saw the announcement of a new base provost marshal: the former corporal, former captain, and now freshly promoted major, Jim. Smitty's own commander was highly pissed when he unlayered the truth and found out how he had been used to set the wheels in motion. But a glowing report from the major stating that Smitty and his three comrades, along with Sergeant Brown, had been instrumental in resolving a homicide had soothed his ruffled feelings.

Frenchy was left off the commendation at first until Sergeant Brown politely pointed out to the major and to their captain that the "old man" who had provoked the entire incident was none other than Frenchy with one hell of a makeup job, a skill he learned from his mother, a former nightclub singer.

Sergeant Brown, when asked about their actions by the captain, had said, "They was just doing what I taught 'em." And the captain himself had announced at final formation that morning that Smitty, LZ, and Frenchy were to be awarded a stripe each, to be on their uniforms in time for pass in review graduation at 1500 hours that afternoon.

All in all, basic seemed to be just another chapter in what had by now become an all too familiar story. Smitty and his friends had done the right thing and endured some personal hardship for it, but in the end it paid off. But as they sat around the barracks waiting for final formation, Smitty couldn't shake the thought that some unseen person was scripting his life.

After dismissal, they all lounged around the barracks listening to a contraband radio that the guy across from Smitty had smuggled in, waiting, and feeling justifiably pleased with themselves. A voice at the other end of the barracks shouted, "Brass coming."

Smitty clapped his hands, and the radio's owner flipped it to him. Smitty glanced quickly down the barracks and saw the captain and Sergeant Brown coming up the steps. He lateraled the radio to Big Walt. "Get rid of this thing."

Walt took this command quite literally. He whirled around and threw the radio out the window into the compound. The two screens and reinforced glass hardly slowed it at all.

LZ stepped over to the window, looked through the holes, and whistled out loud in admiration. "I'll be damned; that radio must be made by Timex. It takes a lickin' and keeps on tickin'. The fuckin' thing's still playing."

No one had a chance to admire Walt's accomplishment further. The captain had just entered, and a crisp bark from Sergeant Brown had brought them all to instantaneous attention.

"I just wanted to take a minute to stop by and extend my personal congratulations to each and every one of you on successfully completing basic training. I know it was tough, but I never for a moment had a doubt that you would all turn out to be fine soldiers." The captain strolled down the length of the barracks.

He paused before Smitty and his friends. "And I also want to acknowledge the special efforts by these three young men, which resulted in their immediate promotions." The captain seemed to stop in midthought, and cocked his head. "Is that a radio I hear playing, PFC Smith?"

Smitty said, "A radio, Captain?"

The captain's peripheral vision caught sight of the irregularity in the screen. He leaned around Smitty to get a better look at the hole. "Make way, Private." Smitty stepped to the side.

The captain examined the hole in the screen and the hole in the window. He caught sight of the still-playing radio in the compound outside and turned back to face

Smitty. "That radio," he said, jerking his thumb towards the window.

"Uh, well, Captain, you see, it was sort of like this," Smitty stammered, his normally quick wit deserting him.

"I'm waiting, Private," the captain said, trying hard to suppress a smile.

Smitty shrugged his shoulders.

"Whoever threw that radio missed his calling," the captain said. "He should be pitching for the Yankees." He walked away from the window and past Smitty shaking his head. "I don't suppose anyone is gonna tell me who did it?"

Suddenly inspired, Smitty raised his arms like the conductor of the Mormon Tabernacle Choir. As he brought his arms down, the entire barracks said in unison, "Waaaaaalter," in the same high-pitched nasal voice that Sergeant Brown had used on Walter during their first weeks here.

As Smitty lowered his arms, thunderous laughter and applause broke out. The captain and Sergeant Brown, Smitty was happy to see, joined right in.

Still chuckling to himself, the captain walked over to Smitty and shook his hand. "Son, you're a pisser. Good luck, and good luck to the rest of you." Shaking hands as he walked to the front of the barracks, he left without a further word, followed closely by Sergeant Brown.

It was a perfect ending. But the next beginning loomed.

CHAPTER EIGHT

"Sergeant Smith, you and Sergeants McCord and Douchet are to report to the base commander's office in one hour," the lieutenant said, leaning into the room.

"Yes, sir, Lieutenant," Smitty said.

"Oh, and Sergeant, I'd suggest you gentlemen put on your best Class A's, be on time, and be on your best behavior." The lieutenant winked as he left their room.

"What's up, man?" LZ said.

"Dunno, man. The Looey said we're wanted in the base commander's office in an hour—in our military best."

"We, I take it, to include Frenchy?"

"That's what the man said."

"Have to go find him, man. He's over at the NCO club. Got the hots for one of the Doughnut Dollies."

"Well, tell that walking hard-on to get his ass back here," Smitty said, playfully popping LZ in the rear with a towel.

"Hey, asshole, watch it. We just got these stripes, wouldn't look too good for us to be knocking heads and lose 'em." LZ made a futile grab for the towel as he rounded the doorway and disappeared from sight.

Smitty watched from the window as LZ exited the barracks and jumped into the "Famous '54." The vehicle was a shared seventy-five dollars, no title, 1954, two-door hardtop Chevrolet. With a silent laugh, Smitty noticed that even though the car was out of sight between the rows of barracks, the plumes of blue smoke were a clear enough trail marker of where it had been.

The four of them—Smitty, LZ, Frenchy, and Big Walt—had left basic training just three short months ago and headed off for advanced infantry training at Fort Benning. They sailed through this eight-week course almost as if on nylon runners. At the conclusion, all were awarded an additional full stripe, making them corporals. Smitty couldn't swear that the "basic MP bashing" had any effect, but it didn't seem to hurt. The good news was that they placed one through four again in their group; the bad news was that they lost Big Walt in the process.

At graduation, they were informed that Smitty, LZ, and Frenchy were to remain for a four-week course in NCO leadership training. Big Walt, whose vision was such that, without glasses, he required a guide dog and a cane to navigate his way from his rack to the latrine, was told that because of this, he was ineligible for further combat training and was being sent to MP school.

Smitty had called Major Jim, who promised that following completion of this training, Big Walt would be assigned back to their basic training stomping grounds. Although he hated to lose the "fourth musketeer," he took some comfort in knowing that the big fellow would be taken care of.

The four-week leadership training had been mildly interesting, and the three former street fighters had done well. The review team had called them natural NCOs.

At the completion of training this morning, Smitty, LZ, and Frenchy were promoted to three-stripers. Making sergeants rated a three-day pass, at the conclusion of which they would be told their next assignment. Smitty was looking forward to his leave with great enthusiasm.

His thoughts turned to Glenda, and he wished he could be with her; but it was not to be. They'd written every day when Smitty had returned to Miami and on through basic, even making plans to get together at the completion of advanced infantry training when Smitty had leave.

But suddenly, Smitty's letters were returned unopened, stamped "return to sender, no longer at current address." Smitty had called her, but the line had been disconnected. Smitty supposed he was just another Dear John.

"Come in, gentlemen, and stand at ease," the base commander, a major general, said, waving them in without looking up from the paperwork on his desk.

Smitty, LZ, and Frenchy entered and assumed a parade rest position directly in front of the general's desk. Thirty seconds passed before the general looked up from his document, stretched casually, took off his glasses, dropped them on the desk, stood up, and walked around to stand directly in front of them.

"I'm General Martin, Ben Martin. First off, let me once again congratulate you gentleman on your completion of the leadership school and your promotions. Bit on the speedy side as rates go, but the army is in dire need of new NCOs. Most of our current billets are filled by men recruited either during World War II or Korea, and they're starting to show their age. When we find young men like you who have youth, mental toughness, and leadership, we try to capitalize on it.

"Which brings me to the reason for sending for you. I've got a little job for you, nobody but you." The general looked at all three of them. His meaning was clear: tell no one.

"I've been looking at your files—what's officially in them and what some anonymous person was kind enough to send me from Miami."

The general held up a hand. "Don't worry. Officially, I never saw it; unofficially, your unknown 'helper' convinced me that you were the men I needed." He reached behind him, grabbed the folder he'd been reading when they entered, and waved it in front of them. All three stiffened.

After glancing at his friends, Smitty said, "Okay, General, we're your happy volunteers."

"I never for a moment doubted it." The general walked back around the desk and fed the entire folder into a shredder located just to the right.

"Oh, by the way, when I called back to verify the source of that trash, I ended up talking to a friend of yours, Sergeant Smith." The general reached into the top drawer of his desk and removed a box, then walked back around the desk and stopped directly in front of Smitty.

"There's a certain assistant chief of the Miami Police Department who said to say hello to you, Smitty. He even sent you a present—off the record." The general handed him the box.

As Smitty lifted the lid, a smile spread slowly across his face. He showed it to LZ, then Frenchy, who smiled back. Smitty lifted the .357 out of the box and hefted it in his hand. The message was clear; all sins were forgiven.

"Mighty good friend you got there, son," the general said. "But as you saw," the general nodded in the direction of the pile of confetti, "you've also got enemies."

"I seem to attract them," Smitty said.

"So does Uncle Sam. And that's where you gentlemen come in. We've got a leak in our munitions boat. We think we know where it is, but we need someone we can trust to go in and confirm it. And as you said, Sergeant, you gentlemen are my happy volunteers."

"Uh, General," LZ interrupted, "is this our next assignment?"

"Your next assignment will not be ready for thirty days. In the interim, I've had you assigned to the adjutant general's office, for 'further specialized military skills enhancement.' Or, to put it another way, you've been drafted into my private army."

"Can't be done, sir," Frenchy said with a mischievous grin.

"Why not?"

"Because we volunteered."

"Okay, son. Then let us say that I convinced you to volunteer to be drafted into my army." Both the comment and the tone left little doubt in Smitty's mind that the general was a man accustomed to having the last word.

"I sort of feel like an informer," Smitty said in a hushed tone.

"Yeah, man, I know what you mean. After spending most of my life running from the law, it sure as hell feels funny to be working for it," LZ agreed.

"Will you two can it? I'm trying to sleep back here," Frenchy said irritably.

"Shhhh!" LZ said grinning, holding his finger to his lips and motioning back at the sleeper portion of the cab. He pivoted silently in the right seat, quietly pulled the curtain back, and unceremoniously dumped the contents of a quart glass of ice water right in Frenchy's crotch.

When Frenchy came up swinging and cursing, LZ dropped the curtain and spun quickly around in his seat.

"You fuckers," Frenchy sputtered. "I'll get you guys for this." He started to lunge forward, but LZ was doubled over laughing, a position Smitty would have been in himself, had he not had the truck steering wheel to hold onto. Frenchy muttered that his time would come, rolled to a dry spot, and lay back down.

All three of them had been issued the new M-16 . . . with extra rounds. In addition, Frenchy and LZ each carried an army-issued sidearm. Smitty was sporting his recently reacquired friend in a shoulder holster that the general had said was "just lying around somewhere."

From Benning, their itinerary had taken them east on U.S.-88 to Strickland, a town so small that the entrance and exit sign were the front and back of the same sign. Then with a slight jog, they followed Georgia Route 183, skirted Macon, and picked up 88 at Barnesville, still headed toward the coast. Somewhere near Collins, following instructions to the letter, they had turned south on State Route 247, which took them directly through the open road of Fort Stewart Army Airfield.

They were just entering the compound now. It was pitch dark, no moon, and eerily quiet. The uneasiness that Smitty was feeling had nothing to do with the fact that he was less than fifty miles from unfriendly hands in Savannah. Smitty thought that compared to what lay ahead, the trouble he'd left behind in Savannah would be as inconsequential as Ma's Wednesday afternoon bridge parties.

They had gone just five miles from LZ's crotch cooldown when Smitty's premonition came true. They were chugging around a blind turn at about thirty when they suddenly found the road ahead blocked by two heavy army trucks. Smitty slammed on the brakes, sliding to a stop less than two feet from the front wheel of the closer one.

Folks in soldier suits seemed to be everywhere. They scurried from the surrounding underbrush like spooked rattlers. They all looked more than ready to use the weapons they were carrying.

Smitty's skidding stop had pitched Frenchy out of his cozy nest like a shot put. He bounced off the seat backs and came up miraculously with his '16 in his hand. The truck had not even stopped rocking when Smitty and LZ were likewise armed. They crouched on the floor, ready for what was obviously an ambush.

"Throw out your weapons and step out of that truck with your hands up," an authoritative voice said from the darkness.

"Fuck, man," LZ muttered disgustedly. "This might be my last stand, but with my dying breath, I'm gonna personally shoot that son of a bitch with the John Wayne lines."

"Let's stall," Smitty said.

"Whatcha got in mind, Smitty?"

"I don't know; let me think a minute."

"Great plan, Smitty," Frenchy said. "What's your follow-up plan, fake 'em out and turn to stone?"

"That's not a bad idea," Smitty responded. "At least it's half an idea. On three, empty a clip into the trees over their heads, then follow my lead."

LZ, Frenchy, and Smitty silently brought their weapons up to firing position. Smitty inhaled deeply, and thought how ironic it was that the first time he would fire his weapon in anger for the government, it would be against his own countrymen. He looked silently at LZ and Frenchy, got their nods, and said sharply, "Three!"

In the close quarters of the truck, the three weapons firing simultaneously sounded like a firecracker convention. Over the smoke and ear-shattering noise, Smitty could see that the surprise had worked perfectly. Everywhere you looked, men in army green were desperately seeking cover, diving headfirst to the ground like Maury Wills trying to steal home or leaping like jackrabbits over bushes.

Instantly after their firing had ceased, Smitty held up LZ's quart cup as though it were a walkie-talkie. In the almost complete blackness, Smitty figured that from thirty feet away they couldn't tell the difference; he could have been talking to his shoe, but they couldn't afford to take a chance.

In his deepest, most authoritative voice he yelled, "Driver to trailer squad, driver to trailer squad, deploy machine guns, repeat, deploy machine guns. Hostile enemy, strength thirty plus, area hot; over."

Smitty passed the cup to LZ, who said in a muffled voice, "Can do. Deploying now."

Smitty motioned to Frenchy and LZ. The three of them used the butts of their weapons to beat on the back of the truck cab, and threw their weight against the side of the cab, making the truck rock. It worked, though not exactly as planned. Smitty was about to shift into reverse and try to get the hell out of there when a voice called out urgently, "Jesus Christ, Captain, these mothers have got live rounds!"

"That's impossible," the captain said. "No one is issued live ammo."

"Well, someone fucked up big time, sir. I've got two wounded diving for cover, and a bunch of others ready to shit their pants."

Inside the truck, Smitty, LZ, and Frenchy looked at each other. It could be a trap; probably was. But they had to be sure.

Smitty nudged Frenchy, who picked up their cup walkie-talkie, held his cap over the top and said in a murmuring voice meant to display distance, "Air recon to truck one, have spotted your field of fire. Mark target with flares and we will engage with extreme prejudice."

"Holy Mother of God!" an unseen voice yelled.

"Can it!" the authoritative voice said again, immediately silencing the wailer. "Captain, I don't know what we got here, sir, but it sure as hell ain't the blue army."

"I concur, Sergeant," the captain answered in a voice that sounded like a creaking bedspring. "I think you'd better find out who before their air support arrives." Smitty couldn't help smiling. The captain had shifted the sergeant's "we" to "you."

In the darkness, Smitty noticed a blur of motion to his right. A flashlight snapped on, illuminating a face that only a mother could love; it had to be the sergeant—officers weren't born that ugly.

"In the truck," the sergeant began. "I'm coming out, unarmed. For Christ's sake, hold your fire." Slowly the sergeant inched forward until he was fully exposed. He advanced toward the truck one cautious step at a time, like a man feeling his way through a minefield, and stopped three feet from Smitty's window.

"You guys aren't from the blue army, are you?"

Holding his weapon at the ready, Smitty said. "No, we're not. We're on a special assignment out of Benning to deliver truck and contents to a specified location."

"What location?" the captain said, as he walked up to stand behind the sergeant.

"I'm sorry, sir, but that information is classified," Smitty said. "Here is our authorization to pass through and receive aid as required at any U.S. military installation." Smitty reached in his pocket and handed across the papers the general had given them.

The sergeant took them from Smitty and passed them back to the captain. The captain took the flash and studied them perfunctorily. "These seem to be official, Sergeant, but I'll have to check." Smitty suspected that the captain had no idea what he was looking at. One quick glance at the sergeant, and Smitty knew he was right.

"Uh, Captain," Smitty said, "I hope you read the part in those orders that said you are not to stop, search, or otherwise detain under penalty of federal prosecution."

"As I said, I have to check," the captain said.

"Well, you've got about thirty seconds," Smitty said. "Then our air support will be overhead, and you and your command are gonna get your shit blown away."

"With you guys still here?" the sergeant asked.

"Those are my orders, Sergeant," Smitty said. "I am not to surrender this cargo under any circumstances, including death. If I deem the situation hopeless and untenable, I can, and will, call for live fire on my position."

Pausing more for effect than breath, Smitty continued, "And that decision point is ten seconds away, so make up your mind, Captain."

"You guys officers?" the sergeant asked.

"No."

"They must be Special Forces, Sergeant," the captain said. "I've heard that they use them for these kind of high-priority security transport missions."

"Well?" the sergeant said, looking at Smitty.

"Who and what we are is classified," Smitty said.

"Gotcha," the sergeant said with a knowing wink.

The captain rubbed his chin thoughtfully for a moment, then folded the papers and handed them back to Smitty. "You gentleman can proceed. I will call in to battalion HQ and inform them of your presence. This will assure that there is no repeat of this incident with the blue army on the other side of the compound."

With a wry smile, he added: "We want to win these games, but not by having you Green Beanies massacre them in the process. The prospects for further promotion for Captain Lewis would be rather dim."

"Thank you, Captain. You've been most kind," Smitty said. With a crisp salute, which the captain returned, Smitty started the truck and waited silently until the road was cleared. As he engaged the gear and drove away, Smitty overheard the captain ask the sergeant, "Do you think they would have called for rounds on themselves?"

The sergeant responded morosely, "Affirmative, sir. Those fuckin' Berets are nuts."

They passed through the installation without further incident. The captain's warning had obviously been heeded. At the blue checkpoint, they were not even stopped, just waved on through. They continued south with Frenchy taking his turn at the wheel.

By sunup Sunday morning, they were about fifteen miles south of Fenalville, on Route 341, the only route through the Okefenokee Swamp. Smitty noticed a signpost: Hilldale was forty-five miles away. Remembering his previous encounters with the state of Florida, Smitty felt uneasy.

Frenchy must have seen it too. His knuckles gleamed white on the wheel. And even the normally imperturbable LZ was tossing restlessly in the bunk behind them.

Frenchy downshifted, and LZ sat up and looked down the road. Frenchy was slowing for a fully loaded logging truck, wheezing and belching oily smoke up ahead.

"Damn," Frenchy said. "With these roads, about all I can do is follow this dude. There isn't clearance to pass."

"Be cool, man, your chance will come," LZ said.

"I know, I know," Frenchy said. "I'd just like to get this shit detail over with."

"Yeah, me, too. But don't let your frustration get you."

Smitty shrugged silently when his friends looked at him for comment. His silence had nothing to do with being noble. It was just that as Dad always said, one bitch feeds on another until you've got a bunch of people sitting around griping and complaining instead of paying attention to the matters at hand, and that's the surest way to end up dead.

They had been following the old mill truck for several miles when Frenchy pointed to the rearview mirror. "Look at that, Smitty."

"Dude's really hauling ass," Smitty said, as a white Caddy convertible rapidly approached.

When the driver had closed up to passing distance, he began alternately honking his horn and weaving out into the oncoming lane looking for a place to pass. Several times, he darted out and had to quickly dart back behind their truck to avoid a certain head-on collision.

"Man's nuts," Frenchy said.

"Nuts or drunk," Smitty agreed, watching another near miss in his rearview mirror, the oncoming driver honking his horn in protest.

"Oh, fuck," Frenchy said. Smitty glanced in the passenger-side rearview mirror only to find that the Caddy was lost from sight.

He looked past Frenchy, through the open truck window as the Caddy shot past them. Carbon smoke spewed out of both tailpipes as the driver made a hell-bent-for-leather attempt to pass both their truck and the weather-beaten relic.

"He'll never make it!" Frenchy shouted in alarm, as he stood on the brakes in anticipation of having to take evasive action.

Smitty, Frenchy, and LZ watched transfixed in horror as the Caddy continued suicidally on, seemingly oblivious of the oncoming eighteen-wheeler closing rapidly.

The Caddy driver, seeming to suddenly come out of his daze, glanced desperately at both sides of the road for an escape avenue, but both were rimmed with canals. Now even with the old truck cab, he was committed to completing his pass. The oncoming trucker flashed his lights and leaned on the horn, but it was too late. At the last possible second, the Caddy darted in front of the logger, missing the truck by a matter of feet. But nobody's troubles were over.

The old truck plowed into the rear of the Caddy with a sickening metallic crunch. The trailer fishtailed across the center lane, striking the semi midlength and sending it on its own arching glide path.

By hugging the shoulder, Frenchy managed to miss the oncoming trailer, but like the truck in front was not able to slow down sufficiently to avoid a collision. A spiky log protruding from the logger truck's rear punctured the radiator, the coolant hissing noisily as it escaped and turned to steam against the hot engine.

"Son of a bitch," Frenchy said in disgust as he brought the truck to a stop. "Of all the stupid things for a man to do. This will probably cost me a stripe." Frenchy rubbed his bloodshot eyes. "Well, I suppose we'd better go find out if anyone is injured."

"Not so fast, Frenchy," Smitty said, laying a restraining hand on his friend's arm.

"Surely you don't think?"

"I'm not sure what to think," Smitty interrupted. "Here we are stuck on the back roads in the middle of shit hole Georgia on a Sunday morning, miles from anywhere, and, for all intents and purposes, isolated. Like my dad always said, if you prepare for the worst then you won't be disappointed. Or unprepared."

"Smitty, I think this army gung-ho shit's gone to your head," LZ said. "You two go ahead and play wet-nurse to a bunch of Southern grits; me, I got better things to do," he said curtly as he jerked the curtains shut and lay back down.

"C'mon, Frenchy, you and I'll go check this accident out," Smitty said, opening the door and jumping down.

Frenchy and Smitty approached the logging truck from opposite sides, pulling on their jackets as they walked to cover the hand weapons; prudently, they had left the '16s in the truck. Frenchy reached the driver's door first, stepped up on the door sill, and leaned in through the open window to check on the driver, who was slumped against the steering wheel.

"You all right, partner?" Frenchy asked.

The driver was a black man who looked to be on the high side of fifty, with a five-day-old growth of salt-and-pepper beard and a Friar Tuck hairline, dressed in clothes that looked like rummage sale rejects.

"Yes, sir, I's fine," the driver said. "And I's sorry."

"Take it easy, pal; the accident wasn't your fault," Frenchy said.

"Thanks ya, sir."

Frenchy patted him on the shoulder and jumped down. He nodded to Smitty and the two of them moved up on the Caddy. Like the truck driver, the man was slumped against the steering wheel, apparently unconscious. Smitty was just about to open the passenger door when he saw a flashing reflection in the rearview mirror.

A police car, with a name that Smitty couldn't make out on the side, slid to a stop in front of the Caddy. The driver, a short, squatty man about forty, stepped out, clapped on his Smokey the Bear hat, and swaggered back toward the convertible. He stopped at the

Caddy and leaned in until he could see the face quite clearly. As his eyes widened in recognition, he straightened up and hitched his pants.

"Mister Lawrence. Owns most of everything worth owning in Charlton County. Gonna go down hard on Ol' Ben. Oh, Ol' Ben's a well-known shiner in these parts. To some folks, he's damn near a legend. Been following him for 'bout ten miles. He's got a load of shine underneath all them logs, plannin' on makin' a run to Jax on a Sunday morning; figures no one will catch on." The officer snapped his fingers at Frenchy. "Hey, soldier boy. Drag that nigger outta the truck for me."

"Drag him out yourself," Frenchy said, stepping out of the cop's path.

The officer spat contemptuously on the ground, then stalked back to the logging truck, snatched open the door, grabbed the driver roughly by the arm, and dragged him out of the truck with such force that he did two tumbling rolls on the concrete.

"Come on, boy. Get your black ass up."

"Yes, Massa," the driver replied, struggling to a kneeling position.

"I'll teach you to go causing accidents with white folks," he said, drawing back his foot.

"Frenchy, no!" Smitty yelled.

"Don't you even think about trying it, boy," the officer spat, as he unholstered his pistol and pointed it directly at Frenchy's head.

"You neither, soldier boy!"

Smitty grimaced in disgust, as he looked to his right and found that he, too, had a pistol pointed at his head. The hand was steady; the voice pure evil. The smile on the face of the suddenly conscious Caddy driver was glacial.

The black truck driver sprang to his feet with the agility of a man twenty years his junior. "Works every time. Been pulling that Uncle Tom routine on you dumb-ass honkies for years." He searched Frenchy roughly and smiled as he relieved him of the army .45.

"Little boys shouldn't play with grown-up toys," Ol' Ben said to the officer.

The officer looked at Smitty and started to speak, but turned away at the sound of running footsteps. "Did it work, Boss?" The driver from the oncoming truck jogged into view.

"Like a charm," he answered back. "They're arming these boys now, but that didn't present no problems. Go around the front, and relieve the angry young man of his concealed weapon, also. Then back the truck up; we'll have our two prisoners unload the truck for us. Dispose of the truck—no traces, no clues." It didn't take a brain surgeon to figure out that Smitty and Frenchy would also disappear without a trace.

A mirrorlike reflection caught the corner of Smitty's eye. As he turned in that direction, he saw Ben dancing a jig, Frenchy's gun waving wildly in tempo. But it wasn't a victory dance. Four shots found their mark, jerking him crazily. He died with a stunned look on his face.

A fifth shot struck just above the right elbow of the officer with such force that he seemed to throw his gun toward the canal like a smoker casually tossing away a spent match.

At the first shot, Smitty dropped below the Caddy door. He was almost too late. The shell from the Caddy driver's gun creased his skull as Smitty cleared his own weapon and hit the ground. He rolled over and shot the approaching truck driver, who was advancing menacingly with pistol in hand, at point-blank range three times, pitching him backward, spinning crazily into the hood of the car, and collapsing lifelessly to the ground.

The quick distraction had been all Frenchy needed. He dove for the pistol, and with a perfectly executed gymnastic tumble, did a forward roll, snatching the gun from the lifeless hand of Ol' Ben in the process, and finishing upright on one knee. The Caddy driver spun around and sighted on Smitty, with deadly intent.

Frenchy's distraction had allowed Smitty recovery time also. Smitty reversed his direction, crawled over the dead truck driver, paused momentarily to remove the pistol from his lifeless hand and toss it aside, then silently moved on to the front of the Caddy. The only real advantage he had was the morning sun glaring down on the windshield. He had hoped the driver's blindness would allow him to get off at least one clear shot.

He never got the chance. As Smitty popped above the hood and prepared to fire, Frenchy shot the driver twice in the head. Smitty sighed briefly and began to lower his weapon. A movement to his right made him refocus his aim. The officer was reaching behind his back with his good left hand.

"Frenchy," Smitty screamed warningly and fired. He emptied his last three rounds in the officer, but he was not alone; Frenchy fired four rounds and a fusillade joined the cacophony.

"Well, bros, you think we got 'em?" LZ said as he walked up, casually ejected a clip from the '16, and tossed the empty onto the trunk of the Caddy. "Oh, by the way, Smitty," LZ continued as he rammed a new clip home, "I activated that new-fangled homing knick-knack the general gave us, so I expect help should arrive shortly."

"Spread out, guys, this ain't over yet," Smitty said. "They could have help of their own on the way."

"Frenchy and I'll take the truck, back there," LZ motioned in the direction of the rig down the road. "You check here."

Smitty waited while Frenchy jogged back to their army vehicle and retrieved both of their '16s and came back and tossed Smitty his before turning and double-timing back up the road to catch up with LZ.

Smitty nodded wordlessly and bent to check the pulse on the truck driver as he watched the retreating figures of his two friends move off down the road in the direction of the truck. First, he checked the other two figures on the ground for signs of life, but found none. He approached the police cruiser, and after assuring himself that there was no one hiding on the floor, reached in and grabbed the keys, noting that the name on the registration above the sun visor did not match the town name decal that had been slapped on the side. Smitty was just about to stick the keys in the trunk when Dad's advice about being prepared caused him to step back abruptly. Quietly, he laid down the '16, reloaded his .357, then crouched down below the level of the bumper, reached up, put the key quietly in the lock, and turned.

The force of the shotgun blast opened a two-inch hole at the crease and flattened him against the ground. He rolled quickly away from the trunk, holstered the Smith and Wesson, rearmed himself with the army's newest issue, and was just about to fire when the mismatched town name suddenly made sense.

If Smitty's guess was correct, the deputy had obviously been knocked out and thrown in the trunk where the riot gun was stored. Why his kidnappers didn't relieve him of the weapon or search the trunk first, Smitty hadn't a clue. Probably knocked him out and thought he wouldn't regain consciousness before they were finished.

"Hey, partner," Smitty called out. "Hold your fire, we're the good guys."

"Fuck you, asshole," a scared voice answered from the trunk.

"Does your mother know you use language like that?" Smitty laughed. "Look, pal, I know you're scared, but we really are on the same side."

"How do I know that?"

"Because if I wasn't, we wouldn't be having this conversation. I'd have just fired a full clip from this automatic weapon right into the trunk and blown your head off."

"You know, you've got a point."

First to emerge from the trunk was the shotgun, a police-issue pump, then the slightly worse for wear figure of a young deputy whose uniform matched the car registration.

"Freeze it right there," LZ shouted as he and Frenchy approached at a dead run.

"Relax, guys, I think he's one of the good guys."

Before Smitty could explain further, the sound of two approaching army helicopters cut him off. They circled the area in two widening arcs apparently searching for other hostile activity before veering back in to land on the road fifty yards away. A squad of troops, led by a first lieutenant, all wearing camouflaged fatigues and full-face black ski masks, dispersed in a way that indicated that they'd done this a time or two before.

"Lieutenant Bartkowski," the young officer identified himself.

"Sergeant Smith, Lieutenant. We're right glad to see you guys."

"Jesus, looks like a Polish Fourth of July party," the lieutenant said. "The general's compliments, Sergeant. He's waiting to talk to you on the radio."

"Yes, sir," Smitty said with a formal salute, which the lieutenant returned with an airy wave.

As Smitty started for the copter, the lieutenant called out, "What about him?" Without turning around, Smitty said, "He's one of the good guys, and after this, he may take up the ministry."

"Gentlemen, the report from my most prized pupil, Lieutenant Bartkowski, was not very flattering," the general said, pacing back and forth in front of them. "You allowed yourselves to be trapped. You allowed them to pick the time and place for the confrontation. And worst, you allowed yourselves to be so outmaneuvered that you were forced to shoot your way out like western desperadoes."

"And despite all those fuck-ups, we managed to survive," Frenchy said.

"Sergeant," the general snorted, "When you get half as smart as you think you are, you'll look back on this incident and realize just how incredibly lucky you were."

He stopped in front of Frenchy. "Hell, son, according to your own statements . . . " The general reached back on his desk, picked up a manila folder and leafed through the papers until he found the page he was looking for. "You followed the logging truck for fifteen miles before they sprang the trap on you," he said morosely, slapping the file back on his desk. "Why do you think we gave you that homing device? If you knew or even suspected you were in trouble, why didn't you use the goddamned thing?"

The general snatched the morning paper from his desk and read the headline. "'Four die in head-on collision on 341.' Now we've got a bloody incident spread all over the papers, and we've had to call in every favor we can to get this mess covered up so the press doesn't even get a whiff of the fact that it was a hijacking and not just a tragic head-on collision on a deserted Georgia back road."

The general reached for a pack of cigarettes from his desk, stuck one between his lips and walked over to Smitty. "Light?"

Smitty fished in his pocket, produced a lighter, and fired the general's cigarette. The general grunted his thanks and as he turned away, Smitty reached for the general's cigarette pack, grinned mischievously at Frenchy and LZ, and shook a smoke out of the pack. He was just starting to raise it to his lips, when the general barked, "Don't even think about it, boy."

Without turning around, he added, "You three gentlemen seem to be laboring under a delusion that the army is some kind of personal shooting club. Well, I'm here to tell you that if you don't start using your heads instead of reacting on your instincts, then you've got a one-way ticket to Arlington reserved."

"Or to hell," Frenchy said.

"Same difference, son," the general said, making no effort to conceal his contempt. "You gentlemen are restricted to quarters until further notice. You will talk with no one about this; I emphasize—no one. Dismissed!"

Frenchy, LZ, and Smitty executed picture-perfect military about-faces and marched smartly out of the general's office.

When they were clear of the building, LZ said to no one in particular, "I bet he'd really be pissed if we'd gotten killed."

"As I understand it, I'll only have the use of you gentleman for twenty-six days. No matter, with the upcoming all-services conferences, and the acute shortage of NCOs to use as drivers for the senior staff, I'm sure we can find a way to keep you occupied and out of trouble."

The last comment was accompanied by a condescending smile, implying that he'd read the report on their recent "specialized military skills enhancement" and the general's less-than-flattering comments. Smitty glanced at LZ and Frenchy, both of whom seemed about as impressed with their new commander as was Smitty himself.

Major Gates was the inevitable result of an overbloated, world power military bureaucracy: what Dad always branded a PPS—a Pentagon paper shuffler. Dashingly handsome, with wavy ash blond hair and matinee idol good looks, he was in his late thirties, tall, trim, and immaculately dressed.

When the major had spent twenty minutes reviewing his distinguished military career, he had pointed out repeatedly that he'd managed to avoid any form of combat or hazardous or unpleasant duty by surreptitiously maneuvering from one liaison or adjutant assignment to the next, leaving the fighting and the dirty work to be done by those best suited to it. He didn't quite say "lower orders." He didn't have to.

He also pointed out, again repeatedly, that this had been made possible by his dad, a former U.S. Senator whose connections kept his son out of harm's way. Major Gates was assigned to the General of the Army's personnel staff as head adjutant. Although he tried his best to make it sound important, after listening to a description of his duties, Smitty thought it sounded more like an MOS—Military Occupational Specialty—for general office boy and shit head . . . not necessarily in that order.

"Are you paying attention, Sergeant?" the major asked suspiciously.

"Yes, sir," Smitty said dourly.

"I take it by your less-than-enthusiastic response that you don't fully comprehend the importance of this assignment to your career.

"You gentlemen have obviously been misled about what's important in the army. Wars come and go, but the army runs on spit and polish. It's the officer or NCO with the most refinement and culture who ultimately gets ahead.

"Look at myself as an example. I graduated from the Point in 1951, avoided the Korean conflict, and even though I've only been in the army sixteen years, I'm up for lieutenant colonel. And what's more, because of my contacts, I know I'm a shoo-in to make it.

"You gentlemen have obviously been sent to me to round off your rough edges. Twenty-six days is a bit of a push, but if you apply yourself, I'm sure I'll be able to write up a favorable report that will carry merit and help you get a quick start on your next assignment.

"Even though it is Friday, I expect you gentlemen to begin your assignment at once. See the motor pool sergeant, requisition a car, and spend the weekend getting to know

Washington. By Monday, I want you to be intimately familiar with all major military routes to and from the Pentagon, all military installations within a one-hundred-mile radius, the shortest direct routes between each, and all of the associated back roads that are usable during congestion. The sergeant will provide maps, as well as anything else you require."

After exiting the major's office, it took them twenty minutes to wind their way through the labyrinth of hallways in the Pentagon to the find the sergeant. They quickly checked out a car, and headed straight for the hotel where they'd booked a reservation. On the way to the hotel, they had a name-the-major contest. All three agreed that LZ's "Feces-Eating-Cluster-Gerbil" was the winner.

After a great weekend in which they'd driven off four tanks of the government's gas just tooling around, reality had set in. They did, in fact, complete their primary assignment, though it required pulling an all-nighter on Sunday night. But they were completely familiar with all the primary routes before returning to Major Cluster-Gerbil's office at 0600 hours Monday morning for their specific assignments. They were to be drivers for visiting officers for the all-services conference. LZ had drawn a navy rear admiral; Frenchy, a marine lieutenant general.

Smitty didn't think too much about it when he was told he'd be the driver for an air force general. But now as he stood outside the gate at Washington National as "his" general approached, he felt a hot flush on the back of his neck. It had to show on his face.

Recognition, Smitty knew, must have been immediate. The greeting confirmed it.

"Hi ya, kiddo, you my driver?" the general asked, as he dropped both his bag and briefcase and shook hands, taking Smitty's hand in both of his.

"Yes, sir," Smitty mumbled, saluting when the general released his hand.

"Aw, knock off the saluting stuff, Sarge. You NCOs been keeping me out of trouble for close on to twenty-five years." He paused and pointed up at his shoulders, "I'm just an old blowtorch jockey who got kicked upstairs to a cushy job, but in my heart, I'll always be a wet-behind-the-ears Looey with a sergeant looking out for me."

"If you'll come this way, sir, I'll show you to your car," Smitty said, pointing to the doors leading to the airport terminal and picking up the general's bags. What should have been a quick trip took close to an hour as the general stopped constantly to say hello to acquaintances in uniform. Didn't seem to matter what branch or rank; the general seemed to know everyone by name, from a navy vice-admiral to a marine gunny. He earnestly asked about their health and families, introduced Smitty to each one, and, after a brief chat, shook hands and wished them well.

When they reached the car, Smitty took the general's case and, after putting both it and his flight bag in the trunk, held the rear door open.

"Son, whenever we're alone, call me Chuck." The general slammed the rear door, opened the passenger's side front door, and pushed Smitty in before him.

"Sergeant," he said after they had pulled away from the curb, "If you expect to make a career out of the service, you'd better learn one fundamental thing."

"What's that, sir?" Smitty asked. Sensing the general's disapproval, he corrected himself, "What's that, uh, Chuck?"

"Treat officers like enlisted men, and enlisted men like officers."

Smitty was silent for a moment as he concentrated on maneuvering out of the airport and joined the traffic on Washington National headed toward the Pentagon.

"I don't understand," Smitty said.

Chuck pulled two cigars from his pocket, lit the first one and handed it to Smitty, then lit a second for himself. Chuck fanned at the fumes. "Ever read 'If' by Rudyard Kipling?"

Smitty nodded.

"There's a line that I really like, goes like this, 'If you can walk with kings but not lose the common touch.'"

Chuck surveyed his cigar at arms length for a moment. "Officers will always do what you tell them to do, because," he returned his cigar to his mouth, and held up his hand as he began to tick off the points on his fingers, "one, it's their duty; two, you're their superior and hold the key to their future 'cause you write their efficiency report; and three, they're the ones who order the enlisted man to go out and get himself killed.

"NCOs and enlisted men, on the other hand, follow you," again he held up his hand and began a second list, "one, because they believe in you; two, because they trust you to do everything possible to keep them alive; and three, because if you don't, they'll shoot you right through the back of the head the first chance they get."

"That's an interesting point of view, uh, Chuck," Smitty said.

"Think I'm full of shit, don't you, boy?"

"Of course not, sir."

"Bullshit!" Chuck looked at his cigar. "You know, there's something you're trying awful hard not to tell me, son," He flipped open his Zippo—which had a Korean War F-86 jet on one side and sixteen red stars on the other—and refired his stogie.

"I'm afraid I don't know what you're talking about," Smitty said.

"Well, lad, I think you're about the worst liar I've come across in years," Chuck said, giving the flame of his cigar much more attention than it seemed to deserve.

Smitty shrugged his shoulders. Did Chuck recognize him? And if he did, would he turn him in to the army? To Dad?

Smitty stole a quick sideways glance at Chuck. If he was concerned, no trace of it showed in his face. Other than an occasional grimace when the cigar smoke curled into his eyes, from what Smitty could see, the general wasn't thinking about much of anything at all.

They completed the remaining short distance to the Pentagon in silence. As Smitty pulled up, Chuck got out of the car almost before Smitty could bring it to a stop, yanked open the trunk, and removed his luggage.

The general slammed the lid and walked back around the car. Leaning into the passenger window, he said, "Pick me up at 1900 hours sharp. In your civvies."

"Yes, sir."

"Then you and I are going to go find us a gin mill and find out just what this big secret is you've been carrying on your sleeve." The general turned and was gone.

Smitty drove off, a badly worried young man.

"Okay, shit-for-brains, spill it," Chuck said.

"I'm afraid I don't know what you're talking about, sir."

"Well, let me just see if I can put you in recall mode, partner." Chuck casually blew out an obnoxious cloud of smoke, much to the annoyance of a buxom young woman who sat at a nearby table with her date and another couple.

"What I'm talking about is the fact that I jump off a plane and who do I find as my driver but the son of one of my oldest and dearest friends. If you were wearing an air force uniform, I probably wouldn't give it a second thought, but to find you as a 'horse of another color,' so to speak, definitely implies that there must be one hell of a story behind it. Knowing, of course, how ambivalent your daddy is on the subject."

Smitty laughed in spite of himself. Dad was so lukewarm on the blue suit, that he'd stated emphatically that when he died, he was to be buried in his air force class A uniform; even if it was fifty years after he got out.

"Uh, how can you be so sure that I'm the son of the man you describe?"

"Oh, I'm sure, Smitty—that is what your friends LZ and Frenchy call you, isn't it?" Chuck gave him a disapproving look and continued.

"You're the sarge's son all right. You're a dead ringer for your ol' man when he was just about your age. I suspect you're like him in other ways, too."

"What do you want to know?" Smitty said.

Chuck reached inside his left coat pocket and pulled out a single sheet of paper, passing it to Smitty. "Got this just last week. I was planning to do some searching when I was here in DC. You saved me the trouble."

Smitty read:

Chuck,

I need your help. My second son, Kevin, has disappeared. The police think he's somewhere on the West Coast and want to question him regarding the slaughter of eight gang members in a warehouse in Miami, last January.

I think the little fart has outfoxed them. I think he's joined the air force and is hiding under an assumed name. He probably has his two friends with him, a muscular young white man and a street-wise black guy.

I know you're headed for the all-services conference next week, and would greatly appreciate it if you'd use your two-star pull to run him through CID on the q.t.

If you manage to locate him, do not arrange to have him detained. Contact me directly and let me handle it from there.

I know this is out of channel, but I ask it in the name of the favor you've owed me since Mission Octagon back in '44.

That boy can be a royal pain in the ass, but like the man said, he's my royal pain in the ass.

I'm desperate, Chuck; please help me.

Sincerely,
Your Ol' Sarge.

"What's Mission Octagon?"

"Uh, that's just one of many classified missions we were on together during WW II." Chuck's casual tone didn't quite ring true.

Mission Octagon again, Smitty thought to himself. Ten years ago in a cold damp office in England, it had been spoken of as a debt with an associated death threat if disclosed. Now it had surfaced again as a marker. Just what the hell was this Mission Octagon? And what was the dark secret that could bind a seven-stripe sergeant to a two-star general for over two decades? Could it be connected to the hidden force that seemed to be keeping Smitty and his friends in the middle of a shit storm? If so, how? . . . How?

Smitty looked quizzically at the general, and was just about to question him further when he caught the general's don't-fuck-with-me stare, thought better of it, and changed the subject.

"Am I really the spittin' image of Dad?"

"You're stalling again, Sergeant."

"We, uh, had a little falling out, so I left and joined the army," Smitty said.

Chuck shook his head sadly, reached into another pocket, and pulled out and unfolded three sheets of teletype printouts.

"Let's see here," Chuck said, and found the passage he wanted. Low-voiced, he read it out.

"Mr. Smith, along with his two friends, Messrs. Douchet and McCord, were most valuable in bringing to a conclusion the three-year-old, unsolved murders of four Cubans and two American teenagers. Mr. Smith, however, believes that it does not end there.

"Mr. Smith stated that he believed that Keith (the deposed gang leader killed in the shoot-out, who, based on the trap set by Mr. Smith, was subsequently proven to be responsible for the aforementioned deaths) did not act alone. Mr. Smith believes that there was a mole, either in the Miami Police Department or the Dade County Government (or both!) who was, in effect, pulling all the strings.

"Mr. Smith's thoughts seem to have substance. I have concluded that there was no basis for the original charges against those three young men. I have been unsuccessful to date, however, in determining who or what is behind this."

Chuck smiled at Smitty and turned the page.

"Sergeant Smith, along with his two fellow sergeants, was instrumental in breaking up a hijacking and smuggling ring that had previously been responsible for the loss of military equipment and personnel totaling millions of dollars and ten deaths over a two-year period.

"Sergeant Smith and his comrades are given highest marks for their performance under combat conditions. However, if their unique skill set is to be capitalized on to its fullest potential, further training in mission planning and combat situational leadership is required."

"There's some more drivel about you and your comrades being the 'cream of the new generation of the army,' but, of course, I assume that you got those positive comments from major what's-his-name, the quintessential aide-de-camp," Chuck said.

"So where do we go from here, General?"

"That depends on you, kiddo," Chuck replied, blowing another cloud of smoke at Miss Cleavage, who coughed loudly, fanning at the haze in a vain attempt to clear the air.

The smoke had obviously gone down the wrong pipe. She bent forward, hacking repeatedly. One of the spaghetti straps slid off of her shoulder, exposing her right breast.

"Nice boob, Miss," Chuck said. He looked at Smitty, jerking a thumb in her direction. "Works on those dumb sperm repositories every time."

Smitty glared at the general, as unamused as Queen Victoria.

Her date obviously did not share Chuck's sense of humor either. He had given Chuck a very nasty stare the first time but was not going to let it go a second. He stood slowly, hitched up his pants, and strode purposefully around the table until he was standing in front of the general.

"Dad, I've about had enough of your cigar."

When Chuck refused to look at him or even acknowledge him, the young man reached out to tap him on the shoulder.

When his hand, with index finger extended, was about six inches away, Chuck reached up with his right hand, and in one continuous motion grabbed his finger at the second knuckle and pulled it forward and down, slamming the exposed end into the table, separating the nail and splintering the bone in the process.

As the young man screamed in pain, Chuck finally looked at him and said conversationally, "Young fella, I'd mind my manners if I were you. You might make your ol' daddy mad."

Chuck smiled politely, retrieved his cigar from the ashtray and blew another cloud of smoke. "I'd get that looked at if I were you."

The young man's table partner started to get up and come to his friend's aid. Smitty cleared his blade, and using it as a bandleader would his baton, shook his head and said, "I wouldn't if I were you," as he made downward motions with his surrogate scalpel. The would-be helper glared at Smitty for a moment, then slowly sat down.

Chuck released the young man, who staggered away, whimpering in pain.

"Now, what were we talking about?" Chuck's manner was so matter-of-fact that Smitty was sure he had done this sort of thing before. Maybe Chuck had staged this entirely for his benefit, but if that was the case, Chuck's face betrayed no trace of it.

"Uh, sir? I think it might best if we finished this conversation in a more private place."

"Lead on, son. I'll follow my driver anywhere."

Smitty stood aside and allowed Chuck to precede him from the bar. As they passed the table where the young woman was bent over her escort, administering first aid, Chuck stopped, leaned down and said, "They really are lovely Miss. Wish young ladies were built like that when I was your age."

"Thank you," she said faintly, her face flaming to match the crimson dress. Her escort looked up, then dropped his eyes without speaking.

"Interesting display, sir. I was duly impressed," Smitty said, finally breaking the silence. "It was for my benefit, wasn't it?"

Chuck fixed Smitty with a cocked eye and removed his cigar. "Yep." He replaced the cigar and said through clenched teeth, "You tell me why."

"A test?" Smitty said.

Chuck lifted an eyebrow, glared at Smitty, and growled, "Don't be stupid. Try again."

"A warning," Smitty said with certainty.

"Bingo. Why?"

"You knew I was coming here. Hell, you probably arranged it."

"Again, why?" Chuck pressed.

"Because enemies are all around. And not always wearing ID tags."

"Those two young men were following you. Their dates were along for window dressing. They've been on our tail since you picked me up."

"Major aide-de-camp?"

Chuck nodded silently.

"Why?"

"Could be a lot of things," Chuck said. He took another long puff on his cigar, brightened and turned to Smitty. "This major, what's his name?"

"Major Gates."

"Name mean anything to you?"

"No, should it?"

Chuck rubbed his chin thoughtfully. "Would it surprise you to know that the major I airmailed home from England several years back also had a last name of Gates?"

"You don't think they're related?" Smitty asked.

"Only by birth," Chuck said bluntly.

"What happened to the other major? His brother, I assume?" Smitty asked.

"Bounced him from the service, ostensibly on a conduct unbecoming. Had a law degree, somehow managed to wangle himself a job in the DA's office in some city in the South."

Smitty shivered. He felt as though someone had just walked on his grave.

"Now, I know . . . "

"What's that, son?"

"Uh, nothing, Chuck, I was just thinking out loud."

"Nothing, hell. Spill it!"

"I said it was nothing, Chuck," Smitty said. "Could we just drop it?"

"Okay, son. But if I was you I'd watch my back. Someone definitely wants to keep you dead center in harm's way."

They lapsed into silence. Chuck puffed on his cigar.

As they pulled into the parking lot at Chuck's quarters, Smitty said, "So, what are you going to tell Dad?"

"I'm going to get back to him and tell him the truth; that I've searched the air force database and I can guarantee that you are not hiding in the air force. I figure you and Sergeant Rock got to work this thing out by yourselves. Give it time, young troop, and it will. Your daddy's a helluva good man."

Chuck slapped Smitty playfully on the shoulder and got out of the car without another word.

The next morning, when Smitty, LZ, and Frenchy checked in, they found the major's office a beehive of activity. Boxes were being packed, files sorted, and a general state of confusion reigned. Smitty couldn't help noticing that one of the bees was a bit handicapped. His right hand was heavily bandaged.

Major Cluster-Gerbil was nowhere to be found. He'd apparently been transferred to another assignment, effective immediately, and had gone ahead to prepare for this task.

Chuck was nowhere to be found, either. Apparently, he'd gone back to his current duty station in Japan. Frenchy remarked how strange it was that all of this activity had occurred in the night. Smitty laughed quietly to himself, suspecting Chuck was involved in the major's sudden travel plans.

Smitty was assigned to another general, a marine major general, for the balance of the conference. The next three weeks passed without incident.

Smitty spent his few brief moments of free time reviewing the meeting with Chuck. It had been too convenient not to have been planned. Obviously, Chuck had something to do with Major Kiss-Ass being banished. To where, Smitty could only guess, but he'd a gut feeling that they'd meet again . . . and violence would be the result.

On the plane to their next assignment, Smitty sat quietly, but his mind was on the move. He now knew that someone had been keeping the school system and the police in Savannah, Chicago, and New Orleans well-informed. Smitty also knew that the fate of his friends was in his hands. They had followed him into the army because of loyalty and friendship; he hoped that his own obsessive search for the truth would not result in their deaths.

The truth came in three parts, he had said to LZ and Frenchy on the bus six months ago. The person who did the dirty work was dead. Smitty now thought he knew the identities of the two above him in the hierarchy.

The general had confirmed what Smitty had long suspected: there were mysterious forces working against him, and those forces intended to keep him in harm's way. Smitty spent several minutes thinking hard on who or what was behind it all, tried to tie Chuck and Mission Octagon into this, but came up empty.

This Kraken had more tentacles than he could identify. Two things were now certain: Smitty knew that until he could harpoon it in the eye, he'd never have peace—and if he didn't, he'd be dead sooner rather than later.

CHAPTER NINE

"Man, it's sure going to be great going on leave for three days," LZ said from the backseat of the Famous '54. The door windows rattled constantly, metal channels long ago devoid of felt. They were the snare drums in the car's fortissimo symphony of bangs, thumps, knocks, and moans that always seemed to threaten imminent self-evisceration. But despite the ominous noises, the old Chevy rolled on, resplendent in a spray-painted rainbow and crowned with a day-glow orange peace sign.

It was true that lately fifty-weight oil was required to keep the oil pressure light from coming on when the car idled. But as long as you kept checking about every fifty miles or so and adding a quart, it ran like a locomotive, black smoke and all. When discretion was required, a couple of cans of STP dumped in the crankcase sufficiently gummed up the rings to inhibit 90 percent of the smoke, which seemed to pacify the cops and the base MPs.

Army General Martin had been right on target. Their next assignment was ready in thirty days, and the last four weeks had been a bitch.

Airborne jump school at Benning in May, with humidity so thick you could cut it with a knife, was no shit assignment. It was definitely meant to separate the boys from the men, and men from their egos.

The day began at 0500 hours with a version of PT that made basic training seem like a high school PE class. Next there was a "casual" four-mile run; motivational singing and hand clapping was required. Then breakfast, followed by the most intensive training Smitty, Frenchy, or LZ had ever been through. Evenings were for hitting the books. Every night they were asleep before the last glow had faded from the lightbulbs.

Two weeks into the course, they made their first live jump. On successive days, the training was stepped up, adding more equipment, different jump heights, halo jumps, and diverse weather conditions.

Incredibly, four weeks later, Smitty, Frenchy, and LZ had been awarded the silver jump wings. There was no feeling of euphoria, only relief at having survived. A third of the class had failed.

The three were in the process of driving to their next assignment. They planned on arriving early to spend the three days before reporting relaxing and getting the area wired. They were going to be there for the next five to six months and were looking forward to it with nervous anticipation.

It was a chance to run with the elite, to be with the best of the best. Midday was stiflingly hot as they drove into the outskirts of a city that had been called "Fayettenam" by just about every soldier who had passed through there.

Fort Bragg was the home of the John F. Kennedy Special Warfare Center. The three of them were going all the way—all the way with the Green Beret. And whether they successfully completed this training or not, their next assignment was a certainty also. It was just a matter of what headgear they'd be wearing when they went all the way "in-country" to Vietnam.

"Say, man," LZ said from the backseat. "What say we start looking for a hotel room?"

"Can do," Smitty replied. He reached out and shook Frenchy lightly on the arm. "Wake up, copilot, we're here. Start looking for a flop, will you."

"All right man, I'm awake," Frenchy said, sitting up and stretching. "Got anything special in mind?"

"Nothing special," LZ said, "just so long as they admit ugly Froggies."

Frenchy turned, and on seeing LZ's grin, gave him a long stare, a grin, and the finger.

The first place they tried was full. Curiously, so were the second, third, and fourth—even though their neon signs blinked "vacancy."

It was as they were getting out of the car to go register at the fifth that LZ decided to remain behind—saying that Smitty and Frenchy could handle it, and he was tired. Smitty and Frenchy had no trouble this time. The trouble began as they were returning from collecting their stuff with LZ.

"HEY! What do you think you're doing?" the desk clerk demanded sharply.

"What are you talking about?" Smitty asked.

"I'm talking 'bout him," the desk clerk pointed at LZ.

"What's wrong, mon ami'? Don't like having guests with bigger dicks than you in residence?"

"If that was the case, he'd be out of business," LZ said, holding thumb and forefinger together in the universally understood sign for a miniature pecker.

The young man with the pale eyes looked coldly across his desk at the three friends.

"Very funny, boy. We don't allow niggers here. You two can stay, but the black boy's got to go," the clerk said.

LZ started forward, pulling his blade in process, but Smitty's restraining hand on LZ's arm stopped him. "Hold it, LZ."

"What you talkin' 'bout, man!" LZ shouted. "Why are you letting that racist motherfucker talk to me like that?"

"Because," Smitty responded, "cutting this redneck fucker won't solve anything."

"Then I suggest that if you white boys want to get along in North Carolina, you stop running with the darkie here," the desk clerk added.

"Excuse me," a haughty voice said from behind them. The man was six-foot-two, lean and muscular, with wavy brown hair, brown mustache, and brown eyes. He carried himself confidently in a manner of one who is used to giving instructions and, more importantly, used to having his instructions obeyed.

"I am the son of the governor of Louisiana. My father had to deal with this racist bullshit all the time in New Orleans." He glared at the desk clerk and his manager, who had come to his distressed employee's aid. "Now, I want this clearly understood. I want a room for these three gentlemen. And, I don't want to hear any crap about who or what you don't admit. Because if I do, I will walk to the nearest phone, call my daddy, who will call your governor, and by the time it gets to you, I wouldn't be surprised if you and your entire staff will be pursuing new careers. Probably in a meat packing plant, which is all I suspect your Neanderthal brain can handle. Or, if you would like to receive firsthand initiation to this new career, I'll be happy to allow these boys to carve you up with the knives I'm sure they're carrying." The man stood and examined his manicure while waiting for a response.

The desk clerk looked nervously at the manager, who shifted back and forth uncomfortably clasping and unclasping his hands. Finally, he rubbed his chin, shrugged, and said, "Do as the gentleman requests, Richard."

"Thanks, uh—?" Smitty extended his hand.

"Ron. Think nothing of it," he said, clasping Smitty's hand. He turned and, as quick as he had arrived, was gone.

"Who's your new pen pal, Smitty?" LZ asked.

"Dunno', said his name was Ron." Smitty answered.

"Who do you think he is?"

"Probably a guy who don't like rednecks any better than we do."

"Uh, sir," the manager said, as he came out from behind the counter with the room keys in his hand. "We have your rooms ready."

As he took the keys, the manager leaned in and whispered in Smitty's ear, "Who was that guy?"

"The Lone Ranger," Smitty said, snatching the keys from the manager's unresisting hand. As they headed toward to the elevator, Smitty added, without turning around, "And I'm his sidekick, Tonto."

The mystery guest, who didn't bother to sign in please, worried Smitty. It meant they were being watched—watched closely. The question was by whom, and more importantly for what?

"Up to now, gentlemen, in spite of every discouragement, your careers have been extremely public. Flamboyant, even. That's all over.

"I'm going to teach you to be ghosts, I'm going to teach you to operate in the shadows, I'm going to teach you how to endure in the worst environment you could ever think of and survive . . . and if you listen closely for the next five months and let me, I'll teach you how to survive Vietnam."

Smitty, LZ, and Frenchy shivered. Knowing about Vietnam was one thing. Feeling it was another.

"Lieutenant Bartkowski," Smitty said in sudden recognition.

"Correct, Sergeant. Ron to my friends,"

"Lieutenant Bartkowski?" LZ repeated, puzzled.

"Dude in black camys and a ski mask who rescued us back at that highjacking," Smitty explained.

"Not dude, soldier, lieutenant," Bartkowski corrected. He smiled wryly. "Or, Lieutenant Dude, if you must be colloquial."

"You've been watching us for six weeks, haven't you?" Smitty mused thoughtfully. "Was General Chuck part of the security check?"

"Nope, he was working on his own agenda, requested you personally be assigned to him. Don't suppose you'd tell me why?"

"Family matter."

"Family matter like an officer in General Martin's company, when he was just a captain, got your mother pregnant, and when she miscarried, your father married her to save Chuck's reputation and career? Or family matter like he was your father's CO numerous times, dating back to World War II, and your esteemed air force sergeant pappy is trying desperately to find you and appealed to the general for help."

"Uh," Smitty mumbled, "little of both."

"Thought so."

The silence was unnerving. Bartkowski obviously knew more than he was telling, and it was a certainty that he knew about Dad, he knew about Miami, and he knew about Savannah. Hell, he probably knew about Glenda—in intimate detail.

Smitty concluded that if the lieutenant knew about him, then he most certainly knew about Frenchy and LZ. He wondered what secrets they were carrying. Would all this disqualify them from the training program ahead?

One thing was sure—Smitty had to find out and find out right now. If the answers were not the right ones, it could be that he, Frenchy, and LZ would have to adjust their plans, even if it meant adjusting themselves out of the army.

"Sounds like you pretty much know everything about me. Was I your only assignment?" Smitty asked.

Bartkowski puffed quietly on his cigarette as he looked appraisingly at Smitty. "Sergeant, you're beginning to annoy me. If you were just one-tenth as smart as you think you are, then you'd already know the answer to that."

"I don't understand," Smitty responded blankly.

Ron rubbed the back of his neck and closed his eyes. "At the start of the Second World War, a certain southern U.S. Senator was the leading candidate to replace the current vice president on the Roosevelt ticket in his fourth election. But surprise, surprise, the senator was not only passed over for consideration, but resigned from the senate and went home to oblivion; why?"

"What the hell does that have to do with anything?" Frenchy asked.

"General Martin was a junior officer then. His daddy was a U.S. Senator, from Tennessee, I think," Smitty said. "I heard Dad talk about it one time."

"The air force two-star you were assigned to at the Pentagon," LZ said, startled.

"Not assigned to—arranged."

"Then the army two-star version would be . . ."

"His younger brother," Ron finished.

"There also was another brother who was killed in the war, and a half-brother and half-sister from a previous marriage," Ron added.

Smitty gave Ron a thoughtful look, but said nothing.

"What became of them?" LZ asked.

"Doesn't matter. Seems they were out of the picture long before the brothers became generals."

"Enough of this trip down memory lane, Sergeant. There's nothing more to tell; the general's background is just a coincidence," Bartkowski said curtly, cutting off further discussion.

"Frenchy," the lieutenant said, turning to face him. "You're with these two for the wrong reason. Moe, you followed Larry and Curly here into the service because you thought you were running away from an irate, well-to-do father whose daughter you'd knocked up back in New Orleans. That about it?"

"Yes," Frenchy said, his voice trembling.

"Could have saved yourself the trouble. You weren't, as she repeatedly told you, the first man she'd ever 'gone all the way with.' Come to that, you weren't even in the top ten. Lost her virginity to two first cousins when she was twelve.

"Daddy was hot for you to marry her instead of one of those limp-dick little rich farts that were constantly hovering around her, because he figured that you weren't bright enough to figure out the truth—that she was knocked up by her own daddy. Our investigation shows that he'd been abusing her since she was five and having sex with her since he 'gave her' to the two cousins to break her in. You were the perfect patsy: big, strong, muscular, and stupid."

Frenchy put his head in his hands and began to cry. It was obvious that no matter what had happened, Frenchy had strong feelings for her and was devastated by this news.

Bartkowski reached out and gently placed his hand on Frenchy's shoulder. "Sorry, son, but those are the facts. Be assured that we have reported our findings to the proper authorities, and your girl is now in counseling and Daddy Bigbucks is in the slammer."

He turned to LZ and said firmly, "And as for you, Numbnuts, you're a first-class jerk who's been giving a saintly woman a real hard time her whole life."

LZ had only begun to reach for the ever-present switchblade, when an army-issue .45 was pressed against his temple. "Don't even think about it, son."

Smitty thought that LZ was going to try anyway.

Bartkowski's icy glare never changed as he pulled back the hammer. "I wouldn't if I were you."

Smitty held his breath. Frenchy lifted his head from his hands and watched anxiously. LZ's eyes darted first to Smitty, then Frenchy, before coming back to stare unblinkingly at the lieutenant.

The silence was broken suddenly by a clatter as LZ dropped the knife. Smitty watched silently as it hit the floor.

Bartkowski retrieved the knife.

"After I finish with you gentlemen you'll wonder why you ever bothered to carry those things in the first place," Bartkowski said.

"We were speaking about you being a jerk. I was referring to the woman who raised you, who was in fact your real mother's best friend, and always told you that she did not know who your father was. You thought your 'mother' was a promiscuous whore who got knocked up by some unknown black GI who left town, never to be seen again.

"The fact of the matter is that your real mother and father were married in San Francisco three days before your father was sent to Korea—and three weeks before you were born.

"Your father did not know that your mother was pregnant, having only known her briefly before moving on to another base. Your mother's girlfriend wrote to him. He immediately cabled your mother to join him in San Francisco, where they were married. Since they were tight on cash, he promised to buy her a ring when he returned from the ROK.

"Your mother died three days after she brought you home from the hospital, when she was hit by a car in San Francisco. The next day, a telegram came to the hotel room. Her husband had been killed on the way to Korea in a shipboard accident. Her friend was the only one there to read it.

"When your real mother died, the woman you call Mom, knowing that the authorities would never give a single black woman custody, took you as her own. She never went back to Chicago; she fled to Miami where she had family and friends, and in memory of her dear friend, raised you as her own son."

LZ looked at Bartkowski and said tearfully, "I never knew."

"Of course you didn't. Maybe when you see her again, now that you know that you aren't a little bastard, you can stop acting like one to that special lady."

"You can count on it, sir," LZ said.

Smitty now understood Frenchy's motivations and LZ's deep-seated anger. His turn would be next. How much did Bartkowski know? Could he shed any light on the dark cloud that had seemed to follow Smitty around his whole life?

He wouldn't have long to wait.

"And now, shit-for-brains, it's your turn."

"You're the worst of the three because you lead the other two stooges into one skirmish after another, with continually escalating tragic results, and for no better reason than that you're trying to stick it to your old man."

When Smitty opened his mouth to speak, Bartkowski waved him to silence. "Yes, I know all about your conspiracy theory. But you know what, Sergeant? I don't give a fuck. And if you want to live until your twenty-first birthday, you'd better not, either.

"By the way, I'm not saying that there isn't some validity there—there are several things that do seem to stretch the boundaries of coincidence—but I'm telling you for your own good to suspend your search, until after Nam, because believe me, you're going to need every ounce of concentration you have to meet the challenge of what lies ahead. Are we clear?"

"Yes, sir," Smitty answered.

"Good. I'm glad we had this private moment together; we'll not have another."

"One last thing, gentlemen: whatever it is that you drive will need an immediate cleanup. It just wouldn't do for members of our most elite U.S. Army unit to be seen motoring around with a peace sign on the roof. Tend to it, will you."

Smitty, Frenchy, and LZ nodded wordlessly in reply.

Lieutenant Bartkowski hadn't been making idle boasts when he talked about teaching them to survive, to say nothing of keeping them out of trouble. He was accomplishing the first with a fourteen-hour-a-day, seven-day-a-week accelerated training program that did not allow time for the second.

Smitty, LZ, and Frenchy were being trained to be replacements, presumably for "A" detachments in Vietnam. Each of them was being taught a different primary skill and cross-trained in each other's skill, with an additional twist where Smitty was concerned.

An "A" detachment was a twelve-man group, commonly referred to as an "A" team. The team comprised a commanding officer, usually a captain, and an executive officer, usually a first lieutenant, plus ten NCOs with specialty skills ranging from weapons to medic to demolitions. These billets were usually filled by hand-picked senior sergeants with seven to ten years' experience.

But because of a combination of combat deaths, a siphoning off of enlisted personnel to regular army NCO assignments, or senior sergeants getting fed up and getting out of the service, the Special Forces noncommissioned ranks were woefully understaffed. There were two—and sometimes three—level grade substitutions, with less experienced and lower ranking NCOs more the rule than the exception.

The officers didn't fare much better. Bartkowski had told them that during his last six months' tour in Vietnam, he'd been involuntarily extended for a second tour. Additionally, he had held an XO position as a second lieutenant, and the team CO had been a first lieutenant instead of a captain.

LZ was being trained as a medical specialist, Frenchy as a communications specialist; both were being cross-trained in weapons and demolitions. Smitty's primary skill was to be weapons, with cross-training in demolitions and communications. Additionally, he was also being given the extra burden of learning intelligence—under Bartkowski's personal tutelage.

Smitty had seen little of either LZ or Frenchy since their training had officially begun in June, three months ago. They were billeted together, but the different training regimens had kept them apart. A week would pass and Smitty would catch only a passing glimpse of them as they dressed and left—like everything else around here—at double-time. The only time they were together was in the hand-to-hand training, the Vietnamese language training, and the live field exercises that seemed to begin with almost clockwork regularity in the middle of the night.

General Martin had talked about the NCO billets beginning to show their age, and that was the reason for the "fast tracking" path that Smitty, LZ, and Frenchy were on. What General Martin had not talked about was the effect it was having on the three of them.

In the darkest corners of his mind, Smitty was torn by the guilt of having led his friends onto a collision course with the war in Vietnam, though the reason had little to do with "sticking it to his old man." As each day passed, and the training got more intense, Smitty was coming to the gut-wrenching realization that not only would he be held accountable to God for the loss of an enemy human life, but also the fear—the certainty—that his dearest friends' lives would be offered up on the altar of his obsessive, narcissistic search for the truth.

He agonized about his friends being wounded and left for dead, facing the slow, painful process of dying over hours or perhaps days. Smitty told himself that if it happened to him, he'd kill himself. No matter what Dad had said about there always being a way out, as long as a man continues to thinking. He just couldn't face it.

Although they'd never discussed it, fear was affecting LZ and Frenchy in the same fashion. LZ's unflappable wit had dried up. Frenchy had not plied his usual roguish charm with any of the PX Popsies.

But their spirit wasn't entirely quenched. They did comply with the lieutenant's directive to paint over the peace sign on the roof of the Famous '54. They then repainted it on the trunk lid, with another on the hood for good measure.

This had been discovered by a "straightleg," a nonairborne army colonel who not only gave them a twenty-minute lecture on patriotism, but assured them that he would be addressing the matter with their training officer immediately.

Smitty got a message that the lieutenant wanted to see him on the double. He could only assume that LZ and Frenchy had gotten the same message. Smitty knew from personal experience with his dad that when a full colonel filed a report, things happened. All of them were bad.

Smitty was right. LZ and Frenchy were there and standing at ease when Smitty arrived. The lieutenant looked up from his desk as Smitty entered, saluted and uncovered. Smitty assumed a parade rest position with his two friends and waited in silence for the dressing-down he knew was certain to come.

"Tenhut," Bartkowski said suddenly, looking past Smitty's shoulder. "Stand easy, gentlemen," a lieutenant colonel said, coming around to stand in front of them.

"I'm Colonel Wilson," he began.

He looked to be in his midforties with close-cropped hair, a granite jaw, and steely eyes. He was lean, and his uniform had nine rows of confetti, a clear enough indication of a seasoned combat veteran.

Bartkowski had walked around from behind the desk and had taken a seat on the front corner with his arms folded, a clear enough indication that this was the colonel's show to run.

"Now then, let me see if I have my facts right," he said, removing three military folders from his briefcase.

"Six-feet-two, 185 pounds, reddish-blond hair, blue eyes, permanent scars chin and neck. You, I take it, are Sergeant Smith," Colonel Wilson said in a businesslike tone.

Smitty opened his mouth to respond, but the colonel cut him off, holding out his hand like a traffic cop, "Hold your yessirs until I'm finished or we'll be here 'til Christmas." He studied Smitty's records for a minute, leafing back and forth as if correlating information from one page to the next. He chuckled quietly to himself several times.

"Lots of fireworks. I expected better from a second generation military man.

"Let's see now. Five-feet-eleven, 220 pounds, brown hair, brown eyes. Sergeant Douchet," the colonel said, moving to face Frenchy. He examined Frenchy's folder, scowling from time to time.

"Glad my daughter's only eleven," the colonel said, passing Frenchy's file across to Bartkowski.

"Six-feet-one, 180 pounds, black hair, brown eyes. Sergeant McCord, I presume," the colonel said, moving again to face LZ.

"You've done more cutting than most second-year interns, son," the colonel said, passing across the last folder.

Turning to Ron, he said bluntly, "You were right, Lieutenant, they are exactly the men we are looking for. Proceed with your briefing." The colonel walked behind the desk and took a seat.

"Yes, sir, Colonel," Bartkowski said, standing up and began to pacing back and forth.

"You three gentlemen have been here for twelve weeks. Your primary training is just about complete. You've crammed six months' training into three, and you'll look back on this time as the easy part of your enlistment.

"You have been picked for a special assignment. This assignment will require you to use every accumulated facet of your training to date and every ounce of your skill and cunning. For the course of this assignment, you are to report only to me or to Colonel Wilson. You will not, I repeat—not speak about this to anyone else. For purposes of cover, you three are 'officially' being given leave. You will depart the post through normal procedure and will be contacted as to the specific nature of the assignment by means to be disclosed by the colonel. Are we clear?"

"Yes, sir," Smitty, LZ, and Frenchy answered together. LZ glanced nervously at Frenchy, who passed the glance on to Smitty.

Smitty shifted uncomfortably and cleared his throat. "Uh, sir, we're going to have a bit of a problem leaving the post."

"Why?"

"Well you see, sir, there's—"

"Sergeant," the colonel interrupted. "Speak plainly, to the point, and do not concern yourself with military decorum and protocol. Time is desperately short."

"Lieutenant, we cannot leave the post by normal means." Smitty glanced quickly at the colonel. "A 'Chicken Leg' impounded our transport."

"Translation, Lieutenant," the colonel said.

"These gentlemen co-own a 1954 two-door Chevrolet that looks like a cross between a psychedelic paint experiment, an artist's temper tantrum, and a Polish pinball machine."

"So?" The colonel impatiently drummed his fingers on the desk.

"A regular army colonel impounded it today because it had what he termed a 'Communist expression,' painted on it."

The colonel looked at Bartkowski blankly. "Peace signs on the hood and trunk, sir."

"I'll tend to it. The transport will be parked in front of the Elite Café at 0500 hours."

"Gentlemen, here are your orders. You will open them and follow the procedure to the letter when you cross the state line." The colonel flipped Smitty a manila folder.

"How will we communicate?" Smitty asked, snatching the folder cleanly with one hand.

"The lieutenant will function in that capacity. Anything else?"

"No, sir."

"Good luck, gentlemen; come back alive." The colonel was gone before they could respond.

Unable to improve on the colonel's parting remark, the lieutenant looked at Smitty, LZ, and Frenchy, shrugged his shoulders, and said with a wave of dismissal, "What he said."

"What do you think, guys?" Smitty asked as they dog-trotted back to their billet to make final preparations.

"What he said," Frenchy repeated, laughing.

Smitty and LZ joined in, but the laughter was a bit hollow. Smitty couldn't help wondering if this would be the spot where their collective luck would finally run out.

Smitty, LZ, and Frenchy packed, bummed a ride to the base gate, then took a taxi to the café. As they loaded the car, they noticed a dark-haired, muscular man watching them from the Elite's window.

As they got in, Smitty said, "Frenchy, watch him from the rear window until we're out of view. Make sure he's not doing anything peculiar."

Frenchy looked over his shoulder and stared out of the rear of the Chevy.

"See anything, man?" LZ asked with a trace of concern in his voice.

"Would that dude reaching in his pocket and talking into a communication device constitute anything peculiar?"

"Yes, it would," Smitty answered. The two-ton slued crazily as he made an emergency right turn, then a quick left into a parking lot, and pulled over and stopped behind a van.

Smitty, LZ, and Frenchy silently got out of the car, dropped to their hands and slid under the van. They peeked up just in time to see a dark sedan go screaming by out on the main road. Smitty had only a quick glimpse, but he could clearly see the erstwhile diner sitting in the front passenger seat cocking an automatic weapon.

"Dude doesn't appear to be on the side of the angels," LZ said thoughtfully. "Perhaps we should take evasive action."

"What the fuck are we into, mon ami?"

"Dunno," Smitty answered. "But if this is the Looey's idea of a final exam, he's got one macabre sense of humor."

"What's our next step?" LZ asked.

"Hot wheels," Smitty answered.

"I'm on it, man. Back in five minutes." LZ turned and trotted away.

He was back in two, driving a brand new metallic blue Camaro Super Sport.

"Hot wheels," Frenchy said. He opened the door, folded the passenger seat forward and climbed in the back, pulling the seat back for Smitty.

"Where to, Massa?"

"I think it's time to let Hertz put us in the driver's seat," Smitty answered. "And fast. We've got a rendezvous to keep."

Even without a reservation, they were on their way in a nondescript beige Chevrolet Impala in less than half an hour. This had nothing to do with efficiency and everything to do with Frenchy's charm.

"You know Frenchy, you're some piece of work, man," LZ said from the backseat. "Ten minutes with you and that titsy kid was ready to procreate."

"Just one of those things, man," Frenchy said.

Once they were on the road, Smitty asked LZ, "Hey pard', what happened to the pimpmobile?"

LZ sat forward, rested his arms on the top of the front seat. "I took care of it, as you requested."

"Okay, Frumpy, where'd you leave the pussygetter?" Smitty asked.

"In a place where it could not help being found."

"Where?" Smitty asked impatiently.

"In the chaplain's parking space outside the emergency room at the hospital next to the car lot."

"Any chance it'll be traced to us?" Smitty asked.

"Naw, man," LZ said proudly, his voice warming to his role. "I wiped it clean, and left a note under the windshield wiper, apologizing for swiping the dude's ride. It said, 'Sorry man, needed your wheels. My car broke, the wife's water broke, and I'm broke.'"

"Good enough."

"I called in to the Looey, told him about the gentlemen following us and the '54. He was calm about it. Told me he'd take care of it," Smitty said.

"What about the five-four?" Frenchy asked.

"Same response. Said not to worry about it; said we'll see it again."

"Strange, huh?" Frenchy said to no one in particular.

"Yeah, strange," Smitty answered in a voice that cut off further comment.

The next two hours passed in virtual silence, with only an occasional comment to disturb the quiet. With each mile closer to the state line, the air seemed to get thicker, and increasingly difficult to breathe.

Five miles from Charleston's state, Smitty wordlessly pulled out his .357, opened the chamber, and inserted a sixth round. LZ and Frenchy silently followed his actions, checking their newly issued army .45s. As they crossed the North Carolina border, Smitty pulled over to the side of the road and stopped. With a nervous glance at Frenchy and a backward glance at LZ, Smitty tore open the envelope and began to read.

It didn't take long. Smitty read the paper, then read it again. With an uncomprehending nod, he passed the note on to Frenchy, who seemed equally confused as he passed the note to LZ. LZ's reaction was much the same.

"Proceed twelve miles to Milly's Restaurant. You will be contacted there," LZ read aloud. He flipped the note onto the front seat in disgust. "Shit, man. Why all the secrecy? They could have told us this before we left Bragg."

"Dunno," Smitty said uncomfortably, "but they must have had their reasons."

"Maybe they didn't think we'd get this far," Frenchy said, giving voice to what they'd all thought.

Smitty pulled back onto the road and they headed south, watching the mile markers tick by until the number eleven passed on the right. A mile or so farther on, the eatery appeared on the left. Smitty pulled into the parking lot, parked, and the three of them walked cautiously inside and took a seat in the booth closest to the door.

A short, pudgy waitress, with her hair in a bun and a pencil stuck in it, ambled over, removed an order pad from her apron, and plucked the pencil from her hair. "What'll it be, boys?"

"Three coffees," Smitty said.

"Check."

As she passed the counter, a huge figure with long, stringy hair and a mountain man's beard rose from his stool at the counter, turned slowly, and began to walk deliberately in their direction.

Smitty touched both LZ and Frenchy on the leg with his foot, and on receiving their confirming nods, braced for the approaching giant.

His clothes seemed to have been made from the Famous '54's paint pattern, from the multicolored holy T-shirt with a peace sign on it, to the bell bottoms with the frayed cuffs and the scruffy biker boots. Obviously, he never learned to shop at Saks, Smitty thought morosely as the big boy walked menacingly toward them.

"Hey, bro, Daddy just found out ten minutes ago about you knocking up his little girl," the imitation Goliath said.

"I think you've made a mistake," Smitty said.

"I ain't made no mistake. Daddy said it was an army asshole who had two buddies; one white and one black. That makes it you." He reached out to grab Smitty by the shirt and jerk him out of the booth. It didn't work.

Suddenly the big man found himself completely immobilized with his arm twisted behind his back and his face pressed to the table with Smitty leaning over him.

"As I said, bud, you've made a mistake. Now why don't you go count your peas and carrots before I get really mad; ho, ho, ho." Smitty launched him toward the door.

"My daddy's name is Big Ron, and you're gonna have to deal with him, now," the hulking mountain man said, slamming the door back violently and disappearing.

"Hey, you don't think . . . " Frenchy said suddenly, as he started to slide out of the booth.

"I sure do," Smitty said, hurriedly throwing a buck on the table. With Frenchy and LZ right on his heels, he ran out of the coffee shop just in time to see Ron's alleged offspring dive behind the wheel of a dark sedan and accelerate out of the parking lot headed south.

Smitty, Frenchy, and LZ were a quarter of a mile behind. Driving with recklessness fueled by adrenaline, Smitty quickly closed the distance to one hundred yards, five cars back from their quarry.

"Take him, man," LZ said.

"Let's think a minute," Smitty said. "If he's leading us somewhere, it's on orders. If he's a good guy, so much the better, but if he's not, then I vote we hang back with enough space and not get trapped."

"I concur, mon ami," Frenchy.

"Yeah, I guess you're right. My emotions kinda got the best of me there," LZ acknowledged.

They covered the next five miles maintaining the same hundred-yard interval, but now only two cars separated them from the rabbit. This bunny obviously knew the hop. He veered suddenly to the right down a tree-lined side road. Smitty followed, maintaining his distance.

The car drove down the road, around the bend until they were out of sight of the main road, then eased to a stop. The big boy got out of the car immediately and stood beside it, raising his hands.

"Weapons ready, but not pointed," Smitty said, as he got out. "Frenchy, one hundred yards up, front guard; LZ, rear guard here. Remember what happened to us in Georgia, stay alert."

"Yeah, the world needs more 'lerts," Frenchy said, as he dog-trotted away, passing the mysterious stranger without so much as a nod and taking up his position.

As Smitty walked warily toward the dark sedan, he couldn't help marveling at the calmness of his friends in a crisis. That thought triggered a revelation. Smitty stopped and looked at the big man, then walked directly up to him.

When Smitty was within three feet of the large lad, he reached up without hesitation and snatched the wig off, revealing a close-cropped military haircut. He tried the same maneuver on the beard, and after some initial resistance, a freshly shaved, grinning face presented itself with sideburns at the top of the ear, military style.

"Hey, bro, Daddy just found out ten minutes ago about you knocking up his little girl," Smitty said, slapping the big man playfully on the cheek. The man grabbed Smitty in a bear hug that almost crushed his ribs.

"W-w-w-w-well, it wa-as the only t-t-thing I could t-think of," Big Walt said.

Walt's grab was misinterpreted by both LZ and Frenchy, who came charging up, weapons at the ready.

"It's okay guys; it's the fourth musketeer," Smitty said, pushing LZ's weapon downward.

"LZ-z-z-z-z-z," Big Walt squealed in delight as he administered the same bone-crushing welcome he'd used on Smitty and then did the same to Frenchy when he arrived moments later.

"How the hell did you get into this, man?" LZ thumped Big Walt on the back.

"I volunteered," Big Walt said. "Right after Major Jim volunteered me."

"Major Jim," Frenchy said with a raised eyebrow.

"Y-y-yes, I-i-i was recruited by him to pick you g-u-uys up and t-t-ta-a-a-k-ke-e you t-t-t-o the rendezvous point," Big Walt explained.

"What happens from there?" LZ asked.

"I-i-i-i don't know. I-i-i-i was just told to p-p-pi-i-ic-ck you up."

"So where do we go from here?" Smitty asked.

"I-i-i'll drive," Big Walt said, opening the rear door of the dark sedan. He slapped LZ on the back, launching him into the backseat and then gestured toward Frenchy, who warily circled around the rear of the car and entered through the passenger's rear door.

"Smitty, shotgun, if you please," Big Walt said. Smitty walked around to the front of the car and got in.

"Back up to the rental so we can get our stuff," Smitty said.

"Check," Big Walt responded.

"What about the loaner?" LZ asked, getting back in the car after retrieving what few possessions they'd brought along.

"T-t-they're number one; t-t-they'll find it," Big Walt answered.

Smitty looked at Big Walt. The lad had changed. He was no longer the gawky doofus they'd left behind after the "Basic MP Bashing." He was more poised, more mature, perhaps even a bit arrogant. Smitty wondered what caused this subtle change.

They covered the next four hours mostly in silence. Smitty, LZ, and Frenchy attempted to make small talk with Big Walt, trying to catch up on what he'd been up to the last five months, that sort of thing, but Big Walt wasn't inclined to chat. They wound their way down U.S.-18, through an endless series of small towns that all looked pretty much the same.

At Mecca, about fifty miles from Savannah, they turned right onto a small state road. About five miles out, seemingly in the middle of nowhere, they turned right onto a dirt road, and followed it a quarter of a mile until it dead-ended at a farm. They drove straight past the main house toward the barn on the left. Big Walt slowed briefly, gave two staccato honks on his horn, and by the time he reached the barn entrance, the door had been swung open by the same man they'd eluded in North Carolina, carrying as expected, an automatic weapon. The Famous '54 was parked in the back of the barn facing forward, looking none the worse for wear.

"How did that get here?" LZ asked, bewildered.

"Your lieutenant called. I had it picked up and delivered here," a familiar voice said from behind the Chevy.

Colonel Wilson emerged from the shadows followed closely by Major Jim. he skirted the old car, patting it affectionately on the front fender as he walked past.

LZ exhaled heavily. "Man, why all this dumb-shit cloak and dagger stuff? Why couldn't you just have brought us down here?"

"Oh, there are reasons, Sergeant, there are reasons," the colonel said softly. "And they're quite valid."

"To start with, we had to make sure you weren't followed, like you were on your first intelligence mission through Georgia. And we didn't need a second Battle of the Little Bighorn, if you know what I mean."

"I think we all know what you mean, Colonel," Lieutenant Bartkowski said, entering from behind. "And I can assure you, sir, that there will be no repetition of earlier events. These men are now highly trained and have inherent self-discipline."

"You gentlemen have passed the first test," the colonel said. "You discovered our surveillance, avoided it neatly, instinctively sacrificed your material possessions—if you're brash enough to so refer to this junkyard reject. You made your rendezvous point on time, discovered your contact, and arrived at the jump-off point undetected. Well done, gentlemen. We're off to an effective start.

"Now, then. There are specific reasons why you men were selected for this assignment. Each of you has a particular talent that is instrumental for this mission, and when you add that together with the fact that you three think and act as one, and that your civilian backgrounds give you more combat time than some Nam vets, it makes you the perfect team to send in.

"As for your particular talents, since this mission requires intimate knowledge of the area, and the Ops area is Savannah, you, Sergeant Smith, will provide that info and function as team leader. The fact that you are, shall we say, not on the mayor's guest list, will, I'm sure, encourage you to take the utmost precautions against discovery for your team.

"Second, since it is our belief that the individuals involved are foreign nationals, specifically of French decent, you, Sergeant Douchet, with your intimate knowledge of French will function as the team's interpreter. Additionally, your, um, expertise with the opposite sex may prove very useful in intelligence gathering."

"Yeah, babe," Smitty said. "I know a little French whorehouse downtown that's just swarming with desperate voluptuous female spies who'll tell you everything they know for carnal knowledge of your gorgeous bod." Smitty clapped Frenchy playfully on the back and noticed that the colonel was not amused. "Sorry."

"If you're quite finished, Sergeant, we'll continue," the colonel said, shaking his head.

"You, Sergeant McCord, will function as the team's liaison. You'll relay and communicate mission status nightly. Since we expect some of the recipients to be poor and black, you will be vital in information gathering."

"Maybe I'll get lucky like Frenchy," LZ said.

"What do you mean?" the colonel asked.

"Who knows, some of these, how did you put it, 'poor and black recipients' could be young and female, in which case I'll make them the vital recipients of my poor black manhood." LZ grabbed his crotch to emphasize his point.

Smitty burst out laughing, as did Frenchy. Lieutenant Bartkowski was chuckling quietly to himself, trying hard—and for the most part failing—to maintain his composure. Major Jim appeared to be genuinely confused, almost as if he didn't understand LZ's double entendre. But that didn't matter; the colonel did.

Colonel Wilson slowly rubbed first his forehead, then his closed eyes. "Lieutenant. I thought you told me this was your number one team. They act more like the Three Stooges than a highly trained combat infiltration squad, motivated and serious about their work. Are you sure they're the right—?"

The colonel never got a chance to finish his statement. With an almost imperceptible nod from the lieutenant, Smitty, LZ, and Frenchy went into action. A lot of things seemed to happen at once. LZ grabbed the colonel, twisted his arm, at the same time arced him in the direction of the Famous '54. As his body made contact with the hood, LZ brought his arm up behind his back, cleared his .45, pulled back the hammer, and brought the gun down against the colonel's temple, pincering his head against the hood.

At the same time, Frenchy snatched the automatic weapon from their erstwhile pursuer and brought his right hand behind his head, grabbing the man by the shirt collar, slamming him to the ground, and forcing his head into the dirt. Then Frenchy dropped his knee into the small of the man's back and separated his hair with his own .45.

Smitty, meanwhile, grabbed Major Jim and had the major bent over the other side of the hood in two seconds flat. As he executed this move, he cleared the .357 and brought it firmly against Jim's temple, cocking it in the same motion.

"Nice set of bookends you got there boys," the lieutenant said to Smitty and LZ as he studied the incapacitated forms of the colonel and Major Jim against the hood of the '54. "How do you like the comedy routine now, Colonel?"

"I think you've made your technical point, Lieutenant," Colonel Wilson responded through clenched teeth.

Smitty, LZ, and Frenchy released their captives and backed slowly away, returning their weapons to their respective places of concealment in the process.

"Larry!"

"Curly!"

"Moe!"

Smitty yelled triumphantly, and first LZ, and then Frenchy responded in turn as they clasped hands over their heads in a triangular fashion.

"Impressive, gentlemen, I must say," the colonel acknowledged. "Perhaps I was a bit hasty, in my, um, initial assessment. Now as to the mission, gather around and pay very close attention." The colonel removed a paper from a folder that Major Jim handed him and began to read from an official-looking document.

"There has been a hundredfold increase in the amount of illegal drugs entering the United States in the recent past. The primary port of entry for most shipments was Miami. Approximately one year ago, a shift in the drug traffic away from South Florida was noted; inroads into the syndicate apparently forced them to change their import tactics.

"After some initial probes into Tampa, Mobile, and New Orleans, the syndicate has now settled on importing through the East Coast. The new primary ports of entry are thought to be Savannah, Charleston, and Norfolk.

"The Bureau has tried to establish links into this activity, but to date those efforts have been met with some resistance, so it is felt by the FBI that infiltration can only be through conventional channels. Conventional in this case to mean that it is recommended that soldiers who would normally be stationed in the local area be given specialized training and posted in the area in order to minimize suspicion." The colonel paused and read more of the report in silence before handing it back to the major and then continued.

"The purpose of this mission is to gather intelligence. I repeat—to gather intelligence. You gentlemen are there to find out what the pipeline is and map it. Under no circumstances are you to take any offensive action. You are there to observe and report."

"What if we're challenged?" Smitty asked.

"I repeat—you are to take no offensive action," the colonel said. "Do whatever is required to avoid this, as it will involve the police and call attention to you. Are we clear?"

"I think you've made your technical point," the lieutenant answered.

The colonel glared, but said nothing. He spread a map of Savannah out in front of him on the hood of the Famous '54. "Here's your operational folder containing everything you'll need, including cover identities, false IDs, and a supply of operational money. Commit the contents of the papers to memory and dispose of them prior to crossing the border into Georgia. Give your wallets and other valuables to the lieutenant before you leave and do not, I repeat—do not take any form of identification with you that will allow you to be traced. The lieutenant will inspect your possessions prior to your departure at 1900 hours.

"Good luck, gentlemen; come back alive." The colonel handed the ops folder back to the major, stepped around him, and was gone.

"I didn't care very much for the last comment," Frenchy said.

"Which one?" LZ asked. "The 'good luck' or the 'come back alive'?"

"I interpreted it to mean that it would be good luck if we did come back alive," Frenchy said.

Smitty, LZ, and Frenchy exchanged looks, shrugged, and went about collecting their operational supplies. In fifteen minutes they were packed and back on the state road. In fifteen more they were back on U.S.-18 headed south in the rolling smoke bomb.

Neither Smitty, LZ, nor Frenchy spoke much over the last fifty miles. At Hardeeville, they turned south onto U.S.-17.

Approximately ten miles from Savannah, they stopped at a nondescript burger joint and ordered dinner. Smitty passed out their IDs and read through the ops order one final time before shredding the contents and burning them in a coffee can that had been provided explicitly for that purpose. Four miles from the border, LZ pulled over and they scattered the ashes in a swampy stream.

Smitty had told Glenda, when he left Georgia to return to Florida, that it was to excise the cancer at its root. He'd thought that the source of the disease was in a police file in Miami, but he'd been wrong. Miami was not a cause. It was, in fact, just another symptom. A symptom that had thrown two more names into the hopper: Stan the Man and Detective Wallace. A good guy and a bad guy—or vice versa? At this point, Smitty wasn't sure which was which. Could one of them be the mysterious mole?

The army, like Miami, and like Savannah before it, was turning out to be just another in a series of incidents that Smitty believed was more than a set of bizarre unrelated coincidences. Someone was after him. But he still didn't know why.

General Chuck must be somehow involved. So, apparently, was his brother General Martin. And both had to be tied in to Dad. And somehow this all had to relate to the World War II Mission Octagon that the general had sloughed off so casually in the bar.

There was also the entry of the new players into the game. Major Gates—what did he know? And what about his brother, the one who had been bounced from the service in Dearfield for humping Smitty's mom? Major Jim, the innocent-looking lawyer with the penchant for being conveniently in the right place at the right time. Lieutenant Bartkowski, a first-class junior officer with a lot of information on a lot of confidential matters. And finally, Lieutenant Colonel Wilson, who was new to LZ and Frenchy but not to Smitty; he had been the LTC on the hearing board when Smitty got hacked in basic.

Behind all of this, was there an anonymous master puppeteer who was constantly pulling the strings on Smitty's life?

Smitty had no physical proof that he could take into a court of law, but enough, in his gut, to confirm that, like Dorothy, he was definitely moving on down the yellow brick road. But Vietnam, though green, wasn't the Emerald City.

He knew that it would take a miracle to reach Oz. Personally, if Smitty were a betting man, he'd be making large wagers on the Wicked Witch.

The sun was already below the western horizon, but it was not yet dark when the Famous '54 chugged up the incline to the top of the Talmadge Bridge over the Savannah River and the panoramic view below.

Seemed like a simple enough assignment on the surface. But then again, 90 percent of an iceberg was hidden below the waterline. Call it ESP, but Smitty'd a feeling that the analogy of the iceberg would prove to be true. It had nothing to do with being back in Savannah; but it had everything to do with leaving it alive.

CHAPTER TEN

So much for James Bond, Smitty thought. So far, he felt more like coolie in a rice field. His back hurt from bending, stooping, and crawling from one bilge hole to another, searching in vain for the elusive drug shipments that were supposed to be there.

Frenchy and LZ were having no better luck. Working on two other ships, they had so far turned up zilch, also.

Getting the jobs had been easy. The shortage of qualified "strong back–weak mind" machinists to crawl around the rusting scows was acute. Repairing the miscellany of leaking valves, ruptured plates, and salt-air-frozen ship components on these rust buckets that came endlessly into the shipyard was child's play compared to the complex weaponry and electronic components of their most recent past. Presenting their carefully prepared forged papers—with recent honorable discharges included—to the hiring office had netted them hard hats and start times on the next whistle.

The foreman at the tool shack was enthusiastic, assuring them that there were "boys here that had been here since they came home from the war. Figure you boys will be around that long, too." After two weeks, it seemed like a lifetime; twenty years would seem like an eternity.

But the trail was cold. They were looking in the wrong place or the stuff wasn't here to be found. They were halfway through this assignment and the only thing they had caught so far was a permanent stench in the pores of their skin from the oily miasma that permeated the entire shipyard. Smitty suspected that there were other teams assigned all along the docks, but he didn't know. It appeared to be a scattershot approach, hoping that some unwitting pig would turn over a truffle.

"Man, this is a shit assignment," LZ said in disgust, flopping down against the tool shack wall beside Smitty and Frenchy just after the noon whistle blew.

"I couldn't agree more." Smitty nodded halfheartedly. "Just think: We could be back at Bragg digging foxholes approved by Good Housekeeping, rather than this."

"Or cleaning the shitters at Fort Polk," Frenchy added.

"Well, Mister Liaison Team Leader, tonight contact that fuckin' Polack, and tell him to get us the hell out of here," Frenchy said. "And to make it PDQ.."

"Consider it done, my brother," LZ replied. "But it'll be Major Jim. The Polack's gone, remember?"

"That's right," Smitty said. "He's going on leave effective tonight for thirty days before he rotates back to Vietnam with a promotion to captain."

"Strange, him being yanked in the middle of the assignment," LZ said.

"Well, call whoever," Frenchy answered. "Anything's got to be better than this, even—"

"Can it!" Smitty hissed. "Do you see what I see?" He nodded in the direction of the yard superintendent's office.

"No, what?" Frenchy asked. LZ looked puzzled, too.

"Look at the eyes, the shape of the nose and the way that dude in the suit is walking into the foreman's office," Smitty said. "We've seen him before. And he's seen us."

Frenchy and LZ were studying the man like a jeweler examining a ten-carat diamond for flaws with a loupe.

"Oh, shit, man, it's that guy," Frenchy said.

"What guy?" LZ asked.

"A certain homicide detective, Detective Wallace, to be precise," Smitty said.

"What the hell is that sadistic asshole doing all the way up here?" LZ asked.

"More to the point, why the hell is he here?"

"Scratch what I just said about this being a shit assignment," LZ said. "If this dude is here, the dope's here and we should be here. That asshole ain't close to being on the side of the angels."

"Or something's here," Smitty said. "It remains for us to find out what."

"Frenchy, see that guy over there by the machine shop, leaning against the wall smoking a cigarette?" Smitty pointed to a round-faced, smiling Puerto Rican man who looked as though he didn't have a care in the world.

"Yeah, so?" Frenchy shrugged.

"I want you to go pick a fight with him—and take your time losing," Smitty said.

"Why?"

"In the confusion, I'll slip up to the super's window and see what I can hear."

"What if they come out, man? They'll want to know what you're doing so close. It could tip them off, make them suspicious," LZ said.

"Chance I'll have to take. Try leading your sparring partner in the opposite direction. It's the first lead we have; there may not be another."

The fight went off pretty much as planned. Frenchy sauntered over to the worker, slapped the cigarette out of his mouth, and with a few well-placed racial epithets, achieved the desired result. The Puerto Rican had only rudimentary pugilistic experience, so Frenchy was able to block and parry most of the blows while looking like he was getting his ass kicked.

With each punch, Frenchy would go down like a pug taking a prepaid dive and roll away, taking the onlookers farther away from the super's office, before he gamely got to his feet for another round.

LZ was lookout, with a prearranged signal that would break up the fight and tell Smitty that the coast was no longer clear.

The fight was not ten seconds into its first round when it had the yard's complete attention. The Puerto Rican hadn't thrown his second punch when Smitty walked casually over in the direction of the office, ducked around the front corner, dropped silently to one knee underneath the office window, and peeked in the bottom corner.

"Thank you for seeing me on such short notice, Superintendent Brinkman," the detective said.

"I must say your call intrigued me, uh . . . ?" the superintendent began, hesitating when he realized he'd not asked the visitor for his name.

"Special Agent Clev Clayborne, FBI special projects, Washington D.C.," Clayborne-Wallace said, flashing what looked like an official G-man badge.

The superintendent nodded, impressed. "As I was saying, Agent Clayborne, your call intrigued me. Do you really think that there is a drug ring operating out of this shipyard?"

"We have positive proof. In fact, several of your employees are involved in the ring. They were planted here by a cartel," Clayborne-Wallace said.

"Whew!" The superintendent whistled softly to himself. "What can I do to help?"

"I'll be sending four of my men in undercover to your hiring office today. Their cover story will be that they just got out of the navy and are looking for a job. I would appreciate it if you could expedite their hiring process so that they are hired and assigned to the work aboard the *Jesus Capri* starting on third shift tonight."

"Consider it done. I'll attend to it personally. In fact, I'll come in tonight to assure that there aren't any slipups."

"The Bureau appreciates the cooperation of citizens like yourself. Without it, we could never hope to stem the drug menace," Clayborn-Wallace said.

Outside the window, as Smitty listened to the pious speech of Beaver Cleaver, he thought he was going to throw up. He thought to himself how odd it was that bad people were so good at convincing the innocent that they were on the side of the angels.

The imitation G-Man lowered his voice and said in a conspiratorial tone, "They'll be here only one night. I hope that won't raise any suspicions."

"People start here, work half a shift, then leave at the lunch whistle because they can't handle the physical demands of the job. Your men leaving won't cause any suspicions. Is there anything else I can do to assist?"

"Thank you, Superintendent. I'll remember you in my report to Washington."

"I appreciate that, sir."

"Mum's the word," Clayborne-Wallace said, holding a finger to his lips. "Forget I was ever here, and forget about my boys."

"Oh, uhhh, of course. I understand completely. It's forgotten already."

Smitty had heard enough. Clayborne-Wallace was already striding across the office to leave when Smitty ducked below the window, stood upright, and walked around the corner of the office back in the direction of the yard fight, pretending to zip up his pants in the process.

"What the fuck are you doing back there?" a leadman yelled suddenly as Smitty came into clear view.

"Takin' a fuckin' leak, asshole," Smitty shot back.

"You just better watch that smart mouth, boy, or I'll be calling you out."

Wordlessly Smitty flipped him the bird as he walked past.

"Next time you use the shitter, boy. Them walls ain't for pissin' on," the leadman hollered at Smitty's retreating form.

"Got it, gramps," Smitty said without altering his stride.

On seeing Smitty's signal, LZ rushed into the middle of the fray, separated the pugilists and said, "Okay, dudes, what say we break this up? Besides," LZ said with an amused glance at Frenchy, "I think the bud's had enough."

Frenchy, who was just getting to his feet after another punch-and-roll routine, held up his hands. "No more, man, I've had enough."

"From now on, you better watch what you say, man," the Puerto Rican said with a thick accent.

"Next time, your friend won't be able to save you. I'll kick the living shit out of you, man," he said, shaking his fist once more at Frenchy, who cowered on cue.

Such lunchtime sideshows were so commonplace in the yard that they were forgotten almost before they ended. Tomorrow or the next day, there would be another. Only the names would change; the frustration, which was the real fuel behind them, would remain the same.

"Whatcha learn?" LZ asked, as Smitty sauntered up and stood next to him and Frenchy. Smitty held out two fingers and brought them to his lips.

Smitty leaned down and plucked the top cigarette with his lips directly from the pack of Pall Malls that LZ had shaken out. As LZ offered a light, Smitty cupped his hands to cover the flame from LZ's lighter and mask his response from any curious onlookers.

"Dipshit got a promotion; at least according to the credentials he presented the yard superintendent. Seems he's an FBI Special Agent now."

"No shit," LZ said, impressed.

"Not only that, but it seems the promotion came with a side benefit."

"Which was?" Frenchy asked.

"A new name. Calls himself Special Agent Clev Clayborne now," Smitty responded. "And it seems we're going to have some new hires. Clev the G-man is bringing in four people undercover on the graveyard shift tonight to work the *Jesus Capri* that just docked yesterday. Ostensibly to look for illegal drugs."

"Yeah, right, and my mama's gonna be the next Queen of the Virgin Prom," Frenchy said.

"Thoughts, guys?"

"Well maybe we just ought to meet them and arrange for a little accident," LZ said.

"Like what, man?" Frenchy asked.

"Like slipping on a bar of soap in the shower," LZ answered.

"Aren't you forgetting our prime directive from the LTC?" Smitty reminded him. "Observe and report."

They stood in silence and stared at one another. Old instincts were hard to break, but the rigorous training was having an effect.

"LZ, don't wait for the shift to end. Walk out to the pay phone across the street from the yard entrance and call in what we've learned and ask for the next directive, signal code Peter-Alpha.

"Frenchy, you're on the *Jesus*. Nose around this afternoon and see what you can turn up without raising any suspicions. I'll arrange to go to the tool shack when the back-to-work whistle blows and see if there are any special tool requirements for the *Jesus Capri*. It could be that whatever we're looking for is concealed, and we may need a special 'can opener' to get at it.

"You guys meet me at the latrine at the 2:30 break, and we'll cross-check our information. Everybody execute plan B; don't take any chances. We're on foreign turf here and we don't know who's a friend and who's not, got it?" Smitty looked at them with raised brows.

"I'm on it, man," LZ said.

"Right behind you, mon ami."

"You guys be careful," Smitty said.

"Yes, Daddy." LZ walked away, flipping him the bird without turning around.

Smitty, LZ, and Frenchy did keep their appointed rendezvous at the 2:30 PM break, but not at the latrine; they kept it at the hospital.

Frenchy was in the engine room on the false bottom of the *Jesus Capri* when a chainfall that had been resting on an overhead valve slipped as he was walking under it and came down on his head and shoulder, knocking him unconscious. Frenchy was being lifted off the ship in a basket when Smitty heard that LZ had been hit by a car as he crossed the street on his way back from the phone booth. And as Smitty was leaving the ship he was working on, he stepped on a ten-inch flexible duct that was connected to a sixty-inch fan with nine ports to pipe air down into the holds of the ship. The duct inflated suddenly, causing Smitty to slip and sprain his ankle.

Smitty was riding in the ambulance with his unconscious friend, wondering about the fate of LZ, who was on his way to the same hospital by another meatwagon.

"Frenchy," Smitty said softly. "Talk to me, man," Smitty said, slapping aside the attendant's hand as he attempted to stop him from touching his friend. Frenchy winced in pain.

Frenchy was quiet for a moment, then stirred and slowly opened his eyes.

"How you doin', man?"

"Okay, I guess," Frenchy replied.

"Got any idea what happened?" Smitty asked.

"Oh, yeah. Of all the stupid things for a man to do," Frenchy replied.

"What?"

"I was walking through the engine room, wasn't watching where I was going, and stepped on a two-inch socket wrench. I started to lose my balance and reached out for the nearest thing I could find," Frenchy said with a sigh. "I grabbed the chain that was part of the chainfall that was laying off the overhead valve. Goddamn thing came down on my head. Lucky I had my hard hat on."

"It sure was, you moron," Smitty said.

Noticing the ice bag around Smitty's ankle, Frenchy nodded down at the shoeless foot and said, "Et tu, Brute?"

"Same church, different pew. Slipped on a duct tube and sprained my ankle," Smitty said. "Like my dad once said, 'some days, boy, you're just ate up with the dumb ass.'"

"That must be why we get along so well; we're both stupid," Frenchy said.

"Yeah, that must be true," Smitty said. "LZ made it a clean sweep."

"What do you mean?"

"Seems that while you and I were doing our very best imitation of Koko the Clown, LZ was trying to do an ole' with an Olds."

"Is he all right?"

"Don't know. Guess we'll find out soon. They're taking him to the same hospital in a separate ambulance."

"Aw shit, man. Not a good day for the three musketeers."

"I think today we're more likely to be compared to the Three Stooges."

"Don't sweat it, man, it was just a series of dumb accidents that happened at the same time."

"You think?"

"Yeah, man, don't sweat it," Frenchy said, yawning before closing his eyes. But not before giving Smitty a knowing wink that the attendant didn't see.

LZ was lying on a gurney wide awake when Smitty and Frenchy were wheeled in. He raised himself up on one elbow, looked at the two of them sadly, and said, "You guys just couldn't stay away from me, could you? Just had to go and get yourself banged up so you could follow me here, didn't you?"

"Yeah, right, man," Frenchy said. "It's definitely a love thing. We just couldn't stand being without you." Noticing the ice pack attached to LZ's hip by an Ace bandage, Frenchy commented, "Looks like the car won."

"Yeah, but I dented it, man," LZ retorted.

"What happened?"

"Stepped in front of it when I turned to run back across the street," LZ said by way of explanation.

"What kind of car was it?" Smitty asked.

"Tell you the truth, I didn't have time to look. It hit me a glancing blow and took off. Guess they don't figure hitting black folks is a crime here in Georgia."

"They consider it sport in Louisiana," Frenchy said.

LZ's silent single digit did not require a verbal response.

Further conversation was cut off as they were separated and wheeled down the hall to examining rooms and on to X-ray. LZ's and Smitty's wounds were deemed superficial, and after being given crutches and prescriptions for pain, they were discharged. Frenchy was admitted for observation of possible concussion and would be released the next day if no further complications were found.

LZ and Smitty waited until Frenchy had been admitted and were on their way to his room when they were stopped by a local policeman.

"Sorry, boys, your friend is being questioned by detectives right now, and you can't go in."

"How long do you think it will be?" Smitty asked.

"Come back in an hour."

LZ and Smitty hopped to the hospital cafeteria. After the first few bites, Smitty decided that army chow was haute cuisine by comparison. They were not halfway through their meal when the officer entered with two detectives and pointed to them.

"Afternoon, boys," the younger detective said, as they both took the seats next to Smitty and LZ. "Wanted to get a little background information on y'all."

"What do you want to know?" LZ asked.

"Well, according to witnesses, the car that hit you had Florida plates; it was a tan Oldsmobile that seemed to start up and make a run directly at you before driving away. You wouldn't have any comment on that, would you?"

LZ and Smitty shook their heads.

"I see," the older detective said. "Don't suppose it could have anything to do with this?" He slid a paper in front of them and said, "I'll have to see your cards, boys."

They looked down to see a year-old photocopied newspaper article about the deaths in the Miami warehouse. LZ and Smitty each gave the article a cursory glance, as they slid out their false driver's licenses—Smitty's was from New York, LZ's from Michigan.

"Don't see what that's got to do with us," Smitty said indifferently. "We're just three ex-GI's working for a paycheck until we can figure out what we want to do with the rest of our lives."

"Got any idea why someone would want to run you down?" the older detective asked.

"Naw," LZ answered. "Lot of rednecks around the yard. Maybe I rubbed somebody the wrong way."

"Well, it's probably nothing, but we have to check. You know how it is," the younger detective said. He glanced at their driver's licenses and noted the numbers on a pad before passing them back.

"Got a tip, thought it might lead somewhere; had to check it out." The older detective stood up. "Be seein' ya, boys." He waved as he ambled away.

LZ and Smitty watched the two detectives leave. The older detective said something quickly to the uniformed officer and nodded in the direction of LZ and Smitty.

"We're fucked, man," LZ said with a trace of panic in his voice.

"Take it easy, partner. They're probably following up on a fits-the-description thing like they said," Smitty said. "Let's not give them any motive by doing something to validate their suspicions."

Forcing down the last of their tasteless meal, Smitty and LZ made their way back to Frenchy's room. The uniformed officer followed behind just close enough to keep them in sight.

They entered Frenchy's room and took seats on opposite sides of the bed. Smitty held up a finger to his lips and then picked up the telephone and held it to his ear. The message was clear: The room was bugged and they were being listened to. But by whom?

"So how's it going, partner?" LZ asked.

"I'm okay, man, I expect to be out of here tomorrow," Frenchy said.

"Great, man, we'll be by early to pick you up," Smitty said, searching the other side of the room.

"Don't show before ten o'clock, mon ami. There's a cute candy striper that volunteered to stop by and give me a bed bath. She said it would be a personal service and that she'd come in on her off day to do it especially for me."

"Hope she wears a body rubber," LZ retorted.

"Fuck you, man," Frenchy answered back.

Smitty waved them to silence. Under the bed frame, lodged in the spring was a small cylinder. Smitty got down on his hands and knees and craned his head around so that he could examine it closely. It looked to be about the size of a quarter and had pinholes on the face.

"What do you think?" Smitty wrote on a piece of paper and passed it across to Frenchy, who glanced at it and handed it to LZ.

"Let's pull it and see who shows up," LZ wrote.

"No way, man, let's leave it and keep up the show," Frenchy wrote under LZ's note.

Smitty thought, waved at Frenchy and LZ to get their attention, and said, "See you later, partner. My foot's starting to hurt, and I need to go back to our room and lie down. Come on, LZ, let Don Juan here get his rest. We'll be by to pick you up at 10:45 PM."

"You mean 10:45 AM, don't you?" LZ corrected.

"Oh, yeah, right. Don't want lover boy to miss his rubdown. Let's boogie, LZ," Smitty answered as he and LZ headed for the door with a final wave, but not before Smitty held up one finger and made a plus sign in the air; a gesture that Frenchy acknowledged silently in return.

With a wave to the policeman, Smitty and LZ pogo'd their way to the hospital exit and grabbed a cab back to their car at the shipyard. From there, they drove the '54 to the front of their rented rooms on Benton Street and went inside.

The one-bedroom apartment had three beds, two in the bedroom and a Murphy bed in the living room/kitchen. LZ and Smitty collapsed onto the two in the bedroom and were almost instantly asleep. But not before Smitty peeked surreptitiously out the window and saw a tan sedan with the two detectives in it slip quietly into a parking place across the street.

Four cars behind them, Smitty noticed another car slip unobtrusively into another parking spot, a dark Chevrolet. Somebody was keeping a very close eye on them. Who was in the other car that was watching the watchers? It was going to be a long night.

It was 11:30 PM when Smitty and LZ slipped quietly out of the rear entrance of the apartment building and walked directly away from the building for two blocks to Channel Street, before turning right one block onto Heard Street. Spotting a dark Chevrolet sedan, they walked straight to it, opened the rear doors, and slid quickly inside. They both seemed to have made a miraculous recovery from their earlier injuries. Smitty walked without the slightest trace of a limp, and LZ showed no traces of his earlier fandango with the GM tanko.

"Evening, boys," Major Jim said conversationally. "Thanks for the call."

"Are our tails still in place?" LZ asked.

"Right where you left them, in front of the apartment. And doing a dandy job of babysitting the police."

"Next time, tell those guys not to cut it so close," LZ said. "Or I really would have been hit."

"Will do," Jim said. "How's the 'sprained ankle' Smitty?"

"Hurts like hell," Smitty said with a grin. "Let's move; Frenchy's waiting."

"Nicely executed Plan B gents. Anyone looking for you will think you're incapacitated. Will Frenchy be ready?"

"I told him 11:45 PM this afternoon," Smitty responded.

The car moved off in silence. Inside of five minutes, they pulled to a stop two blocks from the hospital, the door opened, and Frenchy silently joined them in the backseat. He'd been given a sedative and would sleep through the night, according to his nurse, so no one would be checking on him until breakfast tomorrow morning. Fifteen minutes later, and they were parked a quarter mile from the shipyard. As they exited the car, Major Jim said, "Remember gentlemen, 'observe and report.'" He added as an afterthought, "And don't get dead."

They split up, each man going in a prearranged direction according to the instructions LZ had received when he'd phoned in that morning. They each carried a flashlight for signaling and a miniature set of folding binoculars, but no firearms. Major Jim felt that if they were caught, a trespassing story might hold, but not if they were armed. Also, the absence of weapons would again emphasize that this was an observe and report, not a shoot and escape mission.

The phony injuries, Jim felt, were necessary to get the innocent and the guilty off their tail. The innocent, in this case being the Savannah detectives who'd inadvertently—or maybe not so inadvertently—picked up a scent from the old photocopy in response to investigating the staged hit and run.

The guilty—well, Clev—couldn't very well suspect them if they all had perfect alibis, backed up by the shipyard medical records. Major Jim wasn't sure just who or what was involved but felt it best to err on the side of caution. For once, Smitty had to agree with him. Whatever the real detective or phony FBI guy was up to was unlikely to net him the good citizen of the year award.

Smitty climbed over a fence, reached his observation position, and settled down to wait. He had a clear view of the north end of the *Jesus Capri* and the gangway leading to and from the ship back across the yard toward the tool shack and the superintendent's office. The yard was well-lighted around the work areas but almost pitch dark in the areas in between. Based on what he'd overheard this morning, Smitty was sure that the introduction of the four bogus workers was not designed to look for the drugs, but to bring them out. Nothing like putting in a fox disguised as a chicken to take the eggs right from under the hens.

An hour passed, then two. Smitty was getting stiff, tired, and a little sleepy. He wondered if LZ, who was staged on the south end, and Frenchy, who was inside the yard, were feeling the same.

Surveillance, somebody once said, is hours of boredom, followed by days of tedium. He pondered this point at length. What was the real reason for the three of them being assigned to this mission?

Was it, as their training officer had said, to teach the power of diligence and success as a result of patience? Or did Ron already know that that asshole sergeant would be here and was he just dangling a carrot in front of his nose? Too much coincidence/too little truth for the facts to align by chance in this particular fashion. One thing was certain: Ron and Smitty were going to have to have a heart-to-heart on this in the very near future.

Smitty sat up suddenly and stared more intently. Down below, in yard work clothes, Detective Wallace had appeared from the hold of the ship, supervising the activities of four people as they unobtrusively off-loaded metal cartons that looked to be about the size of a moving box, but were labeled "spare parts—engine room." Although Smitty was one hundred yards away, Smitty could hear the night-carried voices plainly.

"Take these valves over to the machine shop to be serviced," Detective Wallace said to his helper.

"Yes, sir," the helper responded. "Okay if I have Mitch, Freddy, and Billy give me a hand? There's lots of them and they're kind of heavy."

"Yeah, okay," the detective said. "Just haul your asses back here as soon as you're done." It was done so nonchalantly that it did not arouse even the slightest suspicion in the workers around them. It also implied to Smitty that a routine this pat meant that they'd done this many times before.

Smitty watched as the boxes, twenty of them, were loaded carefully onto a flat rusty cart and wheeled away. He watched them disappear into the darkness alongside the dry-dock, then reappear next to a truck parked by the superintendent's office about two hundred yards away. They loaded the boxes into the truck casually.

Every move well-practiced, Smitty thought to himself. *This has got to be a professional operation. A well-established one.* The term "syndicate" suddenly leaped into Smitty's conscious thoughts like a four-year-old jumping up and down, flailing her arms and legs for her daddy's attention.

He thought back to Keith's statements about the peace between the gangs messing up a thriving business of selling drugs, alcohol, and weapons. But what if these were just the fronts for something more sinister? Who were the mysterious "friends" that Keith had referred to? If Clev was the dispatcher, who was the boss, and was there a boss of bosses? And how, or why, was Smitty standing dead center in the middle? More thought and more digging on his own would be required, but not now.

Smitty was just about to signal Major Jim with his flashlight to take over the tracking, when something else caught his attention. The yard superintendent appeared at the top of the gangway carrying a box about the size of a notebook under his arm. The box was made of metal painted a nondescript gray and had a hinge on one side and a lock built into the other side. It wasn't a keyed lock, it was one of those fancy combination spin locks, the kind you'd find on a diplomatic attaché's secure documents box. He hustled down the gangway and quietly handed the box to the detective, who nodded wordlessly and, making no attempt to open it or conceal it, tucked the box under his arm and walked away into the dark.

Smitty wondered about the contents of that box. That the detective hadn't tried to open it implied to Smitty that he already knew what was inside.

Smitty signaled to the major, who signaled him to return. As he was making his way back to the car, he saw the detective exit at the yard's gate, get into a car with the box tucked under his arm, and drive away alone in a southerly direction.

Smitty reached the car and reported this latest finding to the major—prudently withholding his own observations—who nodded in understanding, made a note in his book, and used a car phone to call for a tail on the detective and his men.

The twenty crates had been loaded on a truck inside the yard and were driven out with a yard pass previously signed by the yard superintendent. The truck turned north on exiting the shipyard and was soon lost from sight.

"A good night's work, men," Major Jim said, as they rode back to the hospital. "We've tracked and charted the movement of the shipments very well. I'll consolidate your individual reports and send in my final report. You did very well at observing and reporting." Then he added with a dry smile, "And you didn't get dead."

"And for once you didn't leave a catastrophe in your wake," he added without expression. "There's hope for you morons yet."

Taking no chances that their cover identities had been compromised, Major Jim aborted the mission and ordered Smitty, Frenchy, and LZ back to Bragg for resumption of normal training activity. He told them, in no uncertain terms, that they were not to discuss their midnight rendezvous with anyone else, ever.

When they left Savannah that same morning, Major Jim assured them that there were no loose ends to tie up. As the super had said, such comings and goings of the non-union, workload-balancing scabs were commonplace.

Whatever suspicions the Savannah police might have had apparently were not sufficient to warrant their being detained. While Frenchy was tossing their bags in the back of the '54, the two detectives drove up, seemingly accepted their explanation of drifting north to Virginia to the Roanoke-Norfolk area where there was more yard work with better pay, wished them well, and drove away. The major said a replacement team would be dispatched; he did not say from where.

Smitty was sure that this mission had been a success. What bothered him was that he wasn't exactly sure what they had accomplished. Obviously there was badness afoot, but they hadn't done anything about it except observe and report. Smitty hoped that "They also serve, who only stand and wait" was a true adage. He was sure that their assignment was important to Colonel Wilson: maybe a test of patience, maybe a yardstick for their future survival.

But it had hurt to let that bastard detective drive away. Smitty vowed to himself that he'd see him again . . . if the detective didn't see him first.

"Fort fucking Rucker," LZ said. "What the hell are we doing at this shithole?"

"Orders, mon ami," Frenchy said. "Besides, it's only for four weeks until we 'officially' turn nineteen. Then, like Captain Bartkowski said when he left, we'll get our orders for Nam. Can't send us to a combat zone until we're nineteen and officially old enough to go and be killed; it would be uncivilized."

"Yeah, not old enough to vote or drink but old enough to die," LZ added. "Fuck man, it's almost Christmas, and we didn't even draw leave. Stuck on an army base is bad enough, but to be stuck in the southern part of that racist fucker Wallace's country really sucks."

"If we had leave, where would you go?" Smitty asked. He couched his remarks carefully. Since they'd returned from their special mission in Savannah in midfall, LZ's attitude had seemed to be getting progressively worse. For a man with an excellent vocabulary, LZ was using a lot of repetitive profanity.

Smitty thought LZ was scared; not physically scared but mentally. The kind of scared that makes you sweat in the middle of the night; the kind of scared that comes from imagining the unknown . . . the kind of scared that the fear of Vietnam was arousing in Smitty himself.

Frenchy was just the opposite. The mission in Savannah had seemed to settle him down. Unlike LZ, who had more aptitude, Frenchy was completing his training almost as if on nylon bearings, while LZ was suddenly laboring to get his certification.

Smitty was somewhere in the middle. The Savannah sidebar had seemed to calm his outwardly raging feelings, but the brush with the detective sergeant and the confirmation that there was something there had seemed to give him an inner determination that had been missing in his life. He now understood patience, and had suddenly figured out that he did not have to seek his unknown adversary. It was headed for him at breakneck speed; all he had to do was figure out how to keep from getting killed in the resulting head-on collision.

"Fuck you, man," LZ said. "I sure as hell would get the fuck away from all this army green shit." Pausing to shake his head in disgust at no one in particular, he continued, "Stuck for Christmas in dumb-shit Alabama. I don't know how I ever let you talk me into this. I'll probably get my ass shot off in Vietnam. And for what? A bunch of fuckin' gooks."

"We do get a three-day Christmas leave," Frenchy said quietly. "We could split down to my parents' place in Biloxi, just up the road from New Orleans. Should be a good time happening there."

"Yeah right, I'm sure I'll fit right in," LZ continued in the same dour tone as before.

"Well, there's always the other alternative," Smitty said.

"What's that?" LZ asked.

"Well, like Frenchy said a few months back, we could put you out in the middle of the roadway and see how good the locals are at hitting you," Smitty said, deadpan.

"Fuck you, cocksuckers," LZ said. Turning and seeing Frenchy doubled up in laughter in the backseat, he said in a cooler voice, "Dumb motherfuckers probably couldn't hit a moving target if they tried."

LZ lapsed into silence. They were forty miles from Rucker and the '54 was performing like a badly out-of-tune circus calliope.

In addition to the normal bangs, squeaks, and rattles, the old Chevy had now developed a thump deep inside the engine, which Smitty suspected was a rod knock. Additionally, the "normal" three quarts of fifty-weight oil now had to be supplemented with two cans of STP to enrich the viscosity. It seemed that the old car now ran more on goo than oil, but she ran. Each day that passed put them a day closer to when the Famous '54 would no longer be required. The war would be there waiting for them and for Special Forces; it had been for some time.

It was December 19, 1967, and their training was complete. Smitty thought how ironic an anniversary date it was. It was just six years ago, almost to the day, that a seven-man Special Forces Group had gone active to train a group of local tribesman called "Yards" in Buon Enao in Vietnam.

Ron had been right. They no longer had a need for their cherished switchblades. They were specialists now, cross-trained in counter-insurgency warfare. They knew how to destroy the armaments and facilities used in war and were able to set a charge to destroy a found ammo cache or a bridge. They were also now specialists in how to destroy human life, with a weapon of war in a conventional manner or in the dark of night, silently with a piano wire around the throat of an unsuspecting sentry.

The Savannah mission was the graduate course in the art of patience and finesse. After that mission had been completed in October, they had returned to Bragg by Halloween. The training regimen had not slowed; if anything it had intensified. Completion was to be accomplished by mid-December. The requirements of their individual training meant that Smitty, LZ, and Frenchy were again very seldom together during the last months as each honed his skill specialty to a razor-sharp edge.

The boyish bluster of street gang youth was gone so completely that it was almost as if it had existed in another lifetime, in other people entirely. In its place was a quiet confidence, a confidence in themselves that came from actions trained and rehearsed until they had become instincts—instincts that, as Ron had said, would help them to survive Vietnam.

With Ron's rotation back to Vietnam, the training NCOs and their own level of progress easily took up the slack so that he was not missed. They no longer needed Ron; they were now the trainers—at least in their own minds. Ron had departed with a good-bye note signed at the bottom with the time honored-soldiers' farewell, "Hope we soldier together again sometime." Given the events to date, Smitty was certain of it—and they still had to have that little talk.

After all of the hoopla of becoming a Green Beanie, the graduation itself was as acute an understatement as sending Miss Universe to a Playboy photo shoot in a sack dress. There was no parade, no band, just a simple formation and a short speech by the battalion colonel that ended with a formal salute and a curt dismissal. Of the six hundred who had started six months before, only 150 had graduated. Of those, approximately sixty received their orders for Vietnam immediately, with the report dates varying from ten to thirty days.

Some of those remaining were being siphoned off for further specialized training. The rest, like Smitty, LZ, and Frenchy, were given holding assignments, ostensibly to be followed by thirty days of leave, until their birthdays coincided with the army's decree on when they could go to war.

It took an hour to cover the last thirty miles in stop-and-go traffic. They pulled up to the gate at Fort Rucker, got a pass, and proceeded to post operations to check in. They were assigned to the same barracks room with a fourth person who was not in the room when they stowed their gear. After traveling close to fourteen hours to get from Fayettenam to Rucker in their old rattletrap, they were asleep almost before the lights were out.

"Wakey, wakey, guys," a familiar voice said enthusiastically. After a moment or so it clicked, and Smitty sat bolt upright in the top bunk to find himself staring eyeball to eyeball with Big Walt, the fourth musketeer.

"Where the hell did you come from?" Smitty asked, reaching out and ruffling the big fellow's crewcut, and throwing his pillow at LZ, who was still asleep in the top bunk across from him.

"Somebody's got to look after you big bad Green Beanies, so I volunteered," the big boy said in his high-pitched voice.

"Oh, shit, it's the Jolly Green Fucking Giant," LZ said sleepily. He propped himself up on one arm, grabbed Smitty's pillow with the other, wound up, and fired the pillow back at the big guy like a Bob Gibson fastball. "I thought we were rid of your big dumb ass," He lay back down and closed his eyes.

"How you doin', mon ami?" Frenchy asked from the lower berth.

"Frenchy!" Big Walt squealed in delight.

"What are you doin' here, man?" Smitty asked, hopping down from his bunk and shaking hands with the big guy.

"Same as you guys, I'm waitin' my time out to head to Nam."

"I thought your eyesight made you ineligible for combat," Frenchy said.

"Still does. I'm headed there as an MP. Major Jim arranged it. Got me promoted to private first class, too. Look," Walt said, pointing proudly at his sleeve.

"That's great Walt, just great," Smitty said. His earlier assessment had been right. This was a much more confident Walt. Obviously, the stutter must have been related to his confidence, since he seemed to have no hint of one now.

"Cured your stutter, too," Smitty added.

"Now if the army could just do something about your mousy little six-year-old girl's voice, we'd all be happy," LZ said, turning over in his rack.

Reacting with catlike agility that Smitty did not know he had, Big Walt grabbed LZ by the arm and right leg and plucked him out of the top bunk.

"LZ, I don't like it when people make fun of my voice," Big Walt said, turning and dropping him on his feet.

"Let go, man!" LZ said heatedly, rapping Big Walt on the wrist with his knuckles. "You don't know your own strength." He rubbed his arm to restore circulation.

"Sorry," Big Walt responded sheepishly.

Seeing Big Walt's wounded look, LZ's softened. "It's okay, big guy; I know you meant well."

Smitty and Frenchy watched in silence. LZ had struck a chord that had caused the big guy to react instinctively. It confirmed to Smitty that the maturation of Big Walt in the army was having a side effect. A side effect, that, if left unchecked, like a cancer would only grow over time.

"So you're headed out, too." Frenchy broke the awkward silence.

"Just like you guys, I'm here for helicopter orientation training," Big Walt said. "In fact, Major Jim told me to stick with you guys and keep you out of trouble. "

"There goes the fuckin' neighborhood," LZ said with a grin. Big Walt grinned back.

The four musketeers were together again and apparently destined for the same path. Only time would tell whether they were destined for the same end.

"That was one great weekend, guys," LZ said, settling back in the '54 and lighting a cigarette. "Frenchy, your parents are cool people, and that girlfriend of yours, bitchin."

"Thanks, mon ami, I'm glad you had a good time. My folks enjoyed the visit too. I think it makes them feel better to know that I have good friends around me, especially considering where we're all headed."

"The four musketeers." Big Walt held up his hand.

His hand was quickly joined by LZ's, Frenchy's, and Smitty's. They clasped hands tightly, feeling the emotion pass through them and knew that they would be friends forever.

"Boy, your mom sure can cook," Smitty said, breaking the moment and returning his hand to the steering wheel. "And you didn't tell me about that sister of yours."

"With good reason. She ain't for the likes of you," Frenchy shot back.

"Oh, I don't know, there's a lot there to tempt a man," Smitty said.

"Fortunately, she doesn't look a thing like him," LZ said, jerking his thumb in Frenchy's direction.

As expected, Frenchy gave him the single digit.

"Good hunters eat what they shoot," Big Walt said.

"And that's for your horse, fat boy." Frenchy turned his digit sideways.

They all laughed together. It had been a good three-day leave.

Frenchy had insisted that they all come to his parents' house for Christmas. Smitty and LZ were hesitant at first, but Frenchy's perseverance soon won them over. Smitty was glad it had. He'd eaten better than he had in a year. And if he'd gained five pounds, Big Walt must have gained ten. Smitty'd never in his life seen anyone eat so much.

Frenchy's parents took them to a Christmas buffet at an all-you-can-eat place. About halfway through the meal, Smitty looked down the table at Big Walt's plate. He had chicken legs stacked like cordwood in rows of three. Smitty counted seven stacks, which totaled twenty-one legs, and that was before he started on the potatoes—absolutely incredible. Smitty now believed that Big Walt's parents must have put him in the army because they couldn't afford to feed him.

Frenchy had lived up to his reputation with the female sex, arranging dates for them all that seemed to fit their characters. LZ had a date with a beautiful black college student who was a friend of his sister. Big Walt was fixed up with a girl who seemed to be entranced with his squealing laugh. Frenchy reconnected with his lost love, Sondra, a former beauty contest winner. Smitty was left the "duty" of taking out Frenchy's sister, Trudy, a truly beautiful brunette college sophomore who had the same high cheekbones and beautiful clear complexion as her mother.

They were pretty much an eightsome for the weekend, cramming all four couples into the '54, with the girls sitting on the guys' laps, except for Frenchy, who did most of the driving with Sondra snuggling close by his side.

Smitty discovered Trudy had a playful side when she wiggled her butt against his crotch while sitting on his lap. The more Smitty tried to hide it, the more it became apparent that she turned him on.

Trudy laughed at his predicament, put her arm around his neck and whispered in his ear, "It's okay, you turn me on, too." With her head buried in Smitty's neck, nibbling on his ear, she took his other hand and unobtrusively slid it under her skirt and placed his hand against her wet panties.

When they were alone in the den of Frenchy's house, Trudy wanted things to go further, but Smitty was hesitant. His hesitancy ended when Trudy said she understood his reluctance, she being his buddy's sister and all. Then she stood up, removed all of her clothes, and stood naked before him. She walked into his arms while at the same time unzipping his pants. They made love passionately, the fact that she was Frenchy's sister totally lost in the suppleness of her sinewy and sexy body.

"Hey, bro, what you thinking about?" Frenchy gave him a playful nudge. "You been fuckin' my sister," he said in best Pancho Villa imitation.

This was the first time he had spoken about the events of the weekend since they had left his parents' house six hours ago. They were well into Alabama now, with still about an hour left until they were back at Rucker.

"Yeah, right," Smitty answered. But, in point of fact, that was just what he was thinking about. She was definitely Frenchy's sister; she had the same lust for life and was as beautiful in the female way as Frenchy was handsome, when compared to his masculine counterparts.

She had told Smitty that she was almost a virgin, almost meaning she had only been with one other guy in high school—a drunken high school prom thing that Smitty could certainly identify with, and was by no means promiscuous, and furthermore, would never go this far under normal conditions.

But she had heard about Smitty and LZ from her brother for years, and had formed a secret crush on him as a younger teenager—a crush that, on seeing him in reality, had freed her inhibitions. She had promised to write, and Smitty had promised to write in return. When they parted, she had unobtrusively slipped a pair of her panties into his pocket with a cooing admonition to come back and have them filled—anytime.

"So what if I have," Smitty said.

"You have been fucking my sister. I knew it," Frenchy said in the same accent, slapping his thigh with delight. "Hey, man, it's cool, Trudy's a big girl. What you two do ain't none of my business. Besides, it would kind of be hypocritical of me, considering that Sondra and I broke the bed the other night."

"Bragger," Walt said with grin. "Besides, you act like you're the only one who got laid."

"Our boy has lost his cherry. There'll be no living with this stud now; man will turn into a rapist," LZ said, shaking his head.

"So, did you, mon ami?" LZ's smile was answer enough.

"The four musketeers," Big Walt yelled, holding up his hand, which was immediately joined by the other three.

"Hey man, let's celebrate our common studness by stopping for something to drink," Big Walt said.

"And eat," Frenchy added.

"Good idea," Smitty said. "We need to oil up the old girl anyway. We're still twenty miles from the base."

"There's a spot," Frenchy said suddenly, pointing to a rundown older bar and grill that, according to the sign, had "good food, good beer, and good music."

Smitty noticed the preponderance of dusty pickup trucks as they pulled into the parking lot. They were mostly older Fords and Chevys. Judging by the number of cars in the parking lot, this had to be the happening place in Shithole, Alabama.

"Walt," Smitty said, flipping him the trunk key. "Your turn to oil the old lady. Give her two quarts and a can of STP."

"Can do. I'll be right behind you; order me a beer."

Smitty acknowledged Big Walt's request with a wave. He crossed the parking lot and held the door open to the greasy spoon for first LZ, then Frenchy to enter.

The wall of noise coming from a four-piece country band was the first thing Smitty noticed as they entered. He had barely gotten adjusted to this, when the music suddenly stopped and the room went totally quiet.

They had walked approximately ten feet, when LZ turned, held up his hands in a police crowd control fashion, and said conversationally in a loud voice, "Sorry, boys, I don't think they like poor white trash in their bars."

They made their way to three vacant bar stools and took seats. As LZ sat down, the woman next to him, who had a face like a badly tanned cowhide and a body that looked like what was left of the cow, got up and moved away to a table. Murmurs began at the tables and ceased immediately when Big Walt came through the door. Spotting his friends, he made his way through the crowd, who parted like a herd of cattle for a cowboy drover.

Every eye in the place was on them, or to be more precise, on LZ. The bartender had backed away from the front of the bar, making no attempt to serve them, and seemed to be looking at a man in his forties seated at a table just behind them.

Slowly the man, who could have been the proprietor, the mayor, or just the lead redneck, got to his feet and walked around his table and stood directly in front of LZ. He touched LZ on the shoulder roughly. "Hey, boy, we don't allow no niggers in our bars."

LZ spun around on the bar stool, shaking off the man's arm in the process. "No problem, gramps. Just soon as I find one, I'll throw that black son of a bitch outta here."

"I'm a-talking about you, boy."

"Demander pardon, enculé," LZ said, using the correct French pronunciation. "But I'm not a nigger."

"Jus' what are you then, boy?"

"I am a Mulatto," LZ retorted. "Black mother, poor white trash Alabama shit-kicker father, but Mama tries to keep that part quiet. She doesn't wish to besmirch our family name." He spun back around on the bar stool, slapped the bar twice with his open hand. "Innkeeper, a glass of your best."

"Why, you smart-ass nigger," the older man said, reaching out to grab LZ by the shoulder. Sensing his action, LZ spun around and caught the out-of-shape racist with a judo smash to the throat with his elbow. He dropped like a fifty-pound bag of fresh Alabama cow manure.

The man's drinking mate stood up and immediately joined his friend on the floor, thanks to a well-placed kick in the balls, courtesy of Frenchy's size tens. The two guys at the next table stood and ran toward the foursome only to be returned like two Rod Laver smashed tennis balls, courtesy of Smitty and Big Walt. Although their styles were decidedly different, the result was the same.

Smitty handled his efficiently with a three-punch judo combination to the nose, ribs, and neck that dropped his adversary in two seconds flat. Big Walt showed no such finesse: he simply reared back and backhanded his antagonist with such force that he air-mailed him across a table, which collapsed from the weight, sending beer glasses, dinner plates, cutlery, and condiments smashing to the floor.

Things became kaleidoscopic. The rednecks advanced like a stampeding herd and were dropped as they came into range of the vastly better-trained foursome. The bar-room melee lasted nearly two minutes. The score at the end of the fight was army sixteen, Alabama shit-kickers zero.

Among them, the rednecks had a pretty catholic assortment of injuries. The wounds inflicted by Smitty, LZ, and Frenchy reflected their recent intensive training: mostly pressure points related to collarbones, knees, kidneys, and balls. Big Walt's combatants, on the other hand, were easily distinguishable by the outwardly visible carnage. Broken noses, dislocated jaws, and a few missing teeth made it easy to pick the unfortunates who had come within hailing distance of his huge right hand. The four musketeers did not, however, get off free; Big Walt did break a fingernail.

In colloquial army terms, they kicked ass and took names. As they hurriedly left the bar and unassed the area, the full implication of what had just occurred began to dawn on Smitty. Months of specialized military training and pent up frustration had just been vented. Smitty knew that the army's version of kicking ass and taking names on them was yet to come.

It wasn't long in coming; in fact it came approximately thirty-five minutes later, the time it took the four of them to reach the safe confines of the base driving the Famous '54 at a top speed of seventy-two mph, which was all the old girl had to give. No sooner had they driven through the Fort Rucker gate than the shit hit the fan. Two Jeeps, with four MPs riding in them, met them at the gate and led them straight to the provost marshal's office. Do not pass go, do not collect your two hundred dollars, Smitty thought resignedly as they were "escorted" inside and were motioned with batons to take seats against the wall.

"Good evening, gentlemen," a familiar voice said. The officer strutted briskly into the room, removed his cap and tucked it formally under his arm. "As soon as I was notified by the local police of the near-destruction of a local establishment, somehow a vision of you three gentleman came into my head, although apparently you have acquired a fourth member of your merry little band." He looked at Big Walt with disdain. "And lowered your standards somewhat, as well.

"Obviously my attempts to counsel you back in Washington fell on deaf ears." He turned away, not seeing Big Walt's middle-finger salute. "You preferred, I suppose, to listen to the bravado of that air force major general who, for reasons I cannot begin to fathom, has taken a personal interest in you gentlemen, especially one of you.

"When I attempted to intervene on your behalf, he had his brother transfer me to this hellhole, and my promotion to lieutenant colonel was frozen until such time as I had acquired field, and God forbid, actual combat command experience."

"Who is this fucker?" Big Walt interjected. "Dwight Five-Star Fucking Eisenhower?" Smitty realized that the big boy was acquiring a confidence that now bordered on arrogance, and unfortunately, he also had the mouth that went with it.

The pacer executed a precision about-face and marched three steps back to Big Walt. "Major William P. Gates Jr., at your service, you cretin."

Instinctively Big Walt started to rise from his chair, but Smitty's restraining hand on his shoulder halted him, much to the relief of the major and the MPs in the room, who, it seemed, were not looking forward to the prospect of trying to put the big fellow down.

"Major Cluster-Gerbil to you, Walt," Smitty said.

"Or Major Feces-Eating Cluster-Gerbil if you want to be formal," LZ chimed in.

"I see you gentlemen have not lost any of your rapier wit. I only hope you are able to maintain it in the trials that lie ahead," the major said.

"Like for instance?" Frenchy inquired.

"Like for instance?" he mimicked. "Since I am the camp staff adjutant to the base commander, the recommendation for proper military disposition will be made by me and no doubt rubber-stamped by the general. You had a chance to make a career for yourselves in the military if you had listened to me; now it's too late.

"My recommendation will be for immediate court-martial on conduct unbecoming, a dishonorable discharge, and time in Leavenworth, if it's within my power. I assure you, gentlemen, your two-star blue-suit pull will not save you now.

"The damage you've done to the community goodwill in this area will be with us long after you gentleman are disposed of. You've crossed the line; the army frowns on this kind of conduct. We are professional soldiers, not brawling hooligans."

Stopping to survey them, he added, "Although from what I read in your files that's all you gentlemen are capable of."

"Well there goes my VA money for college," LZ cracked. "Harvard's gonna be pissed."

"Humor to the end, gentlemen. How self-defeating and puerile."

Through all of Major Dipshit's oratory, Smitty had been leaning back in his chair balanced on two legs with his back against the wall, thinking quietly. This looked pretty much like the no-way-out situation that Dad had spoken of many years ago. But Dad always said, "As long as a man keeps thinking and reasoning, he has a chance; when he stops, he has none." Smitty was trying hard to think logically, but there didn't seem to be a logical solution to this mess. The major held all the cards; hell, he owned the deck.

A sudden thought flashed through Smitty, like a lightning bolt hitting the same spot twice, which was not logical. Maybe it was illogical enough to work. Pulling it off would require the complete cooperation of the other three musketeers and was solely dependent on their ability to pick up a fast cue. Major Shit-Eater had to pick it up, too.

"Well, boys, we pulled it off," Smitty said, suddenly rocking forward in his chair and slapping his hands in obvious glee. He winked at his three friends in a way that he hoped said, "Follow me."

"Pulled off what?" the major asked.

"The plan."

"What plan?" the major asked, giving Smitty a withering glare.

"The plan," LZ answered. "Don't tell this motherfucker about the plan!"

"Why not?" Frenchy replied. "It's too late for him to do anything about it now. We've executed our part; now all the army has to do is follow through."

"Yeah, even Major Feces Eater couldn't stop it now," Big Walt joined in. "Remember what he just said. We've crossed the line, there'll be no turning back now."

"Would you gentlemen be so good as to tell me what on earth you are talking about?" the major demanded.

Smitty glanced first at Frenchy, and received his approving nod, then at Big Walt and received an even more enthusiastic nod. Smitty turned back to his left to LZ, who threw up his hands in capitulation and said sourly, "Go ahead. You seem bound and determined to anyway. But I warn you, you're gonna blow it."

"Sergeant," the major asked.

"Well, you see, Cluster Butt," Smitty said. "We aren't as dumb as you seem to think we are. We know that the army's going to ship our asses to Vietnam and that it's better than a fifty-fifty chance that none of us will ever come back any way but toe-tagged.

"As the old expression says, better to live a hundred years as a coward than one year as a hero."

"I think it's the other way around, Sergeant," the major interrupted. "I think the expression is, it's better to die on your feet than live a lifetime on your knees."

"Whatever," Smitty said. "Anyway, we figured out the army's Achilles' heel. Since we don't want to go get zapped halfway around the world for a bunch of slopes, we came up with this little plan to avoid going. Like you yourself said, Major, we'll get courts', an undesirable, and maybe a couple of years busting big rocks down to little ones, but at least we'll be alive; we're not like those other dumb-ass sheep that will go get slaughtered. Then we can just drift on back to Miami and our station in life. For our level of subsistence, a prison sentence is actually a plus. It will give us a reputation; nefarious reputations may be a detriment in your world, but they're vitally important if you have to survive in ours."

"I see," the major said, although it was clearly evident that he didn't. "I see," he repeated, obviously mulling their plan over in his mind and wondering what he could do to thwart it. He paced back and forth several times, rubbing his chin thoughtfully. He stopped as if he'd made a decision, shook his head, and resumed his back and forth mini-sentry walk.

A minute passed, then two. Smitty was sure that the major was determined not to let them get away with their plan. He wanted to do to them maximum harm while doing minimum damage to the army.

The major stopped in front of Smitty and snapped his fingers. "I'm afraid I'm not going to be able to allow you boys to carry out your coward's scheme."

"What do you mean?" Frenchy asked.

"You thought you were going to get out of going to Vietnam; well, you're not." He smiled smugly, warming to his task. "By noon tomorrow, I'll have orders cut for the four of you. Immediate change of duty stations to Fort Lewis, Washington; then on-site camp containment pending first available transport to Vietnam. Once you're there, I will personally recommend that you gentlemen be assigned to the hottest areas.

"You are, after all, as you've so recently proven, our best-trained soldiers. I think it would only be fitting and proper for you to use this expertise in a fashion that benefits the army. Then we'll see how tough you gentlemen really are when you have to fight against personnel as well-trained as yourselves."

"But what about our court-martial and pacifying the locals, and shit like that?" Walt asked.

"I can assure you boys that the general will be able to more than pacify the locals when he informs them that your punishment is being sent directly to Vietnam. Good night, boys; oh, and nice try. Too bad it didn't work," the major said cheerfully. He clapped on his hat and left the room.

As they were being led to a holding cell, LZ said, "Yeah, sure is too bad it didn't work; guess that major's just too smart for lower life forms like us."

"Man that arch was something," LZ said in an appreciative voice. "Too bad it wasn't summer, we could have gone to see Bob Gibson pitch. That dude sure can bring it."

"Yeah, wouldn't have been bad at that," Smitty commented.

"But, at least we got to see the stadium and beat it out of town before the snow came," Frenchy added.

"And we got to go to Las Vegas and went to that whorehouse where we got laid legally," Big Walt said. "Well, at least LZ and I did. You two were too chicken to go in."

"We weren't as desperate," Frenchy corrected.

"Disneyland was neat, too," Walt said.

"Personally, I like San Francisco," LZ said. "What was your favorite part of the trip, Smitty?"

"Watching Big Walt select his lady in Nevada," Smitty answered, eliciting a laugh from everyone but Big Walt.

"Yeah," Big Walt replied, "and what about that Alamo thing in San Antonio . . ."

His friends continued to relive their cross-country experiences as they drove from Fort Lewis to Seattle, but Smitty had tuned them out. It had been quite a trip, and it had been quite unexpected.

True to his word, the major had been diligent in cutting their orders the next day. What he had not counted on was the fact that no sooner was the ink dry on the official orders, than the four of them were given fifteen-day passes with a reporting date of January 10, 1968, to Fort Lewis. Typically, the leave was thirty days, but in their special case, according to the major, they should consider themselves lucky that they got any at all.

It had something to do with a policy of a leave before shipment to a hazardous duty zone. Using the same logic, or illogic, that they had two weeks for one last chance at having a good time, they cashed in their airline travel vouchers, invested two days, plus the weekend in the Famous '54 and set out to drive to their destination, stopping at points of interest along the way.

The Famous '54 now looked rather docile in comparison to its former self. The four of them had worked on the old car with a vengeance at the base garage at Fort Rucker before leaving. The multicolor paint scheme had been replaced by a shiny metallic purple enamel. The rusty grille and bumpers had been painted white, and the engine now ran like a sewing machine, thanks to a quick overhaul. It no longer smoked, although it did still use the occasional quart of oil, but at least it was thirty-weight, and not the sludge of before. Additionally, they put four recaps on, did a brake job, and replaced the shocks and steering components. Together, doing all the labor themselves, they invested three hundred dollars in the old girl, who now looked and ran more like a sweet old lady humming a church hymn than the caterwauling old crone of before.

All the rework was intent on helping the car withstand the rigors of a cross-country trip across mountains and deserts in forced-march time. They planned on selling her to some soldier at Fort Lewis, figuring that they would recoup their investment.

The trip itself had been something that Smitty would always remember. In eleven days, they'd logged close to thirty-five hundred miles going first to New Orleans, then to Frenchy's for a good-bye with his parents—and passionate good-bye kisses and more from their respective ladies.

From there they headed straight north to St. Louis, then doubled back to San Antonio, crossed Texas to El Paso, crossed the border into Mexico, then drove on through Arizona to Tombstone, Los Angeles, and San Francisco, arriving at Fort Lewis on January 12.

The fact that they were two days late checking in didn't seem to bother anyone at all. There was some light scolding but not much else was said.

It was now January 17, and their current status was unassigned, waiting for transport to Vietnam. With the current buildup in progress, they expected to depart within a week. They were told just to keep out of trouble until then by the relocation office and to check in every morning should a transport spot open.

"Hey man, did you hear what I said?" Frenchy asked, touching Smitty lightly on the arm.

"Uh, what?" Smitty responded absently.

"I said, how far is it to Seattle?" Frenchy repeated.

"I don't know. The relo officer said it's about forty-five minutes, so that must make it about the same in miles,"

"What's the name of this place we're going tonight?" Big Walt asked.

"For the third time, the Space Needle, you big dork," LZ said, more than a trace of impatience in his voice. "It's the place where they held the World's Fair in '62 and where Elvis made that movie."

"Okay, okay, don't be so touchy, LZ," Big Walt said.

"Relax, mes amis, we haven't left yet."

Nobody responded to Frenchy's remark, but everyone knew what he meant. The waiting was the worst part. As bad as it was for the three of them, Smitty thought the idle time was the worst on him.

The short time they had been in Washington was too long as far as Smitty was concerned. Frenchy, LZ, and Big Walt had families to write and call. But other than Trudy, Smitty had no one. He couldn't, no make that wouldn't, call his father, and only God knew if he and Mom were still together.

Smitty wondered idly about his brother, wondered if he was happy with Leslie and marriage. Come to that he wondered about the concept of marriage itself. Sure must be nice to get laid every night, but must get kind of boring too, same woman and all.

"What you thinkin' about, bro?" LZ asked, sitting forward and resting his head on his crossed arms on the back of the front seat.

"Oh, I was just thinking about my family. Wondering how they're getting on, even my dumb-shit brother," Smitty said.

"Yeah, it's funny, I've been thinking about my mom," LZ said. "At times like this, you kind of think of them, don't you?"

"You sure do, brother," Frenchy said. He added, "I miss Sondra."

"And I miss Gillian, the girl Trudy introduced me to," Big Walt said with a soft smile.

Smitty smiled to himself. One of the "and more" things that Trudy had given him was a generous tuft of her pussy hair which she snipped off and gave him in a plastic wallet photo envelope that also contained a picture of her in a white micro bikini in which her nipples were clearly visible. On the back of the picture she had written, *37-22-35 inches of hot woman waiting exclusively for you when you get home, Your girl, Trudy.*

"Hey guys, what say when we get back to the base, we all pose for a picture and send it to the folks," Big Walt said.

"Yeah, let's do that," Frenchy agreed.

Smitty and LZ were quiet. LZ smiled sympathetically when Smitty caught his eye in the rearview mirror. He knew that Smitty would not be sending any pictures home; he also knew how much Smitty wished he could.

"Yeah, let's do that," LZ said.

They lapsed into silence, not saying much of anything until they reached World's Fair Park in Seattle.

"Forty-five minutes, guys," the elevator man said. "That's the waiting time to go up for dinner if you don't have a reservation. Here's your number. When they call group seven, up you go. I'm sorry, I can't do anything until then."

"Forty-five minutes," Frenchy said. "Guess we could walk around the park until then."

Frenchy took the group card and they wandered away. There wasn't much left of what had been the World's Fair. The Space Needle and the monorail were the main attractions still there, with a few assorted amusement rides thrown in. As usual, it was raining.

One of the guys in the repo barracks was from Tacoma; he had said that with all the rain they got around here, that cars did not rot, like in snowy climates—they moldered. In the five days they had been there, it had rained every single day—a clammy, misting rain that left you damp to the skin and chilled to the bone.

For want of anything better to do, they took the monorail to Pine Street and walked around downtown for thirty minutes before returning to the monorail station. They were just walking up to the ramp, when LZ suddenly grabbed Smitty and Frenchy by the arms, and shoved them into a business door recess. Seeing the three of them duck for cover, Big Walt followed suit.

"Look," LZ said in a low voice, pointing with a slight nod of his head in the direction of the monorail station.

"I don't see anything," Frenchy said, attempting to shake himself free of LZ's vise-like grip as he surveyed the station.

"Look at the top of the ramp; at the two people talking."

"What the fuck?"

Standing at the top of the ramp in line to buy tickets back to the Space Needle were Major Cluster-Gerbil Gates and Clev Clayborne, AKA Detective Wallace.

"What in the name of God are they doing here?" Smitty wondered aloud. "Too much coincidence for it not to be on purpose."

"What say we go find out?" Big Walt balled up his fist and started to move off.

"Hold it!" Smitty whispered, stopping Big Walt in his tracks. "We need to find out what's up without letting them know we know. Remember Savannah; observe and report, observe and report."

"And no catastrophes," LZ said echoing Jim's words.

Smitty stood in silence, shivering in the cold Seattle mist. How in God's name did they both get here? Were they following them, or was it coincidence? One thing was for sure: they had to find out, and find out quickly without being discovered, and, as Major Jim was fond of saying, "without getting dead."

"Frenchy, you and the big boy here tail them. Get on the last car, and for Christ's sake, don't be seen. LZ, you and I will grab a cab, and get there before they do and tail them from the front when they arrive at the park. Move out smartly, gentlemen, and don't get dead. If we get separated, meet back at the car as soon as you can," Smitty said.

Smitty and LZ flagged a yellow car for hire and they dove in the back even before the car had rolled to a stop. "We need to be at the Space Needle before the monorail gets there. I'll add an extra five to the meter if you can make it," Smitty told the driver.

"No problem, man," the hackney said. Good as his word, they arrived with minutes to spare.

"LZ, you cover them from here. I'm going to gamble that they're headed up the needle and go topside and find myself a listening spot. If they don't appear in ten minutes, I'll come back down. Look for the other two and be careful. Leave word with the elevator dude where you'll be." Smitty didn't wait for a response.

Running to the elevator to the Space Needle, Smitty saw that they were only up to group five. Thinking on his feet, Smitty grabbed a young couple who were just about to board. "Hi, look, I need to tail a guy up to the top who knocked up my sister and split. I want to keep him in sight until the cops get here. Would ten bucks get you to change tickets with me?"

"How about fifteen?" the man asked.

"How about twenty, no questions, and you never saw me." Smitty flipped the man a Jackson and snatched the ticket from his startled wife's hand all in the same motion. He dove through the elevator doors that were already beginning to close.

"Sorry," he said to the attendant, "almost missed the bus."

The ride to the top seemed to take an eternity. He got off the elevator at the restaurant level figuring logically that if they were coming up, it would be to sit and talk unobtrusively over dinner. He looked for a spot to observe—without being observed—and settled quickly on the stairwell to the restrooms located on the observation deck. He closed the door till he could just see through a crack and settled in to wait.

Five minutes passed, then another five. The elevator had come and gone three times. But they had not appeared. Smitty was about to go to the observation deck when the elevator opened and the major and the detective got off.

"We have a 5:30 PM dinner reservation," the major said.

"We'll be with you in a moment, if you'd just take a seat," the maitre d' said.

"My good man, we have a dinner seating for 5:30 PM; it is now 5:32 PM. If you cannot seat us instantaneously, then have your manager appear before me immediately," the major responded indignantly.

"If you'll come this way, sir," he said. He bowed slightly and motioned with his outstretched hand, leading them to the other side of the rotating restaurant. The emphasis on the "sir" was unmistakable. Obviously, Smitty was not the only one the major failed to endear himself to.

Taking a chance that neither Gates nor Clayborne would immediately get up to go to the head, Smitty walked through the door and ambled up to the maitre d' who had just returned. He had a nervous sheen of sweat on his bald forehead and was clearly perturbed by the major's snub.

"I couldn't help overhearing," Smitty said. "That guy's a bit of a jerk."

"He's an asshole," the man said. "We get them all the time. Probably thinks his shit don't stink." Realizing that he had talked out of turn, he said, "Sorry, sir. Sometimes this job can be a little frustrating."

"I can certainly understand," Smitty said. "Turns out, I already know that. He knocked up my older sister and split with her tax return money. I've been following him, hoping to get something on him that I could use to get even."

Smitty held up a twenty. "I don't suppose there's any way I could get you to wander by there frequently and kind of listen in and then tell me what you hear, is there?"

Folding the twenty back into Smitty's hand, the maitre d' said, "Keep it; it would be my pleasure. Where'll you be?"

"Observation deck."

"No problem."

It was past 7:30 when Smitty came down the elevator on the next car after the detective and the major left. He watched discreetly as LZ and Frenchy followed both men without being observed. As they reached the car in the parking lot, the detective opened the trunk, removed a briefcase, opened it and extracted a package that looked from Smitty's vantage point like the case that the detective had carried away from the *Jesus Capri* in Savannah months earlier.

It sure looked the same: metal, with a hinge and the same combination lock, but now it bulged at the sides. It seemed heavy, too. The detective lifted it with both hands, and the major grunted as he took it. The major carried the box to his car, which was parked two cars down from the '54. Thanks to all their diligent attention, the major failed to recognize it. He opened the trunk, laid the box inside, and with a wave to the detective, drove away. The detective started up his own car and left thirty seconds later.

"Frenchy, grab a cab and follow that fucker," Smitty said, pointing to the detective. "LZ, grab another and stay on the major. Big Walt and I will head for the base. Call us there when you can."

Two minutes after the detective and the major departed, Big Walt and Smitty were on the way back to Fort Lewis in the refurbished '54. They drove in silence.

At 9:00, LZ appeared. He had followed the major right back to the base, where he'd changed into a uniform and caught a 9:30 flight to Hickum Air Force Base, Hawaii. At 9:45, Frenchy walked in. He'd followed the detective to Sea-Tac, where he'd caught a commercial flight back to Miami through Atlanta.

Smitty motioned for them to follow him to the '54. They started it up, left the base, and drove a half-mile to a picnic area beside a canal overpass, parked and settled on one of the benches.

"Well, guys," Smitty said, when they were all finally seated, "The maitre d' listened as closely as possible. From what he could get without appearing obvious, the detective was delivering that box we saw to the major, who was in turn to deliver it on to the "usual contact" in a foreign embassy in Saigon. He didn't catch his name; Chezlovic something or other.

"Lot of bitching about General Martin butting in and screwing up his delivery schedule. That was why there was a delay in getting it back and carried on. The major mentioned the bar fight outside Rucker and that it gave him the perfect opportunity to follow the four of us here to Lewis to assure we got expeditiously routed. That was about it.

"The detective wished the major well on his trip. The major said that he really couldn't say more, but would call the detective's 'father' when he returned from Nam in about a month, to arrange to deliver the return mail. The detective said he would pass this on.

"The rest of the conversation was about sports, the view, and general stuff like that; nothing of importance," Smitty finished.

"What the fuck are we on to?" LZ muttered.

"I think it's what we've stumbled into," Smitty said. "Sit tight while I walk to that phone booth over there, call Major Jim, and report what we've found out tonight."

Smitty grabbed the phone and called Major Jim at his home number. Strangely, he acted as if he were expecting his call. The major thanked him for the update, said he'd see that the information was passed on to the proper people, and hung up without further comment.

They sat on the bench in silence, each man lost in his own thoughts. Their time together was drawing to a close. Smitty suddenly realized that the four of them would probably never be together again.

"Hey guys, what say we give the old girl a proper sendoff?" Smitty suggested. "She's served us well." He added as an afterthought, "The three hundred fifty dollars we were going to get from that sergeant for selling her isn't really that important, is it?"

"Whatcha got in mind?" LZ asked curiously.

"Did you ever see *Beau Geste?*" Smitty asked.

"Of course," Frenchy said. "Let's do it."

"Do what?" LZ asked.

Frenchy nodded at the canal.

"Of course, of course," LZ said, as Walt nodded.

"Big Walt, if you'll do the honors," Smitty said.

Big Walt reached through the driver's window, put the '54 in neutral, and as Smitty, LZ, and Frenchy stood at attention, pushed the car into the canal. The four of them watched silently as the car sent up bubbles before finally disappearing from sight, with only ripples to mark its passing.

"Geste, to Geste, to Geste," Smitty said solemnly. He saluted, and the other three joined him in a final formal farewell to their trusty friend.

"The four musketeers," Big Walt said.

They clasped hands above their heads and held them for a long time. Finally, they turned and with a final salute to the friend that had served them so well, walked the half-mile back to the base in silence.

They returned to their room at 10:45. At 11:20, an orderly delivered a priority message with their travel orders. Big Walt was to be ready to leave by 0500 hours the next morning, destination Saigon, by way of Ton Son Nhut Air Force Base. Smitty would follow at 1400 hours, destination Nha Trang, by way of Cam Ranh Bay. Frenchy at 1900 hours, destination Da Nang. LZ would depart at 2300 hours, destination Ton Son Nhut and on to the Delta. The four musketeers were being split apart. Apparently, they were headed to Vietnam as replacements in different parts of the country. Smitty wondered if he'd ever see any of them again—alive.

Smitty was now sure that if Keith was the one who had done the dirty work, then Detective Wallace, AKA Special Agent Clev Clayborne, was the one who had told him to do it. Another piece of the riddle had now been at least identified, if not understood.

Smitty had pieces of the puzzle but had yet to find two that fit side by side. When Smitty was a kid, his favorite jigsaw puzzle was a picture of Saint Peter's Square in Vatican City. Over half of the puzzle was the sky background. After completing the church and the square, there was no other way to complete the sky blue part of the puzzle except to keep on matching one piece to the next in an endless repetition until by chance they began to fit together.

Smitty had a feeling that the reason he could not fit the pieces he had together was that one more key piece, the one who told them where to look, remained to be found. And whoever was it, or whoever they were, they were making an obvious effort to escape detection. The last piece would take a lot of finding.

The names cascaded through Smitty's mind like a waterfall. Air Force General Martin and brother two-star were now suspect; definitely Wallace-Clayborne; certainly Major Cluster-Gerbil was involved. What about Major Jim? He certainly seemed to be expecting his call earlier. And maybe even the good man Stanley. Could he be the "father" the major had referred to?

But they still did not tie together in any reasonable fashion. As he boarded the plane for the Great Asian Vacation, Smitty wondered what the toll of his own obsession would be in human lives. But Smitty was sure he wasn't obsessed; possessed maybe, but definitely not obsessed. It would take a lot of sifting, and if recent events in Savannah, Alabama, and Washington were a benchmark, he better be prepared to dig an open pit mine. But Smitty would do it. If he had to dig to China, he'd find the last part of the puzzle . . . and he knew instinctively that death would be the result.

CHAPTER ELEVEN

The seventeen-hour flight, with refueling stops, had been exhausting. During the entire time, Smitty was sure that there couldn't have been ten words spoken by anyone—none the last hour before landing. As the airplane banked for the final turn into Cam Ranh Bay, Smitty looked out the window and thought idly how serene the landscape was and how much looks could be deceiving. A land of the haves and have-nots; a land of peasant farmers and politically corrupt power brokers; a land where fifteen thousand Americans had died, to date, in an undeclared war that in its most optimistic terms could only be declared a draw.

Before leaving Rucker, the four musketeers had been through the standard Nam-bound orientation, complete with motivational speeches from a multitude of deskbound officers about the Domino Theory, the importance of being American ambassadors of goodwill, and a fluff puff film interview from a four-star general about how we were winning the war of attrition.

The film left Smitty feeling particularly uncomfortable. The four-bagger talked at length about how the American buildup of troops was designed to wear the enemy down to a point where they were unable to sustain their momentum and would just fade away. This would be accomplished by, in his terms, acceptable kill ratios, which, the general went on to explain, meant that for every American killed, the Vietcong would lose some unspecified number; what the good general failed to mention was how long this would take or what the acceptable kill ratio was. Smitty wondered to himself if the old windbag would feel the same way if it were his son that was to be one of the statistics.

After the airplane landed, they filed off the plane and Smitty was immediately enveloped by the mugginess. Before he reached the adjacent building, his armpits and crotch were damp with sweat. The dank Georgia coast or the damp southern Alabama lowlands seemed like the Arizona desert compared to Vietnam.

As they entered, they showed their orders to an officer and were appropriately cued and staged for the next leg of their journey to their final destination. Smitty was to go by truck to Nha Trang, the headquarters of 5th Special Forces in Vietnam, just a few miles up the road on Route 1, where he, along with two other Green Hats would be given their initial in-country orientation and specific team assignments, and would be issued weapons, jungle uniforms, and equipment.

The entire process was well-organized—too well-organized. From the countless stories Smitty had heard from his dad and his uncle about the numerous battles they had been in during World War II, he remembered an ominous comment: "Overorganization is a piss-poor commander's substitute for battlefield victories."

Two hours later, as they piled into the back of a deuce-and-a-half with their duffel bags, one of the Berets next to him said, "Well, at least we'll have some time to get oriented.

The Tet truce is supposed to start in three days."

"You think?" the other Green asked. Like Smitty, the other two were "Shake and Bake" sergeants, a rather derogatory term used by veterans to define those who had achieved NCO rank but were short on the combat and service experience that normally goes with it.

Smitty was uneasy about the trip. The driver and his shotgun were equipped with M-16s, extra clips, and grenades. After they were all in the truck, the last two soldiers to enter and take the end seats were similarly equipped MPs. There were six trucks in total, three with troops and three with supplies. They were to be escorted by MPs in Jeeps with sixty-caliber machine guns mounted on them at the front and rear of the column.

Smitty's initial thought was that he had traveled through a time warp and was part of the Rat Patrol. But this thought died stillborn. The MPs were wearing flak jackets and no-shit, serious-business looks on their faces. Smitty decided to give them the benefit of the doubt.

He fished in his duffel and retrieved his .357, clicked open the chamber, slid in a sixth round, and flipped it shut. He also removed six speedloaders that held six rounds each that could be loaded all at the same time and slipped them in his vest pockets. Last, he opened one of the four boxes of ammunition he had brought with him and put a handful of individual shells into both of his pants pockets.

Noticing this, a 1st Air Cavalry private seated across from him said, "Expecting trouble?"

"Never hurts to be prepared," Smitty responded without a smile, laying his weapon on top of his duffel.

"You Berets," he said, shaking his head in disgust. "You see Vietcong around every corner."

Nodding, Smitty said in a grim voice, "I'm a cautious kid."

"Pfft!" the holder of the horse-with-no-name yellow patch on his shoulder gave a wave of dismissal. He rummaged in his own duffel, brought out a tin of fudge, and offered it around. Intentionally avoiding passing any to Smitty, he said, "None for you, General Patton, you're standing guard."

His smile changed to a look of bewilderment accompanied by a soft plop and a loud crack. The private's head slumped to his chest and he fell forward, the tin slipping from his hands and clattered noisily on the metal floor. Smitty caught him with his outstretched arms, and he saw the blood already creating a red bull's-eye in the middle of his back.

"I guess you can't be too cautious." Smitty cradled him in his arms. He'd never make private first class, and he'd never finish the fudge; with one final gasp, his eyes glazed over and closed and he went limp in Smitty's arms and died.

"Ambush, ambush, everybody out!" one of the rear-guard MPs to Smitty's right screamed as he stood up, unlatching the tailgate. As the truck rolled to a stop, he flinched and fell backward out of the truck, dead before he hit the ground, when several bullets tore his face to shreds.

A small figure in black pajamas appeared suddenly between the truck and the rear-guard Jeep. He fired an American M-79 grenade launcher directly at the rear Jeep, turned even before it exploded, was reloaded by his partner, and sighted on their truck. The rear-guard MP across from Smitty shot him with his M-16. Another Vietcong appeared in view and shot the guard with his AK-47. Instinctively, Smitty grabbed his .357 with his left hand and shot the second Vietcong three times with his hand weapon, using the dead soldier as a shield and wincing involuntarily as several rounds thudded into the body. He released his grip on the lifeless private, grabbed the M-16, unbuckled the dead soldier's web belt, grabbed his grenades and helmet, then leaped cleanly over the side rail of the truck and on impact, rolled to the surrounding cover of a ditch on the side of the road.

As Smitty looked up from his place of concealment, events were unfolding with blurry speed. There seemed to be fire coming from everywhere and all directions. Both Jeeps had been hit, and from what Smitty could tell, none of the soldiers inside were alive. Two of the trucks behind the lead Jeep were already on fire; there seemed to be Vietcong troops everywhere, firing from all positions. Smitty raised the '16 and fired the rest of the clip at two approaching VC, killing both with a spray of rounds. Smitty could hear firing from other GIs as they began to return fire. Grenades exploded somewhere across the road, followed by the sound of men crying out in agony.

For the next ten minutes, the battle was intense as the Americans and the VC exchanged fire. Smitty fired the '16 at anything that was wearing black or appeared to be moving toward the convoy until he ran out of clips. He saw what looked like three regular NVA soldiers move up on the truck that had his duffel, and he threw a hand grenade and ducked. He had no chance to see if he had been on target, as another VC ran right by his place of concealment, and before Smitty could stop him, shot the Green Beret he had spoken to on the ride down from Cam Ranh Bay. He was lying half out of the rear of the truck, his blood dripping and pooling on the road as though he were a car that had just ruptured its oil pan.

Smitty sighted and shot the VC six times with his .357. The dead VC's blood and the dead Green Beret's blood were running together; they both were the same color.

Smitty reloaded the Smith and Wesson and waited, his heart racing. He could hear movement all around him, but he could see nothing to shoot at. Smitty heard, before he actually saw, the deep thumping sound of helicopter rotors. Two Hueys appeared overhead, the door gunners strafing suspected enemy positions beyond the road. The choppers had only made their first pass when the VC fire ceased as suddenly as if a light switch had been flipped. As the soldiers began to come out from their places of concealment, Smitty did also.

It seemed that everyone was in charge and no one was. Soldiers were shouting orders, some contradicting the others, others screaming for help either for themselves or for someone else. Some begged for God's help. Some begged in vain, and some were already beyond it. Eventually a sergeant first class who had been riding shotgun in the third truck took charge, and some semblance of order was restored.

"You okay?" the sergeant asked, snapping a fresh clip in his M-16, misreading the bloodstained shirt.

"Yeah, fine," Smitty replied in a low voice. "It's from that private." He nodded in the direction of the truck.

"That's the way the bastards work. Attack and haul ass before we can do much harm."

"What's the damage?" Smitty asked.

"They hit both Jeeps and two of the six trucks with grenade rounds. They also strafed your truck and another." The sergeant walked over to the VC Smitty had shot, rolled him over with his foot, removed the M-79 from his lifeless hands, and flung it as far as he could in disgust.

"Fuckin' dinks are using our own captured weapons on us, the motherfuckers." The sergeant reached down, grabbed the dead man by the shirt, and dragged him to the side of the road.

Suddenly, and with a practiced motion, he sighted his weapon on the dead VC's genitals and squeezed the trigger. The body convulsed jerkily as he emptied a full clip, literally blowing the balls off.

"Goddamn slope won't have any fun in the next life." The sergeant kicked the now detached genitals away from the mutilated body.

"That kid that fucker killed was short; headed home inside a month." He spat on the dead VC's face in a voice faltering with emotion.

He noticed Smitty's confusion. "Don't worry kid, you're new. By the end of your tour, you'll be doing the same thing, too."

"Maybe so," Smitty said. *But then again, maybe not,* he said to himself.

Six dead and nine wounded. It did not seem to matter to Smitty that there were twelve VC confirmed killed and an "estimated" fifteen others. The estimated kills seemed to be more or less negotiated and agreed to by the sergeant as he was reporting the details of the ambush by radio to his lieutenant at Cam Ranh Bay. *I guess,* Smitty thought to himself, *the estimated were rounded up to fit the general's kill ratio algorithm.*

Ambushes, dead body dismemberment, and exaggerated body counts, Smitty thought, as they were airlifted out to Nha Trang. What kind of fucking war was this? What was he into? What was he to become? The sun hadn't even gone down on his first day in-country.

"You did well in your first live action," Lieutenant Colonel Wilson said in a satisfied voice after Smitty gave him a personal debrief at Captain Bartkowski's request.

"Yes, sir," Smitty said.

"That's a standard VC tactic, ambush a bunch of greens, just in from the States; it creates fear and uncertainty," the colonel continued. "I know it's hard to hear it now, but you will get over this. You'll have to. If you don't, you'll come apart inside."

"Thank you, sir," Smitty responded. "I guess that '7 mutilating that VC kind of got to me."

"Learn from it, and don't let it happen to you," the colonel said with sudden forcefulness. "If you do, you'll cross over, like that sergeant, until the day will come when you'll feel no remorse at the death of another human being, only vengeance.

"Vengeance is more addictive than any narcotic. It leaves you alone in the land of denial and self-righteous indignation, where your enemies become the Antichrist as your humanity slowly slips away. With your humanity gone, you may go home, but you'll never know peace. Are we clear?"

"Perfectly."

"If it is any consolation to you," the colonel said, his voice softening, "I reported it, and I can't guarantee it, but I suspect that the sergeant first class will be private first class within a week."

"Thank you," Smitty said in a hollow voice.

"Dismissed."

As they left the colonel's office, walking to the equipment area for Smitty to draw his gear, Smitty said to Ron, "Was there some reason why the three of us were split up?"

"Absolutely, but it's not the reason you might think," Ron said. "We'd never admit this publicly, but we're woefully understaffed. There are a lot of groups competing for our limited resources. MACV—Military Assistance Command Vietnam—in Saigon sets the priority for our manpower decisions. Some posts require 100 percent fulfillment at all times. As a result, we're operating two, sometimes three levels out of grade in our teams and camps.

"Some of the camps are so short that we may have to close them down. We felt that the three of you had the abilities to be leaders and thought that dispersing you would accelerate your in-country training. Teaming you with experienced NCOs and officers will allow your individual talents to develop and be put to best use."

"I miss them."

"You'll see them again," Ron said. "As it turns out, you'll see Frenchy very soon. Colonel Wilson has asked me to head north to the Special Forces camp at Da Nang. There's a buildup around Khe Sanh. We have a camp at Lang Vie on Route 9 that could be exposed. He thinks that area could become hot during Tet and has asked me to use Da Nang as a staging point for reinforcements.

"You're going along as part of the reinforcement team. Then you'll all be back here for a new twenty-day combat orientation school conducted by the MACV here at Nha Trang. After that, you're scheduled for additional in-country training in counterinsurgency a bit south of here."

"What about LZ?"

"His final destination is the Special Forces Company at Can Tho Air Base. Intelligence confirms that the Delta will be a prime strike area. We've got him slated to replace a wounded man."

"Counterinsurgency training?"

"Secret stuff," Ron answered. "We don't talk about it publicly. We just supply resources—you know, no name, no insignia, that kind of thing. That observe-and-report mission to Savannah was a trial run to see if you characters had that kind of skill also."

"How'd we do?"

"We're gonna give you passing on that," Ron said. He frowned. "I heard you even managed to not shoot your civilian antagonist, that detective, on sight. We had to put you in harm's way and see what would happen. Fortunately, your training took over and you somehow managed not to kill him."

"Anything to that?" Smitty asked.

"Major Jim followed up on your last report from Lewis; Qued me, I checked. Major Gates is due in through Ton Son Nhut on February 7. We'll have him staked, but from initial checking, seems to be nothing more than elephant trophies."

"What?" Smitty asked, totally confused.

"Yeah, seems that Major Kiss Ass, from his cushy Washington staff job, was flying to Nam about every three months on some kind of information-gathering mission for the JCS. What he's really doing is purchasing ceramic souvenirs of elephants and other items for the general's crowd—or to be more precise, the generals' wives.

"Seems to be the hot new fad. That box you saw in Washington had cash in it to purchase them. He has them shipped by boat to Savannah and other ports; that's what the detective was retrieving that night on the dock, elephants and other expensive souvenirs. The box you saw that night was empty, meaning the bank vault was being returned. We could bust him, but for what? If we nailed him, we'd have to nail damn near half the generals in the service for accepting the damn things.

"This is or should I say was his glide path to lieutenant colonel, supplying whatever to higher-ups, hoping that this would get him enough favors to climb the ladder. 'Course that's changed since he tangled with your two-star friend. Seems your buddy turned him in for not having combat experience and for tailing him that night with you in the bar."

"What was the major after that night?" Smitty interrupted.

"That should be obvious," Ron said with a disdainful look. "He was looking for something to use against the general that would neutralize him from blocking the major's advancement in the future. As I understand it, your friend exposed the situation in the bar that night."

"Part of his trip here is to scout around and find himself a nice cushy job where he can meet the general's directive and get his six months in-country and a combat ribbon. He's got two years, then he'll get passed over for the third time, rifted, and dropped from the service."

"What about the phony detective?" Smitty asked.

"Just coming to that," Ron said with a nod. "Checked him out, too; seems he's legit, working undercover on loan to the FBI. They stumbled onto the major's deal through a security check, thinking it was drugs, and recruited him. You verified that it was another blind alley."

"How?" Smitty asked.

"When you stumbled on him in Seattle. The detective was giving him seed money to follow the trail."

"Guess I was way off base," Smitty said.

"I wouldn't sweat it. Although remember, I warned you back at Bragg, didn't I?"

"Lot to learn."

"And I think you'll learn it well," Ron said, putting his arm around Smitty and steering him into the equipment building.

The way Ron explained it, it sure seemed to add up, but what still bothered Smitty was that if you added the facts up differently, it could be something else altogether. One thing was certain, that personal battle would have to wait; his own immediate survival was now the most pressing problem.

Two days later, in the words of Ron the Polack, "The shitski hit the fanski." Intelligence reports started coming in to Da Nang in the early morning hours of January 30 about rocket attacks and fighting in Saigon. Confirmed reports were coming in on attacks on Nha Trang and Ban Me Thuot.

This was not just the 1:00-3:00-5:00 AM shellings that were a frequent VC practice to disrupt sleep and keep nerves on edge. This was a constant bombardment, followed up closely with ground assaults by troops that numbered from two hundred to two thousand. A general invasion of all of South Vietnam seemed under way.

Smitty and Frenchy were asleep when the first reports started to come in. The base was alerted, and the two were assigned to defensive positions on the perimeter. It seemed that every cook, typist, and dishwasher who could hold one was manning a weapon and standing a post.

Smitty first heard the deep rumblings of rockets exploding in the city of Da Nang. Within two minutes, the rockets were walking their way toward the base. From the firing positions, Smitty guessed that they were coming from dug-in VC emplacements no more than eight hundred yards away.

"Man, that was close," Frenchy said with a sigh of relief, as one round passed over their position and exploded three hundred yards behind them.

The next round was closer, two hundred yards, then another landed two hundred yards in front of the fence.

"Target acquisition," Captain Bartkowski said, joining them in the trench with a radio. "They're searching for the range to the wire. Guess their inside intel screwed up on this one. Down!" He screamed suddenly.

The next round came in and exploded fifty yards behind them. They dove for the bottom of the trench and covered their ears. The noise was deafening. His ears were ringing and

Smitty was temporarily deaf; he was sure that his hearing would be permanently impaired.

"That was too close," the captain said, grabbing the radio and directing return fire. "Ten rounds of HE—high explosive—I'll direct."

Instantaneously, a deep whomp occurred every three to four seconds as the return mortars were fired.

"Ten right, fifty deep," the captain barked into the radio as he looked through his starlight night glasses. Five more rounds were fired.

"Right there, right there!" he yelled into the radio. "Stick it to 'em!"

Either his fire control was right on the mark, or the VC had stopped. If they stopped, the question was why? Was this another hit-and-run tactic, or had they stopped because they didn't want to take the risk of hitting their own men who could be perilously close to the wire?

It was the latter. A bugle sounded in the darkness, sending goose pimples down Smitty's spine, followed immediately by screaming as the VC hit the wire. Smitty had no idea how many there were in the darkness. By the sound, there could have been fifty or five hundred. They blew the wire with satchel charges and came pouring through, throwing ladders on the scattered tanglefoot to use as passages. An M-60 opened up to Smitty's right. M-16 fire began to his left in response to the AK-47 fire of the VC.

Smitty stood transfixed, almost as in a daze as the enemy approached.

"Son." The captain touched him on the shoulder, "Are you planning to fire that weapon sometime tonight, or are you going to stare them to death?"

"Uh, yes, sir," Smitty said. He raised his own M-16 and sighted down on the closest VC, who was no more than forty yards away and fired.

Smitty shot the VC, and remembered watching him fall backwards, but from then on it became a kind of frenzied nightmare. Silhouettes flashed into view and were gone again. Smitty had gone on autopilot: fire on the images, eject, insert a new clip, then continue firing. He had no consciousness of time; they didn't measure that kind of time with a watch, anyway.

Screams that can only be made by men dying in agony were coming from all around him. A dead VC fell three yards in front of him, and in his heightened state, Smitty instinctively shot him again.

"Easy, son, somebody already got that one," the captain said between clenched teeth. "Try shooting the live ones."

Smitty had no time to respond. A VC charged directly at him. Ducking instinctively, he avoided the bayonet thrust, pulled out his .357 and shot the VC four times in the chest and head, recoiling as blood spattered his face like raindrops on a spring leaf. The dead VC fell down in the trench against the captain's leg. The captain looked down at him. "Nice shootin', Tex."

Smitty smiled in reply.

A bugle sounded again, and as suddenly as the battle had begun, it ceased. It seemed incredible that a battle could start and stop almost as if turning on a dime. Additional phosphorous rounds showed the VC retreating—not just withdrawing from the battle, but running away. Within two minutes, all firing had ceased, and it had become eerily quiet. Smitty waited in silence as the silhouettes became shadows and the shadows became ghosts.

This was the real paradox of war—any war—moments of sheer terror followed by times of unnerving silence. The only sounds now were the wailing cries of the wounded and the urgent calls of "corpsman" from somewhere in the darkness.

Observing the captain checking his weapon and his extra clips, Smitty did the same. He glanced to his right and was relieved to see Frenchy give him the thumbs-up sign from his position six paces away . . . Smitty'd felt this way before . . . It was going to be a long night.

They stayed at their posts all through the night and into the afternoon of the next day. The base itself was not attacked again, but the city was. The enemy caught civilians in the rocket and small arms crossfire, hoping to draw the U.S. forces into the town for an ambush.

The next day, Smitty and Frenchy had volunteered to join a recon patrol led by Captain Bartkowski for a firsthand look-see at the effectiveness of the fire. Smitty was fine until he saw what looked to be a nine-year-old girl lying in the street next to her mother. *It must have been a rocket round,* Smitty thought to himself, *and it must have been damn close.* The entire right side of her face simply wasn't there. Neither were her right arm and part of her chest. The force of the blast had blown her mother's blouse into tattered shreds; a piece of the little girl's hand was impaled in her mother's left breast.

Smitty tried to hold on but found it impossible; he turned away from the death scene, doubled over, and retched violently.

"Feel better, kid?" a master sergeant asked, laying a hand on his shoulder for support.

Smitty was trying desperately to bring his churning stomach under control. "Yeah," he managed weakly between deep breaths.

"Hang in there, Sergeant, it'll fetch you around," he said.

"I feel like such a candy-ass."

"Well, when the time comes that you don't feel something . . ." he left the statement unfinished. Smitty saw his point.

Smitty walked on like a robot. He couldn't look back, but he knew their image would haunt him for the rest of his days.

They headed straight down the dusty street and were not one hundred yards from the grisly scene when someone up front yelled, "Incoming!" just as Smitty heard the whirring sound of the rocket. He instinctively dove for cover behind a tree and stared in horror at Frenchy, who seemed to be caught out in the open in no-man's-land and had frozen.

"Frenchy, get down! Frenchy, get down!" Smitty screamed urgently. But it was too late; surely . . . a lifetime too late.

The round exploded on impact right beside Frenchy, shot-putting him fifteen feet.

Not caring about possible other rounds, Smitty ran to Frenchy, grabbed him, and dragged him behind a cart to cover.

Frenchy was badly wounded. The shrapnel had torn through his left shoulder and his left forearm looked more like raw meat than a human appendage. Blood was coming from everywhere; if the bleeding didn't stop, he'd be dead.

"Corpsman! Corpsman!" Smitty screamed. "In the name of God, somebody get a corpsman!"

It was probably no more than ten seconds but seemed like an eternity before two corpsmen raced over, shoved Smitty roughly out of the way, and began to apply pressure dressings to his friend.

Smitty crouched, praying to himself, *Please, God, don't let him die! Please, God, if it's a death you want, take me instead. I got him into this; it's my fault!*

"Saddle up, son, and let's move on outta here." The sergeant took his arm to lead him away.

"He's my friend; I can't leave him," Smitty said, shaking the senior noncom off.

"There's nothing you can do for him now, son. The medics will do what they can." He grabbed Smitty by both arms and shook him. "Kid, he ain't the last friend you're ever gonna lose over here. Now c'mon."

Smitty's eyes, wet with tears, never left Frenchy as the older veteran dragged him away. Smitty felt the same hollow emptiness that he had felt on leaving Stan the Man the year before. Two friends down. How many more would it cost before Smitty found his truth?

Smitty had watched from a distance as the helicopter landed and Frenchy was medivacked out to the hospital at Da Nang. When they returned from the patrol, Smitty had gone straight to the hospital, but Frenchy was still in surgery. Smitty could not believe the casualties going through there.

Soldiers were being processed through like automobiles in an assembly line, but this looked more like a human junkyard. This was the real horror of war. Smitty was already sure that the cost of this war in terms of human lives was like the national debt; the American people couldn't even afford the interest.

He fell asleep on the floor and was awakened by a nurse and told that his friend had come through surgery and was in post-op recovery, but was still in critical condition and would be for the balance of the night. Smitty returned to his temporary quarters, sat down on his bed, and cried himself to sleep.

Smitty didn't see Frenchy again. Since he was still unassigned, Smitty was "volunteered" for another recon patrol, a search-and-destroy that was helicoptered in about two clicks from the Mang Yang Pass. They were to link up with a reinforced convoy that was headed to Pleiku across Route 9 to open up the besieged highway. By the time Smitty returned to Da Nang three days later, Frenchy had been medivacked out to Japan, after which he was headed home. For his friend, the war was over, his injured left arm and the shrapnel in his shoulder more than enough to disqualify him from further combat.

The search-and-destroy mission in itself had been an eye-opener for Smitty as to how and why the war was a stalemate. It seemed that the Vietcong had the same idea as the general: if they just dragged the war on long enough, the American public would tire of the war and demand that the troops be withdrawn.

So in reality, it was not a search-and-destroy the enemy but stroll-and-die for the Americans.

The concept of a search-and-destroy mission is to have a helicopter drop off a group of soldiers in a cold LZ—landing zone—then search for signs of enemy activity, munitions, or foodstuffs, and destroy them, engaging the enemy whenever possible and inflicting maximum casualties with minimum losses.

Smitty was helicoptered out to a preselected LZ, the landing process itself making enough noise to wake the dead. Then they were ordered on a predetermined course, sometimes through jungle so thick you couldn't see five feet ahead. They were to look for suspected VC strongholds or to find the enemy, making no effort at concealment or stealth. Even with point leads, they still were creating enough noise that Smitty felt his eighty-year-old grandmother, who was deaf as a fence post, would hear them coming.

Sadly, Smitty's feeling of foreboding proved to be painfully true. On the afternoon of the first day, the VC sprang an ambush, killing four and wounding thirteen American soldiers. The VC then retreated, leaving a smaller group as a delaying force, while the main body escaped safely away. The patrol was delayed while helicopters were called to medivac out the dead and wounded. VC casualties were hard to estimate, for they dragged away as many of their dead and wounded as possible.

In the morning of the third day, the VC struck again with a second ambush. The result: seven dead and twenty-two wounded. A 1st Air Cavalry soldier was hit in the legs as they were repelling fire. Smitty dragged him away from the fire zone, and with another 1st soldier was carrying him to the LZ to be medivacked, when the VC suddenly opened up on the medivac helicopter and the troops attempting to load the wounded.

Smitty was running fast toward the evac LZ when he felt a burning pain in the back of his leg. His leg was momentarily paralyzed, and he nearly fell. The 1st Air Cav soldier who was helping him was cut down and critically wounded.

Smitty got the first wounded soldier on the aircraft, then despite the burning pain and the groundfire, ran back, grabbed the other wounded soldier, and dragged him to the aircraft. After literally throwing the wounded soldier on the chopper, he felt the back of his leg and found it red with blood from a round through his thigh. He had now been bloodied, or, in the words of the vets, he'd lost his cherry.

Since the bullet did not strike a bone and had passed completely through outer tissue, he refused to be medivacked. He was just bandaged and given antibiotics against infection. He gimped along the rest of the patrol with what was tantamount to a sore muscle.

After sleeping off the three-day walk in the woods, Smitty was ordered back to Nha Trang for permanent assignment.

Smitty couldn't think of anything stupider than sneaking up on the VC using the search-and-destroy concept; he was surprised that they didn't attack like the British in the French and Indian War with bagpipes and drums. And even a retarded, crippled newsboy could see that the war was being fought with outdated World War II tactics by generals whose last original thought had probably occurred before Glenn Miller went down.

A platoon lieutenant witnessed Smitty's actions and wrote him up for a Bronze Star, which was approved. The accompanying citation said something about "selflessly exposing himself to repeated enemy fire in order to save wounded comrades."

In that particular engagement, Smitty had witnessed a hundred different selfless acts. It all bore out Dad's belief that it didn't matter how brave you were under enemy fire. Medals were awarded only if an officer witnessed it and was still alive after the battle to write it down.

Despite the seemingly all-out war going on in the rest of the country, Nha Trang had become relatively quiet. An occasional five to ten rocket rounds every day or so and that was it. The Vietcong commanders had gambled that with an all-out assault, there would be a general uprising of the Vietnamese people in support, but that had not happened. As a result, the assault was for the most part being contained.

After initial thrusts, Saigon and Pleiku seemed to have beaten back their attackers. The major fighting now seemed to be in the provincial capital of Hue, where the VC had taken the town and raised their flag over the citadel, and in Khe Sanh, where the VC had laid siege to the camp in a manner similar to that used on the French at Dien Bien Phu a decade and a half back.

The Special Forces camp at Lang Vie was on highest alert and could be hit at any moment. Smitty was now standing by to join a reinforced Mike Force made up of Special Forces and montagnards—local tribesman recruited as fighters, also called Yards.

The casualties from the Tet Offensive, from the VC standpoint, were astronomical; the American casualties heavy. But Smitty was only concerned with one: Frenchy. The only reports he could get said that his friend was "stable and recovering." Smitty had fired off a letter to LZ and Big Walt but had not heard back. LZ was assigned to Delta, Big Walt as an MP in Saigon. Both areas had been hit hard. He hoped they were all right; they were all he had left.

"Gentlemen, the purpose of the Special Forces Combat Orientation School is to teach you all the shit they didn't know how to teach you at Bragg, or in the case of you repo depos from other more conventional units, the shit you never learned in the first place." The master sergeant stood in front of them with his hands on his hips.

"We're going to run live-fire simulation, take what you learned stateside, and extend it with a stiff dose of Vietcong reality. Some of you fives and sixes have been in grade less than a year, so we're going to give you a crash course in experience to match your rank. Any questions?" No one responded. "Split up with your assigned training NCO, and he will take it from there."

Chairs scraped as the forty-odd "green apples" split up and headed to their respective rooms at the combat orientation school at Nha Trang. Some of the information would be rudimentary review for Smitty and LZ, but the actual field experiences of the lead NCO would be invaluable.

Smitty didn't feel like a green apple anymore. Following the three-day search and destroy, he was back at Da Nang only two days when he was airlifted out to reinforce what was left of the Special Forces camp at Lang Vie. The camp had been overrun by regular North Vietnamese army troops using Russian-made PT-76 tanks, and at least a battalion of VC with an estimated strength of one thousand men—mainly because the MACV major sitting on his fat ass in his air-conditioned office in Saigon didn't believe the live field reports that the VC had tanks, despite the fact that the late camp commander had held his mic outside the bunker to let him listen to the live rounds. When questioned later as to why he didn't send reinforcements, he insisted that there was no need, because "the VC have no tanks." When asked about the camp commander's live feed, he explained it away as the last actions of "a panicked and desperate commander."

The camp had been savaged. The command bunker looked like a cross between a crater and scorched earth. Just walking through it made Smitty queasy, especially since he knew that twenty-two Special Forces personnel and more than two hundred Yards had died there. This seemed to be the pattern of the war: hit and run before any real damage could be done—to the VC.

Captain Bartkowski was dispatched with his Mike Force, but again, based on bureaucracy and late intelligence, this was after the fact. Smitty was there for six days but never fired his weapon. Following his return to Da Nang, he and the captain were airlifted back to Nha Trang. Since the orientation class was supposed to start in a few days, Smitty was held from future assignment.

"Sorry about the Frog, man. It must have been rough on you being there and seeing him get hit," LZ said, as they were walking down the hall.

"I've never felt so fucking helpless in my life," Smitty said. "But at least he's out of it now."

"It's been three and a half weeks since he was hit. What's the latest?"

"Last letter I got from him—written by a nurse, as you might expect—he's been shipped to Fort Lawrence, Kansas. He's got some pretty nasty therapy to get through to get his left arm functioning again, although the sawbones is telling him it will never be 100 percent."

"Don't worry, my man," LZ said. "I'm betting that Froggy will recover fully."

A master sergeant was sitting casually on the corner of a desk waiting for them. "Come in, gentlemen, and have a seat."

"My name is Sergeant Andrews. I have been in the army for twenty-six years and have served in World War II and Korea, and two tours in Nam, all in combat assignments. And I'm here to tell ya, Nam ain't for shit like the other two. This is a dirty guerrilla type of war. There are no front lines, only battle zones.

"Your main opponent, Victor Charlie, or VC, is a smart son of a bitch. It's his ball-park, and he's been playing in it for a long time. He knows all the tricks, and just when you think you've got the little bastard, he'll disengage and unass the area so fast you'll think he's got a rocket up his butt. Before you can recover, he's across the border in a safe area, giving you the finger.

"And if you think this is some kind of fuck-off training class, remember one thing: This class was put together to try to bring down the casualty rate for you inexperienced Green Berets, but even with that, for two of the three people in the room, your next assignment is permanent—a one-way ticket to Arlington National Cemetery."

As openings go, it pretty much served the purpose of getting your attention. Smitty felt fortunate that at least he and LZ had gone through Bragg. Special Forces shortfalls being what they were, several of the sergeants and specialists in the room could not even read a terrain map. With only standard military training as a background, they were ill-prepared to operate independently or to meet the rigorous demands that would be placed on them as part of a Special Forces unit.

"Sergeant Smith," the sergeant said, suddenly snapping Smitty out of his daydream.

"Yes, Sergeant Andrews," Smitty answered quietly.

"I understand that unlike most of the men here, you've actually been under fire several times. Care to comment?"

"Well, I, um, was scared shitless and just lucky, I guess," Smitty mumbled quietly.

"Bullshit! If you were, you'd already be dead," the sergeant said bluntly. He picked up a folder from his desk. "This is a report from Sergeant First Class Hastings on the convoy ambush.

"Out of twelve VC killed, you were credited with killing four and wounding two. You shot the first one with that illegal cannon you carry, the next one with an M-16 you took off a dead soldier. You also took his web belt and grenades, and evac'ed the truck for a defensive position. Next, you killed one and wounded two more with a grenade, and then shot another at point-blank range with that .357.

"On your three-day recon patrol, you were in two firefights, shot through the back of the leg, and still managed to assist a more seriously wounded man to be medivacked. Then you refused evacuation, finished the patrol, and were out on a reinforcement patrol at Lang Vie until extraction on the fifteenth.

"You've been in more shit in two months than some people do in their entire tour. I would hardly call your survival luck, would you, Sergeant?"

"No, I suppose not," Smitty answered.

"How did it happen that you had your Smith and Wesson at hand on the truck convoy?" the sergeant asked.

"Well," Smitty said in a more confident and reflective tone, "something just didn't feel right. The MPs were uncomfortable and that made me nervous."

"And?"

"I got out my Magnum, slid in a sixth round, got out six speedloaders, put them in my vest pocket, then put a handful of individual rounds in my pants pocket. I know that it's not the precise military response you're looking for, but that's the best I can do."

"As a matter of fact, son, that's precisely the answer I was looking for." The sergeant nodded, satisfied. "As a result of your training, or civilian experiences"—he said with a knowing wink—"your instincts told you what to do.

"That's what we're going to do here, gentlemen. We teach you what to look for, what the warning signs of trouble are, so that you can instinctively avoid it, and make the appropriate response before it occurs. And who knows"—the sergeant surveyed the room somberly—"some of you might beat the odds and not go home in a tin box."

The sergeant let that sink in for a minute. "Okay, now that the hey howdies are over from me, I want each of you to stand and give me a thirty-second background, then we'll begin with our course . . ."

"Class kiss-up," LZ said to Smitty as they left the classroom for the training field.

"Class clown," Smitty shot back.

The next twenty days consisted of intensive eighteen-hour days that made Fayettenam seem like a walk in the park. Despite VC activities going on at Hue, where a painful house-by-house search by the marines was on to extract the enemy from their fortified positions, and the fact that Khe Sanh was under intensive siege by upwards of fifteen thousand VC, and even with the VC overrun and casualties at the Special Forces Camp at Lang Vie, no one was pulled from the class early as a repo depo replacement.

The sergeant was right. Even with his baptism under fire, there was still a lot for him to learn. At the end of the training at Bragg, Smitty had felt that he knew his primary skill and had learned how to take care of himself. At the end of this training, he felt he understood how the VC were fighting the war, what tricks they had learned from experience, and how they were now using them against the American forces.

Smitty now felt sorry for the grunts who were being led by conventional officers, with conventional battle strategies, against a highly unconventional enemy. They were paying the bill for these misconceptions with their lives.

More than once, Smitty wondered where the roadblock was and who didn't get it. Was it the general and his World War II big-war mentality, was it President Johnson and his containment policy, was it McNamara and his obsessive body count and statistical approach, was it South Vietnamese President Thieu's government that was so riddled with corruption and insecurity as to be totally ineffective? Or was it all of these working together to create a useless, politically insensitive bureaucracy that just wouldn't listen or didn't understand this kind of war?

And what effect would the new President Nixon have on this? He had run for office on the promise of a secret plan to end the war—but he never disclosed what this secret plan was. Well, you'd better hurry up, Dick; one of us needs relief, Smitty had thought wryly to himself more than once.

Toward the end of the training, Smitty was called into Colonel Wilson's office and given the Army Commendation Medal for his impromptu actions in the convoy eight weeks earlier and the Purple Heart for his leg wound on the recon patrol. He was polite but unimpressed.

As a result of these commendations, Smitty was given a three-day pass to Saigon at the end of the training, and told to report to Bien Hoa at the conclusion; for what, he was not told. It was now the end of April and Smitty had been in-country three months. Frenchy was gone, and the letters from LZ and Big Walt had been few. At least it would give him a chance to check up on the fourth musketeer while he was there.

"Excuse me, I am trying to locate a PFC called Walt Wellmen. You wouldn't know where he is, would you?" Smitty asked the specialist five behind the counter at the Military Police building at Ton Son Nhut Air Base.

The MP spun around in his chair, looked up at a Plexiglas wall chart with names listed alphabetically in grease pencil, and traced down with his finger until he came to Wellmen. "He's on patrol in Saigon."

"Uh, could you narrow it down a bit? Saigon is a fair-sized village," Smitty said with a trace of irritation.

The MP gave him an exasperated look, spun again in his chair, studied the chart again, spun back, and said, "Somewhere on Tu Do Street around the Caravelle Hotel. Try there."

"Thanks, pal," Smitty said.

As Smitty was leaving the base, he flagged down two MPs in a Jeep, who looked as if they were on a mission to somewhere, and asked them for directions to Tu Do Street. They were much more cordial, acknowledging that they were headed in that direction, and volunteered to give him a lift.

"Where ya in from?" the younger of the two MPs, a PFC, asked, once they were underway.

"Nha Trang, headed to Bien Hoa," Smitty said, his attention momentarily diverted by the sights and sounds of downtown Saigon.

"Something, isn't it?" The other MP, the driver, was a specialist four who looked to be slightly older.

"It's not like I expected," Smitty admitted, staring wide-eyed at the bustle of the city. "From up north, we heard it was blown to shit during Tet."

"It was pretty messed up, but that was three months ago. Now it's dropped to just an occasional shelling," the older MP said. "But we were pretty busy there for a couple of days, especially when that suicide sapper force breached the embassy walls; the ambassador and General Westmoreland liked to shit a brick. Looks like you've been in the shit yourself."

"Just one of those things," Smitty said. "My friend came in-country as an MP just before Tet. I guess he made it through okay."

"What's your friend's name?" the younger of the two asked.

"Walter Wellmen."

The MPs looked at each other with alarm. The older one said suddenly, "Uh, look, sport, we're not supposed to have you riding with us. How 'bout we drop you here? The Caravelle Hotel is just two blocks up, I'm sure you can find your friend somewhere near there." He pulled to the side and the younger MP held the seat forward so Smitty could hop out.

Without a further word, the younger MP hopped back in the Jeep and they drove away.

That certainly was the bum's rush, Smitty thought to himself as he reached the sidewalk. Checking first to make sure that all his valuables were safely stowed in his breast pockets, Smitty set off toward his destination. It looked like Americanization had taken over.

The street was alive with bars named after American cities or songs, black market sidewalk stands that seemed to be adequately provisioned with everything from American cigarettes to perfumes, fleabag hotels, and dimly lit alleys with arrows illuminated for what Smitty guessed were directions to whorehouses or maybe even drug dens.

On the street, old Renaults left over from the days of the French mixed with every kind of vehicle. Buses, three-wheeled two-person tricycles, bicycles, scooters, carts, and even the odd dilapidated Hillman or two competed for lane space.

Smitty walked on, trying to avoid eye contact, but found that was impossible.

"Hey GI, you want to fuck my mother or sister, original cherry girls?" A young Vietnamese boy who looked to be about eight, going on eighteen, grabbed Smitty roughly by the arm.

"No thanks." Smitty jerked his arm free and walked on.

"I give special, two for one, they fuck you long time." The boy grabbed at him again.

"I said no." Smitty jerked his arm away a second time.

"You fag queer, GI." The boy gave Smitty the finger and ran away.

He was not thirty paces away when Smitty realized something else: his wristwatch was gone. Apparently, the second grab had done it.

Oh, well, Smitty thought to himself as he walked on, *it was just a cheap Timex anyway.* But it was a pretty good harbinger of what the influx of American culture had done to a country ill-prepared to absorb it.

Up ahead on his left, a bar named California Dreamin' was blaring a song of the same name by the Mamas and the Papas. The makeshift doors suddenly flew open and a young marine private came sailing out and landed hard on the pavement in front of him.

"Just because you're on leave don't give you the right to rip that gook's dress, grab her tit, and try to punch me when I try to stop you," a high-pitched voice said.

"Now get your ass outta here, and don't come back," the unseen voice said. A foot and leg came into view and kicked the young marine in the stomach and onto the street where his uniform merged with the untreated sewage water running along the curb.

When the young marine, badly winded but trying desperately to get up, did not move fast enough to suit his aggressor, the full person emerged into view. It was an American MP, a big MP; it was Big Walt.

"Hey!" Smitty said, stopping Big Walt, who was just about to kick the marine in the balls.

"Smitty!" Big Walt squealed, forgetting about the marine, who used the distraction to beat feet outta there.

"What are you doing, man?" Smitty asked. "Don't you think that was a little too much force?"

"Ah, man, you gotta understand how it is here. These gyrenes are the worst. They come down here all full of themselves, talking trash about how much shit they been in, go hog wild, and expect everyone to kowtow to them. I learned my lesson the first night, when I tried to talk to one of them and got a bottle upside my head. Since then, I take no chances; I swing first and ask questions later."

"I wouldn't think they would all be like that," Smitty said.

"Well, fuck 'em. I ain't letting what happened to Frenchy happen to me."

"Frenchy was hit by a rocket on a recon patrol in Da Nang."

"Rocket, bottle, it's all the same to these fucked-up gooks."

"Uh," Smitty began uncomfortably, "what time you get off?"

"2300."

"How about I meet you in the bar at the Caravelle and we can talk a bit?"

"Okay, fine, but let's make it out front. I'll take you to my place. If I'm a little late, it's because I still got a few heads to bust. Wait for me." Walt walked away with an arrogant swagger.

If Big Walt had changed so much, had LZ? Had he?

"You've changed a bit." Smitty and Big Walt sat in ramshackle chairs in the kitchen area of his one-room apartment, holding beers from the small refrigerator that whined incessantly in the corner. In the opposite corner was a straw mattress on the floor. The bathroom was no more than a drain downspout. The shower was a hose hung by a coat hook. In Harlem, it would have been a slum and declared uninhabitable; but in Saigon, it was probably considered middle-class.

"If what you're really saying is that I'm no longer the country bumpkin I was, then you're right," Walt said. "All my life, people been pushing me around and making fun of me. Now the foot's on the other shoe."

"No chance you could be a little over the top right now, is there?"

"None at all," Big Walt said.

At that moment, the door opened, and a Vietnamese girl who didn't look more than fifteen entered wearing makeup that looked like it had been put on with a trowel, a tight red miniskirt, and a white blouse. On seeing Walt, she yelled "Baby" in a thick Vietnamese accent and ran to him.

Walt caught her in his outstretched arms and wrapped her in a big bear hug. He gave her a deep, sloppy French kiss, a kiss she more than willingly accepted.

As he released her, he patted her rear end. "You got nooky for me tonight?"

"You betcha, MP cop," she said, spinning and allowing his hand to slide between her legs.

"Mmmm, baby," she moaned. "You fuck me long time; it your night."

"Your night?" Smitty repeated.

"Who he?" the young girl asked, as she slid behind Walt.

"He's okay, he's a stateside bro."

"You want I fucky sucky him too? I do." The girl peeled up her skirt, exposing a practically hairless genital area.

"How about it, Smitty, want a little pussy? She's young, but she definitely knows how to fuck, my man, and she can suck the chrome off the Famous '54's bumper belles."

"No, thanks, I'll pass," Smitty said.

"You no like Ke'? You lose. After Ke' fuck you, you no want to go home to fat pig American girls."

Smitty sat silently, taking it all in. Obviously, this young hooker was a shared arrangement that came with the apartment or vice versa. Smitty surmised that Walt probably rented this apartment with two or three other guys who worked different shifts, and "shared" the girl. Obviously, tonight was Walt's night.

"I think I'd better go." Smitty stood, drained the last of his beer, and set the can back on the table.

"You sure you won't stay?" Walt rose and shook Smitty's hand.

"No, I wouldn't want to spoil your fun."

"Well, take care, bro. Keep your head down," Walt called out as he closed the door.

On a hunch, Smitty stopped and leaned his ear against the door.

"Who that cocksucker, baby?" Smitty heard Ke' ask.

"Oh, he's some straight-ass Green Beret who used to be a friend of mine," Walt said. "He's a stateside choirboy; you're my friend now. Come here and let's smoke some of that good grass that I took off a marine this afternoon. Then I'll fuck you."

Smitty walked soundlessly away from the door. As he started down the steps, he looked back through the banister rails at the cheap apartment and heard Ke' squeal, "Oh stretch me baby with you big cock." He shook his head, continued down to the ground floor. On reaching the alley he was immediately enveloped by the combined pungency of Vietnamese cooking and raw sewage.

As he made his way through the narrow alley back to Tu Do Street, his thoughts couldn't help drifting back to Big Walt. To paraphrase Colonel Wilson, Walt had crossed over. And if what he had said was true, Walt would never be able to have peace; a piece of ass maybe, but no true peace.

Smitty would not seek him out again; as Big Walt had said, "He used to be a friend."

"Have a nice weekend?" Captain Bartkowski asked as they shook hands at the Bien Hoa operations building and started walking toward the helicopter landing area.

"So-so."

"Find your friend?"

"Yeah," Smitty answered.

"Not what you expected, huh?" Ron said.

"He's changed a bit."

"By that, I take it you mean for the worse," Ron said. "If there was ever a place to screw up your brains, this place will do it."

"Why doesn't it seem to affect you?"

"Fourth tour," Ron said. "But I'll tell you one thing, if you think it will help."

"Fire away."

"You've got to figure out how to hold onto your sanity by yourself."

"Great saying, Captain," Smitty said. "Ranks right up there with, 'There's an Edsel in your future.'"

"Think I'm full of it, don't you, Sergeant?" Ron asked. "Well, I'm not. Everybody goes a little nuts over here, but, as Colonel Wilson said, you have to know when you're close to crossing over, and at the crisis moment, you and only you can call the ball. This is made easier by good military discipline all the way up the command chain, but again, in the end, it's the guy with a weapon in his hand who lives it day to day, and he's the one who's finally responsible."

"What do you mean by discipline all the way up the command chain?"

Ron rubbed his chin. "Based on what you saw of your friend in Saigon, and assuming you don't agree with that behavior, do you think Colonel Wilson would tolerate that kind of behavior in this group?"

"No, I don't."

"Why?"

"Because he lets you know that he's still in control and that you will be held accountable for your actions, as he is for his own," Smitty answered with conviction.

"Right," Ron said. "You know we heard rumbling of a bloodbath just up the road at My Lai last month—ugly stuff, hundreds of civilians, mostly women and children, killed, gruesome stories of army soldiers raping women then shooting them in the vagina—that kind of thing. Even got some intel to back it up, but everyone up to the division commander denies it. Doesn't it strike you as strange that they don't even want to investigate?"

"Yes, it does, if what you say is true," Smitty admitted.

"Care to guess why?"

"Based on what you just said, probably because the breakdown in discipline is so acute that they know it's true and figure, probably correctly, that if they don't cover it up, they'll get tarred with the same brush."

"That's pretty smart for a buck sergeant. I think it deserves a reward."

"What have you got in mind?"

"Well, this, for one," Ron said, unbuttoning his breast pocket and withdrawing a set of E-6 chevrons. "Sew these on your uniform, Staff Sergeant." Smitty stared. "Don't look so surprised, you've earned it."

"Thanks, Captain. When will this be effective?"

"Well," Ron paused and rubbed the back of his neck in discomfort. "It actually came with your Commendation ribbon, but I convinced the colonel that we should hold the new stripe up until I was sure it would fit you."

Smitty stuffed the chevrons in his breast pocket. "Captain, they'll fit."

Ron slapped him playfully on the cheek. "I think so, too."

The thumping of the approaching helicopter rotor blades drowned out further conversation. This Huey was flown by an air force officer—a major, not a twenty-something stick jockey—and it was camouflaged and had no markings or number on the tail, just a picture of the Green Hornet.

"Ah, our chariot awaits," Ron said.

"Where we going?" Smitty said in a voice laced with apprehension.

"Part of your promotion celebration; I'm taking you on a little sightseeing trip," Ron said.

They landed a short time later at Quan Loi just inside the Vietnamese border adjacent to a suspected VC safe area in Cambodia called the fishhook. They waited on board the aircraft, near where another helicopter, an older model Kingbee, a tall and thin '50s version of a helicopter, was autorotating, obviously waiting to pick up passengers; it would not be a long delay.

Nine men, fully loaded with field equipment, walked up to the helicopter and got on. The team, from what Smitty could see, comprised three Americans and six Yards. The Kingbee lifted off with the Huey right behind.

Incredibly, they were headed directly toward the Cambodian border. After only twenty minutes, the Kingbee began to circle while the Huey remained aloft at three hundred feet. It was almost dark and overcast. Smitty thought the LZ would be extremely difficult to spot, but apparently it was not for the other pilot.

With practiced ease, he set the helicopter down only momentarily and was already pulling the stick back to take off as the team jumped from the helicopter and ran toward the cover of the surrounding treeline.

Suddenly, AK-47 fire opened up on the aging helicopter, strafing it with gunfire. The pilot of the Huey banked slightly, pushed the stick forward, and the right door gunner began firing at the tree line in front of the team.

The Huey began to take rounds from the groundfire. The door gunner was hit across the chest but was not seriously wounded thanks in no small part to his "chicken plate"—a piece of ceramic worn across the chest. Often, extras were kept around to sit on to protect your crown jewels.

One of the VC rounds had hit the gunner in the arm, rendering it useless. Smitty climbed over the rear seat into the gunner's space and grabbed the gun, which was swinging freely, suspended from the ceiling by an elastic cord.

Smitty began to fire on the treeline where he could clearly see the VC firing on the team and pinning them in a clearing of elephant grass. Smitty thought that they were all dead meat when suddenly the first team member jumped up and fired his weapon—it looked like a British Sten submachine gun—then sprint to his left. Immediately, the second man did the same thing, then the third, and so on through the entire nine-man team.

This obviously practiced drill allowed them a vital thirty seconds to put out a shitstorm of gunfire and escape into the trees. Smitty continued firing the '60 until the helicopter completed its pass and banked right to come around for a second pass on the left. As the other door gunner fired his '60, Smitty applied a pressure dressing to the wounded gunner's arm. The Huey was completing its second pass as the Kingbee lifted away.

When they reached three hundred feet, they banked away from the LZ and turned back toward the Vietnamese border. Twenty-five minutes later they were back at Quan Loi. The door gunner was hustled away for treatment. Smitty and Ron and a senior team leader who had met them when they landed adjourned to a private spot for, as Ron said, some informal conversation and a lot of beers.

"So, what do you think, Staff Sergeant?" Ron asked.

"Hot damn, the cap's got another volunteer. Welcome to the war with no name." The senior team member, a forty-something sergeant first class lifer with a weatherbeaten face and a receding hairline tossed Smitty a beer.

Smitty caught the Pabst Blue Ribbon, smiled at the sergeant, and said uncertainly to Ron, "Um, I'm not sure what to think. I didn't know that we were engaged in activities in Cambodia."

"And Laos," the sergeant said.

"And Laos," Smitty repeated.

"Well, see, that's the beauty of it. We're not, at least not officially." Ron took a deep pull on his beer. "If you join us, it'll be like joining a military version of *Mission: Impossible;* we go in sterile uniforms, with no insignia or rank, and if you're killed or captured, the U.S. government officially denies that you exist."

"Yeah, kind of like 'Secret Agent Man,'" the sergeant said, starting to sing. "They're giving you a number and— "

"Shut up, Blackbird. If you can't improve on silence, zip it," Ron said. He grinned. "I'm trying to recruit him, not scare him off."

Blackbird stared blankly at the captain for a long moment, took a long pull on his beer, then finally said, "Yes, sir."

Smitty watched the exchange with interest. There was a relaxed informality with Ron that, on the surface, could be misunderstood. There was also no question now as to who was in charge.

"You told me several times that you don't want to get your shit blown away for nothing. Here's your chance to do something that matters. Something for all those grunts out there humping it from one day to the next."

"What exactly is the mission?" Smitty asked.

A smile spread slowly across Ron's face. "Observe and report."

"Just like Savannah," Smitty said.

"Just like Savannah," Ron repeated. "Only here, we do something about it. What your team reports, we follow up on with a shitload of bombs and rockets aimed at destroying what you find. And remember, what we destroy, the VC can't use against us in-country."

"You must have some political clout," Smitty said.

"My boss's boss reports directly to the joint chiefs in Washington."

Smitty sat drumming his fingers on the PBR, thinking. He looked first at Blackbird, who gave him a knowing wink, and then at Ron, who was staring at Smitty expressionless. "Okay, I'm in. What's the next step?"

"The official title of this group is Studies and Observation Group, or SOG. We have ten nine-man operational teams that make incursion missions into Cambodia and Laos, and, when required, North Vietnam. Obviously, not all teams are in the field at the same time. These teams are based at command and control centers in Da Nang for Northern Laos and North Vietnam, Kontum for Southern Cambodia, and Ban Me Thuot for Northern Cambodia and Southern Laos. Although you will operate out of Pleiku, we do share resources when things get tight.

"I am in charge of a forward observation base, FOB, at Pleiku. My job is to house, recruit, and train both Americans like yourself and native Yard recruits who make up the balance of the incursion team. I also supply equipment for the teams. When we mount major assaults of fifty to one hundred men or so, I, or someone like me, will be designated to lead the mission. You'll be assigned to the Kontum center but will billet at Pleiku with my group.

"First, we're going to get you to our secret training facility at Long Thanh, and then you'll be assigned to a recon team as third member. As your experience grows, you'll move up, but not before. We don't stand much on rank here; experience is what counts.

"The conventional marine and army officers typically don't like us, preferring a more conventional war, but they do need us. As I told you several months ago, our intel, which came directly from a mission like this, was ignored at Lang Vie, and you saw what happened firsthand.

"Last, and most important, this group is secret. I repeat—secret. You don't talk about what you do on a mission or even acknowledge the existence of this group to anybody, I repeat—anybody. Drunk or sober, keep it zipped. If anybody asks what your assignment is, you tell them that you're part of a Special Forces Mike Team assigned at Pleiku for standby duty to reinforce hot areas as required. Got it?"

"Yes, sir," Smitty said. "When did you first decide that I might be a fit for this group?"

"Your file first came to our attention after that 'Basic MP Bashing' when Jim sent it to Lieutenant Colonel Wilson. I followed up and watched, and, as you know, we planned several activities as sort of an initiation, at the successful conclusion of which I credited your account, so to speak." Ron said.

"What about Frenchy and LZ?"

"There were plans to add Sergeant Douchet to the SOG rolls, but, unfortunately, he was injured and rotated home. We feel, however, that Sergeant McCord is a bit too impetuous for recruitment at this time, although he is perfectly suited to his current 'conventional' Special Forces assignment."

Seeing his hands empty, Blackbird flipped Smitty another beer. He opened it, pondering everything the captain had told him.

"Okay, Irishman," Ron said with a grin.

"Irishman," Smitty echoed.

"Irishman," Ron repeated. "Your call sign; don't forget it. It's not only your call sign, but it's also your radio identification sign if you're in trouble."

Smitty nodded, somehow sure that this was now not only his SOG call sign, but his moniker. "And you are?"

"The Polack," Ron answered.

"Or the Crazy Fuckin' Polack, if you must be colloquial," Blackbird said.

"It figures," Smitty said. "I'll say one thing, Captain. You sure know how to hold an informal conversation and pick up the bill."

And Smitty had a feeling it would turn out to be quite a bar tab.

CHAPTER TWELVE

The training at Long Thanh, was, in a word, thorough. It was not about firing weapons or combat tactics, although those were certainly addressed. This was about how not to bungle in the jungle.

"We'll teach you how to think like a VC, to move through dense jungle silently like a VC, and to sense danger like a VC. The result of which will elevate your chances of survival in the jungle—just like the VC."

"Remember, the Vietcong that were sent south, and the NVA regular troops from the north have been fighting this war for generations. They're patient; you have to be, too," the instructor had counseled. "Ho Chi Minh went to grad school on Sun Tzu's *The Art of War*. His tactic is to drag the war on at a stalemate until the American public loses interest and demands that we withdraw."

At the conclusion of the instruction, Smitty's basic knowledge of the VC, the NVA army, and their tactics, and perhaps most importantly, the warning signs of what to look for, had improved somewhere around 1000 percent.

Smitty now knew what thousands of U.S. soldiers and officers didn't: how to fight the VC using their own methods of hit-and-run against them, creating fear and uncertainty in their minds just as they had done in the Americans'.

Unfortunately, most senior officers were still fighting their conventional war with their conventional World War II knowledge, led by their conventional American leaders wagging their tongues about the Domino Theory with their "We're trying to stop the spread of communism" repertoire and their bloated egos . . . and young American soldiers were dying weekly by the hundreds as a result.

Smitty now felt sad for the young draftees who were given nine weeks of basic, eight weeks of advanced individual training, thirty days leave to say good-bye to mommy, and then a ticket to Vietnam; the return was often through a hospital or direct to Arlington in a body bag.

But the training was, as they say, just the end of the beginning. This group seemed to exist pretty much as a separate army within itself. It had everything from its own supply of special weaponry to specially designated helicopters, clothes, and other equipment. Smitty's primary Special Forces skill of tactical weapons was a good fit for the team's standard weapons choice, a Colt CAR-15 which looked like the M-16 but with a barrel half the length and a folding stock.

Additionally, the unit had its own special weapons, from a six-inch custom black bayonetlike jackknife, to mini-hand grenades called golfballs and small mines called toetappers; there was a virtual arsenal of weapons from which to choose. Smitty's .357 seemed to fit right in. In fact, it was seen as one of the tamer weapons.

Smitty was learning fast; counterinsurgency was a totally different kind of war.

The nine-man team he was assigned to, Blackbird's team, was comprised of a team lead, Blackbird, who had twelve missions behind him; an assistant team lead named Bulldog with eight missions' experience; a third man, who usually carried the radio, in this case, Smitty; and six Yards, commonly called Nungs, recruited from the surrounding mountain tribes of the area.

Smitty had been with the group for four months since completing his training in late May and had been on four missions: three five-day, the other an eight-day.

Fortuitously, he had been under fire only twice. A slight skirmish on the third mission involved a lot of fire, but with called-in air support, the team was extracted with only a minor injury to one of the Nungs. A full-fledged firefight on the last mission had left Smitty and most of the team with minor shrapnel wounds, but as Blackbird had said, "No autopsy; no foul."

"Morning, Irishman," Ron said, entering Smitty's hooch with an envelope in his hand.

"Morning, Captain, what's up?" Smitty said, not bothering to get up from his rack.

"This." Ron flipped the envelope onto Smitty's chest.

Smitty tore open the envelope to find an official army letter from the Legal Beagle down in MACV in Saigon formally ordering Smitty to appear at Ton Son Nhut, ostensibly to testify, but in reality to act as a character witness for Private First Class Walter Wellmen in his court-martial proceedings.

The letter went on to state that when Wellmen was arrested for assault and battery, excessive cruelty in the performance of his daily assignments, and being absent without leave, an altercation had broken out that had ended with a fellow MP having his neck broken and subsequently dying the next day as a result of the injury. The cause of the injury and subsequent death was a judolike blow struck to the neck with tremendous force by Private Wellmen.

The letter required that Smitty be at Ton Son Nhut Air Base by the evening of September 24 and ready to testify at 0900 hours the following morning.

The last paragraph stated that Sergeant McCord and "certain locals"—or indigenous personnel, as they were formally called in military terms—would also be testifying. Smitty was warned that should he come into contact with them, he was not to discuss the case in any manner.

"What do you think?" Smitty asked, passing the letter over to Ron.

Ron scanned the letter quickly and passed it back to Smitty. "Have a nice trip."

"But what about the mission? We're all set to go on the evening of the twenty-third. We've been delayed twice already."

"And you now will have been delayed three times, Staff Sergeant," Ron said. "This is not an invitation to your high school prom. It's an official subpoena from a military court. Get your ass to Saigon. I'll review your mission with Blackbird, then I'll repo depo someone with equal experience. Are we clear?"

"Crystal, sir," Smitty climbed quickly out of his rack, stood at attention, and cracked off a razor-sharp salute. The captain returned it with equal formality, then spun on his heels and left without further word.

Smitty suspected that the captain wasn't upset with him as much as the army bureaucracy. This mission was deep into Laos to observe and report on the enemy supply buildup. It had been planned and rescheduled for weeks. There was a good chance that continued delay would cause a security leak and cost them the element of surprise, but there didn't seem to be any way around it.

As he lay back down, his thoughts drifted to his stateside friends.

Smitty had been in-country eight months now, and it had been close to five since his last contact with Walt in his apartment in Saigon. He was surprised, but, then again, not surprised by Walt. He'd heard through the grapevine of a sadistic MP in Saigon who performed his duty with excessive zeal. His last two letters had gone unanswered, so Smitty had not written again.

Frenchy, on the other hand, was Emily Post in drag, writing faithfully once a week, even if Smitty didn't. His arm and shoulder had been operated on eleven times and he was not done yet. While the arm was healing, he'd been assigned to administrative duty at the Fort Polk, Louisiana, hospital, riding out his time until an early out, tentatively set for April of 1969.

LZ had written sporadically. It seemed duty in the Delta had been pretty up and down, mostly down since Tet had ended. His last letters implied that he had a little too much time on his hands and was getting bored and had begun volunteering to go on Mekong Delta riverboat missions with the Navy Seals. They thought he was nuts, as these river patrols were extremely dangerous; but casualties being what they were, they took him anyway.

And what effect was it having on him? Smitty was drinking a lot more, that was for sure; his alcohol consumption had gone from one beer a week to two and sometimes four a day when back at base. After his first incursion mission, Smitty had gotten shitfaced and stayed that way for two days. The only reason that there had been nothing said about this was that with this group, after returning from a cross-border jaunt, the entire team got a week to decompress. Comparatively speaking, two days was a fart in a whirlwind.

Smitty also noticed that he was now tense and suspicious of everyone—especially the South Vietnamese. It seemed perverse that the very people they were sent there to save were the ones who bore the brunt of the pain, but he just couldn't get close to them. Hell, he trusted the goddamn Nungs more than any Republic of South Vietnam soldier he'd met to date, to say nothing of the local villagers.

It was a strange war. Nothing in the army's stateside training could prepare you for the reality of the actual conflict. The new commander, Abrams, who'd taken over for Westmoreland in the spring, had pledged to carry out President Nixon's promise to reduce the American involvement by training the South Vietnamese to take over more of the actual fighting themselves.

Some stateside bureaucrat had coined the term Vietnamization to describe it, and the name had stuck with the press. But so far, the results were infinitesimal. Having been trained himself under Patton in World War II, Abrams seemed to be taking the same conventional approach to the war that had failed for his predecessor. Rumor had it that he also was not fond of the SOG mission, believing that wars were to be fought face to face.

It struck Smitty as funny that a marine general had made a statement to Colonel Wilson that they were having trouble locating the enemy; Colonel Wilson replied that they were having trouble not finding them and invited the general to send some of his troops over the border to accompany an incursion team on a mission. The general declined, stating that he didn't believe in this behind-the-lines shit. Colonel Wilson shook his head sadly and walked away. Probably, Smitty now knew, because he understood what the real war was about.

On the surface, it was about the will of the South Vietnamese people to determine their destiny and all that crapola that sold well to reporters, politicians, and other uninformed people who hadn't been there. But in reality, it was nothing more than a dirty little civil war between two halves of the same whole.

The South Vietnamese people were caught in the middle. They were afraid to cooperate with the Americans, fearing reprisal from the VC if they did and from their own government if they didn't. That was the real no-win situation of Vietnam. As it was with every war, the civilians were trapped in the middle.

General Westmoreland's war of attrition and body-count big-win theory had proved, after four years and just short of 25,000 American deaths, to be woefully inadequate. Abrams didn't seem to get it, either.

It all seemed so simple to Smitty and his SOG comrades. Blackbird had said repeatedly in his drunken soliloquies, "If those fat-assed Washington bureaucrats and World War II vintage fighting generals would forget about borderlines and concentrate on supply lines, this war would be over in six months. Take away their supplies; you take away their ability to make war. Then what have you got? Peace." While Smitty recognized that this was an oversimplification, it sure seemed to be a concept worth exploring.

In each of Smitty's missions over the border, they had reported on enemy troop movements, methodology, and in some cases, huge caches of supplies. But by the time the information was filtered through the army chain of command, debated, then acted on, the stuff was usually no longer there. It reminded Smitty of a line from a movie about Korea. "Supply is the enemy's jugular vein, and no price is too high to cut it." What Washington needed was the balls to take a big pair of scissors to the red tape, go across the border, and cope.

But Smitty would keep going, if for no other reason than for all the grunts in conventional outfits, day in and day out helicoptering in to engage an enemy who only fought when he was sure he had a tactical advantage, withdrew after inflicting maximum damage, and then returned only when the Americans were gone. He felt if he could help cut the supply lines, he might save some lives. Most of the men in SOG felt as he did and, as a result, believed fiercely in their cause.

As Smitty boarded the helicopter transport that would take him to Ton Son Nhut, he did so with mixed feelings. He desperately wanted to be with his team, but he also wanted to be there to help his former friend—if any such help was possible at all.

"Attention, the proceedings will come to order. All rise," the court-martial orderly sergeant announced formally. The judge, a no-nonsense full colonel from the adjutant general's office, entered and assumed his seat. He slammed his gavel down twice. "Let's proceed."

The prosecutor, an army captain in his early thirties, rose. "Your honor, if it please the court, the prosecution will show that the defendant, Private Walter Wellmen, did with malice aforethought, violently resist arrest on the night of September 4, 1968, and that as a direct result of the altercation that occurred during that arrest, Specialist Fourth Class Jerome Jackson sustained injuries from Private Wellmen that led to his death the following day at 0950 hours, September 5, 1968. The prosecution will prove that Private Wellmen did premeditatedly plan to kill anyone who tried to stand in his way, thereby justifying the charge and conviction of murder in the first degree.

"The prosecution will further show that Private Wellmen has been under surveillance by the Criminal Investigation Division or CID of MACV Command in Saigon for the last three months, commencing June 6, 1968, for theft of United States goods and services, selling illegal drugs, engaging in acts of procuring prostitutes to U.S. servicemen, and finally, for acts of repeated brutality to military and South Vietnamese personnel. The prosecution will prove that Private Wellmen is guilty of conduct unbecoming a United States Army soldier.

"To support this last charge, the prosecution will offer concrete evidence that

Private Wellmen was given every chance to change his wanton behavior by being repeatedly warned, counseled, reduced in rank, and finally removed from street patrol and assigned to administrative desk duty in efforts to curb his actions—to no avail.

"Finally, the prosecution will show that Private Wellmen left his assigned post on the night of September 2, 1968, without permission and was unreported for two days—justifying the third charge of deserting his post and being absent without leave.

"In closing, I would like to call the court's attention to a statement made by Private Wellmen when confronted by the four MPs sent to arrest him, 'I've been expecting you pussies; if you want to die, come and try to take me.' This one statement alone demonstrates the prosecution's case, and seals the defendant's fate with his own words." With a withering look at Private Wellmen, the prosecutor sat down.

The defense counsel, a first lieutenant who looked to be in his late twenties, rose and faced the court-martial board. "Gentlemen, the defense will show that the defendant is a victim of circumstance and was systematically framed by elements of the United States Army. The defense will further show that the defendant was pressured into deserting his post under threats of physical violence by his peers, and that the attempt to arrest Private Wellmen was a preconceived plan to murder the private by jumping him unexpectedly, and that no chance to surrender was given to him.

"The defense will prove that during that unprovoked attack, the injury to Specialist Fourth Class Jackson was an unfortunate occupational accident. Finally, the defense is confident that as a result of the testimony given and brought out at this trial, the jury will have no other option but to find my client not guilty of all charges." The lieutenant sat down to murmurs of disbelief from the assembled spectators.

With a heavy sigh, the colonel said, "Captain, call your first witness."

The first witness was the young marine Smitty had seen Walt tossing out of the bar back in May. After being sworn in, he recounted his version of the events of that evening. He was cross-examined briefly by the defense counsel, then excused.

The next witness was a navy seaman; he recounted basically the same kind of story with the same kind of cross-examination.

Ten more witnesses followed—three from the army, two from the air force, three from the marines, and two from navy. It took the balance of the day for all the witnesses to tell their tales. All had much the same story to tell. The prosecutor was laying a pattern of abuse through the testimony of all twelve witnesses—and doing it very impressively. The defense counsel tried to break down their stories by pointing out that they were all in varying states of intoxication and that the private was just doing his duty by maintaining order, but even Smitty had to admit that it sounded weak.

The next day, the prosecutor changed direction, calling a succession of local Vietnamese street vendors who fingered Walt as the one who sold them their American products. The defense counsel did cross-examine, asking if they pressured Walt to sell to them under threat of violence or blackmail. One street vendor's testimony was particularly damning in that he adamantly stated that not only was that not true, but that it was Walt who pressured them into buying from him. He said that he had at first refused, until Walt came to his shack late one night, grabbed his thirteen-year-old daughter, ripped her clothes off right in front of him and his wife and threatened him by saying that if he didn't buy from him, he'd take his daughter, first rape her himself, and then put her in his own whorehouse.

Ke' was the star witness the following day. She nodded assent to just about everything the prosecutor asked, even if she appeared to be unsure of the question. When asked if she had had sex with Private Wellmen, her eyes lit up. "You betcha, GI; Big Walty fuck Ke' loooong time." The polite laughter died quickly and turned to frowns when the Prosecutor asked Ke' if she had ever had sex with anyone else at Private Wellmen's request.

"Sure, GI. Ke' fucky sucky three, sometimes five, GIs a night when Big Walty say."

When asked if she was paid, Ke' said, "Big Walty pay all girls. Pay regular ten dollars American, every month. Plus Big Walty give American food and clothes to Ke's family. They sell; make more money. Ke' love Big Walty."

The lieutenant in cross-examination asked only if she charged her clients. "Leave that to Big Walty; I do what he say do."

The four CID investigators, three sergeants, and a lieutenant took the stand. Their testimony took the balance of the morning. Using charts and army records as a backup, they were able to show a pattern of United States items that had been shipped to Ton Son Nhut and Bien Hoa, and how, through comparison to Walt's activities, they were able to establish the trail from Walt to the vendors. They testified as to how they had confirmed this by marking items and tracking them until they ended up in the hands of the black market street vendors.

Finally, in the afternoon session of the third day, the key witnesses testified: the four arresting MPs. One by one they validated the prosecutor's opening statement. As they attempted to put the cuffs on Private Wellmen, he became violent and resisted arrest, striking wildly at the four of them in a desperate attempt to flee. They were compelled to use force to subdue him, striking him with M-16s several times until he was docile enough to be handcuffed.

The lieutenant tried in his cross-examination to prove excessive force was used, but that was hard, considering that Private Jackson was dead and two of the other MPs had sustained a broken jaw and a broken collarbone, respectively.

Following the lieutenant's cross-examination, the court adjourned for the day. Curiously, Walt did not look subdued at all. He had an expression of defiant confidence when he was led away. The defense's time would come tomorrow. Smitty and LZ were scheduled to testify, Smitty thought it would take a miracle for the fourth musketeer to avoid some very heavy time in Fort Leavenworth.

"What do you think, man?" LZ said to Smitty and the lieutenant, over a beer at the NCO club that evening. The fact that the lieutenant was an officer in the enlisted men's club didn't seem to upset anyone at all; neither did the lieutenant seem particularly concerned about the formal "don't discuss" rule. The Big Guy was in trouble and the lieutenant, more concerned with truth than protocol, had appealed to Smitty and LZ in hopes that they might help.

"It doesn't look good, does it?" the lieutenant asked gravely.

"Well," Smitty said, thoughtfully drumming his fingers on his beer can, "I can't deny what Walt's charged with. I mean, I'm sure he did belt the guy, but maybe there's some extenuating circumstances."

"Like what, man?" LZ said.

"Well, my old man always said that no one knows whether you're dumb or smart until you open your own big mouth and remove all doubt one way or the other. Right now, the Big Guy looks pretty clever, I think it's time we made him look a little stupider. So instead of looking at this incident by incident, which makes him look like he's guilty of everything up to and including the Lindbergh kidnapping, what if we step back a ways and look at this from a higher level?"

Both LZ and the lieutenant looked at Smitty as if he'd just lost his mind.

Smitty held up his hands. "Hold on a second, guys; hear me out."

"Fire away," the lieutenant said.

"First off, let's establish a few concrete facts about Big Walt." Smitty took a long pull on his beer while he collected his thoughts. "Nothing personal about the big guy, but I just don't believe he has the gray matter to put together and run an operation this big. I've known him since he was a stuttering doofus in basic. Yeah, I admit he's grown more confident, but that's no substitute for intelligence. Confidence doesn't change your IQ, does it?"

"Go ahead, we're listening," the lieutenant said.

"Well, if the basic hypothesis is inaccurate, then all thoughts from that point on are therefore invalid since they were based originally on that concept. So, if we assume that Walt isn't ingenious enough to put together this operation on his own, then all the rest of the activities are now suspect."

"Except, of course, the actual crime, which is fact," the lieutenant put in. "I mean, Jackson is dead."

"Yes, but suppose he was led to it? You know, the way an abused dog turns and kills its master," LZ said, joining Smitty's line of reasoning.

"What are you guys saying here?" the lieutenant said in confusion.

"One of my dad's other great sayings is you can't kick the dog in the ass all day and expect it to snuggle up with you at bedtime. There's somebody higher up who obviously felt the pressure coming and pulled the ladder up after them to keep their skirts nice and clean and let Walt and others like him take the fall."

"I think you said it the other morning," Smitty said. "Your opening statement was not just false bravado. The big guy was framed, and we've only got the rest of the night to prove it."

"You don't actually think we can pull this off, do you?" the lieutenant asked.

"If you mean get him off scot-free, no I don't believe so. But we might be able to bring to light enough facts to get the charge reduced from premeditated murder to maybe involuntary manslaughter or temporary insanity or whatever the technical term is," Smitty said.

"How?" the lieutenant asked.

A smile spread slowly across Smitty's face. "Well," he began, studying the depths of his beer, "I think there's a lot we can do, but we also need some outside help, and I think I know just who to call."

"Oh, shit," LZ said. "I've seen that smile before. Hold on to your ass, lieutenant. You're in for a wild ride."

There was no session the next morning. The lieutenant asked for, and received, a twenty-four hour delay to "research evidence brought out by the prosecution." When court opened the following day and everyone was seated, the judge said, "Lieutenant, call your first witness."

"Your honor, I'd like to recall the young lady Ke' to the stand."

As she walked seductively to the stand, Smitty suppressed a yawn. He and LZ had been up for two days tracking down some witnesses, and with the help of a few Yankee greenbacks, had gotten quite different stories from those they had told in court previously. Additionally, they had obtained some emergency personnel recruitment assistance from a certain air force two-star general.

"Now then, Ke', you realize you are still under oath to tell the truth?"

"Ke' tell," she responded.

"Very well, then. Would you please tell the court what prompted you to say the things about Private Wellmen you said in court the other day?"

"Sure GI Lieutenant, I tell. Ke' get visit from man. Man no give name, but man say Ke' help Big Walty if Ke' say what he tell her to say. Man give Ke' one hundred American dollars and promise more if what Ke' say end the way he want."

"What did this man look like?"

"Ke' not know for sure. He American, wear uniform. Talk from shadows. Ke' only notice he have gold on shoulder."

"You mean a cluster like this?" The lieutenant crossed the room and pointed to the insignia of rank on a major on the court-martial panel.

"Yes, that it."

"So, the truth is that you had sex with Private Wellmen but were never a prostitute for Private Wellmen. More like a girlfriend kind of relationship, is that right?"

"I good girl, I no fuck for money. I love Big Walty, want to marry, go to America. Do anything he ask."

"Did Private Wellmen ever promise to marry you and take you to the United States?"

"I wish," Ke' said, causing the judge to smile and the court-martial board members to laugh lightly.

"Thank you, you may step down," the lieutenant said.

Curiously, the prosecution did not wish to cross-examine.

The lieutenant recalled all of the street vendors and heard basically the same story. They had been paid, the same as Ke', to tell the story by the same mysterious major; although they couldn't recognize him, either, if pressed. Again, the prosecution was silent.

Next, the lieutenant called a doctor, an air force major who was not on the witness list, to testify. The prosecution objected, but they were overruled when the lieutenant stated that the doctor was being called to rebut testimony given under oath.

"Thank you for joining us, Major. Would you please describe your qualifications?"

"Yes, I have been a practicing physiologist for nineteen years, the last sixteen in the United States Air Force. My specific focus is the effect of mind-altering substances on the human body. I have participated on panels to study the effects of mind-altering drugs on soldiers starting with my first assignment after Korea."

"I called you yesterday morning and asked you to perform a service. Would you please tell the court what that service was?"

"Yes, uh, you asked me to interview Private Wellmen, understand his physical and mental condition, given the time allowed, and to come to court today to share my thoughts."

"I brought in an air force doctor to assure that the results were impartial," the lieutenant said, producing more laughter in the courtroom.

"Would you tell us, in your own words, what you found?"

"Well, with the help of a medical colleague to do the lab work, I found extremely high levels of illegal drugs in the private's system," the doctor replied.

"Such as?"

"Marijuana was the most prevalent. There were also large quantities of mescaline and LSD. In short, Private Wellmen is a drug addict," the doctor said.

"What, in your opinion, would be the effect of all of these drugs on Private Wellmen's system?"

"Well, the most obvious effect would be on his personality. One drug alone would tend to make him aggressive, but the combination would most likely make him lethal, sort of like a ticking time bomb waiting to go off. The closer he got to detonation, so to speak, or the edge of losing control of his faculties, the more assertive his actions would become. Since Private Wellmen is extremely insecure to start with, he would become extremely defensive and hostile when threatened."

"Doctor, I have just one more question." The prosecutor rose and approached the witness. "Is Private Wellmen responsible for his actions?"

"Yes, but I'm fairly certain in his present state he's not consciously aware of them." The doctor stepped down and the judge ordered a ten-minute recess.

"Your honor," the lieutenant said, "I'd like to call Private Wellmen to the stand."

There was a buzz in the courtroom as Big Walt took the stand. After he was sworn in and had stated his name, the lieutenant began.

"Why did you leave the post without proper authorization on the night of September 2, 1968?"

"When I got back to my hooch that night, there was a note on my pillow. It said that 'the man' had ordered me killed to keep me quiet and it was to be done that night. The note was signed 'a friend.' What would you have done?" Walt said.

"The man?" the lieutenant asked.

"Yeah, there was this guy who gave me orders, always by message, never in person. The message usually said I would be paid 'X' amount of dollars for delivering this or picking up that. After I completed the request, money would be left in my boots in my room."

"Where and how did you get started in this?"

"When I first came in-country, I used to hear some of the buds talking about the extra cash they were making on the side doing a little selling. They didn't make it seem like such a big deal. They told me everyone was doing it and told me that if I was interested, they'd set it up for me. I told them I was, and the notes and money starting appearing. Sometimes the payment would be money, sometimes drugs."

"Who were these 'guys,' as you describe them?" the lieutenant asked.

"Just American GIs I met in the bars downtown. I didn't ask their names," Walt said.

"Was beating up soldiers who owed money to this 'organization' part of your extracurricular tasks?"

When the big guy didn't answer, the lieutenant prompted, "Private, remember, you're under oath to tell the truth."

Walt looked down at the floor for five seconds, then nodded his head slowly and said in a sad voice, "Yes, sir."

"So the witnesses presented by the prosecution were, in effect, soldiers that you were sent to beat up or keep silent about the black market activities."

"Yeah," Walt said.

"Private Wellmen, it has been stated by the doctor that you are a drug addict. Do you dispute this?"

"Hell, yes, I dispute it!" Big Walt yelled back defiantly. "And no fuckin' shrink is gonna make me say I am."

"But you do take drugs?" the lieutenant prodded.

"Well, yeah," Big Walt said, with a little less defiance in his voice.

"Marijuana?"

"Yeah,"

"How often do you smoke?"

"I don't know, five, maybe six times a week. It takes the tension off."

"Mescaline?"

"Yeah."

"LSD?"

Walt inhaled audibly. "Yeah, LSD, all right."

"When did you start?" the lieutenant pressed.

"Right after basic with the Mary Jane, the rest when I came over here."

"Why?"

"'Cause I was scared, man," Big Walt said in a voice filled with anguish and remorse. "I mean, look at me, all my life people been making fun of me, calling me names and shit because I stuttered. But once I started to take the stuff, nobody made fun of me no more." He began to sob into his hands. "Nobody made fun of me no more."

"No more questions," the lieutenant said, as he patted Walt sympathetically on the arm.

The judge looked at the captain, who looked at the whimpering private and shook his head. There would be no cross-examination; none was required.

The court was recessed for ten minutes, then both sides gave their closing arguments. But given the unexpected turn of events, they were extremely tame. The judge gave final instruction to the board and they filed slowly out of the courtroom.

They were back inside the hour. As the foreman handed the judge the verdict the courtroom became deadly quiet. The judge looked at the verdict, asked the jury if that was their uniform decision. When they all said yes, he polled them one at a time, then nodded and looked at Big Walt, ordered him to rise and face the board, and began to read the outcome in a solemn voice.

"Private Wellmen, on the charge of first degree premeditated murder, the jury finds you not guilty.

"On the charge of deserting your post and being absent without leave, the jury finds you not guilty. On the charge of conduct unbecoming an army soldier, the jury finds you guilty."

The colonel paused, looked heavily at Big Walt, and continued. "It is the order of this court that you be reduced in rank to private, dishonorably discharged from the United States Army, that you forfeit all pay and allowances due, or to become due, and be transported to the United States Army facility at Fort Leavenworth, Kansas, to serve a sentence of no less than one nor more than three years.

"Reduction of sentence will be solely dependent on your personal efforts at completion of drug rehabilitation program. This court is adjourned." The colonel slammed his gavel, stood, and quickly exited the courtroom.

Big Walt sobbed silently as he was led away. Smitty was fighting back his own feelings of loss. The big guy did it to himself, but Smitty couldn't help feeling there was something he could have done.

"You did all you could, man," LZ said, reading his mind.

Smitty embraced his friend, tears forming in the corners of his eyes. "Take care of yourself, my brother; you're all I have left."

"I will, my man, I will," LZ said with emotion.

"Thanks, Sergeant," the lieutenant said, shaking Smitty's hand. "If you hadn't had your thinking cap on, Private Wellmen would have probably hung. Your call to General Martin sure helped our cause. But one thing still bothers me. How on earth did you ever figure out that something was wrong with the Vietnamese testimony?"

"Oh, let's just say that I was born under a shit cloud. A shit cloud that seems to crap on my friends as easily as it does me."

"I'm afraid I don't understand," the lieutenant confessed, looking bewildered.

"I do," LZ said with a slow nod.

"This shit cloud followed me to Nam," Smitty said, recognizing the inevitable, "and I'm getting right tired of the smell."

Smitty did a little calculation in his head. The four musketeers came to Vietnam together eight months ago. First there were three, now there were only two. If two were gone in eight months, and that was a linear calculation, then LZ and Smitty would be also—before either of them was twenty years old.

Smitty returned to Pleiku that afternoon. When he walked into the NCO club, he found a group of the SOG men drinking beer, toasting a comrade, and singing. It was a tradition that was observed whenever a SOG man was killed. But in this case it was worse; as much as it could possibly be.

Smitty's team had landed in Laos and been immediately ambushed, almost as if the VC had known they were coming. Blackbird, Bulldog, and Smitty's replacement, Whippoorwill, had been killed along with the entire Yard team.

Smitty was still getting over this shock when he had a priority message from LZ. The Seal team he had been working with had been likewise ambushed in the Delta, with similar results: all killed.

Although it could have been coincidence, Smitty did not believe it. Whoever the mysterious major was, he'd framed Big Walt and obviously leaked intel on LZ and Smitty, in hopes of getting them too, not knowing that they both would be pulled at the last minute for Walt's trial.

Smitty discussed his theory with Ron but did not find a believer. "Hell, four hundred Americans died last week, Sergeant. It's quite a stretch to assume that they were singling you and your friend out specifically," Ron said. "Forget it."

But Smitty couldn't forget it. As he had said to LZ, he was tired of the smell.

Dearest, I think it's best if we see other people . . . . First it was Frenchy, then Walt, and now Frenchy's sister Trudy.

Memories of Glenda flashed through his head; it was, according to a statement attributed to Yogi Berra, "déjà vu all over again." First Glenda, now Trudy. In the woman department, he was still at zero.

When Smitty had first come to Nam, he'd written Trudy at least three times a week, sometimes more, and she in return. In one of their early exchanges, they'd talked of meeting when Smitty got his week's R&R—or I&I, intercourse and intoxication, as it was more commonly called. But slowly, the letters had dropped to once a week, then every other. Smitty read the rest of the letter, then tore it into little pieces, and dropped it in the trash can.

Smitty had just finished disposing of the past when the captain approached and informed him that he would be reassigned to another team in the same position as soon as he got back from a recovery mission that Ron had volunteered him for: reclaiming the bodies of Blackbird and his team.

Because of the lack of immediately available experienced SOG men and the anticipated heavy concentration of enemy in the recovery area in Laos, a fifty-man extraction team would augment the traditional ten-man recovery force. The additional team was divided into two twenty-five-man squads, each led by a lieutenant and comprising primarily new SOG replacements from regular Special Forces and conventional army personnel—unfortunately, they had been given the primary extraction mission.

The ten-man SOG force comprised regular SOG members led by an experienced master sergeant. Smitty had been volunteered again as part of that SOG team; Captain Bartkowski would assume overall command of the mission, which was scheduled to leave within the hour.

They landed two clicks from where Blackbird's team had been inserted without incident, which in and of itself seemed strange, considering the area was hot enough just two days ago to claim nine lives in less than an hour. It seemed to Smitty one of the improbabilities of the war that an enemy force of five hundred to one thousand could clear out so fast.

Slowly, carefully, and quietly they made their way to the ambush site. It took five hours to accomplish this in the unfriendly thick jungle and terrain.

"There they are," the captain said, as he pointed to a clearing in the dense thicket about fifty yards from their present position. Using arm signals, the team silently spread out in a flanking formation and approached cautiously. Checking the bodies first for booby traps left by the VC, and finding only rudimentary hand grenades with the pins pulled, they quickly disarmed them and began the onerous task of placing the bodies in body bags for transport.

It had been a slaughter; there was no other word for it. The bodies were riddled with so many bullet holes that they looked more like Swiss cheese than human beings. Whippoorwill had been shot so many times that he had been decapitated; his body was a twisted mass of flesh lying four feet from his head, which gruesomely still had his boonie hat attached.

In morbid fascination, Smitty bent down for a closer look. Curiously, the spinal cord had been cleanly severed, not shredded, which was what you would have expected of a body literally being torn to pieces. Smitty looked closely at the severed head and found the same clean, almost surgical amputation. He turned away from the skull to begin to roll the body over and straighten the torso to remove the web belt and Stabo shoulder harness—a specially designed body harness that allowed SOG soldiers to be plucked from the jungle with a rope when a landing was impossible under fire—when he saw it.

"I got your message, man," Smitty said to himself, patting Whippoorwill's shoulder.

Whippoorwill had not been killed by enemy fire. He was captured, tortured, then killed, but definitely not just killed straight away. But one thing was certain, and that was that he did not die in a hailstorm of gunfire; he was decapitated while alive, then the body riddled with bullets to make it look as though he'd died that way. Somebody tortured him inhumanly to make him talk. He had died in agony, and Smitty would have bet he didn't tell them a thing. How could he? Being Smitty's replacement, he would not have understood the questions they were asking, but Smitty would've.

Smitty looked at the fingers of Whippoorwill's right hand. All were curled except one; the middle digit was raised. He was definitely alive when he gave the VC the finger—and sent Smitty a message.

They had just about completed the gruesome bag-and-tag task when the right flank support team came under heavy fire. Three of the extraction team members died instantly in the initial burst. Smitty had just grabbed his weapon when the left flank was opened on with the same fire, and unfortunately nearly the same results: four dead.

Mortars began dropping with deadly precision, wounding additional team members as they scurried for virtually nonexistent cover. They were in the middle of a targeted ambush. The VC obviously knew they were coming and had laid a well-made trap. Smitty looked desperately for the captain but in the smoke and pandemonium was unable to locate him. He next looked for the closest team lieutenant from B Force, and found him dead ten paces away. Smitty dove to the ground next to the lieutenant's radioman, grabbed the mic, and contacted the air force forward air controller who was bird-dogging them from above in a prop job.

"Fat Cat, Fat Cat, this is Irishman. Over," Smitty screamed.

"Irishman, this here is Fat Cat responding. Over," the FAC answered.

"We're in the middle of a VC shitstorm, taking fire left and right flank, frontal assault pending and could use all the armament you can get to cover extraction. Over," Smitty screamed back.

"Understand Irish, am painting targets now. Try not to crap your britches, Sonny, help is on the way," he responded in the same cool voice.

Smitty looked up to see Fat Cat fly over, marking the suspected VC targets with smoke. Almost immediately, four Hueys followed. The first two made straight passes, but the next two hovered in a 360-degree rotation with the door gunners firing almost directly downward, creating a ring of fire and cutting off the VC from the team.

Next, F-100 Super Sabre jets screamed overhead, throwing up a wall of fire from their nose cannons. A1 Skyraiders followed with cluster bombs. Then F-100 P-4 Phantoms screamed overhead, dropping five-hundred-pound bombs so close that Smitty was sure that several team members must have been hit by the shrapnel.

"The little Commie bastards are pulling back," Fat Cat said. "We've got you an emergency LZ, four hundred yards south of your position. Suggest you guys make like a shepherd and get the flock outta there 'cause I've got two A1s with napalm standing by for when the little mothers raise their heads."

"Already moving," Smitty answered. He turned to the radioman. "Call Lieutenant Henderson, tell him that his A Force needs to withdraw south through the trees to a temporary LZ and to go now with his wounded and secure the goddamn LZ for the B Force."

"Yes, sir."

Smitty ran to find the B Force platoon sergeant, locating him thirty yards away behind a mound, wounded from a round through his leg. "You walk?"

"If I can't, I can sure as hell crawl real fast," the sergeant said with conviction.

"Look, we've got about a three-minute window to get the fuck out of here before Fat Cat brings in two A1s and gives us all a third-degree suntan. There's an LZ four hundred yards south. A Force is leaving now with Lieutenant Henderson in the lead. You follow with the wounded in sixty seconds. Got it?"

"Got it, Lieutenant," the sergeant said, acknowledging his authoritative manner rather than his actual rank.

Smitty ran back to the radioman. "What's the holdup? Why isn't A Force moving?"

"He says he'll get killed if he moves out into open fire."

"Gimme that." Smitty grabbed the mic from the startled radioman and raged into the mic, "Lieutenant, if your fat ass isn't moving your force in the next ten seconds, I'm gonna tell the sergeant to take charge."

"I'm a lieutenant, Sergeant, and—"

"And I don't give a fuck. Move your goddamn ass, or I'll come over there and personally shoot you myself, you chicken-shit cocksucker; now move it!" Smitty roared.

That seemed to break the lieutenant's temporary paralysis. He signaled his force and they began moving rapidly to the south, carrying wounded and dead as fast they could. Thirty seconds later, the B Force with the fast-crawling sergeant was also on the move.

Smitty had detailed the security force to go last, setting Claymore mines and firing on the VC positions as a delaying action to allow the two main forces time to reach the LZ and evac—a technique they'd learned from the VC.

There were six members left; the team lead master sergeant was not one of them; he'd been one of the first killed when the VC opened fire. These six were regulars with code names just like Smitty—thank God.

"Underdog, did you see the captain?" Smitty asked a SOG sergeant as they paused to set Claymore mines.

"Last I saw, he was on his way to that dipshit lieutenant's right flank position when Charlie opened up. I saw him get hit and go down; don't know how bad; that's all I know."

Underdog finished his task and broke into a run. The radioman running beside Smitty called, "It's Fat Cat for you, sir."

Without losing a step, Smitty took the mic. "Initial fire site unassed. A Force and B Force at LZ; security team trailing 150 yards and closing fast."

"Mind your heads," Fat Cat said.

The A1s were already overhead and releasing their napalm canisters even before he could hand the mic back. The napalm hit three hundred yards behind the security team in a magnesium-type flash that sucked in the air around them. Smitty looked back and could only see VC bodies that looked more like charcoal briquettes than human beings.

They broke through the jungle into a small clearing. The evac Hueys were landing fifty yards away.

"Underdog, you and . . . "

"Greg Barber," the radioman answered.

"Greggy are with me. Little John, Graverobber, and Slimedog on the other. Go!" Smitty said, finishing his sentence as he pushed them toward the aircraft, pausing just long enough to check one last time for any enemy trailing them.

Greggy and Underdog were thirty yards from the last helicopter when three NVA regulars burst through the thicket and began firing in the direction of the helicopter with their AK-47s.

Smitty turned and sprayed a full clip from his CAR-15 and killed them. He turned and ran toward the helicopter, and saw to his satisfaction that Underdog was safely aboard, but, to his horror, Greggy lay face down twenty yards away, looking more dead than alive.

Smitty reached him in three seconds flat, just as more AK fire began churning up the earth around him.

"Leave me, man, I'm done for," Greg whimpered.

"Not 'til I fuckin' say you are, you asshole." Smitty snatched Greg off the ground, threw him over his shoulder, and ran for the helicopter as a second barrage of AK fire whizzed all around him, missing him by some incredible stroke of luck.

The helicopter was lifting off even as Smitty threw Greggy onboard. He stepped up on the skids, and vaulted cleanly onto the floor just as the chopper began to rise. Time seemed to lapse into slow motion as Smitty willed the helicopter upward. They reached an altitude of 150 feet and soon were safely at a three-hundred-foot cruising range.

"I'm getting too old for this shit," Underdog, who looked to be all of twenty-one, said to no one in particular as they headed back toward the Vietnamese border.

"Me too, brother, me too." Smitty settled back, closed his eyes and tried to think about anything other than the war as they flew back to Pleiku.

After every operational mission, a debriefing was held to ascertain what had gone right, what had gone wrong, and what they could do to correct it for the next time. Since there were eleven dead and twenty-three wounded from the rescue mission, the colonel had ordered Smitty, Captain Bartkowski, and Lieutenant Henderson to Special Forces headquarters at Nha Trang for a more formal review. As the colonel made his opening remarks, Smitty scowled at the lieutenant, a scowl that got him a raised eyebrow from the captain, and a silent defiant glare from the lieutenant.

"Captain Bartkowski," the colonel said in an even voice, "would you relate what happened, from your perspective?

"Sir, we landed at the assigned LZ, and in five hours were able to proceed to the ambush LZ without incident. As we were finishing the bagging, the VC opened up with fire to the right flank. Since there was not an immediate first response from A Force, I was on the move to the A Force area when a mortar round exploded in front of me. I remember turning to the master sergeant, ordering him to continue to the lieutenant's position and assure that the area was being secured. Then I passed out. Best I can recall," Ron answered.

"Did the master sergeant reach your position, Lieutenant?"

"No sir, he did not," the lieutenant answered. "I had just completed my own assessment of the situation and was just about to contact the FAC when that little buttinsky sergeant panicked and started screaming orders over the radio."

"By that little buttinsky, I assume you mean Staff Sergeant Smith?" the colonel said.

"Yes, sir. And may I add, Colonel, that if Sergeant Smith had followed the chain of command and allowed me to assume command as the senior lieutenant, then I think that I can state with assurance that the casualty rate would have been lower. The sergeant's inexperience led to a general panic, a panic that caused personnel under my command to bolt into the enemy fire, causing additional members of my team to be killed and wounded.

"It was only after I was able to firmly reestablish my command presence with my own force that we were able to complete an orderly defensive withdrawal to the emergency evac. Upon reaching the LZ, we set up a perimeter for the B Force and the regular SOG force to follow, thereby assuring their ability to escape.

"Personally, I would add two things. First, if it were not for my ability to handle the sergeant's hysteria, by humoring him and commanding around it, so to speak, I don't think anyone would have gotten out of there alive."

"I read that in your report recommending yourself for a Silver Star. And the second point, Lieutenant?"

"I think the sergeant should be court-martialed for panicking under fire," the lieutenant said. "In fact, as you'll note sir, I wrote as much in my report."

"That's a pretty serious charge, Lieutenant," the colonel said. "Are you sure that the sergeant's actions warrant that dire a step?"

"Yes, sir," the lieutenant answered.

"Sergeant, your response?" the colonel asked.

"I think the lieutenant is as full of shit as a Christmas goose, sir," Smitty said.

"Well, I cannot speak to the lieutenant's latest bowel movements, Sergeant, so I would prefer your response in a more concrete military form," the colonel said tightly.

"I was speaking metaphorically," Smitty said.

"I see," the colonel said; although it was plain he did not. "Well, Sergeant, just for the sake of argument, what would you recommend the lieutenant do next time to unblock his large intestine?"

"There won't be a next time, sir."

"Why not?"

"Because if I have to go on another mission with that useless West Point son of a bitch, I'll shoot him through the head before we leave," Smitty said bluntly.

"I rest my case, sir," the lieutenant said.

"Fuck you, sir," Smitty said, flipping the lieutenant the bird.

"Gentlemen, I have read your individual reports and all the other reports from the key personnel involved in this mission, and ordered this meeting here to discuss the events in," the colonel paused, "let us say, more detail, than the written reports indicate.

"After this brief, but albeit informative, review, it is clear to me that the views are quite polarized; therefore it is my duty to reach some conclusions, and as a result, make some rather painful decisions.

"Lieutenant, after careful consideration and a great deal of outside personal investigation on my own, I would like you to write up your recommendation into a formal army document."

"Yes, sir," the lieutenant answered, basking in the colonel's attention. "I'll have a formal set of charges on Staff Sergeant Smith written up and on your desk by 1800 hours, sir."

"Lieutenant, I was referring to the recommendation for the Silver Star."

"It would be no trouble to include that also, sir."

"Very well," the colonel said, crushing out his cigarette. He got up from the chair and walked around to where the lieutenant was standing. "Lieutenant, I want a set of documents for a recommendation for the Silver Star prepared and on my desk by 1600 hours today. Take no shortcuts, have it complete and in triplicate for forwarding up the command chain. Once submitted, your full-time assignment will be to hand-carry it from desk to desk as required. Your mission target is to have it approved in ten days so that it can be awarded on Friday of next week."

"Yes, sir," the lieutenant said. Smitty thought for a minute he was going to kiss the colonel.

"Excellent. I expect to see you and Sergeant Smith back here a week from Friday where you, as his commanding officer—well, interim commanding officer, anyway—will present the decoration to the sergeant in my office."

"The sergeant, sir?" the lieutenant asked, the color draining from his face.

"Of course, Lieutenant. As I said, I read all the reports, then flew to Pleiku and talked to several members of the regular SOG team. After review, I'm afraid my assessment supports the facts as recounted by the sergeant in his written report," the colonel said.

"But what about the recommendation for the court-martial?" the lieutenant asked.

"Lieutenant, if I were you, I'd make sure that I completed the assigned task I have given you by next Friday. The sergeant has already told you what he plans to do with you before your next mission together. If you're not ready, I may let him, metaphorically speaking."

"Yes, sir." The lieutenant gave a half-salute, which the colonel did not bother to return, and without another word left the colonel's office.

"Son, you handled yourself right well in that ambush," the colonel said to Smitty when he, Ron, and Smitty were alone. "The opinion of certain second lieutenants notwithstanding.

"Now then, let's talk about you. You just did an incredibly brave thing, however, in reviewing your file to gather background information for your forthcoming commendation, I've found certain facts of which I believe you are quite aware."

Now it was Smitty's turn to have his face change colors faster than the famous Ludowici, Georgia, speed-trap red light. Damn, just when you thought you'd run away from the past, it jumped right out and bit you on the ass. Amazing that even in a shithole like

Vietnam, they'd found him.

"Uh, yes, sir."

"You do know what I'm talking about, don't you, Sergeant?"

"Um, not exactly, sir," Smitty said.

"Let me see if I can help clear the cobwebs, son." The colonel stood up and walked to his desk. He took a file from a drawer, leafed through several papers, and stopped and tapped one.

"As you know, and I've known since your security mission into Savannah, you and your cohorts lied your way into the army by falsifying documents that allowed you to meet the minimum age requirements of eighteen. I have to admit, you provided a very impressive set of forged documents stating that you were remanded to the custody of the United States Army in lieu of civilian prosecution.

"It was that more than anything else that caused us to check a little closer. Since you entered the service from Florida, we sent an inquiry to the Miami Police. The assistant chief of the department, a Stanley Baker, with whom I believe you are personally acquainted, responded to our letter. Would you like to know what the chief has to say?" Smitty did not immediately respond.

"Thought so." The colonel walked back to the chair, sat down, and began to read:

Colonel Martin,

I am responding to your request for information on a Kevin, AKA Smitty, Smith and his two colleagues regarding their disposition to the United States Army.

Short and to the point, this was a complete case of mistaken identity resulting in misapplied blame. Mr. Smith and his two colleagues, Mr. Johnsele Douchuet, and Mr. Lucius McCord, were mistakenly implicated in a teenage gang killing that occurred in Miami during a time of great upheaval when quick blame and even quicker justice were the order of the day.

Initially, Mr. Smith and his two associates were found guilty and banished from the state in the political purges following the riots in mid-1965. That process was reversed and the conditions surrounding the remand removed in August of 1967 by order of the Florida State Superior Court. This was due in no small part to the actions that Mr. Smith, Mr. Douchuet, and Mr. McCord took, at great personal risk, to bring the truth to light.

On a more personal level, I can say that I have known Mr. Smith for four years, and consider him a person of the highest moral fiber. Should the time come when the United States Army no longer requires his services, I would welcome him home to Miami with open arms. There is a badge waiting for him with his name and a corresponding Miami Police Department number assigned to it.

Best regards,
Stan

P.S. If you are in contact with Mr. Smith, please give him this message: "All sins forgiven, come home."

"That seems to clear up a lot, son. Know what the PS means?"

"Yes, sir," Smitty said.

"Me, too." The colonel smiled. "As I said, it clears up most of your problems, but it still leaves us one big one left to solve."

"Such as?" Smitty replied, raising an eyebrow.

"Well, both the captain and I feel that your current skill level is adequate for your current NCO billet. However, if you wish to aspire to the higher NCO ranks or even officer ranks through a field commission and assume the authority you exercised on the last mission, there is a specific thing that will hold you back from future advancement, should you elect to remain in the army."

"And that would be?" Smitty said.

"You forgot, when you forged your papers, to forge yourselves a high school diploma."

"Fuuuuck," Smitty said. "I don't give a shit about that."

"You'd better," the colonel said, "if you ever want to make sergeant first class or master sergeant. It's a fundamental army requirement, no exceptions. Are we clear?"

"Yes, sir," Smitty said. "So I guess I'm a six until after Nam, huh? When I can go back to school with all the other dropouts."

"Not necessarily," Ron answered. "The colonel and I put our heads together and we've come up with an idea to help your educational process along."

"This ought to be just dandy," Smitty mumbled.

"What was that, Sergeant?" The colonel asked abruptly.

"Uh, nothing, sir. That is to say, thank you for taking such a personal interest in me, sir."

"As I was saying before I was so rudely interrupted," Ron said, "the following is the plan of procedure.

"You are on in-country R&R here at Nha Trang until Lieutenant Henderson finishes your paperwork and you receive your well-deserved commendation. Immediately following that, you're to catch the first plane out to Okinawa. You'll be on detached duty until such time as you complete your high school equivalency diploma course.

"Following that, you will be allowed one week's official R&R, tentatively scheduled to start 6 November in Hawaii, and are to return to Nha Trang no later than 15 November, 1968. On your return, the tentative plan is for you to be reassigned as a team lead in your old unit based out of Pleiku. Questions?"

"What if the paperwork runs into trouble because of the Saigon MACV bureaucrats reducing the recommendation like they usually do for SOG teams?"

"Don't see that happening, Sergeant," the colonel answered. "Seems there is a general, General Ben Martin to be exact, who knows you personally, just in from the States. He assured me that he would help speed up the process.

"That's about it, son," the colonel said, rising and extending his hand.

"Thank you for the help, sir," Smitty said, taking the colonel's hand.

"Oh, son," the colonel said, stopping Smitty as he turned to leave.

"On that other matter. Your father will land at Hickum Field in Hawaii on 8 November on his way to Thailand. Maybe the two of you could get together and forgive each other a few sins."

Smitty, speechless, left the colonel's office.

Before leaving Vietnam Smitty had a few quick private words with the colonel. The discussion was fruitful. They discussed, among other things, family relations and how those could be important—in the past, the present, and the future.

Sometimes, when you least expect it, he thought as he boarded the plane, *in spite of everything you personally do to fuck it up or prevent it, events happen that just plain-ass restore your faith in life—either that, or God has one hell of a sense of humor.*

CHAPTER THIRTEEN

Sergeant, the last time anything caused this much chaos on this island, it was a volcano. So you leave me no choice but to invoke the harshest sentence within my power," the night court judge said in a heavy voice. "Since you are the property of the United States Army here on R&R, I'm restricted in what I can officially do."

He stared pointedly at Smitty to let him know what he thought of that arrangement. "Therefore, it is my judgment that you be escorted directly to Honolulu Airport by the police, and take a commercial flight out of the state of Hawaii within the next twelve hours. Should you not comply with my directive, you will be returned to my presence and formally charged with contempt of my court."

"It is also ordered that you are not to return to the territorial limits of the state for a period of no less than three years. We are a young, growing state with an eye firmly on expanding our tourism business. Such antics as yours are a part of our distant past, not our new future. Do you have any comment you wish to make?"

"Well, that still leaves me forty-eight states to get thrown out of," Smitty said with a smile.

Smitty's court-appointed public defender, a clean-cut young man of about twenty-five, elbowed him in the ribs. "Shhh, he's giving you a break, Sergeant. Don't get on his bad side."

The judge picked up his gavel. "Six hours. Court dismissed."

The public defender grabbed Smitty's arm and hastily led him away before he could open his mouth again.

When they had exited the courtroom and were standing alone in the hallway under the watchful eye of two policemen, the junior legal beagle said, "What is wrong with you, Sergeant? He was trying to give you a break."

"Oh, that's what it's called," Smitty said. "I noticed the locals got off clean. Guess the Holy Roller judge is blind to their part in the donnybrook, or maybe he collects a cut."

"I don't think he's blind; I think it's the repetition factor, Sergeant,"

"Could be, could be. Look, uh, thanks for the assist. I know you did your best, uh . . . " Smitty offered his hand, fumbling to remember the lawyer's name.

"Tom Dempster. Thanks, Sergeant, and good luck to you." He shook Smitty's hand, and headed down the hall toward the holding cells.

"Let's go, Sergeant." A police officer in his early twenties prodded him with his nightstick.

Smitty glared silently at the officer and was considering taking the baton away from him and shoving it where the sun never shines, when an older officer said quietly, "Ease up, Jerry. The soldier will move directly. And I don't think we'll be needing the bracelets, do you, son?" The officer looked hopefully at Smitty.

"No," Smitty said briefly. "Not now."

"Good. Take a minute; get your bearings. When you're ready, we'll proceed."

Smitty exhaled and said in a low voice, "Okay, I'm ready, let's go."

"This way, then." The career man led the way down the hall and out of the building. He opened the rear door of the patrol vehicle for Smitty. "Watch your noggin." He went around to the passenger side, opened the door, and slid in.

"Jim, you're supposed to ride in the back with the prisoner," the younger officer said, sliding behind the wheel and slamming his door to emphasize his point.

"I know," he responded, "but I don't think this young fella intends to leap over the seat, attack us, and go tearing off into the night with the siren blaring, do you? Besides, if he did, about the only way you or I could stop him is with our service revolvers, handcuffed or not."

"I can take care of myself," the younger officer shot back.

"That's good to hear, Jerry, but if you want to live to be my age, you'd better start to learn to read people, or you'll be dead before your new baby is old enough for her first training bra," Jim said.

"With your permission?" Jim said politely, as he turned back to Smitty.

Smitty silently waved his consent.

"Jerry, the first thing you need to look at is the sergeant's uniform. Look at the shoulder patch and the combat ribbons. We get young soldiers in here all the time on R&R. How many of them have a Silver Star, a Bronze Star, an Army Commendation Medal, a Purple Heart, silver wings, and Special Forces shoulder patch?"

"Not many," Jerry conceded.

"Right," Jim said. "Now, look at his eyes. This young man has been so elitely trained that there are probably at least ten ways that he knows of to kill you without breaking a sweat."

"More like twenty," Smitty said.

"More like twenty," Jim nodded in agreement. "So the young sergeant has been trained to the point where he's past trying to prove his manhood. So us leaning on him will only make him mad, not intimidate him like the normal lot we usually deal with. So why do it? If we acknowledge his professionalism and give a little houseroom to the rules, then he'll acknowledge our duty to carry out the judge's orders, and everybody will get along fine without any further disagreement; then we don't have to have an altercation with the sergeant that in all probability will only get our asses kicked, okay?"

"Okay," Jerry said.

"Good. Now let's just run the sergeant over to his hotel so he can collect his gear, and we'll be off to the airport."

Jim changed the subject and began to engage Jerry in a discussion on the latest doings of his two-year-old daughter, but Smitty had tuned them out. His thoughts were dialed into another channel—no doubt, he could do it much better now that he was an official high school graduate.

Smitty had left Vietnam by military transport for Okinawa on September 30. The class was not what he had expected at all. It was taught by a civilian instructor, a Filipino civil service teacher who had been specifically recruited for this purpose. There were twenty-two other truants in the class from all branches of the service, including LZ. They had bunks next to one another and studied together after class.

This was no fuck-off civilian time waster. Successful completion of the class had a carrot, a $500 bonus, but perhaps more importantly, early consideration for next promotion. The proposal was a simple tit for tat: we're investing time in you, you invest time and complete the course successfully in return.

Smitty noted that all of the class attendees were similar to him: young folks who had achieved fast NCO ranks through personal dedication and effort and were here trying to punch a ticket, satisfying requirements as fast as they could.

The class was not easy, but all the attendees managed to struggle through successfully in the required thirty days. This was due to two things. The first was that all attendees were restricted to base and, more specifically, restricted to the training building during the week and pulled double guard-duty shifts during the weekend. There was no doubt in Smitty's mind that the main purpose of the double Saturday and Sunday duty fell under the old adage of "busy hands are happy hands."

At the conclusion of the class, Smitty and LZ did manage to quaff a few dozen beers at the NCO club before they parted with the three other members who made up their study group: a couple of navy guys and a marine. During the shitfacing process, everyone bared his soul about future plans after Nam. This assumed, of course, being alive to act on them.

One of the navy guys was going home to marry his childhood sweetheart waiting patiently for him in Kansas and work on his dad's farm. The other was reupping, hoping for a Mediterranean cruise, and the creation of not-to-be-forgotten memories with a bevy of ladies from different countries. The marine was hoping the diploma would punch his next ticket for DI at Parris Island, which Smitty personally thought was about as exciting as a late show at the morgue.

Not by chance, LZ and Smitty were the last to answer. LZ hemmed and hawed before finally answering that if he didn't stay in, and he was leaning that way, that he thought he might go home to Miami and try to become an aircraft mechanic at Eastern Airlines.

Smitty was last. For want of anything better to say, and probably still smarting from his recent dumping by Trudy for a college boy, he said unemotionally, "Oh, I'll probably rotate home to Savannah, be Joe College."

LZ doubled up in laughter and said disbelievingly, "Yeah right, and the first guy to break Babe Ruth's home-run record will be a black man. You got about as much chance of graduating from college as most of the 'brothers' becoming an E-7."

The first part of the analogy didn't bother Smitty too much, but the remark about a black man making E-7 did. Not since their early acquaintance had Smitty heard LZ refer to race so bitterly. He thought unhappily of Walt.

As the plane landed at Hickum field, Smitty had to admit he was both anticipating and dreading it. He was excited about the prospects of a week's R&R, but dreading the contact with his dad, who would be arriving in two days. Smitty had decided not to write to his father. He told himself that he needed more time to think what to say. But he knew that he was really afraid that Dad, forewarned, might decide not to come.

As Smitty descended the ramp, the smell of bacon frying in the flight kitchen pulled him like a siren luring sailors from the sea.

"What'll it be, Sarge?" the mess cook asked, wiping his hands on his greasy apron.

Smitty looked at the grill and saw eggs frying sunny-side up. His quick count totaled up to an even dozen. "I'll take 'em," he said.

"How many?"

"All of them, and the bacon too," Smitty answered.

The overweight mess cook sighed heavily and jerked a thumb in the direction of the sign on the wall, which read, "Take all you want, but eat all you take."

"No problem," Smitty answered.

With a dubious expression, the cook began to ladle them onto a plate with the bacon. While he was doing that, Smitty grabbed a tray, propped his foot on the serving rail, retrieved a knife from inside of his boot, grabbed a loaf of bread in a plastic bag, and sliced cleanly through it at the midpoint.

Next, he filled a pitcher with milk, took the plate from the cook, sat down at a table, and pigged out. It had been a long time since he'd had such a wonderful meal. In fact, after nine months of mostly C-rations in the field, it was the most delicious meal he could remember.

After finishing the eggs and bacon and using the bread to sop up the remains, Smitty returned the plate and tray to the cook, then said, "Look, I've been in Nam the past nine months. Do you suppose the air force could spare the other half of that loaf of bread and another pitcher of milk?"

"It's your's," the cook said holding up his hands in surrender as he backed against the grill thinking, Smitty was sure, that he had a wacko on his hands and it was probably best to just humor him. Smitty left the mess with his hands and belly full and boarded the bus with thirty other R&Rers for the trip to a downtown hotel.

During the drive, an air force lieutenant gave them the mandatory safe sex lecture, the mandatory "you're the service ambassadors of good will" lecture, and the perhaps most important, mandatory reminder of "this is only a week, don't forget to come back" lecture. So far as Smitty could tell, no one listened to any of it at all.

After checking in, Smitty immediately ordered a chilled six-pack to quench his thirst and called down to reserve a rental car—a sporty car that handled well—to go exploring the island the next day. He had two days until he had to face his dad; it occurred to him that a fifth of bourbon would help steady his nerves. With that thought in mind, he picked up the phone and ordered two.

After consuming most of the fifth of Jim Beam and chasing it with the six-pack, for his own version of an Irish seven-course meal, Smitty slept the next fifteen hours. When he awoke the next morning, the sun was shining in through the curtains he had forgotten to draw. He felt rested, having slept the deep sleep of not having to keep one eye open for VC attacks for the first time since he went to Vietnam.

He staggered to the bathroom for a shower, shave, and a change into civvies he'd bought in Okinawa—not forgetting to strap on under his shirt the .357 in the shoulder holster he'd had specially made. For breakfast, he polished off the fifth, and stuffed the other in his bag with a pair of swim trunks.

He ordered a twelve-pack and sandwiches with a cooler from the bar, then ordered the rental car, and went down to the lobby to collect everything. A '68 Camaro SS was waiting with the cooler in the trunk. He signed the papers, slid behind the wheel, and was soon clear of Honolulu, passing Schofield Barracks on his way to the North Shore.

His brother Billy had always talked about going to Waimea Bay to challenge the big waves of Hawaiian surf ever since he could remember. Smitty thought it was poetic justice that he had gotten there first.

The fabled bay was a disappointment. A scruffy-looking surfer, with a cute little beach bunny in a bathing suit that could have been put in a Band-Aid box, informed him that he was too early. The really big waves were in January and February.

Smitty changed into his swim trunks in the car, stowing his pistol in his bag, and spread a towel on the beach next to his cooler, intent on getting a little sun and drinking a lot of beer.

"Kevin?" a female voice said excitedly from behind him. "My God, Kevin is it really you?" the voice asked again.

Smitty turned just in time to catch a voluptuous bikini-clad woman as she leaped into his arms.

"My God, Kevin, it is you," she said again, as she hugged him tightly. She pulled back, and kissed him passionately.

As she broke the kiss and pulled back from Smitty, she removed her sunglasses and said, "Don't tell me you don't remember me? Kristie. The damsel in distress you rescued from the party back in high school in Savannah."

"Um, what are you doing here?" Smitty said.

"I live here. Well, sort of. My stepfather has an old acquaintance that has a house in Honolulu and another on the North Shore as sort of a getaway place. He's letting me live there for a couple of months while I get myself squared away." She kissed him again, and when he made no move to wrap his arms around her, took his arms, and placed them around her waist.

"Get yourself squared away?" Smitty said curiously, as he came up for air.

"I'll explain it to you over dinner tonight, baby," she continued in the same delighted voice as she locked her arms around his neck and hugged him again. "How about you, how on earth did you get here?"

"R&R from Nam."

"Ooooh, a badass soldier, I feel safe now from all the surfer dudes who are constantly trying to hit on me," she cooed in his ear.

"Come on, soldier boy," she said, as she broke the clinch, snatched his beach towel, and ran up the beach. "Grab your cooler and follow me."

Smitty followed Kristie to the parking area, stowed the cooler in his car, and trailed her to an expensive-looking beach house a couple of miles up the road. This was an unexpected turn of events, and from all appearances, it would turn into a delightfully unexpected but eventful evening.

"Thank you for fixing the meal for us, Mrs. Christen," Kristie said, as she gave the gray-haired native Hawaiian lady a kiss on the cheek.

"You're welcome, dear," Mrs. Christen responded. Turning to Smitty, she said, "It was so nice to meet you, Kevin. If you and Kristie need anything at all tonight, just let me know. I live just up the road about a mile," she said, as she moved toward the front door.

"Nice to meet you too, ma'am," Smitty responded.

"Bye, children; have an enjoyable evening."

Smitty and Kristie stood arm in arm and watched as Mrs. Christen got in her car and drove away with a friendly wave, which they both returned. As soon as she was out of sight, Kristie turned, broke away from Smitty, grabbed his bag, and ran across the great room toward a bedroom at the end of the hall. "Follow me, baby, and I'll show you where you'll sleep, maybe."

As Smitty entered the room, he found Kristie sprawled across a king-sized bed in the master suite, clutching his bag to her chest. "This thing is heavy, baby. What have you got in there, a gun?" she asked innocently, as Smitty joined her on the spacious bed, flopping on his back next to her.

"As a matter of fact, I have," Smitty answered.

Kristie rolled up on her knees on the bed, unzipped the bag, and removed Smitty's weapon carefully by the handle. "It's heavy. What is it?" she said curiously, as she hefted it in her hand.

"It's a .357," Smitty answered.

From her kneeling position, she threw one leg over Smitty, straddled him, leaned over and carefully placed Smitty's weapon on the nightstand, and tossed the bag casually on the floor. She straightened, reached behind her, untied the string of her bikini top, and let it fall on Smitty's stomach.

"Since you like to play with heavy things, how about these 38s?"

Smitty sucked with reckless abandon. Kristie freed his throbbing member from his trunks, and pulled the string on her bikini bottom in the same motion. She sat down on him, impaling herself to the hilt on his length.

They made love with the ferocity of youth, Kristie's moves passionate and uncontrolled. As Smitty's orgasm erupted deep inside her, Kristie screamed in reply, rocked forward and bit him on the neck. Like his dad had said, it was still the greatest, most goddamndest feeling in the world.

They slept, awoke, screwed each other again, and then slept again. It was after eight when Kevin heard Kristie padding quietly outside the bedroom. He slipped on his pants as he got out of bed, and left the bedroom to the sound of Kristie humming contentedly in the kitchen as she reheated the meal prepared earlier by Mrs. Christen.

He crossed the open room to the kitchen, and stopped dead in his tracks as he rounded the corner of the partition that separated the eat-in kitchen from the living space. Kristie was bustling around the kitchen naked.

"Hi, baby, you're awake. I was afraid I'd screwed you to death." She posed for him with one hand on her hip, a ladle in the other, and said invitingly, "You like?"

Smitty could only nod in reply.

Obviously enjoying his predicament, she put down the ladle, crossed the kitchen, stopped two feet from him, undid his pants, and let them fall to the floor. She bent down as he stepped out of them, and casually tossed them onto a chair in the living room. As she stood up, she paused to give him a quick kiss, then said suggestively as she rose and wrapped herself around him, "Dessert for later," as she licked her lips.

They shared dinner together, literally. Kristie sat straddling him on a chair and fed both of them from the plate of food located by her right hand. After every other mouthful, they exchanged kisses. It took an hour for both of them to eat, but all things considered, Smitty didn't mind at all.

After dinner, Smitty helped clear away the dinner plates and was starting to fill the sink with water when Kristie said, "Leave them. Mrs. C will do them when she comes in tomorrow." They settled down naked on throw pillows in front of the fireplace and snuggled quietly together until the silence became uncomfortable.

"Kevin, what happened to you?" Kristie said softly, as she turned to face him. "One night you were at my house; the next day you didn't turn up in school. Your father came into the band class the day after, looking for you, and told Mr. Wilkins that if he saw you to call him.

Rumors circulated for weeks, then we heard the news story about those murders in Miami, and everyone said that you had done it and that the police were looking for you. My stepfather not allowing you to take me out didn't have anything to do with any of this, did it?"

"No," Smitty answered with amusement. "Your father showing me the door didn't have anything to do with it. It was more what happened when I got home that night. My dad and I had a disagreement, and I decided to split."

"Anything you'd care to talk about?"

Smitty was quiet for a moment, then said, "No, it's not important now. Check it off to teenage stupidity; just distant memories."

"Are you going to make the army a career?"

"Not sure. I've got to survive Nam first to have any other options."

"How long do you have left?" she said, as she stroked his arm.

"Three months until the end of my tour, then a year to go after that in the army. I went in thinking I'd make it a career, but being over there has made me think twice."

"What do you think you'll do then, baby?"

"I dunno, I found out recently that my friend in Florida has a job waiting for me as a cop. I'm a fair-to-middling auto thief. I could always go back to being an auto mechanic or take up aircraft mechanics like my friend LZ is thinking about," Smitty answered.

"Ever think about going to college?"

Smitty snorted in spite of himself. "Hell, I just got my GED from the army less than a week ago. Besides, can you imagine me as one of those long-haired college pukes I see in the paper?"

"I can imagine you as anything you want to be, baby," she cooed softly, as she nibbled on his ear.

The direction of the conversation was making Smitty uncomfortable. He broke away from Kristie, got up, went into the kitchen, got a couple of beers, lit a cigarette, and came back to the fireplace. As he handed Kristie a brew to change the course of their conversation, he said, "So what's your story? You said earlier you had to get yourself squared away."

Kristie took a long pull on the beer, spiraled up on her feet as Smitty sat down, and threw another log on the fireplace. She stood staring deeply into the fire, the flames silhouetting the luscious curves of her body. The fire cast her face in shadows. The tears that were beginning to glisten from the corners of her eyes seemed as starkly out of place as the pencil-thin six-inch horizontal bikini line scar that Smitty could now see highlighted in the firelight.

"You remember Ricky, the boy who took me to that party that night?" She sniffled, wiping away a tear that had managed to escape down her cheek.

"Yes," Smitty answered.

"Well, my parents, make that my new stepfather, thought he would be a good match for me. His father is one of the most influential lawyers in Savannah. So my new 'daddy' invited Ricky over for a barbecue in the spring, and I guess from there we just sort of started going out on a regular basis. You know how those high school things are; you go out a couple of times and everybody just assumes that you're a couple and no one else asks you out.

"Well, anyway, he was a year ahead of me, same class as you, so once he went off to college, I didn't see him except on holidays when he was home from school.

"This past summer, just as his sophomore year in school started, he called and asked me to go to a college frat party that was being held down at a house on Savannah Beach.

"I guess I had too much to drink, and things went a little too far," Kristie paused, looked at Smitty, and said, as the tears now flowed freely down her face, "No, make that a lot too far. Ricky put something in my drink and I passed out. The next thing I knew, I was tied spread-eagled and naked on a bed, and Ricky was saying, 'There she is, boys, as promised.'"

Kristie wiped her eyes and kneeled in front of him. "They raped me and sodomized me, Kevin. God knows how many of them, some more than once. Then they had this guy, who everyone said had to go last because he was so big. When he entered me, I felt like my insides were on fire. After he was done, something was wrong, far wrong. They were all scared, and I was bleeding onto the bed. I started to pass out, but the last thing I remember was Ricky saying that 'This wasn't part of the deal' and that he couldn't be here for this. Some guy handed him a bag with some pills in it, he popped a couple, took the rest of the bag, and then just left me there.

"One of the girls, who had been told that I was a whore that Ricky had brought to the party as part of his initiation into the frat, called the ambulance and they called the police.

"They took me to the hospital, and that big bastard had ruptured my uterus. They did a complete hysterectomy two days later. Twenty years old, and my child-bearing years are already behind me," Kristie said bitterly, as she ran her finger softly along the bikini line scar.

"My stepfather was livid. He called Ricky's father and told him he was going to have his son thrown in jail. Ricky's father told him that he had discussed the incident with his son first, then a lawyer, and since no one could prove who gave me the drugs, and that since Ricky had not raped me himself, that he had no case. Ricky's father must have been scared though, 'cause he sent his spineless son abroad to college.

"After I got out of the hospital, my stepdad told me that Ricky's father wouldn't even contribute to the hospital bill. Since I couldn't identify anyone, and all the boys were sons of influential people, the whole thing was just hushed up. The police checked it off to 'a whore getting what she deserved.'

"I couldn't show my face in Savannah, so my stepfather arranged for me to stay here until, as I told you earlier, I could get myself squared away."

Kristie leaned forward and softly stroked his cheek. "Do you know that you're the only man I've wanted to touch me? Do you know how special that makes me feel? When I saw you on the beach, I just couldn't believe my eyes. The only man who ever treated me properly was suddenly here." She paused again, wiped away tears from both eyes, and said in a more confident voice, "Because of that vile experience, I couldn't stand to be touched. Until today, when seeing you inexplicably freed me. I guess I went a little overboard when I saw you."

Holding out his arms for her, and feeling the warmth and sensuality of her body when she joined him, Smitty said, "Like I told you in Savannah, you go through life saying hello like that, and you'll never want for friends." It seemed only natural, that from their confided shared loneliness that they made love again in front of the fireplace and fell asleep in each other's arms.

It was a little past 1:00 AM, when a noise caused Smitty to awaken. It was the front screen door slamming shut on its return spring.

"Kristie, my God, what is this?" a male voice bellowed loudly. "Don't look, mother," the voice instructed as the arm came up to cover a female's eyes.

"Daddy!" Kristie screamed, as she jumped quickly to her feet and ran naked into the bedroom.

Awake now, and realizing what was happening, Smitty rolled behind a chair, retrieved his pants, slid into them, sprang to his feet in a defensive stance, and on seeing that there was no immediate danger, relaxed and stayed a safe distance away from the screeching Bernie.

"Daddy, what are you doing here?" Kristie asked in a stunned voice, as she came out of the bedroom wearing a white robe hastily tied at the waist.

"After talking to you on the phone the other day, your mother and I decided to come out and surprise you. It seems you weren't as lonely as we thought."

Attempting to restore some order, Kristie said in a more even tone, "Daddy, this is Kevin, you remember him, the boy who brought me home from that party in Savannah a couple of years ago. He's in the army now, a Green Beret on leave from Vietnam." Kristie blushed and said, "We ran into each other down at Waimea today, and I invited him home for dinner."

"And a lot more, I see," he said.

"So, I see you finally accomplished your goal and got Kristie. I suppose you're proud of yourself; just another notch on your gun belt. When you get back to Vietnam, I'll bet you'll be bragging to all your dope-smoking buddies of how you finally tagged the high school tart whose father wouldn't let you anywhere near her back in Savannah because he knew what kind of person you are," Bernie said.

"Daddy," Kristie said savagely, as she stepped up beside Smitty and faced her stepfather, "it's not like that at all."

"Shut up, you slutty little bitch, I know how to deal with his kind," Bernie said, as he raised his hand and slapped Kristie across the face before Smitty could stop him.

"I'll show you what you need, you little whore," Bernie loosened his belt, pulled it free of his pants, and folded it in two.

"Sorry, Bernardo, time for everyone to cool down," Smitty said, as he grabbed his raised arm, and with a simple twist to the right nerve, removed the belt from Bernie's numbed hand and flipped it into the fire.

"Why you son-of-bitch, I'll show you what a good father does to trash like you," Bernie said, as he charged him like a stampeding bull.

Smitty dropped to one knee, easily avoiding Bernard's futile rush. As he passed, Smitty tripped him, then caught him before he could fall, lowered him softly to the ground, and in the process twisted an arm around behind his back and placed a knee on his shoulder to control and incapacitate him.

"As I said, I think we all need to calm down," Smitty said. "Now, are you going to settle down and act like a nice little middle-aged stepfather, or do we have to do this the hard way?"

Bernie's silence was answer enough. Smitty released his arm and helped him to his feet. Smitty led him to a chair and said, "Sit there, and don't get up." He turned to Kristie's mother and said politely as he pointed at the sofa, "Ma'am, if you please." She sat down without a word.

Smitty next went to Kristie, who was sobbing silently on the other end of the couch from her mother. "Easy, kid, it's all over now."

"It will never be over, not as long as he's around," Kristie said in a shaky voice. "He's never believed I'm a good girl. He's constantly accusing me and watching me. As I told you, honey, you're the first man I've ever been with that I wanted to touch me, and he's got to make even that seen dirty. I hate him."

"Then come with me now," Smitty said. "I can help you."

Kristie's silent reply was a clear enough answer. She'd not leave with him, maybe because she felt she wouldn't know what to do without her parents, or because Smitty had nothing to offer her. But more likely, because she was used to a certain kind of life, a kind that she knew would be gone forever if she left with Smitty now.

Everyone sat silently as Smitty went to the bedroom, dressed—including putting his shoulder holster and Magnum on under his shirt—packed his bag, walked back to the kitchen, and retrieved his beer and bourbon.

They were still in the living room exactly where he had left them glaring at each other silently. He bent down and gave Kristie a peck on the cheek, handed her a piece of paper with his mailing address, straightened and said, "Look, I think you folks have got to talk this out among yourselves." He wished he were anywhere but here.

"Now, Bernard, here's the deal. No more hitting. Try listening for a change instead of accusing and overreacting. And Mom," Smitty said, as he looked at Kristie's mother, "You've got to stick up for her. She's your daughter, and she's a wonderful girl.

"Okay, everybody got the rules down?" Smitty paused, and looked first at Bernard, who nodded, then at Kristie's mother, who nodded also. "Good-bye, Kristie, and thanks for a special evening," Smitty finished with a wink that only she could see.

Smitty walked quickly to the door and let the screen door slam as he left. He started up the Super Sport and drove away, half-hoping that Kristie would come running out the door after him, but knowing in his heart that there was no way she could.

Smitty returned to Waimea Park and found the bar across the gate. The park had closed at sundown. He drove up the hill about a quarter of a mile and parked in a pullout overlooking the Pacific Ocean. He checked the cooler. Eight cool ones left, plus a full bottle of Jim Beam. Not enough to drown his sorrows, but more than enough to teach them to swim.

It was eight beers and half of a fifth of bourbon later at a little past four o'clock in the morning when Smitty started up the car and headed back to Honolulu. He was angry and shitfaced—a lethal combination that caused him to drive the car faster and harder than he normally would.

Curiously, when he started his car, another car parked at the bottom of the hill had started up and dropped in behind him. Smitty had noticed it, but checked it off to coincidence when the car, a Chrysler Imperial, roared by on one of the few passing areas on the narrow twisty road that split the island between the North Shore and Honolulu.

Fueled by anger, rejection, and booze, Smitty was taking the corners like an Indy racer. But alcohol and exhaustion did nothing for his skill.

Smitty saw the sign for the tight S-curve too late to slow down and was already well into the first bend when the light-assed Camaro began to skid. As he turned the wheels in the direction of the skid, he heard a soft plop, followed by a loud bang and complete loss of steering. Smitty was fighting a losing battle to keep the overpowered but under-balanced car under control. It slid horizontally across the road into the roadside underbrush, where the passenger wheels dug into the soft ground. The side pressure was more than the two-door hardtop could stand. The car began to roll on its side, flipped several times, and landed on its roof on the roadway at the bottom of the curve.

Smitty awoke to disorientation and the pungent smell of gasoline. He was certain it was only a matter of time until the leaking fuel encountered a hot engine part, with fire the certain result. He unlatched the seatbelt and lowered himself gently onto the headliner. Taking a second to get his bearings, his first thought was how to expeditiously unass the newest junkyard resident.

Exiting was a simple enough process, even for someone as blitzed as he was. The front windshield was no longer there; obviously it had popped out when the car rolled and was probably lying somewhere along the path the car had taken as it self-destructed. As Smitty started to crawl forward through the opening, his hip struck something hard and cylindrical.

Miraculously, his half-full bottle of booze had wedged itself between the top and bottom half of the front seat and had survived the roller-coaster ride intact. He pried it loose and dragged it along, after doing several half-gainers inside a couple of tons of Generous Mother's finest, a stiff belt would certainly steady his nerves.

Smitty wiggled through the narrow opening between the roofline and the front of the nose-heavy car, now resting on the ground, and got shakily to his feet. He gave himself the once over twice, and in short order, pronounced himself—aside from a few bumps and bruises—in surprisingly good shape. He staggered about fifty feet up the road and sat down heavily with his back against the road sign advertising a dangerous curve ahead. No problem with truth in advertising there.

Smitty noted sadly that there wasn't a straight panel left on the car; the boneyard buzzards would have her now. Smitty felt a deep sense of sadness for the car. No different, he guessed, from the sense of loss he felt when Dad had taken his Husky. Cars were important to Smitty, and he hated to see this one suffer. He grabbed his bottle, hoisted it in a silent toast to his Detroit chariot, and slugged back a good fifth of the remaining contents.

A minute passed, then two, then flames appeared in the front fender wells, blackening the paint as they licked at the twisted body, slowly but surely spreading until it would be only moments before they reached the gas tank.

Headlights became visible from a car coming in the other direction. The car stopped twenty feet from Smitty. He heard a door open and slam. Someone ran toward him, steps loud on the tarmac.

"Are you all right?"

Smitty pondered this ridiculous question at length before replying in a slurred voice, "I expect I shall be."

"Man, your car is fucked up."

Almost as if in response to the stranger's statement, the gas tank blew with a tremendous noise. The good Samaritan winced and ducked. "Well, if it wasn't, it sure as hell is now," Smitty said, grabbing the man's arm to keep him from falling over from the force of the explosion.

"Gotta drink to that," Smitty said, rasing his bottle in a salute and taking another long pull at the bourbon.

"You gotta do something!" the man said, tugging at Smitty's arm.

"Okay, man, don't have a kitten, I will," Smitty said. With great difficulty, Smitty got up, and strolled unsteadily toward the burning vehicle.

A thought began to form in his mind, and as he walked a few steps farther, it crystallized. Smitty turned, smiled at the local, gave him the thumbs-up, continued until he was fifteen paces from his late lamented friend, unbuttoned his shirt, and removed his pistol.

"Sorry, my friend, I can't stand to see you suffer," Smitty said. He sighted his weapon on the car and emptied all five rounds. After the last shell had been discharged, Smitty holstered his weapon, and with a last silent salute, downed the remaining liquid courage, leaving just a small swallow for his late lamented ride, and chucked the bottle into the car.

Smitty turned and walked back, swaying from side to side, to his new acquaintance, who was anything but pacified by Smitty's actions.

"Are you crazy, man, shooting a car?" he screamed.

"Well, you wanted me to do something, so I did; I shot the poor thing to put it out of its misery," Smitty explained.

The man backed slowly away, then turned and ran for his car. He started it hurriedly and, tires screeching, disappeared into the night. Smitty sat back down against the signpost. Nothing to do for the moment, he thought to himself. Help would soon be on the way.

A Hawaiian State Police cruiser arrived ten minutes later. The officer approached Smitty warily with his service revolver drawn but pointed at the ground.

"Good evening," he said in a friendly voice. "A guy stopped me up the road and started babbling at me about an accident and a drunk who was shooting up his car. Well, that's definitely a car that's been in an accident, so I'm gonna take a blind shot here and guess that you're the guy that was doing the shooting."

Smitty unbuttoned his shirt slowly, and holding it open so the officer could see the Magnum. "Don't shoot, Marshal Dillon, I'll come along quietly."

The officer reached inside Smitty's shirt, easily slid the weapon out, flipped open the chamber and verified that it was empty. "Any reloads?" he asked pleasantly.

"Up in smoke," Smitty nodded in the direction of the car.

"Why'd you shoot the car?"

"To put it out of its misery, man."

The officer laughed out loud. "Why is it, son, that I have to run into one of you R&R characters just before I'm supposed to get off?" The officer helped Smitty up and walked him to the back of the police cruiser just as a fire truck arrived.

"According to testimony from you and the officer, and statements taken from a Mr. Katsowa, tonight's events play back like this: You got up this morning, rented a car, drove to the North Shore, met an old high school acquaintance, spent the evening at her beach house until her parents arrived and threw you out. Then you drove up the coast, drank yourself into a stupor, and rolled your car driving back to your hotel. When it caught fire, you toasted it with the last of your alcohol, then shot the car five times with your service revolver. Is that about it, Sergeant?" The judge shook his head in disgust.

"Except you left out the fact that I got laid three times by the luscious stepdaughter before Daddy Big Bucks arrived."

"Sorry," the judge said, rolling his eyes at the court clerk.

"Sergeant, the only reason you are not being charged with driving under the influence, reckless driving, and anything else I can think of, is that you drank half a fifth after the accident, so it is impossible to tell how much alcohol you actually had to drink before the accident, and there's now no reasonable way your blood alcohol level before the accident can be conclusively established. You're a very lucky young man, and, given the fact that you're a soldier on leave from Vietnam, I'm going to give you a break."

Looking past Smitty to the police officer, the night court judge said tersely. "Officer, please take this alcoholic back to his hotel and see that he sleeps it off."

"Yes, your honor."

"And, Sergeant." The judge glared at Smitty. "I don't want to see you back in this courtroom for the balance of your R&R. If I do, you won't like it. Case dismissed."

The officer touched Smitty on the arm and motioned to the side door.

"You're lucky, son. If not for that technicality, he'd have busted your ass," the officer said, as they were driving back to Smitty's hotel. "He's not too fond of service people to start with, and you didn't help yourself by mouthing off."

"How old are you, officer?" Smitty asked.

"Thirty-seven."

"Well, partner, I'm only nineteen, and the odds are better than fifty-fifty that I'll be dead before I'm twenty, so ask me if I give a rat's ass what some by-the-book judge thinks."

"What if you happen to survive Vietnam?" he asked pointedly. "What will you do then?"

"Don't see it happening," Smitty answered somberly. "I figure guys like me are born just to get killed in wars so that rich little college pukes don't have to go."

"Well since you've already written yourself off, I don't suppose you'd do me a favor?"

"You know, partner, the last time I did a favor for a cop, he got shot and I got banished from the other vacation paradise state," Smitty said. "Who you want done and where?"

"It's not like that, exactly," the officer said. "It's just, with your specialized talents, you're in a unique position to help us—how shall I put this?—deal with a local problem."

"What's your name, officer?" Smitty asked.

"Sam Dennison."

"Well Sammy, do you know how to spell point?" Smitty said bluntly.

"Yes, p, o, i—" Sam stopped in midspelling, Smitty could see his neck flushing in embarrassment that he'd fallen for the bait. They drove on in silence, the officer seething at his own gullibility.

Smitty let him stew in his own juices a minute or so, then memories of Stan the Man and the honest and honorable things he stood for flashed to the forefront of Smitty's mind: Just as fate needed a little push, honesty sometimes needed a helping hand. Smitty leaned forward. "Okay, Sam, tell me what you need."

Before the officer could reply, they pulled to a stop in front of Smitty's hotel. The officer got out, came around to the curbside, and opened the door.

"Here, Sergeant," the officer said in a low voice, surreptitiously handing Smitty back his .357 to conceal the transfer from the curious onlookers. "Since nobody told me not to return this to you, I'm giving it back.

"Officially, I'm telling you, put it away in your room and don't carry it on the street, got it? Unofficially, I suggest you reload it and keep it close to your smelly armpit. You might be needing it; especially if you fancy a beer in our seediest clipjoint. It's called The Drunken Sailor."

"Thanks, man," Smitty said, shaking the officer's hand and pocketing the pistol.

"No, thank you," Sam said, with a smile and a wink.

Smitty looked at his watch. It was just after 7:00 AM. With a wave to the departing officer, he entered his hotel. Smitty flipped the rental car keys to the concierge. "Return these to the rental company."

"What about the car?"

Smitty entered the elevator, pushed the button, and as the door closed, smiled and said, "As a friend of mine once said, 'They're number one, they'll find it.'"

Smitty awoke at 3:30 PM. He felt hung over and sore. After a hot shower and a shave, Smitty called the police department, and, after being switched three times and put on hold twice, was able to find out where the rental carcass had been towed. He headed down to the lobby, grabbed the first cab, gave him the name of the impound yard, and on reaching it, told the hacky to wait.

After the briefest of bluffs about retrieving personal articles, he was able to get past the uncaring gate attendant and easily locate the charred black hulk. It was upside down on a flatbed trailer in front of several other wrecks in what Smitty figured was the insurance salvage area of the yard.

There truly wasn't much left. The engine and passenger compartments were completely gutted. Probably the only reason the interior of the trunk was still intact was that the fire department had gotten there in time to extinguish it before further damage could be done. Smitty vaulted cleanly up onto the trailer for a closer examination.

Three tires were partially burned and melted, but on the fourth, the driver's side front, the tread was still attached. But the sidewall fibers were shredded. This must have been where the blowout occurred. Slowly Smitty rotated the wheel, examining the charred rubber for any traces of irregularity. Just between two of the raised white Goodyear letters, where the sidewall was basically intact, there was a puncture about a quarter of an inch in diameter. Smitty stuck his little finger in the hole, and felt the smoothness, almost as if it had been stabbed with an ice pick.

This must have been the source of the accident and also must have accounted for the soft plop Smitty heard microseconds before the tire blew. He must have hit some object that punched the hole and contributed to his losing control. Smitty spun the wheel absently noting its irregular rotation and teeth gnashing scraping as the bent wheel rubbed against the front cross member.

Additionally, there was a rattle of something caught inside the wheel. Smitty took out his knife, slit the remaining sidewall, pulled the tire apart, and stuck his hand inside. At the bottom, he felt a small object and removed it. It was cylindrical in shape and made of lead. It must have been a piece of the lead wheel-balancing weight that had gotten broken off, dislodged, and flattened in the crash. He dropped it into his shirt pocket, stood up, dusted off his hands, and vaulted down.

"Find what you were looking for?" the guard asked, as Smitty walked past.

"Yeah."

"You're lucky to be alive."

"You don't know the half of it," Smitty said, without turning around.

Glancing at his watch and noting that it was only 5:30, Smitty said to the cab driver: "Take me someplace where I can eat that's close to where the beer is cheap and the girls are even cheaper."

It was just past ten-thirty, and Smitty was sitting alone at the bar in the Honolulu dive where the cabby had dropped him. Appropriately enough, The Drunken Sailor seemed to be largely populated by drunk and getting-there seamen on shore leave.

The hostesses had attached themselves to the swabbies like leeches, working them for drinks to run up the bar bill. These hustling entrepreneurs insisted on drinking champagne at four bucks a pop; the fact that it was really colored water that the barman poured from a special champagne bottle with an X on it didn't slow the orders.

Smitty was quietly sipping his third beer when one of the debutantes, whose latest paramour had been hastily and not too gently shown the door when the dollars in his wallet amounted to significantly less than the inflated bar tab, looked around for another mark and locked in on Smitty.

"Hi sailor, you buy me a drink?" she oozed smoothly in a native Hawaiian accent, the layered makeup making her look like she couldn't possibly be more than sixteen.

"I'm not a sailor, and no, I prefer drinking alone," Smitty said.

"Wassamatta, Mac, you don't like the little lady?" the bartender asked. "Her boyfriend across the room ain't gonna like you hurting her feelings."

He caught the eye of a large, overweight Hawaiian, as her "beau" slowly advanced menacingly across the bar. "If I were you, I'd spring for a glass of champagne for the little miss just to show there are no hard feelings. You don't want to tangle with him. I understand he did a stretch in a mainland prison for killing some dude with his bare hands."

"Please, Admiral," the girl begged, "I don't want no more trouble. You buy me one drink, okay?"

"Which part of no did you not understand?" Smitty asked.

"It's your funeral," the bartender said quickly, as the big boy approached.

"You gettin' out of line with my woman?" the "boyfriend" asked.

"Take a hike, you fat fucking pig," Smitty said. He already knew he'd walked into a setup. He'd be damned if he was going to play by their rules. His response was designed to make the man angry. Angry people usually did not have the capacity for rational thought, so the madder he was, the better Smitty liked it. From the goon's reaction, the plan had worked—maybe too well.

The heavy's face colored with rage and his eyes narrowed to cat slits as he lunged at Smitty, raising his hands to grab him around the neck—which was just what Smitty wanted.

Smitty dropped to one knee, formed his knuckles into a judo fist, and hit him with as much force as he could under his ribcage, causing an involuntary gasp as the air rushed from his lungs. While the big gorilla was grabbing his stomach, Smitty straightened up, reached inside his shirt, removed his weapon, and using it like a club, brought it down in a slashing motion on first the left, then the right collarbone, the easiest bones to break. For good measure, Smitty followed with a judo kick to the balls.

The now totally defenseless thug staggered and further lost his balance when he threw a half-hearted punch that wasn't even close. As the fist sailed harmlessly by, Smitty stuck his weapon in his belt, grabbed the back of his shirt collar and the back of his belt at the spine, dragged the lumbering giant across the room, building up a sizable momentum, and slammed his head into the ladies' restroom door. The latch, unable to withstand the weight of a 275-pound battering ram, gave instantly, flying open with a resounding crash as the would-be hero landed in a toilet stall that had long since lost its door, but not its occupant.

The young lady's screams had not begun to fade when Smitty spun and brought his pistol up, freezing the bartender in midmotion. He positioned the Magnum two inches from the bartender's nose, pulled back the hammer and asked, "Need your sinuses ventilated?"

The sawed-off shotgun clattered noisily on top of the bar as it slid from his hands.

"You should teach that asshole better manners. Otherwise some two-year-old with a severe case of diaper rash will get mad and knock him on his butt." He picked up the shotgun, opened the chambers, removed the two shells, closed the weapon, flipped it in the air, and caught it by the barrel end, then slammed it across the edge of the bar, breaking it cleanly in two.

Smitty swung the barrel at the beer taps, shearing them off and spraying three different kinds of beer in every direction. Then he threw the barrel at the back of the bar, shattering the full-length mirror and several bottles of liquor.

Smitty turned and surveyed the room. "Next?!" There were no takers. The tapster was madly dialing the phone. Smitty figured it would be the police on the other end of the wire, and he figured that he'd get the blame. He was right, as usual.

Smitty finished replaying his own personnel R&R highlights in his mind when they arrived at his hotel. It took only minutes to check out and fifteen more to reach the airport. Smitty hit the ticket counter with a first-thing-available-off-the-islands plea as his two erstwhile guards stood a respectful distance away.

"So what'd you get?" Jim asked.

"The only thing I could, an 11:00 AM flight to Sydney, Australia."

"Forty-five minutes from now. Think we can trust you to get on, or do we have to follow you onboard and buckle you in?" Jim asked.

"Oh, I think I'll make it. The natives around here are pretty unfriendly."

"Not all of them," Officer Sam Dennison said, walking up from behind to join them.

Jim turned to his younger partner. "You got that package."

Jerry reached into a bag and produced a gift-wrapped present. Jim took it from him and handed it to Smitty.

"What is it?" Smitty took the parcel, wrapped in pineapple-printed paper, and shook it.

"Open it, dummy," Jim said. "It's a little going away present from the Honolulu Police Department."

"And the Hawaiian State Police," Sam added.

It was a box of cigars. The brand that was frequently advertised by a blonde bombshell on TV who advised, "Pick one up and smoke it some time."

"What gives?" Smitty cocked his brow, and he offered them around.

"Well," Jim said, a smile spreading slowly across his face. "Let's just say that some of us, particularly those of us on the Honolulu Police Department and the Hawaiian State Police, are real pleased that a certain lowlife got his ass kicked in the worst gin joint we have. It seems that whoever did it, and we're not mentioning names here, screwed him up reeeeal good."

"Not only that, but it seems that he believed the Green Beret when he told the bartender that he was coming back with two of his Green Beanie buddies to dismember him, then feed his intimate parts to the sharks on the North Shore.

"Seems he's suddenly decided on leaving the islands on a slow boat for anywhere," Jerry said, joining in. "As soon as he gets out of the hospital."

"That bastard has beaten the crap out of probably twenty or thirty guys. And there were always twenty eyewitnesses who'd say the sailor or soldier started it, and there'd be nothing we could do," Jim said sadly.

"Well, at least this time the witnesses weren't lying," Jim said.

"How's that?" Smitty said.

"The soldier definitely did start it, but this soldier definitely did finish it. A bunch of us just thought we'd let you know that we appreciate your efforts at urban renewal," Jim said.

"You know," Sam added, "that was a good touch to break both of that scumbag's collarbones. Seems that he can't even take a piss without somebody to whip it out for him."

"Personally, I don't think he's got that kind of friends," Jerry said, making them all laugh.

The loudspeaker announced first call to board. Smitty stood up and grabbed his bag. "Look, since we're all such good friends, and I'm now an honorary member of the Honolulu Police Department and shit like that, how about you do me a favor?"

"Name it," Jim said.

Smitty took a folded envelope from his shirt pocket and handed it to Jim. "I need a little information on that accident I was in. My mailing address is on the outside. Just follow up on what's inside, and mail me the results."

"You got it. Aloha, brother," Jim said, as they shook hands.

"Hasty bananas to you, too," Smitty responded, shaking hands with Jerry and Sam also.

"You aren't by any chance related to a hardcase police detective I knew in Miami by the name of Stanley, are you?" Smitty asked.

"Get on the plane, you idiot." Jim laughed and cuffed Smitty playfully upside the head. "All of us who carry a badge are brothers."

Smitty turned and walked silently to the plane. He was just going through the boarding door when Sam called after him, "Sergeant?"

"Yeah."

"Any time you want to come back, my wife makes a great steak."

"Never mind that, does she have a younger sister, and how does she look in a bikini?" Smitty responded with a laugh. "Or better yet, without it."

Jim suddenly snapped to attention and cracked off a crisp salute—an act which Jerry and Sam immediately imitated.

Smitty returned the formal salute, added an informal wave, and turned away.

As he settled into the seat and the plane taxied for takeoff, Smitty was mind surfing through recent events and, after adding up the totals, had come to the conclusion that he had come out ahead.

Sure, he'd missed out on developing something long-term with Kristie, totaled a car, gotten charged with assault and battery, and was being expelled from his second state. And he would miss his rendezvous with his dad.

But, on the other side of the ledger, he'd picked up another sign, and if Jim's information paid off, that clue, comparatively speaking, would become a windfall to help sort out the ghosts from the goblins that were constantly haunting him.

It had been an interesting five weeks, and there were still five days of I&I to go in Sydney before returning to that faraway place and the war that nobody wanted.

CHAPTER FOURTEEN

Smitty flew into Cam Ranh Bay on the eighteenth of November, landing at dusk. His thoughts returned to the incursion missions that went in by design at dusk, to have less chance of discovery. He stepped off the plane into stifling humidity and rain. The war was still here, and Smitty was definitely not glad to be back.

Smitty caught a Huey to Nha Trang to check back in at Special Forces headquarters. With fourteen hours of traveling to get back, preceded by an all-night sendoff from two Australian girls, Smitty was asleep at once.

"Welcome back, Sergeant," Colonel Wilson said when Smitty reported to his office at 0900 hours the next morning.

"Congratulations, sir," Smitty said politely, nodding at the new eagles on the collar, signifying a promotion to full colonel.

"Thank you, son, and the same to you on completing your diploma requirements. Although from the reports I have heard on your recent sojourn in our tropical paradise state, I understand you need not bother to use your newly obtained credentials to apply for a position in the tourist office when your hitch is done, at least not for the next three years."

"Well, sir," Smitty said, "I did manage to avoid the slammer and, in the process, assist the police in dealing with a local problem."

"Yes, I was just reading the report that was forwarded to me by the chief of the Honolulu Police Department. They seem to agree. In fact, they've enclosed a certificate of recognition."

Smitty briefly scanned the certificate, called an Outstanding Achievement Award, noting that it was duly signed by the chief, and that he had rendered assistance to the Honolulu police in solving a felony murder.

Reading from an enclosed letter, the colonel summarized the main points to Smitty, "It seems that the Palooka you went a few rounds with was wanted on a host of other things, but they couldn't pin anything on him until they had him confined and could work on him. Apparently, he copped to a murder that was committed a month back, as well as to enough other crimes that they're able to hold him without bail."

He read silently to himself, tapped the paper, and began to read aloud. "The injuries to the defendant were obviously applied by a professional and meant not only to incapacitate but also to humiliate. With two broken collarbones, the defendant requires assistance to perform even rudimentary bathroom functions."

"Nice touch," the colonel said. "After consultation with the judge, all charges have been dropped and the sergeant's record expunged, but the three-year ban on return to Hawaii remains in force."

"Fuck 'em," Smitty said.

The colonel gave Smitty a long, unblinking stare, shook his head in exasperation, then said, "There's also a sealed envelope addressed to you from an officer named Jim Jenson."

The colonel passed the envelope to Smitty, who surveyed the outside but did not open it. "Thanks," Smitty said. The colonel looked quizzical.

"Procedural information on the car I destroyed," Smitty said.

"Very well. Now then, back to the business at hand," the colonel said. "As per the plan, your new assignment is team lead in the same area as before. Your second and radioman are waiting at Pleiku now. This will be your assignment through the balance of your tour. Should you elect to extend, you will be reassigned to lead a team rescue and recovery force, much as the late master sergeant on your last mission did.

"According to the records, you have one year and approximately three months left on your enlistment. Again, if you extend and continue to perform well, I will consider you for further advancement based on experience and opportunity. Any questions?"

"What if I extend and you're gone stateside? What would happen to the 'consideration for advancement'?" Smitty asked.

"As a condition of my promotion, I have extended one additional year. Therefore, I will be in-country for the foreseeable future. Should I depart early, I have documented the plan for you in your service record. Sergeant, I want to do everything possible to encourage you to make a career out of the military. Your father did very well; you should be able to do even better."

Smitty nodded. The colonel was talking about a future that Smitty honestly had not given any thought to, just assuming that sooner or later he'd end up toe-tagged for Arlington. Nevertheless, one thing was clear: he'd better start giving some thought to his future. Officer Sam Dennison's words were ringing in his ears, "What if you did survive? What then?"

Smitty left the colonel's office, deep in thought. In the safety and relative quiet of his rack, he pulled out and read the information from Officer Jenson. Smitty reread it several times until he had committed the contents to memory; then he tore it into small strips and burned it in the ashtray on the table. The information answered some specific questions. The answers confirmed his suspicions of a wolf in sheep's clothing.

The colonel's meaning was absolutely clear: If he extended, he would have further opportunity. If he didn't, he was a body to be used as they saw fit until he left Vietnam in January of '69—at the latest.

"Fat Man, Fat Man, bring on the rain," Smitty said into the radio.

"Roger, Irishman, downpour coming now. Mind your heads."

Smitty smiled in satisfaction. Fat Man's closing was always the same, and always in that calm, comforting tone of voice that made you think he was a neighbor who's just called to ask if he can borrow the lawn mower, rather than someone calling up more air support for this one incident than had been used in an entire conventional World War II battle.

The cluster bombs seemed to float to the ground, then were lost in the tremendous force of the explosion that followed. The napalm came next, lighting up the hillside with a phosphorous flash that sucked the air from around you and instantly turned the surrounding area into a torrid zone.

Two regular North Vietnamese soldiers popped clear of the tall grass. Smitty sighted, fired, and dropped them instantly. Following long-established tradition, he was, as team lead, the last one on the aircraft. The helicopter lifted away, and Smitty and his team began to breathe again.

They were well back across the border when Smitty's team second, Hogsbreath, asked tiredly, "What's a-happenin' with you for Christmas, Irish?"

"No idea, Two. Might roll down to the safe house in Saigon or Da Nang after debrief and get plastered for a couple of days," Smitty said absently.

"Me," Smitty's number three said, "I'm going down to Nha Trang and get me a local, overpay her, and screw her brains out for three days. When I'm done, she'll walk so bowlegged that you guys will think she's been on a horse for a week."

Smitty's number three, Dogbreath, was a nineteen-year-old specialist four. Like Smitty's friend Frenchy, Doggie was a confirmed pussyhound with rumored pregnant girls in every army post at which he'd been assigned.

"Well, you guys take it easy. Remember, I'm the one who writes the letters," Smitty said quietly.

"Yes, Daaaaddy," Hogsbreath drawled. "We'll be careful and make sure that Doggie Dick has a truckload of them there rubbers made from old Arkansaaaw tractor tires."

Smitty smiled tolerantly at his team's lighthearted banter. They had been on three missions together. And although they had been extracted under fire each time, they had not suffered so much as a skinned knee among them.

The first mission had been to chart and report on enemy supply activity ten miles on the Laotian side of the border; the second, the same, at a different location. The third had been called for Laos, but suspected contamination of intelligence took them to North Cambodia instead.

Each time, the missions had been hazardous, requiring precise planning and split-second timing of the extraction; however, the team had performed flawlessly. This was their last mission of the year. It was mid-December, and they were due for five-day leaves after mission debriefing. Smitty had been told by Colonel Wilson that he would be a team lead through the balance of his first tour. Decision time was approaching. After Christmas leave, he had only twenty-four days to go until his year was over.

"Sergeant, Pleiku is under attack. Should we divert to Ban Me Thuot?" the helicopter pilot asked urgently.

"No fuckin' way," Smitty said, stuffing a new clip in his weapon. "Let's go get the little bastards."

Forgetting how tired they were after seven days in the field, Smitty, Hogsbreath, Dogbreath, and two Nungs began preparing for the assault. They readied hand grenades and golfball mines and looked for anything else they could fire or throw.

Smitty checked his whippet—a sawed-off shotgun lashed to the end of a piece of web belt so that the adjustment hook hung on his waist gear. It was tied down with a piece of parachute lacing cord to his leg, so that he could just untie the cord, pivot the weapon up, and fire, letting the shotgun recoil whip past his leg. He opened the breech, reloaded it, and tied it down where he could quickly bring it to bear.

Smitty also brought out from his pack his new secret weapon. It was a silver-plated model .220 Besson concert trumpet that he had picked up used for a hundred bucks in Sydney, sprayed with black paint, and taped with electrical tape so that it was solid black all over. Smitty had been itching for a chance to use it. He looped it around his neck with the piece of parachute cord he had cut specifically for that purpose.

The helicopter began to bank in toward the base. The door gunners opened up with their '60s. Smitty, Hogsbreath, Dogbreath, and the Nungs opened up with their hand weapons and tossed hand grenades at clusters of VC as they came into view. It looked to be a sapper attack—a suicide squad of one hundred VC that usually had explosives, grenade launchers and small arms that conducted surprise attacks aimed at inflicting maximum damage and creating pandemonium and uncertainty.

They numbered approximately two to three hundred. This was no small hit-and-run attack squad—this was a full-blown invasion. They were heavily armed and, from their movements, had excellent intelligence on the base and the strategic locations. A rough count showed that there were ten to twenty Americans already lying dead or wounded in and around the hospital, which seemed to be the focus of the attack. As the helicopter made its first pass, Smitty noted that an air force cargo transport had landed and had been unloading materials and personnel when the attack started.

Smitty reached forward and touched the pilot on the shoulder. "After your next pass, put us down. It looks like the air force crew is in trouble."

Smitty turned to Hogsbreath. "Bacon, when we land, take the Nungs and see if you can help break the attack at the hospital. Doggie, you and I will head toward the transport." Both nodded and gave the thumbs-up.

The pilot nodded his understanding as the helicopter banked for the next run. The pilot came in low, banked, and made a running landing. Smitty, Hogsbreath, Dogbreath, and the Nungs leaped from the copter before it landed and fanned out.

Smitty ran toward the aircraft shouting for Doggie to check on the crew while he went to the rear cargo area. Dogbreath acknowledged with a wave and ran toward the front of the aircraft.

On reaching the rear, he found the cargo master dead, as was the front loader driver, who was slumped over in his seat. Smitty crouched beside the ramp, looked up, and could see pallets of unloaded material with indistinguishable scared faces looking from behind them. Smitty could smell fuel everywhere and knew that it was only a matter of time until this big goony-bird went up.

"Everybody grab your gear and run for that building over there," a female voice screamed over the shelling and the panic.

Smitty had only a passing glance at a female form in army greens but was more concerned with her direction. To reach the building she was pointing to would require them to cross an open area approximately seventy-five yards away through murderous crossfire while the relative safety of a well-sandbagged trench was no more than thirty feet distant.

Two VC were approaching from her blind side. The fact that they were not firing was sufficient evidence that their intent was capture, not kill. A captured nurse would likely cause the launching of several rescue sorties that the VC would be well-prepared for, resulting in tens, or more likely, hundreds of deaths as American soldiers, spurred on by misplaced chivalry, would move with reckless abandon in an all-out attempt to save the nurse.

A warning yelled over the smoke and the noise would fall on deaf ears; the VC would be on her in less than ten seconds. Smitty took off like a blitzing linebacker after an unprotected quarterback. Figuring that he needed to get the attention of both the VC and the nurse, Smitty grabbed his trumpet and blatted out the loudest noise he could, then untied and readied his whippet.

It worked. The nurse froze and started to turn her head in the direction of the noise. The VC hesitated momentarily, and that moment was all Smitty needed.

He flattened the nurse with all the gentleness of Dick Butkus tackling Bart Starr in a Bears-Packers game, wrapping his left arm around her, physically lifting her off the ground, and driving her into the tarmac in one motion. Then, from his prone position on top of her, he whipped the shotgun upward at the two VC, who were now less than five feet away, and pulled the trigger.

The shotgun blast blew them backward like a halfback clotheslined by Docile Dick. They were dead before they hit the ground.

Smitty rolled off the nurse, grabbed her by the back of her pants and shirt collar, yanked her onto her feet, jerked a thumb in the direction of the trench, swatted her on the ass, and yelled, "Sweetheart, forget the duffels, get these people in that ditch unless you want to see most of them at graves registration."

Smitty's voice had carried enough that most of them were moving in that direction before she pointed urgently and shouted, "Over there."

Smitty ran on toward the front of the plane, not bothering to look back; there wasn't time. Dogbreath had grabbed a maintenance ladder, pushed it up to the nose of the aircraft, climbed up, and peered inside the flight deck. He looked down at Smitty and shook his head sadly.

"C'mon down," Smitty hollered with an emphatic wave.

Doggie acknowledged with a wave and a confident smile, a smile that turned to confusion as he turned and slowly toppled off the ramp onto the tarmac.

Smitty ran to him and turned him on his back. He'd been shot. God knows how many times with AK-47 rounds. Smitty looked around for the shooter, and to his relief saw a VC throw up his hands, not in surrender, but in spasmodic response to a small arms blast from Hogsbreath.

"How's the kid?" Hogsbreath asked, as he joined him.

Smitty's silence was response enough.

"One," Dogbreath said through coughed-up blood, "Tell my mom I love her." He went limp in Smitty's hands.

Smitty hoped that the ears were burning on all the irate fathers who cursed Doggie for knocking up their daughters and wished him a gruesome death. The kid was gone. Smitty knew that none of his young lovelies would be at the funeral. Arlington Cemetery was a long way from anywhere.

The total was now more than thirty thousand killed. More young Americans had died this year than in the all of the previous years combined. How many more would die before the Washington bureaucrats figured out how to feed this dog or shoot it?

The new year was a bad joke for anybody in-country in the beginning of 1969. After seeing to the kid and writing the letter he hated to write, Smitty went to a SOG safe house in Saigon and got teeth-numbing drunk for three days. He'd made contact with LZ, who wangled a three-day pass, and they had gotten drunk together for two more.

The gulf between them had widened into a chasm. LZ now talked openly and bitterly about the mistreatment of black soldiers in Vietnam and the special treatment given to whites. Through large swigs of bourbon, he talked at length about the equality of black men and what he was going to do, not to help them gain equality, but to anyone who tried to stop him. He validated this by pointing out the differences between the two of them. Smitty was an E-6; LZ was now an E-4, having been busted and losing a stripe for "speakin' up for the brothers."

After LZ had drunk himself to sleep the second night in the cheap hotel room they had rented, Smitty had gone to SOG headquarters on the Rue Pasteur and made a direct appeal to the chief of SOG. His emotionally charged argument was to have LZ transferred onto his team as a number three replacement for Doggie.

But Smitty had been turned down flat. The stated reason was that it had nothing to do with his being black, but it had everything to do with his attitude about being black. Also, the colonel had stated that in his experience, having friends on the same team was the quickest way to get both of them killed. That part of the argument was logical and unfortunately historically valid.

Smitty and LZ had argued at length, more so than at any time since Smitty had known him. Somewhere in the process, Smitty realized that he was arguing for their past relationship, which no longer existed. He fell silent and just let his friend rant.

Paradoxically, although he had a distinguished combat record with a Bronze Star and a Purple Heart, LZ had been turned down on his request to extend for another tour and had already received his orders for reassignment to Germany, following a thirty-day leave in the States. With the demand for well-trained, seasoned combat veterans being as acute as it was, the denial of a second tour was tantamount to the IRS refusing a million-dollar payment because they were pissed off about your using the wrong tax forms.

Something was wrong, far wrong, or not being disclosed, and LZ was being evasive about it. When Smitty asked if he was going to stop and see Frenchy, LZ had been adamant in his refusal. To Smitty, it almost seemed like it was a personal thing between them. He had queried LZ along that line but hadn't been able to get a straight answer. They had come to Vietnam a year ago as brothers; they parted with a perfunctory handshake as acquaintances. Smitty wondered idly if the circle would be complete when they next met. Would they be enemies again?

The balance of his leave had been bouts of alcoholic nothingness, followed by bleary-eyed consciousness and nightmare-filled sleep. The linear progression was right on target; the four musketeers had become one. First Frenchy, then Walt, now LZ. By his calculations, Smitty was due to meet his end before his beloved Baltimore Orioles could begin their drive for the World Championship that every sportswriter had predicted was theirs.

Smitty returned to Pleiku and to another mission. Underdog had joined the team as the new number three, replacing Doggie. Underdog, a specialist fourth class like Doggie, was twenty-six, three years into his second hitch, with the intent of becoming a lifer. He was good and steady but was known as a solid team member, not a team leader.

Their mission had gone flawlessly. Smitty was glad. Whether he extended or not, this was his last team lead. If he extended, he'd become a force recovery leader. If not, he'd be going home, in all likelihood back to Bragg as an instructor.

As the helicopter landed it was close to dark. Smitty knew the decision time was at hand; his tour was up in eight days.

There were four MPs, plus Captain Bartkowski waiting for them when they landed. Smitty hoped that their appearance here didn't have something to do with LZ.

"Sergeant Smith?" the lead MP, a specialist fifth class, asked perfunctorily.

"Yes."

"Sergeant, I have a warrant here ordering your arrest and immediate transport to Da Nang to expedite disposition," the MP said solemnly.

"What the fuck for?" Smitty snapped.

The MP exhaled. "You are charged with assault and battery on a superior officer, threatening a superior officer, countermanding the orders of a superior officer in a combat situation, and conduct unbecoming a United States soldier by making lewd, suggestive remarks, and fondling a superior officer. Now then, I suggest if you don't wish me and my team to use force to restrain a disgusting maggot like you, that you hand your weapons over to the captain and come along quietly."

Smitty looked quickly at Ron who spread his hands and shrugged. "It's out of my hands, partner."

"Wait a minute," Smitty said. "Does this have anything to do with that dumb bitch whose ass I saved before Christmas?"

"Sergeant, I have no knowledge of the specifics. A Captain Williams filed the charges. Now are you coming peaceably or not?"

Realizing that it would be futile to resist, Smitty handed his pack to Hogsbreath, his weapons to Ron, and his web belt with his shotgun to Underdog.

"And the Magnum, if you please," the MP said.

Smitty opened his shirt, and removed the pistol from its concealed shoulder holster and slapped it in Ron's hand.

The MP held out his hand indicating their direction, and they were off. They walked barely a hundred yards to an autorotating helicopter, boarded, and were airborne in less than one minute, headed straight toward Da Nang.

Smitty sat in stunned silence. *That's what you get for sticking your neck out,* he thought to himself. He was probably going to end up getting slam-dunked to Leavenworth for doing the right thing. To make matters even worse, the mission they had just come in from had been particularly nasty, requiring them to cross and recross streams used as sewers several times.

Not to put too fine a point on it, but he smelled—literally. And he was bone tired, badly in need of a shave, and in no condition, either mentally or physically, to make a good impression, if that was possible in this situation.

A short time later, the helicopter landed and it began to rain, only adding to his general nasty humor. Smitty was taken to a waiting Jeep and driven to the nurse's quarters next to the hospital. They escorted him to the first door on the right. The sign read Capt. L. Williams.

"Who is it?" a female asked in a baritone voice.

"I have Sergeant Smith here per your orders, Captain," the MP said.

There was a pause of ten seconds, and then the husky voice spoke again. "You and your men can go. Sergeant Smith, you are to assume a parade rest position outside my door and await my next command."

"Yes, ma'am," the MP said. He looked at Smitty sympathetically, imagining, like Smitty, that if the voice was any clue, this Captain Williams must not only sound like a middle linebacker, but must look like one, too.

A minute passed, then two. Several nurses in army greens strolled by, wrinkling their noses at his appearance and aroma.

Finally the voice from behind the door said, "Come in, Sergeant."

He opened the door and stepped inside. The room was sparsely furnished in basic army gray. It had a closet, a double bunk bed, an end table with a small cooler underneath it, a five-by-two desk and two chairs—a straight-backed one in front and a swivel one behind. On the desk was a pile of papers and a picture of two smiling older folks. Smitty guessed they must be the very brave parents. Off to the side was a closed door that Smitty guessed led to a head.

Smitty stopped just inside the door and fell in at parade rest. "Reporting as ordered, ma'am."

"Stand easy, Sergeant, I'll be with you in just a moment," the captain said in the same hard voice. "There's a cold beer in the cooler. Help yourself. The church key is on the table."

Smitty reached down and opened the cooler. He was just removing a cold one when the captain said, "Open one for me, too." Mechanically, Smitty did as she requested.

He opened his bottle and took a long pull, set it down on the corner of the desk and was just opening the second when the door opened.

Smitty almost dropped the bottle.

Framing the door before him was a perfectly proportioned five-foot-something platinum blonde. Normally, army greens did an excellent job of hiding a woman's best attributes—a gunny sack would be more appealing. In this case, it was the exact opposite, or maybe her uniforms had shrunk about three sizes in the wash. The last name clicked in Smitty's mind. He had heard something about a nurse named Williams before.

He had it; his face colored in apprehension and recognition. This was the infamous woman they called Captain Iceberg—rumored to be the Ballbusting Ice Queen of I Corps. According to the stories that Smitty had heard, she was some stuck-up ex-Miss California wannabe beauty queen who joined the army when her adult movie career fizzled.

Supposedly, every soldier from the lowliest private to three-star generals had put the make on her with negative results. A real man-hating bitch who, it was rumored, would on only the slightest provocation, cut your nuts off and stuff 'em down your fucking throat.

"Sergeant," she said, "don't they teach you Green Beanies the fundamentals of military courtesy?"

"Uh, ma'am?" Smitty stammered in embarrassment, reluctantly dragging his eyes from their own personal X-ray examination.

"Weren't you taught to salute the rank, not the person?" she asked.

"Yes, ma'am," Smitty responded.

"Well, then?" Smitty followed the line of her finger as it slowly angled upward—past the mounds of plenty—to point at a set of captains bars pinned to the collar of her fatigues.

"Yes, ma'am," Smitty mumbled, giving her a half-hearted salute.

Walking slowly to her desk, with Smitty watching her every move—and her knowing it—the captain sat down in the chair behind the desk, which, like every other army issued chair, squeaked irritatingly, and motioned for Smitty to do the same.

"No thanks, ma'am, I'd prefer to stand," Smitty replied.

She frowned at him. "Sergeant, do you know why you are here?"

"I know what the charges are. That doesn't say I necessarily agree with them."

"Do you deny that you assaulted a nurse, who happens to be an officer, then grabbed her, fondled her, and slapped her on the rear end?"

"Captain, if a confession is what you're looking for, then okay, fine, you got it," Smitty said. "Next time I'll leave that dumb bitch to fend for herself and let you write the letters and toe-tag the remains." If Smitty was going down, he was going down swinging, and he sure as hell wasn't going to go down kissing Miss Haughty Butt's ass.

The captain drummed her fingers on her pile of papers. "And you're going to stick to that story, huh?"

"Fuckin' A, I am," Smitty answered.

The captain folded up the pile of papers, laid them aside, and picked up a two-by-five-by-half-inch-deep box underneath. Opening it as she got up, she walked around the table. "Attention."

Smitty instinctively snapped to.

"Sergeant, it is my extreme pleasure to present you with the Bronze Star for your brave and selfless actions on 19 December last. Your actions saved many lives, for which I and my nurses will be eternally grateful," she said, as she pinned the decoration to his pocket.

"And on a personal note, I'd like to thank you for, how did you say it, not leaving 'that dumb bitch to fend for herself,' and saving my life. Your captain told me what would have happened to me if I'd been captured." She stopped and shuddered in horror.

"Uh, Captain, I'm totally confused," Smitty said simply. "The MPs told me I was being brought here to face charges of whacking a superior officer."

"Oh, that," she said. "I wanted to get you up here to give you the decoration and thank you myself. But your colonel told me you'd probably tell me to shove it. So we put our heads together and came up with this little scheme to assure that you came along peaceably.

"The deception was your colonel's part. The decoration and the personal presentation were my own idea and way of saying thanks." She impulsively stepped forward and kissed him lightly on the cheek. They made eye contact before she stepped back.

"As I told a high school acquaintance a few months ago, if you go though life saying thanks like that, you'll never want for friends," Smitty said evenly. Spotting the self-doubt in her eyes, he added, "You're quite different in person."

"You mean from the Ice Queen that everyone calls me behind my back. That's because you're the first man I've met in a long time who did something for me before you tried to do something to me."

"I think I understand," Smitty said. Visions of Kristie flashed into his head.

"Do you?" she asked angrily, turning suddenly and causing her blonde mane to fan seductively. "Do you really know what it feels like to be someone like me? From the time I was born, I've been told how pretty I am. Unfortunately, just about every man I've met equated that with short-term promiscuity, not long-term commitment."

She reached back on her desk and fished out a pack of cigarettes, shook out one for herself and one for Smitty, then picked up from her desk a souvenir lighter from New York City.

Smitty took the lighter from her unresisting hand and lit hers, then his own. She nodded her thanks, then began to pace nervously in embarrassment that she had unintentionally let down her guard.

Smitty felt strangely drawn to her and suspected she was to him. Obviously, she needed to talk to someone, and perhaps Smitty did also.

To get her talking again, and for want of anything better to say, Smitty asked, "Has it always been this way?"

The captain blew a big cloud of smoke. "Only from the time I can remember. At six, I was the one all the boys wanted to play doctor with. At ten, it was spin the bottle, at thirteen, I was being groped during the slow dances in junior high. At sixteen, the boys who were brave enough to ask me out wanted to take me to the drive-in. In college, it was the frat boys trying to get me drunk. Even in nursing school, other girls came on to me.

"The army has been more of the same. Do you know how many so-called officers and gentlemen have told me how much I could advance my career if I would just be 'cooperative'?" she said bitterly as she slugged back the rest of her beer then dropped her cigarette butt into the can in disgust.

"Captain, you're not the only one who's been dealt life from the bottom of the deck," Smitty said, thinking of LZ. "I've got a good friend who's had to overcome more obstacles than you would face in ten lifetimes; so you can too. Lady, I myself have been in the middle of a shitstorm since the day I was born, with a black cloud permanently following me around.

"Nursey, it ain't being drop-dead gorgeous that's your problem; it's learning to get along without it. In a few years your looks will be gone, then you'll have to run the man race with the rest of the pack who have to work to get one. Your only problem is that you're used to the attention and afraid to try making it without leading with your tits."

The captain spun on her heels and slapped him across the face. "Go to hell, Sergeant!"

"I've already been there, sweetheart; I got kicked out for bootlegging ice water and sent to Nam as punishment," Smitty said through clenched teeth.

They stared at each other silently as anger masked mutual loneliness. The captain suddenly leaned forward, turned her head up, put her arms around Smitty and gave him a passionate kiss—a kiss that caused a certain part of his anatomy to begin to make its own transition from parade rest to attention, also.

They broke the kiss and stared unblinkingly at one another. If hatred and passion were indeed, as the old expression goes, two sides of the same coin, then Smitty and the captain had just done a mutual flip with a ten-point landing. She kissed him again, taking her hands and using them to place his unresisting arms around her.

After what seemed like a pleasurable eternity, she broke the kiss off suddenly, backed away and wrinkled her nose in distaste. "You know what, Sergeant, you stink."

Smitty opened his mouth to speak, but she cut him off. "Strip off your clothes Sergeant, I'm going to give you a bath." She impishly pushed him down on the bed, stooped, and proceeded to unlace his boots.

As Smitty lay back on the rack with his eyes closed, he enjoyed being attended to. If what he thought was going to happen did happen, he thought, he could still be charged with assaulting a superior officer. But it would be in a totally different context from that for which the statute was intended.

Smitty extended for a year. It was more or less the path of least resistance. He just wasn't ready to go home to a training gig at Bragg. The colonel had not only come through as promised, but surprisingly better. Smitty was reassigned as team lead for a thirty-person recovery force. Since the force was usually commanded by a lieutenant, Smitty was surprised when he was given a reserve field commission as a second lieutenant on his birthday, although his regular army rank remained staff sergeant.

By reserve, it meant that he was being advanced in rank temporarily by the army in times of conflict to fill rapidly depleted billets, based on experience. His regular sergeant's rank, E-6, was the rank he could, and would, probably be reduced to if he elected to remain in the army after the war was over, and there was an oversupply of second lieutenants.

The force deployment could be all thirty men, or as few as five, depending on circumstances. Smitty would also, due to depletion of regular Special Forces ranks, be responsible for augmenting the regular mike forces and base camps when the situation required it. Hogsbreath had taken his old team lead spot, with a yet-to-be-assigned person to replace Hogs in the number two slot.

Smitty's new second in command had the swagger of John Wayne and the demeanor of King Kong. He cursed like a stiffed Times Square hooker. His nose bore evidence of separate breaks and a shrapnel scar ran from the right side on his forehead to the hairline. That scar was from a Nazi tank he single-handedly blew up in the Battle of the Bulge; a second scar, running vertically the length of the right ear, was from a machine-gun nest he eliminated at the Chosin Reservoir; and a particularly prominent third one across the bridge of the nose was from a beer bottle bar fight in a dive outside Bragg.

He was a twenty-seven-year army veteran of World War II, Korea, and one previous '66 tour of Vietnam. His name was Sergeant Mike. He had a last name but, due either to age or custom, was referred to by his rank and first name by everyone from the lowest private to three-star generals.

According to Captain Bartkowski, Mike had made E-8 on three separate occasions only to be busted back to E-7 each time due to "misunderstandings" with the local civilian police. But he was a professional soldier, having earned enough medals in three wars to start his own personal museum—and enough misdemeanor arrests in the peacetimes in between to have a police file as thick as the entire 5th Special Forces Division roster. Apparently, Sergeant Mike was extremely brave and dedicated in a war, but no more patriotic than necessary in the peacetimes in between.

"Lieutenant, we're alerted," Sergeant Mike said, yawning. "Seems a team coming back from Cambodia was just inside the border when their helicopter was shot down. We're going in as resupport."

"How'd you find that out?" Smitty asked.

"Call just came in on the radio. I was covering it for Johnson while he went to the shitter. Poor bastard's got the squirts."

"You know how to operate a radio?" Smitty said.

The sergeant shook his head in disgust. "Lieutenant, that was my original MOS classification when I went in the service in '41. I was parachuting in Europe long before D-Day, running missions with Special Ops as a radio operator long before you were even part of your daddy's hard-on."

Smitty raised an eyebrow. Mike shook his head emphatically. "No, it's not your old team. It's guys from the south command that you probably don't know. The south force is already in Cambodia, and we're covering their area."

"What other units are in the area?" Smitty asked.

"Well, Third Marines sent in a platoon. The VC reinforced, and our team and the platoon are pinned down in a village two clicks from the border. The VC must want our guys or the intel they've got pretty badly to risk an open battle," the sergeant said.

"How soon can we be ready to move?"

"If that fat-assed straight leg one-star general gets off his duff and authorizes the helicopters, we can be ready to go in two hours."

"Let's target for one. I'll call the colonel and see if he can help," Smitty said, reaching for the field telephone.

"Yes, sir," the sergeant said, frowning. He saluted formally, did a precise military about-face, then quickly marched out of Smitty's hooch.

They had been teamed for two months, been on four missions together under fire, and still their relationship could best be termed as strained. The sergeant performed his assigned duties efficiently but with none of the customary warmth and camaraderie that Smitty had grown accustomed to in SOG.

At first, Smitty thought it was him, then he thought it was just squirt second lieutenants he didn't like. But more and more, Smitty was coming to the conclusion that he or his rank had nothing to do with it. Mike was harboring a major pissed-off from somewhere in his past.

Smitty made the call. Colonel Wilson said he'd see what he could do and get right back to him. With half an hour to kill, Smitty decided to finish a letter to Captain Williams, or "Linda, sweetie" as Smitty had now come to know her. In the middle of all this insanity, Smitty had found his first steady girlfriend.

After the first torrid night, Smitty had to admit candidly he had thought of it as a one-night thank-you-for-saving-my-bacon, roll-in-the-hay-and-kiss-off. But it had not died, like so many one night stands over here; if anything, it had intensified.

They came from the same background; her father was a chief petty officer in the navy who'd done his twenty then returned to the Iowa farm he'd left behind during the War. She was a service brat who'd gone to college to major in nursing, then joined the army as a second lieutenant six years ago—a thousand latrine-o-gram rumors of her promiscuous youth not withstanding.

Like Smitty, she had extended for a second tour. Although they'd been together only that one time for that one night, they were exchanging notes like two love-struck teenagers and were already making plans for spending their R&R together.

The phone rang. "Lieutenant," Colonel Wilson said in a hurried voice, "You'll have your transports in one hour. Can you be ready by then?"

"Yes, sir. We'll manage."

"Good luck," he said quickly and hung up before Smitty could reply.

Smitty wrote the last lines to Linda, folded and sealed the letter, and dropped it in the mail bag on his way out, along with letters to LZ, who was with a newly created Special Forces division in Germany, and to Frenchy, who was now less than thirty days from his early out. He grabbed his gear, checked his weapons, and walked over to the supply hut where Sergeant Mike was expertly assembling the team for the mission. Catching Mike's eye, Smitty gave him the thumbs-up. The sergeant grunted in response.

Shaking his head in frustration, Smitty grabbed his supplies and left, preferring to wait out on the tarmac in the stifling heat. It would seem like an icebox compared to the hot daggers the sergeant's eyes were piercing him with now.

They went in prepared for an LZ hotter than a lava pit; they landed on one colder than an Eskimo's igloo. The VC, with their uncanny sense of impending disaster, had pulled back a half-hour before Smitty's team arrived. They landed not to small arms fire but to marines sitting around casually with their M-16s resting across their legs, smoking cigarettes, talking the nervous talk that always comes out after a battle, and walking around the village searching for weapons or just being curious.

"They're gone, huh?" Smitty nodded to a marine first lieutenant who was in charge of the platoon.

"Yeah, but the slimy little dinks gave us a hot time when we landed," he answered in frustration. "They killed six of my men and wounded twelve others. I don't know who your boys are, and why it was so damned important that we get to them, but I hope it was worth it." He spat at Smitty's feet.

"Some of my boys are ready to take out their frustration on anything with slanty eyes. If something did start, I don't know whether I'd be able to control them."

"It was, and you will," Smitty said.

The lieutenant nodded dubiously and walked away to check on his wounded, leaving Smitty standing next to Sergeant Mike, who had already deployed the force to perimeter defense positions, in spite of the apparent calm, and was making preparations to lift the SOG team out before too many questions could be asked.

On the ride over, Smitty tried to engage Mike in conversation, but the one-word answers and nonverbal grunts were evidence enough of his feelings. Since diplomacy wasn't working, it was time for a frontal assault. Smitty had made a mental note to call him in when they got back and have it out privately. Since there was nothing to do here but mop up the mess, Smitty decided the time was now.

"Sergeant, I would like to talk to you privately," Smitty said quietly. He motioned to a spot next to a tree thirty feet away.

When the sergeant grunted but made no move to respond, Smitty added, "Make that an order."

With a withering look, the sergeant slowly followed him to the tall woody plant.

"Smoke?" Smitty offered, shaking out a Camel.

"Got my own," he growled, glowering at Smitty.

Smitty exhaled deeply to keep his temper in check. "Sergeant, it appears you don't care much for me."

"You could put that in the fuckin' plan of the day," he said.

"Why?"

"Lieutenant, I've seen you shavetails come and go. I haven't met one yet that was worth what your daddy squirted to make ya. You lean on sergeants like me to do all the work and run the team, but when the going gets rough, you'll toss me to the wolves for your next promotion and forget about the guy who helped you get there."

"You know, Sergeant, I was an NCO on my first tour," Smitty said.

"That only makes you worse, sir. Now you'll become some promotion-climbing asshole whose only purpose in life is to feather your own nest so you can retire a major or lieutenant colonel no matter how many of these boys you have to sacrifice to get there."

"Mike, I don't think all second lieutenants could be that bad."

"Pfft!" he scoffed. "I've even got you assholes categorized."

"Do tell." Smitty smiled.

The sergeant glared silently at Smitty, obviously debating if he were worth the trouble. After ten seconds, he pulled out a cigarette and waited expectantly for Smitty to offer to light it.

Smitty sensed that this was some kind of are-you-going-to-kiss-my-ass? initiation. He pulled out a cigarette of his own from the pack in his hand, lit it with his own lighter, put the lighter back in his pocket, and blew a thick cloud of smoke directly in Sergeant Mike's face.

With a nod and an amused smile, the sergeant lit his own cigarette. "There's four kinds of second lieutenants. There's lieutenant, sir, with a salute"—Smitty winced involuntarily at that one, as this had been Mike's main means of ending their communication most of the time—"There's lieutenant, sir, without a salute; there's just plain lieutenant; and finally there's LT." Mike blew his own cloud of cigarette smoke back at Smitty.

"Your definitions are pretty granular. What's the difference?"

Surveying Smitty like he was something the cat did and didn't cover up, he grunted and continued. "Well, addressing one of you little pricks as 'lieutenant, sir,' with a salute means I think you're about the most useless piece of shit on this earth. When I do it in the field, it also means I'm pointing you out for any snipers who just might want to know who's in charge." He smiled wryly, "I got rid of some lieutenants with that one in my career, I can tell you."

"If I address you as 'lieutenant, sir,' without the salute, it means I still don't think you're worth a flying fuck, I just ain't deliberately trying to get you killed or in trouble with the brass, figuring that you're such a screw-up that you'll be a doin' it to yourself. I don't hate you; I think you're trying. I just think you're an incompetent fuck."

"If I call you just plain lieutenant, it means that you're not an incompetent fuck-up anymore, and I can at least trust you to wipe your own ass without getting crap on your britches. I ain't deliberately hurtin' your career anymore, and in time, just might try to help it."

"And LT?" Smitty asked.

"Hell, if you're my LT, you can come to my house and fuck my daughter. It also means you got your shit together and I like you. But," he added, "I only had me a few of those. Boys with guts and principle are a rare combination; usually you find one or the other. All principle and they sell you down the river. All guts and they get you killed."

Taking a blind shot, Smitty said, "What was the name of the second lieutenant who fucked you over the last time you were in Vietnam?"

The sergeant gave him a you're-a-lot-like-him look. "His name's not important, since he's not in Nam now, but the useless little puke ordered a village torched after we found a cache of VC rounds and weapons.

"When some bleeding heart reporter did one of those headline-grabbing sob stories for the press, the little pissant covered his shirttails real good and told the brass that I was the one who gave the order. Since he was from some well-connected family, they shipped him stateside to Bragg with a promotion, busted me to E-7, then shipped me directly to Germany through India so I wouldn't talk. Hell, I didn't even get a chance to stop at home and play slap and tickle with my ol' lady for a couple of days. I had to wait for her to get there."

Smitty felt like someone had just goose-stepped over his grave. That must have been what LZ was trying to tell him that night in the hotel room but was unsure of where Smitty stood. LZ had clammed up when Smitty disagreed with him, thinking that Smitty had become, or was in the process of becoming, one of them, too.

LZ must have had the same thing happen to him that happened to Sergeant Mike and couldn't do a thing about it. The parallels were there. Smitty wondered if it could be the same root cause. He made a mental note to investigate privately on his own on his next trip to SOG headquarters in Saigon when there was more time. Misinterpreting Smitty's look of disbelief, Mike said, "I knew you wouldn't believe me. I thought for just a minute you might be different, but you're the same useless piece of shit as all the rest." He thumped his cigarette butt at Smitty's chest, turned, and started to stalk away.

Smitty grabbed him and spun him around. "I do believe you, Mike. You have no idea how much I believe what you just told me. And while I can't make up for the mistakes of the past, I hope you'll give me a chance to correct the future."

Mike attempted to shake his arm free, but Smitty held on with a firm bear claw grip. "I mean it. I need you," Smitty said. They stood eye to eye, neither man wanting to give in to the other.

Finally, Mike's eyes softened. "We'll see, Lieutenant, we'll see." He shook himself free and walked away.

We will see, Smitty thought to himself, but it was only partially to do with Mike and a lot to do with his musketeer friend LZ.

They were evac'ing the village. The SOG team was second out—behind the wounded and before the dead were loaded on helicopters for the long ride to graves registration. Sergeant Mike had gone to the other side of the village to round up the balance of the team, and the marine gunnery sergeant had gone along to pull in his men, also. This was the true futility of Vietnam. Land, fight a battle, suffer casualties, pull out, and the VC would be back in the village by tomorrow.

Smitty had gone in search of Mike and was walking down the main dirt road when he heard a scream. He had left his assault weapon back at the LZ with the radioman and had only his whippet and the ever-present .357. Cursing his own stupidity at leaving his primary weapon behind, he drew his Magnum and ran in the direction of the shriek.

Behind a hut at the end of the village, Smitty heard voices. As he reached the edge of the building, he stopped, dropped to his chest, and peeked cautiously around.

Four marines had grabbed a young Vietnamese girl who was screaming and struggling as they wrestled her to the ground.

"Hold the little bitch still," a marine corporal said. He dropped his pants, dropped to his knees, and began to stroke himself.

"Grab her other arm and leg, man." The second marine, a private, grabbed her left arm and leg, motioning for the third marine to grab and hold the thrashing right arm and leg so that she was now secured and defenseless in a spread-eagle position. The fourth marine dropped to his knees and positioned himself behind the girl's head with his hand over her mouth to prevent her from screaming again. The marine corporal grabbed her shirt and pants, slit them open with his bayonet, then ripped them off, leaving her naked. She had neither breasts nor hair.

Smitty paused, not to consider the consequences of intervening but to figure out how. Four armed marines intent on rape would be angry at being stopped. Smitty doubted he could incapacitate all four of them by himself, so that left out surprise. The only thing left was gall. In order to stop this, he'd have to incapacitate the crap out of the leader in such a way that it intimidated the others into inactivity. So that made the corporal his pigeon.

The marine had positioned himself between her spread legs and was lowering himself onto her, when Smitty took a deep breath to steady his own nerves, stepped from the corner of the building, and approached the corporal from behind. The others were so intent on watching the two-striper that no one saw him.

"You shoot your wad, I shoot mine," Smitty said, pushing his Smith and Wesson against the corporal's ear.

The corporal froze, and slowly reversed his direction until he was now fully back on his knees—his erection protruding vilely from his body like a flagpole looking desperately for the pennant of the Stars and Stripes.

"C'mon, Lieutenant," the marine holding her head said caustically, "she ain't nothin' but a dink. We're just gonna have some fun. If you want, you can go next."

"You know we ain't gonna let you walk away from here you fuckin' shavetail; you may as well join us, cause you sure as hell ain't gonna report us," the corporal added. "How you gonna take all of us? You can't shoot us, but we can sure as hell shoot you. It's four to one in our favor."

"Make that four to two, scumbag," Sergeant Mike stepped from the other side of the building and stuck his assault weapon against the temple of the marine holding the girl's mouth. He said to Smitty, "LT, you want to handle these guys yourself like you usually do, or do you want to give an old man a chance to get in on the ass kicking?"

"Last chance," Smitty said, cocking the Magnum.

The marine on the right had released the girl's arm and was slowly and unobtrusively trying to slide his M-16 off his shoulder. The one on the left had released his hold on her leg and was likewise trying to get to his .45.

Smitty grabbed the marine corporal's shirt collar and jerked him back, bringing the .357 arcing down, pistol-whipping it with full force across his penis. He grabbed his crotch and fell to the ground howling in pain. Then Smitty's Magnum caught the marine on the left with an upward backhand across the face before he could get his own hand weapon out, sending him toppling over backward like an uprooted Georgia pine.

Mike had obviously been waiting for Smitty to act. He had his bayonet in the scabbard behind his back holding it by the blade end. Smitty had just completed his crude attempt at blunt castration, when Mike brought the weapon around and clubbed the marine holding the girl's head on the back of the skull, instantly knocking him unconscious. The fourth marine stood up to run, only to find that he had lined himself up perfectly for a right cross from Mike, who sent him to the ground with a single punch.

The terrified girl jumped up, ran naked, screaming in panic, back toward the center of the village, and was soon lost from sight.

"Pretty good punch for a worn-out old fart," Smitty said.

"Thanks, LT," Mike said, patting Smitty paternally on the cheek. "We did pretty good at that. Scumbag jarheads got no fuckin' class. Thousands of Vietnamese women that can be had for a couple of packs of cigarettes and these pricks have to go and try to rape a kid. Shit, she ain't even as old as my youngest daughter."

The girl's screams had brought reinforcements. Members of Smitty's force, the marine lieutenant, and several other marines were soon on the scene.

"Restrain 'em," Sergeant Mike said to three of their force.

"Look, Sergeant, couldn't you leave the discipline to me?" the marine lieutenant said. "I can handle it internally."

"I'd like to sir, but my lieutenant is a real prick and a stickler for the rules," Mike replied. "If I tried to let these guys go, the little shavetail bastard would shoot me instead."

Smitty called the incident in to the captain at Pleiku. He just couldn't seem to take the path of least resistance. In this case, he was glad he hadn't.

"Nice to be back in the field and not putting up with all that political shit, eh, LT?" Mike and Smitty were on a flight to Ia Drang Valley to reinforce a beleaguered Special Forces camp that was a jumping-off spot for SOG missions into Laos and in danger of being overrun.

Political shit was right. The past three months, Smitty had felt like a turd floating in a presidential punchbowl. Stopping the rape had been hard enough; living with the fallout was a bitch. Much like doing the right thing at the party in Savannah a couple of years back and paying the price, that's what had happened to Smitty: he'd paid the price. The reporting of the attempted rape had set off a chain reaction of events from Da Nang all the way to Saigon.

It had started at Marine Headquarters in Da Nang, and filtered to Nha Trang, with Smitty having to go to the Special Forces Headquarters twice to tell his version of the story. First to an army major, then a marine lieutenant colonel, who ended the hearing by saying, "Off the record, son, you'd have saved us all a lot of trouble if you'd just walked away."

With each retelling of the events, the versions got a little wilder. Linda had written in one of her letters that there was a rumor circulating with the marine doctors in the hospital in Da Nang that the only reason that Smitty had turned the marines in was their insistence that he go last.

At the court-martial in Saigon, the marines' defense lawyer tried, unsuccessfully, to advance the theory that Smitty and Sergeant Mike were in fact the rapists, and the valiant marines were just trying to stop them. The prosecutor laughed so hard they had to adjourn for ten minutes for him to get himself together. Before the trial was over, the phrase "regrettable situation" seemed to have replaced the phrase "attempted rape." The words "deplorable" and "unfortunate" became pretty much part of the standard dialogue of any officer commenting officially on the "regrettable situation."

"Thinking it wasn't worth it, son?" Sergeant Mike asked. "Your crystal ball is working overtime, LT, trust me. This whole thing is just the tip of a very shitty iceberg; they're just after you 'cause they don't like the smell. That, and they're scared shitless that more of this crystallized water will come to the surface, and they're not prepared to deal with it. Especially since they spent years trying to push it down and pretend it don't exist."

"Damn, in addition to everything else, a philosopher," Smitty said.

Mike's reply was a single digit.

"You know, it would seem to me that a master sergeant would have better manners and serve as a better example to young, impressionable second lieutenants like myself," Smitty said.

"If I ever get to be a master sergeant again, I'll worry about it. Until then," Mike again displayed his IQ—"and that's for your horse." He turned his digit horizontal and thrusted upward.

"I'm gonna hold you to that," Smitty said agreeably. He grabbed Mike's right hand, reached in his breast pocket, pulled out a set of master sergeant chevrons and slapped the new rank in Mike's grimy paw.

"Sew these on when we get back, Master Sergeant. Although, considering your checkered history, you probably should attach them with zippers." Smitty laughed

"How?" Mike asked.

"When I was in Nha Trang for the marine depositions for the court-martial, I did a little checking on my own on that story you told me and found it to be true. You were fucked over—so were a good many others. So, I had a private talk with Colonel Wilson and he agreed to the promotion. God knows you deserve it, even if you do have a rating scale for the systematic reduction of whaleshit second lieutenants,"

"Thanks, LT," Mike said humbly. "I'll never forget this." He added, "You little devious shavetail cocksucker."

"Mike, you're about the bravest and ballsiest fucker I ever met. You're good with the troops; they listen and respond to you. So the colonel told me to add this.

"If you can manage to finish this tour without gettin' into any more trouble—which I personally took to mean assuring that a certain second lieutenant is well taken care of—then your next assignment, correction, make that your last two-year hitch, will be as a sergeant major back at Bragg. And if the billet opens, it'll be as a brigade first sergeant if the colonel has anything to say about it."

Mike looked at Smitty in a face filled with feeling. He stuck out his hand. Smitty took it and the two men shook hands firmly—the deal was sealed. In a voice choked with emotion, Mike said, "Anytime, anywhere, LT; for the rest of your life, you call and I'll be there. You can count on me."

Wishing to break the heavy mood, Smitty said, "Cool, does that mean I can now come home with you and have carnal knowledge of your daughter?"

Mike snorted contemptuously. "Yes, sir, Lieutenant, sir." He saluted. "She's eighteen now and legal; just as soon as you marry her, you'll have my absolute permission. Matter of fact, I'll reserve your honeymoon suite 'cause I want to sit in a chair, watch, and see if you little butterbars can even get it up in the first place."

The helicopter was preparing to land and Smitty was sure he'd done the right thing for Mike. But what Mike did not know, and only the colonel now knew, was that Mike was the tip of a very shitty iceberg also. Only this one, when it surfaced, would make Smitty's seem like an ice cube.

They landed hot. AK-47 fire crackled all around them. Smitty and Mike were in the first helicopter. The second was hit coming down and slammed into the ground with a gut-wrenching metallic sound a hundred yards away. Smitty knew he'd be writing more letters tonight—if the captain wasn't writing his.

They moved as fast as seventy pounds of equipment on their back would allow, instinctively firing at anything that showed its face toward the firebase.

"Yooou boys give the recognition sign," a voice drawled into the radio on the back of the specialist four next to Smitty."

Smitty recognized the voice. "Bacon Butt, it's Irishman. Open the fucking gate before I call in a napalm air strike and turn your fat ass into barbecued pork."

"London Bridge is a-comin' down. I hope y'all got the toll," Hogsbreath said.

Smitty paused at the gate to count noses. Twenty-four of them had made it through to the relative safety of the base camp—and four of them were wounded, two to the point of incapacitation. Smitty had a bad feeling about this. It didn't feel right; it felt like a trap; it felt like the VC knew they were coming, almost like they'd been forewarned.

"What's the poop, scoop?" Smitty asked his former number two when they were in the command bunker.

"Weeell, I'll be a-tellin' ya, Irish, I don't like it. The original attack wiped out the captain and the lieutenant and most of the regular Special Forces team. They had them bottled up here for six days, but ain't attacked. It's kinda' like they been a-waitin' for more of us to show up so's they could make a bigger score," Hogsbreath explained.

"Maybe they have," Smitty said absently. Smitty made a call to Captain Bartkowski at Pleiku but was informed that Ron was unavailable. Smitty asked for a patch to Nha Trang. A Major Something-or-Other, the camp adjutant, came on the line and said that he was sure he could handle whatever Smitty needed and refused to connect him, then gave him a lot of double-talk about rules of air support engagement and other hogwash for five minutes before Smitty clicked off. The message was clear: they were on their own. Smitty stood tapping the radio in his hand nervously.

"Think out loud, LT," Mike said.

"Okay, Mike, here's my thoughts in no particular order. One, there will be no air support. We've been set up. Either because of that rape thing to just kill off everyone and bury it or to stage a nice little wipeout of the force to break the back of SOG." Smitty paused to read their eyes.

Hogsbreath and Sergeant Mike nodded knowingly at the last statement. It was no secret that certain senior officers of the conventional army and marines thought of the SOG incursion missions as a wart on their backsides because they repudiated their conventional battle decisions. And the SOG approach was now being lobbied by a former chief SOG in Washington and listened to, it was rumored, by the wiry-haired secretary of state. An embarrassing military disaster would have far-reaching political effects.

"Second, we can't expect any help. We're it. So we need to prepare to fight this to the end, I repeat—to the end. If this is the trap I think it is, then there are probably pretty close to a thousand VC out there. They know that there are less than two hundred of us, counting the SOGS, Nungs, and regular Yards. And probably, because of informers inside the camp, know just what our armament is. If what you say is true Hogs, and I think it is, they'll probably hit us tonight.

"Third, since we're all that's left to command, we've got to act like this is a cakewalk in the park. We've got to leave this bunker like we're king shit. Act like we're going to come through this; then we just might."

"Lieutenant, I don't mind tellin' ya that this one's got me a little bit scared," Hogsbreath said.

"Well, Porky Pecker," Smitty said with a grin, "like my daddy always used to say to me: It ain't being scared that matters, it's what you do when you're scared that counts. The other thing he used to say is that as long as a man keeps thinking, he has a chance; when he stops, he has none."

It was not a statement that called for an answer.

They came at 2:00 AM, mortars first, then bodies—lots of bodies. Looking through the night glasses, Smitty thought that someone had just kicked over an anthill made of people. The VC filled his vision as far as he could see. All the mortar pits began to fire at once, the rounds exploding in the center of the human blanket. Temporary holes opened as bodies fell, only to be closed up again by the bodies that followed. The M-60s began to fire as the VC came into range, cutting down more bodies like blades of freshly mowed grass.

They hit the wire with ladders as Hogsbreath hit the Claymores, blowing the first wave back against the others. The attack stalled temporarily, regrouped, and came on again. Hogsbreath blew the next set of Claymores, hoping that they thought the first round was it. More bodies fell and body parts flew into the air. By Smitty's count, they had cut down 20 to 25 percent, but they kept on coming.

Even with fortified positions, the firebase casualties were mounting also. One mortar pit was out of action—the fire team all dead. An M-60 crew had suffered a direct mortar hit, and the men were sprawled in a ghastly fashion on top of one another. One of every three of the frontline Yards was dead, and the numbers mounted continuously like a running charity donation tally board. By Smitty's count, they had lost 30 percent of their effective force already. Hogsbreath's SOG team had been split to act as squad leaders for the rest. Two of the Nungs on that team were now dead, also.

And still they kept on coming.

By prearrangement, they fell back to secondary perimeter defense positions, continuously firing and continuously dying. The corrugated roof of the team house went up in a blast of mortar fire that sent pieces of shrapnel flying through the air like a swarm of gnats, hitting anyone who was close. Smitty watched helplessly as Underdog, acting as the squad leader, motioned his squad away and fought a one-man delaying action until he was virtually cut in half by AK-47 fire as the left flank defenses were breached. The VC were aiming to cut the camp in half, then surround the smaller separate groups and exterminate them. By Smitty's count, they were now down to 40 percent effectives. Bodies littered the ground like refuse after a rock concert, and the human trash pile continued to grow.

Smitty, Sergeant Mike, and Hogsbreath had divided the original two hundred men into three platoons of approximately sixty-five men, with each of them assuming command of a platoon. Together they now had less than that single number combined.

"If they get the ammo below the Commo bunker, LT, we're fucked," Mike screamed in Smitty's ear. "Nobody will leave this shithole alive."

"I know," Smitty yelled back. "The only way I can think to deny it to them is to barricade it from the inside, and that's a certain one-way ticket."

"So what are we waiting for, Boss?" Mike asked.

Smitty looked Mike straight in the eye. "You sure?"

"Who the fuck wants to live forever?" Mike shot back.

Smitty turned to Hogsbreath and said, "Hogs, assume command of what's left and evac the firebase per the escape corridor as planned. Sergeant Dumbfuck and Lieutenant Shit-for-Brains are going to stay behind with the radio and defend the ammo from the inside."

"Irish, are you fuckin' crazy?!" Hogsbreath screamed in disbelief.

"Yeah, as a matter of fact, I am," Smitty hollered back. He jerked a thumb at Mike. "And it's contagious. Now, like they say, make like a shepherd and get the flock outta here," Smitty shoved Hogsbreath ten feet in the direction of the rear perimeter.

Smitty and Mike opened the hatch that led down a set of dirt steps ten feet to a well-fortified and heavily sandbagged underground bunker. At the bottom of the steps was a sandbagged firewall in the shape of an L to prevent anything from accidentally or intentionally being rolled down and detonating the entire ammo load.

Smitty and Mike used their bayonets to cut a killing hold in one of the sandbags, giving them an unobstructed view of the entrance. They had just completed this task when the hatch was snatched open and Hogsbreath shouted, "Irish, it be me, Pig Breath, I'm a-comin' down."

"What are you doing here, you fool?" Smitty asked when Hogsbreath was behind the wall.

"Y'all forgot your radio, Lieutenant. So I thought I'd just mosey on down here and be a-giving it to you."

"Who's leading the evac?" Smitty asked urgently.

"Superman, my number two. He's a good man and can handle it. Don't worry, LT, he'll a-get 'em out."

They waited in eerie silence as they heard the battle pass over them as the VC chased those able to evacuate across the camp to the rear perimeter. There was a tremendous explosion that Smitty knew meant that the Claymores had been detonated.

Five minutes passed, then five more. Slowly voices became audible as the VC came back into range of the bunker. They heard sporadic AK-47 fire, which Smitty knew meant that the slimy motherfuckers were shooting the wounded and stripping the dead.

The hatch was jerked upward and a VC who looked to be all of fifteen appeared. He started down the steps followed closely by an older VC officer who looked to be in his mid-thirties. They came in complete innocence, assuming that the base had been completely evacuated and that what was left was theirs for the taking—and they died the same way.

The hatch opened again, this time Smitty saw a head peek cautiously around the hatch. Smitty shot him through the exposed temple. The hatch slammed down.

Smitty could hear nervous voices. They were trying to figure out what to do. It was plain that they wanted the ammo. The only question was how much they were willing to pay to get it.

"American," a Vietnamese voice called out. "You come out; you give up. We treat you good."

"Yeah, and my wife will give all of you big sloppy blow jobs," Mike shouted.

Mike turned to Smitty and Hogsbreath. "That ought to confuse the little mothers for a minute or two. It does my wife."

Smitty looked at Mike blankly. "When I ask her for a blow job," Mike explained, "she acts like she doesn't understand English, either." The three of them smiled at each other.

More nervous chatter; then, "What is blow job, American?"

"You be a-suckin' my dick, boy," Hogsbreath said.

"Ahhh," the voice responded, then was silent.

The hatch opened and two hand grenades bounced down the steps. Mike, Hogsbreath, and Smitty ducked. The resulting explosion in the confined space was deafening. The ricocheting shrapnel was worse. It got all of them: Hogsbreath in the shoulder, Mike in the leg, Smitty in the left wrist.

"You come out now, American," the voice called out again.

"Naw, we kinda like it down here. This wolf hole has been approved by Good Housekeeping. We're planning on staying a while," Smitty answered defiantly.

Smitty had his weapon trained on the hatch, watching for the most infinitesimal movement. He saw the hatch move ever so slightly and an arm appeared with two more grenades. Smitty sighted carefully and fired. The round found its mark. Attempting to shove a fresh clip in his weapon, Smitty dropped it nervously.

From his position propped against the wall, Mike said, "Easy, LT. Ain't no sense gettin all upset about this dying thing. You ain't going to get out of this life alive anyway."

Underneath all the training and experience, Smitty was scared and trying damn hard not to show it. There was something about Mike's comment that had been said just the right way and come at just the right time. Smitty was still scared, but at least he wasn't going into vapor lock anymore.

"Yeah, but I'd just like to live long enough to bang your daughter." Smitty hit the hatch with fire from his hand weapon as it started to rise again.

"If you do, I'll deball ya, you fuckin' shavetail," Mike shot back.

More chatter, urgent this time, as the pounding of feet told Smitty that they had done some damage. Smitty grabbed Mike's weapon and, using both of them, began to pepper the hatch again. He heard small-arms fire, a precursor to more grenades coming down while they were ducking.

The small-arms fire began to have a different sound—like an automatic weapon was now part of the firestorm.

"Listen!" Mike said suddenly. "Them's M-60 rounds from a Huey, LT."

They all listened together; it was M-60 fire. It was goddamned M-60 fire.

"You fantasmic mutherfuckers!" Hogsbreath drawled.

The voice from above had stopped. Ghostly silence replaced the noise of the previous hours. Five minutes passed. Five tension-filled minutes during which, to control his own edginess, Smitty treated Hogsbreath's and Mike's wounds as best he could with his own limitations.

He heard footsteps above. It sounded like boots worn by American soldiers, not sandals worn by the VC.

"Anyone down there?" an American voice asked.

"We sure as hell are," Smitty answered.

"Come on up, it's safe."

"Fuck you, brother, we've heard that one before," Smitty said.

"Who is this?"

"Lieutenant Smith, call sign Irishman."

"Just a minute," the footsteps faded. Less than thirty seconds later, the footsteps returned, only this time they'd been cloned. There were two sets of them now.

A familiar voice said, "Irishman, this is the Crazy Fuckin' Polack. If you're not up here in ten seconds, I'm coming down there and hit you so hard your little butt will grow together. And when I'm done there won't be anything left for Stan the Man to offer a cop job to back in Miami."

Ron started counting at one. By the time he got to four, Smitty was there. In less than two minutes, Mike and Hogsbreath were above ground, lying on stretchers also.

"Irish, what's your real name?" Hogsbreath asked.

"Kevin," Smitty lit a cigarette and placed it between his lips. "What's yours?"

"Gary."

Smitty thought how ironic it was that they'd known each other for seven months and never known each other's given names.

The overrun firebase was a total loss. Of the 203 American and Vietnamese originally inside, only thirty-six had survived, and seventeen of them had been wounded seriously enough to require evac. The VC, by a rough count, had lost 750. Smitty wondered vaguely if the head four-star would find this an acceptable kill ratio.

After initial treatment at Pleiku, Hogsbreath, Mike, and Smitty had been evac'ed to Japan for rest and rehabilitation. Hogsbreath's wounds were the most incapacitating, Mike's the most uncomfortable, and Smitty's the most serious.

Hogsbreath's shoulder was a mess, although not nearly as much of one as Frenchy's had been. And after the shrapnel was removed, he required simple rest and rehabilitation of the injured muscles. Mike's shrapnel had checker-boarded his left calf and thigh with thirteen separate pieces that had to be removed, which made even simple walking or, in Mike's words, taking a dump a most painful process. Smitty's were a combination of both. His left wrist had been operated on twice—once to remove the wristwatch and grenade fragments and a second time to reset broken bones. Additionally, Smitty had seven separate fragments embedded in his right forearm.

The three of them had agreed by drunken consensus that Smitty's wounds were the worst, based simply on the fundamentals of bowel movement. Hogsbreath could sit on the can comfortably; Mike could sit on the can uncomfortably; Smitty could sit on the can comfortably, but he couldn't complete the paperwork without standing awkwardly.

Sergeant Mike had joked that most second looeys he knew couldn't wipe their own asses anyway, but Smitty had given literal meaning to the term. After a month, when Smitty could move his right arm sufficiently to complete the process, Hogsbreath had given him a medal made from a toilet roll's cardboard center, with two rubber gloves stapled to it. Both he and Mike had signed the "Royal Order of Shitter Proficiency." It meant more to Smitty than the Medal of Honor.

Smitty had gone to the PX to replace his watch and had instead bought four. He planned on sending one to LZ in Germany, one to Frenchy in Louisiana, and one to Big Walt at Leavenworth. He had them inscribed on the back with their moniker, the four musketeers, and a personal comment for each. He hoped it would remind his friends that no matter what happened to them individually, they had started out as a foursome. But he couldn't bring himself to mail them. That would be like sending a Dear John letter on their friendship. Smitty put them away for a time when he could deliver each one in person.

Six weeks after the firebase attack, Mike's wife arrived in Japan. From Mike's previous descriptions of her, Smitty would have sworn that she would have had four eyes and two heads. But she was a charmingly delicate and sedate woman, no longer girlishly cute, but now possessing the mature beauty of a woman in the prime of life. Smitty felt a special warmth when he was introduced to her by Mike as "my LT."

Hogsbreath, who was not married and had no girl to write home to, had become a favorite of the nurses at the hospital. His country drawl and southern charm had a disarming effect on the female nursing staff.

Linda arrived the following week on a six-week temporary duty assignment, ostensibly for "enhanced nursing proficiency training." In reality, Colonel Wilson had arranged it. It seemed that Smitty required, in the words of Colonel Wilson, "individualized care from a person intimately familiar with his nature and surly fucking personality."

The firebase might have been disaster from a military standpoint. But the army sure wasn't treating it that way.

Out of the firefight, a ton of medals had been awarded, most posthumously. Underdog's mother would receive his Silver Star and Purple Heart—and Medal of Honor, if Smitty's report had anything to do with it. Superman, Hogsbreath's number two, had similar honors bestowed on him, unfortunately, posthumously also, as he had elected to stay behind after the Claymores blew and was killed in a hail of AK-47 gunfire. By Colonel Wilson's decree, every soldier who was in the engagement was awarded a Purple Heart, as everyone had at least one minor shrapnel wound.

The one exception to the commendation parade was Captain Bartkowski. He was reprimanded for being away from his post when Smitty's call came in. It was rumored that he was down in the village getting laid by a local, but that was never proven.

Colonel Wilson had ordered an air observer to do a flyover of the besieged firebase when communications were lost just before dusk. He'd then flown directly to Pleiku and, on the captain's return around 3:00 AM, had ordered Ron to personally to lead the rescue mission.

After the base was secured, and several days after Smitty, Mike, and Hogsbreath were on their way to Japan, the captain was reassigned to duty at SOG headquarters in Saigon with an official reprimand placed in his personnel jacket.

In the case of Smitty, Mike, and Hogsbreath, the colonel, Army General Martin, and a three-star army general had flown to Japan to award their commendations personally. In addition to the Purple Hearts, Hogsbreath, Mike, and Smitty had received Silver Stars—for Hogsbreath it was his first; for Mike his seventh; for Smitty, his second.

Additionally, Smitty was awarded another Bronze Star for bravery under fire on a previous mission. As the general was pinning the medals on his pajamas, Smitty couldn't help feeling a trace of sadness that his father was not here.

After looking at his record and adding in all the combat ribbons with his commendations to date, the three-star had remarked to Smitty that he was collecting a lot of confetti over here that he could use to punch a lot of tickets when he got home. The general's remarks made Hogsbreath roll his eyes and Mike grimace. After they left, Bacon had looked at Smitty and said, "Never be a-trustin' anybody over thirty." Then he caught Mike's nasty glare. "Present company excepted a-course."

Their injuries had occurred in the summer. It was now fall, and Smitty, Mike, and Hogsbreath were sufficiently healed for them to be returned to active duty in Vietnam. They had two more days in Japan before their scheduled departure.

As Smitty returned from his final therapy session to the small apartment he and Linda had rented just outside the base, he had a passing thought about going home and what it would be like to be back in the land of the big PX. He had to admit, his passing thought had to do with Linda and the promise of a future together, not yet fulfilled.

"Linda, I'm back," Smitty said. He unbuttoned his uniform coat, loosened his tie, and dropped both on the chair by the door.

"How did it go today, honey? Are you finished?" Linda asked. She stepped through the door from the bedroom into the open combination living room and dining room.

"Uh, fine, that is, I am," Smitty said, catching his breath and feeling his nether regions begin to stir. Linda stood posing in a black nightie that looked like something straight out of a Playboy lingerie shoot.

"We're going to dinner tonight at 7:00 PM with Sergeant Mike, his sweet wife, and Gary and his latest girlfriend," Linda said. "I just thought maybe you could use a little personal therapy before we go."

Although he was clearly aroused, Smitty hesitated. Linda seemed to sense his hesitation and she went back into the bedroom. Seconds later, she emerged wearing a terrycloth robe.

"What's wrong, babe?" Linda put her arms around him in a maternal hug.

"I don't know, Linda." Smitty inhaled her perfume as they exchanged a light kiss. "I guess I'm confused. Before I met you, I never had much of a life or a plan. I just figured I'd hang in Nam until I got killed. But since I met you, I've started to ask those questions that I pushed away before."

"Such as?" Linda broke the embrace and padded silently to the kitchen to retrieve a beer from the fridge. When she returned, she sat down on the sofa and patted it, waiting for Smitty joined her.

"Like, what's next? I can't stay in Nam forever. The war is winding down. Where do I go from here? Where do I fit? Do I stay in the army or get out? If I stay in, what do I have to look forward to—another battle in the next far-off land? That and the fact that I'll probably be rifted back to an E-6. And if I get out, I just can't see myself returning to the life I had before."

Linda started to reach for him, but he brushed her away, stood up, and began pacing.

"And what about my parents?" Smitty said. "I've been thinking a lot about them, especially my dad. I walked out on them almost three years ago. They don't even know if I'm alive or dead. Come to that, I don't even know if they're alive or dead."

Smitty stood at the window and watched a C-5 land before turning back to her. "And most importantly, what about us? Where do we go from here? Are we just a Nam thing or is there more?"

"If that's a proposal, I accept," Linda said.

"Huh?" Smitty said, bewildered.

"I said I accept your proposal of marriage. That is what you're offering me when you talk about us in the future, isn't it?"

"Well, yes, I guess it is," Smitty responded.

"Then the rest is simple: we'll work it out together." Linda cupped his face in her hands and kissed him. "And when we get back in-country, we'll work out how and when to get married when our tours are over. We'll also talk about what our future is—in the army or out of it, it doesn't matter as long as we work together to get there." She kissed him again. "And after we're married and sorted out, we'll go home and sort out you and your parents. Fair enough?"

"Fair enough," Smitty said, responding to her kiss.

"Are you trying to assault a superior officer?" Linda grabbed his hands, twisted out of his grasp, and skipped off to the bedroom.

"Every chance I get." Smitty followed her in and slammed the door.

Smitty, Mike, and Hogsbreath returned to Vietnam in mid-October of 1969. They had been in Japan slightly over three months but were returning to a different Vietnam and a different war. The reason was twofold: The war was, in fact, winding down, with troop deployment decreasing and with active plans for reductions of personnel as the Vietnamization process picked up steam. The second reason was that Smitty's worry over the general's concern over the firebase kill ratio was now a moot point.

He never got a chance to hear or even care. The overrunning of the base camp passed quickly into insignificance, as a newer story from Vietnam had now become the central focus: Mike's prophecy had come painfully true. The rest of the shitty iceberg had surfaced. My Lai had become public.

It started slowly with a rumor, as Ron had said last year. It meandered by word of mouth for over a year until there was such overwhelming evidence that, incredibly, even some of the conventional army brass began to believe it. Finally, as the truth inevitably does, it had reached the right ear and the army had launched an investigation.

Investigation in the army's terms generally meant "find a sacrificial lamb, toss him to the wolves, complete the report, and bury it in the files," but this report was different. As Mike had prophesied, there was a huge glacial ridge just beneath the surface. As one layer was scraped off, another bigger and uglier one appeared.

Battle reports suddenly became secondary as the army and the American press looked high and low for any tidbit or scrap of information on My Lai and what had actually happened. They scoured the existing in-country battle groups for evidence of any irregularities now or in the past. The army went into full cover-up mode. The press went into full exposure mode.

The army had to take a painful and critical look at the structure of the army itself, which made the effect of Vietnam on the armed forces painfully clear. Draftees and young inexperienced enlistees were in frontline command positions usually occupied by professional soldiers. In times of combat stress, this lack of experience led to breakdowns in command structure. The effect of My Lai was the massacre. The cause was the breakdown in military discipline.

The My Lai report made a recommendation for punitive actions against the entire command chain connected with My Lai. After reviewing the report, the army finally settled on an inexperienced platoon second lieutenant as the scapegoat, as the officers above successfully spin-doctored their way out of the damage path of formal guilt—but not of informal repercussions.

The press was not so easily pacified. Every young reporter looking for a front page byline was out in the battle areas watching, waiting, and looking to interview anyone who had seen, or claimed to have seen, any irregularities. They were not just looking to air dirty laundry. They were looking to turn it inside out and comment on the color and texture of the stain.

One young army platoon lieutenant, frustrated by the repeated question of, "How can you in good conscience rape and kill women and children?" released his pent-up feelings by blurting, "It's easy. It's like shooting reporters. You just lead them a little less." He was instantly removed from his command and hustled stateside before the ink was even dry on his orders.

All divisions of the armed forces were now working in full whitewash mode, hoping against hope that if they sprayed enough air freshener on Vietnam, the sweetness would cover up the smell of the shit. But it didn't. The combined odor was even more nauseating.

The army, bearing the brunt of the guilt, was actively combing each division and ferreting out any irregularities—rapes, drugs, officer killings, self-inflicted wounds, and black-market activities real or imagined—and dealing with them in an abbreviated judicial manner that reminded Smitty of the Miami kangaroo courts.

Similar purges were now actively under way in the marines and, to a lesser degree, the navy and air force, sending the reeling morale even lower. In some cases, soldiers were refusing to obey officer commands.

Eventually, it filtered all the way down to the attempted rape that Smitty and Mike had prevented six months ago.

The marines were now touting the attempted rape, which they had tried for months to hide, as proof of their own no-nonsense stance on civilian personnel crimes. The army reaction was to order Smitty and Mike to sit for an interview for some young reporter with an attitude.

For every question he asked about what happened, he asked ten more about how many times they had personally witnessed these kinds of actions, and why they had done nothing to stop it until now. Noticing Smitty's scarred hands, he even had the audacity to ask if the wounds were self-inflicted to get out of further combat. Smitty had been so tight-jawed that Mike had to drag him away before he went after the reporter.

In spite of all the crapola flying around, Smitty felt more hopeful about the future than at any other time in his life. He looked forward now to living the plans he had made with Linda. But on the dark side, his beloved Baltimore Orioles had blown the World Series to the upstart New York Mets. Smitty hoped it was not a harbinger of things to come, for either the city of Baltimore . . . or himself.

CHAPTER FIFTEEN

That was a nasty one, LT," Mike said, whistling softly.

"Fuckin' A," Hogsbreath agreed in a solemn voice.

"I have to agree, guys, I thought we were done for then." Smitty flipped the cigarette out the door of the open helicopter as it lifted off. He stared blankly down the passing landscape below. None of the three of them was wounded, but a third of the force was.

They had been deployed over the border as part of a joint marine-army operation to land, search for, and destroy VC strongholds of arms and supplies. The supply areas were supposed to be lightly defended. They had walked right into the middle of a shitstorm. There had been two thousand troops in an area that, according to the intel reports from Captain Bartkowski, should not have contained more than two hundred.

This miscalculation could have been due to several things.

First and most obvious, the VC were getting smarter. The missions over the border were now starting to take their toll, and North Vietnam was now assigning additional regular army troops to guard sections of the Laotian supply trail. They now knew that if these missions were successful, B-52 airstrikes that brought death and heavy damage to their supply routes would follow.

Second, there was a security leak. One of Captain Bartkowski's new roles in Saigon was to track and validate where information went once it reached SOG headquarters and at what point the information was disseminated to MACV and the South Vietnamese government—to find where the potential for leaks existed.

Third, the stepped-up North Vietnamese defenses could just simply be a reaction to the change in the U.S. policy on Vietnam. With Vietnamization now the order of the day, the change within the Nixon administration had been slow in coming but was now beginning to shift into high gear. The civilians who now ran the defense department had become full-fledged believers in SOG and its mission and were now telling the military commanders in the Pentagon what they wanted done, rather than just being a doormat for implementation of standardized World War II conventional military battle plans.

Which was another way of saying that they had finally come to understand that the Vietnamization program could not succeed unless they could eliminate the North Vietnamese ability to carry out the war, and that in order to accomplish this mission, they would have to make wholesale command changes to eliminate generals stuck in WW II and replace them with younger, but experienced, commanders who were more receptive to newer creative approaches.

As rotations occurred in the conventional ranks, two-star generals, or in some cases, one-star generals on the verge of becoming two-stars, began to replace older three-stars and so on down the line.

The trickle-down effect of this new thinking had reached Smitty. With Ron's reassignment to Saigon and Smitty's return to duty in October, he had been promoted to first lieutenant and anointed to Ron's position, although his reserve rank had changed only from E-6 to E-7. Hogsbreath had taken Smitty's previous position and was commissioned a second lieutenant.

Colonel Wilson, feeling that Smitty met the new requirement of "younger experienced commander," but also feeling that he needed the voice of an old hand around to bounce ideas off of, had placed Smitty in charge of two assault forces and formed them into a strike company and had appointed Sergeant Mike to a newly created position of group first sergeant. When asked by Hogsbreath what his new job was, Mike had replied, "To shoot the lieutenant through the back of the head the moment he gets too full of himself."

In addition to his existing inherited responsibilities of recruitment and training, Smitty was now in command of two emergency extraction forces. One was commanded by Hogsbreath, the other by a newly transferred twenty-two-year-old second lieutenant whom Smitty had code-named Freckleface. Despite the fact that he had one year of college ROTC, had been through army OCS, and had served nine months in Nam as platoon lieutenant in the 101st Airborne, he still looked fifteen years old. But looks aside, he was highly qualified and on two missions had shown himself to have excellent command presence and to be tenaciously brave.

"Whatcha thinking about, 1LT?" Mike asked.

Smitty smiled at Mike's question. He had begun to refer to Smitty as 1LT a few days after his new rank became effective. When Smitty had asked him why, Mike had replied without expression that Smitty had forced him to revise his rating system for second lieutenants. Smitty had assumed that this new designation was a positive, until Mike had explained with a cynical smile, that 1LT meant that he was the first second lieutenant that he had let live to get promoted to first lieutenant.

"Oh, nothing much, just this and that," Smitty responded absently.

"Thinkin' about going home, and what happens next when you get to screw that hot nursey every night," Mike said shrewdly.

"How did you know that?"

"Pretty smart, Boss. Been around a long time." Mike reached out and touched Smitty lightly on the arm. "Long enough to listen if there's anything you want to talk about."

"It will all work out," Smitty said. Mike couldn't fix what was eating at him. Only he could, and he couldn't fix it from here.

"Here if you need me," Mike said, as the helicopter landed at Pleiku.

With the stepped-up activity on the other side of the border, and with the command change, Smitty now reported directly to Colonel Wilson, who was waiting for him fifty feet away. As the engines died, he came out to greet them and shook hands perfunctorily. "Let's go somewhere we can talk."

As the two of them were walking away, the colonel stopped, turned, and said impatiently to Hogsbreath and Mike, "You two idiots, also."

When they had settled quietly into the colonel's office, he said, "Gentlemen, this has got to stop. Our casualty rates are becoming alarmingly high. Before we leave here, we're going to put our heads together and try to determine why. Now, who'd like to start?"

The silence was deafening. Everybody had ideas, but no one wanted to be the first to speak, especially when the colonel was on a rampage.

"1LT," Mike said. "Why don't you tell Sam"—the use of the colonel's first name by Mike seemed uncomfortably foreign to everyone except Mike—"what you were talking to me about the other day?"

The colonel looked unblinkingly at Smitty. "Well?"

"Well, sir, I have the same feeling that you do, that the casualties are too high—"

"Lieutenant," the colonel interrupted. "Don't waste time repeating what I just said. Get to the point."

Smitty swallowed hard then. "I think we've got a security leak."

"Where?" the colonel asked.

"It's in either SOG or MACV. Someone is tipping the VC off. The only way they could have access to the information is through those two channels. Everything else is internal. It's only when we need air support or to alert other units of our presence that we disseminate information to SOG headquarters where it then gets passed on to MACV, at the senior command level, and to the Saigon government as a courtesy."

"Uh huh, and what's the fix? We can't cut off the information flow. We have to let them know where we are; otherwise they may mistake us for the enemy."

"Structured disinformation, sir," Smitty said.

"Explain?"

"Well, sir, suppose on our next mission we supply SOG command itself with disinformation, then using our radios each of us dummy up some of the mission details and we'll find out who gets it and how."

"That tells us nothing, Lieutenant. We won't know a damn thing more than we do now."

"It does, sir, if we disseminate the information individually and each of us puts a slightly different spin on the details. If the details surface later, we may not know everything, but at least we'll know which branch of the tree is rotten."

"Then what?"

"Then nothing, sir," Smitty said. "We continue to feed disinformation until we find the source. If we can, we can definitely close it down."

The colonel got up and began to pace. After taking four laps, he stopped. "What kind of details?"

"Well, sir, the details have to be juicy enough to be transmitted, but not so outlandish that they aren't believable," Smitty responded.

The colonel sat down on the corner of the table. "And I suppose you've got a few ideas in that square head of yours on how to do it."

"A couple," Smitty said.

"Lieutenant, I'd like to use this area privately to make a call. Please excuse yourselves. Go to the club and have a couple on me. I'll catch up with you there."

The three of them were filing out when the colonel delayed Smitty with a restraining hand. "And Lieutenant," he said in a low voice, "on that other matter you requested, it took a while, but the mistake has been corrected and Sergeant McCord has been repromoted to E-6 in Germany.

"Although my understanding is that he was pleased with the promotion, it has not altered his present stance on racial issues in the military. In fact, it seems to only have made the issue worse." He added, "Incidentally, your friend has already reupped for six years; give you any ideas?"

"Yes, sir, it does," Smitty answered, as he left the room.

Smitty, Mike, and Hogsbreath walked to the NCO club and had a couple of beers. When the colonel didn't arrive immediately, they had a couple more, mixed in a couple of Jim Beams, and then chased that with a couple more brewskis after that, until they had gotten mildly shitfaced.

Two hours had passed since they left the colonel. They got rowdy enough that they were asked to leave. As usual for Vietnam this time of year it was raining heavily. They hardly noticed since they were now laughingly drunk. Exhaustion and the cessation of the stress of their last mission had worked with the alcohol to produce a state of euphoria in which everything seemed hilarious. If someone had told them that the president had been assassinated, they could have made bad jokes and guffawed.

It was a delightful high while it lasted, but it was dangerous, too. Those in it were as oblivious of risk as a cat is of calculus. The only cure was twelve hours' sleep.

"Stand tall, troop, I'll have a word with you," a voice said from behind.

"Fuck off," Smitty said without turning around.

An arm reached out and spun Smitty around before either Mike or Hogsbreath could intercede. Through his drunken haze Smitty was trying hard to focus on who it was, sure that he must be hallucinating. The face that he kept seeing couldn't be there.

Thinking that he'd finally cracked up, he said flippantly, "Hello there, Popster. How they hangin'?"

"I'd prefer that you call me Dad, boy." Smitty's father tightened his grip on Smitty's arm to emphasize his point—and maybe to help hold Smitty up.

"Okay, Daddy-O. How they hangin'?" Smitty broke into laughter.

Smitty hardly felt the sting when his father slapped him with his right hand. "I didn't come halfway around the world to try to hold a conversation with a drunk."

His father shook him with his left hand and was just in the process of following through with the back of his right hand when Smitty's training reasserted itself, and he grabbed the arm with his left hand, stopped it dead, and with pressure on the right nerve, forced the arm down.

Satisfied that it was now going to remain there, Smitty patted his father's cheek. "You know, First Sergeant, you shouldn't go around slapping first lieutenants; it might be misunderstood."

"Not if they're your drunken son," Dad said.

"What's going on here?" Colonel Wilson called out breathlessly, as he ran up to Smitty and his father and separated them.

"Butt out," Dad replied.

"Excuse me, Sergeant, I'm Colonel Wilson. Colonel outranks sergeant."

"Father outranks colonel. Butt out!" Dad pointed to Smitty and then to himself.

"Oh, I see." Turning to Mike and Hogsbreath he said softly, "Come on, gentlemen. I think these two need to talk."

The colonel, Mike, and Hogsbreath walked away and left the two of them alone.

"Is there someplace you and I can talk privately, son?"

"This way." Smitty motioned in the direction of his billet.

When they reached his hooch, Smitty lay down on his cot. "Make yourself comfortable." It was his last conscious thought.

Smitty awoke the next morning with a hangover that would choke a Clydesdale. He sat up on his rack and rubbed the back of his neck to try to clear the haze. Memories from last night were slowly surfacing like air bubbles from an Aqua-Lung fifty feet under the sea. As one of the bubbles popped, he had a fleeting recollection of his dad.

Shaking his head again at the obvious mistake and making a silent vow to never drink that much again—until the next time—Smitty got shakily to his feet and staggered to his desk, where his .357 was laying. Funny, he didn't remember removing it from the shoulder holster last night. As he picked it up, a note was taped to the handle, and the writing came into focus.

"Son, I'll be at the mess hall. Come over when you're ready. Dad."

It wasn't a dream. It was real. His dad was really here.

Jamming his Magnum in the shoulder holster, Smitty double-timed over to the mess hall. He jerked open the door, slowed to a normal pace as he spotted his dad, went quickly through the chow line, then joined his father, who was sitting at a table eating breakfast with Sergeant Mike.

"Good morning, son. How's your head?" Dad asked.

"Morning, Dad. Morning, Mike," Smitty said.

"Hi, 1LT." Mike drained the last of his coffee and got up from the table. "Well, I've got to be going. It was a real pleasure seein' you, Sergeant Smith."

Mike shook hands with Dad, who had stood to accept the offered hand, turned to Smitty, and said, "Sir, the colonel requested that I inform you that you are to take whatever time you need with your father and that he'll remain and see you when you're through." With a casual wave, Mike left without further comment.

"Sit down, son." Dad motioned to the seat across from him recently vacated by Mike.

Wordlessly, Smitty sat down. The butterflies in his stomach had become dive-bombers attacking in formation.

"So, how have you been?"

"Okay, I guess," Smitty murmured. "How's Mom?"

Dad sang, "Gone again, skip to my Lou."

Smitty laughed in spite of himself. "For good?"

"Filed for the divorce a couple of years back," Dad answered without emotion. "She bailed from Savannah. Went home to Atlanta to live with her mother again, last I heard."

Pausing momentarily, as if he'd forgotten something, he held up his finger. "Oh, about her parents. Just before the divorce, your grandfather died. Shortly thereafter, I don't know exactly when, your grandmother fell and injured her leg. I guess they didn't react in time, because the leg became gangrenous, and she lost it just below the right knee. She's now living in a nursing home in the area."

"How's Billy?" Smitty nodded at the news of his grandparents.

"He and Leslie have moved to Cocoa Beach, Florida. He became one of those long-haired surfers and lives in some fleabag on the beach. Leslie's parents disowned her for marrying your brother. They said she married beneath her station." Dad exhaled deeply. "And yes, before you ask, they left town in your Hillman Husky."

"I was wondering when you'd get around to that."

Dad surveyed the depths of his coffee cup. "Okay, son, here it is, short and to the point. I fucked up. I should not have given your brother your car. I took something from you that you had worked for, gave it to your brother in a desperate attempt to pacify your mother and hold on to her. I'm genuinely sorry for the wrong and bad thing I did. It was a mistake—a mistake I won't ever make again."

Smitty was shocked to say the least. He had expected that his dad would get around to discussing the sore point between them but had not expected him to just blurt it out like that and admit it was wrong up front.

On the other hand, Dad had always faced things head-on, so it came as no surprise that he was doing it now. Yeah he'd been wrong about giving away his car. But a desperate man does desperate things, especially when his entire life, no matter how fucked up, was in the balance. Maybe that was what he was doing now.

For over three years, Smitty had rehearsed exactly what, and exactly how, he was going to tell his father off for the deep hurt he had inflicted on him. He had prepared arguments to countermand his father's anticipated defense of his actions and in his mind had seen himself thundering back at the old hardcase in a man-to-man confrontation. Now he'd never get the chance.

Smitty felt like a high school baseball player who had just been beaned. It was hard to be angry when the opposing pitcher had rushed up, apologized profusely, helped you up, offered to drive you home, do your homework, and even offered to have your dirt-stained uniform dry-cleaned to make up for it.

"What happened to the Husky?" Smitty asked.

"You brother let it run out of oil, fried the motor, and sold it to a junk dealer for twenty-five dollars about a year ago."

"Water over the dam," Smitty responded. After a moment he asked, "So you're alone now?"

"More or less," Dad said, his eyes twinkling.

"Hope you remember that protection is six cents a pack in the PX." Smitty remembered all the times that Dad had used that particular line on him.

Smitty pulled out a pack of cigarettes, offered one to his dad, lit both, and blew out a thick cloud of smoke. "That is, assuming that an old fossil can still get it up."

"Oh, I can still manage to rise to the occasion. From what I understand, you do, too," Dad shot back.

"I guess I'm just a chip off the ol' block."

"No, son." Dad reached out and ruffled Smitty's hair. "I think you're a whole new kind of building."

Smitty stared in silence at his father. Could this really be the same man he'd walked out on only three years ago? He seemed so approachable now, so reasonable. Maybe they'd both done some growing up.

Smitty's dad had left that afternoon on a transport back to Thailand. The party line was that he was officially there for a meeting and had just bummed a ride over to try to "catch up with his son."

Smitty didn't for a moment believe it. Dad had flown over with General Chuck, now sporting his third star, who was there for an Air Force Combat Logistics Conference. Dad had managed to wangle himself a ninety-day temporary duty assignment as the general's aide. It was a substanceless assignment that would allow him to hunt for his son.

Over a few beers before he left, Dad had complimented Smitty on his deception in going into the army and his progress, assuming that these were cornerstones to a future career in the military.

Smitty had been evasive in his response. He didn't have the heart to tell him that he was thinking of other options and that the military might be just a stepping-stone in that direction, rather than the foundation for a long-term union between himself and Uncle Sam.

They said good-bye with a handshake, a hug, and promises to write faithfully once a week. Dad also encouraged Smitty to write to his mother. Smitty was noncommittal—a polite way of saying "when pigs fly."

"So 1LT, you do have a father. I thought little pricks like you were hatched." Mike and Smitty were waiting to lift off from their most recent incursion mission in Laos. It had gone remarkably well. The disinformation was working.

"I thought the same thing about limpdick career master sergeants," Smitty shot back.

Mike's response was typical. He flipped Smitty off.

"It's funny," Smitty said. "You know when you and my ol' man shook hands, you said, and I quote, 'It was nice seein' you, Sergeant Smith.' What was implied was that it was nice seein' you again." Smitty eyed Mike suspiciously. "Comment?"

"We traveled some together, 1LT."

Smitty waited for Mike to respond further, but apparently there was nothing more to be said. Smitty surmised that the two of them had probably crossed paths sometime during the war. That seemed to be where most of his father's contacts dated from.

After Smitty's dad had departed, they had met with Colonel Wilson again. He had been in touch with the chief SOG and the plan, now code-named "Honest Abe," was approved. The information conduits to SOG from the central command would be Smitty, Hogsbreath, and Sergeant Mike. Similar plans were to be adopted for north and south, with similar streamlined conduits.

To add to the security level, each person's individual adders would not be disclosed to each other. Only he would know to whom he passed along the information, and specifically what was said.

The process appeared to have worked. Hogsbreath's team had landed without opposition, Freckleface's team the same ten miles away. Their mission was to link up at a major supply area know as The Bra, for the curviness of its terrain, and set up an ambush of the supply trucks from both sides of the road. Smitty and Mike had landed and gone with Freckleface to check him out personally.

The ambush had worked to perfection, with the two teams able to hit the front and rear of the truck convoy simultaneously, immobilizing the convoy until air support had arrived to finish the job, and turning that particular stretch of the supply line into an inferno. Under cover of the resultant chaos, both teams had successfully unassed the area and reached their respective pickup LZ's the next afternoon.

Smitty and Sergeant Mike, Freckleface, his newly transferred-in number three from the Air Cav—a staff sergeant by the name of Patterson—and two Nungs, had been waiting for the last helicopter to come in. Smitty wanted to ride with them to try to get to know the Boy Wonder, who seemed shocked at the casual disrespect that Mike had shown to Smitty but had made no remark.

Mike had just finished disclosing digitally the number of friends Smitty had had before his dog died when an explosion rocked the incoming ship. It veered right and slammed into the earth about three hundred yards from them as the ground around them opened up with VC fire.

Whatever had hit the helicopter had done serious damage. The door gunner and the copilot were dead before the ship hit the ground. The pilot and second crewman managed to make it out alive only to be cut down by AK-47 fire before they had run ten feet from the doomed aircraft.

The first round of ground fire had been costly to them also. The two Nungs were dead. Freckleface, the Boy Wonder, would never grow up to walk in Batman's tights. Most of the right side of his head was now missing.

"Let's go. They got us sighted. We need to get the fuck out of this area," Sergeant Patterson yelled, as he began to run away from the fire.

"No shit, Sherlock," Sergeant Mike grabbed the staff sergeant by the back of the shirt and forcibly slammed him to the ground. "Hang onto your jockstrap, son. Ain't no need to run until we know where to run to." Sergeant Mike held firmly despite Patterson's frantic attempts to flee.

Smitty was on the ground using the now lifeless form of the lieutenant as ground cover. Sergeant Mike and Sergeant Patterson were doing the same with the Nungs. The ground fire was increasing as they had ceased firing on the helicopter and now were firing full force on the three remaining team members.

"Five-second intervals," Smitty said, as he readied four golfball grenades for firing.

Mike nodded his head in understanding and readied four of his own, plus two more he had taken from the bodies of the Nungs. The staff sergeant followed Mike's lead.

"Throw and go, me, Patty, then you, Michael!" Smitty tossed his first two mini grenades in succession, one while the other was still in flight, ducked the impact, then threw his next two farther back and ducked again. As soon as the explosion of his last grenade had died, Smitty jumped up and ran for five seconds directly away from the VC, firing his weapon. He counted five and dove into the elephant grass as Sergeant Patterson repeated the procedure. After the fourth grenade had exploded, Smitty was up and running again, firing his weapon as he moved. Sergeant Patterson moved to Smitty's previous position. Sergeant Mike repeated the process and when he started to move, Smitty had reached the cover of the tree line.

At the count of five, both Sergeant Patterson and Mike dropped as Smitty hurled three additional golfball grenades as far as he could. After the explosions, Sergeant Patterson and Sergeant Mike were on the move again. This time Sergeant Patterson reached the cover of the tree line and together they repeated Smitty's initial process until Mike had made it also.

"Nicely done, children, you make me so proud," Mike said. He turned to Sergeant Patterson. "Now, we set Claymores on a timer. While we're doing that, 1LT will be setting toetappers along the trail here. Then we turn ninety degrees right, cover our tracks, and double back on our trail while they're tangled up in the mines still wondering where the fuck we went."

"Then what do we do?" Sergeant Patterson asked.

"Then we run like a motherfucker for the next couple hundred yards, double back on our trail again, and keep on looping and darting until dark," Mike explained.

"Then what?"

"Then we make like a ghost and vaporize outta here right before their eyes," Smitty said.

"How do we do that?" the staff sergeant asked.

"We flee in absolute quiet, putting as much distance between us and the VC as possible by morning. Then we call for a pickup point two miles from where we'll actually be. While the VC are tied up with the decoy, the trailing chopper will land and pick us up. If not, they'll drop lines, which we'll attach to these here Stabo harness rigs we're wearing and we'll fly right outta here suspended below the choppers like Peter Pan."

"What if all that stuff doesn't work?"

"Then I hope your boots are comfortable, son, cause it's a long walk home," Mike answered.

As it turned out, Mike was a seer. The plan worked as expected—somewhat. They were able to successfully evade until dusk, the sounds of Claymores, toetappers, and screams of pain were clear enough evidence of a successfully executed initial evasion. The distancing in the night part worked to perfection also, as did the numerous double-backs and randomly executed turns to shake the VC off their trail.

The problems came the next afternoon. They had slept away the morning in a hidden lair, after first setting up a false one three hundred yards away. They found that the radio was dead. They could not call for air support.

The second problem was the number of VC. From the noise they were making, there were approximately three to five hundred VC less than two miles away, searching for them with diligence using all means available—physical and psychological.

Physically by foot search, psychologically by megaphones, asking them to give up because they had no chance of getting out of there alive. The psychobabble Smitty had heard before, and normally it didn't bother him.

But this time it had an interesting twist that sent goose pimples running down Smitty's spine. The voice was calling him Lieutenant Smith, encouraging him to give up, as he was never going to get promoted to captain, and get Captain Bartkowski's cushy job in Saigon . . . which was exactly the individual rumor that only he was privy to, since he was the one who had disseminated it in the first place.

It took them nine days to walk out to safety.

Nine torturous days in which they had to battle growth so dense that the sun never reached the jungle floor. Leeches dropped from trees and went down the top of their shirts, despite their best efforts, and every other form of biting and stinging insect imaginable attacked them, covering their bodies with nasty, itchy welts. Nine days of walking and navigating solely by compass in the steaming heat, crossing streams in the rain, then drying out again just in time to cross more.

Nine days during which they wished desperately for the comfort of the choppers that had initially circled overhead, then stopped coming after day three when no contact was made or trace of them found.

Nine days when they had food for four. After starving for two more, they began to eat local vegetation and insects to keep up their strength.

And nine days on feet that had begun to blister at five. By the ninth, they were nothing more than bloody stumps that collectively were just one pus-filled boil.

The perimeter of the firebase Plei Djereng looked like the Playboy mansion and the soldiers Playmate pinups, as they met a recon patrol sent out to get them. Smitty collapsed into someone's arms and accepted assistance after making sure that Sergeant Mike and Sergeant Patterson were in good hands. They were immediately airlifted back to Pleiku and on landing were given a hero's welcome back from the dead, then taken to the hospital for treatment of their injuries and dehydration, fed, and bedded in clean sheets.

"How goes it, son?" Two days later, Colonel Wilson approached Smitty's bed with Captain Bartkowski. Smitty had been under sedation most of the last two days.

"Not bad, sir. How are Mike and Patty holding up?"

"Sergeant Patterson has been evac'ed to Japan. Several of his scratches had become badly infected. Sergeant Mike you can ask for yourself." He pointed to the bed across from Smitty.

"1LT, the next time you decide to go on an extended all-nighter, find yourself another fucking prom date," Mike gave him the finger.

"I will," Smitty responded. "Especially since I ended up carrying your fat butt back from the weenie roast.

"Well, he's fine," the colonel said.

Smitty nodded in satisfaction. "At least he will be. Sir, I need to let Linda know . . . "

"Already handled," the colonel said.. "I think maybe a rest in Da Nang will be in order after the debrief."

Changing subjects abruptly, the colonel said, "Tell me what happened out there, son."

"I will, sir, when I'm a little better rested," Smitty said with a wink.

"Okay, Lieutenant. How about day after tomorrow at 1400 hours in my office in Nha Trang?" The colonel nodded to Mike, and he and Captain Bartkowski left.

"Pansy ass Colonel Kissup," Mike said, after the colonel left.

"Pussywhip," Smitty retorted. Mike gave him the finger for his horse, and he closed his eyes and dropped off to sleep. The idea was catching, and Smitty was right behind him on the road to dreamland.

"Lieutenant, we had choppers crossing back and forth for three days. Why didn't you signal us?" The colonel had asked Smitty and Mike if they were up to answering a few questions. When they had said yes, the colonel had, as usual, gotten right to the point.

The debriefing was not going well, mostly because the colonel was in a bad mood. In trying to locate the three of them and pick up the dead bodies from the LZ, they had lost two more helicopters and crew, as well as six of the rescue force.

But the other factor was the presence of Captain Bartkowski. Since the captain's effective banishment to Saigon, their relationship had been strained. The colonel had accepted the captain's reason for being here—getting a firsthand report for the chief SOG—but that didn't mean he had to like it.

The first half-hour had been spent gathering the factual data. The colonel's tone signaled that the assessment of personal judgment was about to start.

"One, our radio was out. Two, we were constantly on the move and any kind of ground reflective signal would have been seen by the VC that were trailing us. And three," Smitty looked at Mike, who nodded. "You knew where we were because you told the VC."

The colonel stared in disbelief. "What in the name of Christ are you talking about?"

"You told them," Smitty repeated.

"They were calling out on the hog caller for us to surrender, and me specifically by name. They also were using one of my disinformation scuttlebutt lines. Specifically the one about getting promoted to Captain and taking Ron's job in Saigon. You were the only one I made that comment to."

"You're out of your mind, Lieutenant," the colonel raged. "While it's true that I remember you saying that, there could be other reasons."

"As a matter of fact, there are, sir," Smitty rose and walked around the colonel's desk. He picked up his telephone, turned it upside down and pointed to a disk less than an inch in diameter.

"What the hell is that, son?" the colonel asked, as Smitty picked up a letter opener from the colonel's desk and pried the device off the phone.

"You've been bugged, sir," Smitty said, handing him the disk. "They've been listening in to everything you say. "Remember, I told you and Captain Bartkowski my rumor over the phone. So it couldn't be anything else." Smitty paused. "Unless you decided to go over to the other side."

"I'll be damned!" the colonel said in amazement. "I'll be damned. Got any idea who would be bugging me?"

"That ain't my department. I'm sure you'll know better than I."

"Dismissed, gentlemen," the colonel said. "I have to make some inquiries and some calls."

"Good piece of detective work, Lieutenant," Ron said with a satisfied nod. "We've been looking for that leak for a long time. Looks like you plugged it."

"Thank you, sir. Sometimes people trip themselves up on the simplest things."

"Sometimes they do," Ron said. "Sometimes they do. Well, I guess we know now where the leak is coming from,"

"Yes, that's true," Smitty replied.

What Smitty didn't tell Ron was that he now knew who was responsible for creating the leak in the first place. But things being as they were, he decided to keep this thought to himself.

The colonel sent for Smitty and Mike less than an hour later. "Lieutenant, you were away long enough that we had to list you as missing in action. The official telegram notifying your father of your well-being will not arrive for several days. So I've arranged for the two of you to talk to the home folks at 1600 hours from my office. You'll only get five minutes, but it should be more than enough time to assure your father, Smitty, and your wife, Sergeant Mike, that you are okay."

"Thank you, sir," Smitty and Sergeant Mike responded in unison. They walked out of the colonel's office.

"I could use a beer or ten," Mike said.

"Better make it a beer as opposed to ten, Top," Smitty said in a low voice.

"Why?"

"I need you sober tomorrow. We've got another mission to get ready for," Smitty responded.

Mike did not reply. He nodded affirmatively at Smitty and walked away.

"First Sergeant Smith's quarters. First Sergeant Smith speaking," Dad mumbled sleepily into the phone. Dad's voice was comforting, as was the fundamental telephone courtesy routine that both he and Billy had drilled into them when they were children.

Kevin could still remember the first time he had not answered the phone with the standard, "First Sergeant Smith's quarters, second son Kevin speaking. How may I help you?" greeting. Retribution had been swift and certain. The backhanded slap he'd gotten from his dad had assured that he'd never forget a second time. Even Billy, with his rebellious spirit, never violated the rule.

Dad's reason was logical. Because he was a first sergeant and was constantly receiving service-related calls, when the phone rang, it could be anyone from a desk sergeant telling him that one of his troops was in jail to a wing commander alerting him to an ORI. In the military, your ability to control your family situation was a factor in your overall proficiency rating and could affect your future career.

"Courtesy is cheap. It doesn't cost a cent," Dad had preached repeatedly. "Telephone courtesy is a simple way to demonstrate that you understand this basic tenet. It will not be violated in this household." And it never was.

"Dad, it's me, Kevin. I'm calling—"

"You drunken son of a bitch," Dad interrupted angrily. "You call me back at a decent hour when you sober up." The connection went dead in his hand as Kevin's dad slammed down the receiver close to half a world and twelve hours away.

"I got cut off," Kevin said to the MP. The cop, a specialist fourth class, was assigned to monitor the time of Smitty's call in the colonel's office. It was 4:00 PM Vietnam time, which made it 4:00 AM U.S. time, an ungodly hour of the morning, as Smitty's father had just pointed out.

"Sorry. You'll have to get your commander's permission to schedule another call," the MP said.

"But I got cut off," Smitty protested.

"Back of the line," he said.

"But I'm a lieutenant."

"Back of the line, sir," the cop repeated.

"It's no use 1LT, the little prick's just doing his job. And loving it," Mike said sympathetically to Smitty.

Smitty left Mike to make his call, walked down the hall, and found the colonel drinking coffee.

The colonel looked up, startled by Smitty's presence. "Did you make your call?"

"I got cut off," Smitty said. "The little bastard made me go to the end of the line; said you'd have to make another request."

"Consider it done." The colonel picked up the phone, dialed, and spoke briefly before hanging up. "First available time slot is 0400 hours tomorrow morning. Best they could do, sorry."

"Thank you, sir." Smitty saluted. He turned and walked back down the hall just in time to meet Mike coming out.

"Get through?"

"Yeah, my lady said it was a good thing I called. The car was busted and she was just about to let the auto mechanic take it out in trade if her allotment check was held up," Mike smiled. "Poor bastard doesn't know what he'd be in for."

"Come on," Smitty said, pointing toward their hooch. "Lots to do before 0400 hours tomorrow when I talk to my dad."

The phone far away had only begun to ring when it was picked up and Dad's voice said breathlessly, "Son, son, is that you? Are you there, son?"

"Yes, Dad, it's me," Smitty said. "Gee, Pop, whatever happened to telephone courtesy? How come you didn't answer the phone and say, 'First Sergeant Smith's quarters; First Sergeant Smith speaking'?"

His father didn't speak, but there was noise in the background, almost as if there were a struggle going on. Then a female voice said, "Smitty, he's your son; tell him that you love him."

"Shut up, I'll handle this," Dad snapped.

"Well, to date, your methods leave a lot to be desired, Sergeant Rock."

Smitty heard more tussling in the background, then Dad saying, "Give me that!" The female voice shushed him.

"Hello, Kevin, My name is Sally. Your father and I got married last month, so I guess that officially makes me your stepmother.

"I just wanted to tell you how much I'm looking forward to meeting you and also to let you know that after you called yesterday and your father hung up on you, when I asked him who it was, and he realized who he'd hung up on, he reached for the phone so fast that he body-checked me completely out of bed. And he's been on the phone all day long calling every general he knows trying to verify that you are all right."

Sally said impishly, "I'll give the phone back to your father now."

Before she could get away, Smitty said quickly, "Sally?"

"Yes."

"I think I love you."

"Thank you! I look forward to meeting you." Sally handed the phone to Dad and said, "Tell him!"

"Geez, Pop, I didn't know you cared," Smitty said.

"Well, troop, that is, uh, son, it's good to hear your voice. Are you all right?"

"Yes, sir."

"What happened? I was worried as hell when I got the telegram." Dad said, trying hard to contain the emotion in his voice.

"Our helicopter was shot down. We had to walk out. I'm okay," Smitty said.

"Well, that's good, son," he said. "I'm glad you called, though. I was just fixing to clean out your billet and liquidate your leavings."

There was an involuntarily grunt followed by a momentary silence. Sally's elbow in Dad's ribs, he'd bet. If she could take on the old First Shirt and get the better of him, she must be some tough old broad.

"One minute," the line attendant interjected.

"Look, Dad, I'm out of time. You take care, and I'll talk to you soon."

"Okay, son, you take care. And, son," Dad's voice broke with emotion. "Stay safe."

"I will," Smitty said, handing the phone to the colonel.

"I'm glad you got through to your dad. He's a good man." The colonel lit a cigarette.

"Speaking from personal experience?"

"If you're trying to be subtle, Lieutenant, forget it and get to the point." The colonel suppressed a yawn.

"Sir, that bug they found on your phone," Smitty began hesitantly.

"Yes."

"I've seen one like it before."

"So?" the colonel answered testily.

"It was attached to the bedspring of the hospital bed Frenchy was in after we executed the phony injuries to throw off any would-be tailgaters on that observe-and-report mission in Savannah two years ago."

"Go on," the colonel said. But his tired eyes were suddenly alert and clear. He was listening now.

"Colonel, you were the assignment officer on that mission. That means whoever was tailing me then has followed me to Vietnam. It's too specific to be a coincidence."

"I agree."

"So the question is, sir, where do I go from here?"

"Why do you think someone's after you?"

"Hell, Colonel, someone, or a bunch of someones, has been shadowing me since I was ten years old," Smitty answered.

"You still haven't told me why," the colonel prodded gently.

"My guess is that somebody thinks I know something or that information was passed to me, and they're trying to either discredit me or kill me," Smitty answered.

"The term is disassociate," the colonel said. "If that doesn't work, then they'll try to kill you."

"So I'm on the right track?"

"I don't know yet, you need to tell me a little more detail. But before you do that, how are you sure you can trust me?"

"Because of my father. You knew him before, didn't you?"

"Yes."

"And you're part of the same secret that haunted him?"

"Yes."

"And the source is Mission Octagon?"

"Yes."

"What is Mission Octagon?" Smitty asked, hoping to catch the colonel off guard.

"I won't tell you. It's classified." The colonel paused. "But if you figure it out, I'll confirm it."

Smitty drummed his fingers on the colonel's desk in silence. He'd hoped that the colonel would just spill it out to him, but that was not to be. You don't make full bird being a blabbermouth.

Whatever this Mission Octagon was, it must be one hell of a secret.

"What level of classification?" Smitty asked.

"Presidential eyes and dissemination only—the highest classification possible," the colonel answered. "That means that outside of the actual team members, there were only a half dozen people in the government who had a high enough security clearance to entitle them to know the details."

A half-dozen could be a metaphor for a handful, but the question was how many specifically. Smitty thought about that for a moment. He could easily identify four and make an educated guess as to the fifth, but the colonel had said a half dozen. The sixth person baffled him, and that sixth person could be the missing link.

"Do you know who the six people are?"

"Four of them. And so do you."

"Don't suppose you have any guesses on the other two you'd be willing to share?" Smitty asked half-heartedly.

"In a word, no," the colonel answered.

"How many people were on the actual team?" Smitty asked.

"Six."

"Seems I heard my father say that these incursion missions were made up of three-man teams," Smitty ventured, hoping the colonel would confirm it and tell him why.

"This one had six," he repeated. "The term, by the way, is espionage mission."

"How do I go about finding out more?"

The colonel rocked back in his chair, put his feet up on the corner of the desk, and closed his eyes. "Let me think a minute."

A minute passed, then another. The colonel neither moved nor spoke. Obviously, he was trying to figure a way to point Smitty in the right direction without divulging anything more.

Finally, he rocked forward in his chair, crushed out his cigarette, and began.

"Son, you're opening Pandora's box, and once it's opened, there will be no way to close it. Everyone connected with that mission has suffered personally and professionally more than any human being should.

"Second, as you yourself have just said, the fallout affects everyone around you. I know. I tried to piece together why that mission was so important myself back in the late '40s. I got framed for a phony affair, divorced, passed over for captain, and almost thrown out of the service. So officially, I'm telling you to drop it.

"Unofficially, I'll tell you this. In order to get to the bottom of this, you're going to have to become really, really good at piecing together disjointed bits of information and accept the fact that what you're looking for, others are trying as desperately to conceal.

"So, how do you go about it? You have to spy on your friends as well as your enemies and assume that everyone is lying until you personally verify they aren't—including even me. You have to pick up on subtle nuances and turn those wispy clues into hard facts.

"You have to understand and accept that espionage is one of the slowest-developing forms of treason, and that on the faintest whiff of exposure, real or imagined, your quarry will run to ground, sometimes for years.

"You have also to understand that espionage is the purest form of paranoia. It's close-knit and incestuous, with friends using friends and family using family.

"And finally, you'd better understand that they'll come after you and try every way possible to discredit you and, if that doesn't work, kill you. In order to get to the bottom of this, you're going to have to set yourself up as the bait, then maintain another life, and get on with it, just in case you're wrong."

The colonel lit another cigarette and threw the pack to Smitty. "Still want to go on with it?"

"Yes," Smitty answered. "You did."

"Okay, then I'm going to give you a set of rules. On the surface, they may not seem like much, but if you think about them and apply them, they'll guide you in the discovery process. We'll call them, Colonel Wilson's Handbook for Spies," the Colonel said with a smile.

"Rule number one: what they don't know; they can't make you tell.

"Rule number two: never, never, never tell anyone anything unless you think you can benefit by their having your knowledge.

"Rule number three: sometimes you gotta take one to the choppers and never let them know it hurt.

"Rule number four: if you believe in something, you'd sure as hell better fight for it now, 'cause after you're dead, you can't hardly take aim."

"That's it?"

"That's it, son. Good luck in your search."

"Son," the colonel called after him, as Smitty turned and started for the door.

"Yes, sir," Smitty answered.

"I will tell you this. What happened on Mission Octagon is not important. What happened to the participants after Mission Octagon and why it happened is. And as God is my witness, I don't know the answer to that one myself."

"Thank you for the starting point, Colonel." Smitty turned, and without further comment, left the office.

"Everything okay on the home front?" Mike asked, when Smitty joined him and the captain for breakfast.

"Yeah. The old fossil got married," Smitty said.

"Hey, being a pussy-whipped sergeant isn't limited to your favorite army NCO, you know," Mike said with a laugh.

Smitty, Mike, and the captain flew back to Pleiku together the next morning. On the way, Smitty removed his trumpet and started to tootle on it. With a little practice, his high school form was returning, and according to Mike, Smitty's playing was actually starting to sound like something akin to music rather than someone strangling a cat.

Obviously, the captain did not agree. He snatched the instrument from Smitty's hands, and threw it out of the helicopter in disgust. Then just to assure that there would be no reclamation, he assured Smitty that he would call in an air strike for a suspected VC position on the approximate coordinates as soon as they landed.

They flew the rest of the time in silence.

"Captain's pissed," Mike said. "I don't think the desk job agrees with him."

"Probably not, probably not," Smitty agreed. "Either that or he just doesn't appreciate good music."

There could be another reason why Ron was angry, but it had nothing to do with music. It could have a lot to do with singing like a canary.

Smitty had been in touch with Linda and was planning to head to Da Nang tomorrow and stay the night. After which, they had planned a Thanksgiving week R&R in Tokyo to eat turkey and nibble on each other or vice versa. He never got the chance.

He was awakened at 0330 hours with a call from the colonel in Nha Trang. The news was the unimaginable. His dad had suffered a massive heart attack and was not expected to live. He was going home on the first available transport.

Smitty did not actively listen to the travel plans . . . something about getting to Hawaii and that General Martin was lining up a priority flight. He was only thinking about his father. As it always was in times of crisis, the troubles of before seemed utterly insignificant.

Smitty dressed in his best uniform in a daze, remembering somehow to strap on the specially designed holster for his Magnum. He packed minimally. With the funeral arrangements, he figured he'd be gone a week at most. Before boarding the transport from Cam Ranh Bay, he got in a quick call to Linda, who wished she could be with him, but assured him that she loved him and that his future wife would be waiting on his return.

He slept fitfully all the way to Hickum Field in Hawaii, recalling the ups and downs of childhood, regretting all of the bad times and all the things left unsaid, and wishing for just one more chance to say them.

The plane change in Hawaii was like a relay team handoff. He was met, escorted to another plane, and on his way again in thirty minutes. The landing and transfer at the air force base outside of San Francisco was just as efficient, and Smitty was quickly on his way eastward. The general's plane had been dispatched from Hunter Army Air Field in Savannah to pick him up when he landed at Dobbins Air Force Base outside of Atlanta. It also provided the first news update: his father was still alive, no other details were known.

They landed at Hunter, and the general had a car waiting. It took Smitty straight to the same hospital where he was born and where he had recovered from the cartwheel down the garage steps. He hoped against hope that it would not be the place where his father would die.

The car had not even pulled to a stop at the hospital when he was out of the car and running. The closer he got, the more anxious he became. Receiving his direction from the information desk, he raced up two flights of stairs, and on the ICU floor turned left and headed for the room. With his heart in his throat, he reached the correct door and slowly pushed it open.

Dad was sitting up in bed, obviously weak, but awake and being fed soup by a nurse. General Chuck was sitting casually in a chair reading the paper, his uniform jacket hanging on the chairback and his tie loosened.

Dad stopped eating and looked at Smitty like he was someone who had just landed from Mars. "What the hell are you doing here?"

Smitty smiled and couldn't help sighing in relief. "I heard you were sick."

"Well, I was, but I'm gonna be okay now, so you can go on back to where you came from," Dad said with a mischievous smile.

"Smitty, I sent for him," Chuck said, getting up to shake Smitty's hand. "Well, Lieutenant, this is a surprise. I expected you to follow your daddy's footsteps and go into the service, but I always figured you'd wind up in a blue suit." Chuck gave Smitty a wink that his father did not see.

"It's good to see you again, General."

"The last time you saw him, son, he was only a full colonel. Now he's a big shot lieutenant general," Dad said, laboring for breath.

"I'll handle the intros, Sergeant. Save your strength," Chuck said to Dad, who looked relieved at relinquishing the hosting duties.

"How long you here for, son?" Chuck asked.

"Depends on Dad."

"And whether I croak or not," Dad wheezed. "Don't worry, boy, I'll be here."

Just then, a young doctor, a captain, walked in. "General, I think it would be best if you gentlemen left and let the sergeant get some rest. He is still extremely critical and needs to sleep."

"C'mon," Chuck said, motioning toward the door. "Let's let sleeping beauty here get some rest. I'll buy you a beer. We'll be back tomorrow, Sarge."

Smitty walked to the bed and touched his father tenderly on the shoulder. "I'll be back tomorrow. You get some rest."

"Okay, son," Dad said, too weak to lift his arms. "Take care of Chuck."

"I will."

Smitty and Chuck left the room and walked down the hall. They waited in silence until the doctor emerged several minutes later.

"So what's the prognosis, Doc?" Chuck asked.

"Actually pretty good. The sergeant has survived the critical first twenty-four hours. Barring anything unforeseen, like a blood clot, he should make it."

"Anything we can do?" Chuck asked.

"Try not to overstay your visits. Rest is the important thing," the doctor said, "That and the fact that you showed up, Lieutenant. I think that will lift his spirits."

"Thanks, Doc," Chuck said, shaking his hand like a pump handle.

Smitty and Chuck took the elevator to the lobby and walked out to Chuck's car. Smitty opened the door for the general, who grabbed him by the arm, and shoved him in first. "Don't start that shit."

"Where to, sir?" The driver was a young air force staff sergeant.

"BOQ, son. The lieutenant and I have a reservation," the general said.

Smitty thought of offering to have him stay at his dad's house, but realized that it was too far away if anything should happen. It felt strange to be back in Savannah as a reputable citizen, after leaving more than three years before as a delinquent.

Smitty wondered how Sergeant Mike was, and how Hogsbreath was getting on sitting in for him as the acting 1LT. His thoughts inevitably turned to Glenda and even his wayward brother Billy. There were many questions to be answered, but they would have to wait. After three years of running, he'd finally come home. Part of him was wishing, with all of his heart, that he was home to stay.

Smitty and Chuck talked briefly before heading to bed. After sleeping only sporadically during the last thirty hours, Smitty was asleep immediately. He awoke the next morning at 0800 hours to the sound of the general dressing. The BOQ was a quasi-apartment with a common living and kitchen area and two separate bedrooms.

"Sir, have you heard from the hospital?"

"Called them first thing this morning when I rolled out of the rack. No change. Your ol' man is sleeping peacefully and will be, they tell me, until later this afternoon." In a brisker tone, Chuck said, "Look, son, I've got to go do my three-star appearance thing with the base commander, so I'll be tied up until this afternoon. Why don't you take the car and go check in with your new relative and pick me up at the headquarters building at 1400 hours?"

"Thank you, sir. That's awful nice of you. If you don't mind, I'd like to swing by the hospital first just to check. I'm sure the new Mrs. Smith would like to know the latest."

"Suit yourself." The general paused as they headed out the door. "Don't worry, son, your daddy will make it. I ordered him not to die yesterday. And you know your ol' man, he always obeys orders."

They rode together in the general's car to base headquarters. Not waiting for the driver to come around and open the door, Chuck stepped out quickly and leaned in the front passenger window. "Sergeant, this army lieutenant is on special assignment to me. Carry out all orders from him as unhesitatingly as if they were coming directly from me. Any questions?"

"No, sir," the sergeant said.

Smitty had gotten out of the backseat of the car with Chuck. He opened the front passenger door, turned and saluted. "I'll return for you, sir, at 1400 hours, per your directive."

"Thank you, Lieutenant. If I am not waiting for you here at the curb, please come inside and drag me out."

"Where to, sir?" the driver asked.

"First the base hospital. Then we're going to take a little sightseeing tour."

Smitty checked in at the hospital and found that his father was sleeping and would be for some time. Smitty had asked the doctor what he thought had brought on the heart attack. The doctor rolled his eyes. "The sergeant is only five-foot-ten but weighs two hundred fifty-eight pounds, smokes three packs of cigarettes a day, has a highly stressful job, and hasn't been to a doctor in twenty years. The surprising thing is not that he had a heart attack. The mystery is that he lasted this long before he did. If your father wishes to continue to live, he's going to have to make some major changes in his lifestyle, lose seventy-five pounds, and quit smoking."

The doctor looked up at Smitty. "Think he can do it?"

"I don't know, Doc. In his case, the cure could be worse than the disease."

Smitty shook hands with the doctor and thanked him for his time. On the way out, he ducked into a pay phone and put a quick call in to Sally. Seems she had just left the hospital shortly before Smitty had arrived the previous evening, having been there since the wee hours of the previous morning and was just putting on her face before departing for the hospital.

When Smitty informed her of the current status and the doctor's visitation recommendation, she said that she would wait for Smitty at the house. He told her he had a stop to make first and would be there in an hour. Sally had said, "I'll bet you're going to stop off and visit an old girlfriend in your soldier suit and get her all titillated, aren't you? Young girls have always gone for young men in uniform." She laughed pleasantly and added, "That goes for us older broads too, particularly with older sergeants." Her laugh was infectious, and though he'd not met her face to face, Smitty was genuinely looking forward to it. But she was wrong on her point, Smitty was not going to visit an old girlfriend to try to impress her with his uniform; he was going to see why it didn't.

The doorbell at the apartment complex off Wellington Road was answered by a disheveled-looking middle-aged lady in a tattered blue housecoat. Her stringy gray hair hung limp around her sagging cheeks. She had been beautiful in her youth, but the effects of a hard life were indelibly defined on her face. The lines and wrinkles were firmly etched, and the eyes had a permanent sadness.

"Mrs. Jackson," Smitty said politely.

"Yes," she said with suspicion, as she clutched her housecoat tightly against the late November chill.

"My name is Kevin Smith. I used to be a friend of Glenda's. I was wondering if she was home, or if she doesn't live here anymore perhaps you could tell me where I could find her," Smitty said.

"Come in, Lieutenant." She unlatched the chain lock and held the door to allow Kevin to enter.

"Would you like coffee?"

"No, thank you, ma'am."

She motioned to the sofa, then sat in a chair facing him and brushed back a strand of gray hair. "Glenda is dead, Lieutenant. She died two and a half years ago in a traffic accident."

"A traffic accident?" Smitty repeated, stunned.

"Yes. A drunken driver ran a red light when she was on her way home from work late on a Saturday night. The Savannah policeman that came to my door told me the man would be charged with vehicular homicide. But it turns out that my daughter was at fault, so they say."

"I don't understand."

"Well, even though the man who hit her was drinking, the police said later that he was not above the legal limit, and therefore they could not charge him, and that according to witnesses, my daughter was the one who ran the red light." She shook her head in disgust.

She got up, walked to the dining room table, and grabbed her cigarettes and matches from the table. As she put a cigarette to her mouth, Smitty got up and lit it for her.

Mrs. Jackson nodded her thanks, held the pack to Smitty, and shook one out.

"I've got my own, ma'am," Smitty said, as he removed the Camel nonfilters from his vest pocket and lit one.

"You said that Glenda was at fault, so they said," Smitty prodded gently.

"Bastards," she said."I think they covered it up because the guy who killed my Glenda was a cop."

"A Savannah police officer," Smitty said.

"No, he was from out of town, some place in Florida. Orlando or Miami, I think. Boy, those cops, they sure stick together."

"Yes, ma'am, they do." Smitty paused. "I guess, like they say, you can't fight city hall."

"No, but I'd sure like to try. They took my only daughter. And her having already suffered so much," she said. "Did you know her well?"

Before Smitty could answer, she smiled in recognition. "Oh how silly of me. Of course, you're that nice young man that Glen was so fond of back then. I was working days in a coffee shop and Glen was working nights at that drive-in. She told me about you, but we never did actually get a chance to meet."

Smitty crushed out his cigarette in the ashtray, came over, and placed both his hands on her shoulders. "Mrs. Jackson, Glenda was my first love. I was in training in the Carolinas when her letters suddenly stopped coming. At the time, I thought she'd just gotten tired of me, but now I know I should have had more faith in her. After all these years have passed, I still see her smile. And because she was my first love, I'm sure I always will."

Mrs. Jackson hugged Smitty. "God bless you for coming, Lieutenant. You don't know how comforting it is to find out that my Glenda had met such a fine young man as you and that I now know she died happy."

Smitty started for the door, and Mrs. Jackson walked him there with her arm around him. She opened the door and hugged him again. "Lieutenant, thank you for coming. You've made an old woman very happy."

"Well, a woman, but definitely not old, ma'am," Smitty said.

"I can see why my Glenda went for you. You could charm a girl right out of her socks," Mrs. Jackson said, as she impulsively kissed him lightly on the cheek.

"Thank you, ma'am. I'll never forget her." Smitty waved as she closed the door.

"Where to now, sir?" the driver asked when Smitty returned to the car.

"My father's house. I'm sure you already know the way. Then the Savannah Police Department downtown."

"Expecting to find your girl there?" the driver said.

"No." Smitty lit a cigarette and blew a cloud of smoke out of the window. "But I expect to find out who murdered her."

Smitty wasn't a betting man, but in this case he was betting on a sure thing.

The old neighborhood looked pretty much the same, only smaller. The distance from Shade Road to the house seemed closer, the yard shallower, and the house not as big.

At first glance, the home front looked pretty much identical to Smitty's last remembrance. The house was the same color and looked to have not seen a fresh coat of paint since before Smitty left. The infamous Plymouth that had concealed the girdle in the bowels of its glove compartment was still there, parked in the front yard, three years older now. A new car, a gold 1969 Oldsmobile Cutlass four-door, was parked on the driveway next to the porch.

But something was missing. The Hillman station wagon was nowhere to be seen. When Smitty had left that night long ago, the Hillman had been parked in the front yard, where the Plymouth was now. If that was gone, then it was a sure bet that the convertible had done a disappearing act, also.

The driver pulled into the driveway behind the Olds and stopped.

"Sit tight, Sarge, I won't be long. Just want to say a quick hello to the new stepmom, then we'll be on our way."

"Yes, sir," the driver said.

Smitty exited the car, and then remembering Chuck's advice to him almost three years ago, leaned in the window and extended his hand. "Oh, and Sarge, when we're alone, my name is Smitty or Kevin if you must be formal."

"Thanks, Smitty. My name is Allen." The sergeant took the offered hand.

"Back shortly, take ten."

"Well, well, well, aren't we important? Driver and all." Smitty stood up to find an attractive ash blonde woman standing on the porch. She seemed to be in her mid- to late-forties, with fair features, penetrating eyes, and a figure that could still turn a head or two.

"You must be Kevin." She started down the steps toward him.

They met at the midpoint between the house and the car. "Oh, excuse me," she said. She hugged him and kissed him lightly on the cheek. "I understand from your father that you go by Smitty now."

"Yes, ma'am," Smitty answered.

"Oh, don't be ma'aming me, Lieutenant," she said with a charming laugh. "Young soldier boys like you have been calling me Nurse Sally for years. You, Smitty, may just call me Sally."

"So you're an air force nurse?" Smitty asked, as she put her arm around him and began to escort him toward the porch.

"Army, past tense. Got out after twenty-six years little over two months ago." She led him into the kitchen.

Seeing Smitty doing the mental arithmetic, Sally said. "Yes, your father and I got married three weeks after I got out of the army as a major. Had to, otherwise on our honeymoon your father would have been guilty of assaulting a superior officer. Although, from what I understand from your father, that hasn't caused you any difficulty with one of my younger colleagues."

"Chip off the ol' block," Smitty said.

"You're all of that and more, sonny," she said. "Your daddy's been going nuts trying to find you. And now that you have found each other, I hope you two won't get lost again."

Smitty sat down in the kitchen chair as Sally opened the refrigerator. "You wouldn't happen to have a Coke in there for me and an extra for the driver, would you?" Smitty asked.

"Can do, Lieutenant," Sally said, as she reached back and grabbed two bottles and in the same motion opened them from the opener attached to the front of the cabinet. "I'll run it out to him. Make yourself at home." She was gone before Smitty could protest.

He stood and walked to the entrance to the room at the other end of the kitchen. When they were teenagers, this had been Billy's bedroom. It was now a comfortable den. Smitty passed through to the hallway. The bathroom, the only bathroom, was on the left, the far entrance to the other end of the living room on the immediate right.

Smitty glanced quickly at the new den furnishings, which seemed more homey and informal than when Dad had lived there with Mom. The new living room furniture was tasteful without being pretentious, and the new bedroom suite had a queen-size bed. He moved on quickly. The room at the end of the hall was his real destination. Straight ahead was his former bedroom, and the window he'd gone through in the night to begin his own journey to manhood.

The twin beds with the headboards were still there, but the high school trappings were gone. The room was freshly painted and had a sterile guest bedroom quality to it. Absently, Smitty opened the dresser drawer to find the top drawer empty. He closed it in acceptance. He opened the closet hopefully only to find it now full of women's dresses. No doubt it now served as overflow storage for Sally.

"Your dad has your things stored in the attic," Sally said, leaning against the bedroom entrance with her arms folded. "They're waiting for you when you want them. Although, I would guess that most of your clothes would no longer fit."

Smitty turned slowly and said to Sally in a pain-filled voice, "It seems like such a long time ago that this was home."

She opened her arms to him, and he came willingly. "Don't worry, Kevin, it will be again. Only it will be better this time. I promise." After almost three years, Smitty had found in this new stepmother what he had been missing his whole adolescent life: a simple maternal hug.

They left the bedroom and returned to the kitchen. "I'd like to take a quick peek at the garage before I go, then maybe duck next door and say a quick hello to Mrs. Young before I leave," Smitty said.

"Okay. You do that. I'll finish dressing and drive myself to the hospital and just meet you there," Sally said. "See you there, son. And thanks for coming home for your father. He wouldn't say it, but I'm sure it means a lot to him. And it means a lot to me, too."

Smitty went out through the back door, recalling sadly how his mother had taken away his front door key, forcing him to walk around to the back door when coming home from his job in the service station so he wouldn't mark the carpet. He headed for the garage located in the corner of the backyard.

In high school, the garage had served as a parking area for numerous fix-up projects, some running, most not, that had been dragged in there by Smitty and his friends. Smitty and his high school motorhead buddies had turned a lot of wrenches on a lot of cars in this garage, but right now he was only concerned with one, and it wasn't there. He opened the door to find a 1962 Falcon station wagon with imitation wood grain paneling and a Pennsylvania license plate the only resident.

His 1959 Hillman convertible was gone. Gone, too, were any traces that the car had ever existed. No spare parts in the overhead cabinets, no engines in the corner, no miscellaneous items up in the attic. Smitty left the garage and noticed also that the 1960 Hillman convertible parts car was gone from the opposite corner of the yard, as was the assortment of doors, fenders, and hoods from other dismantled Hillman junkers. It looked like a German city that had been totally devastated during World War II, then rebuilt with no trace of the former town remaining. This backyard now looked totally different, like it belonged to some other owner, and definitely like he no longer belonged in it.

Smitty walked around the house past the porch and with a quick wave to the driver. "Be right back. Just want to say a quick hello to Mrs. Young, then we'll be off."

The driver nodded. "Take your time. It's only 1020 hours."

Smitty was halfway around the front hedge to Mrs. Young's house when a snide voice said, "Look what we have here guys, a bad-assed soldier."

Smitty whirled and found himself facing six people: three guys and three girls all in their teens, wearing nondescript faded clothes with patches and hair so long it was difficult to tell which were the girls and which were the boys.

It took a second, but Smitty slowly recognized the male in front as the bratty little kid from across the street that everybody used to call Dinky, whose four-times-divorced mother had a mouth like a salty old marine gunny sergeant and a leatherneck face to match.

"Oh, look guys," Dinky said. "This is my ex-neighbor who ran away from home three years ago. Back as a Green Beret." He glanced around at his friends for encouragement. "I bet you think you're tough."

"I am," Smitty said.

"I'll bet that you got all those medals for kissing some general's ass," Dinky said with a sneer.

"That or kicking it," Smitty said.

"Oh, so you think you're a bad-ass, huh? Well, we know all about you candy-assed baby killers. My friends and I demonstrated against it at college. Let's just see how tough you are with a real man." Dinky reached up and slapped Smitty's Green Beret off his head.

Smitty quietly retrieved his headgear and repositioned it down low on his forehead just above the eyes. "You had your fun, now leave before you get hurt." Unfortunately, like most big-mouthed bullies, Dinky didn't get it.

Dinky balled up his fist and brought it forward in the direction of Smitty's face. The only problem was, Smitty wasn't there; he'd stepped in and to the right. As the fist sailed harmlessly by, Smitty hit Dinky with the back of his hand with a judo smash just above the Adam's apple, remembering just in time to pull the punch so as not to crush his windpipe. As Dinky grabbed his throat, Smitty reached out with his foot, and, like a soccer kicker, brought his leg around, upending the boy like a tight end tackled in midair. He landed solidly and squarely on his butt on the hard tar road.

Dinky's two friends attacked together and went down together. It was actually so simple that Smitty almost laughed. As they charged blindly, intent on grabbing him, he dropped to one knee and punched both of them in the balls. While they were helplessly grabbing their aching crotches, he grabbed them by their manes and slammed their heads together with sufficient force to assure that a numbing, disorienting headache would be the outcome.

One of the girls stepped forward and attempted to slap his face. "Fuckin' baby killer!"

Smitty blocked the blow with his right forearm and slapped her hard across the face with his left. "If you continue to use that kind of language I'll have to wash your mouth out with soap."

The other two girls were apparently not as passionate in their feelings. They backed away two steps and stood silently waiting for their friends to recover.

"I'm calling the cops and your motherfucking ass is going to jail!" a female voice yelled. "I saw the whole thing while I was watering my grass, and I'll press charges against you.

"We ran your goddamn thug ass out of this neighborhood once, and going in the army won't help," Dinky's mother walked up and bent down toward her son. "Don't worry, my little Dinkbug. Mommy saw what that bastard soldier did to her sweet little boy. Mommy will take care of it."

"Did I hear you say you required the services of a policeman?" a voice said to Smitty's right.

Smitty turned and saw a burly City of Savannah policeman approaching. Barney Fife, or Sergeant Beanie, as all the neighborhood kids had called him, had lived on the other side of his dad's house for years. He had a son close to Smitty's age that Smitty had knocked around with some as a teenager. Benny was well-liked, slow to anger, but conscientious in performing his duty. He had extraordinary common sense and was able to quickly size up events.

"You're goddamn right you did. I want this motherfucker arrested."

"For what?" Benny questioned.

"For beating up my son and these other two boys. He's an animal and needs to be caged."

"That there's not quite the way it was a-happenin'." Mrs. Young said, as she walked up from her yard. "Me and Clark were a-sittin' on that there porch and we seen the whole thing, too. And them details Mrs. Hartman's a-tellin' ya is at the very least a stretch of the truth, and the very most, a bald-faced lie." Sara Lee elbowed her husband in the ribs. "Be a-tellin' 'em, Clark."

"It happened jus' like Maw sayed."

"Well, I still want to press charges," Mrs. Hartman said, "And if you don't do it, I'll call your captain."

"If you insist, Mrs. Hartman," Benny replied.

"Dinky, stand up and put your hands behind your back. You're under arrest for assault and battery, inciting to riot, assembling without a permit, littering, and anything else I can think of. You three also." He pointed to the other two males and the girl who had assaulted Smitty.

"You see, Mrs. Hartman, I was on the way to work, and I also saw the whole incident. Frankly, judging by Kevin's combat decorations, you can consider yourself lucky that he didn't kill your son rather than just teach him a valuable lesson about how to be accountable for what comes out of his mouth." Benny snapped the handcuffs with an audible click.

Benny must have called for backup before he came over. Two Savannah police cars arrived on the scene moments later and the four teens were taken away. Mrs. Hartman stomped away in a four-letter snit, vowing to sue everybody who ever lived.

Smitty visited with Mr. and Mrs. Young and Benny for twenty minutes, enjoying the sense of normality that was part of their everyday lives and hoping that one day he might have the same.

When he finally said his good-byes to the older neighbors, and he and Benny were walking back toward the car, Benny asked him where he was headed next. When Smitty told him his destination and why, Benny agreed not only to check on Glenda's accident for him, but also promised to get back to him personally with the details at the BOQ that night.

The car started, and Smitty and the driver left the subdivision the same way they had come. He had long since left home physically. Leaving the memory of it was just as hard.

CHAPTER SIXTEEN

Smitty was back in Vietnam four days later. He stayed one more day to assure himself that his father was out of critical danger then accepted the general's offer of a ride back as far as San Francisco. Before he left Savannah, Smitty had sent a wire to Colonel Wilson, informing him that he was on the way back. When he landed in Hawaii, a response was waiting for him that said he was to report to the colonel directly on his return.

On the plane over to the fiftieth state, Smitty had read the report from Benny. After shredding the report in an ashtray in the chow hall and burning the shreds, Smitty had a hunch, that, like all good gamblers, he was going to play for all its worth.

He hurriedly left the slop chute and placed a call to Stan the Man in Miami. When he explained the reason for his call and his hunch, Stan thanked him for the information and said he'd check it out. He called back in one hour. Smitty's intuition was dead center in the bull's-eye.

Like the report from his Hawaiian friend Sam, it confirmed what he had already suspected—namely, that if the coincidences that were occurring in his life were stretched end to end, they'd probably make a daisy chain he could walk on from Savannah to Vietnam. He was certainly getting more pieces; what he needed was a major breakthrough to start putting them together.

"Sit down, son." The colonel didn't meet Smitty's eyes as they shook hands when Smitty reported to him as ordered. Right after landing at Cam Ranh Bay, Smitty'd caught a helicopter straight to Nha Trang and the colonel's office.

Looking up with pain-filled eyes, the colonel said in a solemn voice, "Son, I got some bad news for you." Pausing to collect himself, he said, "It's the worst."

"Dad?" Smitty asked, alarmed.

"No, son, it's not your father; he's fine." The colonel inhaled. "It's your girl, son, Linda is dead. There was a sapper attack on the hospital in Da Nang the day after you left. It was well-planned and well-executed. Little bastards were under the wire before the first retaliation. Killed a bunch of doctors and nurses. Your girl was one of them."

Smitty sat in stunned silence, too upset to speak or even cry. Coming on the heels of the facts surrounding Glenda's death, it was almost unbelievable. For a moment, Smitty hoped that this was some sort of macabre joke, but a quick glance at the colonel's eyes and Smitty knew it was true. Seconds passed into minutes as Smitty tried to come to grips with his loss. Finally, he said, "I've got to get to Da Nang."

The colonel put a hand on his shoulder. "It's too late, son. She's already been shipped stateside for burial in her parents' cemetery in Des Moines."

The colonel slammed his hand down on the desk. "Another useless death."

"No, sir," Smitty said with certainty, "another purposeful murder."

Smitty stayed drunk at the SOG safe house in Nha Trang for the next two days. He didn't eat, even though someone was delivering food into the room during his bouts of pain-filled sleep. Linda had been so young, so beautiful, and so full of life—it didn't seem right that God would take her. Smitty had nightmares about her beauty, knowing he'd never touch her again and feel her warm caress. He cursed God and swore off his religious beliefs. In a drunken stupor, he cried for her and for himself. He punched the walls, he screamed in rage, and he swore eternal vengeance against the person who did this.

But slowly, as each bout of alcoholic nothingness passed, Smitty's rage was fading, and he knew that he'd have to go on, if for no other reason than for all those grunts out there, for all those who had died . . . and for those who were yet to die.

He awoke with a start on the morning of the third day to Sergeant Mike slapping him back and forth across the face and cursing fluently. "Wake your goddamn drunken ass up, 1LT. It's time to get on with life."

Mike struck him four times—that Smitty could count—before he finally put up a hand in defense. "All right, Mike, that's enough."

Mike slapped him again, harder this time. "It's not enough, in fact, I'm only beginning."

The last shot did it. Like the air strike that sets off a chain reaction, Mike's stinging contact traveled directly to Smitty's alcohol-soaked brain and reached the psychological fight-or-flight instincts buried deep in everyone's subconscious.

Mike's arm was cocked to strike again. As he followed through with the right forehand, Smitty jerked up and blocked it with his own right, then hit Mike on the chin with his balled-up left fist with all the strength his booze-basted body would allow.

Mike staggered backward, bounced off the wall, stumbled, and fell awkwardly to the floor.

"Welcome back, 1LT," Mike smiled from his supine position, as he patted his bleeding lip and started to get up.

Smitty reached down, offered his hand, and he helped Mike to his feet. "Sorry."

Mike shook his head slowly. "Don't be. You got a right to get plastered. She was a nice kid. Had me one of them myself in the Big War. You will get over it."

"Jesus, Mike, I'm not real sure what to do next."

"I am," Mike said. "The colonel wants to see you. He told me to sober your butt up and get you over to his office by 0900 hours.

Smitty glanced at his watch. It was now 0815. "Guess I'd better get my shit together, huh."

"You sure as fuck better," Mike said. "In your present state, you hardly resemble the 1LT that I'd follow to hell and back." He smiled. "Maybe send you, but not want you back."

"Attention!" the colonel barked, as an army lieutenant general entered his office.

"Stand easy," the three-star said. Sighting Smitty, he walked directly toward him and shook hands. "How are you, Lieutenant? I understand you were with my older brother, Chuck, a week or so ago. Sorry to hear about your father and your girl. I know the timing absolutely is the worst, but the army needs your help, and needs it right now."

General Ben Martin was the spitting image of his older brother in both look and manner. He had been a two-star three years back when Smitty, Frenchy, and LZ had run across him at Benning and performed that special trucking mission that had qualified them for Fayettenam, and eventually the real thing.

Smitty had heard that he'd taken over a command in this sector; up until now, their paths had not crossed. But the general had obviously known where to find him.

"Lieutenant, I need you to assemble a team of your own picking and leave on a special mission within the hour. You are to proceed expeditiously to Pleiku to pick up equipment, personnel, and transport."

"What is the mission, sir?" Smitty asked.

"A search and destroy company is trapped by an estimated force of three thousand VC two clicks from Kannack in the area north of the Mang Yang Pass. The company is made up of mostly green kids just in from the States and is under the command of an old friend of yours, Major Gates."

"1LT, isn't that the asshole your buddies nicknamed Major Cluster-Gerbil?" Sergeant Mike interrupted suddenly.

"Exactly," the general said. "He's led a bunch of kids into an ambush, and we have lost radio contact. We need you to go out there, work your way in under the cover of darkness, relieve that idiot of command, and figure out how to get as many of those boys out of there alive as possible."

"Uh, General," Smitty began, "the major and I have a history together that's less than cordial. I don't think he's going to take too kindly to being relieved of command by a lieutenant, and especially by me."

"The colonel and I thought of that also. But you are the best and most experienced man we have for the job at this particular moment. Therefore, we have done two things to help you as best we can. Sam," the general said with a nod to the colonel, "you're on."

The colonel handed Smitty a letter. "Give this to the major if he's still alive, or to whomever is in command if he's not. It's signed by the general and orders you to take charge of the patrol. It specifically states that it will be a court-martial offense to refuse to obey your commands."

Smitty surveyed the letter, noting some of the phraseology. "You are instructed to turn over command at once to Captain Smith."

"Yes." The general reached into his pocket and handed Smitty a matching pair of railroad tracks. "The colonel and I felt that you needed a little more power of rank, so to speak, so we are advancing you, temporarily, to the grade of captain."

"If the major refuses to relinquish command, just how far can I go in dealing with the situation?"

"Captain," the general said bluntly, "how you deal with the major in the event that he refuses to obey the written directive is your business. We want those boys back. Go out there and cope.

"Lastly, your men are to be selected specifically by you, and this mission is secret. I repeat—secret. The press would have a field day if they ever got hold of the details. Time is desperately short. The colonel will brief you on the details in flight to Pleiku. Good luck, Captain." The general offered his hand.

Smitty shook hands with the general and the colonel then left the office quickly.

He was not looking forward to renewing his acquaintance with his "old friend," who wasn't likely to get any older. A whispered message from the colonel had pretty much assured it.

Nineteen-and-a-half hours later, they were in sight of the besieged patrol. Smitty's team had landed under cover of darkness, with covering fire from a forward artillery base near An Khe, and had managed to work their way silently past the VC to the edge of the patrol. They had, by design, come in from the back as the artillery barrage plastered the front.

Smitty had picked his team with care. There were only six of them: Smitty, Sergeant Mike, Hogsbreath, and three guys who were individual team leads themselves. These were Hairless Dick, a twenty-five-year-old, prematurely bald staff sergeant with twelve missions; the Swede, a twenty-three-year-old, six-foot-seven sergeant who had eleven missions; and Tiny Tim, a twenty-two-year-old buck sergeant with eight. They were the most experienced guys Smitty could lay his hands on. Each was a tried and tested operative who had been under fire enough to not wilt under pressure.

They were able to advance silently until they were less than fifteen feet away from the besieged right flank. Smitty could see the fear in the eyes of the young E-2 standing the perimeter watch. He was constantly darting his eyes back and forth as if expecting the VC to be everywhere and their advance to be imminent.

On Smitty's silent command, Hairless Dick made a barely audible noise to the right with his bayonet to distract the sentry. Smitty crawled forward with Mike and quickly overpowered him from the blind side, wrapping a hand around his mouth and whispering urgently, "Be quiet if you want to live!"

The guard was so startled by the unexpected contact that he wet his pants.

"W-h-ho-o are you?" he asked, his voice trembling with fright.

Sensing that he had to lighten the moment before the young man vapor-locked, Smitty said, "I'm Tricky Dicky and this big idiot is Sir Spiro of Agnew." The sentry relaxed slightly. "Captain Smith, 5th Special Forces. I've been sent in to bring you guys out. Who's in command here?"

"Major Gates, sir. He's over there." The young man pointed in the direction of a group of foxholes approximately thirty yards away.

"Thanks, partner. Sit tight and we'll get you guys out of here."

Smitty and his team crawled silently to the command center that the private had pointed out. When they were ten feet away, a voice said urgently, "Billy, the major told you to stay in position, and if you left it again, he'd see to it that you were shot for desertion of your post."

"Unfortunately, son, Billy is the name of my brother," Smitty said. "My name is Smitty, or Captain Smith if you wish to be formal."

In a stunned voice, the young grunt said, "With all due respect, Captain, just how the fuck did you get here?"

"My friends and I heard you boys were in a spot of bother, and since we were just passing through, we thought we might be able to help," Smitty said. His experience told him that to get out of here in one piece, he and the team would have to exude confidence. Otherwise, they'd stampede the herd.

"Where's the major?"

"Over there, asleep, sir." The young corporal paused and said, "I hope you can help us, sir. Since the captain was killed, that major's been issuing orders and countermanding the lieutenants and the NCOs. Sir, he led us into this. With all due respect, sir, that major's an idiot."

Glancing at Mike, Smitty said, "I seem to attract them."

Mike smiled back and flipped him the bird.

"Go wake him," Smitty ordered. Then he nodded to Mike and looked at his watch.

"Tell Tiny Tim to radio for the encirclement barrage to be ready in five minutes—at 0500 hours—on my command."

Smitty duck-walked to the major's foxhole position down in a swale. Noting that it was below the firing line, he stood up just as the corporal was rousing him. The major was scared, but it was worse than that. He was paranoid scared. Smitty could see it in his eyes.

Hell, everybody over here was scared; there was nothing wrong with that, but paranoid scared was different. It was a special kind of fear reserved exclusively for those who had rank and responsibility without the corresponding experience. Smitty had seen it before, mostly in young second lieutenants and in some higher-ranking conventional career officers. It was the kind of fear that made you attempt to mask your own inexperience and insecurity by trying to bluff your way through on ego. If you were lucky and the paranoia was in its early stages, an experienced NCO could usually talk you through the worst of it until your in-country experience grew—as Mike had done for Smitty over the past year.

Unfortunately, in the major's case, the patient was critical—no, on life support. Eighteen years in the army in cushy Pentagon paper-shuffler jobs with no combat seasoning made him very long on insecurity and very short on experience.

Smitty's first instinct was to save himself a lot of time and effort and just cope with the major. But experience told him he had to try—not for the major, but for all the kids who would be watching. Mike had followed Smitty into hell, but these kids would have to believe in him for Smitty to lead them out.

"Major, I have a letter for you signed by Lieutenant General Martin." Smitty passed across the mail.

The major simply stared, so Smitty said, "Sir, that letter relieves you of command and instructs you to turn over command to me effective upon receipt, which means now."

"I have no intention of turning over command and placing the lives of the company in the hands of an irresponsible juvenile miscreant, masquerading as an army sergeant." The major slapped away the letter with his left hand, unread. His right hand went to his .45.

"Sir, that individual you speak of no longer exists. That irresponsible miscreant died in a warehouse on the west side of Miami. That wet-behind-the-ears sergeant changed into a lieutenant and then a captain through many missions and the deaths of many friends."

"You may have fooled the army with your false heroics, but I can see right through you. You may be an officer by rank, but you're definitely no gentleman, nor will you ever be." The major looked around at the company for support, and finding none, unsnapped the .45 holster.

Smitty looked quickly at Sergeant Mike and received his affirmative nod. "Major, I am a captain in the United States army. I paid a heavy price for my rank with a trail of dead American bodies of soldiers, friends, and many enemy killed.

"Right now, what you think of me or I think of you is unimportant. I don't care. What is important is that we get these guys out of here alive." Smitty removed his .357, with the silencer attached, and aimed it directly at the major's forehead at point-blank range.

One of the things that Smitty had obtained when he was stateside on emergency leave was a specially designed silencer for his favorite hand weapon so that he would no longer have to carry a silenced .22 on incursion missions. Smitty thought how sad and ironic it was that his first chance to use it would be on one of his own countrymen.

"You won't shoot me, Captain. There are too many witnesses. Besides, it would do great harm to your precious career."

"Right now, Major, my career don't mean shit to me. My country don't mean shit to me. This fuckin' war don't mean shit to me. The only thing that matters is these guys and getting them out of here alive. And if I have to blow your fuckin' head off to do that, then so be it, and to hell with consequences," Smitty said savagely.

When the major didn't respond, Smitty cocked the Magnum. "Last chance."

"I can't let you, Captain, it will finish my career," the major said in a pleading voice.

It became quiet, deathly quiet. Smitty could hear no sounds, nor was he conscious of any movement. His total attention was focused on the major and his eyes. Smitty knew that the major had no choice. Smitty had forced his hand, called his empty bluff, and could see in those eyes that the major knew it, too.

The major tried to draw his .45 like Billy the Kid, but his inexperience made him clumsy and slow.

The major's weapon hadn't cleared the holster when Smitty fired. A strawberry-colored stain instantly bloomed right between the major's eyes. He fell backward and died, his face a mask of disbelief.

For seconds Smitty stood there. Frenchy had become disabled, Walt had become a junkie, and LZ had become a racist. What had he become?

The colonel's two-year-old warning was ringing in his ears. He had become the worst of the four musketeers: a soulless killer who felt neither pain nor remorse at the major's death. He had crossed over and there was no path back. He could go home but would never know peace.

"1LT!" Mike stepped forward and pried the weapon from Smitty's hand.

"1LT!" Mike repeated in a louder voice, as he put his arm around Smitty's shoulders and turned him away so that the dead major's open eyes no longer mesmerized him.

"Mike, give the orders to the team, then proceed as per plan," Smitty said.

"Captain, you have to call in the air strike personally," Mike said, a trace of admonition in his voice.

"I know that!" Smitty roared back. "Now get the fuck away from me."

"Yes, sir, Captain, sir!" Mike said with a formal salute.

Smitty looked at Mike. "Pointing me out for snipers?"

"If that's what it takes," Mike answered back.

"Okay, Mike," Smitty said. "Hand me that radio."

"You got it, 1LT." Mike playfully slapped Smitty's jaw. He took several steps and turned back. "Oh, and 1LT, if we ever get out of this mess, you can come to my house and fuck my daughter anytime—marriage no longer a prerequisite."

"Git, you idiot lifer."

Mike flipped him the bird as he crouched and scurried away.

It was 0520 hours when Smitty keyed the mic and said urgently, "Fat Cat, Fat Cat, this is Irishman. Come in. Over."

"This here is Fat Cat. How can I help you boys?" The calm response was instantaneous. Someone was keeping a very close watch.

"Fat Cat, Fat Cat, I am saying code word Anastasia," Smitty shouted into the radio in a firm, controlled voice. "I repeat—code word is Anastasia."

"Stand by," Fat Cat replied.

Thirty seconds passed. "Irishman, Irishman. Top Dog requests verification through the major. Over."

"The major's dead. They're all dead and the rest of us soon will be. I repeat—the code word is Anastasia," Smitty roared, his voice tinged with panic.

"I'll confirm, Irishman—"

"You'll confirm jack shit!" Smitty interrupted. "I'm in command here and have made the decision that escape is not possible and am calling for fire on my position. Confirm the fucking air strike. Over."

"Irishman, this is Top Dog!" Colonel Wilson's voice cut in. "Distill your transmissions, this is not a secure line. I repeat—distill your transmissions, this is not a secure line."

"Fuck you, sir!" Smitty cut him off. "We're done for, Sam, and as long as we are, we may as well take as many of the slimy little motherfuckers with us as possible."

"If you keep talking into an unsecured line and tip them off, then they'll pull back and that mission will not be attainable, Captain," the colonel answered.

"ETA to air support arrival overhead, Fat Cat," Smitty said anxiously.

"Five minutes," Fat Cat said.

"Requesting four quadrant barrage, full penetration, from my smoke mark." Smitty opened a smoke canister.

"Roger."

"Top Dog, tell my father I love him." Smitty clicked off before the colonel could reply.

The members of the besieged company who were within hearing distance of the radio transmission had gone rigid from what they just heard.

"Sir?" a young platoon lieutenant asked in a shaking voice. "Did I just hear you call for an air strike directly on our position?"

"Yes, Lieutenant, I have. As you heard, I have informed the colonel that the position was untenable and will be overrun imminently and that we had too many wounded to get out."

"But, sir, that will kill us as well as the VC. Besides, Captain, it's just not true!"

"Keep your voice down, Lieutenant, I know that and you know that, but no need for the VC to know it too," Smitty said. "Sound travels, you know."

"I don't understand, sir."

"Partner, over that radio I just told the world that our position was grave, and we're too heavily damaged to retrieve. Did you believe it?" Smitty asked.

"Yes, sir!" he replied.

"Then if you believe it, do you suppose the VC who are monitoring this unsecured channel will believe it also?"

A smile spread slowly across the lieutenant's face as he nodded and replied, "If I were Victor Charlie, I'd be headed for the hills about now."

"And we're going to be right on their heels before they figure it out," Smitty replied with a grin. "The artillery barrage will start with live rounds in all four quadrants triangulated from our smoke position. Only the south quadrant's rounds will start three hundred yards farther out and after five minutes will switch to smoke rounds."

"And then we haul ass through the gauntlet before they know what's happening," the lieutenant said.

"Right-o, daddy-o." Smitty nodded his head in agreement. "There's an LZ waiting two clicks beyond that with more air support than you could possibly imagine to help us unass the area."

"I'm impressed," the lieutenant said.

"Aw, don't say that to him," Mike said shaking his head gravely. "The little fuzznut's head is swollen enough as it is."

This time it was Smitty's turn to digitally introduce Mike to the number of friends he had before his dog had died, an introduction Mike returned with the usual acknowledgment for Smitty's mythical horse.

Smitty had expected fallout from the incident in the Mang Yang Pass, but the reaction was not what he anticipated at all.

The major's body was recovered along with the other casualties three days later, quietly marked KIA, and unobtrusively sent home for burial in the family cemetery. Officially, not a word was said about the action or the circumstances surrounding it.

Unofficially, Smitty had received congratulations from the colonel and General Martin when he handed back the temporary captain's bars to the general. "I had a chance to shoot that paper-pushing SOB years ago in Korea and didn't," the general said. "Thanks for paying my debt."

The rescue operation had worked flawlessly, catching the VC completely by surprise. They were able to beat feet outta there without any further deaths or injuries. There was to be no formal recognition for any of the SOG team members involved in the rescue because it might raise questions and because, as General Martin said, "You boys were never there." But the general had stated that he was very grateful and that there would be informal recognition, and the general was obviously a man accustomed to paying his markers.

Smitty and the other five members of the incursion team were immediately given fourteen-day leaves and given their choice of destination—anywhere they wanted to go, with the army picking up the bill.

Hairless Dick, the Swede, and Tiny Tim had taken off together for Taiwan, intent on hitting the capital and picking up a little yardage in the local bars and with the local girls. Hogsbreath had airmailed himself back to Japan where one of the lovelies from his injury tour seemed to have captured his fancy. Mike had gone to Hawaii for, as he put it, a fortnight of gruntin' and sweatin' with the ol' lady.

Smitty had resisted Mike's offer to accompany him to aloha land and a platonic meeting with his oldest offspring. Instead, like a homing pigeon, he was headed indirectly to the coop, and that coop was in Savannah.

He still ached for Linda, but her death had taught him to treasure the friends he had because tomorrow was an unfulfilled promise. He had blamed Vietnam for transforming his close friends into distant acquaintances but saw now that he should be reprimanding himself. He resolved to transform right into positive action. Smitty knew he had to touch all the bases on his way home.

The trip became a clean single with a stop at the hooch at Pleiku where he retrieved the four watches he had purchased months ago in Japan for the other three musketeers. He added to the inscriptions to Frenchy's, LZ's, and Big Walt's watches before having them gift wrapped, intent on delivering in person.

It became a solid double when he left Vietnam to deliver the mail.

His first destination when he hit the States was Fort Leavenworth, where he delivered Big Walt's watch, had an emotional reunion, and promised faithfully to write. The big guy looked well and had been, according to the stockade sergeant, clean for six months. He was scheduled for release in January of 1970. Smitty had called Stan the Man in Miami, who had promised that he would help Walt get a job and do whatever he could to help.

Smitty's next stop was Biloxi, Mississippi. Frenchy had been discharged from the army in April 1969 when his rehab was completed at Fort Polk. He had married Sondra five days later and gone to work for Sondra's new stepfather in the family business. His arm was horribly deformed and would be for life. But his attitude was good, he was happy, and Sondra was expecting their first child in February.

Smitty's next stop was Fort Jackson, where LZ was currently assigned. Over a few beers, Smitty listened to LZ's frustrations without making judgments. He promised his own friendship and support no matter what. They parted with a hug, and Smitty felt the closeness of before return. His friend was still there. Smitty was glad he'd found him again.

Smitty rounded third base with a trip to a suburb of Des Moines, Iowa, and a tearful meeting with Linda's parents, where Smitty hand-delivered a check—endorsed by him—for Linda's life insurance. Unbeknownst to him, she had made him her beneficiary. Ten thousand dollars was a year's army pay, but he just didn't feel right taking it. It had nothing to do with being noble, but it had everything to do with being loyal to Linda's memory. Besides, she had confided their financial woes to him and had been sending them money herself. He was sure this unexpected cash bonanza would be put to good use.

After four days, Smitty was finally safe at home in Savannah. He had not called ahead, wishing to surprise them. On his arrival at Hunter, Smitty had called the house. Sally had answered and was exuberant at his return, and told him that his father was not at home, but was attending a company Christmas party while on convalescent leave.

Smitty had gone directly to his father's outfit at Hunter to find him. The Ol' Sarge had responded to questions as to the identity of this army officer with all the confetti by grudgingly acknowledging his presence. "This ain't no fucking officer. He's my son."

Even though he did his best to downplay his feelings, there was no hiding the gleam of pride in his eye. They had spent the Christmas holiday together, talking late into the night, renewing bonds that had been frayed.

As Smitty boarded the plane on the twenty-ninth of December for his trip back to Vietnam, he was at last at ease within himself. He had repaid some past-due debts and credited some new accounts. His friends, one way or another, were getting on with their lives. It was time, as the colonel had said, that he did the same.

Smitty had just stepped off the airplane at Cam Ranh Bay when he was met by a sergeant and ordered to report to Colonel Wilson immediately. A transport helicopter had been arranged, and Smitty was to leave at once. Ninety minutes later, he knocked at the colonel's door.

"Welcome back, Lieutenant," Colonel Wilson said, as they shook hands in his office at Nha Trang. "I trust you had an enjoyable two weeks' leave."

"Yes, sir," Smitty said. "It was nice to see my friends and folks. And thank you for the leave for the team."

"Son, it's I who should be thanking you. If that patrol had been wiped out, there would have been a tremendous loss of human life, but we also would have suffered another public relations disaster at a time when the army can ill afford it."

"I'm afraid I don't understand."

"Well, son, to put it mildly, right now the army's got its tit in the wringer. We're engaged in a very unpopular war that's losing support at home as each day passes. Remember, Nixon ran on a campaign promise to end the war and bring the troops home. He's been in office a year now and, other than some ceremonial withdrawals, hasn't done much to bring the boys home.

"The president is like the little boy digging in the manure pile. When his parents ask him why, he says that with all this horseshit, there must be a pony in here somewhere. The political element is desperately searching for a win, any kind of win, out of this pile of crap to justify all the investment of equipment, money, and human lives."

"If that were true, then why did it take them so long to listen, and why doesn't the president just stand up and tell the American people that the former administration and the former military commanders fumbled the ball and that we are on the right path now?" Smitty protested.

The colonel smiled and said, "Do you remember telling me about that bratty little college student from your neighborhood, the one who tried to jump you when you were home on emergency leave?"

"Yeah, so?"

"Do you think you could convince him that we're doing the right thing now?"

"I get your point, sir."

"If you get the point, then you tell me why we couldn't get through to that boy," he said directly.

"Well, sir," Smitty paused to light a cigarette and collect his thoughts. "I guess because all of the fumbling to date has been so sensationalized in the media that he wouldn't listen."

"Why do you think he wouldn't listen?"

"Because he's never had to."

"Bingo. Why?"

"Probably because his mother has indulged his every whim to the point that he has never had to develop the capability to think for himself. She gave him things rather than thoughts. He's had no practice at thinking, so he just follows the crowd. If all his friends are against the war, then he is, too. He couldn't stand alone against his friends even if he wanted to."

"Why not?" the colonel prodded.

"Because he's more worried about what his friends, or his mommy, will think of him than he is about what he thinks of himself. The consequence of this is probably that he's a deeply unhappy young man."

Smitty looked up at the colonel. "And I'll bet my new watch that he'll go through life unfulfilled and frustrated, never knowing how good it feels to stand up for something he believes in, fight for a lost cause, or tell someone in authority to fuck off and walk!"

The colonel smiled and said lightly, "You mean like telling a certain colonel to fuck off and turning off the radio?"

Smitty blushed and said sheepishly, "Um, yes, sir."

The colonel lit a cigarette, rocked back in his chair, and blew four smoke rings into the air. "Took me a month to learn to do that as a young captain in Korea," the colonel said. Whatever he thought of Smitty's outburst, he was not responding. But he was obviously trying to find out either Smitty's feelings on the home front or his feelings about himself.

The colonel and Smitty smoked in silence, each lost in his own thoughts. Finally the colonel crushed out his cigarette in the ashtray, opened his center drawer, and pulled out a single folded sheet of paper.

"I see while you were home on leave you became a bit of a philanthropist." The colonel unfolded the paper and passed it across.

The letter was from Linda's parents and was dated just eleven days ago. Smitty was stunned to see that it was addressed to the President of the United States.

Basically, it covered the facts of Smitty's visit in the first paragraph. In the second, they stated how grateful they were for the money and that it had come at a most opportune time when their mortgage on the farm was in jeopardy. In the third was a request that the president "find a way to reward such a fine young man for his generosity and his service to his country." They closed by saying how proud they were of their late daughter and their almost son-in-law and just wanted the president to know that there were still young people out there who cared.

Below their signatures, the president, or someone, had scrawled in a response to a staff member, "Margery, we need to do something about this—recommendation in twenty-four hours, please."

Below that was a hand-written distribution list that included senators, the local congressman, and the governor.

"Whew!" Smitty said. "How did this get all the way down to you so fast?"

"Get to me so fast?" The colonel snorted. "Hell, son, a copy of that letter was hand-carried by an army colonel, who couriered it directly from the army chief of staff to General Martin three days ago, and has been camped out on my desk since then waiting for you to return.

"When this Colonel Perkins heard that you hadn't reenlisted, he called the Pentagon, and I understand the army chief of staff liked to have had a conniption. General Martin gave me direct orders to have you met when you landed and brought here the moment you returned in-country." The colonel reached for the phone.

"Um, sir," Smitty began politely, "Perhaps it would be better if you and I talked first before you bring in that brass hat."

"About?" the colonel asked, as he replaced the phone and sat down.

"Well, sir. I don't know how to say this . . . "

"Don't tell me you're thinking about getting out?" The colonel looked up in disbelief.

"Uh, well," Smitty stammered. "That is to say, yes, sir."

"And do what?" The colonel stood up. "Go home to some two-for-a-nickel job or back to the streets from which you came?"

The colonel came around his desk and sat down next to Smitty. "Smitty, why did you give Captain Williams's parents the money?" he asked in a fatherly tone.

"Because it was the right thing to do," Smitty answered.

"It was a tremendous thing to do. Frankly, if I'd been in the same circumstances, with two kids coming up on college, I don't know if I could have been so charitable." The colonel lit a cigarette. "Did you do it knowing that they would write that letter or expecting them to write it, or did you ask them to write it?"

"Of course not!" Smitty started to get up and leave in disgust but was stilled by the colonel's restraining touch on his arm.

"Exactly. So you stand to be the beneficiary of an unplanned event that occurred without your knowledge, correct?"

"Yeah, so?" Smitty replied, tight-jawed.

"So this," the colonel said. "There are literally thousands of young officers in the army right now who have piled up combat records just as impressive as yours and who work just as hard or harder. But no matter how outstandingly and admirably they perform their duties, they will spend their entire careers in anonymity and retire like myself as lieutenant or full colonel."

"So what's your point, sir?" Smitty asked.

"My point is, that through a totally selfless act, you have come to the personal attention of the president, and looking at the distribution list, probably half a dozen U.S. Senators, a couple of congressmen, and a governor or two also.

"The result of this, I'm guessing, is that right now the president sees this as a tremendous media opportunity to showcase an upstanding young American who happens to be a two-tour Vietnam veteran and has performed a selfless act. It's the kind of schmaltz that appeals to the American public and is the kind of media opportunity that is the lifeblood of career politicians.

"Right now, both the senators from Iowa and the Williamses' local congressman are clamoring to climb on the political bandwagon. And I'll wager your .357 that they talked to the senior senator from Georgia, who just happens to be the president pro tem of the senate, and who sure as hell doesn't want to miss out on this opportunity to showcase you to his constituency back in your home state.

"This thing is probably spreading, politically speaking, like a wildfire back home. As I said, the military has a huge black eye with the public right now. You can rest assured that they want to be in favor with the president and the congress and will jump though hoops to please them.

"And perhaps you have no any idea how much." The colonel rose and went around his desk. He opened the top drawer, and pulled out another piece of paper. As he handed it to Smitty he said, "I never showed you this, right?"

Smitty took the paper from the colonel, skipped over the official headers and other military mumbo-jumbo from the army chief of staff at the top, and began to read:

General Martin,

Understand that First Lieutenant Kevin Smith has not signed reenlistment papers as of 2 January 1970. Imperative, repeat—imperative that you attend to this immediately. President is waiting to extend personal congratulations, re: philanthropic incident.

Work directly with Colonel Perkins to whom I have given personal recommendations and guidance to achieve this soonest. Notify this office upon completion. All reasonable conditions required to accomplish objective will be granted.

Smitty handed the paper back to the colonel. "Thank you for showing me that, sir. Even if I never saw it." Smitty paused. "But I don't see that it changes anything."

The colonel slid the paper back into his drawer, came around his desk, and sat back down next to Smitty.

"You know, on my first tour, there were a couple of sergeants who performed one of the first SOG missions into Laos. The chief SOG had them flown to Saigon for a personal briefing with General Westmoreland, who was so impressed that he asked them if there was anything he could do for them. One said he always wanted to be a pilot. So the general instantly gave him a battlefield commission to captain and sent him stateside to pilot school. The other said he'd always wanted to be a combat commander so that he could use his experience to save lives in the field. The general gave him a battlefield commission to captain also, but remembered his reason and took a liking to him.

"Do you know where the two captains are today?"

"No, sir."

"Well the one who wanted to be a pilot is still a captain and will probably retire as a major. But the one the general took a liking to is now a lieutenant colonel, is slated for early promotion to colonel, and will probably retire as a two-star general at least."

The colonel gripped Smitty's arm with sufficient force to cause him to turn so that they were in direct eye contact. "The point is, Lieutenant, this is a chance for you to grab the golden ring. Politically speaking, you play this right and it could net you dinner at the White House. With your record, possibly even the MOH. You can't pass it by."

The general looked at Smitty, frowned, and said shrewdly, "And it might open a few locked doors in your search for the truth. Now, son, before you decide not to reenlist, don't you think you ought to listen to what the colonel and the general have to say?"

"And when do I discuss assassinating the major with the president? Over the salad course? Or do I wait till dessert?" Smitty asked sarcastically.

"Hmm, I see your point." The colonel went back to his desk, picked up the pack of cigarettes and tossed it to Smitty.

"This will require some thought. With your permission?" The colonel gestured toward the phone. Smitty nodded and the colonel picked up the receiver and dialed. Colonel Perkins answered and the colonel asked him to inform the general that Smitty had arrived.

He listened briefly and hung up. "Let's get the general in here and see if we can noodle on this solution together. He's a fair man."

"That's fine, sir, but with your permission, I'd like to call my father and General Chuck Martin first."

"Be my guest, I'll wait outside."

Smitty made his calls and was damn glad he did. Dad told him that this reenlistment would probably be tied to furthering his education and added some sage advice about the situation in general, but General Chuck was more specific. Smitty now knew how to structure the deal, especially when, politically speaking, he was holding all the cards. In point of fact, as Chuck had pointed out, he owned the fucking deck.

"I think we have the makings of a deal, Lieutenant." General Ben Martin leaned forward and stubbed out his cigarette in the ashtray on the colonel's desk. He picked up the tablet on which he had been making notes and began to read.

"You've agreed to reenlist for six years. In return, the army agrees to the following plan:

"Your current tour in Vietnam will be extended for approximately ninety days in your current position at your current rank of first lieutenant. On or about mid-March 1970, you'll depart Vietnam for a permanent change of duty station to the Pentagon as a general's aide for approximately six months, advanced to the reserve rank of captain and a regular army rank of second lieutenant. Commensurate with this duty station change, your security classification will be changed to Q level and your military service records in Vietnam permanently sealed and classified.

"During this transitional time frame at the Pentagon, you will have two primary missions. The first will be to prepare and take whatever preliminary steps are required to gain admission to a university in the fall. The second will be to appear at the White House for a formal dinner with the president, at a time to be mutually agreed upon, at which you will be awarded the Distinguished Service Cross in a preplanned media opportunity.

"Upon your receiving written confirmation of acceptance to a university, the United States Army agrees to place you on paid academic leave, minus two weeks per year on active duty at the army's discretion, until such time as you complete your degree requirements in a technical field. After graduation, a diploma accompanied by transcripts will be the accepted evidence of completion. At which time you will be restored to active service with a regular army commission at the rank of captain."

"And probably be a brigadier general by the time you are forty," Colonel Wilson added thoughtfully.

"And probably be a brigadier general by the time you are forty," General Martin echoed. "Or higher."

"Congratulations, son, and welcome to your new career," the general said warmly, as they shook hands.

"Thank you, sir," Smitty said.

General Martin flipped over a sheet, nodded, and read aloud.

"The following stipulations accompany this agreement:

"One. On or about March 1970, with the rotation of Lieutenant Smith to a Pentagon billet, his replacement is to be Second Lieutenant Gary Garvey, who will be promoted to first lieutenant on assuming this role.

"Two. On or about March 1970, Master Sergeant Michael Billingsly will be reassigned to a senior instructor's position at Fort Bragg, North Carolina, as a sergeant major.

"Three. While he is attending college, the relationship of Lieutenant Smith to the United States Army will, by mutual agreement, remain Q-level classified by both Lieutenant Smith and the United States Army to guard against exposure of the incident in the Mang Yang Pass, and specifically the details surrounding the death of Major William P. Gates.

"Four. The agreements made herein are to be placed in Lieutenant's Smith service record and covered under his new security clearance."

The general flipped the tablet shut and passed it across to the colonel. "Have this typed up ASAP and ready for signature by 1600 hours today. I'll go talk to the Pentagon and fill them in on the details."

Turning to Smitty, General Wilson said, "I must congratulate you personally on your agreement. You were smart enough to know you had the army over a huge barrel and that they would basically honor any request to satisfy the president's political agenda." He paused, then added, "And I was especially pleased to see that you took pains to take care of your friends. Shows selflessness and will probably be the key thing that will seal the deal."

The general patted him on the arm and left.

The colonel blew out a cloud of smoke rings. "You don't have to tell me this Lieutenant, but what did your father and that air force general tell you?"

"Well, sir," Smitty began, "General Chuck pretty much said the same thing as you. That I was in the catbird seat politically and that I should treat this like a union negotiation."

"I'm afraid I don't understand," the colonel replied.

"Ask for twice what you want, and be willing to settle for half. The general figured that if they would send the messenger halfway around the world to talk to me, that it was to do whatever it took to keep me in the service, and create a political win for the army. This agreement satisfies both."

"And your father?"

"Dad was a little more philosophical," Smitty said with a smile.

"And what bit of wisdom did your father impart?"

"When you have them by the balls, their hearts and minds will follow."

"Old sergeants," the colonel said, shaking his head.

"Yes, sir," Smitty said.

When Smitty was alone, he smiled to himself. He felt good about the pact he had just made. The three-month extension was his idea, especially after Colonel Perkins told him that the White House ceremony would not, or could not, occur until the spring due to the president's current agenda. There were military plans in the offing that it would be politically expedient for Smitty to be part of before he left. Also, Colonel Perkins had been adamant that these kinds of events played better to the media if held in the spring when the cherry blossoms and such were in bloom and the country was in an optimistic mood.

Originally, Colonel Perkins had wanted Smitty reassigned within a week—Smitty suspected that he was worried about his getting killed and screwing up his plans—but Colonel Wilson had overridden this and supported Smitty when he stated that he wished to remain until March because he wouldn't feel right about pulling out on Hogs, Mike, and the rest of the team, and leaving them holding the bag. In order to get this condition, he had to agree to the six months in Washington to, as the colonel put it, be available for showcasing on the Washington cocktail circuit.

The college agenda was a given if Smitty stayed in. Colonel Perkins came with that part of the package all prearranged, including the rank and reinstatement conditions. Smitty had added the security classification and the nondisclosure of his army status while there. Based on his brief experience with Dinky at home, if there was one thing he was certain of, it was that he would have a much easier time of it if those spoiled college assholes who were vehemently against the war did not know he was there to "feather his own nest."

The conditions for Hogs and Mike were to ensure that they did not get lost in the vacuum after he was gone. Especially Mike, no matter what, Smitty wasn't going to let Mike get fucked over again.

Smitty knew that it was time to quit hiding out here from life and to go home and face the thing he was most afraid of—the uncertain future. What Smitty did not tell the colonel was that he had no intention of keeping certain parts of the deal he had just agreed to. Specifically, he had no intention of going on to spend four years with those pampered Joe College jerk offs, but had wisely kept silent on this key point for now.

Mainly because, although he was not looking forward to the six months in Washington as a general's aide and did not for a moment believe it was a great career move, the position did have one major attraction: it came with a very high security clearance that would allow him to poke around the military records section and maybe match a few of the jigsaw pieces that had so far remained distant cousins in his life.

"Last mission, 1LT." Mike, Smitty, and Captain Bartkowski were waiting for the evac helicopter that would take them back to Pleiku, where Smitty would finish his packing and be on a transport for the land of the big PX for the last time. Mike corrected himself, "Excuse me, after this you'll be 1CAP."

"1CAP?" Smitty raised an eyebrow.

"You're setting new boundaries, boss. First little prick that I ever let make it to 1LT and now up to captain. I imagine before I die I'll be calling you 1GEN or some such nonsense." Mike spat out the cigar butt he'd been chewing on. "But you'll always be my whaleshit 1LT, no matter what."

"I'll settle for that," Smitty said. "Thanks for hanging back, Captain, and riding out on the last chopper with me."

"Um, yes, I'm glad to do it," Ron answered. Smitty assumed his nervousness came from the unfamiliarity that comes with having been away from the shit for so long.

This moment had been coming for months. Smitty knew it, Mike knew it, and Ron knew it. Unfortunately, Hogsbreath did not.

No sooner had the ink dried on the deal than Hoggie was killed on an incursion mission into Laos. His team had reached the evac LZ and were climbing aboard the helicopter when Bacon Breath, true to the SOG motto of the team lead being the last one on, had taken a round through the back of the head. He was dead before they could pull him onboard.

Smitty was going to miss him, but he'd be in good company. Arlington now contained the remains of a lot of friends he'd made over the last two-plus years in this land, where a war should never have been fought in the first place.

Big Walt had become a casualty of sorts also. He was released three days after the final agreement on Smitty's deal was approved by the Army Chief of Staff—and God knows who else—and immediately took a bus to Miami where Stan, true to his word, helped the big guy find a job and an apartment. Within two weeks he was back inside, busted by an undercover officer when he tried to buy grass. Stan had promised to do what he could, but he had written in his letter it didn't look good.

As the days grew short, Smitty could at least take comfort from the fact that the SOG mission had finally been taken seriously. The invasion of Cambodia, rumored for many months, was finally under way in March of 1970, led by regular army and marine units into VC supply strongholds located just inside the Cambodian border. They were discovering thousands of hand weapons, hundreds of mobile artillery pieces, and hundreds of tons of rice. And if they had been able to clear the bureaucratic Teaberry Shuffle with the dumb-shit Laotian ambassador quicker, they would have captured thousands of VC troops that had narrowly escaped beyond the twenty-five mile incursion limits set by the dickless president.

Blackbird's drunken soliloquy of almost two years ago echoed in Smitty's ears. "If those fat-assed Washington bureaucrats and World War II vintage fighting generals would forget about borderlines and concentrate on supply lines, this war would be over in six months. Take away their supplies, you take away their ability to make war. Then what have you got? Peace."

But Smitty knew in his heart that General Martin was correct; the American involvement in Vietnam would wind down. The anti-Vietnam sentiment was far too strong now to be changed back.

Although the SOG concepts of strangulation of the supply lines, which seemed so foreign two years ago, were now universally accepted, with regular army and marine units participating daily in border incursion missions, Smitty had serious doubts about its long-term success.

The Vietnamization policy would be implemented, but the combination of feudal infighting between the South Vietnamese villages, lack of uniform resolve, insecurity, and the incompetence of the current government compared to the strong will of the North would doom it. The South Vietnamese would hang on, but eventually the South would fall to the North, and the war would be lost

Smitty felt sadness, not only for his friends, but for the thousands of grunts who had died uselessly while conventional-thinking generals and bumbling political leaders based their decisions on archaic battle strategies and played war games with young American lives.

Smitty suspected that it was some kind of perverse mathematical formula that had been replayed down through history numerous times. The politically inexperienced, led by military incompetents, equaled the deaths of thousands of their country's most prized possessions—the young. Of the 150 guys Smitty had gone through Bragg with two-plus years ago, there were not enough left alive to field a good game of pickup football.

"Reminiscing, Lieutenant?" Ron asked.

"Yes, sir, Captain," Smitty said. He thought of Mike's rating system for lieutenants, applying it to Ron. He smiled silently to himself, beating back an impulse to add a salute and another "sir."

"I did the same thing myself after each of my tours. I suspect I'll be doing the same when my last tour ends in June, especially since I know that I won't be coming back this time. 'Course I should brain you, since I'm going to have to take over for you until I rotate home in June, all because your friend Hogs didn't make it."

In point of fact, Ron had already taken over. With Hogs' death and the scale-down in the war, Ron had assumed direct command of the force and would continue in this role once Smitty was gone. The colonel had not deemed it necessary to replace Hogs, electing instead to reconsolidate the positions. Technically, Ron reported to him, but Smitty had not made a big deal of it since he was leaving. But his glibness about Hogs and other Arlington-bound friends irritated Smitty; it was an irritation of which he'd had enough.

Smitty's reaction surprised Ron and happened before either he or Mike could take any preventive action. Smitty spun suddenly, and with the full two years of useless deaths and futility behind his fist, punched Ron squarely on the chin. Given the equipment he was carrying, Ron landed in the elephant grass with all the finesse of a shot-put.

"What did you do that for?" Ron asked, as Mike helped him up.

Smitty looked at the captain coldly, then turned away and lit a cigarette.

"For that good man Porky Pecker," Mike answered. "Captain, if I were you, I wouldn't be making any morgue jokes on 1LT right about now. I think he's a bit wired."

"Sorry," Ron said. "Hogsbreath was a good man and a good soldier. I'll miss him." Ron finished his apology, then walked around Smitty until they were facing each other, and stuck out his hand.

"And a good friend," Smitty added, as he took the captain's hand. "Sorry."

"Okay, girls, do you want to continue to just hold hands or will you kiss and make up?" Mike said with just the right light touch to relieve the tension.

The sound of the approaching helicopters separated them as they made preparations to climb aboard for the last time. The evac was proceeding like clockwork. Smitty, Mike, Ron, and two replacements Smitty didn't know by name were on the last chopper as it lifted off.

The helicopter was only three hundred feet in the air when an explosion rocked it. It immediately starting spiraling downward and crashed into the top of the jungle canopy. The impact tossed Smitty and Sergeant Mike, who were sitting across from each other, out of the aircraft like spent M-60 shell casings.

Smitty bounced through trees, snapping two-inch limbs like matchsticks. He landed feet-first in a stream approximately fifteen feet wide and four feet deep with lush jungle overgrowth on both banks. The last sound he heard was not that of a branch cracking off. It was similar, but it had that hollow internal sound that only a bone breaking can make.

Smitty felt the pain all the way up to his throat. By the sound and the numbing agony, he knew that his left leg was broken, probably in several places.

The ripples in the stream from his forced high dive had barely begun to recede when he heard the helicopter crash in a teeth-gnashing, metal-twisting impact a hundred yards away. It exploded in a ball of flame.

Smitty heard voices to his left, Vietnamese voices shouting loudly in excitement as they ran toward the downed aircraft. Unfortunately for Smitty, they would have to come right past him. The aircraft was to his right and to reach it, they would more than likely traverse the footpath located two feet from the bank of the stream.

Ignoring the pain in his shattered appendage, Smitty silently slid his pack from his shoulders and let it sink to the bottom. He dragged himself awkwardly to the bank's vegetation, praying that it would provide sufficient cover to shield him from the approaching VC.

By their sounds, they were no more than fifteen feet away when Smitty took a deep breath and immersed himself in the water, using the roots growing from the bank to pull himself down to the bottom. He surfaced behind the growth overhanging the water next to the bank, then he let out a breath and waited, his heart pounding like a marching band's bass drum. He was certain that the VC could hear it too.

They were just above him when they stopped. They talked rapidly among themselves, then a burst of AK-47 fire opened up with a nerve-shattering staccato sound no more than three feet directly above Smitty's head. The rounds peppered the stream six feet away, precisely where Smitty had dropped his pack. One of the rounds must have hit one of his canteens. The implosion produced air bubbles which haphazardly made their way to the surface—just like air escaping from a man's lungs if he had been shot.

They laughed sadistically and fired again. The firing continued for five seconds then ceased as suddenly as it had begun. Leaving a guard there, Smitty assumed, in case the body surfaced—no doubt so they could shoot it again—the balance of the patrol moved off. Ten seconds of silence followed, during which Smitty was fighting desperately to control his fear and keep his teeth from chattering.

The silence was replaced by the sound of raindrops falling lightly on the overgrowth. The rain became more focused. Smitty suddenly realized that it wasn't rain at all; the little bastard was taking a leak right into the overgrowth above him. The liquid made loud plopping sounds as it dripped slowly off the reeds and mixed with the water in the stream right by his head.

AK-47 fire erupted from the vicinity of the smoldering helicopter, followed by screams of men dying in agony. More sadistic laughter was followed by the sound of a shouted command. Smitty's erstwhile piss pelter moved off at a run. Smitty was too paralyzed with fear to do much of anything at all.

In the middle of Cambodia, in the middle of the Vietnam War that no one knew how to win, and Smitty didn't want to be in, it was, as his dad had said all those years ago back in Dearfield, the last moment.

He waited in pulse-pounding silence, knowing in his heart that he was soon to become another MIA statistic. They'd never find him. The sound of the gunfire and the shrieks of agony were confirmation that all the rest were dead. With his wounds incapacitating him, all he could do was lie here until he succumbed to hunger or thirst or both. The evac had been at dusk and the jungle was now pitch black, the darkness magnifying every sound and multiplying every fear in his mind.

Smitty was losing his fight to maintain consciousness. He was in excruciating pain, and his leg was starting to go numb. His mind was slipping into the land of irrational thoughts. In what he was sure were the last moments of his life, his thoughts turned to his father and those words said so long ago to a naive kid on a hospital bed in England. Smitty made peace with his God and, as unconsciousness overtook him, prayed that despite all his sins, He would be merciful.

Smitty was having horrible dreams. He'd had them before. Each time he was facing his secret childhood fear, being critically wounded and left behind to die. He'd had the dream many times, and in many variations over the years, but in the end, he would wake up and thank God that it was only a dream. Only this time it wasn't a dream. It was the reality of Vietnam . . . or any other war.

Smitty dragged himself from a pain-racked unconsciousness and glanced around quickly. His first thought was that he had gone blind; ebony blackness was all around him.

But the stench of the river, the fog of incinerated fuel, the pain in his leg, and the smell of death brought him back to reality. He lifted the canvas cover on his wristwatch and could just barely read the time by the light of fluorescent dial: 0440 hours. He'd been out pretty close to eight hours.

Cobwebs, there were cobwebs all around him. Smitty raised his arm and fanned it back and forth in a futile attempt to break free of them; but they were still there. He tried shaking his head to clear them, and almost passed out again from the nausea. Slowly, painfully, he raised his arm, parted the undergrowth, but could see no more than before. The pain in his leg had gone from unbearable to a dull steady ache that felt like the aftereffects of a botched amputation. The rest of his body felt as though it had been used for a blocking dummy. He was still alive and aware of his situation, but one thing was certain: hell had come to breakfast and brought its lunch pail.

In the darkest recesses of the mind is that secret fear of death that no one talks about, and everyone denies steadfastly if pressed. Smitty had reached that point eight hours ago when he was certain that was his last moment of life. He knew that no fear could ever be that bad again.

He'd bottomed out, and even if he did not survive, he knew instinctively that he could never again be that scared. Maybe God made human beings with a built-in switch that fooled the mind into believing that after a certain point, death was a preferable alternative. If that was the case, Smitty was ready. He was afraid, but no longer terrified. He was frightened, but no longer panicked.

His brain was working again, but the big question was, what now? It would be light in several hours. But what then? Smitty was trying hard to think, but purposeful thought kept eluding him. His fantasies were comforting but not helpful.

Smitty was at the point of giving up when he heard his dad's voice from almost a dozen years ago in the hospital in Dearfield:

> *Son, there's nothing wrong with being afraid; it's what you do when you're afraid that counts. Fear left unchecked magnifies itself in your mind until it can quite literally paralyze your thoughts or actions. So, when you feel scared admit it—an admitted problem is half solved—and say to yourself, what do I have to do to resolve it? If you follow that approach, you'll always be able to think yourself out of a tight spot.*

Smitty remembered the words, and his objections, and his father's answer from a simpler time when he was just plain Kevin.

> *You find yourself in a no-win position, and you have made up your mind that there is no way out, you've examined the facts and come to the conclusion that there isn't a way that you can get out alive. So, do the next best thing: make peace with God, then take as many of the bastards with you as you can. And by doing that, a lot of times you'll come up with a solution that you didn't think of before. The point is that as long as you keep thinking and reasoning there's always a chance. When you stop, there's none.*

Dad was right. He wasn't done for, not yet—not by a long shot, not as long as he kept thinking. So, he asked himself, what was the first thing he needed to do? The answer was obvious; his assault weapon had landed God knows where, so he needed to come up with some sort of alternative weapon.

Smitty pushed aside the overgrowth, moved out to the middle of the stream, reached down, and grabbed hold of the shoulder straps on his field pack. He dragged the field pack to the edge of the stream, then fifteen feet to the left, until he felt a small clearing on the bank. Moving in agonizing slow motion, lest the VC still camped in the area hear his movements, Smitty slowly lifted the pack out of the water and set it quietly on the bank.

He hoisted himself up on the bank and dragged himself and the pack across the path six feet to the underbrush on the other side. He reached in as far as possible, quietly snapped off a branch, dragged himself back to the edge of the stream, and used it to cover the traces of his exit and path to his hiding place.

Fortunately, the important contents of his pack were basically still intact. He had spare rounds for the Magnum and shotgun shells for the whippet in waterproof pouches, whose watertight seals had not been perforated when the VC used the pack for target practice. As he suspected, they had gotten one of the canteens, but had not hit the other. The water was a blessing to his parched throat.

He used his knife and cut off the top half of his fatigue shirt, then used it to dry off the Magnum and the whippet, and inserted fresh rounds in both. His next thought was to look around for materials to build a splint, but the darkness and the unfamiliar surroundings discouraged him.

Since he could do nothing more until the faint light of morning, he concealed himself as best he could and asked himself if there were other actions that he could take. On satisfying himself that there were none, he settled down to wait.

The minutes seemed to tick by like hours. Despite his most fervent attempts to stay focused, Smitty found himself once more reminiscing; only this time it was about all the friends he had known and seen die over the past two years.

The nameless GI that had died in his arms on his first day; Blackbird; his first team lead; Whippoorwill, who took his place and died for the effort; Doggie, the ladykiller; Tom Sawyer, so baby-faced and so young; and of course Hogs, who had the courage of a lion but the heart of a social worker. Images of hundreds of others that he knew casually by name or face popped into his head.

His thoughts turned to Glenda and Linda, his first love and his true love—would there ever be others? Frenchy, Big Walt, and LZ and the misfortunes that had befallen them flashed into his mind. No matter what the outcome of his life, theirs would be forever changed. It seemed like a hundred years ago that they had been a naïve young foursome punching out rednecks in an Alabama bar. Could they ever have been that young? Could their lives have ever been that innocent? Never again.

And now, it was Ron and Mike's turn. It seemed that everywhere he went, death followed.

It reminded him of a time when he was younger and had sat outside his father's office as he chewed out a young airman for getting drunk and punching a policeman. The E-2 was trying to alibi his way out of it by saying that if he'd not been drinking then he would not have punched the policeman. Dad would have none of it and said no matter what the circumstances, he was responsible for his actions and therefore also responsible for the consequences of those actions.

That was the thought that brought Smitty back to reality. He was responsible for his actions—in the past, in the present, and in the future. Not his parents, not his friends, not his loves. Time to stop feeling sorry for himself and start figuring a way out of this mess. A quick check of his watch showed that it was now 0620 hours. It was no longer as dark as the Earl of Hell's waistcoat, but only several shades of gray lighter, which was enough to do a visual on his leg and assess the damage to the rest of his body.

The inspection did not bode well. His leg was black and blue well above the knee and was swollen to about twice the normal size. It was about the same color as a bruised banana when it was peeled and just about as tender and mushy. He thought that the tibia and fibula were both broken and his ankle had multiple fractures. The rest of the damage was, comparatively speaking, manageable. His ribs ached and Smitty was sure there were fractures. And though his torso ached, the injury wasn't incapacitating.

But the whole question might be academic. Smitty picked up the sounds of movement about forty yards away. It was faint but distinguishable. Someone was working his way slowly in his direction and taking great pains to disguise it. At first, Smitty thought there was only one, but he listened hard and picked up the sound of a second. Obviously, they knew he was wounded and were taking their time.

Smitty could understand why they were in no hurry. His injuries had affected him to the point that he sure as hell wasn't going to hop up and bolt like Bugs Bunny.

Smitty readied his weapons for what he was sure would be the last fight of his life. He checked the chamber on the Magnum to assure that it had six rounds, then silently placed it on the ground in front of him with two regular grenades and four golfballs that had survived intact and dry. He picked up the whippet, braced himself against his pack for the recoil, and aimed it in the direction of the approaching enemy. Smitty figured that he could get both of the advancing VC with both barrels of the shotgun when they tried to flush him.

Then he could drag himself and his weapons to another spot that he could make out twenty yards away and wait to ambush the reinforcements that were sure to follow the point duo with the grenades. If the patrol were fewer than ten, his odds were fifty-fifty of surviving this first engagement. More than ten, and his chances were considerably less. In the end, he was sure that other VC in the area would get him, but as his dad had counseled many years ago in Dearfield, he was going to take as many of the bastards with him as possible.

Smitty made a vow to himself that no matter what, he was not going to surrender and wouldn't get captured. If he had to, he'd put a round through his own head. The decision time for that resolution was near. Smitty could clearly hear but not yet see his attackers through the dense jungle. By his estimate, they were now less than ten yards away.

They began to move faster, crawling the last twenty feet at twice their former rate. Smitty readied his weapon, braced himself, and prepared to fight for his life.

The growth parted suddenly four feet in front of him and Smitty's finger began to squeeze the trigger.

He stopped.

Kneeling, a head poked itself into his lair and said, "Hi there." The ice-cool voice belonged to a man who was truly living up the nickname Blackbird had given him years back: Crazy Fuckin' Polack.

Smitty didn't fire the shotgun, but neither could he put it down. His body was absolutely, totally frozen, like a Neanderthal suddenly discovered in a block of ice.

Ron crawled on his knees to Smitty, waved his hand back and forth in front of him and said, "Would you mind terribly putting that cannon down? It might go off and give away our position. To say nothing of what it would do for Mrs. Bartkowski's little boy Ronny's matinee idol good looks."

Smitty remained rigid as Ron slowly peeled the weapon from his resisting hands. He opened the breech, checked the weapon, and frowned. "Pointing a loaded shotgun at a superior officer is a court-martial offense. I always knew you didn't like me, Irish." He shook his head. "And this time I've got a witness."

"1LT, what the fuck are you doing sittin' here on your ass?" Mike's face appeared. "I don't mean to usurp your authority, boss, but there's one place we definitely need to be."

"Where's that?" Smitty managed to reply weakly.

"Out the fuck of here," Mike boomed.

"How bad, Lieutenant?" Ron asked.

"Leg's busted, probably in several places," Smitty said.

Ron looked briefly at Smitty's leg and winced at the ghastly color. Mike looked and flinched also. "We don't have time to splint it, Irish. We need to get out of this area. There's a VC patrol of roughly three hundred camped about two hundred yards from here, and they're bringing in more to search for possible survivors as soon as it's light."

"Mike, fuck the formality, pick him up, toss him over your shoulder, and let's move," Ron said.

"How did you find me?" Smitty gasped in pain as Mike dragged him as gently as possible from his hiding spot to a small clearing next to the bank of the stream. With Ron's help, Mike hoisted Smitty over his shoulder like a bag of coal.

"Mike saw you come down, so we knew approximately where to look." Ron gathered Smitty's weapons, did a quick camouflage job on Smitty's lair and quietly lowered the pack back into the water. He set off on the footpath toward where Smitty had heard the helicopter crash.

"From there, I just followed my nose." Mike grunted.

"Your nose?"

"Yeah, boss, my nose." Mike said. "I told the captain I could smell your whaleshit 1LT ass easier than a blue tick hound could find his next quail."

The three of them plodded along for the next two days with Smitty steadily getting worse. His leg was completely numb, although Ron and Mike had tried to set it with bamboo poles as best they could. As a result of his initial injury and the internal bleeding, Smitty was slipping into shock and intermittent bouts of unconsciousness.

To Smitty, it was like those times in high school when he would drop off to sleep during a boring lecture. He could hear what the teacher was saying, but the words and the meaning were lost in an unintelligible jumble.

Mike's descent had left him with bumps and bruises, but no broken bones. He had landed squarely on his ass. Ron, after having been forcibly ejected from the aircraft headfirst, had a broken left wrist to show for his less-than-perfect landing twenty-five yards downstream of Smitty's entry.

They had played cat-and-mouse with the VC patrols, who, after two days, apparently having satisfied themselves that there were indeed no survivors, had ceased their pursuit and circle patrols. Somehow, the pilot had managed to get a radio message off before the chopper went down and U.S. aircraft could be seen crisscrossing the skies. They had watched from a hill as the rescue team landed four miles away and recovered the bodies from the crash site. Ron, Smitty and Mike were the only survivors.

Incredibly, Mike managed to get the attention of the rescue chopper by using his knife from the top of a tree to reflect sunlight. The chopper had flown on by, damping their spirits, but returned three hours later at dusk, on its way back to the original crash site, and dropped them a radio, packed to absorb the impact, C rations, ammunition, and medical supplies.

On its return, after communicating with Ron by radio, the helicopter dropped three McGuire rigs, and Smitty was quickly tied in. Mike and Ron immediately hooked themselves up to the two additional harnesses, and the helicopter lifted off with the three of them suspended below the craft.

The cooler air above the jungle brought Smitty around. He looked over at Mike and weakly gave him the thumbs-up. A response Mike acknowledged, as usual, with the finger.

The lights of the firebase at Plei Djereng were in sight, and Smitty was never so happy to see anything in his life. He made a promise to not miss a visit to the chaplain for a month of Sundays. The helicopter slowed above the landing pad in a stabilized hover so that Smitty, Ron, and Mike could be unhitched.

Through his pain-wracked brain, Smitty heard the sounds of rumbling in the distance, a rumbling that grew louder the closer they got to the ground. Two soldiers were hurriedly helping him out of the harness, when one screamed suddenly, "Oh God, mortars. The bastards are mortaring us."

And then, to paraphrase Billy Shakespeare . . . the rest was silence.

CHAPTER SEVENTEEN

The silence was actually anything but. It started slowly, with a noise here and a sound there, almost like the symphony tuning up for a performance—disparate sounds that had no meaning and built slowly until it was a calliope of noises that together sounded like a combination of a one-man band, a child's first drum set, and a dentist's drill. Or, it could be a cross between twisting metal from a car crash and fingernails scratching slowly down a blackboard. Or, maybe a medley of a screeching baby with an overamped electric guitar, and a jackhammer. These were just some of the orchestrated reverberations that Smitty had singled out in the din.

The accompanying visual part was the worst kind of nightmare. Every time Smitty tried to focus, tiny amoebas raced past his eyes at light speed and then, as quickly as they arrived, were replaced by a different set traveling at twice the velocity of the last ones in a different direction, before he could concentrate on any of them at all. It was like looking directly into the sun at high noon.

Nothing mattered in this personal hell. There was no time, just the pain-filled nausea of a perpetual purgatory, alternating between ear-splitting, mind-numbing clamor and the disorientation of being in the absolute and total abyss of nothingness. Maybe this was death, and given the sins of his mortal existence, this was to be his permanent penance for the transgressions of a life lived amid so much violence and death.

And then, as constant as the collective noise and disorientation had been, it stopped.

The silence was unnerving, the stillness deafening, and then Smitty was awake or, more likely, having one hellaciously realistic dream. But this manifestation was different—it came with side effects, such as fragrance. He could detect a whiff of ladies' perfume. As his eyes came into focus, he thought he must be hallucinating, because he was looking straight at a female ear, a delicately shaped ear with a gold earbob in it. Smitty glanced down and caught a glimpse of a button-down white blouse with a sufficient enough amount of cleavage showing to make Kristie look like Olive Oyl.

Maybe he had passed through some type of heavenly portal and was now in the land of promise on the other side. Or maybe this was his true reward for a life spent doing the right thing and fighting for lost causes. Forget the heavenly harp crap, he'd take an eternity's supply of booze and oversexed broads, throw in a T-bone or two, and a couple of beers, and he could get used to this death stuff.

Instinctively, like a drowning man grasping desperately for the last life raft, Smitty reached for her bursting chest and was instantly dismayed to learn that this particular apparition came with a set of rules.

"What are you doing, Lieutenant? Stop that!" a female voice said indignantly. Smitty learned that his sense of touch was now working also as he felt the sting on his wrists as she slapped his hands away. The voice softened to one Smitty would have imagined went with the elegant lobe. "Besides, you'll pull your IVs if you keep that up."

From somewhere in the background came a heavier authoritative voice that, in Smitty's stupefied state, sounded like a football coach barking signals to a forlorn team. "Why don't you lighten up a bit, nurse. The poor son of a bitch is going to die anyway."

Smitty felt as though someone had just marched hobnailed over his grave. Whoever said that, Smitty swore he was going to find him and make him eat his words. He vowed angrily to himself that he wasn't going back to sleep. That was a certainty. He wasn't through yet, not by a long shot, and as long as he stayed awake, he couldn't die.

His angry internal tirade was interrupted by that same feminine voice. "I'll be right back."

Smitty watched from glazed eyes as the platinum blonde nurse seemed to disappear into a haze of fog and cobwebs. Moments later, the nurse reappeared like a plane suddenly flying free of the clouds and explained, "I had to wait until the doctor left so I could close the door."

She leaned in over Smitty's face, undid four buttons on her blouse, reached inside and unsnapped the clasp on her bra. As her huge breasts tumbled free, she cooed softly, "There you go, Lieutenant." She took his hands and placed both of them on her chest. Smitty could feel the nipples grow on contact but could not get his hands to move or caress them.

The symphony was tuning up again, apparently for the "William Tell Overture." He could no longer feel her softness, nor see her beauty. The materialization was fading like a desert mirage. The disorientation of before was returning.

The hallucination of the nurse faded into insignificance as the hullabaloo cranked back up to a crescendo. It made "Seventy-Six Trombones" sound like a hymn on Palm Sunday.

But one thing was certain: Smitty was not going to sleep, even if he was already dead and his penance for eternity was to have to live with this cross between the "Anvil Chorus" and Woodstock running amok in his head.

Eventually, the all-out free-for-all of calamity in his head began to dim. It softened to a low, irritating hum. Eventually, the buzz began to develop a pitch, with high and low tones. The tones began to take on a melodic, voicelike quality.

Smitty was suspicious. He'd been lured once into the land of imagination by what he was sure was the devil and was mindful of the fact that the second trip would be fraught with greater temptations. Smitty was sure that there was a mind game going on here.

Maybe the melodic tones were VC, maybe he'd been captured and drugged, maybe a lot of things, but he was sure that he was going to understand what that tone was, why it was there, and exactly what it was trying to get him to do before he let on that he knew it existed.

He focused all his thoughts on that tone. Gradually he began to make out sounds of letters, then words, then phrases and eventually whole sentences. He had it now—it was a voice—and it seemed to prattle on incessantly like a manic three-year-old.

The voice was saying words and sentences, but they didn't seem to make sense, and Smitty was having a hard time understanding. Using the same technique of identification that had worked so well before, Smitty again focused exclusively on the words, trying to pick up just one that would give him an insight into who this asshole was who seemed to talk incessantly and not be able to shut the fuck up.

This was a harder task. It seemed to take twice again as long as it did to identify that it was a voice in the first place. It came painfully, total focused concentration causing the philharmonic to start up again for short periods. But Smitty was determined. He just had to know.

His first breakthrough came some indeterminable time later when he was suddenly able to distinguish the fact that it was a male voice. A male voice that he could almost—but not quite—identify.

His next insight came when he understood the meaning of the first word, "Homestead." A short time later, he absorbed his second, "Dearfield" that seemed to be the key that unlocked the door to his mind. The words and meaning came more rapidly now, and Smitty didn't know where he was but was sure he was somewhere safe. The voice was methodically reciting Smitty's entire life story—from Savannah to England to Miami, then back again to Savannah.

This voice seemed to have personal insight. It was recounting his life quite accurately. Too accurately, with too many microscopic facts, to be some brainwashing technique of the VC. But it seemed to be stuck on replay as Smitty began to recognize the same story over again. The question was, who would know that many minute details, and why was he constantly repeating them.

The answer came to him so quickly that he was angry with himself for not getting it sooner. The voice belonged to Dad. Now that he had it, the dam burst.

He tried desperately to tell his father that he could hear and understand. He could swear his mouth was moving, but the voice would make no sounds, and the words just wouldn't come out. Maybe he was injured and couldn't talk, or maybe the whole thing was a ghoulish nightmare.

That must be it, Smitty told himself. The whole thing was just a surreal bad dream, and all he had to do was go take a little snooze, wake up, and the whole thing would be over. Smitty willed himself to shut out the familiar voice of his dad, not to dream, and go back to sleep. He wasn't afraid of dying now, because when he awoke, the whole fuckin' thing would be over, his dad would be there, and he'd be fine. He was sure of it.

Smitty was awake. Although from first appearances, he thought he must be awake in the hereafter. Everything within the field of vision of his eyes was white—solid white.

"I'll be goddamned. Everything in heaven is white, but where are the fucking angels?" Smitty said out loud, feeling the absolute euphoria in hearing his own voice for the first time and knowing that he was truly awake—wherever he was.

A shadow with two horns loomed into his field of vision, followed closed by the head that had made it. "You're not in heaven, Lieutenant," a craggy-voiced woman said. Smitty made out a pointed nurse's cap, a chubby framework, and a face that could stop an eight-day clock. The woman smiled, which only made her seemed uglier. "You're in Walter Reed Hospital outside of Washington."

Smitty said with drug-induced honesty, "I know I can't be in heaven 'cause they wouldn't let no ugly bitch like you in there."

"That will do, Lieutenant," she said. "The fact that you're injured does not give you the right to be disrespectful to a superior officer."

"If I'm going to look like you, I'm not sure I want to grow any older." Maybe they had given him truth serum. He seemed to be saying whatever came into his mind.

The nurse glared at him and opened her mouth to respond, when a hand on her shoulder halted her.

"That will do, Major Swanson. I'll take over from here," a male voice said from behind.

The major turned and bowed slightly. "Yes, sir," She marched out of the room, her back ramrod straight.

"Good afternoon, Lieutenant." The speaker was an army doctor with a Friar Tuck hairdo, the beginnings of a midlife budge, and the rank of lieutenant colonel on his uniform collar under his white coat. He had a kind smile and a warm demeanor that Smitty found instantly disconcerting.

"Hi," Smitty said. The hovering doctor meant that this was serious, just how serious, Smitty needed to find out.

"I'm Colonel Evans. I'm assigned to your case. I overheard Major Swanson tell you where you are. I'm sure, Lieutenant, that right now everything seems totally confusing and disoriented. But it will come back to you a little bit at a time, I assure you. You seem much better today than when we talked before. Do you remember when that was?"

"Yesterday?" Smitty answered. He hadn't the faintest idea but he figured he might as well guess.

"Actually, Lieutenant, it was six days ago. In the interim, you've been awake off and on but only just momentarily. When I was sure you were out of the coma, I let you sleep as much as possible to build up your strength."

"Just how bad off am I?"

"Well, Lieutenant, we'll get to that in a moment. A few simple questions just to start, then we'll let you rest."

"Okay," Smitty said in a lifeless voice.

"Now then, the major told you that you were in Walter Reed. Do you know where that is?"

"Outside of DC, a few clicks from the five-sided military idiots' zoo," Smitty answered weakly.

The colonel chuckled. "Got any idea how you got here?"

"You tell me."

Ignoring his request, the colonel asked, "What's the last thing you remember?"

"Reenlisting last week," Smitty answered. A fit of coughing took him.

The doctor waited patiently for the hacking to subside. "And when was that?"

"Second week in January," Smitty said.

"I see." The doctor nodded and made notes on a clipboard. "Do you have any idea what today actually is?"

"Give me a hint," Smitty said.

"April 12, 1970."

"No shit?" Smitty began to breathe heavily just from the energy required to give such a forceful answer, and he could feel a sheen of sweat form on his brow.

"Exactly." The doctor made some more notes on his clipboard and signed it with a flourish.

Suddenly feeling his own incapacitation, Smitty asked, "Why can't I move?"

"Some of your shrapnel wounds required that we tie you to the bed to keep you from moving your head." On seeing the alarm rise in Smitty's eyes, the doctor patted him on the arm comfortingly. "Nothing to worry about, I assure you. Get some sleep. We'll talk more tomorrow." He left without further explanation.

Smitty lay in the bed in total confusion. How the hell did it get to be April 12? If the last thing he remembered was from January, what the hell had been going on the past four months? As he focused on this time warp, the band began to play again.

Smitty slept on and off again for the next week, getting stronger every day and remaining awake for longer periods of time. His bouts of consciousness had extended from a few minutes to several hours at a time. His sleep was painful, filled with disjointed ends of different events ramming themselves together in dreams. Some of the dreams made sense, some did not, but collectively they all were contributing to his memory recall, which in the past week had improved remarkably.

Sometimes he would awaken in the middle of a dream and answer a question from a past vision, almost like a person with an amputated leg who would wake up scratching the itch on the long-departed limb. Some of the dreams were horrific revisitings of the many missions and the many dead that were the result of being too young, with too much responsibility in Nam. He awakened from them in a screaming frenzy.

Others were erotic, recalling teenage lust with Glenda, momentary unbridled passion with Kristie, and that best of combinations when lust and passion merged in that all-too-rare union called love with Linda. Smitty had several times in the past week awoken in a cold sweat to find he had answered a cry from Hogs or a question from Linda, only to discover the attending nurse staring at him blankly from over the top of her magazine.

Smitty continued to have dreams about the nursey with the blonde hair, the delicate earlobes, the gold accentors, and the Jayne Mansfield chest. All of his dreams so far had been based on some reality from his past. Smitty was at a loss to understand why and where this particular phantasm came from. Was it the stimulus of Smitty's search for a perfect woman or merely the offshoot of an overworked and weary imagination? In his latest one, she was leaning over him smiling with her folded arms resting on the bed railing, which seemed to frame her most luscious assets and cause them to bulge even farther out from her torso.

"Hi, Lieutenant, welcome back," she said. "I'm Claire, Claire Simmons."

"My God, they're real," Smitty realized too late that he had awoken to a much nicer ghost this time. Involuntarily, his vision focused on the protrusions from the tight-fitting uniform, the delicate neck, the friendly smile, and ultimately, the silver captain's bars on her collar.

"Sorry, Captain, I, uh, meant to say, you're real." Smitty felt the heat on the back of his neck and the flush of his face turning red. "I seem to remember you from a dream, one of my better ones."

She blushed and leaned down into his ear. "Shhh, let's keep that between us, okay? I've never done anything like that before. I thought you were dying and just wanted to give you a little final comfort. I didn't think anyone would ever know."

Smitty was now fully awake and said appreciatively, "If I had known the Big Walter provided that kind of resuscitation service, I'd have gotten myself injured a long time ago."

"Lieutenant, I can see I'm going to have my hands full with you," she said. The hauteur wasn't quite convincing.

"Fair's fair, Captain," Smitty said with an impish grin. "I seem to recall I've already had my hands full of you."

"Yes, but like a typical man, you fell asleep before you could finish what you started," the captain replied in a tone that implied that she'd had quite enough of this conversation, and wished it to go no further. "And I'd appreciate it if you would call me Claire; Captain sounds so formal."

"Sounds like the voice of lots of experience, Claire."

"Lieutenant, I've been married for four years," she said, holding up her left hand and pointing to her engagement and wedding rings. But there was no hiding the traces of redness returning to her cheeks.

"Was, I mean. He died in October," she said in a tone that left no doubt that she still missed him. "He was a navy pilot. He got hit on a mission over North Vietnam and crashed into the sea while trying to nurse his aircraft back to the carrier."

Smitty understood. Her husband was now one of the forty-odd thousand who had become a statistic known as KIA. Vietnam had claimed another young life. And although Smitty had never met him, he knew instinctively that he would have liked him. The look in her eyes spoke volumes and said he was the love of her life. Smitty knew that look; he'd worn it like a comfortable pair of shoes himself since Linda died.

"Sorry," Smitty said quietly, then added, "Mine was a nurse, a captain like you. She died in a VC attack at Da Nang in December."

They exchanged looks. In some ways, it was a closeness greater than physical intimacy and surely just as sensual. In the strangest of places, Smitty had found friends. He felt he had just found another.

She broke the uncomfortable silence suddenly by leaning over the bed and kissing him lightly on the cheek. "Thanks, Lieutenant." She stood upright just as the doctor entered the room followed by two others.

"Thank you, Captain, please stand aside." The doctor assumed her position by the bed.

"Lieutenant, there's some folks here who want to say a quick hello," the doctor said, as he moved away.

"Hi, troop, I heard you were sick," Dad said, trying hard to fight back the tears forming in the corners of his eyes.

"Well, I was, but I'm gonna be okay now, so you can go on back to where you came from," Smitty smiled weakly, remembering what Dad had said to him in similar circumstances.

"The doc here says not to overstay our welcome, so I'll see you soon." Dad's voice began to break up and he wiped away a tear and stepped back from the bed.

"Hey, kiddo, how you doin'?" General Chuck said. "You get yourself well, hear, son, cause your next assignment is waiting for you here in Washington."

The doctor stepped forward. "Now that your father's here, let's talk about you." He inhaled heavily then exhaled. "I don't believe in beating around the bush, Lieutenant, so here it is.

"As you and I have discussed over the past two weeks, you have shrapnel wounds to the head, neck, chest, and pelvic area. Additionally, you have sustained a dislocated hip, and compound fractures in two places below the knee and six places in the ankle."

"Tell me again how all this happened," Smitty said. In the last two weeks, he'd been able to fill in a lot of blanks but the last mission was still a complete zero. Not only was he not able to recall it, but he was also unable to retain it. His mind would instantly erase the message as some kind of pain-blocking device.

The doctor looked exasperated at having to tell Smitty again. "You first crash-landed in a helicopter, breaking your leg, then received mortar wounds when you were brought in on the evac chopper."

"Am I going to be all right?"

The doctor glanced at Dad and the general, making no effort to conceal his irritation and chagrin at having to constantly restate his conclusions. "Frankly, Lieutenant, as I've said before, you should consider yourself lucky to be alive. The shrapnel wound to the head alone put you to sleep for three and a half weeks. And the injuries to the neck and chest will cause you some discomfort, but the injury to your pelvis was damned lucky."

Smitty's looked at the doctor blankly. "It's a good thing you tuck your penis on the left side of your shorts; otherwise you'd be singing soprano right now. There was a piece of shrapnel that went right beside your scrotum and missed your family jewels by centimeters."

This Smitty had not heard before. He was damn certain of it. He didn't think he would have forgotten. He glanced quickly past the doctor to the captain, who Smitty was sure had heard it, but was busy examining the ceiling in a very professional manner, pretending to have a severe case of temporary deafness.

"Same question, am I going to be all right?" Smitty asked, a trace of irritation in his voice.

"Mentally, yes. But whether or not you'll be able to recover full use of your leg is questionable. The damage is quite severe, and it will require several more operations to reset the broken bones that were not properly aligned in time. The process will be long and difficult and with the calcium deposits that could possibly build up, it could take as much as two years for complete rehabilitation to occur."

"Huh, sounds to me like you're trying to tell me that I'm going to be permanently disabled."

"That is a distinct possibility. Rather more of a probability."

"Yeah, well, don't write me off yet, Doc. If I can short-sheet the grim reaper's bed, I can beat this rap, too."

"I admire your spirit, Lieutenant," the doctor said. "I just want to temper it with reality."

"Colonel, are you a betting man?" Dad asked, stepping up to the bed.

"On occasion, hospital football pools and such."

"Well, here's fifty bucks that says my son will be back one year from today and beat you in the fifty-yard dash." Dad opened his wallet and threw two twenties and a ten on Smitty's chest.

"Sergeant, while I admire your optimism, I must again caution you that we must be realistic," the doctor said.

"Make it a hundred." General Chuck added his cash to the pile.

The doctor was silent for a moment, then said quietly, "Lieutenant, you're up against long odds." He started to reach for his own wallet.

"Make it one-fifty," the captain said suddenly, as she leaned around Dad and added twenty—two tens and two fives. "I believe in the lieutenant, too."

"It would be worth it to see you do it, Lieutenant." The doctor added an equal amount of money to the pile.

"You don't know my son, Doc," Dad collected the money into a pile, folded it in half, and handed it to the doctor. "You hold the stakes and give the winnings to him." Dad pointed to Smitty. "And the original stakes back to us."

Dad turned, glanced at the general and at Claire and asked, "You two okay with that?" Both the general and the captain nodded their agreement.

"Okay with what, Sergeant?" the doctor asked, as he put the folded wad in his pocket.

"The best way to get my son to do something is to tell him it's not possible for him to do it."

He winked at Smitty and said with absolute certainty in his voice. "Don't spend the loot, Doc. 'Cause in April of '71, my boy will be back for his cash."

"We'll see. Now I think the lieutenant has had enough for today. We need to let him get his rest." The doctor ushered them toward the door. Turning to the captain, the doctor said formally, "Carry on, nurse."

With a wave from his dad and Chuck, the three of them left without further comment. Smitty listened quietly until their footsteps faded and he was alone with the captain. The silence was unnerving. Finally, he asked, "What made you do that?"

"Instinct," she said, approaching the bed and leaning softly on the rail. "The colonel can be a bit pompous at times, especially given the VIP clients we usually deal with.

It was nice to see someone stand up to him." She reached down and softly took Smitty's hand. "Think you can do it?"

"Care to make a little side bet, Captain?"

"I think you can, too." She ignored his innuendo and squeezed his hand.

The captain headed to the doorway, then leaned back around the corner. "And as for the side bet, Lieutenant, I never bet on a sure thing."

He had been at the Palace, as the military doctors called Walter Reed, for six weeks and was, as of today, considered ambulatory. Most of the shrapnel wounds had healed sufficiently so that now they just looked like big ugly red welts with scabs. His hair was starting to grow back and cover the hole from the piece of steel that had penetrated his skull, although there would always be a narrow gash where no hair would grow. He was sleeping normally and had been going to therapy daily for the past two weeks. His hip was still sore but functional. So far, one operation had been performed on the leg and both of the compound fractures had been reset. Additionally, he had had two of the six bones in his ankle broken, pinned, and reset in the same operation.

The cast extended from his toes to his crotch. With all the follow-up operations set six weeks apart, the cast was not scheduled to come off permanently until the fall. But at least by late June, July at the latest, it would be down to a walking cast below the knee.

In recognition of his convalescent status, his uncle had come down from Steelton, Pennsylvania, and, along with his dad, had loaded him in the back of a station wagon and taken him to Smitty's grandfather's house for the weekend.

Smitty suspected General Chuck had a lot to do with getting him out on a pass but didn't mention it to his father. After meeting and receiving all of the concerned aunts, uncles, cousins, and nieces, Smitty's dad, his uncle, and his grandfather had gotten on with the serious business of how to get Smitty drunk.

They wanted to take him to the tavern just across the street, but how to transport him in the cast was a problem. A problem Dad solved by disappearing out into his father's workshop and returning moments later with the welding cart—minus the torch bottles. Smitty was quickly strapped to this and wheeled across the street where, for the next five hours, a serious drinking binge occurred.

A problem arose when the bar closed at 2:00 AM. His uncle, his dad, and his grandfather were too drunk to wheel him home. Some of the local regulars solved this by carrying Smitty back to his grandfather's on top of a bar table and placing him gently on the Murphy bed in the living room. En route home, a city police officer noticed them, stopped, and, after being apprised of the circumstances, stopped the traffic so that the "rescue mission" could cross the street without being hit.

His uncle departed, and Smitty's father passed out in the easy chair. As Smitty's grandfather was attempting to lie down on the extra sofa, he lost his balance, rolled drunkenly onto the floor, and began hollering loudly for his wife.

She came down the stairs, slowly rubbing the sleep from her eyes, and in a voice tinged with irritation asked what he wanted. Smitty's grandfather asked her to help him get up. She came down the steps, grabbed the afghan and the cushion off the sofa, and dropped them on his chest, said "Get up yourself, you drunken old fool," and went back upstairs to bed.

The rest of the weekend was not so eventful. But mentally, the visit home did Smitty a world of good.

Slowly, Smitty's memory was returning. He could recall events into March now. But try as he might, he could not retain the accounts of the last six days he was in-country. A headshrinker that the doctor had sent over had told him not to worry, that the mind was still healing, and it would come back in its own time—a form of selective amnesia, he called it.

The initial injuries had been treated at Da Nang, then, due to the coma and a little three-star interest—he had been sent to Japan. When stable, he was air-expressed to Walter Reed for recovery, courtesy of General Chuck, who now had Dad assigned to his staff until his retirement from the air force, currently scheduled for June.

On Smitty's arrival, Dad had talked to an army shrink who told him that sometimes when people are in a coma, their minds lose their bearings and need a light in the window to follow back.

Dad had come up with the original idea of spending eight hours talking to Smitty about his childhood and tape recording it as he spoke. Then when he was away, he would turn on the tape recorder, so that his voice was playing endlessly in Smitty's ears. That must have been the noise that blazed the trail Smitty was able to follow. The quack had said it was all just hogwash and was just Smitty's own fight or flight self-resolve coming up heads, but if the tapes didn't help, they sure as hell didn't hurt.

Smitty had wondered about Sergeant Mike and Captain Ron. Incredibly, Ron had escaped the mortar attack without a scratch and was now completing his fifth tour, currently scheduled to end in June. He had written that he was unsure of his next posting but would keep in touch.

Sergeant Mike was both lucky and unlucky at the same time. Lucky in that he received only minor shrapnel wounds, but they were the million-dollar kind that got him shipped stateside to Bragg, where he was currently on convalescent leave before assuming his next and final assignment as a sergeant major.

It was a certainty that in his twenty months left until retirement, he was at his last post, and his time in war zones a thing of the past. After his lifetime spent fighting and adventuring over most of the globe, it was nice that the Ol' Sarge would make it home to his sweet lady alive.

At the same time, Mike was unlucky. His wounds, which he had received while trying to carry Smitty to safety, were in a most embarrassing place. After being evac'ed to Japan, he'd written in his letter that he had two pieces of shrapnel firmly lodged in the left and right cheeks of his buttocks. His army cronies had started saying that he had now become a real pain in the ass instead of a metaphoric one, and the name had stuck. This had been shortened to PA, and his nickname changed to match.

When Smitty had talked briefly to him, when he had reached Bragg a week ago, Mike had said sarcastically that he always knew that his relationship with a certain whaleshit first lieutenant would end on a sour note. He pointed out that when he had first met Smitty, everyone called him Sergeant Mike out of fear and respect. Now everyone smiled politely and called him Sergeant PA.

Mike had further added that his wife had shortened it to just PA. He vowed vengeance for having his distinguished career, built on toughness and survival, end on such a pantywaist note. He did not elaborate on the specific method or form that revenge would take, saying that it was yet to be determined, but that it would occur some time in the future was a certainty.

Smitty had written Frenchy, LZ, and Big Walt with an update and had heard from Frenchy and LZ, but not Big Walt.

Frenchy had named his first-born Johnsele after himself. Additionally, he had saddled the little tyke with two middle names, Kevin and Lucius. Smitty was pleased and proud. LZ was settled comfortably into his career as an NCO and basic training instructor at Jackson, and would be assigned there until at least June of 1971. Big Walt had gotten six months for the grass charge but, due to his war record, the judge had suspended the balance of the sentence to time already served, after which the big guy had promptly unassed the area for parts unknown.

In accordance with the deal Smitty had made in January with Colonel Wilson and General Martin, his promotion to captain was being held until such time as he was ready to resume active duty. This would be reviewed in June after the second operation on his ankle, at which time he should have a walking cast and available for a noncombatant staff position in the Pentagon.

Things were changing for those he left behind in Vietnam also. Colonel Wilson was headed home from Nam in May with a rumored early promotion to one-star sometime next year and a choice assignment in the Pentagon.

Army General Martin, and his entire division, were to leave Vietnam in the fall. The war was slowly winding down, and despite the all-out protests of the senior military command, the troops were now being scheduled to come home based on seniority, leaving the least experienced troops to bear the brunt of the ground war.

Smitty was glad and also anxious. The war had been a convenient place to play hide-and-go-blame with his life. Now he'd have to come out in the open and face the reality of an uncertain future . . . like thousands of returning soldiers from every armed conflict that the United States had ever been in.

"Lieutenant, good news on the ankle. We were able to reset the last two bones as well as the original two we planned at the same time," the doctor said. "We've reset the leg in a walking cast and you should be able to be up and around soon. Once we establish your therapy schedule, we'll talk about your release date. I'm sure you'll be glad to get away from this place."

"You said it, Doc," Smitty replied.

"Nurse, would you mind going down to my office and asking the secretary to pull the lieutenant's file. Then stop by X-ray and bring the latest pictures," the doctor said to Claire.

"Yes, Doctor." She left instantly.

When the door was closed, the doctor leaned on the bed railing for support, hunched over until he was no more than a foot from Smitty's face and said in a low voice, "Can I ask you a straight-from-the-shoulder question, Lieutenant?"

"Fire away," Smitty answered.

Glancing at the door nervously, he turned back and said, "Just who the hell are you?"

"What are you talking about?"

"Well, Lieutenant, since you showed up here three months ago, more or less in a body bag, I've got more people checking on you than we had when Hoover was here for his gallbladder surgery."

"I'm not talking about the regular visitors like your father and his boss, that air force three-star, or that army Green Beret colonel who comes every night and calls you son. Or even those Secret Service goons sucking around here constantly checking up on you—which, to rate that kind of scrutiny, I assume, must have something to do with the fact that you're the president's illegitimate son, or if not, humping one of his daughters or some such secret thing."

"Seems you're trying to go somewhere with this, Doc. Stop dancing," Smitty said.

"Okay, here it is. I was summoned into the presence of the surgeon general yesterday and asked your current status. After completing my report, which was that, barring complications, you should be able to return to limited duty status in the fall, I was pretty much given a verbal order to fail you on your physical for return to duty status after convalescent leave."

"You were what?!" Smitty said, his voice rising.

"Quiet, Lieutenant. Keep your voice down. Someone will hear." The doctor leaned in closer to the bed and made downward motions to keep Smitty quiet.

"There's more you should know, Lieutenant." He paused, obviously a man struggling with his conscience. "I was told that if I didn't fail you that my career in the army was over." He shook his head in disgust. "Bastards."

"So what are you going to do?" Smitty said.

"More to the point, what are you going to do, Lieutenant?"

"Oh, that's already been decided," Smitty said. "What I need to do is to minimize the damage path for everyone else." Smitty was quiet for a moment, then said, "Any chance you could stall it for a while, like maybe report that, in your professional opinion, unexpected complications have come up, you'll require more time, that kind of technical drivel?"

"How long?"

"Six weeks, two months at the outside. I need time to work a few things out, and I require the cover of the army to do it."

The doctor shook his head slowly. "Eighteen years of faithful army service, and now I'm going to end it for a wet-behind-the-ears first lieutenant."

He smiled sadly. "You've got your two months. There's one other thing."

Smitty waited for the sawbones to continue.

"That captain with the big jugs who has sort of attached herself to you."

"Yes."

"She joined the staff three days after you were shipped in here. Before that she was posted on loan for a special assignment. Care to take a wild guess as to where?"

"Surgeon general's office."

"Dead on."

"A Mata Hari?"

"That would be my guess."

"Thanks, Doc." Smitty extended his hand.

"I'm a friend of man," the doctor replied as he took Smitty's hand in his own and shook it briefly. He was headed for the door when the nurse returned.

"Oh, thank you, nurse, I won't be needing those X-rays now. It turns out there was a slightly older set at the nurse's station and I was able to get what I needed from those."

The doctor gave her a friendly pat on the shoulder, turned sideways, and slipped past her, managing to miss rubbing against her large breasts by sucking in his own chest.

"What a pompous asshole, sending me all that way for nothing," the captain said, as she slammed the paperwork and X-rays down in a chair in disgust.

"Yes, he is, isn't he?" Smitty said with an innocent smile. He yawned loudly. "I'm feeling a little run down. I think I'll take a nap."

The captain approached the bed, leaned over the rail, and as had become her custom when they were alone, leaned down, took his hand in hers and caressed it softly and gave him a kiss on the cheek. "Remember what we talked about. On your first hospital leave, dinner at my place."

"Looking forward to it," Smitty replied. Then added, "Does that include dessert?"

"Oh, dessert's a sure thing," she said with a seductive wink.

Maybe it is, Smitty said to himself after she left, but then again he suspected that his brand of dessert was very different from what her enticing wink implied.

Seven hours later, at 3:00 AM, Smitty awoke, slipped out of bed, and, using his crutches, hopped to the nurses' station. "I couldn't sleep. I'm going out for a smoke."

"Be careful, and don't fall," the night nurse replied. "If you're not back in ten, I'll come looking for you."

Smitty nodded and continued out to the main lobby and the pay phone located just beyond. He dialed a local number, and on the third ring, a sleepy male voice answered, "Hello."

"Anastasia, I am saying again, Anastasia." Smitty covered the receiver with his mouth to obscure his lips from the guard who was sitting ten feet away, casually reading a paper with his feet propped up on a desk.

"Confirm, Anastasia. Suggest directive?" The owner of the voice now sounded fully awake and alert.

"Ten hundred hours, tomorrow."

"Confirm, Anastasia. Out." The line went dead in his hands.

Smitty hung up the phone and with the best speed he could manage was back at the nurses' station within the required ten minutes.

"Enjoy your smoke?" The night nurse asked.

"Yeah, nothing like inhaling a future case of cancer to make you sleep like a baby," Smitty said.

"I'm addicted, too," she said with a friendly wave, as he disappeared down the hall. "Sleep well, Lieutenant."

Smitty was tired by the time he settled down in his rack, but he didn't sleep. As General Chuck had said not too far from here three years back, "Enemies all around, and not always wearing ID tags." Some masqueraded as military officers, some as FBI agents, and some, it seemed, as would-be girlfriends.

"Good morning, son."

"Morning, Colonel." Smitty smiled. "Sorry, I mean, Doctor." Colonel Wilson had entered the room dressed in a doctor's smock, and had even managed to stick the medical insignia on his collar as part of his disguise.

"Figured it might be a good idea. Never know who you'll run into in these corridors," the colonel explained.

"Thanks for coming on such short notice."

"You pulled the fire alarm, Lieutenant. It's your nickel," the colonel said.

Smitty relayed the contents of the conversation with the doctor the previous day, including the role of Miss Lung Warts.

"Hmm," he said, thoughtfully rubbing his chin. "Based on what you've told me, there are two possibilities. One, you screwed the pooch when you got wounded, and Tricky Dicky has moved on to another marquee soldier who photographs better. Or two, someone is applying pressure up through the president to have you dropped from the service."

"How?"

"I would suspect that your records were leaked to the president, and knowing how paranoid he supposedly is, he got cold feet. It would be political suicide if the president handed you the DSC, then the press found out about what really happened in the Mang Yang Pass to Major Gates."

"Any idea who would do this, or why?"

"No, but thinking out loud for a moment, whoever could set this chain of events in motion would have to have some pretty high connections and be pretty firmly entrenched to reach all the way into the Oval Office."

"Firmly entrenched?" Smitty asked with a raised eyebrow.

"Yes, this isn't just some hairbag young reporter looking to trade favors by leaking information in return for his first scoop. Whoever did this is deeply embedded in the Washington power base, and has been for years, maybe even generations."

"They obviously see you as a threat, so they must feel that they have to completely discredit you. It's guilt by association."

"That would seem to lend credence to your thoughts of it being generational, Colonel." The colonel looked pensive. "Why else would someone that important be after a know-nothing lieutenant like me?" Smitty glanced out the window briefly, before turning around. "The generational thing must involve someone older than me, and whoever it is must think the information was passed on to me, so the only thing to do, as you said, is to discredit me so that any information I have is of no value.

"If that's true, son," the colonel said, "then again, the question is why?"

Both men were silent, alone with their individual thoughts. As a sudden inspiration struck Smitty, he looked up and said in a hesitant voice. "Sir, when I first met you back at Bragg, as I recall, you said to me that you expected better from a second-generation military man."

"Yes, so . . . "

"Colonel, you said in Nam you met my father face-to-face during the war."

"We traveled some together," the colonel said.

Smitty started to answer, caught himself and remembered the colonel's rule number two. "Sir, Dad's part of this secret, isn't he?"

"You're warm, Lieutenant, very warm, but, two questions: One, why is this so important to you? And two, again, like I said to you in Nam months back, what makes you think you can trust me?"

"I'll respond to the second question first. I can trust you because you and I are looking for the same thing. As you counseled me, Colonel, I checked up on you. You had an older sister who committed suicide during the war. You're looking for the cause of her death—or who's to blame for the events that triggered it. I think your quest and my journey are related. Tell me I'm wrong, sir," Smitty said.

The colonel nodded his head slowly in understanding. "Okay, just for the moment, let's say I believe you may be on the right track. How do you narrow it down?"

"Well, I think I have to start by getting clear of the hurricane's path. So clear that whoever is after me no longer considers me a viable threat and moves on to the next target and forgets about me," Smitty concluded. "And like you said, successful espionage is the result of patience. I have to go on with my life, if for no other reason than to convince the mysterious 'them' that I really don't know anything."

Smitty gave the colonel a knowing look. "And as for trusting you, that part is easy. The key to what I'm looking for rests with you. I know it. So do you."

The colonel started to protest. Smitty raised his hand, motioning the colonel to hear him out. "Colonel, I didn't say you were the cause. I said you were the key, even if you don't know it. I did a little research on you. You were one of the original Jedburgh members from World War II. It was the forerunner of the ops teams we operated under in Nam.

"You were personally responsible for originally suggesting the teams in Nam using only code names to each other, making it a court-martial offense for any of us to disclose his real name or any details about our personal lives." Smitty smiled faintly. "Despite the fact that all of us violated it all to hell and back."

To soothe his rasping throat, Smitty took a drink of water from his glass. "What did you call it? Colonel Wilson's Handbook for Spies, golden rule number one: 'What you don't know, they can't make you tell.'"

"I don't understand the connection from the Jed teams to the SOG ops teams," the colonel said.

"The hell you don't," Smitty said irritably. Seeing the colonel's anger, he added a respectful "sir."

"Go ahead, Lieutenant," the colonel said.

"The connection is that the Jed teams operated in the same fashion. For security reasons, the operatives didn't know each other's real names or anything about their personal backgrounds.

"Your entire military background has been counterintelligence. The connection is too real to be coincidence. And from what I've been able to dig around and find out, some of your World War II comrades, like William Colby, are now holding down some pretty high-level positions in the CIA and Defense Department and hold you in great esteem."

Smitty paused, and went on in a voice filled with certainty, "You are the connection, sir. You came up with the Jed three-man operational methodology in the Big War and Korea, and you refined it for operation in Nam."

Smitty took another sip of water. "Deny it, sir."

The colonel grunted. "As I told you in Nam, do you know what kind of sacrifice you'll have to make to do this?"

"Yes, sir," Smitty answered. "But if I don't, not only will I never have any kind of long-term peace, but neither will anyone else who comes near me. That means I can never marry or settle down, because this cloud will always be hanging around, and sooner or later, it will rain on my parade."

The colonel stood up and extended his hand. "Okay, Lieutenant, you've found yourself a partner. What can I do to help you?"

"Three things. One, confirm when I'm right and keep steering me onto the correct path when you can or back when I'm wrong. Two, back me up on what I come up with, no matter how extreme or bizarre it seems, and three, if I live," Smitty looked up at the colonel hopefully, "be there at the end to help me settle the score. Even if I'm not."

"How will I know when you need help, and how will I know it's you?" the colonel asked.

Smitty was quiet for a moment. "My security password got you here. Suppose we both use it as an activation code both ways."

"And my uncle's wife's middle name will be my countersign," the colonel said.

"And like I said, whatever this thing is, and whoever is behind it, you've been looking for it, too, either for yourself or for someone else. But I think the problem is that it's like fighting the mythical giant squid. To kill it you've got to stab it in the eye, and you can't get close enough because of all the flailing tentacles that constantly keep you fighting nonessential targets just to survive. I was thinking that maybe if I lopped off a few, then they, whoever they may be, might become a little more vulnerable."

Smitty paused and exhaled deeply. "It will take some time, maybe even years, until whoever it is no longer considers me a threat, but there's a bill due and I intend to collect on it."

"A bill due," the colonel said.

"Yes, sir," Smitty said. "A bill for Gena, Jimmy, a bunch of Cubans who got killed innocently, Glenda, Frenchy, Big Walt, Blackbird, Whippoorwill, and Linda, to name just a few. Not to mention my dad, you, and the hundreds, if not thousands, of people whose lives have been destroyed in the Mission Octagon cover-up."

"Don't suppose you'd be willing to share what approach you've got in that flat head of yours, would you?"

Smitty smiled. "Colonel Wilson's Handbook for Spies golden rule number two. Never, never, never tell anybody anything unless you think you can benefit by their having the knowledge."

"Funny, I thought you forgot that lecture," the colonel said with a wry expression as the door began to open.

As Claire entered the room, the colonel said suddenly, "You know, your goddamn Orioles look like they're going to win it all this year."

Smitty looked at the colonel as though he'd just lost his mind and then caught his sly wink. "Yes, as long as their pitching holds out."

"Oh, I think their pitching will hold out. It's their big stars I'm worried about. They're only masquerading as frontliners. There's a lot of insecurity present in the team leaders and if you scratch the surface, their backup is pretty weak." The colonel stood up. "Good luck, Lieutenant," he said, and headed out the door.

Smitty smiled again. A smile the captain mistook as being for her.

"Who was that?" she asked, leaning down and kissing him on the cheek.

"The sawbones who fixed my wrist a couple of years ago in Japan," Smitty answered with a yawn. "My dad should be stopping by in a few minutes." The implication that he wished to talk to him alone was obvious, he hoped.

"Okay, sweetie. I'll go do a few things then stop back," Claire said, as she smiled. With a friendly wave she was gone as fast as she had come in.

Smitty knew that to get to the bottom of whatever this turned out to be, he'd have to go on the offensive, and thanks to the colonel, who'd not only finally agreed to help, but had given him a location and a first step, he now knew where and how to start.

But he needed one more little bit of information from the military before the army informational news channel went off the air for good, and he knew just the person to give him that extra addition.

"Hi, Dad, thanks for stopping by on your way home from work."

"Yeah, it's my last week," They shook hands and he sat down heavily in the chair beside the bed. "God, I'm going to miss it."

"You've been in a long time, haven't you?"

"May of '39. I got a special deal from the recruiter, he let me enlist then go home a week later so I could be best man at my older brother John's wedding," Dad said. "Seems like only yesterday,"

Dad reached over and ruffled Smitty's hair. "The report is that you're going to defy the odds and recover."

"Yeah, I guess I'm just a chip of the ol' block," Smitty said.

Dad smiled. It was said that people enjoyed their work the most when they were doing what they loved. Being a first sergeant was Dad's calling. He had received superior ratings since first being assigned to the position in the mid-'50s. His reputation was as a firm but fair disciplinarian who went the extra mile for the good of the service and, more importantly, for the individual airman.

Most of his commanders saw him as a father figure to his men. Most of the men saw him in a slightly different light—as strict parent who tolerated no breach of the rules and never accepted any excuse for breaking them. But he could be softhearted and incredibly kind in moments of personal crisis. Funny, but that pretty much summed up Smitty's own opinion of his father.

"You were right about the last ten years, you know," Smitty admitted. "Especially considering what you went through with Mom when you did finally reenlist after twenty years."

Dad chuckled in spite of himself. "You remember that, huh?"

"I remember you coming out of the bedroom with smoke coming out of both ears and wanting to slap the crap out of me for listening through the walls," Smitty recalled. "Hell, the way you and Mom were yelling at each other, a deaf person four blocks away would have heard you."

"If it makes you feel any better, your mother wasn't exactly interested in playing snuggle bunnies that night."

"From what I've heard you say about your marriage to Mom, it was more of an ABC type of marriage anyway."

"ABC?"

"Yeah, anniversaries, birthdays, and Christmas. No wonder you spent so much time in the workshop," Smitty said.

Dad's response startled Smitty. He grinned evilly, gave him the finger, and said sadly, "I wish." Then he said, "Thanks, son."

Smitty patted his arm in reply. "Any regrets?"

Dad was thoughtful for a moment. "Only one—that I didn't do what you did. I had an offer to go to OCS in the '50s and didn't take it. God knows your mother wanted me to, but when I talked to Chuck, he more or less talked me out of it.

"He told me that I'd have to eventually take time off to go to college and I'd just come back from almost three years in Korea, been gone four years in the war, and was tired of being away from your mother and you boys." Dad got up, paced around the bed, and looked out the window. He was not looking at the view but reflecting, Smitty suspected, on what might have been.

"Oh, well, as Chuck said after I'd made my decision, good NCOs are hard to find, and damn good NCOs are damn hard to find." Dad walked back around the bed and resumed his seat. "Besides, Chuck was right, I'd have had to go to college and it just isn't for me."

"Why not?" Smitty asked.

"Son, college is for a different kind of person. I'm just the son of a Pennsylvania dirt farmer, who GED'd in the military."

"So, does that make you any less qualified to go than anyone else? Hell, in my book, it makes you more so. You've got thirty years of life experiences to draw on."

"Just drop it, okay? It's a dead issue," Dad said.

Smitty took a deep breath. "You know what I think? I think deep down you've always wanted to go—no, make that regretted not going—to college fifteen years ago and the reason didn't have anything to with Mom or Billy or me.

"I think you were scared that you might have to break out of that cocoon of comfort that Chuck, and every other officer, had convinced you was your station in life. You didn't want to stick your face into the wind and take a chance. Don't try to lay off any of this blame on anyone but yourself. Remember what you always told me? It ain't bein' scared that counts; it's what you do when you're scared that matters."

Dad glared at him, and said in a frustrated voice, "Son, I'm too old and just don't have the basic schooling skills. You're younger and fresh out of school. It's much easier for you to go back than someone my age."

Smitty stared back at his dad and chose his tone of voice most carefully. "Dad, look. I know you're having a hard time of it right now. Leaving the service after thirty-one years and venturing off into the land of the unknown is scary. But don't sell yourself short. If you're afraid that the regular courses might be too much for you, there are remedial courses that you could take first to get ready for the regular curriculum. All I'm asking is that you think about it, okay? Besides, what are you going to do when you get out?"

"Well, I haven't just sat right down on that. I know I'm headed home to Georgia where Sally is waiting, and we'll see from there. I thought I might take a couple of months and get caught up on things around the house." Dad said in a more conciliatory tone, "Then I might just look into your idea."

"What about your heart?"

"Well, the doc says that as long as I watch myself, I should be able to putter along for the next five years or so," Dad responded. "Besides, if I had to have a heart attack, at the end of my career was a good time to do it. The general fixed it so that I was no longer fit for duty and could retire on a 70 percent disability, which means that only 30 percent of my retirement is taxable," Dad said half-heartedly, "Pretty sweet deal, huh?"

Smitty smiled. Dad would gladly trade it all for another year—or even another day—in the blue suit.

"You and the general have been together a long time, haven't you?" Smitty said.

"Yeah, he was just a wet-behind-the-ears first lieutenant like you when we hooked up in '43. 'Course he'd only been in the service since early '43," Dad said in a reflective voice.

"What was your MOS in those days?" Smitty inquired.

"Aircraft maintenance. Your old dad was considered a specialist in dismantling downed aircraft and cannibalizing and crating the remains."

"Was the general your first commander?" Smitty probed lightly.

"Him? Naw," Dad said, shaking his head. "He was just a whiz kid, had a degree from MIT or some such think tank.

"He went to Italy and racked up a bunch of kills as a fighter pilot. Became one of the youngest aces in something like four months, then became one of the first double aces on jets in Korea five years later. I'll tell ya one thing, kiddo, Chuck knows his way around the inside of a jet plane." The appreciation was evident in his voice.

Dad roused himself from his trip down memory lane. "Say, enough of this morbid stuff. I am here as a messenger. The general heard that you're recovering and wanted to know if you can accompany the two of us tonight for some good food and maybe a beer or twenty."

"Sounds great. What time?"

"His car will be here in an hour and a half. Can you be ready by then?"

"Sure can," Smitty said.

"Okay, we'll pick you up at seven." Dad waved as he left, passing the captain on his way out. "Good evening, Captain," he said with a crisp salute.

"Your father sure looks sad. I don't think he's ready to get out," Claire said, crossing the room and kissing Smitty on the cheek. She paused and kissed him on the mouth as her hands caressed his head softly.

As their tongues began to meet, she suddenly broke off the kiss and stepped back. "I'm sorry, I've been wanting to do that for a long time and finally just got up the nerve to go for it."

Smitty smiled. "As I've said before in similar situations, if you go through life saying hello like that, you'll never want for friends."

Her cheeks turned red and she took his hand in hers. "Did I hear you say something about going out with your father tonight?"

"Yes, he and his boss want to take me out for dinner and a few beers. I think it's a dual first-night-out, retirement-get-together kind of thing," Smitty said.

"What time will you be back?" she asked hopefully.

"'Bout in the eleven to twelve range, I expect."

"I'll be at home. Have them drop you at my place for the rest of the night and we'll have a more intimate celebration." She rubbed the back of his hand against the tightness of her uniform. Smitty could not fail to notice the hardening nipple inside her snug bra.

Smitty smiled. "I'll be looking forward to that."

"Bye, sweetie. See you tonight." Claire glided out of his room.

The scent of her perfume was still in Smitty's nose when he swung his legs out of bed and began to dress. It was shaping up to be an interesting night and maybe a more interesting morning.

"Here's to old comrades—gone but not forgotten," Chuck said, his speech slurring. The three men raised their glasses in the latest of a series of alcoholic salutes to anything and everything in the same gin mill the general had given a young soldier his version of a manicure and manners lesson nearly three years ago. Over the past three hours, there had been a lot of toasts and a lot of beer consumed, with the occasional Jim Beam chaser thrown in.

"Hear, hear," Dad said, taking a long pull on his beer.

"To you, General, and you, Dad," Smitty said, raising his glass. "Dad told me a little bit about how long you've been together when he was reminiscing this afternoon."

"Thanks, son. What's your ol' man have to say about his favorite general?"

"Nothing much. Just that you were one of the fastest to become an ace in the war, and that underneath that folksy exterior you're a college super-dweeb who knows a whole lot more about jets than he lets on."

"Well, got to maintain my touch with the common soldier," the general said. "Let's not talk about all that boring stuff. . . . To old comrades."

"To old comrades," Smitty echoed, draining his glass. Slamming it down on the table, he slapped the counter loudly. "Barkeep, another pitcher."

"Shhh, son. You don't want us to get thrown out of here, do you?" Dad asked drunkenly. He lay a restraining hand on his son's arm. "That bouncer and the folks around us have been eyeing you for the past hour. Let's not have our night of celebration end on a bad note."

"Fuck 'em!" Smitty said indignantly, jerking his arm free. "Who cares what a thick-headed Neanderthal or bunch of long-haired college pukes think?"

"Sir, I'm going to have to ask you to quiet down or leave," the bouncer said, as he walked up and gently touched Smitty's arm.

"Okay, no problem. We're outta here." Smitty stood up, using the table to steady himself, and began to reach for his crutches. "Besides, it's 2315 hours. I'm due to get my balls screwed off by a titsy nurse at midnight."

"Can it, Lieutenant!" General Chuck said.

"Sir, I'm afraid we're going to have to ask you to leave now." The barroom peace enforcer grabbed Smitty's crutches and held them so that Smitty could easily take hold of them.

Smitty slid easily onto the sticks, then smiled that goofy grin that only alcohol can produce. "Thank you, my good man. My chauffeur will settle the bill." He jerked his thumb in the direction of the general.

"Let's go, buddy." The big boy took his arm firmly.

Smitty had been waiting for him to do just such a thing. He balanced himself on his crutches and using them like a fulcrum, jerked his right knee upward, forcing the bouncer's balls northward to somewhere in the vicinity of New Jersey.

The bouncer lived up to his name. He did indeed bounce when he hit the floor in agony. Other assistants arrived, and before it was over, Dad and the general had become involved in the bar fight when they were mistakenly seen as trying to assault the owner's security force. In reality, they were only trying to restrain Smitty from causing any further harm.

Eventually, the MPs were called, and the three of them were escorted from the bar. Due to the general's rank, they were not taken in, just taken home. "We'll talk about this tomorrow," the general had said firmly when the MPs removed him from their van and began to walk him back upstairs to his room. But it didn't sound like he was planning a talk, more like a reprimand. A reprimand that would end up pretty much like Smitty's ill-fated night with Kristie's father three years ago in Savannah.

He was going to be given a first-class lecture, then quietly but firmly shown the door . . . which was exactly what Smitty had anticipated would happen.

CHAPTER EIGHTEEN

"Mr. Smith, oh, Mr. Smith, are you awake behind those sunglasses? If you are, perhaps you could tell the class who the first emperor of the Roman Empire was?" The professor's tone was haughty.

Smitty came fully awake the second time his name was called and heard the question quite clearly. He took off his sunglasses. "Attila the Hun." The students around him laughed out loud.

"Mr. Smith, please see me after class."

"No problem, Teach," Smitty said.

The history professor fluffed his shoulder-length hair. "Mr. Smith, my name is Professor Strickland. I will readily admit I do not mind being called professor or doctor. But I am not now, nor have I ever been, 'Teach.' That sounds like some informal address to a derelict high school shop teacher, which I have no doubt is where your last experience with formal education ended." The class erupted in a chorus of laughter and scattered applause.

"No problem, Doc." Smitty saw the unsympathetic looks of his fellow students, put his glasses back on, and reclined his head back against the wall. Obviously, the good doctor didn't care for him, and Smitty surely had to admit that the feeling was mutual.

Smitty approached him after class one day and had been embarrassed when the teacher interrupted him in the middle of his question and suggested that he go wash his hands. When Smitty had tried to explain that it was ingrained grease from his job as an auto mechanic, the professor had cut him off again, saying that, for the life of him, he couldn't understand, "why a manual laborer would require a college-level course in world history, unless it was to work on antique chariots." The other students had laughed derisively and Smitty had left the room red-faced and tight-jawed. He hadn't asked a question since.

The professor turned to a prim, overly madeup, and too-well-dressed woman. "Mrs. Hargrove, perhaps you could answer the question correctly."

"Certainly, Professor Strickland. It would be my pleasure," she said with a disdainful look at Smitty. "The correct answer is . . . "

Smitty had tuned little Miss Goody Two Shoes out before she could answer, wondering to himself if she ever let her husband on top. Mrs. Celia Hargrove was one of many little college pukes who truly pissed Smitty off.

Although only twenty, she had married her high school sweetheart last year in, according to her, a wedding whose pomp and circumstance had rivaled a presidential inauguration.

Smitty suspected that the real reason for the early wedding was that her gawky-looking hubby's father was one of the most successful car dealers in the city, and Missy knew the distinct financial advantages of being a missus. She wanted to marry him before a college cutie horned in on her territory—his looks notwithstanding. She had a bright, effervescent personality that made you want to choke her ten minutes after you met her. Personally, Smitty wanted to do it in five.

Of course, maybe his wanting to do in Darla Debutante had something to do with what his dad had termed a bad attitude, or maybe it was just that right now, he simply thought that life sucked.

To pass the time until the end of the hour, Smitty did what he usually did to help the time drag by—went over in his mind, not for the first time, how things had gotten so fucked up in such a short period of time.

It was now almost October 1970. He was in the last place he ever suspected he would be—sitting in a college classroom at Barnstein State College back in Savannah, surrounded by a bunch of students who were roughly his own age but with whom he had absolutely nothing in common.

They were, for the most part, violently anti-Vietnam. After listening to some of their mindless rhetoric, Smitty concluded that they were not against all wars, just the latest one. Smitty suspected that the fact that the males were eligible for service had a lot to do with their ardor.

It would probably come as a complete surprise to them to know that Smitty was against the war also but for a very different reason, one that, if he had he tried to explain, would only serve to widen the gulf between them.

The differences were more than philosophical. His short hair and overall neat appearance were so vastly different from their scruffiness that he stood out like a female dog in heat surrounded by a pack of wild rabid mongrels.

Barnstein was a relatively new campus located southwest of Savannah. Since it was a community college and had no dorms, the vast majority of the students lived at home and attended the college during the day. One of the ex-military guys he had met in a bar down the street had referred to it by the rather derogatory title of "Barnyard High," because it was where the uppity Savannah roosters and hens dropped off the little chicks.

Smitty's low opinion of the school was based primarily on the fact that 99 percent of the students were white, middle class, and incredibly naïve—which was another way of saying incredibly spoiled or overindulged. Smitty thought that the name "Barnyard High" fit. His initial impression was that the college seemed to function as kind of a glorified extension of the local high schools for parents to use as a post-twelfth-grade day-care center for otherwise idle teenagers.

Most of the local businessman felt the same way about the students that Smitty did, owing to the fact that few of the students lived in the area. Since they experienced only incidental business from them, they pretty much saw them as more nuisance than boon. Since the students had no money of their own, they were always looking for the local businessmen to "cut them a deal."

Smitty was more than a different kind of student. In effect, he was a different kind of person. Strangers had no idea that he was originally from Savannah, and if asked, he steadfastly denied it. After arriving in Savannah in the early summer, Smitty had gotten a job as an auto mechanic in the local service station, a couple of miles from the college. It was not as life-threatening as his previous military career, but that did not mean it was any less stressful.

Weekdays, Smitty attended classes from eight until two. Afterward, he went straight to the service station and worked until eight as the second mechanic, except for Wednesday, which was his day off. On weekends, he worked ten hours on Saturday and eight hours on Sunday. After work, he would drive the fifteen miles or so back into Savannah in his recently purchased 1960 Chevrolet two-door station wagon, usually stopping for fast food, then taking it home.

Home in this case was a second-floor, ten-dollar-a-week rented room on Gleason Street, not far from where he, LZ, and Frenchy had shacked up three years before on their intelligence training mission. The room had no TV, but there was a common family room downstairs where eight roomers tried, mostly in vain, to reach a consensus on which of the three stations to watch. Smitty skipped these turf wars, preferring to stay in his room, listen to the radio, and try to study.

The Chevy was a '54 déjà vu, only six years newer. He had bought the car with a blown straight six cylinder engine from a Barnstein student for seventy-five dollars. An ex-army buddy had given him, for free, a well-worn, oil-slinging 283 cubic-inch V-8 and Muncie four-speed manual transmission that they had stripped from his totaled '64 El Camino just before the insurance adjuster came to haul off the wrecked remains. In the evenings, mostly after the station closed at eight, and on weekends after he got off, Smitty had worked on the engine swap, then traded the straight six to a junkyard owner for the dual exhaust manifolds and other miscellaneous parts required to complete the changeover.

Within two weeks of arriving in Savannah, despite the fact that he was handicapped by a walking cast on his lower left leg, he was "air mobile" again. In the following weeks, as he became known and trusted by the local clientele, his commission checks went up as a result. He had slowly made improvements to the old wagon, adding a set of curtains to the side and rear windows for privacy, a new set of Goodyear raised white letter tires, and a set of Cragar SS Mag wheels—with wheel locks, of course.

His most recent purchase was a radio with a built-in eight-track tape player, and four stereo speakers, which he had installed in the front doors and the rear tail panels. As more money became available he'd plans for redoing the upholstery and renewing the front and rear suspension, then ultimately, a new paint job and rebuilding the motor.

His reasons for choosing the old Chevy were partly circumstance and partly necessity. Since he had neither car nor place to sleep when he first came back to Savannah, the car had served as his sleeping quarters when parked behind the service station in its initial, nonrunning position.

Additionally, the '60 served as warehouse for his few meager belongings, which consisted mostly of army fatigues and boots, faded work uniforms, and a toolbox with an ever-growing collection of tools—thanks to the friendly credit arrangements of the local Snap-On tool man.

Smitty's boss was delighted with him. His last three mechanics were let go for drinking up their commissions then showing up late for work or not at all. A wrench-turner who showed up for work sober and on time, who was fast, efficient, and good with the customers, was worth his weight in gold. In some cases, the mechanic was, in fact, the cornerstone of a successful service station business, as most owners couldn't stay afloat making two cents per gallon of gasoline sold. Besides, the owner was an old World War II vet himself and was sympathetic to Smitty's desperate efforts to restart his life and so had bent over backwards to help him out.

This radical change in lifestyle was unintentional and courtesy of the United States Army.

Colonel Wilson had called it right on the mark. Whoever was after him had, from Smitty's perspective, pretty much scored a direct hit. He had expected retribution from the bar incident but not total annihilation. The altercation in the bar in Washington in June had been just the impetus, or perhaps the correct term was the final straw, the army was looking for. Smitty was hustled out of town before the orders had been cut, based solely on the newspaper reports of the incident in the bar, to Hunter Army Airfield in Savannah.

The effects were instantaneous and long-reaching.

They took no action against Dad because he was getting out in three days and it would have been bad publicity to attempt to tarnish a spotlessly clean thirty-one-year record of a highly decorated veteran. But the general, and as a result, Smitty, were altogether another story and bore the brunt of the military's retribution.

At General Chuck's level, the competition for the coveted fourth star was so intense that the slightest blemish could disqualify a hopeful from the race. Getting plastered and starting a fight in a public place might not have been so damaging, would have been laughed off, and maybe even considered roguishly masculine, if it occurred at some distant army post. But to do it in Washington, virtually under the president's nose, and three miles from the Pentagon, was tantamount to suicide from a career standpoint.

The reaction was immediate. The afternoon after Dad's morning retirement ceremony, the three of them departed Washington—the general for an obscure command in Alaska, and Dad and Smitty for Savannah. Dad was headed home to an unwanted and forced retirement; Smitty was headed home to nothing.

The army not only rescinded its offer on the deal he had agreed to in January, but informed him that he was being dropped from the service effective when his last cast was removed, which turned out to be eight weeks. Until that time, he was being placed on paid leave of absence, with access to the base only permitted by visitor pass to the base hospital for treatment as required.

All other military privileges were either revoked or denied. Smitty was reduced to his former rank of staff sergeant and denied barracks accommodations on his arrival at Hunter. Additionally, all the previously negotiated conditions of his deal were off, except one.

Because he had served in a secret organization that could not be publicly disclosed, the Q level clearance on his service records was being maintained, which basically meant it would be a violation of the Federal Secrets Act for him to officially disclose, or even hint, his military service record to anyone in any shape or form. Unfortunately, this condition applied to application for veteran's benefits for college or any other service-connected benefits.

Colonel Perkins, who had negotiated the original deal in January, had delivered the official death sentence in person two days after the incident. He stated quite clearly that the president was already leaning against following through on his original proposal due to the fact that Smitty's shrapnel wounds, although healed, remained ugly red welts on his neck and forehead, giving him a battered pug look that, according to the colonel, the president felt would not play well on television or the Washington reception circuit.

But Smitty's getting involved in a public display that discredited the army and more importantly, the administration, at a time when antiwar sentiment was at an all-time high, had made the president extremely angry. Moreover, according to the colonel, he wanted "that little Communist bastard" to feel the fullest effects of a democratic sword of justice.

The army, battered and bruised by the Vietnam War already, with morale at an all-time low after the killing of six students in an antiwar protest at Kent State in June, was again jumping through hoops, so to speak, in their efforts at presidential pacification and public damage control.

When Smitty balked at this, Colonel Perkins smiled evilly and responded in a voice reeking with arrogance and contempt that if Smitty wished to protest these conditions publicly, either by asking for a court-martial or through a lawsuit against the army, then the army would retaliate by seeing that the events surrounding the death of Major Gates became front-page news in the *Washington Post.*

He further explained that the army was being extremely lenient in that, due to his combat record in Vietnam, the army was generously not going to prosecute him for fragging the major, but a team of psychologists met, reviewed his actions, and had attributed it to extreme combat fatigue and mental instability, and had so entered it on his permanently sealed military records.

The army was taking no chances with anyone who came in contact with him either. They had Colonel Evans, Smitty's erstwhile personal physician, airmailed to an evac hospital in a hottest section of Vietnam, and the captain with the bodacious ta-tas disappeared also—mysteriously to her colleagues but not so enigmatically to him.

Smitty did not keep his rendezvous with her that night, nor was she on duty at the hospital the next day. When he inquired as to her whereabouts, he was informed in a rather perfunctory tone by Major Elkins that she had been reassigned to another area of the hospital.

But when he went to the apartment address she had given him the afternoon of the next day on the way back from getting the official kiss-off from the colonel, the woman who answered the door in sweaty clothes with a hammer and picture wire in her hand, although cute, more closely resembled Twiggy than Claire. A quick check with the super was no more revealing. He had found the keys in his drop box when he got up the previous morning, with an attached typewritten note stating that Claire had left town. She also left her security deposit and no forwarding address. Apartment shortfalls in the Washington area being critical, a new tenant snapped it up immediately.

In the girl department, Smitty was now 0-4-1. He only put Claire in the tied column because nothing had happened between them, as it had with Glenda, Trudy, Kristie, and Linda. And knowing his luck, he figured he'd never get the opportunity to decide the issue one way or another.

The retribution had not been confined to official channels. Smitty was feeling it personally as well. The wrath of the army was bad enough, but it was a wart on an elephant's butt compared to what he was feeling from his father. To say Smitty's dad was angry with him was as big an understatement as referring to Brooks Robinson as some obscure major leaguer who played a so-so third base for the Baltimore Orioles.

The lectures had turned quickly to screaming tantrums as Dad blamed him for ruining his best friend's career and for ending his on such a shameful and embarrassing note. When Smitty countered by complaining about the raw deal he was getting from the army, Dad had told him that it served him right and that he had gotten exactly what he deserved.

Dad carried it a step further, banishing him from his house and informing him that he had twenty-four hours to get his ass over there and pick up whatever personal belongings he wished to keep or they were going in the trash—minus what Dad called "those Communist pinko records that I've always hated and have already disposed of directly."

Since Smitty did not go, he assumed that any childhood keepsakes had joined his collection of music by such radical groups as the Fifth Dimension, and were now the property of the city dump.

Tired of hearing the arguments and the constant fighting and with the isolation and depression starting to take their toll, Smitty had begun to drink quite heavily again, racking up a DUI that he could ill afford, as well as numerous citations for speeding and reckless driving.

As if that weren't enough, his last letter to Ron had gone unanswered and was marked "return to sender; no longer at this address." Smitty was certain that the captain's new address was permanent—Arlington Cemetery. Due to his own anger and alcohol-fueled bouts of despondency, he had avoided his father so completely that even though he lived only six miles away, Smitty had not been in contact with him for nearly six weeks.

Even his enrollment in college was a ruse. He had enrolled in the beginning of September, the week before he was dropped from the army's payroll, and fooled them by using his army ID card for verification, so the army not only picked up the bill for the tuition and the books, but also, due to his evident injury, listed him as disabled, entitling him to a monthly subsistence allowance from the VA. Smitty figured that eventually he'd get caught and the trickle of monthly cash would stop, but a little was all he needed to get by the next few months while his leg healed.

Although the final cast on his left ankle had been removed the following week, the leg looked scaly and the muscles had atrophied horribly, causing Smitty to walk with a limp, and he required a cane to balance and steady himself. The cane had a dual purpose. It not only provided balance and support but was also useful to help him push the clutch down on his Chevy because his left leg just wasn't strong enough. The leg was badly in need of physical therapy, but the army had made it clear that it was now his problem to solve, as they wished to be rid of him as quickly as possible. The Washington sawbones was right; the fifty bucks they had bet was water over the dam now.

So far, college was also proving to be a ghastly mistake. He didn't fit in with the students, the professors, or the environment. However, in Smitty's mind, the mistake was easily correctable, either by dropping out at midterm or sticking it out for the monthly stipend until the end of the quarter in mid-December. By then, Smitty hoped that both he and the Chevy would be in good enough shape to split for Florida . . . and the promise of a job from a friend made not so long ago.

"Polack!" Smitty screamed as he realized that the sight of the captain suddenly walking right by the door of the classroom in civvies was too real to be a mirage.

"Irishman. Yo, Lieutenant," the familiar New England voice called out in return.

Ignoring the curious, incredulous, and sneering looks of his fellow class members for disrupting their Harvard education at the hands of Mr. Faggo, Smitty leaped from his desk in the back, and with the best speed his gimpy leg would allow, headed for the exit like a heat-seeking missile.

Smitty was five steps from the door when Ron rounded the entry like Frank Robinson rounding third, hell-bent for home, and repeated, "Irishman!"

They ran to each other like long-lost lovers finally reunited, hugging, and pounding each other on the back in mutual elation. After the last six months of being surrounded by alien acquaintances, it sure was nice to be with a true friend.

They separated briefly, ruffled each other's hair, and hugged again.

"How you doing, man?" Smitty asked, as tears began to form in his eyes. "When you didn't respond to my last letter, I thought you were dead."

"Hell, no, man. Us Polacks just look like that from the day we're born," Ron said. "I've been looking all over for you, Smitty. I went to Washington when I got back, expecting to find you as some assistant in some big general's office in the Pentagon, but they said you'd gotten out and gone home to Georgia. What happened, man?"

"Let's talk about it over a beer," Smitty said, nodding curtly at the scowling professor.

"No, let's talk about it over several dozen beers," Ron corrected, turning his head back to Smitty as he let himself be pushed toward the door.

"Um, Mr. Smith," the professor said, as they were stepping through the entryway.

Smitty turned and said in an insolent voice, "Whaddya want, Teach?"

Ignoring his belittling address, the professor said, "You were supposed to see me after class, or have you forgotten?"

"Later, Teach," Smitty said, pushing Ron out into the corridor. "My captain and I are six months late for a big drinking date."

"How curious," the professor said. Smitty left the classroom behind Ron.

"So, Smitty, what happened, man? I thought you were supposed to have some candy-ass job in some general's office in the Pentagon and then go on to be a general yourself by the time you were thirty-five." Ron drained the latest in a series of beers at a rundown watering hole at Savannah Beach. He slapped the bar loudly with his palm. "Two more, my good man."

Smitty waited in silence while their glasses were refilled by a truculent, balding barman. "It just didn't work out."

"So?" Ron replied.

"I'd prefer not to talk about it. Let's just say that me and the army didn't see eye to eye on a few things," Smitty answered in a tone that made it quite clear that he did not wish to discuss this further.

"Suit yourself, bro," Ron answered, injured. "I was just trying to help."

"Look," Smitty said, his voice beginning to rise in irritation. "For the past four hours, interspersed between homespun Polish jokes, you've been asking me the same question, in one form or another. I appreciate what you're trying to do, but it won't help, okay? Short and to the point, I fucked it up, just like I seem to fuck up everything in my life. It's over now, and like I just said, forget about it."

Smitty chugged the entire freshly poured brew and slammed the glass down on the bar. "Fuck 'em!"

"You soldier boys are going to have to hold it down or split, man," the bartender growled thickly. He glanced at the clock and announced, "Last call!"

"Fuck off," Smitty snapped.

"What did you say, man?" The bartender removed his apron, threw it against the back of the bar mirror and signaled the bouncer as he came charging around the bar as fast as his portly body would allow.

The run-down gin mill was the last in a series that the two of them had hit in a nine-hour drinking binge that started at the bar close to the service station where Smitty worked, continued in a bar downtown, and migrated to the beach with two quart bottles of PBRs each to avoid dehydration during the exhausting half-hour drive.

They'd been there for most of the last two hours, ordering the six-ounce beers two at a time and chasing them with shots of Jim Beam. The bartender, who apparently didn't like service folks to start with, had become the butt of their drunken jokes. He'd had enough.

"You're about to get you're ass kicked, gyrene. We know how to take care of you so-called bad-asses." He charged at Ron with a full head of steam.

Ron motioned to Smitty to watch out for the reinforcement. Then he turned and ducked the roundhouse right intended to smash his face, and with three quickly applied blows to strategic points, the fat man hit the floor with all the gentleness of a dropped bowling ball.

"The proper term is marine, my good man," Ron said to the now unconscious barman. "Saying gyrene to a marine is like calling his mother a whore."

Ron grinned at the barmaid. "'Course if you call his mother a prostitute, he's extremely flattered. That way he can say he was raised in a professional environment."

The bouncer, who Smitty assumed from his looks must be the brother of the bartender, made a terrible mistake—a mistake he paid for when he assumed that because of Smitty's gimpy leg Ron was the only source of trouble. He joined his kin on the floor after Smitty picked up the spare and handled him as expeditiously as Ron had his comrade.

"Time to go, gyrene." Ron glanced around at the barmaid as she reached for the phone.

Smitty eyed her briefly as he started for the door, noting that even as drunk as he was, she still looked butt-ugly. He waved courteously. "Hope you find a blind guy who don't know Braille." Alcohol usually improved a woman's looks but not in this case.

They scurried toward the door past the poorly thrown glass of beer that sailed harmlessly over Ron's head. "Fuck you, man!" she screamed, as they put distance between them with the best speed Smitty could manage.

"I'll follow my captain anywhere," Smitty said. Ron ran forward to the door and held it open for Smitty to limp through, leaving the closing duties to Smitty. Ron ran around to the driver's side of his car and the engine caught at the first turn. They were moving down the beach road almost before Smitty could slam his door.

Savannah Beach was like millions of other sleepy little beachfront resort towns that were strung along the Atlantic coast, with one exception. There was only one way on and off the beach. That was via the bridge over the marshes, then an eighteen-mile drive west on Highway 80 past Fort Pulaski, across the Bull River, through Wilmington Island, and across the bridge into the first mainland town of Thunderbolt. The barmaid's reaching for the phone was an omen, an indication that help in the form of a Savannah Beach policeman would soon be on the way.

"If we get across the bridge we might have a chance," Ron said, his eyes glued to the road. As the speedometer glided past seventy, the car flicked past a legal speed limit sign that said half as much. "We might be able to take the alternate road when we cross the river into Wilmington Island and lose them in the back roads, then come out the other end and sneak across the river into the mainland when they give up.

"We'll make it." Smitty tightened the seat belts attached to the roll bar. "Don't forget about the ninety-degreer to the left coming up."

"No sweat, man, I see it." Ron said. Then he looked in the rearview mirror and said, "We've got company."

Company it was. Only in this case it was not exactly the kind you wanted to invite to dinner, at least not under present circumstances.

Smitty heard the sound of the police siren behind them before he could eyeball the car in the rearview mirror. Obviously, they had fast cars, too. Ron was doing well over eighty and the cruiser was slowly gaining, and they would have to slow down soon. At the end of the beachfront, the road made a no-shit, ninety-degree left turn back toward town, and the speed limit slowed to twenty-five miles per hour accordingly.

Ron braked hard and downshifted as they entered the turn doing at least sixty. He spun the wheel all the way to the left and stepped on the emergency brake, locking the rear wheels. The car skidded into the turn then spiraled out, spinning lazily in a seemingly slow motion three times before coming to rest two feet from the curve on the wrong side of the road, but miraculously, with the nose pointed in the right direction.

Smitty had never seen anyone try to take that turn at more than thirty-five without the tires squealing in protest. Any faster was suicidal. Ron quickly disengaged the brake with his left hand and engaged first gear with his right, paused momentarily, turned, grinned at Smitty and said smugly, "Polish U-turn."

Too frightened to answer, Smitty wordlessly pointed toward the west. Ron was just letting out the clutch when a bone-jarring metallic, wood-splintering crash made both of them turn their heads in the direction of the noise.

The Savannah Beach patrolman was obviously not as adept at making like Richard Petty as Ron. He missed the turn completely, jumped the curve, and airmailed his patrol car thirty-five feet into the first floor of a beige two-story house located on the corner. Fortunately for him, the house was built to withstand the anticipated storm surge of a hurricane and as a result, the first floor was nothing more than a screened porch.

The car sailed completely through the porch area, scattering patio furniture, a portable TV, a portable barbecue, and miscellaneous other odds and ends like tornado refuse before exiting the other side. It traveled an additional ninety feet before plowing into a sand dune, spewing sand crystals thirty feet in the air like a snow blower throwing off snowflakes, and finally came to rest with the front end completely covered up.

Ron looked quickly at Smitty, and on seeing his assenting nod, shifted the car into reverse and with the tires barking in protest, backed quickly across the road to the curve. The dust had not even begun to settle when Smitty was out of the car before it stopped, limping his way around the shattered house and toward the cruiser with the best speed he could manage. Even if they got caught, their military training had kicked in. They wouldn't leave an innocent man hurt and helpless, even if he was the enemy, so to speak.

Smitty jerked open the door, and to his relief, was pleased to see that the patrolman was wearing a seat belt, and other than bleeding freely from a nasty bump on his forehead, was obviously dazed but otherwise unhurt.

"You okay, partner?" Smitty helped him from the car, wrinkling his nose at the pungent smell of gasoline. The patrolman looked up at him silently with glazed eyes in return.

"I think your gas line ruptured. We'd better get you away from here." Smitty took his arm as Ron arrived behind him and took the other. They half-carried him away from the car to the edge of the house. Smitty leaned down, righted an overturned lawn chair, and they gently lowered the stunned officer into it.

"What the hell happened?" an elderly man asked from the darkness at the top of the stairs.

"Call an ambulance," Ron barked at the shadowy figure.

"My house," he said.

"Screw your house. This dude's hurt. Get help," Ron said, as the patrol car started to burn. "And call the fire department." The screen door slammed as the owner went back inside.

"You guys better get out of here," the officer said.

"You'll be okay?" Smitty asked in a concerned voice.

"I'll live," he said.

"Take care, man." Smitty started for the car with the best speed he could manage.

"You only got about fifteen minutes' head start at most before the chief and the County Mounties start arriving here in force. If it was me, I'd make the best of them." He touched the bleeding cut on his forehead and winced. "Thanks for digging me out."

Ron patted his shoulder. "Semper Fi," he said. With a final wave, he ran back to the car, helped Smitty in, and they were again on their way to the Savannah mainland at breakneck speed. They crossed the bridge off the island in less than a minute; a minute more and they were racing past the entrance to Fort Pulaski and turning into Five-Mile Run.

Five-Mile Run was so named by the locals because that's exactly what it was: five straight miles of filled-in swampland sufficiently wide enough for the two-lane road and a row of palm trees evenly spaced about ten feet off the road and twenty feet apart on each side.

Since there was no place for the police to hide, it was frequently the scene of many late night drag-racing grudge matches, and unfortunately it was also the spot of many deaths, as inexperienced racers lost control of their cars and found out too late that palm trees sufficiently rooted to withstand the force of hurricane winds easily absorbed the impact of a couple of tons of a Motown Chariot—which generally collapsed like a squashed beer can against the tree.

Smitty glanced over at the speedometer and was sorry he did. The needle was on the dark side of 120 miles per hour and climbing. In the early morning mist, the palm trees were flying past them like pickets on a fence. One mistake and they would join the long line of casualties who had met their untimely end on the road that did not forgive.

When they made it across the Bull River Bridge, Smitty knew, as Ron had said previously, that they could lose their pursuit in the maze of roads on Wilmington Island or hide out there for the night. But in the end, the only road off Wilmington Island was across the river to the mainland. One way or another, that was the only route, and if they were to successfully run and evade the police, they had to cross it.

And run it would have to be. Flashing lights were visible in the rearview mirror, no more than two miles back. Ron was only half a mile from the curve and gaining on it incredibly fast. As he rounded the curve, the road depressed to divert onto the new concrete bridge, temporarily hiding them from the pursuit.

Good thing. They blew by the turnback onto the new bridge so fast that Smitty didn't even see it. They looked at one another in acceptance and began winding down the windows. Driving like Mario Andretti maneuvering his way around a ten-car pileup at Indianapolis, Ron braked quickly without losing control and steered the car between palm trees, down an incline, and onto an access road that led to a small parking area at the river's edge.

The curve at the end of Five-Mile Run had been christened "Dead Man's Curve" by the locals. Evidence of its danger was plainly visible in the hulks of crumpled, stripped, and abandoned automobiles that could be seen from the road in the daylight rusting quietly, half buried in the bog. They were clear enough evidence of the flatness of the curve and a constant reminder of the consequences of misjudging its treacherous centrifugal effects.

Lately, it had become even more hazardous because the center swing section of the old narrow metal bridge had been removed as the entire bridge had been replaced by a new concrete structure located just to the side, but the mating access road was not complete. As a result, it required an immediate Z-type maneuver to get on the right bridge from the old road. It was a turn that was treacherous in the daylight and potentially deadly when you were on the run late at night—as they had just found out.

Smitty estimated that they were doing only about forty-five or so when they sailed off the end of the embankment and belly flopped into the Bull River, spraying water forty feet up the first pylon of the old bridge.

The latest safety advertisement for cars was that seat belts saved lives; Smitty instantly became an ardent believer. The lap belt was standard Detroit issue, but the self-adjusting shoulder belts—five-finger-discounted from a U.S. Army helicopter—and roll bar that Ron had installed held both of them more snugly in place than Jane Russell's Eighteen-Hour Cross-Your-Heart Playtex Living Bra.

Smitty was convinced that if they had not been wearing the reinforced belts, they would have been shot-putted through the front windshield by the sudden impact and rapid deceleration, probably would have landed in the marshes on the other side of the river headfirst and, like as not, gone undiscovered in the marshy reeds for days, if they were ever discovered at all.

"Time to go, Irishman," Ron said, as the water rushed over the top of the windowsill.

Smitty hit the quick release mechanisms on the seat belts, and as the water came in and the car started to sink, he floated through the open window and kicked free of the suction and swam to the surface. It was just like the old army inverted downed aircraft drill. He broke the surface and looked around to see Ron bobbing beside him fifteen feet away.

"Over there," Ron said, pointing at the first pylon on the bridge. If they missed grabbing it in the swift current, they would have to float completely under the new bridge and try to wade ashore in the marshes, snake-infested and boggy enough that a single misstep could swallow you.

Smitty reached the support first, grabbed a maintenance tie-up ring firmly, reached out, grabbed Ron's hand with his other, and pulled him in. Quickly Ron climbed up on the small concrete island and as quickly helped Smitty out of the water. They climbed the rusty ladder up to the top of the bridge, climbed over the rail, and lowered themselves onto the pavement of the old bridge.

"Damn, and it's not even Saturday night," Ron said.

Smitty fished in his soaked vest pocket, pulled out a pack of equally soaked cigarettes, delicately extracted one, placed it at a roguish dangling angle, looked at Ron and said, "Light."

Before Ron could reply, four police cars went screaming by up on the new bridge, obviously not aware that their quarry had stopped for a rather extended car wash.

Ron started to laugh, then Smitty started to laugh with him. Both were laughing at the same thing. How ironic it would have been, after all the wounds and close calls in Vietnam, to end up drowning in a car accident, shit-faced in Georgia.

After a short rest, Ron and Smitty had put their collective brains together on first how to get off the island, then what to do about the car. Getting off the island turned out to be unexpectedly easy, retrieving the car was an altogether different matter.

Ron went quickly back down the ladder and, not without a great deal of effort, managed to swim across the river to a seafood restaurant located just on the other side. He called his wife from a phone booth in the parking lot. She came out in their VW Beetle and picked them up. She'd brought a change of clothes for both of them, since Ron and Smitty were about the same size.

By the time Ron's wife, Candace, who looked to be of Glenda's pleasingly plump proportions, had arrived two hours later and they had finished drying off, changed clothes, and cleaned up the car's entry point to hide its presence, it was close to 5:30 AM. They made a U-turn, got back on the right bridge, crossed over into Wilmington Island, went on the circular road that led to a shopping center, and had breakfast at a local diner. They left at 6:30 AM and drove back into Savannah. There was no sign of the police and no road blocks, if there had been any in the first place.

Ron dropped Smitty at his rented room, where Smitty showered, changed clothes, and went on to work on Saturday morning, even managing to show up a few minutes early, just as if nothing had happened.

The car remained in its watery garage until Sunday. Ron made arrangements with an army buddy, who was a scuba nut, to borrow his tank and flippers. Smitty borrowed the service station wrecker, and Ron brought along his engine chain hoist and a generous amount of extra chain.

As on their SOG missions, they met at the landing at dusk to attract the least amount of attention. If challenged by the local police, the cover story was to be that he and Smitty were out there fishing, left the emergency brake off, and the car just rolled into the water. Such accidents were so commonplace at the numerous boat ramps and landings around the coast that the story seemed entirely plausible.

The car rescue was difficult but was accomplished without raising any official eyebrows. Inside of two hours, they had the car in tow behind the wrecker; another two hours and it was delivered right to Ron's home, where the tearing apart would begin.

It took a month, but eventually the wild horse was roaming free again. Since the car was at Ron's, and Smitty felt duty bound to help, he had pretty much become a fixture at Ron's trailer after school and in his free time after work. Within two weeks, Ron had offered the spare bedroom to Smitty, which he accepted immediately—an acceptance that Smitty could see did not please Mrs. Polack one little bit.

The police never found them or, to be more accurate, the car, principally because they didn't know what they were looking for in the first place. According to the two-paragraph article in the *Savannah Morning News,* the Savannah Beach police officer had told his chief that the car he was chasing was a light-colored Camaro with out-of-state plates with two guys in it who had made the curve and fled the scene at an extremely high rate of speed. He further added that he thought they were in the military because he was sure he had seen a marine bumper sticker, but apparently didn't bother to mention the fact that they had stopped and pulled him out of his cruiser.

The barman's wife confirmed this, adding that, in her opinion, they must have been marines, because none of the little army soldiers she had seen had ever been able to put her man down.

For the next several days, any Camaro that even remotely resembled that description was stopped, and the driver questioned. But as the days passed and no valid suspects turned up, the incident faded into memory and became part of local beach folklore. The police concluded that whoever was driving the mysterious Camaro had fled the state, and they chalked it off as just another in a series of unsolved car chases. In a military town full of transient soldiers, they were all too common.

Smitty and Ron's narrow escape was not ironic. It was, in fact, just plain damn lucky. Many other Vietnam veterans were not so fortunate. The fatal accidents on the beach road and everywhere else in Savannah were mounting at an alarming rate. The army base at Hunter and its sister base, Fort Stewart, forty-five miles away, were filled to overflowing with Veterans returning from Vietnam with hoards of money on the books and even more pent-up testosterone.

Toss in mass quantities of alcohol, mix in a little loneliness and depression, and you had a lethal combination just looking for the right place to explode. And in Savannah you didn't have to look far. Every bridge abutment to and from the beach, along with a fair number of the three-foot-wide oak trees planted in Colonial times that lined Victory Drive, was marked with human blood

Service guys in cars of every shape and kind cruised the drive-in circuit that started at one end of Victory Drive and continued through three other greasy spoons down to the drive-in movie. Most would then do a U-turn, come back to a turnaround at Daffin Park, and start again. On one of the drive-throughs, inevitably, car taunting would start, which would usually turn into a challenge drag race with, more often than not, tragic results.

Those who weren't cruising looking for other "motorheads" to impress were downtown on the seedy waterfront drinking and getting shilled out of their money by the bar girls. The only difference Smitty could see from when he was in basic three years ago was that the colored panther piss that the girls called champagne was now $4.50 a pop. One separated paycheck through that gauntlet was more than enough to convince Smitty that he had better uses for his meager funds.

It was said that Savannah was the only Southern city that had more gin mills than Baptist churches and that the major reason they were tolerated was the tax revenue generated from the liquor licenses. That, and the resulting endless series of DUI arrests contributed a hell of a lot more to the city tax coffers than all the fire and brimstone houses of the God squad combined.

The fact that the soldiers didn't care much for the civilians or their nervous and intolerant fathers could pretty much be put in the plan of the day. The GIs referred to the local women as GRITS: Girls so Retarded their brains were Interconnected to their TitS. The name became a universally accepted acronym by the soldiers when referring to a date with a local who, if she didn't spread her legs by the second date, was not likely to get asked out for a third. When a marriage did occur, it was usually dismissed scornfully as "a base gate GRIT hooking an allotment check."

Ironically, the local small town girls were flattered to be referred to as GRITS. Smitty didn't understand this until he saw a local Southern cutie wearing a T-shirt that had the term embossed on the front in big letters across her boobs. Underneath was an explanation: Girls Raised in The South.

True, it was a derogatory term to refer to their naïve ways and mannerisms as being as colloquial as the predominately Southern breakfast food it mocked, but it also implied the transient nature of the relationship and what its ultimate goals really were. It was a truism that one of the things soldiers liked best about Southern women was that they talked so slow and acted so refined that by the time they said "I won't," they already had.

Because of this cavalier attitude, the God-fearing parents didn't like the army soldiers dating their daughters much, either. Smitty had seen a sign on the front lawn of a house close to the base that seemed to pretty much sum up their collective feelings. It read simply, "GIs and dogs stay off the lawn." Underneath, in smaller print, the owner had added, "Neutered dogs OK."

Smitty was sitting in the student center at Barnstein reviewing his midterm grades after reading about the latest accident involving three services guys who hit a bridge abutment doing ninety. They were all dead, of course—just like his college grades. Two C's, an F, and an incomplete. The C's were in English and algebra, and the F was, of course, from Mr. Strickland in history. The incomplete was in physical education, which was a freshman requirement; a requirement that with Smitty's mangled and gimpy leg, he had no way to accomplish, so he just skipped it altogether after the first-day orientation.

Besides, he said to himself as he deposited the grade slip in the trash on his way out the door to his car—snugging his faded army jacket around his neck to ward off the late October rains that were steadily spattering around him—*it didn't matter, since this was strictly a one quarter thing anyway.* He was leaving after the current semester ended and splitting to Florida.

He'd already been in touch with Stan the Man, who had promised that if he moved to Miami, he'd help him get squared away and, more importantly, get the therapy his leg so desperately needed. Smitty was looking forward to it. He hated these spoiled little Joe College pukes going to school on their daddies' money. He'd be glad to be shed of them.

Now that he was living at Ron's, which was only ten miles from the college and on the way to and from work, his life had gotten a little easier. He had a routine established, had a good job, a good set of mechanic's tools now paid for, and was pleased with the current progress of the Chevy.

He'd finished the front and rear-end rebuilds and had even rebuilt the Muncie and put in a new clutch. The upholstery and interior repaint, although not perfect, was now done to his satisfaction. He was saving cash for an engine rebuild scheduled for December as the final thing to do before he bugged out of town.

Even though the engine used a little oil, it started at the first turn and ran smoothly. Smitty backed out of his parking space and was circling toward the exit when he saw a car with its hood up. As was his custom, he stopped; it turned out to be a mistake.

The dead Dodge Dart belonged to none other than the PE teacher whose class he had been avoiding.

"Hi, son, thanks for stopping," the instructor said in a friendly fashion.

"What's the trouble?"

"I left the lights on this morning, and it killed the battery. You don't happen to have a set of jumpers do you?" he asked.

"As a matter of fact, I do." Smitty pulled his car next to the Dart in a vacant parking space, stepped on the emergency brake, and left the car idling.

Smitty opened the rear tailgate, reached under the floor into the spare tire well, grabbed his cables, and on beginning to hook up them up to the dead soldier, noted that the positive terminal was extremely dirty. The instructor stood back, allowing him to proceed with, Smitty noted, a sympathetic look at his gimpy leg.

"Better clean these first." Smitty walked back to the rear of his car, retrieved his post and cable cleaner, and a pair of offset battery pliers from his toolbox.

"This may be most of your problem." Smitty quickly removed and cleaned both terminals and battery ends in an efficient manner that indicated to the teacher that he had done this many times before. After tightening the last cable, Smitty connected the jumpers. "Try it now." As he waited for the instructor to get back in his car, he noticed that it had started to rain harder.

The trusty little slant-six turned over and fired on the third turn.

"Thanks, son," the instructor said, as he got out of his car, shielding his eyes from what was now a downpour. "What do I owe you?"

"Forget it, ain't no big thing."

"Well, it is to me." He stuffed ten bucks in Smitty's shirt pocket. "Would have cost me twice that to have someone come out. And they would have probably tried to hit me up for a new battery as well."

"Fred Fieldman," he said, offering his hand. "Physical education instructor and one of the basketball coaches."

"Smit—uh, that is to say, Kevin Smith," Smitty said, taking his hand.

"Kevin Smith, Kevin Smith," the instructor repeated, not letting go of his hand. As the name recognition hit him, he wrinkled his brow. "Kevin Smith as in you-haven't-yet-come-to-my-class, Kevin Smith?"

"The same," Kevin answered.

He let go of Kevin's hand and he clapped him on the shoulder. "Come and see me tomorrow afternoon after your last class. We'll talk."

"About what?"

"About you and about what we're going to have to do to get you to come and participate in my class." He gave Smitty a friendly wave as he got in his car and drove away.

"Hi, son, come in," Coach Fieldman motioned to a seat in front of his desk. The coach was not alone. Seated on a sofa behind him was another man, who looked to be about midthirties, and was eyeing Smitty with great interest.

"This is a friend of mine, a doctor who specializes in physical therapy. He's the man who supervises the rehabilitation on our student athletes. After our chance meeting yesterday, I called him and asked him to attend. I hope you don't mind."

"Doctor Silverman."

"Now, son, to come straight to the point, you don't have to answer this if you don't want to, and even though your records don't say anything about it, my guess is that those welts on your face and that limp are the result of wounds suffered in Vietnam that have not been properly rehabilitated."

Smitty glared at him in silence, afraid to officially acknowledge the obvious.

"I'll take your silence for a yes. Further, I'll bet my next paycheck that's why you've been ditching my class because you know you can't do the things the course would require, or you'd rather sit in some bar and whine about your bad luck."

Again, Smitty only glared in silence.

"I thought so," he said. "Well, son, your running days are over. It's time to come home and join the human race again."

He looked at the doctor, who nodded. "First, my friendly sawbones is going to examine you. Then between us, we're going to design a rehabilitation program that you can follow.

"From now until the end of the term, I expect you to be here every day to participate and get with the program. Without strengthening that leg, it will never get any better. I know; I had the same problem after World War II, and all the civilians who stayed home didn't give a crap about me, either. You stopped to help me out of the goodness of your heart. Now it's my turn to return the favor. Questions?" He came around the desk and offered his hand.

Smitty shook his hand firmly. "Thanks, Coach."

"Doctor, he's all yours." The coach patted Smitty on the shoulder and left the office, slamming the door.

"Well, Kevin, suppose we start with a complete physical so I know where to begin. Then I want you to tell me about your injuries as completely as you can." Silverman nodded in the direction of the door, then added, "And remember, there's confidentiality between a doctor and his patient. So what you tell me, nobody else will know." He looked Kevin straight in the eye and offered his hand.

As Smitty took the doctor's hand, it was part handshake and part lifeline. He'd given up hope of ever walking normally again. Had resigned himself to being one of life's totally fucked. Then, in the last place he'd ever expected to be, in the last place he'd expected it, he'd found people who cared.

Maybe this college thing wasn't so bad after all; maybe even his initial judgment—no, make that lifelong attitude—about Joe College types had been a little harsh. Maybe all the students weren't immature college pukes either.

As Smitty removed his pants so the Doctor could get a first-hand look at his leg, he thought how ironic it was that, once again just as it had with Linda's parents, a selfless act had stepped in to alter his destiny when he least expected it.

Maybe that was the way life worked for normal people: good deeds were returned tenfold. Either that or once again God was displaying his macabre sense of humor in remunerating the flute-player.

Smitty knocked lightly at Professor Strickland's door. "Hello, Mr. Smith. Thank you so much for coming. Have a seat." Strickland motioned to a chair directly across from him. "I'll be with you in a second. I'm just finishing grading the last of the test papers."

While he waited, Smitty glanced idly around the small office, noting the numerous diplomas on the wall, the bookcases full of past and present textbooks and research materials, and what seemed to be endless piles of paper stacked everywhere.

Smitty's leg was bothering him but less and less every day. He was still feeling the effects of the most recent operation two weeks ago to repair a pretty badly torn cartilage and remove numerous fragments in his left knee, which, according to the X-rays taken by Dr. Silverman, was one of the primary reasons that his leg was not healing in the first place.

The injury was old, apparently missed by the army when the original diagnosis was done last summer. When Smitty'd raved disgustedly about the army and army doctors in particular, Dr. Silverman was extraordinarily calm, stating matter-of-factly that based on what Smitty had told him to date, with all the swelling and other life-threatening injuries, it was probably just an honest error of omission.

Three days after the operation, Smitty was at the doc's clinic doing muscle exercises and other therapy in accordance with a strict program, which he had made plain he expected Smitty to follow to the letter—with or without his personal supervision.

When told of the need for another operation on his knee, Smitty had originally declined. The doctor, guessing accurately that he had no money to pay for it, dismissed him with an airy wave saying that they would work something out.

The leg was sore, but it was a different kind of soreness. It was the soreness that comes from therapy to heal, rather than atrophy of acceptance and disuse.

"There, that's all done," Professor Strickland set aside his latest set of papers, reached for a cigarette, and offered one first to Smitty—who broke the filter off with a disgusted look and thumped it in the direction of the trash can—then took one himself. The professor grabbed the lighter on his desk, lit first Smitty's cigarette, then his own, settled comfortably back in his office chair, and blew out a cloud of smoke.

"Mr. Smith, I get the distinct feeling that you don't like me very much."

Smitty snorted in reply.

"I thought so." He leaned forward in his chair and tapped his cigarette delicately in the ashtray. "Well, I suppose that's somewhat normal considering our dissimilar backgrounds. But the reason I asked to see you is to see if it's possible to come to some form of mutual understanding where we might be able to, shall we say, coexist with each other."

Resisting the urge to tell him to fuck off and then leave, Smitty folded his arms in exasperation, and resigned himself to sitting quietly until Sister Mary got through whatever she had to say.

"Mr. Smith, let me first begin by saying I owe you a very great apology. From the minute you came into my class, your demeanor was so different from that of all of my other students that it made me uncomfortable, and as a result of, I guess you would call it, my own insecurities, I embarrassed you when you came to me earnestly seeking help, and I'm truly sorry.

"Also, I regret to say that my initial judgment of you caused me to be, shall we say, somewhat less than objective in my feelings toward your submissions on tests."

"So what are you expecting me to do, say thank you and a give you big kiss?"

"No, actually I was hoping that we might be able to work out something where I would be the one who was thanking you."

"Sorry, professor, I've already got a roommate," Smitty said. "And he's a damn sight more attractive than you."

The professor smiled and blew out a cloud of smoke. "So have I, and I think he is, too." To Smitty's scowl, he said patiently, "Please, let me finish."

"Okay, Teach, get it over with."

"As I was saying, your background is very different from that of the average student we get in this class. I have to candidly admit that I didn't know just how different until I had a short conversation with Coach Fieldman. Although you're approximately the same age as most of the students in my class, you're years ahead of them in actual maturity and life experience.

"Yeah, so?"

"So I was hoping that I could convince you to accept an extra-credit assignment that would allow me a chance to reevaluate your classroom performance."

Smitty stared at the professor in silence. This was not at all what he had been expecting when he walked in here. He had expected this conference to be the one where the prof tossed him out of the lifeboat. And here was a lifeline.

"What have you got in mind?" Smitty asked without expression.

"I would like you to give a series of lectures to all of my classes on your experiences in Vietnam. Most students here, and most of the faculty, including myself, know about the war only from what we've read in the newspapers or heard secondhand. It would be most enlightening to hear about it from someone who's experienced it firsthand."

"A series of lectures," Smitty said.

"Yes, I've taken the liberty of speaking to your other instructors. They are most willing to allow you to omit their classes for a day and spend an entire day, shall we say next Monday, lecturing to all my classes."

"Professor, what does my service in Vietnam have to do with your history class?" Smitty asked, confused.

"Well, Mr. Smith, the purpose of this course is to study the various cultures and customs of the past so that we might learn from them in the future. I'm sure that you have acquired many firsthand facts about the people and the cultures of Vietnam that would be of interest to the students. To say nothing of your firsthand observations on the way the actual war is being fought."

"How would I go about it?" Smitty protested. "Look, I'm no professor. I can't get up in front of a bunch of students and lecture for a whole hour."

"Well, I was thinking that I might do a short introduction, then I suggest you start by giving a short review of your background, what led you to join the army, then quickly review the highlights of your time in Vietnam, then throw the floor open for questions." He snubbed his cigarette out in the ashtray. "I expect the students will be rather curious and keep your mind working for the balance of that hour."

Smitty drummed his fingers on the desk, thinking. He reached for the professor's cigarette pack, shook one out, broke off the filter and nodded his thanks for the proffered light.

The professor pulled another cigarette from the pack, ceremoniously broke off the filter and flipped it in the trash can. He settled back in his chair prepared to give Smitty whatever time he required to think it over.

Smitty's mind raced rapidly through the events of the past like someone flipping the pages of one of those rag mags that always seemed to be conveniently positioned at the supermarket checkout stands to test your impulse-buying restraint.

Why was the professor going out of his way to help a student he'd already made plain that he didn't care for? Could he really be serious? Were the students that interested, or was it an elaborate ruse to embarrass and humiliate him again? Smitty wasn't sure; he sounded sincere, but Smitty was leery. He had to ask.

"Professor, is this some kind of trap to embarrass me again, like you did before?"

The professor leaned forward in his chair, looked Smitty straight in the eye and said bluntly, "Mr. Smith, I give you my word that such is not my intention."

Seeing the doubt in Smitty's eyes, he added. "Mr. Smith, just because I have a different sexual outlook from you does not disqualify me from being a man of my word with honorable intentions."

Smitty puffed his cigarette in silence. Of all the things that had ever happened to him, this was by far the most bizarre. Although Smitty had disclosed to no one that he'd been in the service, again everybody seemed to know. Maybe it was plastered all over his puss, and he was wearing it on his face and in his eyes. When you had the thousand-yard stare, you didn't need official verification.

Was he violating the rules of his U.S. Army separation by speaking out in an informal manner? Smitty suspected that if he bothered to check, the answer would be yes. As he saw it, his choice was a simple one: He could beg off and cover his ass, which would be the right thing to do. Or . . . he could take a chance, do the right thing, and maybe save somebody else from making the same mistakes he did.

Smitty crushed out his cigarette in the professor's ashtray and inhaled nervously. "Okay, Teach, I guess I'm your clay pigeon."

"Splendid. Shall we plan for this coming Monday?"

"Okay." Smitty stood and shook the professor's hand, hoping that he was not walking into a trap where all the students were armed with verbal slings and arrows. When properly applied, they could be much more deadly than guns.

"Students, Mr. Smith has already stayed well past the hour, I'm afraid we'll only be able to take one more question," Professor Strickland said to a chorus of regretful murmurs from the last class, which, from Smitty's estimate seemed to number six times the normal allotment of thirty.

The attendance at each of the classes had grown hourly as news of Smitty's "lecture" spread quickly by word of mouth across the campus. The last three classes after lunch had been so well attended that Professor Strickland had moved the students to the lecture hall on the first floor. The hall was filled far in excess of the fire code occupancy safety regulations. This last class was already forty-five minutes past its official fifty-minute duration. Students were sitting in every available seat, on every step of the aisles, and were standing in every space in between.

It seemed that the students were not only more than curious, but they genuinely cared. Every question seemed to start with, "My brother is in the army and has served in

Vietnam." Or, "If I lose my deferment, how long before I get drafted?" And, "Is your experience typical?"

They asked good questions about the people of Vietnam, their makeup and what the war was really about, and why had it gone on so long. They listened attentively and respectfully as Smitty described the events and nodded in acceptance of his conclusion that it was now too late for the war to be won. Smitty could see they were touched as he told of the fates of his friends and the effects the war had on each of them.

There was, of course, the odd question from a radical student. "How does it feel to be a baby killer?" But Smitty was amazed to find that most of the students were quick to rush to his defense to the point that the heckler was shamed into silence. After the second class, those kinds of questions had ceased. Smitty suspected that uninformed muckraking was playing second fiddle to firsthand knowledge, and those with an axe to grind had decided that their own peers would not allow Smitty to be used as the sharpening stone.

"Kevin, I'm not trying to put you on the spot, and you can refuse to answer this if you wish, but could you possibly try to tell us what it feels like to take a human life?" A cute blonde female student halfway up the left aisle asked politely.

The room became deathly silent. The students who were making preparations to leave stopped in their tracks and turned back to hear how Smitty would answer.

The professor stepped forward quickly in Smitty's defense. "Miss Sanders, remember the ground rules. We agreed that certain topics were out of bounds. Notably, asking Mr. Smith to be accountable for his personal actions was one of those areas."

"Sorry, Kevin," Miss Sanders answered sheepishly, her face turning red.

Smitty sensed her embarrassment and said to Professor Strickland, "Um, Professor, if you don't object, I'd like to take a shot a giving some kind of answer." He noted the relieved look on Miss Sanders's face at being taken off the spot.

"If you're comfortable, please proceed," the professor said with a slight bow.

"Well, I think the first level thing we need to understand is that war hasn't changed since the first recorded conflicts in ancient times. We've just gotten much more efficient at it. But although the technology has improved, I suspect that the feelings of the people involved in wars have remained pretty much the same."

Smitty paced four steps to his right, collected his thoughts, and paced four steps back. "It's not the feeling of taking a human life that has to be rationalized; it's living with it afterward."

Smitty looked up and saw that he seemed to have their undivided attention. "To explain a little further, less than four hours after I landed at Cam Ranh Bay, the truck convoy I was riding in was attacked by the Vietcong. At that point, it didn't matter a whole lot what I felt or thought about the concept of taking a human life. When the guy across from you is pointing a weapon at you, your choice, driven by fear, training, instinct, and adrenaline is a simple one—either you get him, or he gets you. Rationalization happens afterward, in the early hours of the night, in the darkest corners of your mind.

"My boss over there, a colonel whom I respect greatly, said that if the time ever comes that afterward, you don't feel even the smallest sense of remorse at the taking of a human life, then you're already dead from the neck up, and the rest of your body just doesn't know it yet." He added in a voice filled with pain, "You can still come home, but you'll never know peace."

Visions of Hogs and the baby-faced Boy Wonder flashed into Smitty's head, and he smiled sadly in remembrance. Tears began to form at the corners of his eyes. "I'm sorry, that's probably not the answer you were looking for, but it's the best I can do."

Miss Sanders stood and started to clap. Instantly she was joined by most of the students present. Smitty was stunned by the standing ovation.

With the passage of a minute or two, the applause stopped. Mr. Strickland stepped to the podium. "Students, Mr. Smith was doing this as an extra-credit assignment. I think you'll agree with me that he's earned an A." A chorus of yeses and scattered applause filled the room.

"No, Professor, I do not agree," Miss Sanders said, as the noise died down.

"You don't think he deserves an A for this extraordinary effort, Miss Sanders?"

"I was thinking more of an 'A-plus."

As others nodded and clapped, the professor spread his hands and conceded with a smile, "The majority has spoken." He turned and offered his hand. Smitty readily took it and they shook hands.

It took Smitty another thirty minutes to get out of the auditorium as students crowded around to ask more questions, shake his hand, slap him five, or in the case of several lovely young ladies, give him a kiss on the cheek. A couple of the kisses were accompanied by notes with phone numbers.

The professor had been right—Vietnam when viewed from his perspective had been, and was, a historical current event that his students were most interested in hearing about.

When Smitty arrived at his car, he found Miss Sanders waiting for him.

"Hi," she said in a friendly fashion. Smitty couldn't help noticing the way her sandy blonde hair seemed to glisten in the sunlight. "I just wanted to wait until you were alone to tell you how much I appreciated your taking me off the spot."

"No problem," Smitty said. Talking to a class impersonally or propositioning prostitutes on Tu Do Street was one thing, but exchanging polite conversation with a nice, pretty girl from a normal American family was something else altogether. Smitty was woefully short on training and experience for this kind of engagement.

She seemed to sense his embarrassment and smiled warmly. "I really enjoyed your talk. I guess because my younger brother wants to join the army, and I wanted to try to understand what he'd be up against." She fidgeted awkwardly, then said shyly, "I don't suppose you would be interested in coming over for supper Sunday and talking to him firsthand?"

"Well," Smitty said uncomfortably, "I work until three."

"That's okay. We don't usually eat dinner on Sunday until five." She giggled infectiously. "Or sometimes later if my dad doesn't play well on the golf course and has one too many at the nineteenth hole."

She opened her purse, fished around for a paper and pencil, and quickly wrote down her address and phone number. She folded the paper and slipped it into the pocket of his shirt.

"We'll expect you at four-thirty. Bye." As she walked away to her car, Smitty noticed how attractive she looked in her tight bell-bottom pants.

"Hey, what's your first name?" Smitty called out. She pirouetted gracefully and walked back with a smile, giving Smitty a chance to see that she looked as good coming as going.

"Carla," she said. Leaning up and kissed him lightly on the cheek. "Don't be late."

Smitty got into his car and headed the big Chevy away from the campus and toward work.

He found himself laughing inwardly at his lifetime of energy misspent on forming half-baked opinions of his fellow students and of college itself. It seemed strange to him that in the space of three short months, he could now see the differences among them and, for the first time, saw each of them as unique individuals.

Once you got past their hair and dress, they were not so unlike him after all. Different in some ways, but alike in many others . . . all insecure youth bumbling their way to adulthood the best way they could.

He thought of his earlier insight that, in the last place he'd ever expected to be and in the last place he'd expected it, he'd found people who cared. Smitty now had to add to that . . . from the last kind of person he would have ever expected to help. How curious.

CHAPTER NINETEEN

Smitty wiped his forehead with a damp rag as he pumped gas into the tank of the big Chevy four-door land yacht parked at the front pump.

It was mid-March, and Savannah was caught in the grip of an early heat wave that left many of the locals desperately trying to find ingenious ways to keep cool. The intense dampness was supposed to be with them another three to four days, then more temperate weather would return, bringing seasonable weather for the annual St. Patrick's Day bash scheduled for next week.

Smitty had not gone to Florida as he had planned in December; there was now no need. Thanks to the extensive therapy program, his leg was 100 percent better than it had been just six short months ago. He was walking normally and was now even able to use his left leg to depress the Hays's high-pressure clutch that he'd installed when he rebuilt the Chevy engine over Christmas break. The rebuild had been made easier with the aid of his new assistants, Doctor Silverman's teenage sons, whom Smitty coached through the rebuilding process as payment for the operation on his knee.

Smitty was so far ahead of the coach's program that he'd starting jogging in the gym when the winter quarter began in January and was now running two miles a day and lifting weights. He now considered himself 90 percent combat ready.

Christmas was a bad time for him. His mind was awash with memories of a year ago. The major he'd been forced to kill, the friends he left behind, and Linda's untimely death were painful reminders of the past that infusions of alcohol couldn't seem to numb.

But on the positive side, his final grades were two C's and two A's. Not bad for a dropout who'd GED'd his way to a high school diploma, thanks to the army. Not surprisingly, the A's were from Professor Strickland and the coach. He was secretly proud and pleased, and although he'd never admit this to Ron, Smitty was starting to sense that Ron resented his sudden intense interest in higher education, since Ron himself had been field commissioned in 1966.

With every day that passed, Smitty's opinions of Barnstein and college in general were changing. Unlike the army, where you had to earn your stripes and people helped you only if you asked and it coincided with their best interest, here in college, the instructors seem to have an uncanny ability to sense when you were confused or unclear. And they insisted on going out of their way to help. Maybe it was something peculiar to a small college or just to Barnstein, but it sure left Smitty with a nice feeling.

Thanks to a generous Christmas bonus from his boss at the service station and the money he'd already saved, Smitty was easily able to come up with the price of a first-class hopped-up rebuild of the Chevy V-8 and the cost of his January tuition and books in cash. But the painful unreconciled memories were still there, not drowned by the considerable amounts of alcohol that Smitty and his buddies put away every Friday and Saturday night.

The pain was lessened somewhat by Sally, who tricked Smitty and his dad into a face-to-face Christmas dinner meeting by making the arrangements with each separately. Dad came to the restaurant thinking he was taking Sally out to dinner; Smitty came thinking he was introducing Sally to his new girlfriend, Carla. The meeting was tense, formal, and on the surface nonproductive, as Smitty and Dad scowled at each other across the table.

But underneath, Smitty could see that his dad was pleased with Smitty's transition from Green Beret to college freshman and even went so far as to smile sheepishly and comment politely that "in order to keep getting up in the morning, a man has to have something to look forward to." Sally, always the facilitator, volunteered that Dad had told her that he would himself be taking his Number Two Son's advice and would be enrolling at Barnstein for the winter quarter.

For Smitty, January was a tough month. The weather was bitingly cold, making working at the station arduous. The courses he had signed up for were harder, and he had the additional social burden of having his dad in two of his classes. Their relationship was so formal that most of the students had no idea that they were father and son.

Although he hid it well, Smitty was suffering internally from his own personal turmoil, in that it was just a year ago that the army had offered him the deal of a lifetime, and in the same month he'd lost his friend Hogs on a mission that, like all of what went on over the border, the general public would never know about. And if they did, Smitty was quickly coming to the conclusion that they wouldn't care.

Smitty stayed busy right through February and the end of the quarter in March. He worked, he went to class, he studied, and he went to bed. His life had become as monotonous and regimented as a prison routine and he was glad. What precious little time he had left over he saved for Carla and occasional drinking bouts with Ron—when he could get away from his overbearing and nagging wife.

"Seven dollars," Smitty said to the owner of the Chevy.

"Thanks, son. Here's ten, keep the change as my way of saying thanks for stopping to help my wife, then fixing her car so fast last week. It runs great now."

Smitty turned and was halfway back into the service bay, when a car honked behind him.

To his pleasant surprise, it was Sally, who stopped her car quickly and was out of it and running to him enthusiastically before Smitty could cover half the distance to her.

"Hey, sweetie, how ya doin'?" She hugged him without hesitation, not put off by the dirty work clothes at all.

"I'm fine, Sally," Smitty answered with a smile.

"Come in the office, and I'll get you a cup of coffee." Smitty took her arm and led her inside. It was Friday evening. Smitty was caught up on all the mechanical work, and he was looking forward to getting off. He'd a hot date planned with Carla. Her parents were away for the weekend, and she'd invited him to help her house-sit—on her personally, and the house, if there was time after.

He opened the door, nodded to a seat beside the desk, and poured for both of them.

"Sugar and cream?" Smitty asked without turning around.

"One of each, please."

They sipped in silence, blowing lightly on the scalding java. Finally, Smitty said, "What brings you around this side of town? Little off your range, aren't you?"

"Yes, I am." She moved the chair a little closer to the desk.

"I have a message to deliver to you, and given the gulf between you and your father, I thought it best if I came while he's busy visiting with his brother, who was in Atlanta on business this week and has come down for the weekend. Your father has gone to the airport to pick him up."

She set her face in a deadpan imitation of Dad's first sergeant glare. "I'm supposed to be getting the guest quarters squared away."

"Shoot." Smitty smiled at her humor. Smitty might have had, and apparently always would have, his differences with his father, but Sally was the genuine real thing. Smitty wondered idly what a woman so refined and charming ever saw in a feisty old first sergeant like Dad.

"Kevin, you need to go to Atlanta; you need to go this weekend. Your grandmother needs your help. Your Aunt Belinda called your father and tried to explain, but he cut her off and hung up. I don't know what it's about exactly, but she was most insistent that you come up at once. She said the reason that she didn't call your trailer was that you don't have a private phone, and she didn't want to leave a message."

"And she didn't say why, huh?" Smitty asked, taking another sip of his coffee to cover his own anxiety. It had been nearly six years since he'd last seen his grandmother. "Sally, I have to work this weekend. I can't just drop everything and go. People are depending on me," Smitty protested, not wishing to disclose his real reason. He didn't want to give up his weekend of playing slap and tickle with Carla, as Sergeant Mike would have said.

"Are they, or are you just using that as an excuse?" Sally asked.

"Are you using what as an excuse?" Smitty's boss, the station owner, entered the office from the back.

"Um, Jake, this is Sally Smith. She's my, um, stepmother," Smitty finally blurted out.

"Pleased to meet you, ma'am."

"How's my boy doing?"

"I'll tell you one thing, Mrs. Smith, your stepson is one hell of a mechanic." He walked to the back door of the office that led to the service bays, peeked around to make sure no one was within earshot. "And I'll tell you another thing, he works rings around my bolt-on day mechanic. If he wasn't in college, I'd make him my main day mechanic in a heartbeat."

"Bolt-on, what's that?" Sally said in a confused voice.

"Your son here understands the theory of an internal combustion engine and the concepts behind how all the support systems, like brakes for example, work. So when a car comes in, he analyzes what's wrong, and fixes only what needs to be replaced.

"Hal, my other mechanic, doesn't have this understanding. As a result, he tends to guess and just bolt on replacement parts until he stumbles onto the fix. It runs up the customer's bill, and although they pay, they usually don't come back.

"Last week, for example, a customer came in with an electrical problem; his car was hard to start. Hal replaced the alternator and the regulator and couldn't find it. Your son looked at it for ten minutes and tightened the main cable to the starter solenoid, and that fixed the problem. I had a hard time explaining that bill to the customer, I'll tell you that." Jake shook his head sadly.

"So he's pretty valuable to your business, huh?" Sally said.

"Absolutely."

"Valuable enough that if I asked you to let him off this weekend for an urgent family matter he would still keep his job?"

"Certainly," Jake answered immediately. "Smitty is my most honest and hardworking employee. He shows up for work on time, sober, or at least not hung over, and my customers like him.

"Take whatever time you need. As a matter of fact, I've been meaning to give this young motorhead some paid time off, so take the two days on me."

"Well, there you go, son. I told you he wouldn't mind." Sally smiled innocently.

"Okay, Stepmother." Smitty sighed. "Since you sweet-talked my boss out of the time off, I'll go."

"Thanks son. I suggest you leave tomorrow morning after getting a good night's sleep. And don't drive that rocket of yours too fast." She got up and started for the door.

Smitty walked her to her car and opened the door. "You always get your way, don't you?"

"Oh, come on, sonny, be a good loser. You're a dependable young man and a good employee." She kissed him in the cheek and hugged him. "Besides, you're trying to do the right thing for yourself, and people naturally will want to help. It makes them feel good, too. Let them."

She got in the car and rolled the window down. "Bye, sweetie."

Smitty watched her drive away with a wave then turned and went back to work, shaking his head in wonderment.

"What do you mean you're going away for the weekend?" Carla demanded angrily. "I'd planned for us to spend the entire weekend together playing house and doing you-know-what."

"Carla, I'm sorry," Smitty said. "But from what Sally said, it sounds like I need to be there."

"Look, I put up with the fact that you're always working at that damn service station and can only see me on weekends. The weekends after you get off work are supposed to be my time," she pouted.

Smitty stared at her in silence. There was nothing more to say. They had been over the same ground since Smitty had arrived at nine. Well, not exactly at nine, more like nine forty-five.

Carla had answered the door in a rather fetching negligee. She kissed him passionately as soon as the door was closed and dragged him straight to her bedroom. Their youthful fires of passion burned out of control for most of the next hour.

It was in the hour after, as they rested and sipped expensive scotch from her dad's liquor cabinet, that Smitty had started to build the case for why he wouldn't be staying the rest of the weekend. A case that, no matter how many times he told it and how he tried to justify it, did not soothe the hurt feelings of a very pissed off girlfriend.

"Well then, I have an idea. I'll go with you," she said suddenly, putting her arms around him and turning her head up for a kiss. Smitty's lack of response spoke volumes.

"Why not?" she asked in a hurt voice.

"Because I don't know even know what I'm walking into. I haven't been there in six years. I don't think this would be the right time to introduce you. So I think it would be better if I went by myself."

"What am I supposed to do while you're busy doing your family thing? Just stay home by myself and put my hair up in curlers?"

"I'm sorry. I know we had plans. We'll do it some other time," Smitty said, trying to say anything to placate her.

"Get out, you bastard." She began to sob and ran from the room.

Smitty listened to her bare feet pad quickly down the hardwood floor of the hallway and the loud slam of her bedroom door. He walked down the hallway and knocked lightly on her door and called her name softly.

"I said get out of here, you bastard, or I'll call the police."

Slowly, Smitty walked back down the hallway and left by the front door.

On the drive back to his side of town, Smitty realized that he couldn't even go back to the trailer. When he told Ron he would not be home that weekend, his wife was ecstatic and had been busily planning an intimate weekend for two.

He steered the car in the direction of the service station. On arrival, he backed the Chevy behind it into the secluded space that it had occupied before it ran, folded the backseat down, unfolded the army blanket wrapped around the pillow that was in the back and settled down for the night. He thought sadly that almost nine months had passed since he arrived in Savannah, and here he was, still sleeping in his car. It was a problem Smitty vowed to fix—permanently.

Smitty was ninety miles from Savannah, cruising the rolling hills of the two-lane blacktop at sixty, ten miles below the speed limit, and he was pissed.

It had nothing to do with the fight with Carla last night, a fight that he was sure would further depress his girl record to 0-5-1, but it had everything to do with the asshole in the smoking Corvette in front of him. Every time he tried to overtake the red '64 Roadster, it would speed up just enough that he would have to slow down before completing his pass and duck back in behind, and then it would decelerate to sixty. He had done it twice. This would be the third time, and one way or another, Smitty was going to make it the proverbial charm and be out of there.

Interstate 16 was only completed thirty miles out of Savannah. From there, it was State Route 46 and a combination of other back roads until you picked up the interstate again outside of Soperton, sixty miles from Macon and the junction to I-75 to Atlanta. The nursing home was just a short hop up the interstate to the north.

Smitty had called Sally and confirmed that he was going after taking a shower at the service station that morning. She added the fact that Smitty needed to get to the nursing home by 1:00 PM, as, according to what she had overheard, that was the time Aunt Belinda had said they would be meeting—whoever they were. Whatever was up, it was preplanned. Smitty hoped that it would be a meeting and not an ambush.

"C'mon, asshole, move it over," Smitty muttered in disgust, glancing at his watch. "I'm gonna be late." He'd slept fitfully in the car the previous night, awoken late, and was still trying to catch up with that most elusive of all bandits: time.

The land on the right was open farmland; the left was undeveloped woods. Smitty noted there was a curve ahead that arced down the side of a hill and slowly up the other side, which was plainly visible from the top of the rolling hill he was on. He slowed the Chevy to fifty-five, downshifted to third, and as they started down the hill, poured on the coal and fired the booster rockets.

The big Chevy shot past the startled driver like it was fired out of a cannon. At the bottom of the hill, Smitty glanced down at the speedometer and noted that it had just ticked past ninety. Then, a blur to his left startled him.

Backed off the edge of a dirt road about twenty feet, completely hidden in the access road cut through the woods, was a state policeman. As Smitty went blasting past him at the bottom of the hill, he hit the lights and siren and began to pull out, almost broadsiding the desperately trailing Corvette in the process.

Instinctively, Smitty put his foot in it, causing the cylindrical speedometer to inch even higher. It was now closer to meeting its origin at zero, but from the other side. Smitty went over the top of the next hill feeling the temporary weightlessness as the car became airborne before crashing to the pavement with a teeth-gnashing sound of bottoming-out cross frames and scraping mufflers.

As he reached the bottom of the hill, he glanced back in the rearview mirror and saw the state mate pull the 'Vette over and sprint to the car, preparing, Smitty knew, to snatch his keys and license. Then he'd be back in the big Dodge with the 440 tri-power, intent on catching him.

Smitty was going to make him work for it. The speedometer kept climbing. It was halfway back around to zero from the last numbered speed indicator of 120 miles per hour. Smitty roughly calculated his current velocity to be somewhere between ludicrous and light speed, where a prayer book was a much more functional tool than a workshop manual. Smitty had no idea how fast he was going, but the telephone poles beside the road were blurs, flashing past like the railroad signal posts seen from a speeding train. Smitty hoped God liked fast old Chevys. If he didn't, Smitty was going to be the new chariot mechanic in heaven, or more realistically, turning wrenches on Satan's fire wagon in hell.

They covered the next several miles in minutes, with Smitty slowly pulling away from his pursuer. After they had gone nearly ten miles, the officer slowed, turned off his lights, and made a U-turn. Smitty slowed immediately also, expecting a police roadblock to be just beyond the next turn.

The road was clear, as was the next mile and the mile after that. Smitty fired the retro rockets and slowed to something near the posted speed limit as he entered Soperton and the relative safe haven of the interstate located just beyond.

No local police, no county mounties, and perhaps more importantly, no state mates.

Smitty chugged on through the town and got on the interstate a mile beyond. Within two miles, he was back up to his normal cruising speed of eighty and breathing again. He had no idea what had happened to the red Corvette or the state policeman, but knowing his luck, he figured he was bound to cross paths with both them again.

Smitty peeked around the corner of his grandmother's nursing room door at 1225 hours. "Sonny boy, git yourself in here," she said in her deep Southern drawl. He temporarily startled her before a wide, infectious grin spread over her face as she recognized him and welcomed him excitedly.

"How you been there, boyyo? Let me look at you." She held Smitty at arm's length after he bent over her wheelchair and hugged her warmly. She was about five-feet-nothing when standing, with gray hair fading to white, and was having no trouble filling out the seat of the wheelchair. In short, she looked just like everyone's grandmother: short and squatty, with a smile that could light up a dark room.

"The last time I saw you, you were just a skinny teenager. Why, you've become a handsome young man." She took his hand, and patted it affectionately. "You look just like your grandfather when he was your age. God, he was gorgeous."

"Sit down on my bed where I can see you without straining my neck, and tell me what you've been up to."

Smitty sat down and spent the next ten minutes bringing her up to date on the main activities of the last half-dozen years, which consisted of brief descriptions of life in Savannah, followed by highlights of his time in the service, his current activities in college, and his job. Judiciously, he omitted most of the details about Vietnam, telling her that he had some safe job as a staff flunky at a base near Saigon.

"So, how do you like college?" she asked with genuine interest.

"Well, I didn't care much for it at first. But I'm warming up to it. It seems to have merit, although I'm not sure just what I'm going to major in yet." As the image of professor Strickland formed in his mind, he smiled and said, "I have to admit, you sure get exposed to a different group of people than the environment that I grew up in."

"Well, at least you're out and about. Since they took my leg off three years ago, I'm not as mobile as I once was, and I'm stuck here in this darn nursing home. That and the fact that after pappy died five years ago, life just doesn't seem to be as much fun," she said with regret, sighed, and added, "besides, since my daughters only come to see me when they feel like it, I'm a virtual prisoner here."

On his way to the nursing home, Smitty had veered off the interstate and took a drive through town. Like Little Red Riding Hood, he had gone by Grandma's house, where many childhood memories were formed. With the exception of her house and two others, all the rest were gone.

The only thing that would make the picture complete was the appearance of the big bad wolf. And if Aunt Belinda's call was on the up-and-up, Smitty suspected he was prowling somewhere close by, hiding not in Grandma's jammies, but masquerading under that all-inclusive new political term "urban renewal."

From the rumors Smitty had heard, this project, like many others going on in cities across the country, was mired in a political quagmire of payoffs and kickbacks as inept city administrators desperately attempted to revive decaying downtowns by destroying the older established neighborhoods in the name of progress.

"Well—"

"Mama, we're here," a female voice called out from down the hall in what sounded to Smitty like an artificial tone. With catlike reflexes, Smitty leaped off the bed and stepped into the three-foot hallway to the bathroom, holding a finger to his lips.

At first, Smitty did not recognize the woman who rounded the door and walked purposefully straight to Grandma, giving her a businesslike peck on the forehead. But there was something distinctly familiar about the click the high heels made as they heralded her arrival.

This lady was different from the one Smitty remembered. Thirty pounds heavier, hair obviously colored, and the face carrying more life baggage. But the extravagant clothes, the stiletto high heels, and the makeup applied in layers were a dead giveaway: these made her Smitty's mom.

"John is parking the car." Mom opened her handbag and brought out a snack wrapped in wax paper.

"John and I stopped at that barbecue place you like so well and bought you a pork sandwich." Mom set the sandwich on the table. She busied herself attaching the tray to the wheelchair, and poured water from a jug on the nightstand beside the bed. Obviously, Mom assumed Grandma was ready to eat. Either that or she apparently thought her mother was a pigeon in the park constantly in search of food and was to be fed on sight.

"Did you by any chance bring me a Coke?" Grandma asked hopefully as she started to slowly unwrap the sandwich.

"Now, Mama. You know what the doctor said: sugar is bad for you," Smitty's mom said.

This brief dialogue had Smitty's radar clanging like a Claxton on a submarine in one of those World War II movies as the captain yelled excitedly. "Dive! Dive! Dive!" Grandma's wants appeared to be secondary to mom's desires. Of course, to understand a person's needs, you had to be listening in the first place.

"Now, Mama, you hurry up and eat your lunch so I can clear away the serving tray. When John gets here, we've got some things to go over with you."

Smitty had heard enough. It was time to reintroduce himself to she who had birthed him. He quietly stepped from the shadows. "If you'd like, I'll go down the hall and get you a Coke, Grandma."

Smitty's mother almost jumped out of her skin, her body recoiling instinctively in anxiety and fear.

"Who are—" She stopped in midsentence as recognition spread across her face.

"Oh, my God, it's my son." Mom walked around the bed and hugged Smitty, kissed him lightly on the cheek, and patted him on the back like a socialite dealing with an unwanted guest by smiling politely and feigning interest. Smitty could see by her reaction that she was secretly hoping that he'd get the hint and leave or at the very least have the common decency to fall down an elevator shaft on his way to the soda machine—without making a scene, of course.

"What on earth are you doing here?" Mom asked, clearly flabbergasted.

"I've been meaning to get up here . . . " Smitty left the sentence unfinished, remembering the colonel's rule number two. He said evasively, "I had a free weekend, so I took a shot that Grandma wasn't off at one of those senior orgies."

"Oh, son, what a terrible thing to say about your grandmother." Mom's face colored in embarrassment. "Isn't that right, Mama?" She looked to her mother for support.

"I wish," Mama said. Then she looked at Smitty with a sly grin. "Do you know where I can go to one, boyyo? If you do, get me a man about sixty to sixty-five what's still got his functional equipment."

Smitty laughed. The disapproving look on Mom's face only made him laugh harder.

Mom spun on her heel and strutted across the room to the window. She pulled back the sheer curtains and waved urgently.

On receiving whatever signal she was waiting for, she nodded and marched back across the room. "I'll be right back. I left something in the car." She flounced out of the room in a pouting stalk, her high heels clicking in time.

Smitty listened to the sound of her retreating footsteps until they were out of earshot and held out his hand. "Way to go, Grandma. That ought to set her back a bit."

Mama took his hand and shook it. Smitty withdrew it quickly. "No, Grandma, slap my hand like this," Smitty motioned for her to hold out her hand and slapped it lightly. Then he said, "Now slap mine. It's the way some of the black guys in Nam used to greet each other. They say, "Gimme five."

To Grandma's confused look, Smitty prompted, "A swinger like you doesn't want to seem old fashioned, do you?"

Grandma smiled mischievously in reply.

"Look, I think I'll drop on down to the Coke machine and pick us up a couple. Back in a few." Smitty casually walked to the door, and then broke into a fast trot toward the main entrance and the Coke machine located in the other wing.

It was not that Smitty was dying for a Coke, but since the machine was located just the other side of the main entrance, it might provide an opportunity to do a little eavesdropping on Mom and the mysterious John and maybe find out what sent her flying out of the room like an arsonist fleeing a blaze before the fire trucks arrived.

He walked quietly to the entrance and noticed Mom and a distinguished looking man, gray at the temples, talking animatedly in the front seat of a brand new white Chrysler New Yorker. The card had a Fulton County sticker. Fulton County was the main county of Atlanta. So that must be where the old girl was shacked up at the moment.

Smitty walked back through the lobby, turned right and purchased two Cokes from the machine. He stepped to the other side, using the machine itself to block anyone from seeing him as they came in the entrance, and leaned against the wall to wait.

A minute, certainly no more than two, went by before Smitty heard his mother's voice talking urgently to someone as they entered the lobby.

"This may not be as easy as we thought it would be, dear. My son is here, and he and Mother have always had a special bond. She'll listen to him and if he objects, she could make this difficult." Mom apparently did not know that the combination of enameled sheet-rocked ceilings, walls, and tile floors although sanitary in intent, also made a dandy echo chamber.

"Not after he hears what your mother did," John said, as they went quickly down the hallway.

Smitty stepped quietly out from behind the machine, and padded silently until he was ten paces behind them, then purposefully clicked the Coke bottles together noisily. When both turned around he walked up holding out his hand. "This Grandma's date for the orgy?"

"I'm John." The man ignored Smitty's opening remark and they shook hands firmly.

"Um, dear," Mom began in an embarrassed voice, "This is my husband. We've been married almost two years."

Smitty nodded his head. "You always did have a thing for older men."

John glanced quickly at Mom, who nodded with disapproval. "I see you're living up to the reputation I have heard about from your mother. "

"You know what natural born smart asses us college students are."

"If my daughter or son talked to me that way, I'd . . . " he left the sentence unfinished, and lapsed into silence.

"If you tried that with me, Johnboy, you'd end up with your head sticking out of your asshole."

"Son, I can see you're upset by my marriage to John, but life has to move on. Your father and I just weren't right for each other." Mom was hoping to change the subject, and, as usual, totally misinterpreting what was really happening.

"Oh, Mooother!" Smitty said in an exaggerated voice. "I've never objected to any of the men you've been with." Dad always said, "If you don't sleep with somebody, it ain't none of your damn business." Smitty had absolutely no idea of his mother's sexual history, but figured that it was worth firing for effect. He could clearly see he had scored a direct hit on John.

John inhaled sharply, preparing, Smitty knew, for action. When he noticed Smitty's Mom emphatically shaking her head, he exhaled slowly.

"Young man, your manners are atrocious. You're rude and arrogant. And you seem to possess not even the slightest trace of the niceties required to coexist in polite society. God knows how you get along in that college you attend."

"Yes, everybody says I have my father's looks but, unfortunately, my mother's manners," Smitty said.

"Um, dear, how about if you and I take a quick walk outside and you try to calm down," Mom took John's arm and led him back in the direction of the door. John turned and scowled at Smitty until they disappeared around the corner.

As openers go, probably not one you'd find in the latest book of etiquette, but it served the purpose Smitty wished, which was to get John angry and upset, so that he wouldn't be able to think clearly and would be offguard.

Smitty hustled back to Grandma's room, handed her the Coke, and exchanged low- then high-fives. As an inspiration struck him, he called Aunt Belinda's phone number collect, and not surprisingly, the charge was accepted.

After thirty seconds of exchanging pleasantries on what he'd been up to since they'd last seen each other. Aunt Belinda filled him in on the reason for the urgent phone call to his father. Smitty listened attentively for three minutes, offered his thanks, then hung up.

Smitty told Grandma the details of his initial meeting with John on his way from the vending machine—omitting all the other details. Grandma rolled her eyes, a clear enough indicator that her feelings for John were similar to Smitty's. They sipped their Cokes and waited in silence for Mom and the new "stepdad" to return.

Thanks to Auntie, Smitty now knew what this was really about. As a second inspiration struck him, he reached for the phone and again made a collect call to an ex-service friend. Not surprisingly, his caller not only accepted the call, but seemed to be expecting it as well.

They spoke briefly on the phone about what Smitty believed were the real circumstances behind Auntie's call. Even though it was Saturday, his friend promised to get right on it and call back within one hour. As Dad always said, service friendships were temporary; they only lasted a lifetime.

Thirty minutes passed before Mom and John returned. Smitty could see that his opening remarks to John had had the desired effect. He was still tense and angry and he greeted Grandma in a tight voice, then settled in a chair across the room from Smitty, his arms folded.

"Mother," Smitty's mom said, "I'd like you to tell my son about your recent arrest."

"Oh, pooh," Grandma said with a wave of dismissal. "That ain't nothin'."

"Well, maybe not," Mom said, "but I'd like you to tell him just the same."

"Well, if you think it would be best." Grandma reached out and took a final swig from her Coke. She cleared her throat and turned her wheelchair to Smitty, who was reclining comfortably on her bed propped up on one arm.

"Well, sonny boy, you know that I've lived on my own my whole life, until I lost the leg and couldn't walk around so good anymore."

"And couldn't bathe yourself or go to the bathroom without help," Mom interjected.

"Dear, do you want to tell this story or do you want me to?" Grandma spun her wheelchair around like a top and glared at her youngest daughter. Mom didn't say a word. "Thought so," Grandma said. She spun back to face her grandson once more.

"Now, where was I? Oh, yes, I was telling you about the getting used to living here.

"Well, the food is just God-awful, so the last time Doris was down, she and that sweet husband of hers brought me a hot plate for the room so I could cook, or at least heat up things like soup and so forth.

"The problem was that sometimes your Aunt Janet, who now lives in Doraville, doesn't have time to get over every day, and sometimes I get hungry. So one of those times the nurse wheeled me out to the back patio for some fresh air and left me there. She promised to come back in thirty minutes.

"Well, I was sitting there and suddenly got a yen for some bacon. See, they won't serve it here cause of the fat, and they say it's bad for our hearts." Grandma shook her head sadly, a clear indicator of what she thought of that particular rule.

"So I decided to just take myself on a little road trip across the overpass to the 7-Eleven on the other side for some groceries.

"I didn't have any trouble getting to the market. It was getting back that was the problem. I had this bag of groceries on my lap and the damn chair got caught in one of those joints in the bridge and stuck. While I was trying to free it, the bag fell off my lap and landed on the ground.

"After I got the chair unstuck, I picked up the bag and some of the eggs I had bought were broken, so I threw them over the side and went on back to the nursing home. The next day, two nice policemen showed up, asked me a few questions, then told me that I was under arrest for malicious mischief. I guess because of my age, they didn't haul me down to the pokey. They just issued me a summons. I have to go to court next week.

"For the life of me, I can't understand what all the fuss was about. I mean, it was just a couple of eggs."

"Neither can I," Smitty said, sensing there was more to the story than Grandma knew.

"Your grandmother left out a few important details." Mom walked over and looked at her mother in disgust.

"Such as, that the eggs she threw over the side hit a lady who was a passenger in an open convertible and caused the driver to lose control. That resulted in a nine car pile-up on the interstate."

Smitty burst out laughing; he just couldn't help it. And seeing the irritated look on his mother's face only made it funnier. Especially when he knew she was more concerned about the damage the incident had done to her social standing, than about anything else, such as bodily injury or bent sheet metal.

The madder Mom got the funnier it seemed. And when Mom stamped her foot in frustration and huffed, "This is a serious matter. Would you try to set a good example for your grandmother?" Smitty had a laughter blowout.

Try as he might, Smitty just couldn't hold it in and began to laugh uncontrollably. His laughter was infectious, and when grandmother joined in, he lost it, and rolled off the bed onto the floor. Ignoring the menacing stares of both his mother and her husband, they laughed together for several minutes.

As their laughter finally subsided, Grandma said, "High-five, boyyo."

"Anybody hurt?" Smitty slowly got up from floor, wiped his eyes, and exchanged high-fives with his grandmother.

"Fortunately, no," Mom said. "But the car belonged to a very influential local citizen and it sustained considerable damage, to say nothing of the damage that was done to his reputation."

Smitty was not sure what one point had to do with the other, but nodded.

"So I think you can certainly agree that your grandmother is no longer capable of making responsible decisions." Mom looked at Smitty with raised eyebrows, expecting him to agree.

"Well, no, actually. I haven't reached that conclusion at all. To me it just seems like an accident. I mean, Grandma did throw away the eggs, but her intentions were not malicious at all." Smitty paused, and a comical thought came to him.

"From a certain perspective, Grandma was just being a good citizen and picking up her own litter. Since there's only a pedestrian crosswalk on the left side, that would mean that eggs landed in the southbound lane, and since she was on the far side of the bridge, then it follows that she had no realistic way to tell if there was a car coming or not since the overpass is forty-five feet across."

Smitty looked up at his grandmother. "Grandma, if you'd known there was a car coming, would you have thrown the eggs?"

"Oh, good heavens, no," Grandma said, blushing.

"Well, there you have it," Smitty said simply. "Sounds like a pretty responsible answer to me."

"Aren't you even embarrassed that the judge will convict you on this?" Smitty's mother asked.

"Dear, you were always the most beautiful of all my children, but sometimes you're such an Airedale," Grandma said. Then with an impish grin, she added, "Would you like to be the judge who convicts a seventy-seven-year-old, one-legged great-grandmother on this? They'd laugh him right off the bench."

"The term is 'airhead,' Mother."

"Not in your case, dear!" Grandma shot back. Smitty had to admire the way the old lady gave as good as she got. In her youth, she must have been a handful. Come to that, she wasn't bad now.

"This is getting us nowhere." John stood up in disgust. "Your appeasing approach to your son is not going to work."

He reached for his briefcase, snapped it open, removed a set of papers, and set them in front of Smitty's grandma.

"Sign these," he said.

"What are they?" Grandma asked.

"Mother, these will allow John and me to act in your best interests. What John calls a power of attorney," Mom said in a soft voice.

Smitty's grandmother looked at Smitty. "What do you think?"

Smitty never got a chance to answer. The ringing phone cut off his response. Grandma picked it up, listened attentively, and handed the phone to Smitty. "It's for you, boyyo."

Smitty listened quietly for several minutes, made some capacious notes on a newspaper that was lying on the nightstand, thanked his caller, and hung up.

Smitty picked up the newspaper and glanced at his notes. "No, Grandma, I don't think you should sign them. In fact, I think you should tell your daughter and son-by-law to go to hell."

"Now just a minute." John started in Smitty's direction. "I've had more than enough of you."

"If you come within my reach, you'll be having more than you bargained for, Johnboy, and, unless I've lost my touch, you'll leave horizontally." John stopped abruptly.

"You know, Mom, your mother isn't the only one who left out a few details. You did, too." Smitty watched her shrink back into her chair as John went and stood beside her.

"Now then," Smitty said. "Let's do this in the proper fashion: pointers first, then proof.

"Grandma, what your darling daughter and my dear sweet mommy, failed to tell you was the details of how the accident occurred. Either that or the hubs there didn't tell her." Smitty stopped and stared at both of them, hoping one would rat out the other, but that was the problem with rats: they all looked alike.

"I don't understand," Grandma admitted, scratching her head.

"Well, you see, the eggs in and of themselves didn't cause the accident. The female inside did. At least, according to the police report." Smitty glanced down at the notes on the newspaper and began to read.

"The driver sustained 'multiple circular contusions four centimeters above the base of his penis that required five sets of three stitches each to close.'" Smitty shivered involuntarily. "Oooh, that must have hurt."

"So, obviously, the eggs must have hit her while she was in the process of administering oral therapy, so to speak, startling her enough that she obviously took a big bite on the ol' hotdog; that was what actually caused him to lose control. The fact that the young lady who was performing this particular therapeutic massage was not his spouse only seems to add a certain touch of irony to the whole thing." Smitty smiled and continued, "A fact that I'm sure his wife found particularly upsetting.

"Mom is right, though. Because he is an influential businessman, they managed to keep these minor details out of the paper. But the incident itself conveniently allowed them to allege that you were mentally unable to manage your affairs.

"Your darling daughter and Johnboy were going to use this fact to force you to sign over your power of attorney to them so that they could gain control of your money."

"But I don't have any money, just my monthly social security check," Grandma said, "and that goes to the home."

"Well, maybe I should rephrase that. It's not the money you have; it's the money you are going to have," Smitty said.

He paused and looked at his mom, who was trying desperately to look innocent, and failing, and at John, who muttered, "Oh, shit," under his breath.

"Mama, that house you and Gramps lived in, how much did you pay for it?"

"Thirty-eight hundred dollars when we bought it in 1932," she answered.

"Would it surprise you to know that your house is now dead square in the middle of an urban renewal project for the new mall, and that property has a fair market value of somewhere between three and five hundred thousand dollars, according to my friend who just called?

"As soon as your loving daughter and son-in-law got your power of attorney, my bet is that they, with the help of the influential businessman with the Frankensteined pecker, were going to have the house condemned, pay you the condemned price for pennies on the dollar, then sell it to the realty group from New York for a small fortune."

Smitty paused, and jerked his thumb in John's direction. "And you'll never guess who the local lawyer is who's handling the legal transactions for the Yankee boys from up north. And also using the influential businessman to do his dirty work by feeding him inside information so he can then put pressure, or bribe the local politicians, to condemn the properties they need."

"Him." Grandma raised a bony finger and pointed it directly at her son-in-law.

"Congratulations, go collect your sixty-four dollars."

"Once you were paid, your other children would be none the wiser, and John and Missy would be gettin' kinda richy." Smitty paraphrased the last few bars of the Mamas and the Papas song to emphasize his point.

Grandma spun in her wheelchair and looked levelly at her daughter. "Is this true?"

"Mommy, I can explain." Smitty's mother retreated into her little girl's voice.

"Don't even try." She spun her chair around and looked at Smitty. "What now, boyyo?"

"My friend in Washington has called an old law school study group buddy who now lives in Atlanta. He'll be here first thing Monday morning to help you. My friend says he's honest and will treat you right. He'll charge you a fair price and in return perform a fair service.

"And I expect that if you ask him, he'll probably be able to handle the arrest business discreetly also, because if I were a betting man, I bet that my mother here was partially responsible for your accident by constantly pumping you up about how you need to become more self-sufficient in your wheelchair, that sort of drivel." Smitty glanced at his mom, who wouldn't even look at him.

"Go, child, and never darken my door again." Grandma pointed toward the door.

As his mother and John rose and started to leave, John turned and looked at Smitty. "You bastard son of a bitch."

Smitty smiled, looking at his mother. "That's true, but in my case, a mere accident at birth, in your case, a full-time profession." He looked John directly in the eyes. "Besides, you shouldn't be demeaning your wife and my mother that way, especially since she had the best business on the block."

Smitty turned and winked at his grandmother. "But, as it turns out, extremely poor taste in whom she let hump her in the orderly room in Dearfield."

Now it was Johnboy's turn to lose it, although it wasn't to laughter.

John snap-hooked a right, trying to catch Smitty from the blind side. After two-plus years in Vietnam, Smitty's senses had become so acute that he could hear the fingers ball and the thumb wrap around them.

Smitty leaned left as the fist passed harmlessly six inches in front of his face, and continued until it came into something that would alter its present trajectory, like the cinder-block wall. Smitty had to admit that it was a good punch; at least it sounded that way from the solid thud it made and John's instinctive, "Oh shit," exclamation of pain as he grabbed it with his left.

"My turn." Smitty brought his knee up to John's groin, making his eyes bulge like an overinflated tire.

While Mom was grabbing John in a desperate attempt to stop him from falling over, Smitty picked up the papers from the table and tore them into shreds. He walked to the bathroom toilet, dropped them in, and flushed.

They left in silence—Mom supporting a hunched-over and obviously distressed John—their eyes filled with hate. Smitty was not much on exchanging parting threats. He didn't have to.

"High-five, boyyo." Grandma raised her arm and they exchanged greetings. Smitty hugged her. "Aunt Belinda was right on target."

"Boyyo, I've been meaning to ask, just who is Aunt Belinda? Belinda's not the name of any of my daughters."

"No, but it is the name of my very special friend's aunt. He uses it for a recognition signal. He sort of watches out for me and keeps me informed about things that are happening, or potentially going to happen to me or to friends of mine. Or if need be, I can call him," Smitty said vaguely.

"How does he know who's trying to harm you?" Grandma asked.

"Well, it just so happens that your son-in-law and I have had a bit to do with each other through a mutual acquaintance. So my friend sort of keeps tabs on him."

"How do you call him?" she asked with even more curiosity.

"Grandma, what's your middle name?"

"Anastasia."

"That's how I call him," Smitty answered, ignoring her confused stare.

Smitty was glad for the tip-off and even happier that his former service friend Major Jim, now working in Washington for the justice department as a lawyer, was willing to help.

That wasn't all Smitty knew about Johnboy. He knew how John's older brother had actually died in Vietnam. The only reason Smitty knew this was that he had personally shot him right between the eyes a little over a year ago.

Eventually, Smitty had a feeling that Johnboy, whose last name was Gates, would find out what they had in common. And when he did, Smitty was certain of two things: sometime in the future, Aunt Belinda would be wanting a return favor, and as a result, his Mom would look awful frumpy dressed in black.

"Stand tall, troop, I want to talk to you," Dad bellowed, slamming his fist repeatedly on the trailer door with all the gentleness of a pile driver.

Since the front door was next to the panel that separated the living room from the spare bedroom, the one Smitty slept in, Dad's knock had woken him out of a sound sleep, a sleep he seemed to have only just started.

He looked at the clock. Having gotten back late Sunday evening from his trip to Grandma's, he'd been asleep only a little over an hour. It was just past one.

"Hold on, hold on," Smitty yelled back in a voice that he hoped was loud enough to be heard through the wall. He stepped hurriedly into his pants and opened the door as he snapped them.

"What's going on?" Ron yawned as he came out of the bedroom in his shorts but holding an army issue .45.

"Don't know," Smitty answered. "My father's outside. He seems to be extremely upset about something. Go back to bed. I'll handle it."

"I wished he'd get pissed at you at a decent hour." Ron stretched and went back into the master bedroom, closing the door behind him.

Smitty unlatched the door and saw his dad standing there with his hands on his hips and an angry expression on his face.

"Hi, Popster, what brings you out at this hour? Let me guess, your lady tossed you out of the sack tonight 'cause you couldn't get it up, so you felt the burning desire to drive all the way over here to take out your frustration on me," Smitty said.

Dad was momentarily at a loss for a response. One thing most people usually do not expect when they're angry about something is for the other person to become aggressive. It throws them off. Sometimes it can cause them to do a quick internal snapshot and realize how ludicrous their conduct is. Other times it just pisses them off even more and they punch your lights out. Smitty was counting on Dad acting in the former way, but he was prepared for the latter.

"Um, I want to talk to you," Dad finally sputtered in a more moderate tone of voice.

"Come in." Smitty held the door open, then closed it once Dad was inside.

Smitty walked to the kitchen, got a couple of PBRs from the fridge, and slid one across to Dad as he took a seat at the kitchen table.

"Now then, what's got you so worked up that you felt the urgent need to come hawking all the way out here in the middle of the night?" Smitty asked.

"Your mother called me and said that you embarrassed her in front of her mother, to the point that she asked her to leave, and brutally attacked her husband as they were trying to get away from you. And, if that wasn't enough, you meddled in the middle of a business deal he had going and got him fired from his job." He took a long pull on the beer and set the can down emphatically. "I thought we agreed your mother was my problem to deal with."

"You know, for a smart man, you seem to be a sucker when it comes to that imitation Scarlett. What are you trying to do, reform 'er?"

Dad inhaled sharply. Smitty knew he was about to cut loose with a blast of seafaring language that would make a chief petty officer blush.

Smitty beat him to the punch. "Dad, this has got to stop. As usual, Mom gets you all riled up with some fairy story, sets you off, and then you seem to fly into some kind of blind rage.

"Don't you get it yet? The woman is playing you like a finely tuned Stradivarius. She plucks; you react."

"So, tell me your version," Dad said, ignoring what Smitty had said.

Now it was Smitty's turn to take a long drink. He considered his reply. As Smitty saw it, there were two problems to be addressed. The first was that Smitty needed to get out of the crossfire between his dad and mom and the endless cycle of spite as they kept trying to hurt each other using him, and perhaps Billy, as the primary weapons. The second was that Dad had to get over the fact that Smitty was not his little boy anymore, to be ordered around at will like one of the young troops in his outfit.

Since Dad had lost his objectivity and wasn't going to take kindly to anything he said, the obvious solution to Smitty was a frontal assault—with a bunkspacer . . . metaphorically speaking.

"Look, Dad, every time you get a mad-on for something that happened between you and Mom, you come tearing over here, hell-bent for leather to chew me out. Well, that ends here and now.

"Like I've told you and told you, I've got my own problems to resolve with my mother. I don't want to be involved with your problems with your ex-wife anymore, not now or ever again in the future."

Smitty took another swig of his beer. "And I would speculate that Sally doesn't care much about your tantrums concerning her, either.

"Second, stop talking down to me. I'm not your whipping boy. Remember what you always said to me: sometimes in life, the good people get fucked, too. Deal with it; I have. All my life, I seem to have been getting dealt from the bottom of the deck, and I'm handling it, I think, fairly well, despite the world's record for bad breaks. My plate is full; go deal with your own serving and leave me alone. Are we clear?"

Dad drummed his fingers on the table, a mannerism Smitty knew from experience was tantamount to counting ten. "I told you I want to know what happened between you and your mother. I'm prepared to sit here all night if need be until you tell me."

"Bullshit," Smitty said bluntly. "Why don't you tell me what's really got your asshole puckered?"

"I don't know what you're talking about," Dad replied.

Smitty got up and flung the door wide open. "Get out, First Sergeant!" He pointed to the street. "Before I throw you out!"

Dad finished his beer, slammed the can down on the table, and silently got up and left the trailer. He walked to the back of his Falcon station wagon, slammed the tailgate down, yanked an army footlocker clear and let it drop to the ground.

"Your colonel sent your stuff home after you were wounded." Dad dragged the trunk clear of the back of the car, walked around to the driver's side and got in. He started the Falcon and rolled down the window. "And tell 'Aunt Belinda' to handle his own dirty business and leave you the hell out of it from now own."

Smitty smiled and said, "Come back when you think you can ask me how I'm doing rather than demand it."

"When hell freezes over, sport." Dad mashed the gas and spewed gravel as he backed onto the asphalt.

"See you there, Popster," Smitty said softly, as he watched the car's taillights until they were out of sight. He hauled the remnants of his army issue to the door of the trailer, bumped it up the steps, and dragged it across the carpet and into his room.

Smitty was becoming quite a student of human nature, thanks mainly to Dad and his self-developed methodology for getting to the bottom of a problem. He always said that if you ignore a person's tantrums and outbursts and just let him talk, then sooner or later he'll tell you what's wrong. But you have to be listening real close, because the answer usually comes in the middle of a fusillade of emotional eruptions that you can't take personally.

But it was nice of Ol' Sarge to come all the way out here in the middle of the night to deliver his trunk and the warning—the real reason he came in the first place, Smitty thought to himself as he unscrewed the eight screws that held the cover in place. Mom had just provided the incidental impetus.

Smitty folded aside the miscellaneous items and rooted around in the trunk like a pig trying to uncover its favorite truffle until he found what he was looking for.

Dad gave him the answer, and he heard it. Unfortunately, he couldn't sever the connection to his favorite auntie. He was Smitty's lifeline to the truth and the peace and tranquility that perhaps lay just beyond the storm clouds ahead.

Smitty had a feeling that Dad knew it, too. Why else would he have picked this particular moment to deliver a trunk that he'd had safely tucked away for almost nine months? A trunk that, among a host of other odds and ends, contained his favorite friend from Vietnam, a friend that could best be described with the numerals three, five, and seven?

CHAPTER TWENTY

It was now September 1971, and Smitty was sitting in a dive on Bay Street, trying to figure out what the next step would or could be. Up until the beginning of the summer, Smitty had been on the road back from the psychological debacle of Vietnam.

He had completed his spring semester at the "Barnyard" with a grade point average that was inching toward a 3.0, and by taking extra courses during the previous two quarters, was actually an entire quarter ahead and was planning to enroll for the fall. With no declared major to date, Smitty was just continuing to take general courses that were a core requirement for any degree until he could make up his mind.

Smitty had continued the therapy program for his leg, arranged for him by the coach and set up by the doctor, straight through to completion at the end of the term in June. His left leg now functioned as well as his right, although it was still prone to occasional swelling, usually from overexertion. For the rest of the damage, time had indeed been the healer. Smitty couldn't remember the exact day, but just the fact that one day as he was shaving, he suddenly realized that the shrapnel scars were not as noticeable. Others began to not comment on them also as the red pigmentation began to fade and the normal skin color returned.

Through the efforts of a proxy race, arranged and participated in by the coach, Smitty had won his year-old bet with Doctor Evans, who was now working as a physician at the Hayes Point, New York, Veterans' Hospital since his retirement from the army in May. Thanks to the magic of a few strings pulled in the right place, principally with the help of a U.S. Senator and colonel, now Brigadier General Wilson, Evans had been able to retire with his twenty years.

On receiving the entire $300, Smitty had sent $50 to Dad by mail, sent $50 to General Chuck in Alaska by mail also, and put $50 in a bank account for the mysteriously vanished chesty nurse Claire. Smitty was still convinced she would surface again someday. The $150 in winnings went into the kitty for his new home.

In the beginning of April, Smitty had stopped to help a lady who was broken down on the side of the road in a driving rainstorm. He made running repairs to her car, then led her to the service station, and, discovering that the part would not be available until the next day, took her home in the '60. The lady and her husband, who turned out to be a general contractor, showed up at the service station to thank him the following day. They struck up a conversation while Smitty replaced the water pump on the Fairlane. One thing led to another, and two hours later, Smitty had worked a deal with the husband to tear down an old elementary school out on Whittier Island in return for all the materials and a half-acre of land a mile away.

The contractor filed all the permits under his license and helped Smitty understand the maze of paperwork and forms required to get the project started. Then with the help of Ron—who now had plenty of free time since his wife had upped and departed for Vermont—and two other buddies, they had dismantled the cinder-block school, brick by brick and room by room. They then recycled these materials into a forty-by-forty four-bedroom house on the half-acre lot.

The house had a simplistic design. Each of the four corners was made into a sixteen-by-twelve foot bedroom with the space in between used to form individual half-baths, complete with sinks, toilets, and urinals savaged from the school, connected by a common bathtub and shower area. The sixteen-by-forty area in between became a common living room and kitchen, with the kitchen furnishings made up exclusively of items savaged from the teachers' lounge. On the back of the lot, they had built four one-car carports, separated in the middle by a twenty-by-twenty building that would become a common shop.

By reusing the old cinder blocks, toilets, sinks, cabinets and anything else they could salvage, they kept the out-of-pocket cost to about $2,300. The cash outlays were mostly for the items they could not scrounge, trade, or reuse, which included things such as shingles, plumbing supplies, copper pipe, carpets for the floor, and paint—lots of paint.

Smitty had chosen his roommates with care. Lenny and Billy were buddies he knew casually from Nam who had just recently gotten out of the service in Savannah and were working locally until, like every other vet, they figured out what they wanted to do with the rest of their lives. Lenny's dad was an electrician and Billy's a plumber, and that they had apprenticed their offspring helped address two of the critical skills needed.

Ron, who had been a draftsman prior to entering the service, drew up the plans, and Smitty acted as the overall straw boss. The deal was struck on a simple handshake agreement that the last person to leave the house would sell it, split the profits four ways, then send each party an equal share.

Thanks mainly to the tireless ambition of youth and the unpaid assistance of scores of young Nam service vets who had excessive amounts of idle time on their hands while waiting for their enlistment to end—unpaid in this case meant providing beer, food, and the promise of a huge party when it was finished—the house was completed by the Fourth of July. At completion, the contractor had bought the surplus lumber and miscellaneous odds and ends for $600, and that money was then used to hold an open house in celebration of their new bachelor abode. The resulting blast lasted from Friday night to Sunday afternoon.

Scores of service buddies, friends of the four of them, and every neighbor in a one-mile radius attended. Smitty's boss at the service station closed up early on Saturday night so that he and all of Smitty's coworkers would not miss the party. The coach, the doc, and even Professor Strickland from the Barnyard showed up, although the prof discreetly elected to not bring his roommate. The party was such a monumental success that the neighbors' dogs two blocks away got drunk from the fumes.

Unfortunately, like the big egg on the wall, he'd then had a great fall. It seemed to not only affect Smitty, but his parents and their respective partners, also.

The crash occurred in July, just after the open house and when some good things were finally starting to happen for Smitty. The late-night run-in with his father had resulted in a total severing of their already-strained diplomatic relations. In the months that followed, Smitty'd not heard from him at all. They'd pass each other on campus without so much as a nod, like two freighters passing in the night without even a blast of acknowledgment from the ship's horns.

It wasn't that Smitty didn't want to tell his father his version of the events surrounding his mother that weekend, it was just that right now it served a more useful purpose for Dad to have only Mom's version of the truth, for whomever he would repeat it to.

Smitty's only communication with his father in the last four months had been through the tireless mediation attempts of Sally. The latest had been an emotional plea that he come to dinner on Tuesday evening, since he was off work on Wednesday. He accepted with much trepidation and nervousness that was peaking as he turned into the driveway of their home.

"Hello, sweetie. How's my boy?" Sally dropped the hose she had been using to water the rose bushes and bounded across the lawn to give him a bone-crushing hug.

"Fine, Sally. How've you been?" Smitty returned her hug with equal fervor. Maybe it was the fact that she had been a nurse, or maybe it was just the fact that she was a good person, but Smitty genuinely liked her—sadly, even more than his own mother. She was good to him, and Smitty suspected even better for his father, although the old bear would be the last to admit it.

Glancing around the yard and seeing Dad's Plymouth missing, Smitty asked, "Where's Sergeant Rock? Send him to the store?"

"Oh, he sold the Plymouth back to your mom. She's living in Savannah with that horse's ass of a husband of hers. They're out on Wilmington Island now in one of those snotty subdivisions with an unlisted zip code." Sally wrinkled her brow in disgust.

"I don't know what it is about that woman, but he just can't seem to let her go. Even though they're divorced, and she's screwed him from here to hell's breakfast . . . " She left the sentence unfinished and brightened. "Let's talk about something else. I'm beginning to sound like a nag on the rag."

Smitty blushed and she said, "Oh, come on now, sonny boy, don't tell me your ol' stepmom has you embarrassed. You do know women have periods, don't you?"

A smile replaced the redness. "To quote my old man, 'women spend one week getting ready for it, one week having it, and one week getting over it, so they're only in their right minds 25 percent of the time.' So the safest solution is never to try to understand a woman; just love her and let it go at that."

"Smart ass. Sounds like something he would say and you would repeat." Sally playfully slapped his jaw. She put her arm around him and escorted him toward the door.

"Your father's inside. I told him I was going out to water the flowers before we ate." She preceded him up the steps, and she opened the door to the family room. "I didn't tell him you were coming. I was afraid he'd leave. Watch yourself, he's stubborn, but he needs your help."

"For what?" Smitty asked with concern.

"Ask him how school is going," Sally answered quickly, as the door opened before she could turn the handle.

"Hi, sweetheart, did you get the . . . " Dad stopped when he saw Smitty over Sally's shoulder. He pushed her aside so that he had a clear view of his son and could block him from entering the house.

"What are you doing here?"

"I invited him for dinner." Sally showed surprising strength by shoving Dad roughly back inside the house and away from the door.

"Then I'm leaving." Dad began to turn away.

"No, you're not, First Sergeant," Sally said. "If you don't want the bed tonight to be colder than your ex-wife's ass, you'd better sit your butt down. Your son came at my invitation. It's my house, too, now, and I expect you to be courteous to my guest."

Dad stared at Sally, then at Smitty, backpedaled four steps, and slowly lowered himself down into his easy chair.

Turning to Smitty, she said, "And you, Lieutenant, park it right there." She pointed to the recliner that was probably hers, separated from Dad's by an end table.

"Now then," she said in a softer voice, "how about if I get you both a beer and you two talk, civilly, I emphasize civilly, to each other while I finish preparing dinner."

Sally walked to the kitchen and returned with two beers poured in frosted beer glasses. "You two boys remember to use the coasters. You're not in some rumdum joint in Saigon."

The tension in the room was so tight that a cat hair landing on the tile floor would have sounded like a 747 doing a wheels-up landing into O'Hare on an icy night. A minute passed, then two. Neither man spoke, both looking straight ahead, not wanting to be the first one to break the silence or give in.

The Mexican standoff was finally broken by Sally, who peeked around the corner of the kitchen. "It's awful quiet in here. I've heard more noise in a conversation between two signing deaf people."

She turned her head in the direction of the TV, so that her right eye was not visible to Dad. "Honey, why don't you tell your son how you're doing in school, since you both go to the same place."

"Pfft," Dad snorted contemptuously. "That was a stupid-ass pipe dream; I ain't going back."

"Why?" Smitty asked evenly.

Dad glared at his son, grunted, then lapsed into silence.

"Probably because he's failing," Sally answered. "And you know your dad, Kevin. First sergeants never fail at anything; they know it all."

"Sally—" Dad started, but seeing the scornful look in her eyes, did not finish his thought.

"Don't use that superior first sergeant's tone with me, buster. I'm not some young private fresh off the farm."

Now it was Dad and Sally's turn to glare at each other in silence. Remembering Sally's opening comment, and Dad's absolute stubbornness, Smitty decided that he'd better intervene on Sally's behalf.

"Um, Dad," Smitty began hesitantly, "do you know why you're failing in school?"

Dad was silent for a moment. "No, I don't. I go to class every day and take hundreds of pages of notes and read the assigned material, but the class moves so fast, and the professors skip around from one chapter to the next."

Sally cupped her left hand over her cheek and silently mouthed "thank you," before quietly withdrawing to the kitchen.

Dad fired his pipe and shook his head. "If I had tried to hold a maintenance course on the B-52 that way, the goddamn thing would have crashed on takeoff."

"Have you talked to the professors about it?" Smitty asked.

"Hell, yes, I've tried to talk to one of them, but he just won't listen. I've told him that it's confusing to me and impossible to follow, and even related my B-52 analogy, but he wasn't sympathetic at all," Dad answered, frustration in his voice.

"Dad, maybe it's your study methods that need some fine-tuning."

"What do you mean?" Dad asked, his voice beginning to rise. "Are you trying to tell me I'm not smart enough to learn?"

"Look, Dad, you and I have some things in common," Smitty said. "When I was at Bragg for six months, I studied and learned everything about my skill, because I knew that even the smallest thing might be the one that saved my ass in Nam.

"When I went in-country, there were field-level, graduate-level courses taught by specialists who'd actually been through it. Everything was critical, because people were dying, or maybe would die, if I didn't know my job to the minutest detail. Just like your maintenance guys had to know the minutest detail of the B-52s so that you could repair them instantaneously during an ORI."

"Yeah, so?"

"So, what you or I think about a professor or that way he teaches his class is unimportant. What is important is that you study, learn, and comprehend the things that he, or she, thinks matters, commit them to memory, and be able to regurgitate them back on demand."

"Yeah, but if I do it that way, I forget half of what I learned within three months," Dad objected.

"But you retained the other 50 percent, right?" Smitty said. "So in aggregate, you're now half-smarter than you were. And based on the six-striper I know, for a crusty old sergeant to be half-smart would be a wonder, wouldn't it?"

Dad shrugged and laughed in spite of himself. "Fuckin' shavetails."

"1LT, First Sergeant," Smitty corrected, thinking of Sergeant Mike's christening.

"Even worse."

"Well, like somebody I knew once said, 'that ain't no fucking officer; he's my son,'" Smitty said with a smile.

"Dinner in fifteen at 1800 hours, boys." Sally walked in carrying two fresh beers, and winked at Smitty. As she was walking away, she came within reaching distance of Dad who swatted her on the rear end affectionately.

Sally turned. "Pretty smart stepson I've got there, huh?" she asked, amused.

Dad eyed Smitty and smiled. "Not bad at that."

They ate dinner in a cheerful mood, Smitty and his Dad playing catch-up on each other's activities the last six months, the relief of tension in Dad clearly evident. After clearing away the dishes, Smitty sat down at the kitchen table with his father to review his study habits with him.

Proceeding carefully, lest his father become defensive, Smitty was able to give him a crash course in how to outline textbooks, and how to study what the professor thought was important. They spent the balance of the evening with Smitty doing most of the talking about the process of studying and giving Dad inside tips about what he had learned.

It was past midnight, when Smitty and his dad had finished. As Smitty rose to go, Sally took him by the arm. "Come with me."

She walked him through the living room, back through the hall to the bedroom that used to be his, a long, long time ago.

"Have a good sleep, Lieutenant," she said, closing the door.

Smitty stood in silence feeling both discomfort and, at the same time, warmth in being back in the bedroom he'd not occupied in close to five years.

He lay on the bed without undressing and as sleep began to fill his eyes, he thought how good it felt to be home again. Three of the four members of the original family were now back in Savannah, but the players and relationships were different. And with all this friction around, sparks were an inevitable by-product, and there was certain to be a fire.

Smitty was relaxing the next day on a blanket in the front yard, working idly on acquiring a tan for his repaired limb. With a cool towel folded over his eyes, his thoughts inevitably turned to his friends. Changes had been happening to the other three musketeers also—good for Frenchy but bad for LZ and Big Walt.

Frenchy had a daughter in July and appeared to be doing well, but LZ was now back in Nam, with a regular army unit, busted to an E-5 again, and dismissed from his DI duties after punching a white recruit who called him a racist nigger.

Smitty had driven over to see LZ before he shipped out from Benning. Although his friend had regretted the incident, he didn't appear particularly penitent. When Smitty questioned him on this, LZ had remarked in a nasty voice that although he knew Smitty was trying to help, his major problem was that Smitty was starting to sound just like one of those college smart asses that he used to hate, that Smitty just didn't know how it felt to be a minority, and until he did, he'd better just shut the fuck up.

Big Walt had surfaced in Jacksonville, where he held up a liquor store at the point of a gun, got sixty-eight dollars for his trouble, and a four-year prison sentence for armed robbery when caught two days later. Smitty did not go down for the trial; the big guy was beyond any help and support a friend could offer.

Smitty's thoughts were interrupted by pain. Someone had kicked his left leg.

"Well, well, well. Look who it is: the big bad Green Beret baby killer."

Smitty removed the towel, opened his eyes, squinted, and looked up from his supine position.

Smitty did not recognize the person who starred back at him. He saw grimy shoulder-length hair that appeared to have not done a close-order drill with a comb in at least a year, a scraggly beard with patchy bare spots, faded torn bell-bottom pants with matching worn-out beach clogs, and a ratty, holey, surfing shirt two sizes too big with the name of some surfboard company on it. Smitty realized that this misrepresentation of a human being must be his brother Billy.

He was deeply tanned and his skin had a leathery look to it. Sally had surprised Smitty and his dad at breakfast that morning with the news that Billy was on his way and scheduled to arrive in the late afternoon. She was excited by the prospects of a family reunion. Smitty was not. They'd not parted as friends, and Smitty was perfectly happy with the status quo.

Smitty glanced at his watch; it was only noon. Obviously, his older brother had felt a burning desire to arrive early so he could pick up where he left off five years ago. He had literally caught Smitty napping.

"Billy," Smitty said incredulously. He had not seen Billy since that fateful night almost half a decade ago, and hadn't been sure what to expect when his brother showed up, but this abomination was more than he could have imagined.

"That's right, little brother, it's me—your older brother, Billy." He kicked Smitty in the left foot again, sending shooting pains up his still-tender leg. Then he turned to the two equally unkempt looking buddies he had with him. "Jimmy, Jeff, this is my baby brother.

"He ran away to the army after he lost the battle for favorite son with my dad and almost killed himself trying to become some kind of big bad hero so Dad would like him. But it didn't do him any good." He smirked, and kicked Smitty in the leg again, harder this time. "Dad still prefers me, doesn't he, baby brother?"

"Billy." Smitty propped himself up on one arm and prepared to scissor-trip his brother if he tried to touch him again. "Please listen very carefully. I'm not the same little brother who left here years ago as a gawky teenager. You're right, I became a Green Beret, and I'm damn proud of it. And the lessons I learned at Bragg I applied in two-plus tours in Vietnam.

"Not only do I have a great deal more experience than you in the art of physical combat, I'm six inches taller and outweigh you by at least fifty pounds now. Unless you want to have your teeth sticking out of your asshole, I'd go away and leave me alone."

When his brother made no move to leave, Smitty looked first at his brother's two friends, who, sensing trouble, judiciously backed up a step, then at his brother, and said bluntly, "Billy, I realize that you're used to shooting your mouth off and being a big man with your surfer buddies, but I must tell you, I have a lot of stored up animosity toward you. Please don't make me prove it."

"Big talk, little man," Billy said. "But I know it's all bullshit. You try me on and you'll get your Green Beanie ass kicked. I ain't some weak-ass cowering Vietnamese villager like we saw on the news." Billy kicked Smitty in his sore leg for the fourth time.

Smitty's hatred went on autopilot as a lifetime of stored anger toward his brother exploded like dynamite. He brought him down with a judo-type leg kick. From there, the rest was a kaleidoscope of instinctive reactions, fueled by hatred and experience. Somewhere in this process, Smitty totally blacked out, losing track of time or conscious thought, as he pummeled his brother unmercifully.

The next things he could identify were the sounds of a siren receding in the distance, a fierce aching in his head, and his father standing over him screaming at the top of his lungs with a three-foot piece of two-by-four in his hands.

"I think you're out of your fucking mind!" his dad screamed. Smitty's blurred vision came into focus. "What the hell got into you, brutally attacking your brother then going after his two friends?"

"What happened?" Smitty asked in a voice that he only vaguely recognized as his own.

"What happened?!" his father repeated, barely containing himself. "You've nearly killed your brother." Dad paused to catch his breath. "And you would have if I hadn't seen you attack him. I came out of the shop and dropped you with this." He waved the two-by-four threateningly in front of him

"How bad is he hurt?" Smitty asked, shaking his head to try to clear the cobwebs. He regretted it immediately. His vision blurred and his equilibrium temporarily left him.

"How bad is he hurt?!" Dad sputtered. "Bad enough to take him and one of his friends to the hospital in the ambulance."

"You didn't see what happened, Dad—"

"No, and I don't want to hear it," Dad interrupted. "You're a professional soldier, at least you were. You should have better sense than to be chivvied into a go at fisticuffs by some jealous amateur, especially if that envious novice is your own brother."

"Remember what you always told me, Popster, when I was a kid and I appealed to you for help when Billy beat me up?" Smitty asked, scorn in his voice. "'A man has to be able to take care of himself in this world. If you don't want Billy to keep beating you up, pick up something and even the odds.'"

Returning to his normal voice, Smitty said, "Well that's just what I did, Popster. So fuck you; you can't tell me what to do." Smitty got slowly to his feet.

He was immediately returned to the ground, courtesy of Dad's haymaker. The punch stunned Smitty more than hurt him, but now was not the time to discuss Dad's lack of physical fitness.

"No, fuck you, boy," he said, wildly waving the piece of lumber like a club. "Are you too stupid or so far gone that you don't know the difference between teenage fisticuffs and felonious assault and battery with intent to kill? A judge would carve you a new asshole, son."

Dad exhaled deeply, brushed back the few remaining strands of hair on the top of his head, and continued in a more controlled but still threatening tone.

"Now I am going to tell you what to do, and God help you if you don't do it."

Using the wood like a classroom pointer, he poked Smitty in the chest. "You're going to get in that rocket you call a car, drive down to the hospital, and sit there in the emergency room while they tend to your brother. Then you're going to accompany him to his room, and when he's awake, you're going to tell him how sorry you are for this.

"You're going to go now, and if you don't do exactly what I told you, then you'd better stick your head between your Green Beret ass and kiss it good-bye, 'cause the rest will belong to me. Are we clear?"

"Yes, sir." Smitty got to his feet. He was not sorry for using his brother for a judo demonstration. What scared the hell out of him was the fact that he'd lost control.

As Smitty walked to his car and got in, Dad called after him, "Son, someday you'll thank me for this."

"I'll look forward to that day," Smitty said. He started his car and pulled away, being careful, even in his anger, to observe the twenty-five mile per hour posted speed limit, lest he further incur his father's wrath.

Smitty did as his father requested. He did go to the hospital, did sit in the emergency room, and was sitting in his brother's room when he came awake later that night.

Smitty said superficial things like, "Hope you'll be all right. Sorry that I lost my temper," that kind of thing, but he was only mouthing words he did not feel. His brother had brought to the surface feelings and emotions that were festering just below, emotions that he had thought were neatly filed and stored away under control.

Smitty did agree with one thing that Dad had said. He had taken out his own feelings on an untrained civilian. That was appalling. He felt no personal regret for Billy, who was pretty much a dead loss for Homo sapiens, but he was frightened at the realization of just how much anger simmered in him and how ready it was to erupt.

The incident with his brother seemed to open the floodgates on his pent-up feelings. It served as the catalyst for unleashing a host of nightmares and emotional tantrums that had been held in check since his return from Nam and continued long after his brother was discharged from the hospital and had gone back to Florida.

Smitty began to wake up in a cold sweat, sometimes on the other side of the room. His demeanor changed from pleasant to angry when out of the public eye, so much so that, within two months of moving in, Lenny and Billy moved out, telling him to send the money when he sold the house. And, to drown the atrocities and the ghosts of his deceased friends, Smitty had begun to drink again heavily.

The reactions were severe enough that Smitty made a call to Dr. Evans in New York, who listened, then got a colleague, a psychologist, on the phone. The head doctor agreed with everything Smitty had said, which was that basically Smitty was carrying around a lot of rage and that it had to come out.

As to why it was coming out now instead of last year, when Smitty was freshly returned from Vietnam, the good doctor was of the opinion that last summer Smitty had been concerned with his physical and mental survival in a different kind of war, the battle with one's own insecurities when faced with the challenge of an uncertain future. With those needs now being met, his mind was now releasing its pent-up emotions.

Smitty remembered psychology class last term. They had discussed Maslow's hierarchy of needs. Smitty's emotional volcano seemed to be the result of his mind's determination that his basic survival and safety needs had been met. That he was now ascending to the levels of personal acceptance and esteem did not, at present, seem to be a fair trade.

Smitty did find it interesting that the advice he'd given his father had, in effect, come home to roost on him. He didn't remember much about that psych class, but one thing that he'd learned and remembered was benefiting him now. Smitty discussed these thoughts with Ron, but he dismissed them with a scoff, saying that all Smitty needed to do was just suck it up—whatever that meant.

In the weeks and months of that summer of 1971, Smitty began to live two lives. By day, he was the congenial Dr. Jekyll, a studious college sophomore who was working his way through college as an auto mechanic. But by night, he became the evil Mr. Hyde, prowling the sleazy bars of downtown Bay Street and the riverfront, drinking to excess, fighting at the slightest provocation, forcing his attentions on uninterested bar girls, and waking up the next morning with a mighty hangover and empty pockets, sometimes in a strange bed.

By the beginning of August, Smitty'd already been in several nasty rounds of fisticuffs in the local bars and was acquiring a nefarious reputation both with the local bar owners and the police.

In one of these, Smitty, Ron, and two of his other friends got into an altercation with what turned out to be a bar full of marine recruits on their first leave from Parris Island, just up the road in South Carolina. There were upwards of forty marines in the bar and Smitty and his friends eventually lost the battle, but they won the war in the press.

The story published on the lower half of page one in the local newspaper was headed, "Army 22, Marines 4." The story implied that if the army contingent had been one man stronger, it would have won.

In the details of the article, all four army combatants were listed by name. Smitty was named as "Kevin Smith, son of civic leader Mrs. J. G. Gates.

The article appeared next to another, naming Smitty's mom as head of some civic garden club project and, according to her scathing phone call the next day, caused her permanent social embarrassment from which she would never recover. She ended the phone call promising retribution, reminding Smitty that despite his thwarting of their plans with her mother in Atlanta, her husband was well-connected politically and was just looking for a reason to settle the score.

It didn't take long. The fallout hit Ron first. The army barred his reenlistment for conduct unbecoming an officer, ending an anticipated promotion to major, and an eleven-year career that Smitty was sure Ron had intended to go to twenty or maybe more. Smitty was next. He received a letter from the Barn in early September informing him that he was not welcome to enroll for the fall term, coincidentally, for conduct unbecoming a student.

This only deepened the pattern of bad booze and bad women for Smitty. Every altercation seemed to lead to another. With every dispute, Smitty's anger got worse. He had alienated just about everyone he knew who cared about him.

Nearly eighteen months after coming home from Vietnam, Smitty was still living with the effects, with no relief in sight.

"Another beer," Smitty said sullenly.

The bartender looked quickly at Smitty, saw his menacing stare, then nodded his head slowly, and silently refilled the glass.

Smitty sipped in silence, spinning around on the bar stool as he did so, surveying the room for possible carnal contacts.

The pickings were slim. There were only four women in the bar. Two were in their forties, looked it, and were talking quietly at a table, apparently comfortable within their own circle. The third was the server, a woman in her thirties, whose pudgy ass looked revolting in her spandex hot pants and braless halter top that displayed her sagging breasts amply.

The fourth held some possibilities. She looked to be in her early- to mid-twenties, with strawberry blonde hair. She was conservatively dressed, with a good figure, and a pleasant smile. She had come into the bar alone and was sipping her Pink Lady delicately.

Smitty picked up his beer and moved down to the stool next to her.

"Hi," he said in a friendly fashion.

She smiled faintly in return and took a sip of her drink. "Hello."

"I haven't seen you in here before."

"That's because I haven't been here before. I just came to Savannah from a little town outside of Metter two weeks ago looking for a job. Not a lot of opportunity for a girl when Metter is the big city," she said candidly. "Not unless you want to marry the local farmer's son and slop hogs or pick peanuts."

"So what's a person with your ambition doing in a place like this?"

"I could ask you the same thing."

Smitty was quiet for a moment, then answered honestly, "Just lonely, I guess."

"Me, too," she said in a low voice. "I've been cooped up in that rented room for two weeks and just thought I needed to get out. And I got tired of sitting in the den arguing with the other roomers over which TV program to watch."

Smitty was silent. This was not going at all as he planned. He was looking to get laid tonight, not find a nice girl. Besides, Smitty was still zero for his lifetime with nice girls, and, after Carla, had made a vow to give them a wide berth.

"Well, good luck finding that job." Smitty grabbed his mug and slid off the barstool and headed back down to the other end. "Maybe I'll see you in here again sometime," he said without turning around.

"I hope so," she said.

Smitty returned to his spot at the other end of the bar, glancing away quickly whenever the Nice Girl, as he had christened her since he didn't know her name, looked his way.

Any normal guy would have been asking for her name and then asking her out for a date, but Smitty was not normal. Besides, he had the bitter experiences of the past to go on. Nice girls were not meant for people like him: he'd just screw them up, or perhaps screw them over, just like he'd done all the others, or get them killed.

Smitty drained the rest of his beer and left the cocktail lounge. He decided to leave his car where it was parked, just around the corner from the bar, and walk down the block to the next joint, Hard Hearted Hannah's, to see if the pickings were better.

Two hours and five beers later, he was ready to leave. There was nothing in this slop house that even closely resembled an eligible female, or even an ineligible one for that matter. He left the bar in an irritated mood, feeling the emptiness of every lonely person starved for warmth in the middle of a crowded city.

He paused at the door of his more familiar haunt, noticing four Hogs in front. It was past twelve, and he should be headed home, but the memory of her smile lingered, and Smitty found himself turning the handle.

The blast from the jukebox was almost physical. It howled like a kennel full of torturers. A shattered barstool lay across the unconscious body of the bartender. A gash on his forehead had masked him redly.

The pudgy, weathered bar girl was dancing topless on the stage in her panties as her freed breasts flopped up and down, shaping and reshaping themselves like shaken water balloons. The look of terror on her face was sufficient evidence that the impromptu striptease was not her idea.

The nice girl, frozen with horror, was sitting on the lap of a scruffy biker. One greasy hand mauled her right breast, uninhibited by the remnants of her torn blouse and bra. The other was forcing her head down between a mass of beard to the sadistic lips located somewhere underneath. He paused and looked at Smitty.

"Come in if you dare, asshole." He turned and threw a glass of beer at the dancer, soaking her hair, face, and breasts. "Keep dancing, you fat-assed slut. And get them panties off. I want to see your fuckhole and your butt hole before me and the boys try them out for size, bitch."

There were five of them, four males and a female. The four males were sitting around a table next to the stage; the female was on the stage, coaching and taunting the conscripted dancer.

Smitty knew that if he stayed he'd have to take them out with extreme prejudice, just like the marines trying to rape that kid in Nam. Only this time, there'd be no Sergeant Mike to back him up, and no firearm either. His cherished Magnum was safely locked in his footlocker.

Smitty was scared. This was altogether different from his time in the service. Over there, he'd always had some form of backup. Here he was all alone, and all the intensive training he had endured would now be given an immediate graduate test with death the certain result of failure.

Or he could run. He could turn his back on all he'd been taught and all he'd thought he'd become, back out the door, be around the corner, and in his car in a flash and be gone. Then he could flag down the cops, let them handle it. That would be the safe approach—to do what's right. 'Course by then it might be too late for the unconscious bartender and for the bar girl and the nice girl, but at least he'd be safe.

It's what you do when you're scared that matters, Smitty remembered. He took a step forward, his decision made to do the right thing—even if it cost him his life. He surveyed the bar for, as his dad would put it, "something to even the odds."

"Asshole?" Smitty asked. "Asshole?" he repeated as he took another step into the bar, focusing on the armament available, which consisted mainly of chairs, stools, beer mugs and glasses.

"You don't know me well enough to call me an asshole." Smitty hoped he sounded infuriatingly calm. He wandered toward the stage in what he hoped was his most casual manner.

The bikers seemed content to allow him to do just that. *Rabbit taking the bait,* Smitty thought, as they watched in amused silence, all but licking their collective chops in anticipation of rearranging his anatomy. No wonder. Five to one, they figured they had all the time they needed to kill this fool. May as well enjoy letting the fucker squirm.

Smitty was stalling for time, while military lessons, drummed in until they had become instinctive, but rusty from disuse, made their way to the forefront of his brain. He recalled the lectures in hand-to-hand at Napalm Hill at Bragg about the concept of the gang of four. All gangs were endlessly repeating hierarchies of four in terms of ability and willingness to fight.

He remembered the paradox of leadership: that the leader was 100 percent willing, but only 75 percent able, while his lieutenant was 100 percent able, but only 75 percent willing.

From there, the percentages dropped significantly. The third person was 50 percent willing and able. The fourth was only 25 percent in both categories and could be classified as a hanger-on. If the first three were dispatched quickly and efficiently, and he saw his chances of sustaining personal injury go up significantly, the odds were that the fourth would turn and run.

The litmus test for this was fear. Fear can be hidden in a mask of false bravado with practice, but you can never hide it in your soul. And the eyes were the key to the soul.

Smitty made eye contact with each of the four, checking them like an engine dipstick, estimating who was running on full, three-quarters full, half-full, and who was operating with the warning light on. He prayed silently that his estimates were accurate.

He reached the stage and he nonchalantly held out his right hand. "C'mon down from there, sis."

She stepped nervously down from the stage. Smitty slowly removed his army flight jacket and draped it over her shoulders. He looked at the hard case with the nice girl on his lap. "I don't even allow my older sister to call me asshole, or her husband either, for that matter." Smitty nodded in the direction of the recumbent bartender. "And I've known both of them all my life."

He walked slowly around the table until he was standing in front of what his visual scan had told him was the leader, with his second and thirds in the pecking order located to his right and left respectively. The leader, though no more than thirty-five, had a receding hairline that a dirty bandanna did little to conceal.

"You're about to die, motherfucker," the man said, as his switchblade appeared from nowhere and he began to rise.

"Try a comb-over, grandpa." Smitty snatched the kerchief off. Holding it to his face, he wrinkled his nose in disgust.

As the leader stood up, unceremoniously dumping the nice girl squarely on the floor, Smitty knew he was literally in the fight of his life.

Smitty had reached for the half-full pitcher of beer on the table with his right hand, even as he was removing the leader's cover-up. After sniffing it, he flung it into the face of the man across the table, temporarily blinding him.

He brought the pitcher around with every bit of centrifugal backhand force he could muster, tossing most of the contents into the skag to the right of the leader. He continued his arc until the pitcher came to a definitive stop. The thick glass shattered against the leader's jaw. He dropped his knife and sank to the floor, dripping and screaming.

With only the handle of the pitcher left in his hand, Smitty reversed his direction, brought it forward, and raked the face of the man to his left with the jagged end.

Different asshole, same result, Smitty thought, as the man pitched sideways out of his chair, clutching his freely bleeding face with both hands and sobbing.

Smitty stepped up on the chair recently vacated by the leader and launched himself directly at third dude, the one with the beer shampoo, with all the finesse of a battering ram. He toppled over backwards from the chair and crashed to the floor with a bone-jarring crunch.

The crunch knocked the wind out of him, stunning him and rendering him temporarily unthreatening. Smitty made that status permanent in short order by stomping on both of his collarbones, nodding in satisfaction at the snapping sounds and his shrieks of torment.

Smitty turned quickly and was just searching for the other two, when one of them found him. The female leaped on his back from the stage, locking her arms and fingers around his face like a Boston crab, put her knee in the small of his back, forced his head back, and screamed urgently, "Billy, cut this fucker!" to the fourth and last standing member of the gang.

She was stronger than most men Smitty knew, as he soon found out when he tried desperately and unsuccessfully to break her grip.

Smitty heard the distinctive sound of a switchblade snapping open. In desperation, he kicked backwards with his right leg, striking her solidly in the shin with his heel, more by luck than skill.

Her grip slackened infinitesimally for just a moment, but a moment was all Smitty needed. He punched her elbows furiously with his left fist; with his right, he reached over his head, grabbed a hunk of her greasy yellow hair, and yanked it with all his might.

She howled in protest and pain as she released her headlock and grabbed at his wrists in a desperate attempt to stop him from making her as prematurely bald as her leader. Using her hair like a tether, Smitty spun her around until she was between him and the fourth man.

Wasting neither time nor gallantry, Smitty punched her hard in her right breast, and was just drawing his fist back to punch her in the jaw when she suddenly grunted, and with a bewildered look, suddenly went slack, hanging with her full weight suspended from her hair like a puppet on a string.

She opened her mouth to speak, but the words would not come out. Her eyes rolled up and she passed out as Smitty grabbed her under the arm and lowered her to the ground, noticing as he did, the switchblade embedded in the middle of her back. A switchblade that if he'd not spun her around, most certainly would have been imbedded in his chest.

So much for the fuckin' army theories, Smitty thought as he let her settle on the floor and turned to face the last man standing.

Smitty advanced toward him, pausing next to the leader, who was making attempts at getting on his feet, and kicking him squarely in the head.

The fourth was backed against the wall with fear in his eyes. "Please don't. I didn't mean to kill her. I wasn't even going to kill you, just slash you a little so that we could get away."

"Yeah, right." Smitty grabbed him, and smashed him in the throat. The knife wielder grabbed his neck in a desperate attempt to continue breathing.

Locking his right arm around the man's hands, Smitty brought his knee up and smiled savagely as his eyes fluttered. As Smitty let go of him, he slid down the wall and settled on the floor with all the style of a worn dishrag.

"And the next head of the NAACP is going to be Lester Maddox," Smitty said in disgust as he watched him fall.

The bar girl now rushed to the aid of the downed bartender and began to administer first aid to his wounds as best she could.

"Call the police," Smitty commanded. "And tell them to send an ambulance."

Whatever else she had done in life, she knew how to follow orders. She ran behind the bar, grabbed the phone, and began to dial.

Smitty walked over to the nice girl, who had judiciously retreated under a table ten feet away. "You all right?"

"I expect I shall be," she said in a shaken voice, as she accepted his hand and got up.

Smitty couldn't help noticing that she was recovering her composure quickly and didn't seem to suffer from any schoolgirl modesty about the state of her clothes. Smitty judged her as a lady who understood that there were things more important than whether or not Smitty got a look at her naked body.

"I'll go see what I can do to help the bartender," she said softly, confirming his thoughts.

The police arrived within minutes, the ambulance shortly thereafter. For the next two hours, the bar swarmed with policemen, detectives, medics, and the coroner.

The biker babe died on the floor of the bar, the bartender a short while later at the local hospital. The leader and his two henchmen were quickly transported to the hospital for treatment. The fourth man was sitting in the corner groggily holding his head in his hands and begging to be sent to the hospital. The detective in charge refused. He wanted some answers first.

The police held Smitty, the bar girl, and the nice girl for an hour and a half at the bar, having them tell and retell their individual versions of the events numerous times, then asking them to come down to police headquarters in the morning to sign statements.

The bar girl and the nice girl were given treatment on the spot then were free to go. Smitty was finally excused at 3:00 AM, only to find when he got to his car that two of his expensive Goodyears had been slashed.

Smitty returned to the bar to call Ron to come and get him. Curiously, he did not answer. Maybe he had gotten lucky with a local girl who had seemed to hold his interest lately and was spending the night. Smitty slammed down the phone in disgust, uncertain of what to do next.

He looked up to see the last man standing more conscious now and talking like a person who had been injected with truth serum. He was telling the police everything in a scared voice, including his role in his unfortunate female colleague's demise. And telling them, in no uncertain terms, that the fight had been the result of a planned hit on Smitty. The leader had assured them it would be easy to carry out, since Smitty was, in his terms, "just some over-the-hill deranged alky Vietnam veteran."

Now the slashed tires made sense; there must have been a spotter who could tell the culprits when to arrive at the bar. The tire-flattening was insurance that if Smitty came back and did not go in for a nightcap, he would have to return to the bar in any event. It was the closest place to use a phone to call for help.

"So what are you going to do now?" The nice girl slid onto the barstool next to Smitty, now wearing his coat.

"Well, since my ride's disabled, I guess I'll call a cab," Smitty said.

"My room's only two blocks away, you could stay there for the night. I have a double bed," she said.

Smitty raised his eyebrows in surprise. Maybe his barometer was all wrong about her.

"I meant, to sleep," she said pointedly, her face turning red.

"Best offer I've had all night." Smitty got off the barstool and held out his arm. "Miss, uh—"

"Susan, Susan Hopkins," she said, looping her arm in his.

"Smitty Smith," he answered.

As they left the bar arm in arm, the police were questioning the fourth man thoroughly about the source of the hit, but he was adamant that neither he nor any of the other four knew. The contact had been by phone, and the payoff, five crisp brand new Benjamin Franklins, by blind drop.

They walked the two blocks in silence then tiptoed up the stairs to her room. As she closed the door, she switched on the overhead light and opened the closet door, which shielded her from Smitty's eyes as she changed out of her torn clothes.

She stared at him unblinkingly. "I meant what I said. This is not an offer of sex, just a place to sleep for the night."

"Don't sweat it, Susan. When I came into the bar, picking up someone and getting a piece of ass was the only thing on my mind. After what just happened, it's the last." Smitty lay down on the bed fully clothed. "Although a little snuggling together might help."

"That I can do, and it wouldn't exactly do me any harm either." She closed the door, then appeared before him in a faded football jersey that was about four sizes too big, but not so big that Smitty couldn't see that she had extremely nice legs.

"My older brother's. I've slept in it for years." She walked around to the foot of the bed, stopped, removed Smitty's shoes and placed them quietly on the floor, then continued around to the other side of the bed, snapping off the light on the way.

She slipped under the covers and when Smitty did the same, she rolled to him and kissed him on the cheek in a sisterly-like fashion. "Thanks for the rescue, soldier."

Smitty did not answer as she nestled close to him, with her head on his shoulder.

Within moments, her rhythmic breathing was a clear sign that she was asleep, as was the feel of her firm breast rising and falling as it brushed against his side through the flimsy material.

Smitty slept fitfully that night. Maybe the police didn't have a suspect, but Smitty did. Matter of fact, he had a couple. And he was going to pay the primary one a call tomorrow, just as soon as the big Chevy was airmobile again.

It was just past 9:30 PM when Smitty parked his Chevy in front of the expensive-looking estate out on Wilmington Island. It wasn't the biggest one out there, but a golf cart would come in handy when going to the mailbox. It was a good one-iron from the front door—a Jack Nicklaus one-iron.

To use one of his dad's World War II terms, 'the joint was jumpin.'" There seemed to be a continuous line of Caddys, Continentals, and New Yorkers stretched the entire length of the driveway, with the odd limo thrown in for good measure.

He walked up the circular driveway toward the house, surveying his surroundings. The crowd made Smitty nervous, but he was a man on a mission from which he would not be deterred, even by a few snooty witnesses.

As he reached the front door, he glanced sideways into the open four-car garage. The first stall contained a brand new E-type Jaguar convertible, the second, a white Chrysler New Yorker. But it was the third and fourth that caught and held his interest. The third stall was occupied by the old Plymouth. The fourth contained a red Corvette, an older model that looked just like the one Smitty had met months ago on his way to Grandma's house.

Smitty rang the bell.

The door was answered by a distinguished-looking black man in a formal butler's uniform, who looked like a cross between Uncle Remus and Al Jolson in blackface. "Good evening, sir," he said. "May I see your invitation please?"

"I, um, didn't know I needed one," Smitty said, bluffing. "My mother told me to just drop by if I had the time."

"Oh, you must be the missus's son, the one that so infuriates her," he said.

"Yes, sometimes," Smitty said with a smile.

"She's in the living room, sir. Have a pleasant evening." He took Smitty's old army coat, stepped back, and bowed slightly.

Smitty walked across the expansive foyer but had not yet reached the living room, when a loud voice to his right said, "Father, Father, it's him."

"Who?" Smitty recognized Johnboy's voice coming from behind a crowd of people.

"That guy who tried to run me off the road, then ran from me and the state police when we were both trying to catch him." Same scraggly beard, same sneering face. Somehow his being Johnboy's jerk-off son just seemed to fit.

The conversation in the room died as quickly as if someone had flipped a switch. Smitty caught his mother's, "not again" look as he advanced into the living room, his self-assured swagger and snaggletooth's indictment assurance enough that every eye in the place was squarely focused on them.

"You owe me $250, asshole," the bearded one snarled.

"For what?" Smitty said.

"For that incident out on the road a couple of months back, the one where you tried to run me off the road, then ran away like the coward you are when the state trooper and I tried to chase you."

Ah, now it all made sense in a peculiar sort of way, Smitty thought. "I recall the events differently."

"What's your version?" John stepped through the crowd.

"Well, I came up on your son, here, and every time I tried to pass him, he'd speed up. So when I saw a passing space coming up, I slowed down, downshifted, then shot around him.

"At the bottom of the hill, a state policeman was sitting on the side of the road. He pulled out, almost hit your son, then pulled him over and ran up to his car, I assume to take his keys. Then he came after me. After a couple of miles, he turned around and went back. That's all there was to it, John."

John looked sharply at his son and saw him flush. "Frankly, Kevin, your version sounds a lot more plausible than the fairy tale my son told me." He smiled, and said reflectively, "Well, I guess he got what was coming to him. The policeman came back and told my son that since he couldn't catch his racing buddy, he was going to give him two tickets, one for reckless driving and the other for speed in excess of one hundred miles an hour, and when he caught up with you, you could split it."

John continued, "The judge didn't believe my son's story either. Fined him five hundred dollars and suspended his license for six months."

"Shoulda had a faster car," Smitty said. Seeing his opening, he seized it. "Don't you wish you had known the truth before you paid those thugs the five big ones to have me hit?"

"What!" John shouted, as gasps and murmurs rolled through the crowd like thunder.

"You heard me," Smitty said, his voice rising.

"Oh, John, no," Smitty's mom said, as she came to stand beside him.

"I don't have the slightest idea what your son is talking about." John turned to face Smitty's mom.

"Well, maybe this will refresh your memory, Johnboy," Smitty said angrily. As John turned to face him, he punched him on the jaw with all of his strength, snapping his head backward and knocking him flat on his back.

"When he wakes up, tell that bastard daddy and husband of yours that if he ever tries that again, he'd better hire better people and pay them more 'cause they're gonna earn it," Smitty said to his cowering stepbrother and thoroughly stunned and embarrassed mom.

He turned and walked quickly from the room, the crowd parting as obligingly for him as the Red Sea had for Moses.

"I can see that your visit was fruitful, sir. Thank you so much for coming," the butler said cheerfully, as he insisted on helping Smitty on with his faded jacket.

He grinned, and shoved him gently onto the front porch. "If I was you, sir, in the words of my old daddy, I'd be lightin' out of here before the man comes. I'll hold them off from callin' the authorities as long as I can. You best git."

"Smitty Smith, sir," Smitty said, offering his hand.

"Ben Young." He took Smitty's hand firmly. "Y'all come back now, hear?"

With a friendly wave, Smitty turned and trotted down the driveway, wishing he in fact had the golf cart or at least a fast skateboard. He reached the Chevy in thirty seconds. It fired on the first turn, and with a spraying of gravel and dirt, he was gone.

Smitty'd only just regained the main highway to the mainland when the police lights appeared behind him no more than half a mile back. Smitty accelerated away, which didn't make the lights disappear, only multiply. He blew through the stop sign back onto the main highway, narrowly missing an oncoming car on his way to the Wilmington Island Bridge and the relative safety of the multiple roads beyond.

But it was not to be. The drawbridge was up, and there were at least five police cars waiting on the bridge. Smitty slowed and slid to a stop approximately twenty feet from them, shifted into reverse but never let the clutch out. Five police cars had blocked the bridge behind him. He shut off the big Chevy and prepared for the inevitable.

The policemen ran forward, jerked open the car door, and ordered him out with their nightsticks drawn.

"On the ground, asshole," an officer ordered, as he hit Smitty against the side of his head with his nightstick.

Just as it had with his brother, a lifetime of hatred and frustration came bursting through like a ruptured dam as Smitty snatched the baton from the startled officer's hands, and hit him back with a good deal more force than the policeman had used on him. What happened next was short and ferocious.

His next feeling was of pain as he looked blearily through protective steel mesh from the backseat of the patrol car at his bruised and bloody face in the rearview mirror. His shirt was completely red.

Police cruisers and ambulances were everywhere, with uniformed officers and white-coated medics scurrying around like people fleeing from a just-kicked hornet's nest.

Smitty could feel unconsciousness overtaking him. As he slumped down in the seat, he had a revelation and a final demoralizing thought.

Bending Johnboy's beak had been satisfying, but more importantly, informative in that it supplied another clue to the mystery. And he knew now how Custer must've felt at the Little Big Horn when faced with his own certain mortality. Smitty wondered how many of them he'd killed.

The results were predictable, the fallout catastrophic. The assault charges on the police alone were enough to keep the court recorder busy for the better half of a day. There were eight policemen on the bridge at the time that Smitty was jerked out of his car. By the time he was subdued, there were twenty more involved. When all the votes were tallied, on the "Last Stand on Wilmington Bridge" as the press had called it, Smitty was facing serious trouble.

He had begun by disabling the officer who had hit him and the next two to approach. Then he had dumped them all into the river. This set off a mad state of confusion as some of those left on the bridge began concentrating on fishing their colleagues out of the swift current and not on subduing Smitty. By the time reinforcements arrived from the bottom of the bridge, two more boys in blue had joined their colleagues for an unscheduled dip, further adding to the chaos.

Smitty was finally subdued in a bloody confrontation when eight police officers tackled him en masse and basically beat him into unconsciousness but not before he'd sent four other officers to the hospital with disabling injuries. That no one was killed or drowned in the melee was nothing short of a miracle.

Smitty had a policeman to thank for his life. A police officer, his own frustration and rage boiling over, had drawn his service revolver and, without warning, was sighting to fire on Smitty at point-blank range when he was disarmed by one of his own. According to the reports, this further added to the bedlam when the two officers actually got into a fight with each other, causing other officers to intervene, and taking more policemen away from their primary objective.

The final tally was twenty-two counts, with the most serious being the multiple assaults on the police, and then as usual, to beef it up for the press. The police and the district attorney ran up the charges, like a football team running up the score on a hapless opponent, by adding a series of inane charges, the last of which was "criminal trespass on a bridge."

But it played well with the press and they kept busy with juicy, gossipy stories for the next couple of days. These tied together well with the recent barroom fracas and resultant killing that Smitty had been involved in. If you added up all the allegations from the numerous newspaper stories, Smitty was convinced that he now knew who really killed Kennedy. He must have.

All of the family skeletons came marching out of the closet two-by-two. His entire family, and all their individual trials, tribulations, and transgressions, were now exposed and magnified in articles and television interviews. The Sunday edition had interviews with at least six people who Smitty had not been in contact with for years, who were reciting in lurid details for their fifteen minutes of fame their personal contact with Smitty and the disastrous result. Former high school acquaintances and teachers were in their glory telling tales that were at best slanted, at worst just bare-assed lies to conveniently alibi and cover up their own misconduct.

There were no like interviews with any of Smitty's former professors at the Barn. A spokesman issued a one-sentence statement that read simply, "We have a policy against commenting on the activities of former students while they were in attendance at the college."

Through all of this, Smitty's parents and stepparents were eerily quiet. Neither of his parents or their respective mates gave interviews. Curiously, there was no charge related to knocking Johnboy flat on his ass. Smitty suspected that his mom had something to do with this.

She had probably told John in no uncertain terms that if he increased her embarrassment by filing charges against her own son, then the marriage bed would become colder than an igloo's wall art. When confronted by TV cameras, they simply said, as one, "No comment," and walked on.

Since the incident had occurred on a Friday night, after being treated at the hospital and released to the police, Smitty was taken to jail and held until arraignment on Monday morning. Smitty was quickly bound over for trial, and bail was set at $4000. Smitty was able to arrange it through a bail bondsman by paying him the standard 10 percent in cash, which he had saved for his school tuition.

Even if he could find another college to admit him, there would be no school this quarter. Not only did he now not have the money, he did have a possible one-to-five sentence to worry about.

The conditions of his bail were severe. He was not to leave the state, was to strictly observe a twelve o'clock curfew, was forbidden to drink alcohol or enter any establishment that mainly served alcoholic beverages, and was to report to a court officer once a week to review his movements for the previous week. Worst of all, he was ordered to beach the Chevy and was not permitted to drive any automobile that had a V-8 engine in it until his case was handled in the courts, which, given the current backlog, might be months.

When Smitty was released late Monday afternoon, he took a cab to the house, only to find a note from Ron informing him that he was moving back into his trailer with his current girlfriend, Bunny, and that he would call in a few days to arrange moving the rest of his stuff out.

Smitty called his boss, expecting to be fired, but found him not only understanding, but even willing to help with his current dilemma. He and his son would be around tomorrow morning to pick Smitty up and go get his car out of the impound yard, then his son would drive it home. He also had an old four-banger Renault that he'd picked up for $100 that Smitty could drive for free until he got squared away.

Smitty was humbled by his support, said so, and thanked him profusely. Jake would not hear of it, saying no thanks were necessary because, even if half of what he'd read in the papers was true and his stepfather had done to him what he'd done to Smitty, he'd have done more to him than just knock his beak out of joint. He further added that he'd done some wild things himself when he came home from his recall to Korea and that Smitty should not worry about it and should keep his chin up.

Smitty immediately went straight to bed, feeling better about the whole thing for the first time in days.

"Young man, I want you to know that you present me with quite a paradox. According to a visit I had from a General Wilson, you piled up a helluva combat record in Vietnam and have made excellent progress in your transition to college student. Your activities in the bar, electing to intervene against what would be for most people insurmountable odds, are most laudable and I'm sure appreciated by the two young ladies involved."

The judge took a sip of water and continued in a more somber tone.

"However, I must tell you that I cannot in good conscience ignore the other side of the ledger. You've been involved in numerous barroom clashes, have been issued multiple tickets for abuse of the traffic laws in that drag racer you refer to as a car, and in this latest incident have caused several officers to be wounded while trying to take you into custody.

"Additionally, if I look back on your record, it is filled with numerous acts of violence and clashes with the authorities that to me represent a pattern that must be broken if you are to coexist as a useful and peaceful member of society." He looked up over his reading glasses. "Not to mention crashing a party and assaulting one of our leading citizens, who for reasons I can't quite comprehend does not wish—indeed, adamantly refuses—to press charges.

"It is mainly due to that that you are not going to jail. Since there is officially no probable cause for the police roadblock, their response in jerking you from the car is unfounded and excessive use of force, against which, as the record shows, you more than adequately defended yourself.

"Additionally, I was swayed by the testimony of the two young ladies and believe them wholeheartedly when they say they feared for their lives. At the very least, a brutal assault would most certainly have followed, had you not intervened."

Smitty glanced quickly with a raised eyebrow at his defense attorney, Glen Thompson. The lawyer had shown up on Smitty's doorstep as a pro bono gift from Major

Jim. He had been adept in establishing quite a few points that Smitty had a feeling the judge would have preferred not to think about.

Glen shook his head, indicating that it was not yet time to smile in relief.

"Mr. Smith, you need to hear this plainly, and I need to tell you that despite your impressive combat record, your equally impressive attempts at working your way through college as an auto mechanic, and your, one can only term it, discriminating sense of right and wrong in rescuing damsels in distress, the law is now working against you.

"I sentence you to a fine of $2500 for the provoked assault on the numerous police officers, which, thanks to your lawyer, is about all we can charge you with, and hereby direct that you be placed on a one-year noncombative order.

"During the course of this year, you are forbidden to consume alcoholic beverages in public or to enter any bar—for any reason—and the twelve o'clock curfew will remain in effect. Any traffic citation received during this period will require you to appear before me personally in chambers for explanation. You are to undergo mandatory court-ordered anger counseling and alcohol rehabilitation. You are to report, once a month, to a court officer who will monitor your progress and compliance with these conditions. Any absences from the state or changes of address are to be reported and approved in advance.

"Lastly, I am aware of your current financial shortfall. If you do not have the wherewithal to pay the entire fine at this time, the court will grant you thirty days to arrange payment and you will be released on your own recognizance. If you cannot arrange the payment in this time period, you will be taken into custody until such time as the payment is received, with the custodial time not to exceed one year."

The judge closed the legal folder and handed it to the bailiff. "Do you have any questions on any part of this sentence?"

Smitty shook his head in silence.

"Do you have anything you wish to say?"

Smitty glanced at Glen, then at the judge. "I guess you might as well take me into custody now, your honor, 'cause the prospects of me coming up with $2500 in thirty days are almost nil. Even if I sold everything I own."

"Are you requesting the court to forgo the thirty-day grace period and incarcerate you right now?"

"No, your honor, he is not," Glen said, placing his hand over Smitty's mouth before he could open it and stick his foot in any further.

"My client is merely commenting on the extraordinary amount of the fine and the arduous task of obtaining the required funds in the specified amount of time."

"He should have thought of that before he sent several of our police force to the hospital and a larger number for a swim.

"Anything else?" the judge asked, raising his gavel.

"I'd like to pay the entire fine now," a voice said from the back of the courtroom. The assembled crowd turned curiously.

"And you would be?"

"His father," Dad said, as he stepped up and stood beside Smitty.

"See the bailiff," the judge said. "Court dismissed."

Smitty stood uncomfortably as Dad wrote out a check for the entire amount, and they left the courtroom in silence.

As they were descending the steps, Smitty thanked Glen for his help. The lawyer shook his hand and with a friendly wave, said briskly, "Call me if I can help again." He turned and headed toward his car, leaving Smitty alone to face the music; music Smitty didn't think would be a lullaby.

"Thanks for the rescue there, Popster. I can catch a cab back to my place," Smitty said with a lightness he didn't feel.

"Car!" Dad pointed toward his automobile in the parking lot.

The drive back toward Dad's house was not that long, but seemed like an eternity in the tense silence. Smitty avoided eye contact with his dad.

When they were within a mile of Dad's house, Smitty said in a quiet voice, "Thanks for the rescue and the ride. Just drop me at the phone booth there and I'll call Ron to come and pick me up."

Dad ignored him, accelerated, and drove on to the house.

As Smitty got out of the car, Dad said curtly, "Inside."

Smitty made no immediate move toward the door. "That was not a request!"

Dad preceded him into the house, dropped his coat on the sofa, and pointed at Sally's easy chair. "Park it, troop. You and I are gonna talk.

"Proud of yourself?" Dad settled comfortably in the recliner across from him.

"I'll pay you back."

"Oh, that's already been decided. You've got ninety days. That gives you until the end of January 1972. The judge was only going to put you in jail if you didn't pay. I'll put you so far under the jail that you'll need an oxygen line to fart."

It wasn't a threat, it wasn't a promise—it was a certainty.

Dad leaned forward in his chair and looked directly at his son. "Son, do you mind if I give you a little advice?" Dad began to fill his pipe.

Smitty folded his arms and waited for the inevitable.

"You need to understand a basic truth."

"Which is?"

"Today's hero is tomorrow's fool."

Smitty shrugged. "Think I'm full of it, don't you, boy? Well, sport, you better start to believe it, or you're going to end up that way. Ten years from now, nobody will remember your war or care. Twenty years from now, Vietnam will be nothing more than an idle curiosity for people who weren't there. Thirty years from now, people who evaded this war will be touting it as an example of their vision and a qualification for public office.

"If you think that's not true, sport, just look at the past. World War II survivors marching in Veterans Day parades are already mocked and looked on with disdain by today's youth. By the time you have kids the Day of Infamy will probably pass without so much as a mention in the local newspaper."

Smitty had heard enough. Just because Dad had bailed him out sure as hell didn't give him the right to rag him like this, especially when he was the root cause of it in the first place.

Smitty rocked forward, compressing the footrest back into place. He leaped out of the recliner and headed into the kitchen with Dad hot on his tail.

Smitty went to the fridge for a beer and continued on through the back bedroom toward the bathroom. The closed door, obviously a sign that it was occupied by Sally, cut off his last line of retreat. Smitty did a U-turn, just in time to meet Dad head-on. Dad shoved him backward into his old bedroom and closed the door.

"Boy, there is nothing sadder than some thirty-something veteran with a rapidly receding hairline, rapidly expanding beer gut, and alcohol-glassy eyes sitting on a barstool in a faded field jacket telling anybody who'll listen what a hero he was in the last war." Dad grabbed Smitty's arm and twisted it painfully until Smitty had no choice but to look him directly in the eye.

"And the more times he tells it, the bigger the exaggerations get. When the lies catch up with you in one town, and there are no more barflies who will listen to your outlandish tales, you move on to another town, and another, and then another. Eventually you crash when some younger bar thug second-guesses your lies, and you try to defend your honor and fight it out.

"In your mind you think you are that heroic young man of nineteen and your pickled brain now believes your own lies. But in reality, the alcohol has diminished your abilities to the point that you have the physical stamina of an octogenarian. And so you die, namelessly, buried in some local cemetery, and nobody knows but the gravediggers and whoever records it for the county."

"I call that bold talk from a man who was so pussy-whipped he sacrificed his own honor—the thing you always taught me was your highest value—and his younger son for a long-haired freak who can't stand to be in the same room with him and a slut who can't stand to be in the same bed with him," Smitty roared back savagely.

"Boy, only a person, who is afraid to face the present on his own, drags up the mistakes made by others in the past. Insecure people blame others for their lot in life. Real people accept responsibility for their own destiny, regardless of the errors made by others with the best of intent.

"I've already admitted that the decision I made years back was wrong. I can't change the past." Dad released his grip on Smitty's arm and smiled. "The real question is, are you strong enough to overcome them in the present?"

"Fuck off." Smitty jerked his arm free and stepped around Dad, reaching for the doorknob.

He never made it. Dad grabbed him, spun him around like a top with his left hand, then delivered a right cross that knocked Smitty backward against the wall hard enough to crack the drywall from floor to ceiling.

Dad advanced menacingly, intent on delivering a second blow.

Smitty reached out and backhanded his father with a forceful slap shot that buckled his knees, forcing him to sit down on the bed.

He was up immediately. The look in his eyes told Smitty he'd better make out his will. If Dad hit him again, his anger might make the blow a lethal one.

The bedroom door burst open and Sally entered wrapped in a too-small towel.

"What's going on in here? From the yelling and the thumping, it sounds like two buffaloes trying to hump each other."

Sally looked first at Smitty. She reached up slowly and dabbed at the blood that was dripping freely from his nose. She rubbed it distastefully between her fingers as she turned to Dad, who was breathing heavily. "You want to explain this, First Sergeant?"

Dad glared angrily at Smitty and was just about to respond when Smitty said suddenly, "You know, Sally, you ought to get that throw rug tacked down. I slipped on it and hit my chin on the corner of the dresser."

Staring at Smitty in disbelief, she turned and swiped the blood running out of the corner of Dad's mouth. "And I suppose you slipped on a bar of soap in the shower, First Sergeant?"

Dad frowned, and growled, "I tried to catch him."

Sally's eyes darted first to Smitty, then back to Dad.

"Sally," Dad said, "your stepson and I are having an adult conversation. Leave!"

She did. But the interruption had served its purpose.

When it became evident that there would be no more fisticuffs, Smitty handed Dad a Kleenex and took one for himself. Slowly Dad's heavy breathing subsided, and with the passage of a minute or so most of the bleeding stopped.

Motioning for Smitty to follow him, he opened the door and they walked back to the kitchen. Dad grabbed a couple of cold ones and flipped one to Smitty. They sat down again.

Dad sipped his beer in silence for several moments and collected his thoughts.

Smitty had a startling thought that this was probably new territory for both of them; neither father nor son had ever had to resort to diplomacy because physical outrage that caused certain injury had become the accepted form of debate. Maybe this was a breakthrough for both of them—if they were smart enough to listen.

Finally, in a more controlled tone, Dad continued.

"Son, time passes and life moves on, and if you're smart, you'll do the same. Especially since we're going to lose that war because of the incompetence and bungling of our civilian and military leaders. They seem incapable of understanding, or they've forgotten, the basic lesson of World War II. Inhibiting the enemy's ability to make war is fundamental to winning.

"Vietnam veterans are already unappreciated by kids your own age—if you want an example of that close to home, just look at your brother. Very soon, as soon as they see the war is going to be lost, people my age—who are in the position of responsibility—are going to stop being sympathetic to you guys and turn on you like a pack of hungry wolves.

"Short and to the point, son, you got fucked. It's not the first time life is going to be unfair and it sure as hell isn't going to be the last. The question is, what are you going to do about it? Are you going to let something that happened to you at twenty screw up the next fifty or so years of your life? I hope not. I thought you were a better man than that.

"But I will tell you one thing. This self-destructive path you're on is not the answer, and you're not going to find any cosmic revelations of what's gnawing at you in the bottom of a bottle of alcohol. You'd better shape up, troop. Either that or go reserve your unmarked grave in some small patch of weeds 'cause you're on a predestined path to fill it."

What Dad had said made Smitty mad; the fact that it made perfect sense only made it worse. Smitty reached out and extended his hand. "Thanks."

Dad took his hand in his and nodded his head in satisfaction. "You're welcome."

"One question. Why?" Smitty said.

"Oh, let's just say I have a soft spot for well-meaning idiots who think they're Sir Lancelot." He paused to light his pipe and stared down into the flame. "Not to mention ex-lieutenants with a pretty good left hook, especially when it comes to their ol' Dad's ex-wife's husband.

"Now I've got one for you, sport." Dad looked up from his chore and stared Smitty directly in the face.

"Fire away."

"Is this the end of this internal annihilation phase you've been so hell-bent on carrying out for the past six months, or is there more?"

"Yes, sir," Smitty said. "This is the end."

"I hope so." Dad tapped the ashes out of his pipe on the rim of the ashtray on the table. "You know, if I didn't know better, I'd swear this was some kind of planned effort to discredit yourself."

"Remember who you're talking to, Pop. It's me, your son, the whaleshit lieutenant," Smitty said. "Us butterbars ain't that smart."

"Aunt Belinda must think otherwise. He provided the cash." Dad tapped his pipe one final time. He waved toward the kitchen. "C'mon, 1LT, let's eat."

Smitty watched his father as he got up and left the room. He wasn't sure where his father got some of his strange notions sometimes, especially when they were so close to being right. So close to being right that Smitty would have hated to make a living on the difference.

CHAPTER TWENTY-ONE

Sergeant Mike was manning the watch outside the hotel room. "You have a visitor," he said into the two-way radio. "He's still there. He's been leaning against the wall down from your room for fifteen minutes casing the joint."

"Let's hope he wants to get acquainted." Smitty slid into the next hotel room through the connecting door, almost closing it behind him. Leaving the door cracked was risky, but Smitty deemed it an acceptable gamble. Whoever was planning to enter his room at 2:30 AM wasn't going to be concerned about the occupants of the next room, especially when the room was listed as empty on the hotel records.

As Smitty peeked around the corner curtain from the adjoining room, the outline of a shadowy figure could just be seen against the Miami skyline.

"If he enters, take up blocking position as per plan," Smitty whispered into the mic. "And apprise MC and LB to stand by for cover action."

"Roger, lLT; standing by, will advise as per your request."

Smitty strained his eyes to identify a recognizable shape or form but was unable to do so. Whoever this guy was, he wasn't on the side of the angels. 'Course he could just be a second-rate second story man, but Smitty didn't think so. He was after him, and what Smitty hoped he didn't know was that Smitty was waiting with open arms—to welcome him to the reality of death.

"Aunt Belinda" would not have activated the team without provocation. The scumbag they were after was coming here because he knew Smitty was here. Smitty was the bait to reel in a piranha with shark's teeth that had been responsible for tearing Smitty's friends to bits.

People had been killed to accomplish a goal or from personal depravity or both. The reasons were always the same and rather simple: for personnel gain, for retribution, or for fear. The retribution went hand in hand with the fear. Killing sent a message, spreading fear and uncertainty in those left behind. Sometimes not killing someone was more effective, the near-miss creating anxiety that the mind would magnify in the darkest hours of the morning, but that would not be the case this night.

The executioner didn't know it, but he was going to be executed—with extreme prejudice.

It was now August 1973, and it'd been two years since Smitty'd been on active duty. But Granny's marker had been called in from Aunt Belinda; he only hoped his reflexes were still good.

With his eye firmly fixed on the figure in the night, and his Magnum firmly fixed in his hand, Smitty allowed his mind to wander.

Smitty had slowly made his way through the labyrinth of bridges and turn-backs that made up the I-95 "express route" through Jacksonville. He was headed south to Miami in the hot August sun. Ostensibly, he was returning to the land of his teenage banishment for a vacation, just a nondescript college senior taking a little breather between the end of summer school and the start of his last two quarters at college. But in reality it was more; it was a chance to refresh some memories, a chance to heal some old wounds, and a chance to settle some old debts.

A Chevy in the other lane got cut off by the car in front of him and flipped the driver off. Smitty smiled quietly to himself in amusement, remembering a time when he would have done the same thing. That was two years ago, during what Dad had come to check off as the dark times of the summer of 1971. Two years was a long time back, especially to Smitty.

In that two-year span, he'd turned his life completely around and acquired a new circle of friends. Unfortunately, some of his old friends had not.

The four musketeers were now three. Big Walt had shown up unexpectedly at his house at about this time last year riding a brand new Harley Chopper, looking like some kind of Dennis Hopper stunt double in Easy Rider, but acting more like the geek played by Jack Nicholson.

From the chain belt with Bowie knife prominently on display to the mutton-chop sideburns, the stringy mustache and rapidly receding hair now pulled back in a long ponytail, he sounded, and acted, like someone who had a chip on his shoulder the size of a California redwood. He made it perfectly clear to Smitty that those who got in the way of his single-minded view of the world would suffer the consequences—even if they were ex-service friends.

His mood became hostile when Smitty refused to let him stay at his place until he could get settled. They had a quarrel, during which Smitty told him that he needed to get his act together, that Nam was in the past, and that he needed to move on. It turned into a shoving match and would possibly have escalated to a violent confrontation had it not been for the fortuitous arrival of Smitty's relatively new roommate, Fred Clark, driving his state police cruiser home. Seeing the police and thinking that someone had called them, the big guy mounted his Hog and sped away.

That was the last time Smitty saw him. Two weeks later, he received a call in the middle of the night from Fred, informing him Walt had been killed, execution-style, with a .45 round through the back of the head, and his body—with a hash pipe stuffed in the jacket pocket—unceremoniously thrown into a dumpster behind some cheap bar on Belfry Street.

Later details confirmed the obvious: Walt had escaped from a prison work detail and had killed the owner of the Hog, his recently paroled cellmate, by slitting his throat with his own Bowie knife. He had also killed the biker's girlfriend in the same grisly fashion, but not before raping and sodomizing her repeatedly, according to police in Florida.

From the best information Fred could come up with, Walt was executed when a drug deal had gone south and he'd tried to rip them off. The Savannah police confirmed it after a short investigation, and the case was quickly closed although no suspects were ever arrested.

No one showed up to claim the body and Walt was quietly buried in an unmarked grave in a state cemetery in a simple cheap coffin. The only people in attendance were Smitty, his new roommates Susan—the Nice Girl from the bar fracas—and Fred, and two Savannah detectives whom Smitty suspected were there just to see who else showed up.

Since Smitty was the only attendee who had known the deceased, they gave him Walt's effects, which consisted of a wallet that contained a driver's license from Kansas which turned out to be false, a ten, two one-dollar bills, and the wristwatch Smitty had given him when he visited him at Leavenworth years before. There were no other clues to the enigma that was his life. No family, no friends, no past. Maybe he'd been running all his life, and the army where they'd met was only a temporary layby.

Not much to show for a man's life, Smitty thought sadly, as he dropped the wallet and the watch in the "keepsake" footlocker in his study, especially when it had started so promisingly in basic.

Smitty had also lost touch with another of the original musketeers, LZ, soon after his return to Vietnam in 1971. Smitty had written to him and received a terse note stating that he'd "only hang with the brothers now," and would not be corresponding with any "honky muthafuckahs" any more. Smitty wrote one more letter, but it came back unopened. He'd not written again.

Frenchy and Sondra now had two kids, and he'd settled into his job at her stepfather's company comfortably enough that he'd bought a house. Smitty talked to him every couple of months by phone, although they'd never quite been able to connect in person.

Smitty was glad to hear that his ami was doing so well, although Frenchy still complained about his arm. He said that when he tried to mount Sondra the arm just would not support his weight. But Frenchy, as always, was philosophical about it; it was just as good with her on top.

Smitty's dad and Sally were now comfortably married but still cavorting like newlyweds. Thanks to Sally's untiring efforts, Smitty and his dad had slowly reestablished relations—after Smitty had repaid the two-and-a-half big ones, which, Smitty assumed, Dad had repaid to General Wilson. He accomplished this two weeks in front of the deadline by working nights in the shipyard on second shift and weekends, collecting off-shift premiums and time-and-a-half.

Over a period of the following six months, their relationship had slowly normalized. Smitty now reserved his Wednesday nights off for his dad; conveniently, that was Sally's bridge night. Sometimes they'd go out to a movie or to dinner, or sometimes they'd just sit at Dad's house and talk or work on a project together in the garage.

More than once, Smitty had found himself thinking how, when he was seventeen, he thought his father must have been the dumbest human being on the face of the planet. Now, at twenty-three, he couldn't quite understand how the old man had gotten so smart so quick. They now both looked forward to spending time together. They avoided the tender areas and focused on the things they had in common, which turned out to be more than either had thought, as a couple of events made clear.

The first occurred during the healing days in the autumn of '71. Smitty had worked late on Saturday night, and decided to stop for a late breakfast at the local Waffle House. He was sitting quietly, minding his own business, when an altercation, or more correctly, a queer-bashing, occurred. Several drunken teenage rednecks were taunting a person with long wavy hair sitting quietly in a chair at the counter bothering no one, so far as Smitty could see. When he turned, in response to the leader's taunt of "Stuck-up Faggo Butt Fucker," Smitty was shocked to see his friend, the prof.

The next taunt of, "I'm going to cut your balls off and stuff them in your own queer ass," was accompanied by the click of a switchblade. As the loud-mouthed tough stomped menacingly past Smitty, he stood up, and with a quick judo punch to the left kidney, a kick to the left knee, and a slamming of the head on the booth table, dropped him for the count. Before the teen hit the ground, Smitty had grabbed his blade, wedged it between the wall and the table, and snapped it cleanly at the hilt.

As the other three got off their counter stools to come to the aid of their fallen comrade, Smitty threw the handle of the knife at the closest one, hitting him squarely between the eyes, and KO-ing him like a George Foreman right hook. Seeing the odds no longer in their favor, the last two standing stopped and one yelled at Smitty, "You must be another homo queer!"

Smitty smiled. "No, as a matter of fact, I'm not."

"Then why are you sticking up for that faggot?"

"Because we've got this dandy little document called the Constitution that guarantees his right to be one."

"But he ain't even a real man," the first teenager said.

Smitty turned his head quickly to the prof and winked. "Just because he's different than you does not preclude him from being a good man, or perhaps more importantly, a man of honor. I'm not a homosexual myself, Bubba, but I'll defend to the death his right to be one."

The police arrived before more words could be exchanged, and after hearing the details from the manager, called the meat wagon for the first two and the paddy wagon for the latter.

Smitty and the prof shook hands. "We're even."

"Not yet, Kevin," the prof said, "But we shall be."

The second occurred when Smitty was on his way home from the shipyard in the early morning hours between Christmas and New Year's in 1971, when he noticed a car with a flat tire stopped on the road ahead. As Smitty drove by he saw that the windshield had been smashed and a rather well-dressed, attractive black lady was cowering behind the steering wheel holding what turned out to be her grandson tightly to her. She was being circled by six white rednecks, who were bashing the car with tire irons and screaming racial slurs in a drunken rage.

With his rebuff from LZ still fresh in his mind, Smitty unclipped his .357 from the special support bracket he had designed to hold it up under the driver's seat of the Chevy, spun the Chevy around, flipped on the high beams' five hundred thousand candlepower helicopter landing lights he'd installed, raced up to the car, slammed on the brakes, skidded to a stop, stepped out, and fired two warning rounds into the bank behind the car, dispatching them fleeing into the night in their pickup truck.

After assuring the understandably doubtful lady that he was only trying to help, Smitty had them ride with him to a phone booth, where he called the wrecker. The service station had one on call now that they were a twenty-four-hour AAA affiliate. Then he returned with her and her grandson and waited with them until the wrecker arrived and she was safe.

A week later a distinguished-looking black man in a suit and tie introduced himself to Smitty as a Mr. Rollins. He had come to the station to thank Smitty for rescuing his wife and grandson.

At first Smitty took him for some kind of traveling encyclopedia salesman. Like a good salesman, he had done his due diligence prior to making his sales call. He knew that Smitty had been dropped from the Barnyard and plied him with questions about his plans for the immediate future. To Smitty's noncommittal responses, he kept emphasizing the importance of having goals for his life, pressing Smitty to take a long look in the mirror and ask himself if he wanted to be doing the same thing in twenty years.

In the midst of this high-pressure sale, Smitty managed to refrain from telling him that his primary goal at that moment was to work his butt off to pay back the fines from his recent pugilistic encounter with the boys with the badges.

But the cheerfulness cleverly hid a burning desire just below the surface. The man was not a seller of general reference works but rather a purveyor of specific knowledge, and he was passionate about it.

His mistress was his job, or his job was his mistress. It really didn't matter which way you said it; he was single-mindedly and doggedly dedicated to his position as head of the engineering department at the primarily black Silverston College and at doing whatever was required to make it the finest college in the state of Georgia. That included beating the bushes and rounding up all eligible students—flesh tones notwithstanding.

Smitty was understandably suspicious, but "Doc" was more than adequately prepared to "operate on his patient" and obviously knew how to close the sale.

He came with brochures, school history, and a dizzying plethora of supporting information on the fully integrated faculty, the plans already in place for formal accreditation of the engineering program by the National Engineering Council, and hooked Smitty with a constant barrage of flattery on his technical background, the fact that it was a hands-on engineering technology program, and that it would fit him perfectly.

Once he'd hooked his prospect, he reeled him in. Immediately after Smitty half-heartedly agreed to give it a try, the good doctor reached in his briefcase, produced enrollment forms, and sat with Smitty until he had filled them out, promising to walk them through the admissions office personally to assure that Smitty was registered for the winter quarter, which was to start in two weeks.

He then sat down at the desk and wrote out a complete course plan for Smitty from memory for a mechanical engineering major for the next year, and the next year, and the one after that until graduation.

He volunteered that he'd obtained a copy of Smitty's transcript from the Barn, courtesy of an extremely helpful history professor who had written a glowing letter of recommendation, which, to his mind, outweighed the official expulsion recorded in his transcript, and this had been the deciding factor for the admissions board to accept Smitty . . . how curious.

When they were shaking hands as he was leaving, Smitty said that he was surprised the doc hadn't talked to his dad. The good doctor smiled warmly and said laughingly that was his next stop, but he felt that he had to have Smitty signed up first because his dad might feel more comfortable attending a black college if he knew his son would be there for support.

According to rumors at Barnstein, Silverston was where the white students went in the summer to pick up a couple of easy credits, implying that the grading system had been scaled down to meet a perceived lack of gray matter on the part of the average black student. But whoever started that rumor never sat through the doc's drafting class. On Smitty's second day in class, a black student raised his hand and asked a question whose answer would have been obvious if the student had completed his reading assignment.

Doc walked back to his desk, and with a Cheshire cat grin asked if that was his textbook on his drafting table. When the student answered yes, Doc suggested that he turn to page fifteen, about halfway down on the left side of the page, and get a little return on his investment.

Smitty quickly learned that all of the other professors at the college were just as dedicated. As a result, he studied harder than he had at the Barn because a student's best effort was the only thing acceptable to the head prof. Smitty found that his natural mechanical inclination gave him an edge over the average student, and as a result, Smitty's attitude went up, as did his grades. So did those of his father, who was majoring in industrial arts.

Smitty's life had come together on the personal side also, thanks to two things. Daily events seemed much less traumatic now that they were not being distilled through massive amounts of cheap alcohol, and Susan, the nice girl, had become a mainstay in his life.

It had been a month after the incident in the bar. The story had, like all news stories when there were no fresh angles to sensationalize, faded into memory. Smitty had not yet gone to trial and been slapped with the heavy fine when Susan walked into the service station and asked to see him. When Smitty's boss asked why, Susan had replied confidently that, "I'm his girlfriend. He just doesn't know it yet."

Since she had no car, she had taken the bus out to the service station in the hope that she might take him to dinner, as a way of saying thank you for the rescue, after which she was hoping he would give her a ride home.

She waited patiently for over two hours, while Smitty worked overtime to finish a head job on a Mustang, then they walked across the street to a local pizza place and spent the next two hours talking and getting to know one another, after which he took her home.

On the way back to her room downtown, Smitty found himself glancing at her and noticing, not for the first time, that under her clothes was a body with bumps in all the right places. He wondered idly what it would be like to kiss her and explore the private places reserved only for lovers and had even gone so far as to arrogantly assume that was to be part of the night's gratuity.

He found out in short order that he was wrong. When the car stopped in front of her rooming house, she leaned across the seat, kissed him lightly on the cheek, said good night, hopped quickly out of the car before he could even shut off the motor, skipped off to the door, opened it, and was quickly inside.

In the light of the next day, Smitty found a note that Susan had left on the seat with a message, which read simply, "I hope you'll call me for a date sometime." Underneath, she had written the number of the telephone in the lobby of the rooming house.

Smitty had let a week pass, lest he seem too interested, before he gave in and dialed her number on Friday just before he got off work. When Susan came on the line, Smitty asked her out for a late bite to eat. In a pleasant and sweet voice, she said she had been waiting for his call, and had, in fact, not eaten in anticipation of his calling her.

From that point on, they were pretty much a twosome. Smitty found himself able to open up to her, and tell her his secret fears, and for the first time since Linda, he talked openly about his past, a past that she seemed to accept nonjudgmentally.

When Smitty was hit with the heavy fine and was short of cash, Susan had moved into the third bedroom, recently vacated by Lenny. Within two weeks, she had moved across the hall as his bunkmate.

Smitty had not intended to have another housemate, but Fred sort of invited himself in, much like Smitty had done with Ron a year or so back. He had knocked on Smitty's door to identify himself as the officer who was chasing Smitty that day out on the road with Johnboy's son. He didn't know who Smitty was until the incident on the bridge, when he'd recognized the car. It turned out that Fred was the officer who had prevented one of his city colleagues from aerating Smitty with his service revolver and had wound up with a broken nose for the effort.

To Smitty's alarm, he said that was not the reason he stopped. He was passing Smitty's house on route patrol, had seen the car and had to stop. He said, "You disappeared from me so fast that day, I thought my patrol car had started to suddenly run on four cylinders. The reason I turned around was I thought you might be running shine, and once discovered, the car would be trashed, and I'd never see it again." He paused. "Partner, I just got to know what you've got under that hood. Would you mind showing me?"

Leaning on the fenders over the car, Fred and Smitty had an in-depth automotive discussion on Fred's SS Chevelle, which was currently serving time in his apartment parking lot with a blown motor. Smitty offered to let him bring it to the house to work on, and as Fred started spending more time there, he began to stay over, until one day at Susan's prodding Smitty invited him to move in.

More than once, Smitty had thought how ironic it was that, after a lifetime of running from the law, his new best friend should wind up being part of it. With Smitty's work and school schedule, Susan's work schedule, and Fred's rotating schedule, Smitty and Susan had ample time to themselves.

Within four months of moving in, Fred had managed to find himself a bunkmate also, a petite girl by the name of Ginger. She was a county police officer, who Fred met at the Barnyard. She'd answered a car burglary call while he was attending class studying for a degree in criminology. The four of them took to each other at once, spending free time together in addition to being roommates.

Since Fred was pursuing a degree also, that only added to the things they had in common. Susan and Ginger—understanding their need for study time—spent hours together.

Smitty's former service friends had faded from his daily thoughts and from his daily life. Ron had been out of the service almost eighteen months, had bought a service station, and was, in Smitty's opinion, in the process of running it into the ground.

He had taken up with the racing crowd, who were now hanging around the station, intimidating and ultimately chasing off the average customer, the lifeblood of any successful business. There were rumors that Ron was drinking heavily, and that his business was in money trouble, but Smitty had not talked to him personally since he'd moved out.

When Ron had left, he'd moved back into his trailer with Bunny, who had an angelic face and a crowd-stopping hot body that made Raquel Welch look like a twelve-year-old in a training bra. She had been married three times already, even though she was only twenty-one, and was rumored to be a nymphomaniac. Smitty wondered if she wasn't using her body as trade bait to a BBD—a bigger and better deal—since she'd gone to bed with Ron the same night he'd met her, and started making requests of him to move out of the house and back to the trailer almost the next day.

Along with the screw bunny, Ron had acquired a lot of other new trappings. He'd bought a new top-of-the-line Pontiac Grand Prix, a twenty-foot ski boat, and a new double-wide trailer. He'd developed an appetite for squiring Bunny around to the expensive restaurants in Savannah, so much so that he was considered a regular at the trendy Pirate's House downtown.

Knowing the service station business as he did, Smitty had no idea how Ron was affording all of this but suspected that credit was a cornerstone of this new extravagance.

The three-star Martin brothers were still on active duty but, according to General Wilson, were both destined to stay at their current rank, having been passed over for the coveted fourth star. As a result, they were given less responsible command positions as an encouragement to make the transition to civilian life.

Smitty's old friend Sergeant Mike had retired as a sergeant major at the end of 1972. Smitty and Susan had driven up for the retirement ceremony and listened as Mike talked about the farm in middle Georgia that his wife had inherited from her father. Mike said he intended to spend the rest of his days as a gentleman farmer, as far away from dumb-shit lieutenants as possible. It had been good to see his old friend and to know that Smitty was exempt from Mike's generalized judgment of lieutenants.

General Wilson had gotten his second star in late 1972 and was rumored to be targeted to be one of the department heads of a new counterespionage unit being formed in the Pentagon to address the torrent of leaks of military information that were now free-flowing in the wake of the Watergate break-in.

Smitty'd not used his call sign "Anastasia" in almost two years. And during that same period, "Aunt Belinda" had been quiet also—until a week earlier, when his favorite aunt had called one night when Susan was home. She picked up the phone, listened briefly and handed the phone to Smitty with a curious look. "Honey, there's a lady on the phone who calls herself Aunt Belinda. I don't remember you talking about her before." She handed him the phone and walked back to the kitchen.

"Smitty, the code word is Anastasia—I say again Anastasia," a male voice said. It was not General Wilson's voice.

Smitty switched the phone to his other ear and turned his back on Susan, then said in a low voice, "Continue."

"Depart for Miami tomorrow at 1000 hours, you will be joined by a cousin and two stepfathers. Your stepfather SM will brief you on the plan." The mysterious voice added, "A fox has found your lair. Lead him into the arms of temptation and cope."

"Perhaps this fox might feel chatty," Smitty answered in a muffled voice that Susan did not hear.

"Inconsequential. This particular animal is an orphan."

"Acknowledging. Anastasia out." Smitty hung up the phone.

Several hours later, as they were lying in bed talking after an intensive love-making session, Smitty announced to Susan that he needed to go to Florida for a week because his Uncle Stan and Aunt Belinda needed to see him. Naturally, Susan offered to go, and was somewhat put out when Smitty told her that he needed to go alone. Despite her brooding, Smitty packed for the trip and left that morning on schedule, promising to take Susan along on the next trip.

As he waited in silence in the stillness of the early morning darkness, he hoped that his aunt's tip would not be a wild goose chase and that it would be a clue that might start the river of information flowing again. Whatever the outcome, he wouldn't have long to wait. The stranger was moving.

Smitty shook his head free of the cobwebs of the past and focused on the present, lest there be no future at all.

Unlike a conventional thief, this one didn't seem to be looking for anything. In fact, he appeared to be carrying a package. He quietly approached the door to Smitty's hotel room and within ten seconds was soundlessly inside.

He went silently to the closet and pushed the package deep inside Smitty's old army duffel bag where it would not be casually seen but might be easily found if a room search were conducted later.

He turned and stared at the recumbent figure of a sleeping form in the lone king-size bed with the covers pulled up over its head.

He paused, as if hearing or sensing something, walked soundlessly to the window, pulled the curtain aside ever so slightly, and peeked out. Ten seconds passed, then he silently returned to the bed, removing something from his inside coat pocket as he did.

He sighted the silenced pistol and fired six times, the weapon emitting silent thumps in response. "That's from my father, asshole." The man walked to the bed and jerked back the covers.

"Surprise! Surprise! Surprise!" Smitty said loudly in his best Gomer Pyle voice. He snapped on the overhead light and entered the room. Smitty nestled his Magnum against the back of the head of a man dressed entirely in black, whose face was concealed by a black hood with only two slits cut for the eyes.

"I wouldn't move if I were you," Smitty said.

The figure froze.

"Hey, Andy," Sergeant Mike said, imitating Barney Fife. He entered by the door and shoved a .22 with a silencer into the middle of the mystery man's back, then reached up and pulled off the wool hood.

"Well, if it isn't Detective Wallace as I live and breathe," Smitty said.

"Little off your range, aren't you, Detective Wallace? Or Special Agent Clev Clayborne, or whatever you're calling yourself these days." Smitty went roughly through his pockets and found, as he suspected, nothing.

"Fuck you, maggot," Detective Wallace said. "You're a dead man. We know you're onto us, and I was sent to eliminate the threat. It doesn't matter what you do to me. In the end, we'll still win, because we're too deeply imbedded in the government and have bribed enough people in positions of authority to protect us from your paltry efforts. You're just scratching around the surface like a cat in a litter pan. You're a nuisance, but that's all you are."

Smitty smiled and said, "If that were true, you'd just have killed me off long ago. No, you guys must think I know a lot more than I do and that I've talked—or been talked to. Otherwise you wouldn't be going to such great lengths to discredit me and go after my friends and arrange for them to be in harm's way."

"Harm's way?" Mike said.

"Yeah, SM. Harm's way. You see, it's not enough for them to merely kill me off. That would be too simple. They have to discredit me to the point that any thoughts or theories that might have been brought up or passed to you or anyone else would be considered nothing more than the ravings of a madman."

"All the things that happened to me in the summer of '71 were real, but were also a rather convenient way to convince the mysterious "them," that I'd totally lost it after Nam and was no longer a threat. Thank God, my father figured it out and talked to General Wilson, so Aunt Belinda came up with the fine."

"What's the next step, boss?" Mike said.

Smitty stepped forward until he was inches from the sergeant's face. "I have a message for you from Louie the Forger."

The detective's eyes widened in recognition.

"That's for Gena." Smitty removed the bayonet from its scabbard on his thigh and plunged it under the detective's rib cage straight into his heart.

Smitty watched without emotion as his eyes glazed over and he slowly spiraled down to the floor and died.

"Louie the Forger?" Mike asked, perplexed. "Who is he, and what's he got to do with this?"

"He wrote the papers that allowed me, LZ, and Frenchy to lie our way into the service. Gena was his granddaughter.

"On the night a police detective named Stan the Man found her with a metal rod driven through her, there was a set of prints on the rod that nobody could match. For a long time, I though that a Neanderthal named Keith was responsible. I was wrong. After we ran into Dickless here in Savannah on that training mission, I put him on the bad guy list, and starting putting two and two together.

"But it really didn't come together until I was sent home for Dad's heart attack almost two years later.

"I went to see Glenda's mother. She told me her daughter had been killed in a car accident involving a policeman from down south. I asked the neighborhood cop for a copy of the accident report, and sure enough, the detective here was the other driver. I called Stan with my suspicions on my way back to Nam. He called back within the hour and verified that the set of prints on the metal bar belonged to Wallace. They went to his quarters to arrest him, but he had already vanished."

"Isn't that right, MC?" Smitty asked, as Stan the Man, now a Miami police commissioner, and Major Jim, LB—Legal Beagle—quietly entered the room.

"We've been looking for him for six years," Stan said. "He surfaced in Savannah with the phony FBI credentials and vanished before Jim could follow the trial that you boys started."

"He was also a bit of a tourist," Smitty said.

"What do you mean, 1LT?" Mike asked.

"Seems he likes the paradise state, and likes to rent Chrysler Imperials. He had a go at me in Hawaii when I was on R&R, but it wasn't meant to kill me, only discredit me. That wad I found in the tire was from a high-powered rifle—a rifle this asshole bought from a firearms store the day before my accident, according to my friend the Hawaiian police officer."

"Then why kill him, 1LT? If everything you said is true, then we could have bled him dry for information on this, turned him over to the authorities, and watched him fry," Mike said.

"Two reasons," Major Jim answered. "One, he's not the brains, he's only the executioner. Two, when he's gone missing, they'll have to change a bunch of plans because they'll assume we've got him and that he's talking his head off." He smiled prophetically. "Or, lying his head off."

Smitty lit a cigarette. "And there's another thought, they'll have to replace him, and replacing a deep cover agent that they've spent years turning into an assassin won't be easy.

"The late detective didn't know it, but this was a suicide mission either way. If he gets me then they're rid of me, but they'll see that he takes the fall for the murder. Blood feuds play well for those sucker reporters who just love to sensationalize everything.

"If he doesn't, then the police show up . . . " Smitty walked to the closet, opened his duffel bag and removed the package. Wiping the blood from the bayonet on the late detective's pants, he used it to slit open the bundle and held it up for Stan's inspection.

"Cocaine." Stan eyes widened in amazement.

" . . . and nail me as a drug runner," Smitty said. "And it diverts suspicion away from them."

Smitty remembered something. "Just like Big Walt."

"Next steps, boss?" Mike said.

"Carry the body into the next room and change the mattress. Jim, Stan, set up the diversion as planned, and sanitize the room quickly. My bet is that the regular cops are already on the way."

They scurried about like ants who'd just discovered the picnic fried chicken left unattended. Within five minutes, all incriminating evidence had been removed, the table set up with ashtrays full of butts, and the room littered with empty beer bottles to make it look as it they had been playing cards the entire night.

Exactly nine minutes later, the hotel room door was kicked in and the room flooded with Miami policemen dressed in SWAT gear and armed to the teeth.

To say that the lieutenant in charge was somewhat taken aback by the sight of a police commissioner calmly sitting playing cards in a room that was supposed to be the meeting place for a drug deal would be an understatement. Especially when the other players were introduced as his brother, a retired army sergeant major, his nephew, a Wall Street lawyer, and his best friend's son, a college senior who was visiting his "Uncle Stan."

The team dutifully searched the room and the closet, specifically Smitty's duffel bag, intensively but found no traces of drugs or any other evidence of criminal activity. With faces blushing a deep crimson, they sheepishly said that they must have gotten an incorrect tip, apologized profusely, and beat feet out of there, promising to have the door repaired as quickly as possible.

It had taken six years for the late detective to surface. An innocent couple's grisly killing and an old girlfriend's murder had been avenged: Gena and Jimmy and Glenda could sleep in peace.

Smitty was no longer angry about the way the detective had spinelessly killed Glenda in that hit-and-run in an attempt to draw Smitty out, just sorry. Sorry that he hadn't known how big the stakes were, or how widespread the corruption, because if he had, then he might have been able to prevent it.

But the late unlamented detective had given him a clue. Whoever "they" might be, they were, as he said, embedded in the government, which said they must be doing great harm to the very Constitution that was protecting them. Smitty wondered idly if the father the detective had spoken of avenging and the mysterious string-puller were one and the same.

The question still was why? Was it money, or revenge? Smitty suspected that it was a little of both. No, make that a lot of both. That led to a logical conclusion that whoever was giving orders to Aunt Belinda must be providing not only protective radar, but sentries to watch over Smitty also. And it didn't take Smitty but a minute to figure out who they were.

"Mrs. McCord?"

"Yes?" A frail-looking black woman peered through the two-inch crack in the door the safety chain would allow. Smitty stood illuminated by a bare light bulb in the dingy hallway of a rundown apartment building on Miami's west side.

"Mrs. McCord, my name is Smitty Smith. I was a friend of your son, LZ, in the army and before."

The door closed instantly, and for a moment, Smitty thought she'd slammed the door in his face. But the chain scraped, the door was flung wide open, and she leapt into his arms.

"Hello, son." She wrapped her arms tightly around him.

"Mrs. McCord, I need to talk to you about LZ." Smitty managed to get out between her squeezes.

Keeping an arm around his waist, she escorted him into the dingy apartment and to a small, neat living room with rundown furniture, and a portable black and white television that, like everything else in the room, had seen better days.

On a shelf in the corner was a picture of LZ that looked like it was his basic training picture and next to it a picture of the four musketeers, which had been taken when they were all together in Seattle the night before they shipped out for Vietnam.

The faces mugging for the camera looked so young, so innocent, and so confident. Smitty wished that somehow it could still be so.

"Sit there." She placed her hand on his head and forced him down into the overstuffed faded sofa that, Smitty found out too late, was badly in need of new springs.

"I'll get us coffee." Mrs. McCord disappeared into the postage stamp-sized kitchen. The apartment was familiar because it was a duplicate of the one he had grown up in, except that Dad's had an extra bedroom.

She returned moments later with the coffee. "Cream and sugar?"

"Yes, ma'am, little of both, please."

She dutifully attended to Smitty's requests, then passed his coffee across. "I know why you've come. To check up on my boy." She took a sip of her coffee. "And your brother."

"Not so much to check up on as just check on, Mrs. McCord," Smitty said.

His smile disappeared as she reached inside the pocket of her sweater and pulled out two envelopes.

"My son is dead." She passed them across.

With trembling hands, Smitty opened the first envelope. It was an official telegram from the United States Army that began, "The president regrets to inform you that—"

Smitty didn't read the rest. He didn't have to. He'd read too many of them himself. In the blur of meaningless words that followed was a lame attempt by the government to explain away and rationalize her son's death. Smitty recognized only the phrase "siege at Au Lac."

He let the telegram slip from his hands, noting as he did, that the wire was dated some day in June of this year. He didn't care which particular day. It didn't matter. His circle of friends had now been greatly diminished by one who never would and never could be replaced.

His eyes wet with tears, Smitty looked at the second envelope. Surprisingly it was addressed to him. LZ had written, "Ma, when my bro Smitty comes looking for me, give him this."

Underneath, LZ had written, "Open it on the flap side, you dumb-ass honky."

"The envelope came with his last letter. LZ said you'd understand," Mrs. McCord said with a tearful smile.

Smitty's laughter instantly turned to choked-back tears, and he had a lump in his throat the size of a grapefruit. When he turned the envelope over, he saw that just below the flap LZ had written, "Remember always that I love you, my brother."

Smitty was no longer able to contain himself. He began to cry uncontrollably for his friend. Mrs. McCord pulled him to her and cooed softly in his ear, whispering comfort to him like the mother of a six-year-old who had just skinned his knee.

Minutes passed like hours as years of pent-up emotions, carefully held in check, boiled over in uncontrollable sobs. Compared to LZ, his own brother seemed like a fourth cousin twice removed. Smitty knew that even though he was gone, he'd never, ever forget him. His sarcastic grin and superior smile would forever be etched in his mind. As would his sense of humor and his rapierlike wit, to say nothing of his fencing abilities with a switchblade.

Eventually Smitty's emotional outburst began to subside, and he lay passively on LZ's mother's shoulder for several minutes, occasionally sniffling to himself. Finally, he raised his head and said to Mrs. McCord, "Mom, what say we see what my brother has to say."

Using the handle of a spoon, Smitty very carefully and neatly slit the end of the flap and removed the two-page handwritten letter, dated May 5, 1973.

My Brother,

I am including this letter in one to my mother because it would not look good to the other radical black soldiers in the platoon for me to be seen writing to a white man.

That Detective Wallace character from Miami is here in Vietnam, only now he's wearing an Air Force uniform and calling himself Major Williams. He has some kind of fancy liaison title at the U.S. Embassy in Saigon. I couldn't find out anything else, but that pouch we saw that time when we were on that special mission in Savannah is here. I personally saw it sitting in the back of his Jeep when I spotted him in Saigon coming out of the American Embassy when I was down there for a three-day R&R.

I don't know what it means, but I hope that it helps you find the truth that you so highly value.

And in closing, let me speak a little truth at you.

You're not just any white man but someone much more special that I'm proud to call "My Brother"—now and forever.

Unfortunately, I got all messed up along the way thinking that who's a brother has something to do with the color of a man's skin. Until I came back for my second tour, and extended for a third, I didn't realize that a brother is that special someone who cares about you, no matter what you do or where you go, and has nothing to do with your flesh pigmentation or background.

I had planned to come find you when my current tour is up in August of 1973, and apologize to you in person and ask your forgiveness for my reprehensible behavior. But if you are reading this letter, it means that I didn't make it back.

Do not grieve for me, my brother, or blame yourself for my passing. Frenchy and I elected of our own free will to follow you into the service, and I alone decided to reenlist.

You should know, and hear me when I tell you, that I would have followed you through the gates of hell, for no other reason than you are my one true brother.

My only regret is that I will not be there to deliver these words in person.

Good luck with the rest of your life, and rest assured that when your mortal life ends, I'll be the first one in line to shake your hand at the gates of heaven.

God Bless you and keep you, my brother,
Your friend forever, LZ

With tears streaming freely down his face, Smitty read the letter again silently to himself, smiled, and folded the letter and handed it back to LZ's mom.

She pushed it back to him. "No, my son, you keep it. Your brother sent it to you." She rose and went to the jewelry box on the dresser in her bedroom, returned, and handed Smitty LZ's watch; one of the four Smitty had bought for his friends and given to them in person.

"Here, son, you take this as a keepsake of your friendship with your brother," she said. "I'm sure LZ would have wanted you to have it."

Smitty took the watch and slipped it into his pocket. In doing so, he symbolically accepted LZ's death, although he knew he would never forget him.

For the next several moments, they made polite conversation.

Finally, LZ's mom stood up and said briskly, "You'd best go. It'll be dark in an hour, and you need to be well away from this neighborhood before then."

"I'll write to you," Smitty said with sincerity.

"Of course, you will. A son should always keep in touch with his mother." She kissed him lightly on the lips and opened the door.

"Good-bye, and thank you," Smitty said.

"You be good," she answered quickly and closed the door.

Just on a hunch, Smitty leaned his ear against the door. As he suspected, she was crying. Smitty was tempted to knock, but restrained himself, knowing intuitively that she needed to be alone with her grief.

He descended the stairs of her fourth-floor walkup, and ignoring the menacing stares of the local neighborhood kids, started his car and drove quietly away, knowing in his heart that the death of his friend was something that he would never get over.

After the gut-wrenching meeting with LZ's mother, the rest of the "vacation" was relatively uneventful. Smitty spent the next day as a guest of Stan the Man, then set off for home.

Dad had always said that no matter how a death occurs, some good will come of it if you let it. Smitty was going to make that proverb come true.

As a result of Dad's second, and relatively mild in comparison to the first, heart attack, Smitty had begun to stay over at Dad's house several nights a week before heading off to work, giving Sally a much-needed breather. Smitty was sacked out on the couch when a woman's scream woke him out of a sound sleep. He leaped off the sofa in his underwear, grabbed his Magnum from the holster on the coffee table, and went running into the hall in the direction of his old bedroom where his sister-in-law Leslie was currently sleeping.

The door to Dad's bedroom was suddenly yanked open as Smitty snapped on the hall light. Dad was standing there in his skivvies with an army .45 in his hand.

"You hear that, troop?" Dad asked urgently.

"Yeah, Pop, seemed to be coming from Leslie's bedroom." Smitty nodded at the bedroom door that was standing ajar four inches.

"Leslie, we're coming in." Dad grabbed the handle, and in one swift motion, shoved the door fully open against its stop as Smitty and he locked and sighted their weapons.

Smitty could see that Leslie was sitting upright with her back against the headboard with the bedcovers pulled up tightly around her neck.

"Leslie, are you all right, kiddo?" Dad asked with concern.

"Something crawled on me. It was like a big rat or something," Leslie said, her shoulders shaking.

Smitty and his father entered the room and turned on the light. Smitty glanced quickly around the room and on finding what he suspected, started to laugh. He nudged his father, who, on seeing the "rat," started to laugh also.

"It's not funny," Leslie said angrily.

"Leslie," Smitty sputtered, "you see that towel on top of the headboard? Take it and lay it beside your pillow next to the window."

Looking at him with an exasperated glare, she silently did as he asked.

She had not even gotten the towel in place when Smitty's boyhood friend, a jet black tomcat named Clyde, hopped off the top of the portable TV where he had retreated when Leslie screamed, padded silently across the bed, curled up on the towel, and settled down with a contented purr.

"Leslie, the rat you felt was Clyde. That's been his sleeping spot ever since he was a kitten. He was just taking the most direct path when he walked over you," Smitty explained.

"Well, someone should have told me," Leslie's cheeks began to turn red.

Smitty and his dad began to laugh, but not at her overreaction. They were laughing in relief that it was not something more serious, as there had been several break-ins in the neighborhood.

"It's not that funny," she protested.

"That depends on your viewpoint," Dad said.

"Well, you might have at least put some clothes on," she said huffily. She suddenly noticed the weapons. "You guys sure have big guns."

Smitty and his dad looked at each other standing there in the bedroom in the late evening hours, armed to the teeth and wearing only their underwear. Grinning, they recited in unison:

"This is my weapon, this is my gun. This is for fighting; this is for fun."

Each grabbed his weapon and patted his own "gun."

"You know, Pop, I remember when Sergeant Brown ordered me to approach ten officers, salute, and recite that as punishment for calling my weapon a gun. The last one was a WAC captain who shook her head and said, 'It seems like more of a cap pistol to me soldier,'" Smitty said, totally ignoring the flustered Leslie.

"And I don't know how many times I ordered little pricks like you to recite it," Dad answered.

"If you two are quite finished reliving your macho days, I'd like to go back to sleep," Leslie said.

Still laughing at their private joke, Smitty turned out the light and he and his father left the bedroom and closed the door. Before either one of them could speak, Sally's voice called out suggestively from the master bedroom. "Sergeant, how's about you bring that big gun of yours back to this bed."

Dad smiled roguishly at Smitty and handed him his firearm. "Carry on, Lieutenant, I don't think I'll be needing this particular form of weapon the rest of the evening."

Adrenaline and sleep are diametric opposites. Too tired to sleep, Smitty decided to dress and go on to work early. Laughing to himself again as he started to think about the "rat," Smitty removed the clip from the .45 and laid both clip and weapon together on top of the stereo and closed the door quietly as he left.

Because he needed more study time, Smitty had changed his hours at the station to the eleven-to-seven graveyard shift. He earned less money, but it gave him more time to study since the only folks out after two when the bars closed were the night people on their way to work in the early morning hours or the occasional late drunken doofus trying to find his way home.

As Smitty was driving to work, he started to go over in his mind the things that had been bothering him the last six months since his trip to Miami in the summer. Mostly they affected other people and not him.

Dad's second heart attack had been in early December, just after General Chuck had passed through Savannah on his last visit. He was talking mournfully about retiring in two years, now that the fourth star was no longer a possibility.

His brother, the army three-star, although several years younger, was likewise planning to retire when his thirty years were up in August of 1975. He was destined, it seemed, to likewise end his career one star short of the top.

General Chuck's visit was just about the time that the local paper had run an article on Smitty and his dad and their upcoming joint graduation in June.

Not surprisingly, the article focused heavily on Dad, as it was quite an accomplishment for a man with a tenth-grade education to return to college and graduate in his mid-fifties. The fact that both were graduating from a black college made it all the more rare, although Smitty had to admit that after being there almost two years, he felt just like any other student. So much so that he had begun to feel comfortable enough to skip the occasional class and had begun to lead lunchtime forays to the local 7-Eleven for a few quick cold ones after the morning's classes. The result was that they returned with an entirely different outlook on the afternoon labs, if they returned at all.

Smitty didn't feel he was entitled to any special consideration. Dr. Rollins confirmed that this was so.

Smitty was walking up the corridor the day after the article had appeared when he was suddenly yanked into a deserted classroom by Dr. Rollins, who slammed the door after him. He paced up and down the floor for a moment, obviously angry but wanting to collect his thoughts before speaking when upset.

"I want to say something to you, and I want you to remain quiet until I'm through. Do you understand?" Doc asked.

Smitty nodded in reply.

"Son, you and your father have done wonders for this college in ways you can't even begin to imagine. Not only are you the first white students to enroll here full-time, but you're going to be the first to graduate with technical degrees and, in the eyes of the regents, give our school curriculum equality with our cross-town, mostly white rival. You've endured and overcome segregation, name-calling, and in some cases threats on the part of the black students.

"But much more importantly, since a lot of our students come from small Southern towns where racism is still very much alive, you are in some respects much more important to us than your father. You are the first young white man that a lot of our students have known who has treated them as an equal.

"We took a chance on you when Barnstein turned its back after that mess two years ago. I, and a lot of professors and staff, staked our careers on you so that you would have a chance to gain a higher education. You owe this university system, and so far you're not living up to my expectations."

Doc stopped talking and started pacing again. Smitty started to speak, but Doc held up his hand and stopped him like a cop halting traffic at an intersection. Out of respect, Smitty sat down on the desktop and waited for him to continue.

"And what I mean by that is that you're providing the wrong kind of guidance and direction. What you've done as a student is fine, but it's not enough. I want more. I expect more out of you. You're older, we know you've been in the service and have held positions of responsibility, so you know what effective leadership is."

"What is it you want from me?" Smitty asked.

"I want you to stop acting like a smart-assed freshman. I want these lunchtime drinking binges stopped. And I want you to start to lead the students in the right direction."

"Aren't you asking an awful lot? I mean, I'm not their keeper; they're over twenty-one. It's not like I'm forcing them to go. Besides, I do help out with some other things you may not know about," Smitty said defensively.

"I know that you've done things for the students, repairing their cars for free, or at the very least for just the cost of the discount parts. I know that you've loaned them money when they were short, but it's not enough. You attend here, but you're not part of here. I want the students to make you one of their own. They'll never do that from your actions to date because, ultimately, your legacy will become the yardstick that black students will measure all white students against in the future.

"You have a responsibility to them to set a good example. I can't afford for you to become just another college student. There's too much at stake here, both for the university and for you."

"Are you trying to tell me that if I don't do what you say, you'll kick me out?" Smitty hopped off the desk and stood defiantly with his hands on his hips as he felt his temper begin to rise.

Doc came and stood directly in front of Smitty. "Yes, I am."

Doc was a man of conviction. With the exception of his dad, more so than any other man Smitty had ever known. Smitty knew that one thing was certain, he was going to do it Doc's way, or he'd be hittin' the highway. As much of an embarrassment as it would be to the college and the directors, Doc would do it.

"Okay, Doc, I guess we'll try it your way," Smitty conceded, "but that doesn't mean I have to like it."

"Mr. Smith," Doc called after him. "What would I tell the Georgia Board of Regents if they came on campus to audit our integration policy and you weren't here, Smitty?" Doc asked with a friendly smile.

Smitty smiled in spite of himself.

"You could tell them I'm in class," Smitty answered. "And from now on, I will be. Every damned day," Smitty muttered under his breath.

Smitty was also, without meaning to, continuing to distance himself from his former Vietnam colleagues. His erstwhile former Vietnam bro Ron had, in effect, vanished from Smitty's personal radar screen. Smitty had not seen Ron in over two years. He had heard that he was now working at the Ford garage as a mechanic, his service station and all his toys gone in the wake of a mysterious tip to the IRS that resulted in their taking the station, the car, the boat, and the mobile home for unpaid business taxes.

Not surprisingly, Bunny was gone before the first foreclosure. She was now married to Johnboy's son, who could keep her in the style to which she wanted to become accustomed.

Smitty had likewise jettisoned his interest in Johnboy and his mom. Smitty would see their picture from time to time in the society pages at some gala, but like Ron, he had not talked with or seen either of them since he rearranged John's beak almost three years ago.

Aunt Belinda had gone into another dormant phase, as Major Jim had predicted. The death of the shooter, although never officially confirmed by anyone, seemed to have stopped, for the moment, the mysterious forces at work against him.

Fred and Ginger, his erstwhile housemates, had gotten married, moved out in September, and gone on together to their next assignment near Atlanta. Smitty was fairly certain that the two of them, or at least Fred, had been assigned by Aunt Belinda to act as his personal protectors and had moved on when the obvious threat of Detective Wallace had been removed, but he was sure he'd never be able to prove it.

Susan, on the other hand, seemed not to be part of the invisible protective force. She was saddened by the break-up of the foursome but had made no attempt to leave, and Smitty hadn't wanted her too, either.

In the fall, before Dad's heart attack, Smitty and his dad had enclosed the side windows on the Chevy and painted it fire engine red. Shortly before Fred had left, he'd been hit by a drunken driver and had totaled his Chevelle. He and Smitty had yanked the engine, hopped up the big 454, and installed it in the old Chevy, giving it a throaty roar when idling and a running speed that was faster than that of some low flying airplanes.

This last was a thorn in the side of a certain Savannah police detective, who was known by just about everybody as Gumdrops, a derogatory reference to the general belief that the best part of him, namely his brains, must have run down the corners of his mother's mouth courtesy of his daddy, the police lieutenant.

In one five-day period, the officer had Smitty stopped by a patrol officer, who harassed him and tried to goad him into assaulting him or into any action that would allow him to arrest him and impound his vehicle, which he had told Smitty was not for the street.

The end result was always the same: a ticket for loud exhausts and a warning that he would be waiting for him tomorrow night.

Fortunately for Smitty, the detective had shown up drunk at the station one Sunday with his partner, who was a friend of Smitty's boss. He had leaned out of the passenger window and said nastily, "Ha, ha, ha. I wrote that motherfucker a bunch of tickets," in front of at least five witnesses.

When Smitty's court date came, he showed up in court with the five witnesses and a flock of receipts proving that he had changed the mufflers after each of the tickets to a more restrictive exhaust. Smitty's efforts to correct the car impressed the judge, but the five witnesses reciting the detective's conduct on Sunday when no bars were open was a clincher.

He was out in five minutes with the case dismissed and an apology from the judge, much to the detective's dismay. But it had created bad blood between them. Why, Smitty didn't know, but he'd a feeling that, as usual, the reason would make itself clear.

As Smitty pulled into the station, he saw that a faded blue 1965 Mustang with a bashed-in rear quarter panel was parked in front of the office, the spot usually reserved for his Chevy. At first he was pissed, then he remembered he'd been meaning to change the oil on the big block anyway. Smitty drove right in to the first service bay and shut off the engine.

As he walked into the office, he noticed the uniform of a Savannah police officer first. His nemesis, Gumdrops, apparently now reduced to patrolman, was waiting for him, and he was not alone. With him was Jimmy, the skinny freckle-faced nineteen-year-old who worked the evening shift before him, and his former close friend Ron.

"Hi, Ron, long time no see." They shook hands casually, all hint of their former Nam closeness now gone.

"How are you, Irishman? You seem to be doing well."

"I'm keepin'," Smitty responded. He sighed scornfully and jerked a thumb in the officer's direction. "What's with the meter maid? You two swappin' spit in the showers now?"

"If you wish to be arrested for verbally abusing a law enforcement officer, just make one more comment, smart ass," Gumdrops said. "I came here to follow up on a tip, and if you know what's good for you, you'll answer my questions."

"Smitty, you'd better listen to him. This is serious," Ron said.

Smitty shrugged his shoulders in silence.

"What are you doing here so early? Your shift doesn't begin until eleven," the officer asked.

"Came early to confuse the stalking highwaymen. The roads aren't safe anymore. They seem to be filled with city traffic court revenue collectors masquerading as police officers."

Gumdrops pursed his lips in an obvious effort to control his temper. "Do you know a former Miami detective by the name of Wallace?"

"We've bumped into each other occasionally," Smitty answered vaguely. He hoped his voice and body language matched his casual demeanor. He wondered to himself what shit head here would have said if Smitty had blurted out, *Not since I gutted him like a fish with a bayonet in a hotel in Miami.*

"Well, according to your former captain, you were more than just casual acquaintances. He was the only one who had guts enough to stand up to you teenage thugs and was rewarded by being offered a position with the FBI in the late '60s."

"So, what's it to you? He your long-lost boyfriend or something?"

"So this, smart ass, he's my cousin, and he's been missing for the last six months. You wouldn't happen to know anything about it, would you?" Gumdrops asked.

"Naw," Smitty said casually. "Ain't seen that asshole in years." He paused to light a cigarette. "Although based on the way your purse your lips, I can definitely see the family resemblance."

The policeman glared at Smitty silently, obviously trying to decide what to do next. Police Intimidation Technique 101 hadn't worked. Smitty waited patiently while the little peckerhead decided on his next approach.

"Well, according to information from our source, that's not true. He was last seen in Miami last August just about the time you were there. That puts you in the same city, and knowing your history, it gives you a motive."

"For what?"

"For eliminating him."

Smitty burst out laughing. "Brilliant reasoning, Flatfoot. With that kind of deductive power, I'm surprised J. Edgar isn't ringing you personally from his grave to disclose what really happened in the Lindbergh kidnapping."

"This is no laughing matter, you bastard," Gumdrops said, angrily grabbing Smitty by the arm.

"I'm going to give you three seconds to take your hands off me, officer, then I'm going to show you how it's done," Smitty said. There was no mistaking the threat in his voice.

Looking quickly at Ron for support and finding none, he released his grip and stepped back three steps. "Sorry."

They glared at each other in silence for a moment, before the officer turned slowly. "This is not the end of this." He swaggered out the door, got in his patrol car, and drove away with tires squealing.

Smitty and Ron stared at each other silently, neither wanting to be the first to speak.

"I guess I'd better be going," Ron said finally. He turned and headed for the door.

"Captain?" Smitty asked. Ron froze. Then he shrugged his shoulders in resignation, opened the door, and walked purposefully to his beat-up car, worried it to life, and, with a loud backfire, engaged the transmission and drove away. The car sounded more like a braying jackass on its last legs than its muscular namesake.

Smitty left the office and watched the smoke trail until it was out of sight. Then he walked into the first bay to attend to the needs of the big Chevy.

It was just past 2:00 AM, and Smitty was pretty much on schedule. From eleven until about one, there was usually a fairly constant stream of customers at the gas pumps. After that, things slowed considerably and Smitty was able to get the daily clean-up chores done and settle down at the desk to study the rest of the night. He was interrupted only occasionally by a drunk or a bar girl on her way home from a late night until around six when the early morning customers would start to roll in.

Because of changing the oil on his car, he was running a bit late. He'd yet to clean the heads located on the right side of the building. As was his custom, he cleaned the women's restroom first, then the men's. Their doors were separated by a Coke machine.

There was a third restroom located around the corner at the back of the building. But it was now closed, although the label "Colored" could still be clearly seen through the whitewash. Smitty flashed back to the redneck bar in Alabama years ago and what LZ had said. He smiled to himself. He thought that discrimination in the South was still pretty much like the restroom: a thinly veiled coat of compliance couldn't cover up the lack of true acceptance.

A car door opening made him to pause in his cleaning efforts. A second door opening made him lay aside his mop and walk out of the ladies' can. He paused at the soda machine and glanced around warily.

A '65 Chevy four-door sedan was parked in the alley behind the station. A black man was leaning in the opened back door and retrieving something. Curiously, he was reaching through the pockets of his long wool coat, which seemed to be cut out. A second black man in the rear handed him a sawed-off shotgun, which he tucked under his coat so that when he stood up, the weapon was completely concealed by the coat flaps.

The second man then exited the rear on the other side, tucking a .22 caliber snub-nose revolver in his waistcoat pocket. A third black man remained behind the wheel.

Smitty's first instinct was to run, but there wasn't sufficient time or space. The Chevy was in the first stall with the service doors closed and locked. There were seventy-five yards of open space between the service station and the closest building across the street. However, these lads didn't look like they were stopping to ask for directions. Smitty realized he was out of options and would have to fight it out.

Soundlessly he retreated to the office and moved quickly through it to the Chevy in the first bay. He quietly opened the driver's door, retrieving the Magnum and an extra speed loader. He straightened up, stepped up to the doorway to the office, leaned against a stack of oil cartons, crossed his arms so that the Magnum in his clenched left fist was just out of sight, and waited. Smitty knew it would not be long.

Fifteen seconds later, the two men entered the office from the door on the other side. The man with the pistol looked to be about twenty. He had a twitch and bulging eyes. He stepped nervously to the side, giving his partner a clear view of Smitty and a clear field of fire.

The other man was the one that Smitty was primarily concerned with. He was older, perhaps in his thirties, with a calm manner and a cigarette dangling rakishly out of the corner of his mouth. This was his profession, and his scarred face showed his dedication to his calling.

Smitty knew that this was a hit, cleverly disguised as a robbery. The options were few, just like in Nam. Either he got them, or they got him.

"Hey, white boy, how's about giving me change for a dollar, so's we can grab a soda." The younger man enthusiastically held out a bill with his left hand and kept a firm grip on the pistol in his coat pocket with his right.

Smitty ignored him. His focus was on the older man and his eyes. They locked in on each other, silently appraising, each trying to guess the other's thoughts. The older black man's eyes seemed to be saying, "Nothing personal, just a job." Smitty hoped his own eyes reflected the same glacial harshness.

"Hey, man, did you hear me?" the younger man asked, momentarily distracting Smitty.

When Smitty looked again, the older man had dropped the cigarette on the floor and was lazily crushing it out with his foot, as if it were his decision-triggering device. His choice now made, and his die now cast, he slowly began to raise the shotgun from under his coat.

"Please don't." Smitty stepped to the side, concealing all but the top of his head and his firearm, and brought the .357 to bear. He propped it on his right hand, and sighted on the older man's chest.

The older black man suddenly flipped the shotgun up until the barrel protruded evilly from his waist like some kind of huge, vile erection.

The sound of the high-powered Magnum discharging sounded like a blast from the battleship New Jersey's giant sixteen-inch guns in the confined space of the glassed-in office.

This was followed immediately by the sound of shattering glass as the mortally wounded black man pitched backward through the window. The shotgun clattered to the concrete floor.

"Next!" Smitty sighted the Magnum on the younger black man.

"Don't shoot me, white man, don't shoot me!" He yanked his right hand clear of the pocket, leaving the pistol behind, and raised both hands high in the air.

"Okay, sport, we're gonna play gook. Interlace your fingers in your hair and back slowly through the window into the middle of the driveway. Then sit down and cross your legs," Smitty instructed.

The man did exactly as he was told. Smitty had a feeling that the young man would have stripped and danced a hora if Smitty asked.

"And if you so much as twitch, I'll blow your shit away." Smitty squatted and felt the older man's neck for a pulse with his right hand. As he expected, he found none. It was a move that probably saved his life.

As Smitty was kneeling by the late shooter, a gunshot ricocheted off the metal pole above his head.

Smitty was still flinching when he heard the sound of tires squealing and an engine being gunned.

Cursing himself for his own stupidity, Smitty dropped to the ground behind the body and, using the chest as a brace, sighted on the speeding getaway car and fired three rounds in the direction of the driver's window.

The car, which was accelerating away rapidly, slowed, jerked violently to the left, then even more violently back to the right, as the driver attempted to overcorrect. Apparently one of Smitty's rounds had found its mark.

He almost made it, almost. He clipped the right rear corner of a parked new Cadillac and careened into the path of an oncoming garbage truck. The metallic gnashing of metal that followed as the sixteen-ton vehicle effectively compacted the much lighter car head-on was sickening. The only way the driver would talk now was through a séance.

"Okay, pal, in about two minutes, this place is going to be crawling with cops." Smitty turned his attention back to the remaining gunman.

"Yeah, so," he said sullenly.

"So, dipshit, that means you've got about a minute and a half to live. Unless you tell me who hired you and how much they paid you, you're going to get accidentally shot before the posse arrives to cart your ass away.

The young black man stared back at Smitty in insolent silence.

"Oh, I forgot to say please." Smitty cocked the Magnum and held it tightly against his forehead.

"I don't know who it was," he began in a faltering voice laced with fear. "We never saw him. He came up to Leroy from behind in the dark and told him that he knew he had a record and would pay him a thousand dollars for doing you.

"Leroy hired me and my brother to help. I'm the setup guy and my brother's the wheel." Looking down the street at the crumpled wreckage, he added, "Was the wheel, I mean."

There was something vaguely familiar about that method. Hadn't Big Walt been approached in the same way back in Nam by the mysterious major? It could just be coincidence, but Smitty didn't think so. But it couldn't be Detective Wallace/FBI Agent Clev Clayborne/Major Williams unless he had been reincarnated.

That meant another mole had been activated, or maybe been active all along and Smitty in his arrogance had missed him entirely. Maybe someone else with less experience had been assigned the job. Either way, it would be interesting to hear Aunt Belinda's thoughts when Smitty talked to him, right after he cleaned up the mess here.

"Where's the thousand dollars?" Smitty asked.

"In Leroy's back pocket. We was goin' to split it after we capped ya, and then we was going to blow out of here for Charleston 'til this thing cooled."

Smitty walked over to Leroy, rolled him on his side, fished in his back pocket, and produced ten crisp, new one-hundred-dollar bills. With a satisfied nod, he returned Leroy to his former face-up position, folded the Ben Franklins and put them in his pocket. It must be inflation; the price on his head had doubled over the last three years.

As Smitty walked back to the terrified third man, he could hear the sound of police sirens in the distance.

Smitty knelt in front of him. "If I were you, partner, I'd skip what you told me and just tell the police it was an attempted robbery."

"Why?"

"Cause if you tell the cops what you told me, whoever hired you will come after you; they don't like witnesses to misses. And if they don't, I'll take this cash and hire someone else to finish the job on you."

The young man shivered violently. Smitty was sure that he'd not talk. Well, make that pretty sure—a thousand dollars sure.

The service station was closed the next two days as the place was crawling with cops and detectives of every kind. Smitty stayed home from both school and work those two days to avoid the flood of reporters. His father and Sally visited and strongly advised him to quit, as did Susan.

Smitty listened to the opinions of all three but was not swayed. The papers were still reporting it as a robbery. Only Smitty and his surviving assailant knew the truth. An assailant who was mysteriously discovered hanged in his cell the next morning by none other than officer Gumdrops. The other two were also dead, and dead men tell no tales. The police seemed perfectly willing to believe it was just a robbery, and Smitty was perfectly willing to let them believe it. Since such service station robberies were commonplace, by the time the station reopened on Saturday, the story had been dropped from the front pages and was already disappearing from people's minds.

But although the story was dropped, the service station did not stay out of the public's mind for long. The very afternoon it reopened, a young black Vietnam veteran who was a student at Silverston was killed in the intersection in front of the service station. If it had been a traffic accident, it probably wouldn't have been noticed, but the fact that the man died when he was pulled under the tires of a car driven by four white teenagers, who tried to snatch his collection can for a black charity out of his hand, turned it into a political hot potato that no local politician, black or white, could touch without getting singed.

All of the long-simmering Southern racial tensions just beneath the surface rose to a boil as the predominately white city administration asserted that four upper-class white teenagers would not commit such a senseless act unless provoked.

The NAACP spokesman seemed to think exactly the opposite and accused them of trying to cover up the crime by shifting blame. It was rumored that Jesse Jackson would fly to Savannah to personally attend the funeral.

Smitty knew firsthand about the façade of racial equality from his black friends in school. He'd stopped to visit one of them when he was passing through his small Georgia hometown last summer.

His normally congenial friend was nervous and edgy, telling him he'd better leave before the police chief showed up. He'd only been there ten minutes, when the white policeman pulled up in front of the house, walked directly to his friend, shoved him against the wall, grabbed him by the shirt, slapped him across the face, then started demanding that he tell him what he had done that would require a white boy to come to his house personally.

When Smitty intervened, the shocked policeman let go of his friend and pointed his finger directly at Smitty. "Any white boy that would be friends with a nigger is nothing more than poor white trash and don't deserve to be treated no better. You best git."

After assuring that his friend would be okay, Smitty beat feet outta there, with the chief's deputy following him to the city line, pulling him over just outside it and reminding him that, "you'd best not come here again."

Smitty suspected that the truth in this death, as usual, lay somewhere in the middle. The teenagers had probably intended a nasty prank, not a death. That made them racists, but not murderers.

The fact that it occurred on the same corner as the double killings a few days earlier was not lost on the eagle-eyed press who seemed to somehow tie the two incidents together as evidence of racial injustice, or at the very least inequity. Conveniently, they seemed to ignore the fact that Smitty was also a student at Silverston, although the faculty and students themselves were not so unaware.

"Where you going, honky?" A huge black student, surrounded by a group of ten to twelve black brothers from a local fraternity, blocked his path.

"To see the dean," Smitty answered coolly. It was the Tuesday afternoon before finals and the dean had asked to see him. One thing was certain; Smitty was not going anywhere until this big guy decided he was going to.

"I don't think so, white bread." A student just to his left produced a switchblade.

"Considering the medical profession?" Smitty placed his hands behind him in what he hoped was a nonthreatening gesture of openness. It was also a not-so-obvious gesture that put him within reaching distance of his Magnum. Given the current circumstances, Smitty had decided to carry it in a holster clip covered by his jacket.

"Yeah, white boy, starting now. Grab him, Benny." This, to the man mountain barricading his pass.

Smitty reacted quickly. He backpedaled two steps, successfully eluding Benny's grasp, and in the same motion unclipped the Magnum, brought it around, held it with the barrel pointed toward the ground, flipped open the snap catch with his thumb, and as the holster dropped, caught it with his other hand.

Smitty smiled confidently. "Surprise, Tinkerbell."

Benny, big as he was, was no fool. He'd obviously been raised around firearms or knew enough about them to know that at close range the Magnum would blow a hole through someone, even someone as big as he was. He backed up two steps. His actions seemed to guide the rest, who backed up also. Including, Smitty was pleased to see, his would-be surgeon.

Taking a deep breath to control his nerves, Smitty said, "Now look, guys, I know you're pissed off about the black guy getting killed, and the papers have led you to believe that the two guys that got killed in that robbery attempt are in some way related, maybe making you think I'm a racist or something. But nothing could be further from the truth. And if you give me two minutes, I can explain."

No one answered immediately. "If you want to fight it out after my explanation, we can still do that, but you should know that I have pointed this Magnum at another human being, pulled the trigger, and taken a human life. And in a close group like this, I can personally guarantee that I'll get at least six of you before you get me. And if the survivors aren't damn quick at getting to me before I use the speed loader, I'll get six more." Smitty paused for effect and surveyed the crowd, who had prudently backed up another two steps. "Isn't the prevention of all that bloodshed worth two ticks of the clock?"

Smitty was silent. The odds were fifty-fifty that they would just jump him and beat him to death. The sad part was that if they did, Smitty would have to just let them, 'cause he knew in his heart of hearts, he sure wasn't prepared to go shooting innocent students, black or white.

"Proceed," Benny said.

"First things first. The robbery. The facts are that two guys tried to hold me up. One had a pistol, and the other had a sawed-off shotgun. It didn't matter that they were black. I'd have shot them if they were white, black, brown, or little green men from Mars. It was either them or me. It's that simple."

"Go on," Benny said.

"Now as to the black guy getting killed, I'm just as sad and just as angry as you are. He was a Vietnam veteran like me, just trying to put his life back together and better himself. I was raised in the military where race doesn't exist—well, at least less than in the civilian world. I've been going to school here for two years and I'm one of you.

"Last, violence is not the answer. It only leads to more violence until it gets out of control. I learned that in the street gangs of Miami. If you don't believe that, after you kill me, go down there and look up a black lady by the name of Mrs. McCord.

"Her son and I were best friends during my teenage years. We went in the service together and all through the first year of training until we shipped out for Vietnam. He let his anger against the white race consume him until the day he died at Au Lac six months ago.

"He was my best friend, and I'll miss him until the day I die," Smitty said, his eyes welling with tears.

"So if your friend there's rage is so strong that he needs to extract revenge, let him start with me." Smitty took a deep breath and put the Magnum back in the holster, reclipped it on the rear of his belt, and dropped his hands to his sides.

Benny stood silently appraising him. Fifteen seconds passed, then fifteen more.

Finally, Benny nodded silently in satisfaction. Misinterpreting this, the surgeon wannabe with the imitation scalpel stepped forward, raised his arm, only to have Benny arrest it and remove the knife from his resisting hand. He folded the blade and slipped it casually into his pocket, holding out his hand. "It's cool, brother."

Smitty slapped him five, which Benny returned before stepping aside. The remaining fraternity members did the same, parting like a crowd of curious onlookers for the man. Smitty walked through the gauntlet, still half expecting to get a sharp knife stuck up his lily-white ass.

He was ten paces beyond them when he heard someone from the group say, "That's one ballsy muthafuckin' white boy."

When Smitty turned, Benny said with a smile, "No, he's just a student, like us. And we need to take care of our own."

Benny was right. Smitty was a student, just like him. But unlike him, he had skeletons in the closet. Skeletons that had now come marching out two by two and made a renewed, but bungled, attempt to kill him. The next time he was sure they would be more skillful.

As 1973 drew to a close, Smitty had to admit that on the credit side of the ledger, he was now an official college senior, one-quarter short of graduation with an engineering degree. On the debit side there was the death of his friend LZ, and the fact that, although they'd eliminated an assassin who'd killed three of his friends, he'd made no further progress toward finding the mysterious string-puller.

But then again, as the late Detective Wallace had found out, it had taken six years, but there were ways around these legal roadblocks . . . and Smitty was sure the time was approaching when he would have to use those methods again.

CHAPTER TWENTY-TWO

"Surprise, Tinkerbell."

Smitty looked up as Benny, leading six other black guys, who were close to his size, headed toward him, effectively blocking the hallway outside of the engineering building. It had been six months since the incident with him on campus. Feelings appeared to have cooled to the point where Smitty no longer felt it necessary to carry his Magnum to class. Smitty suspected that Benny had a lot to do with that, but had never bothered to check.

"Listen, man, I need you to take a ride with us," Benny said quickly. When Smitty didn't respond immediately, Benny repeated, "I need you to take a ride with us, right now." Then added as an afterthought, "Please."

"Why?" Smitty asked, more curious than alarmed.

"No time to explain." Benny took one arm and another huge black guy took the other and they effectively walked him down the open corridor to the parking lot, more or less shot-putted him into the back of a waiting older Cadillac limousine. The door was not yet closed before the limo sped off with tires squealing, which was a remarkable feat considering that it was transporting close to two tons of beef on the hoof.

Quickly, the big car was clear of the campus and headed for downtown around Olsen Street, a predominately black neighborhood, consisting of older homes that had been converted into apartment houses.

They opened the door, escorted Smitty into a rundown white building, and up the stairs to a three-bedroom apartment that turned out to belong to Benny and two roommates.

"Let me guess, you guys are showing me the place hoping that I'll become a roommate." Smitty hoped his tone covered his nervousness.

"Not a chance, brother," Benny said with a smile.

"So why are we here?"

"We're waiting for a phone call," Benny said in a clipped tone that cut off further conversation.

An hour passed, then two. The number in the room grew by one, as a truly stunning black girl, who turned out to be Benny's girlfriend, joined them.

Ten minutes later the phone rang. Benny listened briefly, and hung up without saying good-bye.

"Let's go." Again they escorted him from the room and back to the waiting limo.

The trip back to the campus seemed to be faster. They pulled up next to Smitty's car, unceremoniously ejected him from the limo, and quickly drove away.

Still not understanding the reason for the mysterious kidnapping and the two-hour detainment, Smitty walked back to the open corridor intent on being early for his two o'clock class.

He never made it.

Another entourage, but this one was more official.

Dr. Tarleton, the school president, accompanied by Dr. Rollins and two campus security guards, were approaching. They had serious and grim looks.

"Mr. Smith," Dr. Tarleton began. "We've been looking for you for over an hour. Where have you been?"

"Off campus for the last couple of hours," Smitty answered truthfully.

"Humph!" he scoffed.

Glancing at Dr. Rollins, Dr. Tarleton said, "Mr. Smith, you are suspended from school pending the finding of a school inquiry. You are to leave campus immediately, and if what has happened turns out to be by your hand, you will be expelled."

"You mind telling me why I'm being suspended fifteen days short of graduation?" Smitty asked in a stunned voice.

"Young man, I think you know," Dr. Tarleton answered.

"Amuse me."

He sucked in his chest and was just beginning to answer when Benny, his girlfriend, and six friends sauntered up, stopping him before he could answer.

"Afternoon, good doctors, afternoon Smitty. That was quite a lunchtime jam, wasn't it?" Benny said in a syrupy voice.

"What?" The president's head snapped around.

"That's right, sir," Benny's girlfriend said. "We invited white bread back to our place after his morning class for a jam. He's been with us for the last two-and-a-half hours."

Benny's girlfriend walked up to Smitty, put her arm around him, kissed him wetly on the cheek, leaving a perfect set of red lip prints. "And I can tell you personally, that after spending some private time with him, based on the size of his drumstick, there sure must be some dark meat in his family tree."

The members of Benny's group laughed.

"Based on their statements, Dr. Tarleton, Mr. Smith could not have possibly have had anything to do with the incident," Dr. Rollins said. "Do you still wish to suspend him?"

"Uh, no. That is to say, let's forget about it." Dr. Tarleton stalked off up the corridor.

"Good thing you had an alibi," Dr. Rollins said.

"Yeah, good thing," Smitty said. "What happened to set him off?"

"Well, as I understand it, two of our students went to see the president this morning and complained that your father was receiving preferential treatment from one of his professors, who happens to be white. Within two hours, or shortly after twelve, the two students had hoods thrown over their heads and were beaten up behind the gym.

"Frankly, I told the president that you were one of my student leaders, a poster boy Joe College type, and would never do such a thing, but he was insistent. He said he had received a report on you that was quite inflammatory, and it convinced him that you would have no problem executing violence and revenge.

"I was glad to hear that you were with black students during the time it happened." He looked around at the seven of them and said shrewdly, "Sure was lucky you had an alibi."

With a friendly wave, he departed without a further word.

"Sure was lucky I had an alibi," Smitty repeated, looking sheepishly at Benny.

"Hey, brother, we take care off our own." Benny and Smitty exchanged high-fives.

An hour later, as Smitty was heading to his lab, he passed Doc in the hallway. Without breaking stride, he held out his hand, and slapped Smitty five as he passed. "Mission accomplished, Lieutenant."

When Smitty had first seen Doc, his breath caught in his throat. After Doc's remark, he began to breathe again as he realized that he was in fact, shortly going to be a college graduate.

The last six months had provided some interesting twists of fate for both Smitty and his friends.

With all his credits accrued through attending classes the last two summers, Smitty had only to take one homework subject each of the last two quarters to fulfill his degree requirements. This gave him ample time to interview with the host of recruiters who came on campus. After the interviewers—who were primarily black—got over the shock of seeing a white student attending a black college, the interviews seemed to proceed well. In fact, Smitty was fairly certain that this seemed to be a point in his favor.

Smitty had taken four interview trips, but settled on a job as an engineer with the largest aircraft-manufacturing defense contractor in the country at its design headquarters in upstate New York. Smitty thought that, considering how many of the damn things he'd seen shot down, it would not only be a useful position, but also something of a payback to his Nam buddies to help engineer the beasts to be safer.

General Chuck had offered to grease the skids for a civil service position with the Defense Department, but Smitty had declined, wanting to make a complete break from the past.

After the on-campus interview, the actual site meeting seemed to be a mere formality, with a job offer made by the personnel department before he left at the end of the day. Since the salary was 25 percent higher than the nearest offer, Smitty accepted it immediately. Smitty was still pinching himself when he thought about starting a job, with no experience, at a salary that was $2000 more than his father had made at the end of his thirty-one year military career.

Accepting the job had its drawbacks and, unfortunately, its casualties.

It meant Smitty would be moving over a thousand miles to a strange place that had long, cold winters and short summers. It also meant he'd be going alone.

Susan could not understand why Smitty did not just take an engineering job with one of the local companies. During the course of Smitty's interviews, they had begun to argue for the first time in their relationship. Smitty had assumed, somewhat myopically it seemed, that he and Susan would get married and move north together.

On the day he returned with the news of the job offer in New York—and his acceptance—Susan had packed her bags and moved into an apartment with a girlfriend. Smitty had tried to see her to work it out, but it was not to be.

Smitty would also be a thousand miles from his father and Sally, but the fact that Dad was from Pennsylvania would shorten the distance during his summer visits.

All of these things were farts in a whirlwind when compared with the fact that he was now the sole surviving musketeer.

It happened in February during Mardi Gras, when Frenchy was going to work. His car was broadsided at an intersection by a Mercury driven by a drunken reveler. At the time, Sondra was seven months pregnant with their third child. Smitty'd always assumed that he'd have time to go see his friend, and now that time was no more.

Considering all the things that had happened to Smitty, LZ, and Big Walt, Smitty checked it out, and found that it was what it seemed, just another tragic T-boner; what a waste.

At the funeral, Sondra had given Smitty the fourth watch. Smitty was now the caretaker of his teenage friends' memories, and they were his only link to his checkered past.

His other Vietnam link had disappeared also. Ron had left town sometime in March two steps ahead of the IRS, who wanted him again for unpaid taxes. Five years back, Smitty would have walked through the fires of hell for the Polack. Now he didn't have to. Ron had assigned himself there of his own volition.

His former division commander, Lieutenant General Ben Martin, was now among the missing also. Having somehow wangled himself a last staff adviser assignment in Vietnam before his retirement, his transport helicopter had gone down in heavy storms while shuttling to a meeting on a navy aircraft carrier in the South China Sea. Neither the wreckage nor the body was ever found.

The cause was checked off as a mechanical failure. Helicopters and crews could be replaced, but three-star generals with Martin's courage and dedication were damn hard to find. Smitty would always have a soft spot for him because he had helped him when times were bad.

His older brother, Dad's friend General Chuck, was still on active duty, although it could only just be called that, in that he had some staff job in the Pentagon. According to General Wilson, he was merely delaying the inevitability of retirement in the ever-dwindling hope of a fourth star.

Changes had happened locally also. The oil embargo had finished the service station owner for whom Smitty had worked since his return to Savannah three and a half years ago. Smitty had quickly gotten a job as a night watchman on a graveyard shift where all he had to do was stay awake and show his presence as a deterrent. The job was dull and routine, but it provided ample free time to study.

In anticipation of moving, Smitty had sold his house for ten times what had been invested in it, split the money four ways, and sent the shares to each of the original foursome. He surmised that since Ron left town right after receiving his payment, the money had been used for traveling cash.

Smitty was now living his final weeks in Savannah with Dad and Sally, an arrangement that seemed to suit all of them and was convenient to his night job guarding tugboats on the Wilmington River just a few miles away.

But it was also a time of nervousness and trepidation. Dad didn't want his son to go. Smitty was hoping desperately that nothing would happen to screw it up.

"Hi, son, how was school today?" Sally was standing at the sink washing dishes. She was excited about the prospect of "both of her boys" being college graduates, and was making no bones about it to anyone who would listen.

"About normal." Smitty entered the kitchen, kissed her lightly on the cheek, grabbed a beer from the fridge, then settled into the kitchen chair right next to it. "I think the last days are the hardest. I'm excited that I'm going to graduate. But a little afraid of the path ahead."

"I know exactly what you mean. I felt the same way when I graduated from nursing school and went into the service during the war. After the briefest of army orientations at Bolling Field outside Washington, I found myself on a ship headed to the Philippines. Then before we knew it, the islands fell into Japanese hands, and I was a prisoner for two years."

"I never knew that," Smitty said, leaning forward with sudden interest. Dad was stationed at Bolling at just about the same time. His father had married Mom in June of '44 while he was on recuperative leave from that Octagon thing, so that meant that they must have known each other before his parents met!

Smitty felt a surge of adrenaline, knowing that he had stumbled onto something. But to get more information, he was going to have to be extremely careful and somewhat devious. Sally was no bubblehead. As long as Smitty kept her in a nostalgic mood, she might provide a conduit to the past without even knowing it.

"That must have been rough. Especially if it was anything like what was depicted in that Hollywood movie I saw on the late show the other night," Smitty responded.

"It was all that and more," Sally said, nodding her head. "Boy, the stories I could tell you." She slammed a pan into the dish rack on the counter. Her body language betrayed her true feelings—the ones Smitty really wanted to know about.

"Sounds like quite a story." Smitty tried to figure out just how to make her mad enough to talk, but not so angry that she stalked out of the room.

"Which one of the little tojos tried to jump you?"

She slapped the dishrag in the water and spun on her heels. "They all tried."

"Any of them succeed?"

Sally walked purposefully across the kitchen and took a long pull on Smitty's beer. She set it down on the table, then picked up the bottle again, drained it and slammed it down on the table. "Only one. And the little Nip bastard ran off in shame when he dropped his pants and I started to laugh and told him to come back when it grew up."

Sally smiled at her own story. "The problem was it already had."

Laughing with her, Smitty reached around the side of the refrigerator to grab two more cold ones. He opened them and slid one across to Sally.

Still laughing, she caught the bottle before it could skid off the table. She held the brew up for a toast and they clicked bottles. "Down the hatch," she said.

They finished the beers and slammed the bottles down on the table together, grinning like two mischievous children. Sally looked at Smitty, her eyes twinkling, and walked to the icebox for two more. She opened them and she slid one to Smitty. "To all our old comrades who never made it back."

In two minutes, Sally had inhaled two and a half of Milwaukee's finest. The flush in her cheeks was clear enough evidence that the alcohol was starting to have an effect.

Smitty reached into the refrigerator again, only this time he brought out four. He opened them and set two in front of Sally who had dropped into a chair next to him.

"Down the hatch." Smitty picked up a beer in both hands and started to take alternate swigs from both bottles.

"To windpipes the size of trombones." Sally's speech was already starting to slur.

Thirty minutes and four beers latter, Sally was bombed. Her speech was slurred, and her normally neat hairdo was falling down around her face. She had become loud, boisterous, and was laughing uproariously at her own jokes, most of which were damn funny.

". . . So when this young lieutenant nurse said she was pregnant, I said, 'Do you know who the father is?' She replies, 'Someone in the 2nd division.' When I asked her which soldier, she scratched her head, and said innocently, 'All of them.'" Sally cackled at her own story.

Smitty had always liked Sally when sober, but drunk, she was a downright hoot. Her stories seemed to come alive right before your eyes as she exuberantly told of a life lived and enjoyed to the fullest.

Not that Smitty was feeling any pain either. He figured that if he was ever going to learn anything about her past life with Dad, now was the opportune moment, one that might never come again.

"Say, Sally," Smitty began slowly. "Did you ever tell Dad about the little Nip who tried to rape you?"

"Oh, good heavens, no," Sally said, her cheeks turning crimson. "Your father would never understand. Besides, your father could only be the same size as that little coward if he folded it in half." Sally blushed and began laughing. Between fits of laughter, she added weakly, "No, make that thirds."

Smitty wrinkled his brow in amazement. "Lets me know what I've got to look forward to when I get to be his age," Smitty said in an impressed voice.

"I wasn't talking about the last four years, I was talking about when he was young." Shaking her head in remembrance, she added, "I was sore for the next two days. I told all my girlfriends that I'd been riding over the weekend and was saddle-sore, which was sort of true—if you know what I mean." She giggled like a schoolgirl.

"You knew Dad before Mom did?" Smitty ventured gently.

"Sonny boy, if it hadn't been for circumstances, I would have been your mom."

"Really," Smitty said in amazement. "Such as?"

"Well, your father and I were quite an item early in the war while I was in nursing school. When I was suddenly shipped out for the Far East, then captured, we lost touch. When I got released in '45, they were so desperate for nurses that I was immediately assigned to a hospital in Japan. Hell, I didn't even know he was married to your mother until I accidentally bumped into him at a MASH unit in Korea in '51."

"What happened? You two seem perfect for each other."

"I thought we were," Sally said. "I don't really know all the details. But as I understand it, your mom got knocked up by some officer from a very influential family. They set your dad up on a blind date with her and pretty much told him how perfect she would be for him and all that crapola. And how, since she was this pristine Southern debutante, she would help his career. Bullshit like that.

"As I said, I don't know all the details, but I do know that your father was all set to marry your mother in early '43 'cause he thought that he was responsible for her being preggo."

Smitty did a little mental arithmetic in his head and it did not compute. This was seven years before his brother was even born.

"Did Dad ever find out the truth?"

"He sure as hell did, and boy, was he pissed. I understand he damn near wanted to kill your mother. He flew into a rage and told her that he wouldn't have anything to do with her or a child that wasn't his. Then he found the officer he thought was responsible, beat the hell out of him, and damned near killed him. The funny part was that the officer your dad liked to have killed wasn't the one responsible.

"Some other officer had your dad transferred to some secret covert group and shipped out immediately to save his career."

"What happened to the baby?"

"Babies. As I understand it, there were two—two boys, I think. Your mom put them up for adoption and wrote your father that she had miscarried."

"And he believed her?" Smitty asked in an incredulous voice.

"Why wouldn't he?" Sally staggered to the fridge and retrieved two more cold ones. She set them on the table, plopping back in the chair with all the finesse of a woman eight months pregnant.

"You see, sonny boy, things weren't like they are today. Communications were not so fast and letters were our only means of keeping in touch. Sometimes it would take months for them to catch up to you and for you to respond. Your father was gone for over two years with letters his only lifeline. Your mom started writing to him, and I guess he was lonely and started writing back. I think during that time, he sort of fell in love with your mother all over again. Then the war ended for him when he was wounded and shipped home. I think he just forgave her, they got married, and their life went on."

"Any idea what happened to my half-brothers?" Smitty asked curiously.

"I haven't the foggiest," Sally slurred. "But your father knows. He found out the truth about their existence sometime when you were posted overseas in the early '60s, although I don't know how. But I do know that from that point on, your father's marriage to your mother was basically over. The damage was permanent; the trust was gone and couldn't be restored. They split up and she went home. I know they tried to get back together again a couple of years later, but it didn't take. There's more to the story, but your father won't tell me. Every time I bring it up, he changes the subject."

Smitty perked up his ears and listened hard. The sound of Dad's Falcon wagon could be clearly heard as the valve-rattling six cylinder pulled underneath the carport. Time to change the discussion and the mood.

Smitty jumped up from the table, grabbed a whisk broom and straddled it. "I just thought of the perfect gift for your next birthday."

"What?"

"A kick-starter for your broom, you soused old witch." Smitty made stepping motions.

"You smart-assed little bastard, I'll get you for that." Sally struggled to a standing position, and began to chase Smitty through the back room into the hallway. They changed positions as Smitty began to swat her on the rear end with the broom. She ran through the living room laughing gleefully, and shrieked for him to stop. He chased her into the kitchen where they met Dad coming from the family room.

"What's going on here?" Dad asked. He saw the dozen or so empties, and nodded his head in understanding.

"Your son and I are forming a more meaningful relationship," Sally said happily, as she hugged Dad.

"I can see that," Dad said. "The question is what kind of relationship?"

"Oh, I was just telling your son what a stud you are, darling." Sally kissed him and began to nibble on his ear.

"And I was just telling her that I'm a chip off the ol' block, Pop," Smitty said.

"Oh, he's all of that, honey," Dad said. "All of that and more."

And thanks to Sally, Smitty now had the chance to be so much more than that. He now knew the key to a thirty-year-old mystery. All he needed now was the proof, and if what he suspected was true, he knew just how to get it, whom to enlist to help him get it, and again, thanks to Sally, whom to set up to get it from.

Smitty and his dad had made it. They were sitting in the auditorium in their caps and gowns looking as ridiculous as most people do in those rigs, while trying to get through the pomp and circumstance of graduation. They were just coming to the part where the graduates rise to form up like a chow line for their diplomas when the president announced the rarity of having a father and son graduate at the same time and asked that they please come up to receive their diplomas together.

As Smitty rose, stepped politely by fellow graduates, and walked toward the stage, a burst of shouts of encouragement and clapping caused him to glance to his right and smile warmly. It may not have been what most folks referred to as family, but they were all he'd ever need, and more than most people would ever have.

They were seated together, his friends who, when banded together, had become the circle of family that had helped him along the way.

A college degree may be a taken-for-advantage expectation in some families, but to Smitty, it was a goal that had seemed so distant when he was a teenager as to be the pot of gold at the end of the mythical leprechaun's rainbow. As a result, Smitty's own insecurities had magnified it into an object that was virtually unattainable.

Through everything that had happened to him in his life, the one thing Smitty had learned was that fears were like bullies. They could be conquered if you faced them head-on. His dad's advice had pulled him out of many tight spots.

His friends were here to celebrate, his friends were here for support, or maybe his friends were here because they had the same dreams either for themselves or for their children, dreams that had for one reason or another gone unfulfilled. By celebrating Smitty's achieving his goal, they felt that they had taken a lease on his dream. Smitty suspected that down through history it had always been that way.

But even so, Smitty had sent out the invitations with great trepidation. Helping him fulfill his dream was one thing, but traveling in some cases hundreds of miles, to attend his graduation at a black college was something else altogether. His uneasiness was rewarded with 100 percent attendance. He was elated that they came.

They were there in the center of the first three rows, whooping it up joyously like cowboys at their first rodeo.

LZ's mom, Linda's parents, Glenda's mother, and Hogsbreath's dad were seated in the middle of the group, smiling proudly and yelling words of encouragement from the front row. Next to them sat Sondra and her three little ones, the oldest of whom was Smitty's godson.

On the other side sat Sergeant Mike and his wife, the old sergeant beaming like the father of a newborn. Behind them in the second row, were General Wilson; Major Jim; Stan the Man and his wife; Fred and Ginger; his boss from the service station and his wife; and several of his former coworkers. Directly behind them sat Dr. Evans, the coach from the Barn, Dr. Silverman, and Professor Strickland and "housemate."

Ironically, seated next to them, were Kristie and her husband, Ricky. Smitty couldn't tell whether Ricky was more uncomfortable being surrounded by a sea of black or uneasy over come-hither looks from Professors Strickland's housemate.

Smitty's friends from the past were with him in spirit also. In addition to his own watch on his left arm, on his right, he wore the three watches that belonged to Frenchy, LZ, and Big Walt in tribute to the memories of his friends. Around his neck, he wore the locket Linda had given him while they were in Japan, and the spare key to Ron's Mustang. On his right little finger, he wore Glenda's class ring.

Seated right next to them, Dad had his own cheering section, comprising Sally, Smitty's 'Aunt-Grandma' from next door, Benny and his wife, eight of Smitty's uncles and aunts who had driven down from Pennsylvania, fifteen assorted friends, and twenty-odd former soldiers, including General Chuck, who had flown in for the ceremony.

Trancelike, Smitty ascended the stage side by side with his father, and accepted his diploma and handshake from the president. He stopped to shake hands with Doc, who said, "Mission accomplished," before resuming his seat.

The parade of the rest of the graduates took another forty-five minutes. The keynote speaker then rambled on for thirty more about the opportunity of the future.

Smitty was reflecting on the events of the past, and the incredible trail of death and destruction, and the steps around, or more often than not through it, that had allowed him to persevere from the streets of Miami to the shithole of Vietnam to here.

All of Smitty's extended family was invited back to Dad's house for the graduation party, which started to break up about ten. Which was just as well, since Smitty had to be at work at his guard job at the docks by eleven. Smitty'd given his notice. This was to be the start of his last week, and then he'd be gone to his white-collar job in New York.

It was 1:30 AM Sunday, and Smitty was making his rounds of the tugs. He tended to make irregular circuits, lest someone start to time him and plan a break-in. His last circuit had been just twenty-five minutes earlier, and things had been extremely quiet. The bars closed at 2:00 AM, and the usual parade of Saturday night deckhands returning from the local gin joints, in an intoxicated but generally happy mood to sleep it off on the boats, had not yet begun.

As he walked along the docks, shining his flashlight up on the rigging of the tugs and across the decks, the spotlight suddenly illuminated a man standing on the top of the pilot house of a white fifty-footer—naked.

The man looked to be in his mid-twenties. He had short brown hair and was clean-shaven and extremely muscular. Obviously, somewhere this dude had pumped his share of iron and been professionally coached on the development process.

Temporarily stunned, Smitty did a double-take, shook his head, closed his eyes, and opened them again, still not believing what he had seen. When he looked again, the man was giving him the finger with his left hand, stroking himself with his right, and tilting his head back and making baying sounds like a coyote howling at the moon.

"Hey, sport, where did you come from?" Smitty called out as he approached the boat, reaching for his illegal, but highly effective, Brooklyn special—more colloquially known as a blackjack.

"I'm warding off the evil spirits. If you bark, they can't get you, man."

"Why don't you come on down from there and let's get you something to put on before you catch cold?" Smitty fingered the handle of his Magnum that he had substituted for the standard issue police .38.

"Auntie Em, I can fly." The man leaped from the top of the roof screaming like a banshee. He hit the deck, did a forward roll behind the steering house, and vanished into the darkness.

Smitty stepped onto the deck flashing his light back and forth like a prison searchlight, hoping to find his elusive quarry.

From out of the darkness he came, charging like a rampaging hippo, catching Smitty from the blind side. The force of the blow knocked Smitty ninety degrees sideways. His head hit something hard, almost causing him to lose consciousness. His shoulder ached fiercely and his lungs felt like all the air had been sucked out of them with a gigantic Hoover; and that might not be the worst of it.

When the man launched himself, he landed on top of Smitty, grabbed his throat with hands the size of shovels and began to squeeze. Alternating between semiconsciousness and flashbacks as his entire life began marching double-time before his eyes, Smitty knew he had only moments to live.

In desperation, he lashed out at the behemoth, striking him once, twice, and then twice again across the forehead and the bridge of the nose with the truncheon. He struck with all his might, but he might as well have been hitting him with balsa wood, for all the effect it was having on the lunatic.

On the fifth try, the leather split, and the lead insert in the end of the sap bounced off his skull and went spinning over the rail of the boat like a sinker. Smitty thought to himself how ironic it would be if the last sound he ever heard was the plop the one-pounder made as it splashed into the river below. And just when he thought it couldn't get any worse, he felt a hand reaching for the Magnum. In a perverse twist of fate, the nutball was zealously trying to work the sidearm free of the holster, while Smitty was furiously trying to keep it in. In a panic, Smitty reached for his mace canister and began to spray it directly into the man's eyes.

The good news was that the hulking stranger had abandoned his quest to secure Smitty's sidearm; the bad news was that he had wrapped one of his monster paws completely around Smitty's hand, and was turning the can and Smitty's wrist completely around so that the can was now spraying him—directly in his eyes.

And then, as suddenly as the pressure on his windpipe and the spraying had started, it stopped. The man let go of Smitty and the tearmaker and rolled on his side, sprang to his feet, emitted a guttural growl, and charged the three drunken tugboat deckhands who had given Smitty a temporary respite by clubbing his assailant with a block and tackle.

Smitty was shaking his head trying to clear the cobwebs. Fortunately, the maniac was otherwise occupied. He was busy doing to the three of them what he had been doing to Smitty.

Smitty called for assistance on his two-way radio, which summoned the police, rolled over onto his knees and vomited violently. As he was wiping his mouth on his sleeve, he heard the faint sounds of a police siren off in the distance. Smitty heard a second, then a third. And for one of the few times in his life, he was damn glad.

For the next several minutes the dock area swarmed with lights and motion.

Eventually, it took eight police officers to subdue the maniac. The first two to arrive on the scene suffered a fate similar to that of Smitty and the three rescuers. Finally, the man's face looked more like a piece of raw meat than anything human. Incredibly, he had not lost consciousness and was now handcuffed to the restraining bolt in the backseat of a police cruiser while the boys in blue were trying to find out just who he was and what the fuck he was hopped up on.

"How you doing, partner?" A police lieutenant came over and placed a hand on Smitty's shoulder.

"I'll live," Smitty said. "But I'd sure as hell like to know what that dude's taking."

"I know what you mean. After he worked you over, he beat the crap out of those three deckhands and two of my officers. Excuse me." The single-bar acknowledged a brother officer's urgent wave and hurried over to take the radio call.

He listened briefly and walked back to Smitty shaking his head in disgust.

"You'll never believe it, bud," he said, gloomily thumping his cigarette in the river. "This psycho we have here is an escapee from the county loony farm. The docs there say he's an ex-college lineman who didn't make it in the NFL and went nuts. From the symptoms, the doc says he probably ingested PCP, which makes you feel like you're burning up so you rip your clothes off, and it intensifies your physical strength tenfold; as if this big prick needs it.

"And now you want to hear the stupidest part? My captain said I'm to take him back to the nuthouse personally. He's afraid that if I allow one of the officers to do it they might injure him.

"Since your rent-a-cop company won't cover the cost of the ride in the meat wagon and the county hospital is right next door to the nuthouse, how about if I drop you off there after I dump the wacko, and we have a sawbones look you over, even though you told me you're okay."

Smitty climbed into the front seat of the lieutenant's cruiser, and with the lights and siren going, they were soon speeding toward their destination.

They were not four blocks from the scene of the melee, when the sleeping giant came to life. He began rocking back and forth, alternately hitting the back of his head on the rear window and lunging forward, screaming obscenities in their ears, spitting on them, and, using his head like a battering ram, repeatedly banging the restraining screen between the seats.

He continued this all the way through downtown and well into the suburbs. The rear window was already cracked from the force of the blows; and the incarceration screen and the controlling bolts were starting to give under the force of the onslaught.

If this dude got loose here in the historic section of neatly trimmed and restored colonial houses inhabited by the well-to-do, there was no telling what damage he might do both to the local citizens, their property, and the reputation of the lieutenant transporting him.

"Hold tight." The lieutenant floored the big Impala, and Smitty watched the speedometer needle climb past a hundred. When the hulking giant was lurching forward after punching a hole in the rear window, the lieutenant slammed on the brakes. With the sudden impact and the restraint of the rest of his head, Smitty would have sworn he could see the man's nose sticking through the partition, sufficiently elongated by the G-forces to look as though it belonged on Pinocchio after he'd told a whopper.

The giant lapsed into semiconsciousness, remained docile throughout the rest of the fifteen-minute journey, and came along obligingly when they removed him from the car and walked him in from the parking lot to the admittance area.

Five minutes passed while they waited for the on-duty doctor to arrive after attending to an emergency elsewhere in the hospital. Smitty was hoping he would arrive soon. His head was aching fiercely, and his eyes were still teary and burning.

"My God, what have your storm troopers been doing to my patient?" A shaggy-haired man wearing a doctor's white burst through the doors and went straight to the bloody mess sitting on the examining table.

"Take these handcuffs off immediately. They're intimidating my patient."

The lieutenant glowered at the doctor, glanced at Smitty, pulled out his key and flipped it to the shrink. "You do it yourself, Doc. I'll stop back by and pick them up after I drop the guard off at the hospital.

"C'mon, son," he said to Smitty. "Let's get out of here before I start intimidating the doctor."

They left the admittance area, walked the 150 yards to the general parking area, and were just opening the car doors when the sound of police sirens halted them.

Three county police cars came speeding into the lot and slid to a tire-screeching stop.

"What's up, officer?" the lieutenant asked the county mountie closest to him.

"Some nut broke free, beat the living shit out of a doctor and two orderlies, and has barricaded himself in a bathroom," he said, as he raced past them.

"You think we ought to go help?" the lieutenant asked half-heartedly.

"Naw, we've done intimidated that fucker enough," Smitty said in his grandmother's best Southern drawl.

Chuckling to themselves, they drove away.

"Lieutenant, do you mind if I ask you a question?" Smitty's voice sounded firmer to him all the time, although it was hard for anyone else to tell, because the cotton balls stuffed in his nose made him sound as though it was being strained through a trumpet's mute.

"Shoot."

"What's the deal with your son?"

"You mean Gumdrops?" The lieutenant rolled his eyes.

Smitty raised his eyebrows. The lieutenant said, "Of course I know what everybody calls him. Little twerp. He probably cost me my chance at captain."

He crushed out his cigarette in the sand ashtray next to a bench just outside the emergency room and shook his head. "I sure made a mistake on him. I guess I was looking at him through the eyes of a father rather than a police lieutenant. He doesn't have the temperament for this line of business.

"Unfortunately, I only recognized it after he tangled with you and got himself demoted to patrolman. God knows how many citizens he screwed over before I found him out."

"Did you know he showed up at the service station where I was working a few months ago in his patrol car and as much as accused me of killing a former acquaintance from my teen years, a Miami detective by the name of Wallace?" Smitty ventured.

"Yeah, I heard about it. Frankly that was the last straw. It convinced me that he wasn't fit to wear the uniform and we booted him off the force."

"Surely you checked it out?"

"We did. A Miami police commissioner, who was Wallace's captain at the time, phoned back and stated emphatically that you were there visiting him the whole time and had nothing to do with it. But for some strange reason, Theodore remains convinced that you were responsible for Wallace's death."

He glanced at Smitty uncomfortably, and when he realized that his explanation had created more questions than solutions, he continued in a weary voice.

"You see, the late detective Wallace was my adopted brother, or claimed to be, although I never really knew him because my father died early in the war when I was just a young teen and he was just a grease spot, not even out of diapers. Since he was adopted, and my mother felt like she couldn't handle two small kids alone, he was sent back to the orphanage. I stayed with my mother, who remarried and later had another child, a girl with my stepfather. Eventually, my new father adopted me and since we moved around a lot, I lost contact with my late brother.

"For some strange reason, the detective showed up here several years ago wishing to reestablish contact. Theodore was at that impressionable age where he took a shine to his newly-discovered uncle that almost bordered on hero worship. He maintained that idolization even after my esteemed adopted brother got drunk and killed a girl in a traffic accident."

"Is Theodore your natural son? He sure as hell doesn't look like you," Smitty said.

"No, he's not," the lieutenant said. "I adopted him during the Korean War when I found out the wife was sterile. If I'd known he'd turn out to be this much trouble . . . "

"Where's your son now?" Smitty stood up and waved at Dad, who was just pulling up under the emergency room drive to pick up his son. Smitty had called him over an hour ago and didn't want to miss his ride, but he sure as hell didn't want to miss the answer either.

"He's living over in some trailer on the east side with a Nam vet and working out at the sugar plant."

"Well, sorry it didn't work out for your son with the police. I hope he's happy with his job now." Smitty offered his hand.

"Good luck, son, and thanks for the conversation. It helped to talk it out."

Dad had left the car idling when he got out, and as Smitty approached, put his arm around his shoulders. "How ya doing, sport?"

"Okay," Smitty answered.

Dad tilted his head until it was in the right light for him to see the massive bruise above Smitty's eye. "I can't wait to see the other guy."

"I don't think you want to, First Sergeant." The lieutenant offered his hand. "He liked to beat the crap out of all of us."

"How are you, Lieutenant?" Dad asked, as they shook hands. "Long time no see."

"Things just haven't been the same with the boys we pick up since you retired, Sarge. When you had the watch, we picked them up, but only once. Now we see the same guys two and sometimes three times. We sure do miss your disciplinary methods."

"Times change," Dad said philosophically, glancing sideways at his son to see if Smitty got the message and nodded in satisfaction as Smitty's cheeks began to color.

"Well, Smitty, I understand you'll be leaving town shortly to go to work as an engineer up north. Best of luck." The lieutenant walked back inside.

On the ride back downtown to pick up his car, Dad questioned Smitty on the events of the evening, and Smitty answered in noncommittal clipped tones. It was not that he didn't want to talk about it. He was just plain tired. It was now four-thirty in the morning. Smitty's head ached, his eyes were still watering, and he just wanted to go home and go to bed.

"Um, son, I know you've had a tough night, but I was wondering if you'd do me a favor?"

Smitty looked at him suspiciously and Dad added quickly, "And a favor for the folks in the neighborhood as well."

When a first sergeant asks you to do him a favor, he's really giving you an order that he expects you to agree with wholeheartedly, carry out expeditiously, and implement immediately.

"Fire away," Smitty said.

"Well, we're having a little problem in the neighborhood that I think calls for assistance from a man of your particular talents. As Dad began to explain what he wanted, Smitty became uncomfortable. When he'd finished explaining it, Smitty was downright pissed off. What Dad wanted was against the law and sure to get him caught and cost him his new job in New York.

"No fucking way, Popster." Smitty got out of Dad's car and slammed the door. They'd reached the parking spot downtown where he'd left his own car when he came to work the night before.

"Son, sometimes in order to correct an injustice, a man has to set himself above the law."

But before Smitty could voice his concerns, Dad had driven off, leaving him alone to contemplate his last statement.

Smitty started his car, lit a cigarette, and despite solemn vows to block it out of his mind, found himself reexamining Dad's request on the drive back to the house.

What Dad was asking of him was to do what's right, rather than just doing the right thing and then wringing your hands in helplessness and whining about your best efforts not being good enough. Apparently, the latter had been the action to date. Dad was, for one of the few times in his life, asking Smitty for help. Somehow he felt that if he didn't give it, then he'd be no better than the little Dutch boy if he'd jerked his finger out of the dike and gone home only to find that the levee gave way as a result.

Dad had lectured him when he was a kid about this country's governing principles being founded on the tenets in an essay called "Common Sense" by Thomas Paine.

Paine had said that when common sense is taken away or destroyed, anarchy reigned.

Maybe Dad was giving him one last test or more likely one final life lesson before he left town.

Smitty rubbed the sleep from his eyes, nodded his head absently, and said cheerfully, "Okay, First Shirt, you found yourself a pigeon butterbar."

"1LT." Smitty could almost hear Sergeant Mike correct him with a satisfied smile.

Smitty shut off the engine and the lights of the big Chevy two blocks from the house, removed the dome light so he could open the door without being seen, and coasted silently into his parking spot in front of the house. It was twenty minutes to six, and would be light in a few minutes. He would need to wait for the clock to strike six times, or a few minutes after, to take care of the favor he'd agreed to handle for Dad.

When the car stopped, he got out as silently as possible, and crouched behind the left front fender. In this position, his presence was hidden and undetectable by anyone passing by in the neighborhood except his dad, who had only to glance out of his bedroom window.

Smitty waited in silence, his weapon drawn, knowing that the firing opportunity would be brief, and that if he was off by the narrowest of margins, he might hit his father instead.

At five minutes to six, Smitty saw the sheer curtains in Dad's bedroom pulled back ever so slightly, as Dad peeked around and nodded his head at his son in satisfaction.

Ten minutes passed, then five more. It was becoming lighter now. Smitty could see the surrounding houses clearly.

The door to the house catty-corner from Dad's opened, and the owner, Mrs. Hartman, the one with a face like a splattered bug on the windshield of a semi and a hot body that seemed to attract men like flies, came out in a transparent negligee, accompanied by her latest paramour, a handsome young stud who didn't seem to be much older than Smitty and whose mannerisms seemed strangely familiar. He stood under the cover of the four-foot roof overhang that covered the front porch, took her in his arms, and kissed her passionately, pulling her nightie up in the process and fondling her now-exposed butt in his hands.

He whispered something in her ear, causing her to smile coyly, drop to one knee, and unzip his pants. Obviously, they assumed they would be unobserved.

She began her oral ministrations and continued for several minutes until Smitty saw his shoulders tense as he muttered an unintelligible guttural sigh of satisfaction.

She immediately zipped him back up, kissed him lightly on the cheek, and waved enticingly as he started to walk shakily away. When he reached his car, he turned and blew her a kiss. She quickly raised her gown to her neck, then lowered it seductively. He started his car, and with a good-bye wave, departed.

Mrs. Hartman turned, and on reaching her door, held it wide open so that her dog, a collie and German shepherd mix, could exit for its early morning trip to its favorite tree in the front corner of the yard.

Someone else was watching also. On seeing the dog exit, Dad let the curtain fall back into place. Thirty seconds later, the front door was opened just enough for Dad to slip through. Dad stood on the front porch, holding the Australian terrier that Smitty had given to him after winning the dog in a crap game several years before.

Smitty could also see that the little pooch was encased in the full restraining body harness that Dad preferred to a simple collar leash. Anybody who's ever owned a terrier of any kind would appreciate the wisdom of this. Terriers are born with bedsprings in their asses, and this one was certainly no exception.

"Rover, go find Kevin. Rover, go find Kevin," Dad whispered, as he lowered the dog gently to the ground.

Rover bounded down the steps, yapping and bouncing excitedly in the direction of his favorite rubber-bone-throwing playmate.

The half-caste across the street heard it too. Despite Mrs. Hartman's urgent plea to stop, the dog came racing across the street, past Smitty's car, and into Dad's yard, making a beeline for his tenfold smaller adversary.

Just as the dog passed Smitty's car, Dad jerked the leash backwards, literally yanking poor Rover back into the house, then stooped and gathered him in his arms.

The big cur was now on the sidewalk directly in front of the door. Sensing the trap, he turned and was just starting to run, when Smitty's .357 shell found its mark. The mortally wounded dog pitched backward against the front steps and died.

Dad was right; it was a shot that called for a man of his particular talents. One second too soon, and, because of the upward angle of fire, Smitty would have struck his father; one second too late, and his quarry would have fled and been out of sight for a straight-on shot.

In the absolute stillness of the early morning neighborhood, the Magnum shell sounded like a howitzer discharging.

No sooner had the shot been fired than Dad winked, and quickly stepped back inside the house, silently shutting the door in the process.

Benny's bedroom light was already snapping on, and a light popped on at Mrs. Young's, as Smitty approached the mutt to assure it was dead.

"You motherfucking bastard," Mrs. Hartman screamed, as she came barrelling across the street at a dead run. "You motherfucking, cock-sucking bastard." She charged him like a toro on steroids, trying desperately to scratch and claw at his face in a totally out-of-control emotional outrage.

Smitty quickly tucked his pistol into the rear of his belt and prepared for the onslaught.

It was brief and basically nondestructive. Smitty slapped away her wildly raging claws, then punched her directly in the stomach, knocking the wind out of her and sending her spiraling to the ground where she settled with her head resting on her dead companion's shoulder.

"What happened here, Kevin?" Sergeant Benny approached wearing his uniform coat thrown hastily over his pajamas, his police .38 was in his hand.

"Well, I was just getting home from picking up my car after an incident at the docks last night that sent me to the hospital to get checked over . . . "

"Yeah, yeah, I heard about that on my way home last night. I'd just gone off duty and turned in my car, otherwise I would have been there," Benny said.

"I know you would," Smitty answered.

"Well, anyway, I just got home and got out of my car when, from out of the dark, the mongrel came charging at me, and I shot it in self defense."

"That's a motherfucking lie," Mrs. Hartman whimpered.

"Where's your firearm, son?" Benny asked.

"Right here." Smitty removed it from his belt and passed it across.

Benny opened the chamber, smelled it, and noted that there were two open chambers. "I assume, since you only fired once, that you carry it with the trigger chamber empty," Benny said.

"Absolutely. I don't want to accidentally drop it and shoot my foot off."

Benny nodded his head in satisfaction as he tucked Smitty's sidearm in his coat pocket. "You'll get it back after it's been tested," he said.

The front door was jerked open and Dad was standing there in his robe and slippers with his army .45 in his hand. "What happened? I heard what sounded like a gunshot."

Exhaling heavily, Benny said, "Your son killed the neighbor's dog. He said it tried to attack him. Even though he claims it was self-defense, I'm still going to have to arrest him for discharging a firearm illegally inside the city limits and for willful destruction of private property."

"That motherfucker murdered my dog. His father helped. He lured my pet into the yard using his own dog as bait." Mrs. Hartman sprang to her feet and pointed a bony finger accusingly at Smitty's dad.

"Mrs. Hartman," Sergeant Benny said, "I suggest you go home and put some clothes on. If you don't, I'll arrest you for indecent exposure."

"Fuck you all. You're all in on it. It's because none of you like me. The truth of the matter is you'd all like to get into my panties, but you're too pussy-whipped to ask." Mrs. Hartman gave them all the bird and stalked away muttering to herself.

"This isn't the end of this, Kevin. My boyfriend's father is a big man in this town. He's not afraid of your fucking Green Beret macho tactics," she called without turning around as she continued across the street.

She paused as the paper man went speeding by in his car delivering the morning news, and treated Kevin, Dad, and Benny to the site of her fully exposed butt as the wind from the auto blew her nightgown up once more.

"You know it ain't nice to say, but that dame's got a screw loose," Benny said, shaking his head.

"Naw, I think she's just a loose screw," Dad said.

The three of them laughed as she crossed the street, opened her door, and slammed it so hard she shattered the glass in the middle.

"I rest my case," Benny said. He turned to Kevin and said, "Look, partner, I don't like doing this, but I'm afraid I must.

"Son, I'm placing you under arrest for the charges specified. I assume you'll come along quietly," Benny said.

"No problem," Smitty said, obligingly holding out his hands.

"Well, we'll just stand right here and wait for the on-patrol officers to arrive, and then we'll head down downtown to fill out the paperwork."

"It looks like you have the situation in hand, officer, so I'll be going back to bed," Dad said innocently. "Call me, son, after they finish processing you and I'll come down and arrange your bail." Dad ascended the steps and closed the door.

After the door closed, Benny looked at Kevin. "Pardon me for saying so, but if you were my son, I'd be more concerned about you being arrested than to just go on back to bed."

"Oh, he is," Smitty said. "Dad just doesn't believe in running around waving his arms aimlessly and shouting forecasts of doom. He subscribes to a different theory."

"Which is?"

"Walk softly and call in an air strike."

"C'mon partner," Benny said, as the patrol car arrived. "Let's get you downtown and get this handled, so you can get home to bed. I know you've had a long night."

"And so, your honor, I'd like to again point out that the defendant has a long record of trouble with the law. This latest incident is only the last in a series of events that have dotted Mr. Smith's record his whole life.

"I, as well as society, demand that he be taught a lesson. The charges stemming from this latest escapade carry a possible sentence of one year in state prison. I ask that your honor sentence the defendant to the maximum penalty."

The slick-looking lawyer sat down amid a chorus of silence, excepting for Mrs. Hartman who thumped him on the back heartily. "Way to go honey. After we burn this little bastard in court today, I'm going to leave rug burns on your sexy buns tonight."

The lawyer shushed her irritably. Smitty was not sure whether he was more upset by her comment or more afraid of the consequences he'd face tonight.

The case had naturally made the front pages and all the local television news stories. The headline that Smitty thought was particularly imaginative was the one that said, "Ex-Green Beret graduates from college with father; celebrates by killing neighbor's dog." Because of the interest, and Smitty's impending departure from the state, the district attorney had requested an expedited process. The case was heard the following Thursday morning.

Smitty had hoped the case would be thrown out or dismissed. A personnel specialist from the company Smitty was planning to go to work for was sitting in the front row. In their brief conversation, he had made it perfectly clear that a conviction, no matter how unfair, would result in a withdrawal of the job offer.

Not for the first time, and Smitty suspected, certainly not the last, he was shaking his head in disgust and disappointment that despite the fact that his records were supposed to be sealed, with access granted only by special circumstances, it seemed like every time he tangled with someone, his past was brought up as the root cause. And not just subtly either; it was more like a Roman trumpeter blaring the arrival of Caesar. It was an all too constant reminder that until he found the source, he'd never be able to plug the leak.

The city ambulance chaser's case summation was filled with superlatives and bluff. Now it was Smitty's lawyer's turn.

"Your honor." Glen rose from his seat beside Smitty, buttoned his coat, and approached the bench. "Perhaps Mrs. Hartman would be happier if we just had Mr. Smith keelhauled."

The assembled courtroom gallery burst into laughter and scattered applause. This was quickly stopped by the judge's gavel, which he had to rap twice to get the room's attention. "Proceed."

"Your honor, since my learned colleague insists on constantly dragging up Mr. Smith's past as predicator for future punishment, then perhaps I should do the same.

"It has been pointed out, based on the previous testimony of eight witnesses, that Mrs. Hartman's dog had developed a taste for blood and had killed seven dogs in the neighborhood. Not to mention knocking a little girl off her bicycle, who would have been seriously harmed, if not for the intervention of Mr. Smith's father, who shooed the dog away with a garden rake, but not before it snapped at him, also.

"You've also heard how each time after the vicious attacks, the dog ran back in the owner's yard and how irate owners approached Mrs. Hartman, who steadfastly denied that her dog was the one causing the problem.

"Furthermore, you've heard how Mrs. Hartman used loopholes in the law to prevent the Humane Society from picking the dog up, and how the police were powerless to act unless they caught the dog in the act.

"So there is a precedent for the dog, which was let out every morning at about the time Mr. Smith got home from work, to suddenly attack and force Mr. Smith to, regrettably, kill the animal in self-defense."

"That's all a bunch of bullshit and my boyfriend Ricky can prove it," Mrs. Hartman said, suddenly jumping to her feet in outrage.

"Order," the judge pronounced, banging his gavel. The lawyer again shushed her to silence as he pulled urgently on her arm to get her to return to her seat.

"Your 'boyfriend,' Ricky, as you called him is the son of Mr. Richard Roberts, the senior partner of our largest legal firm in the area—is that correct?"

"Yes," she answered, low-voiced and sullen.

"What could the son of such a distinguished businessman add to this discussion, and perhaps more to the point, what was a young man in his twenties, married to a beautiful young lady the same age, doing on the front doorstep of another woman? A woman dressed in only a translucent nightgown. A woman who, according to Mr. Smith, was on her knees in front of him at six o'clock in the morning? I'm sure the judge would be most interested in that point, now that you've brought it up, Mrs. Hartman."

"So the fuck would I." Kristie stood up in the back of the room next to an unhappy Ricky, who was here only because of a subpoena, and was holding his head in his hands desperately wishing he were anywhere else.

When Ricky didn't answer, Kristie looked down at him. "You bastard, I must have been crazy to let your daddy pay my stepfather off for you and those frat rats gang-banging me. And I must have been even crazier for believing you when you said you'd changed and I agreed to marry you. I don't care if my stepfather does lose his cushy job with your daddy's company. You'll never touch me again, you psychotic asshole."

"Kristie, I can explain," Ricky said, rising to his feet.

"Explain this to your lawyer, you bastard." Kristie kneed him in the balls with all the force she could muster, nailed him across the face with a purse that looked like it weighed ten pounds, and stomped out of the courtroom to the accompaniment of hoots of laughter and cheers from the assembled audience.

Smitty, feeling no sympathy, watched her go. Years back, Kristie, or perhaps her stepfather, had made her choices. Smitty wasn't good enough for her. They wanted someone who could provide a ready-made life, not someone she could work together with to build one. Kristie had accepted the BBD. Only she was now paying for the path she had chosen.

Smitty had a feeling that the blow job Ricky had received from Mrs. Hartman might well turn out to be the most expensive head he ever got, after Kristie's lawyer got through with him.

"Order, order," the judge repeated. "One more outburst, and I'll have the courtroom cleared.

"Counselor, please continue."

"Well, that's all there is to it, your honor. My client was in fear of his life and fired in self-defense."

"Very well," the judge said. "I'll let the court stand in recess for ten minutes while I consider this," he said, as he banged his gavel hurriedly and seemed to be scurrying for the relative safety of his chambers.

During the recess, Dad, who had been keeping a low profile during the whole event, suddenly appeared with all of the neighbors who had suffered a loss. They took seats that Glen had apparently been saving for them, and waited patiently like everyone else for the judge to return.

Seven minutes later, he did. After the court was seated, the judge put on his glasses and began. "I have considered all of the evidence and have reached a conclusion—"

"Excuse me, your honor," Dad's longtime neighbor Jim said. "My neighbors and I were held up by traffic. Could you please tell us how much the fine is?"

"I haven't gotten to the verdict yet. Why is it a concern to you?" the judge asked suspiciously.

"Well I, um, that is to say, we . . ." he said, as he spread his arms, "the seven people, who lost our dogs, are here to pay the fine."

"But you don't know if there's going to be one or if there is how much it's going to be."

"Your honor, do you mind if I say something in my son's defense?"

The judge waved Dad up with an open palm. The look on his face said that he would not be surprised if a troupe of dancing bears showed up.

"Well, Judge, it's not true that this son of mine iced the lady's mutt because it attacked him. The fact is, I asked him to do it, which is another way of saying I talked him into it. I used my dog as a lure, just like Mrs. Hartman said, and yanked Rover back just in time for my boy to get a clear shot.

"Now don't that make you stop and think, Judge? That if my son was willing to risk everything just to do the right thing, well, isn't that what this country's all about? Have we become so entangled in legal pettifoggery that we have no room left for human judgment?

"All his life, my son has been in one scrape or another, mostly because he listened to his jackass father, who kept telling him to stand up for his principles, and do the right thing, rather than merely do what's right. That's what this case is really all about, isn't it?

"I think personal integrity and individual courage should count for something. I asked him to do it, but he made the decision of his own free will." Dad patted Smitty proudly and pointed his finger at the judge. "And if you don't know that, you're no judge."

The judge leaned forward and rested his head on his hand. "Mr. Smith, what would have happened if your son had shot you instead?"

"Your honor, my son is an excellent marksman. If my boy meant to kill me, then I'd be dead."

The judge looked at Smitty and asked, "Mr. Smith, if I let you go on this, how are you going to feel?"

"Unrepentant as hell," Smitty said.

The judge smiled at Smitty and shrugged his shoulders. "Frankly son, so would I. Case dismissed."

The judge's banging of his gavel was lost amid the shouts, backslapping, and whoops of delight from the assembled neighbors.

As Smitty was making his way from the courtroom, the representative from his future employer said, "We'll look forward to seeing you sometime around the first of July."

Smitty thanked him and promised to be on time.

As Smitty was driving home with Dad, he smiled, thinking how nice it was to have a father who could, when the occasion required it, call in an air strike for support, and when the circumstances warranted it, drop a neutron fucking bomb.

The remaining two weeks in Savannah passed without incident. Smitty made the rounds one last time, saying good-bye to friends who had helped along the way.

He stopped by to see Dad's doctor, concerned because he would be so far away, and was glad he did. Dad had started to complain lately of stomach pains and was taking antacids by the carton, in addition to the usual supply of nitroglycerin pills he took on a daily basis.

After the usual patient-doctor confidentiality line of crap, Smitty at least got him to confirm that Dad's heart, which had been his primary concern, was now in good shape. He had other concerns and discussed them with the youngish sawbones. Since he did confirm what Smitty had long suspected about Dad's health, he left the office in a much different mood.

There was one call he did not make, however. He turned down a last-minute call from his mom to come to a farewell party she was hosting, figuring that the party would go on with equal fervor whether the guest of honor was there or not.

Seven days before he was due to report in for his new job in New York, he began to pack his car and hitch up the Renault with the tow bar. Five days before, he departed with his dad, who'd agreed to ride along as far as his own father's house in Pennsylvania.

As Smitty gunned the powerful Chevy up the Talmadge Bridge headed north, he couldn't help thinking of the friends who had helped him get there, the friends he was leaving behind, and the friends who were no longer here.

Smitty could sense their presence and could almost see the Famous '54 heading in the other direction, just as it had on that fateful day almost seven years before.

Those ghosts and all the others would be with him, Smitty was sure, until he unraveled the mystery behind the person or persons responsible for creating their phantasmal form.

CHAPTER TWENTY-THREE

Smitty and his dad had left Savannah on schedule and, aside from one minor breakdown, rolled into Pennsylvania without incident. Smitty dropped off his father and, not knowing what he would be getting into in New York, stashed the Chevy in his grandfather's barn and drove the "Ragnault" on to New York to get the lay of the land.

Smitty arrived on Sunday the thirtieth and checked in to a nearby hotel for the night. He showed up at the personnel department promptly at 8:00 AM on Monday in his only suit and tie, spent the first two hours going over the company policies and the company rules, and filling out paperwork with a personnel specialist. One of the forms Smitty chose not to fill out was the Veterans' Disclosure Form. Dad had advised against it.

Dad's crystal ball must have been working overtime several years back when he'd "counseled" him on getting over Nam, and predicted what people would think of the war in the future. Vietnam veterans were now looked on with disdain and had become typecast as the avenging psychotic husband of the unfaithful wife, the raving madman just waiting to snap, or the deranged serial killer in just about every TV crime show or suspense movie.

The wisdom of Smitty's decision to close the book on the past was driven home to him when he met his new boss, who was not the person Smitty had interviewed with but to whom he had been assigned after the original manager was promoted to another job.

On reviewing his paperwork in their initial meeting, and noting that Smitty was twenty-four, he asked for an explanation of Smitty's late graduation from college.

Smitty replied evasively that he'd worked for a few years after high school to save up the money to go, which was the truth, just not the whole truth.

"That's good," his new boss, William-not-Bill, replied. "I was afraid you might have been in the military and that we'd hired some closet Vietnam veteran psycho like you see on TV, and we'd have to get rid of you."

Earlier in the morning, the personnel specialist had made a specific point of saying that the company's affirmative action program was second to none in the industry. But the reality was in the departments, where the real people worked and were managed on a day-to-day basis.

Smitty had learned his first lesson in corporate politics on his first day on the job. He harkened back to the wise counsel of General Wilson years before about never telling anyone anything that you don't want him to know. To which Smitty could now add a corollary: and later use against you.

He was assigned to a temporary cubicle with three other new hire engineers. One was a second-generation company employee whose father was a toolmaker in the machine shop. He seemed to come from the same blue collar environment as Smitty. The second was a nice guy from a Midwestern university who was rumored to be a Mensa member. The third was a loudmouth whose father was a senior manager.

The loudmouth seemed to make a point of letting everyone know his opinion on everything, including a rather effeminate-looking male new hire who had joined the department the week before. More than once, Smitty's ears had picked up the word "queer" in his description of him in his phone conversations with his former college frat buddies.

Smitty was cool to his new acquaintances, but it had nothing to do with their mannerisms. It had more to do with his own social inadequacy. Smitty had spent his life so far on two things: surviving his own youthful mistakes and trying to find out who or what was behind all the mysterious circumstances that seemed to be controlling his life. Whatever time was left over was more than used up eking out a living one day at a time.

He was ill-prepared for the social repartee that he could plainly see would be a fundamental requirement of this position. So, he had decided to "put a zipper in his lipper," observe, and emulate what seemed to work for others.

After three days, the next two days were holidays in observance of the Fourth. Smitty returned to Pennsylvania, where his dad had agreed to wait. On the four-hour drive back, Smitty had begun to cultivate a plan. What had worked with Sally might work with his father.

Over the seventh beer at the corner booth of the bar Dad had taken him to on his first leave from the Big Walter, Smitty began to execute the plan he had rehearsed over and over during his two-hundred-mile drive back to his ancestral home.

"Say, Pop, do you mind if I ask you something?" Smitty began.

"Fire away, troop." Like Sally's voice a month before, Dad's was already beginning to sound different.

"When I was a kid, I inadvertently listened in on you and Mom having an argument in Savannah before we shipped out for Dearfield. You said that if it wasn't for then-Colonel Martin's protection, you'd have been kicked out of the service a long time ago. I need you to tell me what he's protecting you from."

"I don't know what you're talking about," Dad said too quickly, averting his eyes.

He was on the right track. He could see it in his father's eyes. And Dad was totally ignoring the titsy young thing bending over with practiced ease as she served the drinks doing her dead-level best to attract his attention to her deep cleavage, in hopes of a tip to match her bra size.

"I'm talking about the fact that you feel indebted to the colonel, and I need to know why." Smitty hoped the mere shock of his knowing would pry open Dad's mouth.

"I still don't know what you're talking about," Dad said evasively. He took a long pull on his beer, then turned and held up two fingers. That was fine with Smitty. If his dad wanted to drink, Smitty surely wasn't going to stop him. Drunken lips divulge tips.

Smitty reached up, and not without some effort, turned his father's head back toward him. "Dad, I need you to talk to me about this. I need you to do it without asking why, and I need be sure that afterward, you'll talk to no one else about it." Smitty took a swig of his beer. "I emphasize—no one."

Dad folded his arms and glared at his son in silent defiance.

"Dad, our time is short and we may never have another chance. You need to trust me. I know it goes against your military background, but I need to know what this marker is. And I need you to tell me now!"

"In a word, NO!"

Thirty years of military decorum was a virtually impossible hurdle to overcome, but as Dad always said, you get bloody screwing a virgin, but even with the mess, it's a whole lot more satisfactory than trying to hump a rock. Smitty ordered two more beers, inhaled deeply, and waited.

Dad continued to stare at him coldly, but made no effort to get up and leave. Better than Smitty could have hoped. At least his curiosity was sufficiently piqued that he wasn't stomping out the door.

Dad reached for his tobacco pouch and pipe and began to fill it without looking at his son. Smitty knew from experience that meant that Dad was thinking and was just stalling for time.

Even though his dad was still seated, it was fifty-fifty that he'd get up, tell him to fuck off, and leave. A minute passed, then another in utter stillness as his father sat staring blankly at his offspring. If Smitty was a betting man, he'd be placing his money on successfully scoring with the untouched female, rather than Rock of Gibraltar there. You don't always play the odds, but it's usually the safest bet.

"I had to kill a man," Dad blurted out suddenly. "During World War II, I was part of a covert ops group known as Easy Does It. Because of the nature of these covert ops, we all were assigned code names, and had no clue as to each other's real identity. During one of those incursion missions, one of the team members was fixin' to rat us out to the Germans. I caught him red-handed with a letter naming all of the team members by name, with their rank and serial numbers, and offering to expose them publicly in return for one hundred thousand dollars American and safe passage to Switzerland, after the others were captured and executed. This would have exposed the Easy Does It structure and rendered the entire unit useless.

"I stashed the letter in my field pack. During our extraction, the letter was lost when I had to drop my pack when we made a run for it to the escape aircraft.

"After the mission, the details of his death surfaced, and since the hard evidence was gone, and I was the only one who knew the truth, the review board stated that, based on the evidence presented, the shooting was unjustified, and they court-martialed me for killing a superior officer.

"At the court, they found me guilty, and I was expecting to go down for twenty long in the Sunflower State at sentencing the next day. But the sentencing was postponed to the next day, then the next. On the third day, when I stood for sentencing, incredibly, the presiding judge stated that new evidence had surfaced that verified my version of the facts, that all charges were being dismissed, and my record was to be cleansed.

"Several days later I found out that Chuck had created a counterfeit letter that backed up my version of the events, and left it in the judge's chambers where it could be easily found."

"Why would Chuck go out on a limb like that?"

"Chuck said that he was certain that the man I killed was a Nazi double-agent, but he just couldn't prove it."

"I don't understand," Smitty said, "How the hell could he know that?

"Because the man I executed was Chuck's brother," Dad answered bluntly. "Chuck said he'd been under investigation for some time by the FBI. And he couldn't let me go down because of some bullshit technicality to save the reputation of a traitor, even if it was his own brother."

"Oh, Jesus," Smitty said. "No wonder you and the general are so close."

Smitty paused, lit a cigarette, blew out a big cloud of smoke, and added, "Pop, I'm sorry. Sorry that you had to do it, and sorry that I had to make you relive pain by telling me about it."

"Son, part of me wants to ask you why. Of all the things that happened on all those covert missions, why is this one point so important?" Dad tapped the pipe on the ashtray and refired. "But I'll not. In answer to your earlier challenge, I do trust you. I trust you enough that I'm not going to ask; and I trust you enough that I'm not going to talk."

Smitty looked at his father and held up his beer glass for a toast. "Here's to you, my friend. Thanks for being my dad."

"Good luck in your quest, troop. I hope you find what you're looking for." Then he added, "And aren't you glad now that I was a tough dad?"

Smitty smiled in response as they clinked glasses. He'd never felt closer to his father than at that moment.

Smitty wasn't sure that his pop had any idea why that point was so important to him. And it was far more important, he was sure, than his father could even begin to realize.

Years back in Miami, Smitty had told LZ and Frenchy that there were three people he had to get—the person who did the dirty work, the person who told him to do it, and person who told them where to look.

The first two parts of the puzzle were solved. The Neanderthal Keith, who did the dirty work, was dead, and so, too, was Detective Wallace, who was the mole in the police department, who was, in effect, telling them to do it. The person who told them where to look was harder to identify.

Smitty now had the edges and a good part of the jigsaw puzzle filled in, and the face in the center was becoming clearer all the time. All Smitty needed to do was wait for him to get paranoid enough to arrange a time and place to ambush him. Smitty would be waiting.

Smitty returned to New York the following Sunday evening. He hugged his dad, and drove away, noticing in his rearview mirror that his father was wiping away a tear from his eye.

The months that followed passed quickly. Smitty found himself a second floor walkup in a private home, ten miles or so from work, and settled into his new routine. In September, he was reassigned within the department to an engineering line support group that seemed to be more suited to his hands-on type of experience.

Smitty was sure that it was meant to be a punitive action for his speaking out at department meetings and voicing opinions different from those expressed by the majority—and his boss. Since it was a split-shift assignment, Smitty was forced to rotate between first and second shifts every two weeks.

Since things were a lot less hectic on second shift, particularly after ten, it gave Smitty a chance to wander the plant, learning the corridors and hallways of the mammoth facility until they were second nature.

Slowly, Smitty had overcome his nervous apprehension and had started to make friends and blend in. Except with his new boss, whom Smitty and three of his department peers, who seemed to come from the same blue-collar background as he, had christened "Jackass Jeff."

Mainly the moniker stuck because Jeffy had a habit of assigning to them the engineering problems requiring real work, and assigning to the others—who kissed up to him—the staff work that required reports that, from what Smitty could see, were never read. Smitty had quickly named the group the Four Musketeers, although he'd not bothered to inform them that this was the second time around for that distinguished name.

One of the four good guys, Smitty's officemate, was the effeminate programmer and the butt of the queer jokes of his macho colleagues—specifically the Italian kiss-up from his former department. Although he was excellent at his profession, he was a strange sort of loner, whom his boss could just barely tolerate. And like Smitty, he would have been gone in a moment, if it were not for the fact that he had excellent technical skills. Remembering the life lessons of Professor Strickland, Smitty went out of his way to spend time with him and try to cultivate his friendship.

An early snowstorm in the second week of November paralyzed the county, straining to the limit even the local snow emergency crews. Smitty remained at home on Friday as work was called off due to a county order requesting everyone, except emergency and snow-removal personnel, to stay off the icy roads.

The county mandate was to remain in effect until six o'clock that evening. Smitty had slept in, then frumped around the apartment, trading phone calls with work friends to pass the time until the 1800 hour deadline, then set off in search of something to eat. The pickings were slim. The only places that seemed to be open were the bars and the diners. Smitty opted for the latter; especially since he'd agreed to meet his cubemate later on for a cold one at a local gin joint across the river. They were set for 9:00 PM.

Smitty bought a paper, settled into a booth against the window, and ordered dinner. Suddenly he remembered that today was Sally's birthday, and made a mental note to call her when he got back to the apartment, then settled down to read. He was halfway through the sports section, when a dimness of the surrounding lighting caused him to glance up.

"Captain Simmons," Smitty said. The last time he'd seen her, she'd been an overly madeup blonde bombshell. He thought to himself how much better she looked as a fresh-faced brunette.

"Not anymore, it's just Claire, you big silly."

She pulled him to her for a hug.

"My God, they're real," Smitty said, echoing his words of many years before.

"Easy, Lieutenant, or this girl will be jumping you right here in the booth."

"How did you get here?" Smitty asked.

"Well, I'm a nurse at the hospital just down the road, and was starving for something to eat. So I guess like you, I just left my apartment and went looking for anything that was open. How about you?"

"I just started working in the area a couple of months ago after finishing college in Georgia," Smitty answered in a daze, still not sure that she was real.

"How long have you been in the area?" Smitty said, his voice tinged with doubt. He was getting over the shock fast, and as memories of their last meeting and the covert actions behind them started to flood into the forefront of his brain, Smitty was becoming more distant. He was suspicious.

"Oh, I've been working here since I got out of the army in '72. My aunt lives just a couple of miles from here, so I guess I just came home."

"What about your uncle?" Smitty said.

"Oh, they were divorced years ago when I was just a little tyke."

Smitty smirked. "Somehow the image of you as a flat-chested toddler in diapers seems as unfathomable as Betty Ford calling herself First Mama for the CB crowd."

"Speaking from a wet dream fantasy, no doubt."

"Memory," Smitty shot back.

"Well maybe you should take me back to your place and we'll see if reality is still as good as your reminiscence."

"Check," Smitty called out to the waitress.

They left the eatery together and Claire followed him in her Jeep Wagoneer back to his apartment.

"I've been waiting four years for this." Claire leaped into his arms almost before Smitty had the door closed.

Dad was right. When you meet your one true soul mate, the one you were supposed to be with, clothes are shed like a zippered snake skin. They hurriedly stripped each other bare and fell backwards on the bed, kissing and fondling one another passionately. First Smitty had explored her body with the ardor and giddiness of an archaeologist who'd just unearthed a lost pyramid, and then she was in the process of doing the same to him, when the phone rang.

"Let it ring, darling, I've waited too long for our postponed date," she said.

"I can't. It might be my father," Smitty answered, rolling off the bed.

"Cellmate," the caller said with difficulty. Cellmate was the recognition signal that Smitty and his office co-worker, the programmer, had for each other.

"What's wrong?" Smitty said, alarmed by the sound of his voice.

"I n-need you, man," he said.

"Where are you?"

"'Cross the river in a phone booth at the corner of Johnson and Seventh."

Smitty glanced down at the bed. Claire was slowly rocking seductively back and forth on her back, spreading her legs wide.

Smitty could hardly believe he'd found her again, and to even consider leaving her in the throes of passion like this was almost unthinkable.

But, as Pop always said, "Friendship is not about what you get, it's about what you give," and the litmus test is will you do the right thing in times of trial?

Smitty had been trying hard to cultivate his officemate's friendship, and although the timing of his call stank, he couldn't say no. That would be what an acquaintance would do. And if Claire were to become more than that, she'd understand.

"Cellmate, I'll be there in twenty minutes. You stay near there, and try to stay warm."

"Twenty minutes," he repeated quickly. "Thanks, man." He sounded relieved that help was on the way.

Smitty hung up the phone, turned to find Claire leaning seductively on one elbow, but with a look of worry, not passion on her face.

"What's up, hon?" she asked, concerned.

"A friend of mine's in trouble and needs help. I told him I'd be there in twenty minutes." Glancing down at the luscious naked woman in his bed, he sighed, shaking his head in dejection as he started to dress and added morosely, "And you don't know how sorry I am to be leaving you."

"I'll come with you." Claire hopped up from the bed, stepped into her slacks without underwear, pulled on the heart-stopping sweater and fluffed her hair. "Let's take my car. It'll be better in the snow." She added suggestively, "We can finish this later."

No whining about him leaving, no stalling while she freshened her makeup, and no bitching about an evening interrupted. Just jump into your clothes and go. Claire was obviously a girl who had the innate common sense to make quick decisions and focus on what was important. Smitty was impressed with the fact that such a ravishing creature was, apparently, so low maintenance.

They quickly put on their overcoats and started for the door. On the way, Smitty reached behind the dresser, and removed his .357 with the belt clip, a speed loader with six additional rounds, and the repaired Brooklyn special. He shoved the blackjack in his rear pocket, then attached the pistol to rear belt, and deposited the extra six rounds in the left jacket pocket.

"Even here?" Claire said.

"Especially here," Smitty said firmly, closing the door behind them.

"Claire, you need to talk to me," Smitty said, as the car turned onto the bridge across the river.

Her hospital explanation as a reason for bumping into him was too real to be contrived. Now that the unbridled passion had passed—unfortunately unfulfilled—the reality of her mysterious appearance here and disappearance from the Big Walter was quickly taking over more of Smitty's conscious thoughts. Before they started picking out matching towels, Smitty had to know what her role was back then, why she was doing it, and who she was doing it for, then determine if what she told him was the truth.

"I know. I owe you an explanation for Reed," she answered. "You want to know what my job was, and who was I working for, correct?"

"Exactly." Smitty lit a cigarette, blew out a cloud of smoke that hung in the frosty air. "And why."

"I was assigned to a secret department of the army called the Special Justice Section—or SJS for short. They deal with the threat of acts of treason and terrorism against the United States government by infiltrating their ranks, obtaining the plans, and taking preemptive measures . . . if you get my drift?"

Smitty got it all right. It meant that suspected enemies of the government that were planning acts of harm accidentally slipped on a bar of soap in the shower. Smitty wondered idly who the judge was for what constituted an act of harm, and perhaps more important, who was the arbitrator to assure that it did not get out of control.

"My assignments required that I infiltrate specified targets, ingratiate myself with them to the point that they trust me, get them to open up to me, then report my findings back to my superiors."

She paused. The what seemed pretty logical. Hell, Smitty had sort of done the same kind of thing in Nam. But, obviously now that the what was out of the way, Smitty suspected she was coming to the why and, more importantly, the who.

"Now comes the hard part," Claire said, the corners of her mouth tightening in a nervous smile.

"My specific assignment at Walter Reed was you. I was 'loaned' to the Surgeon General's office because they needed someone who had practical experience as a nurse, and was easy on the eyes. Since I have a nursing degree, and was a nurse for one tour in Nam before joining the SJS, I had the appropriate technical requirements." She lowered her head and smiled demurely as her cheeks began to color. "And since I started wearing a training bra at eight, they figured I had the rest of the requirements that fit the bill, also.

"I was ordered to go heavy on the mascara and red lipstick, dye my hair that ridiculous blonde color, and wear uniforms a size too small. Then they had me posted to the hospital and arranged it so that I was assigned to you.

"My specific assignment was to gather information on you, your habits, your dreams, your weaknesses, or anything else. I was told to report anything and everything. I was not told why." Claire paused. "And, believe me, I asked."

"I guess I just assumed that you were some sort of spy who had passed information on to the enemy in Vietnam for money, and that I was to do whatever was required to get it out of you."

Seeing Smitty's sharp glance, she winced. "Yes, seducing you was part of my assignment if that's what it took to get you to talk."

"Fuuuuck," Smitty said in a disgusted voice. He rolled down the window, and thumped his cigarette over the rail of the bridge.

Smitty wondered idly if, in fact, the democratic form of government really was nothing more than a hollow shell where men of power existed clandestinely within the framework, manipulating, and killing at will for their own personal gain.

Were there other monsters out there in the lake, or was Nessie the only one? The analogy of the Loch seemed most appropriate, since sighters of the infamous creature were quickly scorned and branded as having a vivid imagination, at the very least, or as crackpots. Based on what Smitty could piece together to date, it would be naïve to assume he was chasing the only ogre in the lake. Others must see it, too. What other possible reason could there be for Sam, and Chuck, and Jim, and Stan to agree to help him in his quest? Maybe they did it on orders, maybe they did it because they were all searching for the same demon, or maybe they did it because they were trying to keep him going in circles, because he was getting too close.

"Who ordered it?" Smitty said bluntly.

"I don't know. Although, technically, I reported to a colonel in the SG's office, my assignment orders came from a phone booth a block from the hospital. I called in once a week and reported what I had. They listened, and curiously, never made any comment, except to say keep up the observation, then hung up."

"Why did you leave so suddenly?"

"I received a call at my apartment at 1:30 AM on the night you were supposed to come over but didn't show up. I was told that I was being disengaged from the assignment immediately. I was to have no further contact with you, pack, and be ready for transport in one hour.

"I was picked up in one of those tan government vans with no windows that say U.S. Government Inter-Agency Pool on them, and told that I had failed to discover the right information in the allotted time frame and, as such, was being returned to general nursing duties. I was driven to Andrews Air Force Base, put on a plane, and thirty-six hours later, I was in the middle of the shit at an aid station in Nam.

"Before I was dumped at the airport, I was told by a guy wearing a mask that, under threat of being court-martialed for treason myself, I was never to contact you again. But, despite that, when I returned from Nam in early 1972, I did try to make discreet inquiries about you when I was stationed at Benning.

"Two days later, a major showed up, said he was your commander in Nam, and that you'd been killed on a mission into Laos in late 1971. When I asked how, he told me the mission details were classified, and that, as a result of my request, I had violated the National Secrets Act and he gave me two choices: I could voluntarily leave the army quietly as a captain with an honorable discharge and my records classified or as a private and a year in Leavenworth with a dishonorable following a general court-martial for treason. He scared me so badly that I agreed to the voluntary discharge. Three days later, I was out-processed, handed a piece of paper that said honorable discharge on it, and escorted off the post.

"The next morning, I received a call at my apartment before I left town informing me that my records had been sealed, and that the army would deny that I'd ever served or even existed."

Smitty lit another cigarette and tried to think. He could sense the truth in Claire's voice. Her army career had been short-circuited, and her records shredded, and like Smitty, she had been used as a cog to turn the bigger wheel. By whom?

"What was your contact code word?"

"Anastasia," Claire answered innocently.

"That's kind of a unique word," Smitty answered calmly. Inside his brain was screaming, *What the fuck!*

Nevertheless, Smitty kept his emotions under control. Ironically, it was Aunt Belinda's rule number three that saved him.

Smitty smiled quietly to himself as he remembered the lecture, and the appropriate actions that could best be summed up by General Wilson's Handbook for Spies, golden rule number three: "Sometimes you gotta take one to the choppers without flinching and never let them see how much it hurt."

"Hmm, same thing happened to me," Smitty said, thinking out loud. "My dad and General Wilson are tied into this also. When I talked to my pop the other day by phone, he told me that when I come home for Thanksgiving, we were going to sit down and chat about some of the mysterious circumstances that seem to keep occurring in my life." Smitty paused, and said, "Maybe yours and mine are intertwined."

"I hope so." Claire blushed and said, "I can't wait to be intertwined with you."

"Anything else?" Smitty asked.

"There's just one more thing," she said softly.

"What?"

"I fell in love with you," Claire answered.

As the car turned onto Seventh, Smitty stroked her chin and smiled, "I'm glad; I think I did, too."

Much later, Claire would get a practical demonstration of the good general's third order; but not before Sammy boy learned about it firsthand from Smitty, at a time of Smitty's choosing.

"Cellmate, Cellmate where are you?" Smitty called out quietly.

Claire had pulled to a stop right in front of the phone booth. He'd found a lot of blood on the receiver, but his work comrade was nowhere to be found. Smitty searched the surrounded area for thirty yards in a circular direction, but he simply wasn't there. Smitty and Claire expanded their search, going in opposite directions, Smitty up the street, Claire down, with no luck. Whatever the emergency, they may have been too late.

Claire waved urgently from two hundred yards down the street. Smitty ran as fast as the treacherous footing would allow, and joined Claire at the entrance to an alley beside a furniture store. The alley was dark and littered with trash, boxes, and miscellaneous pieces of pipe and wood. It was an ideal place to ambush someone in the light of day, or dispose of a perfectly good human being in the dark of night.

From out of the darkness, Smitty could hear moaning. Someone was in pain, someone might be dying, and Smitty had that sick feeling in his gut that someone was his friend.

Using the flashlight Claire had brought with her, they cautiously proceeded down the alley for thirty yards. The moaning became louder. There was a blood trail that led to a pile of boxes next to a dumpster. Two feet, wearing fashionable cowboy boots, could be seen sticking out from under the heap. Smitty knew those boots. They were the ones his friend wore to work all the time.

Gently, but rapidly, Smitty removed the boxes that had been hastily thrown over him.

He had been badly beaten up. His face was a swollen mass of bruises, his shirt was torn completely off, and the tears on his pants were evidence that he'd been dragged to his present location and dumped like a basket of laundry thrown haphazardly on the spare bed to be sorted at some other time.

Then Smitty saw it. On his chest, someone had carved the letters FAG with a knife. Once more Smitty had to remember Sam's rule number three, lest he lose control and do something stupid like punch the wall.

Claire pushed Smitty out of the way and immediately began to attend to the wounds with practiced ease. Along with the flashlight, she had brought along a first-aid kit that contained an assortment of ointments and bandages.

Working quickly, she bandaged the cuts and stopped most of the bleeding within five minutes.

"I've done everything I can, but we need to get him to a hospital." Claire said. "I know he's got at least two broken ribs, and those cuts are going to require stitches to close."

"No," Cellmate whispered hoarsely. "No, no hospital, they'll ask too many questions."

"We have to get him to a doctor, hon." Claire grabbed Smitty's arm. "He's lost a lot of blood and needs a transfusion or he'll die."

Smitty tuned her out to think. They had to get him to a hospital all right, but the cops would ask pointed questions about that stenciling on his chest, pointed questions that most certainly would cost him his job at work.

"You stay with him, I'll be right back." Smitty ran back down the alley and sprinted to the phone booth a block away and made a call.

Smitty was gone only five minutes, but that was enough. Voices in the alley caused him to stop before rounding the corner.

There were three of them, from the sounds, and from the volume, it was obvious that they were drunk. But not so drunk that they'd not set a trap, which Smitty had left Claire in without protection.

Cursing himself for not leaving her his weapon, he began to advance soundlessly behind them.

"Hey, man, a bonus. First we get to beat the shit out of the queer, then we get to bang his sister when she comes to pick him up," the man in the front said menacingly, as he grabbed his crotch.

Smitty assumed from the remark that Cellmate must have told them his call was to his sister for pickup when they caught him, apparently, while he was dialing for assistance from the phone booth.

Seeing Smitty, and knowing a distraction was required, Claire responded in an outraged voice, "I don't think so, scumwad. It takes a real man to handle these, not some insecure little boy who has to beat up a homo to make himself feel important." She unzipped her coat and yanked her sweater up, exposed her bountiful breasts, then added, "These are man toys; insecure little boys need not apply."

They licked their lips in anticipation. Smitty didn't have to worry about being quiet now; he could have marched in like a brass band and they wouldn't have noticed. They were so focused on her that a building could have fallen down right beside them and they wouldn't have even flinched.

"I can't wait to get me some of that," the third man said, stepping forward and, like his leader, grabbing his crotch.

"Oh, yes you can," Smitty said, as he laid him out with a blow to the back of the head from the sap. The second man turned and caught the barrel of Smitty's .357 across the bridge of his nose with a vicious swipe that assured that he'd be spending just about as long in dreamland as his friend; except when he woke up, he'd require a nose job.

That left only the leader. A hollow click, one that Smitty had committed to memory long ago on the west side of Miami, halted Smitty's advance. Even in the semi-darkness of the alley, the switchblade gleamed evilly.

"Back off, asshole," he said, waving the blade wildly back and forth.

"Asshole, you don't know me well enough to call me asshole." Smitty pulled the hammer back on the Magnum, making an equally loud, deadlier click, and remembering with a smile, that he'd used that line before, under distinctly similar circumstances.

The leader dropped the knife. "Hey, man, no need to get upset. It's just some queer."

"Well, asshole, like I said once before in a similar circumstance, I may not agree with his lifestyle, but I'll defend it to the death." Smitty brought the pistol to bear and applied the same treatment that he had to bachelor number two.

The leader landed face-up in the snow. Claire approached and applied the finishing touch, a well-placed kick to the balls. The force of the blow caused the man to convulse involuntarily in pain, unconscious though he was.

"Bastards," she said, as she walked back to Smitty's friend.

Smitty's mind was racing. They needed to do three things, and they needed to do them immediately. They needed to get Cellmate treatment without leaving a blood trail, they needed to get out of here without being seen, and they needed to sanitize the area to leave no trace of their passing. He added a fourth: they needed to assign blame so nothing could be traced back to them.

"Claire, go bring your car up but don't come in the alley. Make a U-turn and park across the street. Signal me when the coast is clear, and I'll carry Cellmate to you."

The first part went smoothly. Inside of two minutes and they had him safely laid across the backseat and resting as comfortably as possible. As long again, and they had policed the area using a cardboard box to carry away scoops of blood-stained snow, pieces of torn clothing, and wrappers from the bandages. A torn-off piece of the lid was used to rake the snow back and forth to erase their footprints, smooth out the snow and leave no trace of their passing; but not before Smitty used the leader's blade to leave both a little departing memento and a pointer to who did it.

They waited until no other cars were visible on the street and drove away, not turning on the lights until they had turned right onto Ninth Street.

The rescue was a sign that meant Smitty's past had reared its ugly head once more; and once more, Smitty had managed to get off with a glancing blow.

The test case of the general's third rule had been implemented. The practical application of it was, in effect, a check yet to be cashed.

"How is he, Doc?" Dr. Evans emerged from the treatment room at the Veterans Center wiping his hands on a towel.

"He'll be all right. It will take some time for those knife wounds to heal, and even then, without plastic surgery, there'll still be scars." He shivered to himself involuntarily. "I'd sure like to get the bastards who did this under my scalpel for a few minutes and put my signature on them."

"What does the term artificial insemination mean to you, doc?" Smitty said.

The doctor looked without expression, smiled, nodded his head slowly in understanding, and stuck out his hand.

"You're welcome." Claire stepped in front of Smitty, shook his hand, and smiled mischievously.

"My girl, the pecker punter." Smitty put his arm around Claire and gave her shoulder an affectionate pat.

"Ouch." Dr. Evans grimaced. "I take that to mean that between the two of you, you managed to extract a fair measure of retribution?"

"And maybe a little more than that," Smitty said.

"They are still alive, aren't they?"

"Yeah, but by the time this is over, they may wish they weren't," Smitty said with a mysterious grin.

"Well, look, I have to go take care of my patient, a Mr. Kevin Smith—one of those deranged Vietnam veterans like you read about in the paper who tried to kill himself by running his car off the road—as you know.

"So you two get out of here and get on back to what you were doing." He paused. "On a night like this, I hope it was humping each other's brains out."

"Sounds like a plan," Smitty said.

"It sounds like a certainty," Claire corrected.

"Um, Lieutenant, could I have a quick word with you privately before you go?"

"I'll go warm up the car," Claire said.

Smitty joined her five minutes later. As he closed the door, he said, "Back to my place driver, and don't spare the horses."

Claire slammed the car into gear, stomped on the gas, and with tires spinning in the snow fighting for traction, they were moving. They had driven in silence for five minutes when Claire suddenly swerved to the side of the road and stopped. She turned and faced Smitty. "Look, buster there's something you and I had better get straight right now. I helped you tonight. I knowingly aided and abetted in the commission of a crime and the cover-up."

"Yeah, so?" Smitty wondered to himself if she wanted a medal or a gold-plated brassiere or something like that.

"So, that makes me an even partner, not some oversexed schoolgirl caught in the backseat at the drive-in to be dismissed and sent to her room while the adults talk in private with the cop in the living room. Get it?"

Smitty smiled, and said, "Yes, I do. I'm sorry. You see, the doc was the one who tipped me off to you when I was at Reed. Called you a Mata Hari as I recall. He was somewhat surprised when you showed up with me as, you'll forgive the expression, one of the good guys, and just wanted to understand our relationship. That's all." As he said it, Smitty elevated the doc up a notch on his dependable list. Obviously, he'd heard of the general's third rule also.

"Oh," she said. "And what did you tell him?"

"That you were just some piece of ass I picked up for the night," Smitty said.

To her angry glare, Smitty added, "That I would dispose of in fifty or sixty years," Smitty said, grinning, "if she didn't treat me right."

"You should live so long," she said, as she pulled back on the road.

"You're right about that," Smitty said. "You surely are right about that," he repeated in a voice she did not hear.

A queer bashing in the little sleepy upstate one industry town like this was big news, and the local paper, made the most of this prophecy. With the banner headline, "Friend's Propositioning of Friends Has Dire Consequences," the story and the related sidelines occupied most of the front page.

It told in lurid detail how three friends started out for a night of friendly drinking and carousing, and how it ended tragically when one friend propositioned the others, and a fight ensued in which all three suffered injuries.

According to police reports, the scuffle took place in a dark alley when one of the members, his courage buoyed by alcohol, propositioned another. His former friend kicked him in the groin in disgust, and, in fear of his life, the propositioner hit him across the face with a metal bourbon flask from which they had all been drinking, then dropped it. Police theorized that the third man tried to run, and that he was laid out by the first with a length of pipe found with his fingerprints on it near by.

The police believed the second man, recovering consciousness, picked up the flask, and hit the first with it. Then he pulled a switchblade knife and carved the word "queer" on the unconscious man's chest before himself passing out. The knife was found in his unconscious hands.

The three defendants steadfastly denied these accusations, stating that they were propositioned by "some homo," and were in the process of giving him what "those kind of people deserve," when they were viciously attacked by his sister and her husband, beaten up, then set up and framed.

Police Chief Dawson scoffed at this. "This here boy just got liquored up enough that his inhibitions freed up and the other college boys didn't like it."

"Besides," he added, "if they were the victims here, they had a knife, a piece of pipe and lots of loose two-by-fours to defend themselves. Not too many people I know could have walked away without injuries from taking on three armed men.

"But, just to be sure, we did make the rounds of all the local hospitals. But no one with the kind of injuries they said they supposedly inflicted was admitted for treatment," he finished, rolling his eyes in disbelief.

"Say, Kevin. You busy at lunchtime?" Kevin's boss, Jeff, walked into Kevin's office and dropped casually into Cellmate's chair.

"No, why?" Smitty looked up from his latest engineering change project for a tester on the manufacturing line.

"Well, your officemate called in this morning. Seems he wrecked his car over the weekend and is pretty banged up. He's going to be out of work for several days and is staying with his 'girlfriend.' He wanted me to bring some computer printouts over for him to work on. He said you would know what they were, so I thought you might like to accompany me when I go visit him at lunchtime."

"No problem," Smitty said. "I'll round up the stuff and be ready to go by twelve."

"Good." Jeff got up to leave the office, then leaned back in around the door frame. "I'll be interested to see what kind of 'girlfriend' he has. To tell you the truth, I always thought he was one of those, myself."

He left before Smitty could reply.

"Hi, I'm Claire, Johnny's girlfriend." Claire opened the door to Johnny's apartment barefooted, dressed in tight fitting black slacks and a white scoop-necked sweater that accentuated the fullness of her breasts.

"I'm, uh, that is to say, I'm Mr. Johnson, but you can, uh, you can call me Jeff," Smitty's boss managed to stammer as he desperately tried to recover his composure and drag his eyes away from Claire's chest.

"Oh, yes, Johnny has spoken of you often. Please come in," Claire said, shaking his hand politely. "Johnny's in our bedroom." She led the way down the hall.

As they entered the room, Smitty could see his boss's eyes dart back and forth from Claire's sexy nightie left lying casually on the dresser, to Johnny's pants and shirt, left hanging over a chair by the door.

Cellmate himself was altogether a separate point of interest. By the light of day, he didn't look too bad; not any worse than if he'd gotten into a head-on collision with a bulldozer. He was bruised but smiling in his pajamas as his boss entered.

"Thank you so much for coming, boss. The doctor says I'm going to be a little sore for the next few days, so I don't think you'll see me until next Monday or maybe a little later."

"No problem," Jeff said. "Take whatever time you need. What happened?"

"I was following Claire home Friday, and I guess I tried to imitate the maneuvers of her four-wheel-drive Jeep, lost control, skidded across the road down into a gully, and flipped over. Claire fished me out and brought me home. Her father is a doctor, so he stopped by, checked me over, gave me a prescription for pain, and told me to stay in bed for the next week or so."

Such accidents were so commonplace in icy conditions that they didn't raise any eyebrows. In fact, Smitty was sure that there were probably fifty or so in the past few days of near whiteout conditions.

And Cellmate's story was verifiable. In the early morning hours of Saturday, Smitty and Claire had retrieved Cellmate's car from across the river and driven it to a spot a mile from Cellmate's apartment. They put it in gear at an ice-slicked corner, and watched as it slid down into a gully, landed nose first at the bottom, then flipped on its side; the police had found it Sunday morning

Johnny brightened and looked up at Smitty. "Hey, Cellmate, thanks for bringing my printouts. Hopefully I'll have time to look at them." He looked roguishly at Claire, who batted her eyes affectionately in return.

"No problem." Smitty laid them on the bed.

Jeff exchanged pleasantries with Johnny for the next several minutes, but his eyes were constantly darting to Claire, who had sat down quietly on the bed next to her boyfriend and was stroking his forehead softly and intentionally leaning forward to give Jeffy a clear view of the Valley of the Dolls.

"Well, look, I better let you get some rest." Jeff slowly backed out of the bedroom, never taking his eyes off Claire. "Take care, and we'll see you soon."

Claire walked them to the door. With polite good-byes, Jeff and Smitty soon departed.

When they were back inside Jeff's car and driving the short distance back to work, Jeff whistled softly to himself. "Kevin, do you know why I wanted to have you accompany me?"

"No."

"You know that disgusting business in the paper?" Smitty's nodded. "Well, I got a call from the police. That faggot with the word queer stenciled on his chest is the son of our general manager. Obviously, in an attempt to shift the blame from himself, he told the police that the guy who propositioned them was John. They asked me to kind of check it out on the QT and report back to them. I wanted you along as a witness."

"So, what are you going to tell them?"

"Are you kidding?" he asked. "That chick makes the Playboy Playmate of the Year look like a ten-year-old in her first training bra. Man, if my wife looked like that, I'd keep her under lock and key and guarded twenty-four hours a day by a Navy Seal team."

He winked at Smitty conspiratorially. "I bet you wish she was your woman. I'll bet she could turn a man every way but loose."

"I'll bet you're right," Smitty said. "I'll bet you she could."

And sometime in the very near future, Smitty hoped he would get the chance to prove it.

The rain was beating down incessantly in a steady, bone-soaking chill that even numerous layers of clothing could not seem to warm. The tears would come later. Right now Smitty felt only anger—anger that he was not here at the end, anger that he'd not seen it coming, and anger that he'd not been able to do anything to stop it.

A young airman first class made a less than perfect attempt at playing Taps. At the conclusion, the honor guard of military pallbearers folded the flag into a triangle and handed it to the officer in charge, who handed it off to the widow, who had tears streaming down her face.

"This flag is presented to you on behalf of a grateful nation." He saluted in slow motion and slowly walked back to the grave.

The honor guard raised their rifles and fired three times, then assumed a parade rest position. That was the final act in the military honors funeral procession.

Awkwardly, each not wanting to be the first, people who were seated stood and began to shake the hands of those around them. Those standing behind offered sympathetic words, handshakes, hugs, and gestures. At these times, faced with their own mortality, people grope for answers and band together in mutual support and fear of the unknown.

Military funerals are especially solemn. At the viewing, the Ol' Sarge looked sharp in his military dress uniform. With eleven rows of combat decorations and other uniform insignia, you'd swear he was a general, until you looked at the stripes on the sleeve. Each one was a testament to a hitch served in multiple places, and a reward for multiple dangers survived. Smitty stood, ran his hand over the top of the casket, and said lovingly, "Good-bye, old friend."

The procession wound its way slowly back to the waiting limousine and the line of cars that had followed from the funeral home. The uniform that Smitty had not had on in over four years felt cumbersome and unwieldy but, as newly promoted three-star General Wilson had said, "It's the least you can do for the Ol' Sarge."

The people who knew Smitty only as a civilian, mostly friends that Smitty had made since the war, stared at him and all the chest confetti throughout the entire procession. Even the local sales manager sent by Smitty's New York employer was unable to contain his inquisitive nature, saying haughtily, "I wasn't aware you were ever in the service, much less in Vietnam. I was led to believe you were a new hire straight out of college."

"This uniform paid for my college," Smitty responded curtly. His terse response was in part due to the circumstances, in part to the man himself.

He looked to be the perfect picture of a white-collar manager. Expensive three-piece dark blue suit, dark blue tie, immaculate white shirt, polished wingtips, perfect manicure and mannerisms. But his pleasant smile was not able to hide his true feelings for the military or those schmucks stupid enough to serve in the great Asian Vacation.

In uniform, Smitty obviously looked as strange to them as he felt. He found himself glancing down occasionally at his own shoulders, staring at the captain's bars that the general had pinned on once he saw him. "You never knew this," the general said, "but I had your inactive rank advanced to captain. I felt it was the least I could do for the royal butt-fucking you got from your own government."

The limo started and headed back to town. It would be a lengthy ride, which meant Smitty had a long time to think—of the circumstances that had surrounded the death, and perhaps more importantly, to think of a way to exact revenge.

Funerals seem to bring out the best and the worst in people. Unfortunately, in this case, there had been a little of both.

The worst had come four days ago, the evening after Smitty and his boss paid Johnny a visit, with a phone call that came, as bad news always does, at 1:30 in the morning.

Smitty's father had died of a heart attack at 12:30 AM.

The attack was very sudden. Dad and Sally had been out to a late movie, and he had just finished showering and had laid down on the bed to wait while Sally showered. Fifteen minutes later when she came out, he was gone.

At first, she thought he had just fallen asleep. But he was cold when she touched him. Sally called next door for Benny, who called the paramedics, but it was already too late.

In that darkest hour of Smitty's life, the best occurred also. Smitty called Claire immediately. She climbed into her trusty Jeep and drove twenty miles through the blinding snow to be with him, then insisted on driving him the ninety miles for his flight from LaGuardia.

As she was kissing him good-bye, she informed him that she would be on the evening flight later that day, as soon as she could make arrangements for a colleague to watch Cellmate. To Smitty's grateful acknowledgment, she had remarked, "It's the most natural thing in the world for a woman who has a fifty-year lease on her man to come and take care of him."

The flight home had been the longest of Smitty's life. Without meaning to, Smitty relived the last phone call he'd had with his father on the day after Sally's birthday.

Dad had told him that he was feeling well and was in such good health that the local banker had given him regular insurance on the new car he'd just bought, so that if he died before the loan was repaid, the car would be paid off by the insurer. According to Pop, he did it solely because Dad looked so fit, so hale, so hearty, and so alive.

That's what made the heart attack so strange. General Chuck was there just two days before Dad's death and also said that he'd never seen him look better when they'd been out to dinner and had a few beers, hoisting one to Smitty in absentia.

Smitty thought, too, of the life lessons Dad had instilled in him through his rigorous set of standards, his high ideals, and his single-minded focus on being a father first and a friend second. Did other fathers act that way? Smitty suspected not.

Dad had always said that raising kids was like planting corn: if the seed is not properly cultivated, your crop will not turn out like you want—and you're stuck with what you have, because it's too late to make corrections. How many times—a hundred probably—had he listened as his dad pointed out the fact that if you can't control your kids at six, you got no fucking chance at sixteen? Dad was right there, as his brother was living testament.

One thing Smitty would always remember was Dad's statement in his teenage years that he needed to be more concerned with the consequences for breaking his rules than with the ridicule of his peers for not going along with the crowd. Or, as Dad would always counsel, any breaking of the rules and Smitty would regret it to his dying day—if he lived that long.

Idly, his mind strayed to that fateful flight home from Vietnam years before; only this time, there would be no miraculous happy ending. But Smitty consoled himself by focusing on the better times, better times that would surely have to be enough because there would be no more.

When he'd reached the house, chaos reigned. Sally was crying uncontrollably, and Leslie was trying desperately to get her husband to act like the responsible older brother and take charge, but such was not Billy's makings.

Sensing this, Smitty slowly, gently, began giving Billy tasks to complete without making it obvious. By the end of the day, without ruffling feathers, all the arrangements had been made, and Billy was comfortable acting as the official meeter and greeter for the host of relatives and friends who were streaming in both by car and plane.

Smitty had the unpleasant task of going into his father's bedroom and removing his wallet and other personal items from the clothes he was wearing the day he died, and getting his last uniform out for burial.

As he searched the jacket pockets, he found Dad's bottle of nitroglycerin pills. Absently, he slipped the bottle into his pocket.

Claire was the last to arrive on a flight that got in around midnight. It was a thirty-minute drive to the airport, but Smitty left at 8:00 PM and made a stop at the funeral home along the way. There would be no autopsy because his father had died at home of natural causes, but Smitty needed to be sure.

With great trepidation, he'd used his code word with Aunt Belinda, from a phone booth, just before he boarded the plane in New York.

Sergeant Mike was waiting, along with Stan the Man, Major Jim, and Dr. Evans. They spent the next three hours in the building. For part of it, they assisted Dr. Evans, when needed, in attending to his duties, while exchanging stories to ease the discomfort that comes with the sacred rites of death. For the balance of the time, they tried in vain to comfort Smitty, based on what Doctor Evans had found.

During the course of this, Smitty discovered the bottle of pills that he'd stashed in his pocket, intent on disposing of them.

The colonel opened them, sniffed, and slid them in his pocket, promising to dispose of them properly.

Smitty left them at 11:30 PM to pick up Claire. They went to a hotel room instead of back to Dad's house to sleep, but they did not make love. His favorite uncle, who they called "Uncle Deadstick," for obvious reasons, said that his aunt liked kissing and hugging just as much. Sometimes a warm caress and a comforting partner to snuggle with can be more satisfying than great sex. This was one of those times.

They'd not yet had the time or the place to consummate their relationship. But Smitty wasn't worried. Besides, as Claire had said, she had a fifty-year lease on her man; they had plenty of time to get around to that.

"Penny for your thoughts?" Sally laid a hand on Smitty's arm as the limo sped down the interstate toward Dad's house, interrupting his musings.

"Oh, I was just thinking how if Pop was here, he'd have had that airman's ass for screwing up Taps."

Sally laughed in spite of herself. "How come you always know how to make a girl laugh?"

Smitty looked directly into her eyes. "Probably because I've made so many others cry."

Well, it looks like you found a keeper now." Sally reached across the limo and patted Claire on the knee.

"Thank you, Mrs. Smith. I'm fond of you, also," Claire responded politely.

When the limo dropped them at the house, Smitty went quickly inside, dialed Cellmate, and talked briefly with him just to check in. He seemed to be in good spirits, due mainly to the excellent treatment he'd received while masquerading as Smitty in the VA hospital for two days. That, and the fact that he was giddy with excitement at the latest news item in the local paper. Coming on the heels of the recent sensationalized news story, it almost seemed anticlimactic.

The banner headline in the local paper, that ran down the left side of the page read, "House Cleaning at Upstate's Largest Employer." In one of the great plays on words, the headline located directly underneath, related to the break from the near-blizzard conditions of the last two weeks, read, "Relief, At Long Last, Relief."

It was the top story that generated all the interest. It seemed that the long-time general manager had retired in the wake of a scandal involving hundreds of thousands of dollars in travel expenditure irregularities and kickbacks from vendors, notably government contractors. The scuttlebutt said the actual numbers were much higher, maybe even in the millions. Smitty was sure there must be some fire in all that smoke for the reaction to be so swift and dramatic.

The story rambled on about the history of the long-time resident and his amazing rise from entry-level data clerk to general manager. It noted his valuable contribution to the business and how those efforts would be missed. The last paragraph ended with a statement from the new general manager, wishing him well in the future.

Cellmate laughed and said contemptuously, "The new general manager must have his sexual preferences, but we're just more subtle about it."

When Smitty asked what he meant by that, Johnny replied that as far as he was concerned it was like when someone came over to his apartment. First you thank them for their coming, then you get on with the butt-fucking.

The reporter who wrote the story said in his closing statement that he did question the new general manager as to whether the incident related to his predecessor's son had anything to do with the shake-up. The new GM quickly answered, "No comment." Then he added tersely, "It is company policy not to comment on the private affairs of former employees—father or son."

When Smitty got off the phone, most of the graveside attendees had arrived at Dad's house for an old-fashioned Irish wake.

General Chuck and General Wilson seemed to spend an extraordinary amount of time together reliving past days of glory. They talked as they walked, mingling freely with other guests who were somewhat awed by the site of two three-star generals in their presence.

Eventually, they drifted toward Sally, Smitty, Claire, and Billy, who were sitting together on the living room couch for mutual support, to exchange condolences and murmur words of encouragement.

Billy was sitting next to Sally on the other side of Smitty and Claire, trying to control the tears that just would not stop. Although Smitty had a lump in his throat, the tears would not come. They would come later, he knew, in the darkest hours of the night.

"General Martin, how are you, sir?" Billy jumped to his feet and shook the general's offered hand like an air pump handle. Smitty thought for a minute that his brother was going to kneel and kiss Chuck's air force ring.

"Just fine, Billy, and how are you?"

"I'm doing as well as can be expected, but don't you worry, sir, I'll make sure I take good care of Sally," Billy said. "After all, I am the older brother, and it is my responsibility."

"Captain." General Wilson reached for Smitty's hand and shook it firmly. "I'm so sorry."

"Not as sorry as you're going to be." Smitty stood up, gripped his hand firmly, yanked him forward, then reared back, and brought his left from his heels, making a solid connection with his left fist—to the general's jaw.

The blow made him stagger backward. He tripped over the coffee table, sending snacks, ashtrays, and knickknacks flying in every direction and scattering well-wishers like ninepins.

Whatever they were doing, whatever they were saying, the assembled crowd froze. No one spoke. No one moved. Arms that were raising coffee cups remained frozen in midair. People in the kitchen and the family room jammed the doorways in an attempt to discover the source of the sudden noise. To put it nicely, Smitty had the total and complete attention of every single person in the room.

"Captain, what's wrong with you? Have you lost your mind?" General Martin asked savagely, as he let go of Billy's hand, turned, and grabbed Smitty firmly by the arm.

"No sir, General, as a matter of fact, I'm just starting to get it back," Smitty snapped in return, shaking himself free. He noticed as he did, that for all his brother's earlier bravado, he had positioned himself behind the general.

"Honey, what's got into you?" Claire asked in disbelief, as she stooped over and began to examine General Wilson. "You just belted the man who has gone out of his way many times to help you."

"Well, when he wakes up, sweetpants, you ask him why," Smitty said with disgust. He stepped over the recumbent general, grabbed his coat, and started for the door.

"I don't know what you're talking about," Claire said, as tears began to form in the corners of her eyes.

"I'm talking about your assignment when I was at Reed and your improbable reentry into my life. I made a few calls, and your story just doesn't quite check out."

"Honey, please," Claire said.

"It's a nice routine, Hot-to-Fuck, but it won't work twice. When he wakes up, you and the general discuss why you withheld the fact that the man who's been keeping me dead center on his personal shit list for most of the last ten years is your asshole employer. And you might want to ask your dear boss why."

The crowd parted as Smitty stepped briskly to the door. He turned back and said to Claire, "And while you're at it, you can tell your Aunt Belinda that, although it took four years, you failed to accomplish your mission once again; your target metaphorically fucked you before you could fuck him, literally.

"Tell him your victim bugged out before you could enslave him to you like you did a string of the others—at least according to your records. And you can start with the navy pilot husband who was supposedly shot down in Vietnam, six months before we met. Hard to be widowed when you've never been married.

"Lastly, you tell him that if he ever comes near me again . . . " Smitty raised his thumb and pointed his forefinger like a gun at the recumbent general's forehead, making shooting sounds with his mouth, fired, then held his "gun finger" up and blew on it satisfyingly. The message was clear as a crystal mountain lake. Next time the gun would be real, and so would the bullet.

Smitty opened the front door, stepped through, and slammed it closed. He walked diagonally across the yard, opened the trunk, and ejected Claire's bags onto the front lawn, started the car, and headed up the street. He smiled ironically to himself as the thought struck him that even now, his father's lessons were being practiced. He made sure he did not exceed the fifteen miles per hour neighborhood speed limit.

Seven years had passed, and in reality, things had not changed at all. It might just as well be 1967 'cause he was still getting fucked and still responding to it by heading up the street and running away. Only this time, there'd be no Glenda to call.

And sometime in the more remote future, when the time was right, Smitty would apologize to his friend in New York for letting him take a senseless beating—and almost lose his life—because Smitty should have seen it coming and taken steps to stop it. The loud-talking leader of the pack had, in fact, been right. It had been a setup; he just had the wrong target.

But as his former friend General Wilson had counseled, sometimes you gotta take one to the choppers, no matter how much it hurts, to which Smitty could now add . . . no matter how much it hurt others also.

CHAPTER TWENTY-FOUR

After his exit from his father's funeral in late November, Smitty opted not to make a reappearance at Christmas. He left the hand-holding chores to Billy, who was much more suited to those kinds of things anyway, and accepted General Chuck's invitation to spend the holiday break at his "little hovel" in the Virginia hills and was glad he did.

Smitty went, expecting to find a two-room log cabin. Instead, it was a 350-acre spread that could only aptly be described by the term big palatial ranch.

According to the general, it had been in his parents' family for over a hundred years, the ranch being the remnants of what was once one of the largest plantations in Virginia before the Civil War.

The original plantation house was still standing, having survived the brutal conflict by serving as the headquarters for first a Confederate general, then his Union counterpart when the South's fortunes reversed. Additions had been made over the years, with the add-ons faithful to the original architecture. In 1974, it was a ten-thousand-square-foot, eight-bedroom mansion sitting regally on a hill, visible for miles in the Shenandoah Valley.

It was now self-sustaining, having been turned into a boarding ranch for upwards of two hundred horses for the Washington elite. The general had joked that on any given Sunday when Congress was in session, a quorum call for the Senate could be held just from the members who could be found riding the wooded trails, idly searching for some small relief from the never-ending pressures inside the beltway.

To handle this, the ranch had a full-time foreman who handled the day-to-day affairs, plus eight handlers and attendants who, like the foreman, lived on the grounds. Although the ranch had no inn, there were fifteen guest quarter cottages that could be reserved, and usually were. According to Chuck, seven of them were rented on a yearly basis, with the others weekly or monthly as the season dictated. The rentals and the boarding fees covered the operation costs, with what little profit left over used to maintain the house.

Smitty was staying in a guest room at the house with Chuck. He lived in Washington in quarters provided for him at Fort Myer during the week, and when he was not around, he left the place in the care of the housekeeper, two maids, and a black lab named Fighter Pilot.

They had enjoyed a quiet Christmas, exchanging small gifts and toasting Smitty's father's memory with very fine Napoleon brandy. Chuck was sitting comfortably in his easy chair in the den, while Smitty was draped across the sofa. Their earlier dinner conversation had lapsed into sporadic silence as each enjoyed the relaxing atmosphere, the crackling fire, the hooch, and the Cuban cigars that Chuck had said were a gift from a former Russian comrade from the war.

"I'll tell ya what, son," Chuck said in a relaxed voice, "This is the life. After I retire next year, I plan to spend the rest of my days right here, doing nothing but watching the sun come up in the summer and the snow fall in the winter."

"Sounds like a dream," Smitty acknowledged quietly.

"Yeah, it's just too bad that my brother didn't live to enjoy it with me," Chuck said.

He took a puff of the cigar and watch the smoke curl. "We had big plans for our golden years, until he went and got himself shot down in the South China Sea a couple of years back."

"Yeah, I was sorry to hear about that. I met him several times. He was a good man," Smitty said.

Smitty blew out a cloud of smoke himself, then ventured gently, "You come from a large family, don't you?"

"Yeah, kind of. There were four of us: three brothers and a half-sister from a previous marriage. The half-sister kinda screwed up my daddy's political ambitions."

"How so?"

"He was a senator, see. From what I understand, he was all but set to accept the VP's slot for Roosevelt's fourth term when the political tricksters uncovered the fact that Shelly, that was my sister's name, was illegitimate.

"Seems Dad had a fling with a woman when he was a young man stationed at some army camp during World War I, and didn't even know about Shel' until after he came back from overseas and met and married my mother.

"After he found out, he tried to do everything he could to put it right. He paid, or maybe I should say overpaid, for her care and well-being. When Shelly was ten, her real mother died. Dad brought her to live with us, then adopted her."

"Where are your brothers and sister now?" Smitty asked.

"They're all gone. My older brother died in the war." Chuck looked suspiciously at Smitty. "I assumed your father told you all about the circumstances surrounding that."

"Naw, Dad never talked about what he did in the war," Smitty answered matter-of-factly. "The times that I did ask, he would brush me off with a half-hearted response that always went something like, 'it was a bunch of boring stateside maintenance support crap.'"

"Mmm," Chuck nodded. "Thought maybe he had. Well, anyway, my sister became a nurse. She bought it at a medivac station in Korea. And my other brother you know about."

"Thanks," Smitty said.

"For what?"

"For telling me." Smitty changed his tone. "You know, I've sort of been idolizing you from afar, since I was a ten-year-old kid in Dearfield."

"Hero worship can be a dangerous thing, son," Chuck said.

"Why?"

"Once you put someone on a pedestal, it can blind you to his real faults."

"Meaning?" Smitty asked.

"Well, take your army general friend, Sam Wilson." Smitty raised an eyebrow. "You've been pretty smitten with him since Nam, according to your father. Then at the Ol' Sarge's funeral, you found out he's been playing you all these years and using those two mountainous tits with a girl attached to them as the bait."

"Everybody's got a right to be a sucker once," Smitty said. "And you've got to admit, there are worse ways to go."

"Well, just watch yourself. You've made a dangerous enemy."

"Why?"

"The shithouse rumor has it that his family is well connected politically. That's how he managed to jump from an obscure twenty-something year colonel to three stars in less than five years."

"I see," Smitty said.

Chuck walked to the fireplace and tossed the butt of his Cuban special. "Now I've got a question for you, partner." He smiled, and added, "Off the record, of course."

"Go ahead," Smitty said with an open-handed wave.

"What's the deal with you and your brother? I've never seen two brothers who are only two and a half years apart be so different."

"Oh, I don't know," Smitty replied. "I guess he was raised mostly by Mom and I was raised mostly by Pop."

"If I didn't know better, I'd swear it was by different parents," Chuck said.

Smitty nodded slowly in response. From outward appearances, Smitty could see his point.

Physically, they were not even close to being the same. Smitty towered over his brother by seven inches and outweighed him by a good fifty pounds. Not to mention the fact that Billy's insecurity and mannerisms made him a charter member of what Smitty termed, the 'Hoover Club' for his vacuum-packed head.

True, Billy did have his problems, but he was still his brother, and much like his friend, Johnny, he accepted him for all his faults, as he was pretty certain Billy did the same with him. But he wasn't sure it was a thought that called for an answer, at least not by him. Smitty shrugged his shoulders noncommittally in response.

The general stretched, then said in a tired voice, "I think I'll hit the rack."

"Sleep well," Smitty said, getting up from the couch and crossing to the fireplace to shake his hand. "I think I'll read a bit before turning in."

"Goodnight," General Chuck said, as he yawned and started up the steps. He turned at the third tread. "There are plenty of books in the study if you're looking for something new." Smitty listened as the door closed then wandered down the hall to the study and browsed the shelves.

He spent the next thirty minutes arduously searching before he found exactly what he was looking for, then spent another hour entranced by it before heading upstairs to the guest room.

Guest room, in this case, was an understatement. This was more like a two-room suite in the finest five-star hotel in London. Hell, it was bigger than Smitty's entire apartment.

As he was brushing his teeth for bed, he reviewed in his mind his conversation with General Chuck—and his responses.

He was not totally honest with the general, but that was all right—neither was the general with him. The reasons, Smitty suspected, were diametrically opposed. The general probably did not go into the details of how his brother died in World War II because it was a classified mission. Or more likely, because he considered it a private matter which would have caused him or his family great embarrassment.

Smitty's reasons were more diabolical. They had nothing to do with being embarrassed but had everything to do with the application of one of the primary rules found in his former friend General Wilson's Handbook for Spies, rule number two. A rule that Smitty had long since committed to memory that began, "Never tell anyone anything unless—" He left the balance unfinished, mainly because he shorted the rule down to this half sentence anyway.

It was pleasant there, and Smitty wished he could have stayed forever, instead of just two more days. But the time was well spent. It was relaxing, restful, and informative.

Smitty stared at the TV screen with tears streaming slowly down his face. He had a feeling he was not alone. All over America, people were watching the craziness being broadcast around the word and staring back in stunned disbelief. He was angry and frustrated.

First, his friends were lost, then the cause was lost, and now the war was lost.

Vietnam was falling. It was late April of 1975, and Smitty watched helplessly as hordes of panicked civilians and Vietnamese army solders surged against the fence of the American Embassy in Saigon in a desperate attempt to climb the walls and somehow force themselves onto the last rescue helicopters that were departing from the roof.

Elsewhere around the city, the panic was just as bad. In the harbor, children and mothers with small babies were trampled to death as thousands of terrified people surged for the few seaworthy boats and sampans left, in a last-ditch attempt to reach the safety of the American navy ships anchored just offshore.

Few were going to make it. Many more would be left to die in the debacle of the failed American intervention in Vietnam. America's involvement in its longest war was ending. But for fifty-six thousand soldiers who had served there, it had ended long ago with death coming in ones, twos, fives, and sometimes tens at a time in the endless rice paddies, dense jungle, and precipitous trails of a land far away. For many more, the wounded who made it home, the emotional suffering would go on long after the televised embarrassing end had faded from people's minds.

It would for Smitty. There was not a day that went by that the face of a former friend in green didn't flash before his eyes. Their faces were as fresh as the day they died, frozen in time. Inevitably, his first thoughts were of his friends who were now permanently assigned to angel detail. LZ, Hogsbreath, Whippoorwill, and the Boy Wonder flashed before him. Next, his thoughts turned to those he'd left behind, like Patty and their spotter Fat Cat. He wondered idly where they were, and if they made it home. Were they watching now? Did they feel as he did? Smitty suspected so. To lose a friend, or even someone whose name you did not know, for no valid cause left you with a sickness that no doctor's prescription could cure.

Then there were those who made it home, but only physically: Big Walt, Ronny, and in some ways, Frenchy.

Last, he thought of Linda. Even after all these years, he could still see her face and feel the warmth of her smile. He knew that he would feel the burden of her death to the end of his days and always savor the taste of her kiss and the warmth of her touch—and the pain of not being there when she died.

The flag being lowered from the Embassy did it for Smitty. He snapped off the TV in disgust, stalked out of the room to the kitchen for a beer, changed his mind, and grabbed an untouched bottle of bourbon from the shelf, cracked the seal and took a long pull. That one tasted so good that he had another.

He took the bottle, headed into his bedroom, and flopped onto the bed, intent on finishing the bottle and getting totally shit-faced. Smitty knew that no matter how much he tried, he could not drown out the rage and sympathy he was feeling, not only for himself, but also for every wife, every mother, father, sister, and son, who lost a loved one in that fucking war. He hoped Nixon, McNamara, Westmoreland, and all the rest of the incompetent political and military fuckups would sleep well that night.

No, that was not true. What he really hoped was that they spent the balance of their days in a state of screaming agony. Maybe if they'd lost a son, they'd understand.

It was his last conscious thought that night.

The next morning, Smitty dragged himself out of an alcohol-induced sleep, showered, shaved, dressed, and was on the road south by 9:30 AM. He had a week off, although it was more a duty call than a vacation. The final destination was Savannah and Sally and Dad's house for the last time.

Sally had sold the house and was moving back to her girlhood home in Macon. Ostensibly, Smitty was going down to help clean out the house and pack up Sally's belongings. In reality, he was going to rescue the tools in Dad's garage. What remained in the rest of the house really didn't matter to him at all.

Three hours later, Smitty was beyond the madness of New York City area traffic, and cruising comfortably down the Jersey turnpike with the cruise control set, and his car operating perfectly.

A car next to him sped past; giving him the thumbs up. A signal Smitty returned with a satisfied smile.

One of the things Smitty had treated himself to after he was promoted to engineer in the early spring was a "slightly used" new car.

Smitty had purchased the car—a Hurst/Olds which sold new for $6,800—with six thousand miles on it for $2,800 from a local who bought it new less than eighteen months ago. When the air conditioner stopped working, and the tape player broke, the owner decided the car was a dog, threw a tantrum, and garaged it for nine months. Smitty heard about it from a friend of a friend at work. His friend took him to see the car on a Saturday and Smitty bought it on the spot.

When Smitty got the car home the following week, he immediately repaired the broken accessories and added some new ones. The air-conditioner fix took about thirty seconds. He replaced the fusible link next to the compressor at a cost of two dollars. The tape player took about two hours to remove and repair. He replaced the single-core radiator with a heavier duty four-core and added an external transmission cooler and a Class III trailer hitch.

With his next paycheck, Smitty made a few enhancements that dramatically improved the handling. The GM standard-issue pansy-assed shocks and bias-belted fourteen-inch tires with five-inch rims were exchanged for heavy-duty Monroes, fore and aft, and fifteen-inch wide radials with fifteen-by-nine-inch Mag wheels.

Then the real fun started. One of Smitty's new friends in the office owned a farm thirty miles away with a huge barn that was also a well-equipped workshop. With the onset of spring, they spent the better part of two months reworking the piss-poor original GM body design that tapered in six inches from the top of the front and back wheel wells to the rocker panels into a custom bumper-to-bumper flaring that replaced the dorky looking add-on mud guards.

After removing the side body trim, the wheel well trim, and the black snakeskin roof, they sanded the entire car and repainted it in the original metallic brown. The additional bodywork, wider rims and lower sidewall tires gave the entire car a sleek California street rod kind of appearance. As a finishing touch, they painted a gold Oldsmobile rocket emblem on the added panel of the lower doors. Last, Smitty took the car and had it professionally treated for rust protection.

The new car looked and ran great and was now a real head turner, especially in the small upstate community where custom cars were seldom seen. Oldsmobiles always were great riding cars, and the addition of the Hurst package and the modifications Smitty and his friend had made only made it that much better.

When the project was completed, Smitty sold the "Ragnault" off for $400, because it just wasn't seaworthy enough to withstand the harshness of the New York winters as a primary car.

But all the work on the car was merely a distraction that kept his idle mind from brooding about his father's death and his break-up with Claire.

Smitty missed his father. He missed his smile, he missed his laugh, and he missed his sage advice. It was most painful during the holiday season. It was that, more than anything else, that had caused him to accept the general's offer to spend Christmas with him rather than return to Savannah.

At the funeral, General Chuck had said that his father was one in a million; Smitty couldn't have agreed more. They both had lost someone special. The fact that the someone was the same person only seemed to draw them closer.

Since November, they had spent considerable time together, when their respective schedules allowed, and consoled each other out of mutual loneliness.

For the general, Smitty suspected that Dad's death had been a reminder of his own mortality. For Smitty, it had been a sobering reminder that, despite all the death and destruction he had witnessed, a family death was a hundred times more painful and a thousand times more lasting.

"Well, Lieutenant, um, I mean Captain, I guess it's time to go." Sally walked up to Smitty in the empty living room of Dad's house and put her arm around him lovingly.

"I thought I would never see this day come. It hurts."

"I know it does, sweetie, but life goes on and so will you. In time, you'll remember your dad fondly. You'll forget the times he wailed the tar out of you, and as you grow older, with the passage of a few years, as you see the permissive parenting of your friends and peers, you'll even begin to remember the discipline respectfully," Sally said, trying to comfort him.

"I guess," Smitty said.

"C'mon. What say we drink a quick one to the Ol' Sarge then get the hell out of here before I start crying, my makeup starts running, and I look like the bride of Godzilla."

Sally pulled a couple of cold ones from a Styrofoam ice chest, popped the tops with a church key, and handed one to Smitty.

They clicked bottles as they faced each other, Smitty said, "To the popster."

Sally grinned, "To my favorite bed buddy."

Smitty laughed in spite of himself. "Speaking from lots of experience, no doubt."

Sally's face hardened. "Not as many as you think, Mr. Smarty Pants stepson." She took a swig of her beer. "Other than your dad, there have been only two others, and one of them raped me."

"Did you turn him in?" Smitty asked.

"Humph!" Sally snorted. "He wasn't the kind you reported. Leastwise, if you didn't want your career in the shitter."

"Why not?" Smitty set his bottle on the windowsill, folded his arms, and leaned forward, suddenly interested.

"Because, my nosy stepson, he came from some very influential family that let me know, through their family lawyer, what would happen to me if I did," Sally answered shortly.

"Such as?"

"Well, I guess since I blabbed part of it, I might as well tell you the rest." Sally took a long pull on her beer and wiped her mouth. "You remember I told you there had been two others? Well the other guy, my boyfriend, was a jet jockey in Korea. He had seven kills and was well on his way to becoming a double ace until he ran into a passel of MIGs over the Yalu River and was killed.

"A month later I found out I was pregnant. You understand, sonny boy, that back then, being unmarried and pregnant was big trouble. If the army had found out, they would have forced me to resign my commission and had me hustled stateside and out of the army before the ink had dried on my orders. I was one shook-up first lieutenant, I'll tell you."

Sally grinned nervously. "Now comes the embarrassing part. Out of desperation, I told my boyfriend's commanding officer. He told me that his family had connections and could help me out of my fix if I just cooperated. When I asked him what he meant by that, he laughed sadistically, then stuck his hand down the front of my shirt and ripped it. He started feeling me up. I pushed his hands away and fought him off as best I could. Finally, when I could see that what I was doing didn't work, I slapped him as hard as I could across the face.

"He became enraged, punched me in the jaw nearly knocking me unconscious, then raped me. "Afterward, I started to cry. Both from my situation and the shame of what that bastard just did to me.

"He grabbed me by the hair, pulled me to my feet and slapped me twice across the face, then sneered at me with that superior grin and said that he couldn't understand why I was so upset, it wasn't like I was a virgin or anything. And since I was already knocked up, he was just running up a little mileage, like using a parking space with time already on the meter. "He told me that if I ever told anyone, my career in the military would be over, he'd see to that. But if I played ball, he'd see that the whole thing was taken care of."

"So what did you do?" Smitty asked calmly, suspecting he already knew the answer.

"I did what they said." Sally said. "I had no choice. I was transferred stateside and reassigned for one year as a civilian assistant to a member of the government."

Sally looked up and said quickly, "And don't ask me to who, 'cause I won't tell you."

"What happened next?" Smitty asked in a low voice.

"For the next eight months, I had some drummed-up job that really didn't exist. The local office people were told I was assigned out of the country as a special envoy, when in reality, I was on maternity leave. After the baby was born, a quiet adoption was arranged, and one month later, I returned to duty in Germany with the army."

Sally finished her beer, turned, dropped the empty bottle angrily in the ice chest, and added, "I've often wondered what became of that baby and how he's doing."

"I'm sure he's doing all right," Smitty walked over and put his arms around her. "I'm sure that you did the right thing."

Sally buried her head in his arms and began to sob. Crying, Smitty was sure, not only for her lost husband, but for a child she'd never seen. When a child dies, there is a sense of closure, but when a mother lets her child be adopted, it creates an open wound that never closes. The unknown questions and heartache will remain with her the rest of her life.

Almost as if she was reading his mind, Sally said, "And it's the not knowing that tears me apart."

"Well, take heart," Smitty said brightly.

When Sally looked up, Smitty grinned. "He could have grown up to be just like me."

"Now there's a thought that will make me euphorically happy with my decision." Sally dabbed away some errant eye makeup lightly with her finger. "Thanks, sonny boy. I would have been proud if my son turned out to be like you."

"C'mon, let's git," Smitty said, "or you'll have me crying, too."

They went through the front door, Smitty pulling the door to behind them. He glanced to his left, waved a last good-bye to Sara Lee, then to his right, and did the same with Benny. He and Sally descended the steps and he escorted Sally to her car. As he opened the door, he noticed the Wicked Witch of the North standing defiantly on her patio across the street with her hands on her hips. As they made eye contact, she gave Smitty the singular digit salute, spun on her heels, went inside her house, and slammed the door.

"You take care." Sally started her car and put it in gear.

"You too, Mom." Smitty patted the car door.

She backed out of the driveway and headed up the road, the moving van dropping in behind her. It was a three-hour trip to Macon and another half-hour to the suburb located fifteen miles beyond. She would be at her new home well before dark.

Smitty would have accompanied her, but cleaning out the garage and crating the tools had taken longer than Smitty thought. Billy was supposed to have shown up to help, but he arrived two days late after all the real work had been done, collected the portion left to him by Dad, and departed the next morning.

Smitty had packed the balance of the tools into Dad's hand-built enclosed trailer and, with some spillover into the trunk of the Olds, managed to get everything in.

Smitty turned, and with a last wave to Sara Lee, got in, started the motor, and was two minutes behind Sally, but headed in a different direction.

Sally was headed west a couple of hundred miles; Smitty was headed north a thousand. But the long trip had been worth it. Smitty would have driven ten thousand miles through the smoke of hell's kitchen to rescue his father's most personal keepsakes. And Sally had given him the last missing piece to the puzzle.

"'Who comes in three parts," Smitty had preached to LZ and Frenchy many years ago on that rickety bus to basic training. "The person who did the dirty work, the person who told him to do it, and the person who told them where to look."

Smitty now knew who that third person was. More importantly, he now knew what was behind it. All he needed to expose him was the right set of circumstances for the tortoise to come out of his shell.

Unfortunately, that time would not be of his choosing. It would occur when his bashful friend thought he had an edge, which in reality meant when he thought he felt he had enough of an advantage to set a trap to kill him.

"Hey sonny boy, how you keepin'?" Sally asked when Smitty picked up the phone and said hello.

"Fine, you old reprobate," Smitty said. "What's got you all excited?"

"I have some wonderful news," Sally said.

"Let me guess," Smitty interrupted. "You're pregnant and want me to be the godfather."

"Very funny, smart ass. If I were, you sure as hell would be the last person I'd tell. Let alone be the godfather."

Smitty laughed easily in reply. He enjoyed teasing her good-naturedly and Sally enjoyed it also, giving back as good as she got.

"Okay my little pissant captain, try to get that minuscule Irish brain of yours to focus for a few minutes," Sally said. "This is your major talking, and I'm only going to say this once, so pay attention."

"Yes, ma'am!"

Sally exhaled and announced happily, "The air force is going to name a building after your father."

"Wow! That's great, Sal," Smitty said. "How'd that happen?"

"Well, you know with the bicentennial coming up, and everyone getting excited about it, the air force is trying to do something special to cash in on the event and get a little PR for the boys in the blue suits.

"So when I heard about it a couple of months ago, I wrote to the local contact at the air force base near here, then that General What's-His-Name at the Pentagon called and told me about it too."

"You mean General Martin?" Smitty asked.

"Yeah, that one. Anyway, the combination must have worked. This coming June, they're naming the Service Club at Johnson Field after your father. Isn't that great?" Sally asked breathlessly.

"Yes, Sally, that is great. You should be pleased and very proud."

"I am, sonny boy, I am."

"Did you call Billy and tell him?" Smitty asked.

"Not yet." Sally hesitated. "I was kind of hoping you'd do it."

"Sal, it's your good news. You should make the call," Smitty said.

"Well, if you think it's best."

"I do."

They spoke for several more minutes, exchanging updates since their last call a couple of months back before Sally hung up.

Smitty had barely set the phone in the cradle before it rang again.

"Captain."

"Hello, General, how are you?" Smitty asked, recognizing Chuck's voice.

"Hear the news?" General Chuck asked.

"Yes, sir. Sally just called."

"It's a great honor," the general said. "And fitting," he added.

"Yes, sir." Smitty said, waiting patiently for the general to get to the point.

"Um, son. Given any thought as to how you'd get there?"

"Not yet."

"Well, if your fat civilian ass will still fit into that uniform you wore to your dad's funeral, I could arrange to smuggle you on the air force plane I'll be taking down," the general offered.

"That's very nice of you, sir," Smitty replied. "I'll have to let you know, General. I haven't called my dad's family in Pennsylvania yet, and I'm sure that they'll want to go, so it's likely I'll end up as part of a convoy to Georgia with them."

"Yeah, I never thought of that," General Chuck answered, failing to hide his disappointment. Smitty suspected that the general wanted Smitty along because it would be his last hurrah in the air force. He was getting out in August, and this tribute to his lifelong friend would be one of his last official military functions, or maybe a last unofficial military act, depending on your perspective.

Having the son of that friend along for companionship would have made the trip a little less painful and a lot less lonesome.

"Well, let me know if things don't work out. I'll leave the invitation open," Chuck said, and after a few pleasantries, they hung up.

Smitty was busy the balance of the evening making calls. The dedication was open to all members of the family and friends. Smitty did well on the family, not so well on the friends.

Thinking maybe it was time to bury the hatchet, Smitty had nervously dialed General Wilson's number. The conversation was short and to the point. He would not be attending and, based on their last meeting and the broken jaw he had to show for it, he tersely requested that Smitty not call him again—for the balance of his lifetime.

Obviously, the word had gone out. Smitty's calls to Major Jim, Stan the Man, and Colonel Evans were likewise as terse, and just as short. The only one of his former friends to break rank was Sergeant Mike.

When Smitty called him, Mike informed him pleasantly, that he would be delighted to attend, saying snidely that he never trusted that three-star idiot anyway, so being on his shit list was an honor he would more than willingly share with Smitty.

Smitty was glad. He and the Ol' Sarge had been through some bad and bloody times and survived. Having Sergeant Mike there would be the next best thing to his father being there in person.

The ceremony was scheduled for mid-June of 1976 and was the first in a series of events culminating in a Fourth of July celebration of the country's two hundredth birthday. The local base commander, a two-star general, would preside over the ceremony, which, it turned out, would be part of a basewide celebration, posthumously honoring other selected servicemen. The dedication would be on a Saturday afternoon, with a formal party to follow that night at the very club that was to be named for his father.

Smitty had a month to prepare, which seemed like a lot of time on the surface, but, with everything going on in his life at the moment, time was the one thing that was in short supply.

No sooner had the New Year's baby with 1976 stenciled on its diaper arrived, than Smitty made some major life changes, both professionally and personally.

Smitty had been with his present employer just short of two years and had already been promoted three times. The first was a promotion to engineer from his hiring qualification position, shortly after he returned from his father's funeral in December of 1974. The fact that Smitty was the first of his incoming class to be promoted would turn out to be more significant than Smitty realized.

Nine months later, after completing his next engineering assignment in August 1975, Smitty was promoted again to engineering specialist. Two months later, he was appointed a manufacturing manager, a lateral move designed to enhance young engineers' prospectives on their final design objectives.

With Smitty's hands-on and military leadership experience, this seemed to be a natural fit, and Smitty took to the job at once. So much so that when his current boss had been offered a promotion to head up the entire manufacturing operations at a sister facility in Arizona last month, he had offered Smitty a promotion to the next level of management at the same site. Smitty had accepted at once.

Smitty had to pack, move, and be on-site and ready to start his new assignment by July. That meant not only putting in overtime on the job but doing the same at home as well.

In January, Smitty had bought a house after the owner had lost his job on Friday and cut the selling price on Sunday by half. Although it had generous square footage and was situated on four acres of land, it was sufficiently run-down that it could be referred to as a fixer-upper at best or a total wreck at worst. Visualizing the ultimate capabilities, Smitty had bought it on the spot.

The house was a ranch-style design. The previous owner had taken this to heart, keeping a thoroughbred horse and two goats in the two-car garage located in the half basement underneath. It gave the entire structure a permanent horsy kind of aroma that Smitty swore could even be tasted in the food in the filthy refrigerator.

The surrounding landscape was not much better. The trees were desperately in need of trimming, and the yard was badly overgrown with weeds, with what grass remaining having been pretty much eaten to the roots by the goats. But since the horse grazed on the same lawn, at least fertilizer was not a problem.

The house became Smitty's hobby and his obsession. After disposing of the contaminated basement structures and all the first-floor carpeting so he could move in, Smitty had pretty much started at the level of a flood victim. He tore the house completely apart, then went through the rooms one at a time, repainting walls, revarnishing peeling woodwork, recarpeting, and repairing mildewed bathrooms and leaky kitchen faucets.

With the passing of April Fool's Day, and moderate weather, Smitty had turned his attentions to the outside, and by June, he had reseeded the lawn, trimmed the trees, removed the weeds, and even cleaned up the spring-fed pond so that now the house looked more like a countryside park and more than respectable in the neighborhood.

Smitty was halfway through painting the outside structure in May when the new job and the move to Arizona surfaced. With a little extra effort, Smitty finished the recoating in time for the company appraiser's estimate and was rewarded for all his second-shift effort with an appraisal that doubled the price that Smitty had paid for the house, less than six months before.

Best of all, he'd not have to split the profits four ways. He'd already been to Arizona on a house-hunting trip, and purchased a home upsized in price and neighborhood to what he could now afford.

The trip home to see Sally and the honor for his late father were icing on the cake. Over the next few weeks, Smitty had arranged it so that the trip to Macon would just be the first leg to his returning to Tucson. He'd always wanted to drive across the country and this would provide the perfect opportunity.

His few pieces of furniture were packed and on their way across country. His beloved Chevy and the little Dodge Colt import he'd bought—to survive the latest oil embargo—for $2000 were in transit also.

During the first week of June, Smitty went around the plant saying good-bye to the business associates he'd worked with and the friends he'd made in his brief tour of duty in New York. He made a special point of stopping in to see Cellmate and taking him to lunch. They parted with a warm hug of friendship and a humorous good-bye request from his friend, that if Smitty ever decided to cross over, he should call him first.

He stayed in a hotel his last night there with his new dependent, an old reddish, fluffy-haired tabby cat that Smitty had named Pussycat Smith. PS had wandered up to his house on a cold February day and decided that if he was lost, this was the place where he wanted to be found.

They'd adopted each other immediately, becoming great pals, making the empty house seem not quite so lonely. It was only natural that Smitty would take his buddy with him to the new home, especially since he had nothing of the female persuasion to bring along.

Claire was gone again. As soon as Smitty returned from his dad's funeral, he'd gone to her apartment straightaway, finding it had been vacated only days earlier, and, according to the apartment manager, she had left with no forwarding address. Smitty was not surprised by this fact, either.

She bounced in and out of his life like a yo-yo, dropping in, entrancing him, then pulling back after he'd been smitten. She'd done it to him twice; she'd not get a third chance. As LZ would have said if he were here, "Three strikes and you're out, Titsy."

Smitty could only guess at what she'd been sent to find out this time, but he had a pretty good idea, and it didn't require the use of a lot of gray matter to figure it out. She'd again failed to get anything useful from him, and although she'd come desperately close, the main course of the seduction had not occurred.

As Smitty crossed the Tappan Zee Bridge in the Olds and turned south on the Jersey Turnpike for the last time, he found himself reminiscing about doing exactly the same thing only two short years ago when he'd departed Savannah and headed north.

Then he'd seen the ghosts of LZ, Frenchy, and Big Walt in the Famous '54. Now his visions were of his father and the last ride they'd shared together in the '60 Chevy.

In the aggregate, the two years had been enormously successful professionally but a disaster personally. His father was gone, his girl was gone, and his friendship with General Wilson was gone. The only thing he had left was his life, and Smitty had a feeling that the next time—and there would definitely be one—that he met either of the latter two again, that either his life or theirs would be gone also.

CHAPTER TWENTY-FIVE

"So you're no closer to the truth and finding out who this mysterious person is or what's behind it?" General Thompson asked casually as he stretched, and glanced at his wristwatch, noting the two hours since Smitty had started to talk.

"No. During my two years in New York, the trail went cold, especially after I decked General Wilson at Dad's wake," Smitty answered truthfully.

"Yeah, I heard about that." Barney snapped his fingers twice impatiently and Smitty flipped him both cigar case and lighter.

He fired off a fresh one and as he was puffing his cheroot, said in mild reproach, "A young captain can find his prospects for further promotion rather dim if he goes around rearranging the bridgework of three-star generals."

Barney blew out a thick cloud of smoke. "'Course now if he was only a brigadier, it would be an altogether different matter. I'd probably figure he got what he deserved."

Smitty laughed at the general's wit. He was obviously a man used to power and comfortable using it. A man so sure of his position that he needn't be concerned about what he said about whom. A dangerous man, whom Smitty suspected was the hidden power behind a very big, secret military throne.

"How'd the ceremony go?"

"Real nice, sir. All the relatives were pleased and happy. And other than one minor snafu, no problems."

"Snafu?"

"Yeah." Smitty chuckled. "One of my uncles got a little soused, and when the base commander ventured out to the men's room, he took off after him. As soon as he came back out he announced to the whole room in a loud and drunken voice that he'd just been in the can with the general, and that, based on what he saw, that if the general was a two-star, then he should be at least a three-star."

Barney broke into a fit of belly-shaking guffaws. "I know the base commander, and your uncle's right. I've seen pygmies that are better hung."

Smitty laughed out loud himself. That made the general a very dangerous man. He was obviously comfortable making jokes about fellow officers also. But Smitty could tell by his expression that it was only intended to be a joke and was nowhere rooted in first-hand knowledge.

"Did that hard-assed sergeant friend of yours show?" Barney asked.

"Sergeant Mike? Yeah. Said he was glad he came."

Smitty paused and blew out a cloud of smoke. "He looked tired. Mentioned the reason as being worn out from a six-week tour of Europe. I asked him if he had time to drop into Switzerland and clean out a few unlisted bank accounts. He laughed and said he'd done just what I suggested first, then traveled first class the rest of the way."

"Um, how'd your day in Savannah go, m'boy?" Barney asked.

"'Bout as expected. Saw the old homestead, visited with the old neighbors, then rode through some old haunts," Smitty said.

"Have any surprises?"

Smitty stared at him for a minute, then realized the futility of keeping anything from him. Hell, he'd probably had him tailed from the moment he left New York.

"Yeah, as a matter of fact I did. When I stopped in at Sara Lee's, there was a note there from my old Nam commander Ron. It was dated about three weeks ago. The note said he was back in town and that if I came through again, I should give him a call at his apartment over on the west side."

"Did you?" Barney asked.

"I don't know," Smitty answered, "Did I?"

Sighing in exasperation, Barney reached into his left inside coat pocket and pulled out a three-by-five top-spiral-bound notebook, flipped the cover and several pages over, removed his cigar, and began to read:

Captain Smith placed a call to his former Captain Ron Bartkowski from the home of Sara Lee Young at 1134 hrs. Captain Smith and Captain Bartkowski agreed to meet for lunch at 1230 hrs. at Big J's on the corner of Peterson Expressway and Cross River Road.

Captain Smith entered the eatery at 1222 hrs. Captain Bartkowski entered the establishment at 1232 hrs. The two shook hands then proceeded together to a booth in the back corner of the restaurant, ordered from memory from a waitress named Charlene, then chatted about general things, mostly the changes in Savannah over the last few years, for the next twelve minutes.

At 1243 hrs., two young Army soldiers (your agents, sir) entered wearing Red Berets down low over their right eyes in a cocky fashion. Captain Bartkowski commented to Captain Smith caustically and wondered "if we ever looked like that." Paused, then answered his own question by saying ironically, "Naw."

Captain Bartkowski and Captain Smith exchanged pleasantries on each other's general whereabouts and activities over the last three years. Captain Smith described his business successes and his successful house venture. Captain Bartkowski explained away his three-year disappearance as "hiding from the IRS" until he could get enough money together to broker a deal with them, which Captain Bartkowski stated was finalized in February of 1976.

Lunch was served at 1249 hrs. Captain Smith had a hamburger, fries, and a coke; Captain Bartkowski, a club sandwich, fries, and a coke. Over food, Captain Bartkowski asked Captain Smith his plans for the rest of the day. Captain Smith stated that he was "just going to ride around, reminisce, then stop at a florist on the way out of town and buy flowers to put on his father's grave." Captain Bartkowski replied that was a nice gesture, and that if he stayed over, he was welcome to stay with him.

At 1257 hrs., Captain Bartkowski complimented Captain Smith on his accomplishments, then commented that because of all that, he must be doing pretty well. Captain Smith nodded but made no verbal reply.

Captain Bartkowski then made a hesitant, uncomfortable request for Captain

Smith to loan him $1800 to help stave off creditors who were threatening to take his car.

Captain Smith considered this for a moment, asked questions about other possible sources of funding, shrugged his shoulders in resignation, then reached into his back pocket, brought out his checkbook, and wrote Captain Bartkowski a check for the full amount.

Captain Bartkowski thanked Captain Smith, who nodded, then stated that he 'owed' him, for hauling him out of the jungle.

Captain Bartkowski commented that Captain Smith sure knew how to pay his bills. Captain Smith added that, "this bill is now paid in full." Captain Bartkowski nodded his head in understanding.

Captain Smith and Captain Bartkowski made small talk for the next thirteen minutes. Captain Smith paid the lunch bill, totaling fifteen dollars and thirty-six cents, then left a two dollar and a half tip. Captain Smith and Captain Bartkowski departed the restaurant at 1314 hrs.

Captain Smith and Captain Bartkowski shook hands in the parking lot and promised to keep in touch with each other. Captain Bartkowski left turning right and headed south. Captain Smith departed turning left, headed north back into town."

"I can tell you where you went from there, if you'd like, but I'm sure you get the idea," Barney closed the book and stuck it back in his inside pocket.

"Where did the captain go, and what did he do with the money?" Smitty asked.

"Paid his bookie," Barney answered immediately. "By the way, the tab was only twelve hundred. He euchred you out of the rest."

"It was a bill that was due; at least it's paid now," Smitty said philosophically. But he wasn't feeling philosophical about the general's report. To have that kind of information, that fast, boggled the mind.

"You're a mighty broad-minded young lad." Barney got to his feet and dusted off the rear of his pants.

He walked the fifteen steps to Smitty's father's grave, snapped to attention and saluted Dad's headstone. "I've got to go, Sarge, I've got an appointment."

He thumbed his left hand towards Smitty. "And so does he."

Barney turned and strutted back to Smitty. "Captain, even though you are not in the service anymore, if a four-star general, like me"—he patted his own chest with his left hand—"and your dad's lifelong friend, gave you an order, would you obey it without question?"

"Yes, sir." Smitty got up and snapped to attention himself.

"What do you think; is he ready?" Barney glanced sideways at Dad's headstone, almost as if he were expecting him to answer.

"I think so, too," Barney answered.

He reached inside his right coat pocket and brought out a plain white envelope. It was not particularly thick, looking as if it contained a two- to three-page letter. He passed it across.

"What time is it according to that cheap keepsake of yours?" Barney asked briskly.

"Six, uh, that is 1812 hours, sir," Smitty answered, his heart racing in his chest as he took the envelope.

"Depart from the cemetery at exactly 1815 hours. Follow the directions inside. Proceed exactly as directed, and do not stop for any reason, not even to take a leak."

"Yes, sir," Smitty answered quickly, biting his tongue to keep from asking what came next.

Following the general's come-with-me motion, Smitty dropped into step beside him and walked purposefully back down the path to an air force staff car that came from the roundabout drive in the back of the cemetery and pulled to a stop precisely at the moment that the general reached the end of the walk.

The general waited patiently while the driver, a sergeant who looked big enough to go bear hunting with a switch, got out, jogged around the car, opened the door, and assumed a standard attention pose.

The general shook hands with Smitty, started to step into the car, stopped and turned back to Smitty. "M'boy, there's just one more thing."

Smitty felt it before he saw it. The general had caught him completely off guard and decked him with a pretty good right cross. Smitty backpedaled three steps, stumbled over a gravestone, and landed flat on his ass.

The general leaned over and pointed his index finger at Smitty. "And by the way, we four-star generals don't like getting knocked on our asses any more than our three-star counterparts." He straightened up, and as he got in the car, called out, "And you know what the object lesson here was, I'm sure."

The door closed, and the driver hustled around the front of the car, got in, put it in drive, and drove swiftly away.

Smitty knew damn well what the lesson was all right, it had to do with the Boy Scout motto that General Chuck had plagiarized into his own advice to Smitty years ago in a bar in Washington . . . which, when translated to his current situation, equated to a deadly warning that Smitty should be damn careful because whoever was waiting for him at the end of these directions was not planning on letting him leave alive.

Not for the first time, Smitty glanced at the directions and second-guessed himself. And not for the first time, Smitty fought against the urge to exit stage right and get the hell out of there—as any sane person would have.

A sane person would have given up long ago and gone on with his life when the wispy clues and the faint echoes seemed to be fading. But going on, when he was this close to his quest, was not any option. Smitty had followed the trail from a scent, to an odor, to a full-blown stink, for fifteen years on a trek that had taken him through three towns, three states, three countries, and three continents. He'd believed when others thought him crazy and journeyed on when the price of admission was great personal sacrifice, and the bill was paid in the immeasurable cost of human lives. Most assuredly, Smitty was not sane. He was possessed.

Following the general's instructions to the letter, he departed exactly on schedule, and, as per instructions, returned to the interstate and headed west. The afternoon sun was lower in the sky than when he first stopped at the cemetery, but Smitty knew, based on the written instructions before him, that he would reach his destination well before dark.

He smirked and consoled himself with a passing thought that if it ended here, at least he'd avoided his scariest nightmare of dying in a war in a land far away in the dark of the night. Had it been only seventeen years since that boyhood fear had materialized in his father's house?

The interstate ended thirty miles from town and, again following the directions to the letter, he transitioned on to State Route 46 and continued in a westerly direction for the next twenty-five miles. He turned south on U.S. 301 for ten miles, then back west on State Route 79. At the junction of State Route 222, he turned south. Three miles down this road he turned right onto Clayton Road.

Again following the directions to the letter, he stayed on the road when the pavement ended and the name changed to Johnson Farm Lane. The one-lane path continued for about two miles before it dead-ended with a sharp right turn into a rustic looking white farmhouse that looked as if it had been there since the Civil War and was the entry point for a rural farm that looked to cover hundreds of acres.

More by training than instinct, Smitty pulled into the dusty driveway, did a U-turn, and backed the car off the driveway onto the lawn. It was a perfectly idyllic setting—miles from nowhere and the perfect place for an ambush. If the need arose, Smitty wanted to be able to unass the area most Ricky-Tic—to use an old Nam expression.

He shut off the motor and stepped out of the car, mentally checking to assure himself that the Magnum and the extra rounds were concealed in their normal location, and the blackjack and the bayonet he'd hidden weren't causing impressions that might be visible through the back of his jacket. It was too hot to be wearing his old army field jacket, but it did conceal his weapon and the extra items Smitty deemed necessary for what lay ahead.

Smitty was halfway to the farmhouse when the front door was suddenly jerked open.

"Howdy 1LT," Sergeant Mike said somberly. He was wearing farmer's jeans and a long sleeve flannel shirt. He stepped casually over the sill, across the porch, down the steps and met Smitty halfway with an extended hand. "Have any trouble with the directions?"

"Nope," Smitty answered shortly, taking his hand. He looked around, and for want of anything else to say, asked, "Johnson Farm Lane?"

"Yeah." Sergeant Mike laughed easily. "It's my lady's grandfather's name. The family's been here for over a hundred years."

Smitty glanced around dejectedly. Of all the places, why did it have to be here, and of all the people, why did it have to be him?

"Um, Mike. I met up with an air force quad-star at Pop's grave. He gave me an envelope with directions that led me here," Smitty said, disbelief evident in his voice.

"I know," Mike said. "Barney called, and told me that you'd be stopping by." Mike paused, then concluded, "I had the feeling when I saw him at the dedication yesterday that he was going to call."

"Yesterday at the dedication," Smitty said. "I didn't see him there."

"That's because you'd never met him until today and weren't looking for him." Mike said. "But he was there. He's always been there."

"Know him long?" Smitty asked.

"We've traveled some together," Mike answered.

Smitty stared at his former sergeant, who eyed him back without blinking. Whatever this was about and whatever was going to happen, Smitty was going to have to ask, because Mike sure as hell wasn't going to volunteer.

"So where do we go from here?" Smitty asked.

"Not we, 1LT, you," Mike corrected. He pointed in the direction of the woods about a half a mile away, and to a barn that looked to be just in front. Mike reached in his pocket and handed Smitty a key. "Here 1LT, you'll need this."

"Key to the barn?" Smitty asked.

"No, you dumb ass, it's the key to that tractor over there," Mike said with a playful head-slap. "It's a good half-mile and too hot to walk. Follow that path beside the field and when you get there, go up the hill and around to the doors in the back.

It's a three-story barn. The first floor is an earth barn for the cattle, the third is the loft. What you're looking for, 1LT, is located on the second floor."

"Why aren't you coming with me?" Smitty asked suspiciously.

"Because I follow orders, too," Mike replied flatly. He turned and walked purposefully toward his automobile.

Smitty stood nervously in front of the tractor. He had just started to step on, when Mike called after him, "Oh, and 1LT, as soon as you get there, shut the old girl down. She's got a bad head gasket, and I don't want her running hot and seizing up."

Smitty waved his acknowledgment. Mike started his beat-up pickup truck, drove out of the driveway, and was soon lost in a cloud of dust.

Smitty was sure he was now alone, totally alone. He started the tractor, engaged the gear, and set off. With each yard closer to the barn, his adrenaline and heartbeat edged up another notch. Despite the wind in his face, his brow began to bead with sweat, and moisture started to form in the small of his back. The end was in sight, both figuratively and literally. It would take him five minutes to bump his way up the dusty path beside the fields, but it had taken a lifetime to get here.

Smitty pulled around behind the barn next to a set of double doors approximately equivalent in size to an airplane hangar's entryway and stopped. Located next to it was a single entry door that, judging from the cobwebs, hadn't been opened for a long time.

Nervously, with his heart racing almost as fast as the tractor, Smitty stepped off, shutting off the motor as Mike had requested, removed and cocked his Magnum, and put his hand on the doorknob.

He stopped. His military training kicked in, and he retreated to the safety of the nearby forest, and settled down to wait. After five minutes, convinced that no one was following him, he retreated fifty yards into the woods. Smitty did a 100-yard-by-100-yard grid search, listening attentively for the slightest sound, to convince himself that no one was close by waiting to ambush him.

He exited the woods and circled the barn looking for signs of recent entry but found none—not a footprint or impression. He was totally alone, or maybe whoever was in there had an accomplice who had covered up his entry. Either way, Smitty was taking no chances. He circled around to the front and slipped quietly through the front access door and closed it silently behind him.

The barn was eerily quiet, almost like a tomb. The light, what little there was, came through spacing between the warped and shrunken slats, and the occasional broken-off plank. The whole barn smelled of manure and was dank and musty.

Smitty waited thirty seconds for his eyes to get accustomed to the semi-darkness then began to look around. Immediately to his left was a ladder that seemed to go to the second floor and possibly the loft. It was hard to tell in the darkness. Remembering his military take-the-high-ground training, Smitty began to climb, making certain that his steps were like rose petals falling on a velvet carpet and would not create a stress crack that would squeak and give away his own advantage.

He reached the second floor, but was not able to reach the loft as the ladder ended there, and paused to look down. The first floor was some fifteen feet below. Above it, the second floor was only half the area of the first with a balcony running diagonally across the middle and ten feet around on both sides to the front. The third floor loft above was actually two lofts, located on each side of the barn with two catwalks that crossed back and forth, double doors on each end with a beam, and a pulley on the front end obviously for raising and storing the hay. Based on the rust and cobwebs, the pully appeared to have not been used for that purpose in years.

Smitty's first thought was to search the loft, but he quickly abandoned that idea. The only ladder was located next to the railing overlooking the first floor, or it used to be. There were age discolorations and impressions on the planks denoting its former path, but the ladder itself was nowhere to be found. Obviously some time in the past hundred years, it had rotted away to the point of being unsafe and had been removed.

The second floor beyond the balcony was semidarkness. Smitty caught an odd reflection and was puzzled by the ghostly shapes. He nervously sighted on it with his Magnum. Glancing to his left, he saw a light switch with bare wires which seemed to run upwards to sockets, with no shades, hanging from the beams of the loft. Surmising that whoever was waiting for him would be set up for him to come in the back, Smitty switched on the light, and as he did so, crouched—with his weapon at the ready—behind a rusty tractor engine located just to his left.

The barn was immediately bathed in light as sixteen two-hundred-watt bulbs completely illuminated the second floor and most of the first. Smitty laughed at his own nervousness. The reflections were headlights, grilles, and bumpers refracting light off their fading bright work.

From Smitty's vantage point, he could see lined up across the front a couple of Chevy pickups—a '35 and a '49, as best he could tell. Next to them was a '50 Mercury fastback that had been chopped so that the roofline was lowered to the point that the windshield was no more than twelve inches high, probably by Sergeant Mike when he was Smitty's age.

All had flat tires, and a thick layer of dust and grime that indicated that they had not moved from their present positions in many years. As Smitty approached them, a second row of cars behind them caught and held his eye. Not believing what he was seeing, Smitty skirted the first row of classics and stopped in front of the second, stunned with his mouth hanging open.

The car directly in front of him was a foreign car and not just any import. It was a Hillman, a 1960 two-door convertible, with the seats removed, and the top down, that was crammed with spare engines, transmissions and boxes of miscellaneous parts. Next to it was a 1959 Hillman convertible, his convertible from high school. Smitty's eyes began to tear as he approached the last car, a Hillman also, but a station wagon, or estate car as it was known in England when Dad purchased it many years ago in 1959.

Smitty advanced slowly, touching the dusty old car with all the reverence and delicacy of someone touching the frame of the Mona Lisa. His mind was racing with questions. How did they get here, how long had they been here, and why hadn't Sergeant Mike told him about them before?

By the dust, they'd been here a while. Smitty circled the cars, noting as he did that the license plate on his convertible said 1966, and the one on Dad's car 1968. He advanced to the driver's door of Dad's car, brushed the dust off the driver's window, and peered in. Inside, taped to the horn button was an envelope addressed in Dad's handwriting; the envelope said simply "No. 2 son," Dad's pet name for Smitty when he was a kid.

Smitty opened the door and slid into the seat. With trembling hands, he detached the envelope, opened it, and began to read:

29 January 1969

Son,

Today is your nineteenth birthday and having you here to share it with me would be the ideal present. Since you're not, I'm giving you the next best thing; I'm giving you a present. I'm stashing these rusting buckets of bolts that mean so much to you here in the barn of one of my World War II buddies in the hope that one day you'll come back to claim them.

I hope that one day I'll be able to tell you in person how wrong I was in giving away something that was not mine to give to your brother.

You were right that night in the garage. I was a pussy-whipped old windbag, but no more. As of today, and from this day forward, I'm going to emulate my son, do the right thing, and stand up beside him.

I told myself that if I did this horrible thing, I could make things right with your mother. She has a lot of baggage that I am accountable for, and I thought that this would finally make her see that I truly loved her.

But like I always told you, a man can bullshit everybody but the face he shaves in the mirror every morning, and that's just what I was doing, shitting myself.

I guess the real reason was that I was jealous of you. You were sixteen, and everything I always hoped I would be: young, fearless, and willing to risk your life for nothing more than a principle. More to the point, you saw through the sham of my marriage and phoniness of my own teachings, challenging me to come forward and stand beside you. I chose instead to retreat behind the skirts of a woman whom I was never truly meant to be with.

The two most powerful human emotions are jealousy and hate—Siamese twins that fuel and feed on one another. People with creative drive who strive for greatness cause envy in those who are willing to settle for half. Left unchecked, the envy turns to jealousy and eventually to hatred. Hatred controls their emotions as they devote all their waking hours to plotting and scheming to get even for some imagined evil.

And believe me, they will. They'll rally others with weak minds like them and stir up a mindless panic that will accomplish their short-term aim, but leave them unfulfilled, still searching for their ultimate goal.

In constant search of this elusive emotion, they move on to the next person of fortitude, driven to smash him, obsessed with the fact that they must crush what they can never have—which is intestinal fortitude, and what they'll never know—which is internal happiness.

The one saving grace in all this is that there will always be people who will recognize your greatness. These people are rare, but they are the true leaders of the world. In answer to the question of how do you look for them; don't worry, they look for you. They'll recognize your individuality and will rush to include you in their elusive circle. A circle whose stalwart belief is: "Do the right thing, not merely what's right."

The difference? Most people do what's right. Look at most politicians. They tell the masses exactly what they want to hear and are rewarded with election to office, promotion, fame, and money, as their result.

But the real heroes are usually not found in the public eye. They operate discreetly, laboring in anonymity for the good of their fellow man. Their yardstick is a much more meaningful measurement of friends, their reward, the self-satisfaction that only internal tranquility can bring.

You are such a person. Through the balance of your life, you will achieve great things but be constantly pulled down by those who would seek to destroy you to hide their own mediocrity and weakness.

Do not let their hatred become your anger, otherwise you will be consumed, judge solely on accomplishment and not on personal preference. Seek out others like you and encourage them when they are down.

Interact with the people of artificial purpose, but do not be disappointed when your efforts to change them are not achieved. Do not judge them or hate them. Merely pity them the treadmill of unhappiness they are trapped on and encourage them and welcome them openly, if they should try to change.

At the risk of sounding two-faced, let me say that I am taking the advice I am now giving you.

Years ago, early in the war, there was a girl named Sally that I truly loved with all of my heart. But, I took the noble path, and let her slip away. As a result, I condemned myself to a lifetime of unhappiness with your mother.

As you foresaw that fateful night, your mother was not pacified by my pitiful efforts concerning you, and in fact, began to despise me for giving in to the very thing she had told me was so desperately important to her.

I know that you blame her for this, but the fault was mine. We were meant to be married, just not to each other. If I had learned this earlier, I would have been happily married to Sally for the last thirty years.

But the nice thing about life is that God, in his infinite wisdom, is always waiting there to give you a second chance. All you have to do is ask for it.

As of this writing, your mother is again threatening me with leaving—as you might guess—if I don't find you and put right what I did to you. Well, she's in for a shock, in that, this time, I'm going to stand up to her like my Number Two Son did to me several years ago and won't stop her.

I'm giving up looking for you, troop, mainly because I already know where you are. General Thompson has been keeping me well-informed on your progress and has assured me that he will look after you. To that end, he's having Mike recalled from Germany and assigned as your platoon sergeant. Since I can't be there myself, I've arranged to send you one of my lifelong friends as the next best thing.

But the one thing I did not, and will not, do is ask Barney to keep you out of harm's way. You'll have to take your chances in Vietnam and throughout your life the same way I did. The goal of parenthood should be to raise a child who becomes a self-sufficient, fully functional adult, not a sniveling lifetime dependent on the parents that bore him.

See that's what I would do for you, if I was trying to do what's right; rather than do the right thing . . . I know on the surface, that may seem cruel, but then again, I raised Billy by the former methods, and you by the latter. You'll have to measure the results for yourself.

In closing, let me say this to you.

The source behind what you are looking for is Mission Octagon. Every person that was connected with that secret sortie has suffered. Careers have been ruined, reputations tarnished, and lives have been lost. Additionally, family members and friends have been framed or killed on the slightest rumor or merely from guilt by association. But I can honestly say I do not know who is behind it. There's a very powerful man who I believe does . . . He'll find you when the time is right and lead you here.

Good luck, Son,
Dad

Smitty laid the letter delicately on the seat and wiped away the tears that were now flowing freely down his face. He glanced around the dusty car, groping for anything that his father had left behind to touch as comfort. He found it on the package tray between the steering wheel and the door.

Dad had left a cigar box with the lid removed. There was a note attached that said, "Smoke 'em if you got 'em," and a pouch of tobacco, with his favorite pipe lying inside.

Laughing to himself at his father's forethought, Smitty opened the pouch, filled the pipe and fired it off.

The transistor radio that Dad always kept hanging from the rearview mirror since the original car radio became inoperative long ago was still there. Out of curiosity, Smitty switched it on, and to his surprise, it crackled to life, emitting snippets of country music between the static. Smitty switched it off with a smile, unslung the radio, and casually dropped it in his pocket.

He rolled down the window to air out the smoke and was glad he did. Smitty jerked the pipe from his mouth and listened. Smitty could hear the crunching of footsteps. Someone was coming, and not making any attempt to be subtle about it either.

Through the cracks in the aging barn Smitty could see the light being blocked by a human form that was walking quickly toward the rear of the barn, and from the sound, stumbling, slipping and cursing on the rutted path that led from the house.

Smitty got out of the car and closed the door silently. He quickly, and quietly, moved around to the front of the car, cursing himself for his emotional lapse in judgment. Smitty removed the Magnum, attached his silencer, propped his arm on the valley between the passenger's fender and hood, and waited.

He'd already decided that, if whoever it was entered with a gun in his hand, then he would kill him just where he stood.

The door was jerked open and a figure entered grumbling and muttering to himself. "Of all the fucked up places to hold a payoff, the asshole has to pick this God forsaken place." His demeanor totally opposite the air of diplomacy and tact that he'd displayed in their meetings in the past.

"Surprise, Tinkerbell." Smitty stood up and pointed the Magnum straight at the man's head. The intruder froze like he'd just been sprayed with liquid nitrogen.

"You!" Johnboy said. "You're the motherfucker who's been blackmailing me all these years?"

"Assume the position," Smitty said. "And I'm sure being a former district attorney for the city of Miami, you know what I'm talking about."

Johnboy snorted and walked to the side of the barn, leaning in at a thirty-degree angle. He slapped his hands against the planks loudly, and pointedly stomped each of his feet in slow motion, like a sumo wrestler, as he placed them wide apart.

"I knew it was you all along," Johnboy said. "I tried to tell that idiot police captain that you were the source. But did he believe me? Nooo."

"Stepfather," Smitty said, cutting him off, "at the risk of seeming like a disrespectful stepson, I suggest you shut the fuck up. I'm not the one who's blackmailing you, but I know who is. At least I think I do and I know why." Smitty patted him down, and found as he expected that Johnboy was not armed.

Johnboy was barely able to contain his rage.

"You see, Johnboy, the person who set this up, arranged it so that you'd show up here and, knowing our, shall we say, strained relationship, was counting, or is counting on, I should say, me eliminating you.

Smitty inserted Dad's pipe in his mouth and relit it. "Your lifetime is now measured in minutes and solely dependent on your being completely honest with me and answering the questions I'm going ask you absolutely truthfully. Are we clear?"

Johnboy looked over his shoulder at Smitty and nodded his head. He'd walked in thinking he was making another payoff, but he now realized that it was a trap and meant to be a kiss off. He was scared. Smitty could see it in his eyes, but that was okay. Smitty was scared too but for a different reason.

He knew that if he didn't quickly get what he needed and dispose of John, that whoever sent him would be coming to investigate, and he would not be coming alone.

"You were the lawyer, the major that Chuck sent home from Dearfield?"

"Yes."

"Because my dad caught you and my mother humping in the orderly room, and the popster belted you one," Smitty said.

"More than one, he damn near killed me," John said. "The colonel had me shipped stateside PDQ to the Pentagon. He told me that if I didn't go, he'd nail me on a conduct unbecoming charge. I had no choice. But the air force got me anyway. Your mother showed up in Washington several days later unannounced, and we ended up at my apartment."

"For a game of gin rummy, no doubt," Smitty said.

John ignored the remark. "I didn't intend for anything to happen. I just wanted to talk. But you know how attractive your mother is and how seductive she can be when she wants something. Things just sort of got out of hand."

Smitty nodded his head in understanding. What John was saying had the ring of truth to it. Dad always said that down through history, more bar fights, skirmishes, battles, and wars had been started by that little thing between a woman's legs than anything else. John was absolutely right, and knowing his mom's manipulative ways, it probably occurred exactly like he'd said.

"And then the CID or FBI or some such enforcement group busted in, arrested you, and told you they would nail you if you didn't immediately resign from the air force for the good of the service. That about how it happened?" Smitty asked.

John nodded his head.

"What happened next?"

"Well, the ink wasn't even dry on my separation orders when I got a call from someone in the mayor's office telling me that they heard I'd just gotten out of the service, and would I be interested in a wonderful opportunity in the DA's office in Miami.

"I was thrilled, accepted immediately, and settled into the new job with enthusiasm. About a year later, I received a call in my office late one night. The unknown voice said that if I'd look the other way at the right time, they'd not disclose my sordid past, and that there'd be lots of money in it for me in return."

John turned around and held his hands out helplessly. "I agreed. What choice did I have?"

"You could have told them to fuck off and walked."

"You're right, son, and I should have, but by then it was too late. Events were spinning out of control and had begun to take on a life of their own. I was on their payroll, and we're talking about a lot of money here. Once you've sold your soul to the devil, you can't buy it back."

"What exactly did you do?" Smitty asked.

"Mostly, I acted as a tip-off man both inside and outside of the department. A voice would call and say that on such-and-such a date a 'shipment' would be coming in. I was to assure it wasn't located by misdirecting the department's resources away from the actual area. Or if a major bust was coming down, there was a number I would call to tip them off.

"Within a couple of days, there would be an electronic transfer of funds into a special savings account in my name, and paperwork would arrive to match the total for legal assistance or some such sham to throw off suspicion."

"How did you zero in on me, LZ, and Frenchy?"

"According to a Detective Wallace who came to see me, the American teenagers were causing trouble for the Cubans, and you were leading it. When the killings started to occur, again, according to the detective, the police captain was scared to act boldly. When those Cubans murdered that young American girl and boy in that ghastly fashion, the mayor hit the panic button, declared a martial law, and called out the National Guard.

"I asked for the names of the biggest juvenile delinquents and gang leaders from the captain in charge. When he refused, I called the detective. He gave me a list of the biggest troublemakers. I presented it to the mayor, and he agreed with my plan to banish all the agitators from the state in one fell swoop rather than waiting for the arduous and lengthy judicial process."

"And my name was on the list?" Smitty asked.

"Son, your name was right at the top. Along with that Negro and that muscular white guy with the big forearms."

"Why didn't you try to screen the list? Out of the 150 names, about half of them never did anything worse than be caught out after curfew."

"There wasn't time. According to the mayor, some very heavy pressure was being brought to bear by the military. They argued that, after essentially saving Miami's ass during the Cuban Missile Crisis, this outbreak of violence, and the prominent newspaper article highlighting the NonComs street gang as being made up of air force NCO dependents, was causing their image to be tarnished, affecting their local recruiting and morale at other southern bases. But most importantly, it was hurting their appropriations currently before congress. Also, the tourist bureau was screaming bloody murder that the riots were screwing up the Snowbird trade."

Smitty glanced at his watch and began to detach the silencer from his Magnum.

"There's one more thing you should know." John nervously eyed Smitty readying his weapon.

"What's that?" Smitty grunted.

"I tried to save you. I did! I made a call to your mother and convinced her to agree to take you before your dad ever called." His voice was shaking. "I did it because I loved her."

"I know that, John," Smitty said. "And because of that, I'm going to make this quick and easy." He took a long puff on the pipe and pointed his weapon directly at John's head. "Just like I did for your brother."

Smitty fired, drew back his weapon, and fired again. The force of the shell striking John's forehead spun his body around and bounced him off the wall of the barn like a slap shot caroming off a handball court wall, before he collapsed into that dishevelment that only a dead body can achieve.

As Smitty grabbed him by the collar and dragged him forward until he was lying face down beside the old pickup. He stared at the body.

It occurred to Smitty that he'd forgotten to ask the most important question, which was, who was blackmailing him. But, on the whole it was not that big a mistake. It would have just been a confirmation of what he already knew.

Dragging the body had left a distinctive blood trail. Smitty was sure Sergeant Mike wouldn't mind the mess, especially when he learned the reason.

Ten minutes passed, then ten more. Smitty's sweat glands were starting to work overtime again, and he was beginning to think he'd made a mistake. If he was right, he'd be calling Sally from Mike's farmhouse and telling her not to hold dinner. If he was wrong, she'd probably not know for several days, until a missing persons report was filed by somebody, probably his employer when he didn't turn up in Arizona. Turn up was a key point, because Smitty was sure that if his thoughts were in error, and they did get him, no trace of his body would ever be found.

Scolding himself for his own self-doubt, Smitty refocused his attentions on what lay ahead. It was too late for second-guessing. Seventeen years of piecing together microscopic and disjointed clues could not be wrong. He was here, and the path to living until the sun set on this day was solely dependent on who walked through that door—and he wouldn't have long to wait; someone was coming.

But unlike Stepdaddy, he was making every effort at being stealthy. He was advancing from the other side of the barn, so that his shadow would not be reflected through the openings in the wood. Even though he was trying to be quiet, to Smitty's heightened awareness, his footsteps sounded like a brass band marching down a cobblestone street with horseshoe taps on their marching boots. Smitty could hear every footstep and mentally pictured his advancement.

The same rules applied; if he entered holding, he'd be leaving folding. Because Smitty was going to blow his balls off first and ask questions later.

Smitty assumed his position by the front of the old car and waited. He patted the hood of dad's car comfortingly, and said in a low voice, "Don't worry, Popster, your little boy ain't gonna vapor lock now. I'll get the man who murdered you. I swear it."

The door opened slowly and a head peeked cautiously around, stood motionlessly for five seconds, then gingerly stepped through the door. It was a man in uniform with eleven rows of combat ribbons, three stars on each shoulder, and a blue suit. Blue instead of green. As the thoughts registered in Smitty's brain, he stood up, lowered his weapon, and stepped clearly into view.

"Jesus, General, you scared me to death," Smitty said, his voice filled with relief. He wiped the sweat from his brow.

"Hi, son," General Chuck said. "Who were you expecting?"

"Well to tell you the truth, sir, I kind of thought it might be General Wilson." Smitty said pensively.

"Got him fingered as the bad guy?" Chuck asked.

"Well, sort of," Smitty said.

"Me, too. I overheard General Thompson making some arrangements with him by phone yesterday at the dedication and thought you might be headed for trouble. So I put in a call to Sergeant Mike last night. He told me you would be here this afternoon to reclaim your dad's car, and about what time, so I decided to drive down and see if you could use some backup."

"Thanks for coming," Smitty said. "It means a lot."

The general reached inside his coat, pulled out a cigar and lit it. "Least I can do for my godson." He frowned. "What's it all about, son?"

"Well, General, I'm not completely sure. But I have a clear enough picture of the puzzle I think, to piece together the rest," Smitty said hesitantly.

"Why don't you tell me what you know, then let's see if we can noodle this out together."

"Well, so far, I know Dad was part of a secret special operations group in World War II, code named Easy Does It. Its purpose was extremely hazardous and dangerous missions behind enemy lines in Europe. To observe and report, sort of like a spy would be today behind the Iron Curtain or like my training mission in Savannah years back.

"The group was a splinter group of William Donavan's OSS, using army personnel on detached service. Their purpose was to steal German secrets, then pass them on to the Pentagon to adapt them for our use or understand well enough to plan countermeasures. Because, like Dad always told me, intelligence is the swizzle stick that stirs the toxic drink of warfare.

"Each man was a specialist with an unequaled core skill. It meant advanced promotions, more money, and of course more peril. Since the casualty rates were quite high, sacrificing their love life as membership dues was expected, which meant, none was allowed to be married.

"Dad was selected because of his unique, highly skilled background in dismantling, crating, and shipping downed aircraft quickly. It was a skill that was very, very valuable to the military. If a new type of German plane crashed into a field in England or behind enemy lines in Europe, Dad was part of the team that was sent in to inspect, and crate for airlift, the valuable parts of the plane. His other task was to review all available spy photos taken of German planes for possible advancements.

"Dad had been part of this group for a year when he was hand-picked for a specific mission that was probably one of the most important of the war.

"The team spent three months training for it at a secret base in America, then two months in England totally sealed off from the rest of the Allied forces, just waiting for the right circumstances to be inserted. The mission was so vitally secret that it's still classified."

"Do you know what the mission was?" the general asked.

"It had something to do with jets. Intelligence reported in late '41 that the Germans were working on a new rocket-propelled plane that could change the course of the war if they got it operational."

"That wasn't exactly a secret, son," General Chuck objected. "Hell, every latrine-o-gram had that rumor."

"Yes, sir, but what made this mission so secret was, this was not your typical—though still highly dangerous—go in undetected, photograph the plane, sketch trace, or photograph the blueprints, then turn them over to the authorities kind of spy foray.

"The Allied experts, and the generals in Washington, knew that if the Germans completed this plane, the Heinkel 280, it could change the course of the war. And they knew something else. This kind of technology was so advanced that they'd have to have a real plane in order for it to do them any good. Pictures and prints wouldn't do, and it couldn't be a snapshot in time. The team would have to be inserted and have time to study the plane, which meant they'd have to actually work and be around the aircraft for some time.

"The key question was how. To gain the Germans' confidence and establish their own credibility, the team would have to have firsthand knowledge of our latest technology, which meant giving them our own innermost secrets. There could be no evasion or ruse, because it would be too easy for their spies to check. So in effect, the mission was to become traitors, and the only way that could be accomplished was to make it real.

"It was the hairiest of missions. The team members selected were told in advance that they'd have to break off relationships and start laying a trail of deceit, so that their arrest and escape would be seen as a progressional next step when the German spies checked, which they most surely would.

"While the rest of the Allies were trying to destroy the Germans' advanced aircraft bases, this mission, code named Mission Octagon, was exactly the opposite. The team was to set themselves up to be arrested for acts of treason by the conventional Allied Command, escape, flee to Germany by way of Sweden, get captured, then help the Germans—aid and abet the enemy—in completing the plane, then fly the completed model out of there back behind Allied lines.

"They were told that once they were inserted, if they were exposed, the government would deny their existence, and their records would forever show them to be traitors to their own country. Also, if the mission went sour, they were not to get captured and, if for any reason a team member was compromised, they were to eliminate him."

"Go on," Chuck urged.

"The team comprised six men. An airplane maintenance specialist responsible for understanding their technology. An electronics and equipment specialist responsible for understanding the planes' systems, and also acting in the capacity of radioman. An intelligence specialist responsible for compiling the data, coding it—since he was the only one who had the Allied code transmissions memorized—and passing it on to the Allies. The fourth man was the team security specialist who was responsible for assuring that cover stories were airtight and, should the mission require it, serve as the team's demolition expert.

"If I assume that Dad was the maintenance specialist and that Sergeant Mike, who told me in Nam that his original skill was electronics specialist, knew my father and was running classified ops in World War II, then that makes him the second man on the team. That would make Lieutenant Wilson the intelligence specialist and it's not too far a stretch to fit Stan the Man in as the security specialist. But that leaves two unknown to me."

"Got any leads on the other two?" The general dusted off the front fender of the Hillman. He rested his rear on it comfortably and crossed his arms.

"A couple," Smitty said.

"Think out loud."

Smitty laid his Magnum on the hood beside the general, stretched, and walked several paces toward the door to think. He held his hands to his forehead and rubbed it, leaning against his Hillman.

"Well, sir, there had to be someone on the team with aircraft engineering experience who could understand the technical specifications and requirements. Like maybe a specialist in aircraft design, borrowed or drafted from a leading stateside airplane designer—so that would make five.

"Additionally, there would have to be a pilot to fly out if, improbably, the mission succeeded. My guess is that since these teams were normally made up of seven men, and since this one only had six, that would make the sixth man the team lead. The lynchpin to Donovan and the few generals and the president, who knew the truth," Smitty lowered his hands, clasped them together, and stretched.

"When you described the first four members of the team, you were able to make an educated guess as to their names. You've told me what you thought the roles were of the last two, but haven't ventured a guess as to the names of the individuals," General Chuck said shrewdly. "Why?"

"Well sir, several times when I'd ask former commanders, like General Wilson or friends of mine, notably Sergeant Mike or Stan the Man, if they knew my father personally, they'd all get a distant kind of stare and respond the same way: 'We've traveled some together.'

"At first it didn't mean anything to me, but after spending my own time in the military, it seems to have come up too many times for it not to be something else."

"Like what?"

Smitty looked at General Chuck thoughtfully. "Like maybe a recognition response for this secret covert operation."

"I don't understand where you're going with this, son," General Chuck said, with a trace of irritation.

Smitty relit the pipe and looked hollowly at General Chuck. "General, I heard my father use that same recognition code only once, in the hallway of the headquarters in Dearfield the day I first met you back in 1959; Dad used it in reference to you. That would make your late brother, the one you told me was killed in the war, who was, in fact an aircraft designer, the fifth man."

He removed the pipe from his mouth. "That makes you the pilot and the team lead." Smitty tapped the pipe on the side of the barn to remove the ashes. "That also makes you the traitor and the master puppeteer who I've been hunting for the last fifteen years."

CHAPTER TWENTY-SIX

For a minute, Smitty thought Chuck hadn't heard him and was just on the verge of repeating it, when the general slid off the fender and picked up Smitty's Magnum; the .357 was now pointed directly at his heart. "Used to be pretty good with one of these things in Korea. Reckon I can still hit what I aim at, if need be."

He puffed heavily on his cigar. "I hate to do this, son, but I'm afraid I'm going to have to turn you over to the authorities for violation of the National Secrets Act and threatening to expose classified and potentially embarrassing information to the public."

"And let me guess: on the way in, I'll accidentally slip on a bar of soap in the shower and break my neck before anyone can question me. Is that about it?"

"Something like that." All traces of the genial general were gone.

"But first, I suppose, you'll want me to talk?" Smitty asked.

"Oh, I insist," Chuck said.

"You're holding the weapon. Are you sure that thing's loaded?" Smitty asked.

"Let's find out." He pointed the weapon directly at Smitty's knee from a distance of six feet and pulled the trigger.

In the absolute quiet of the barn, the noise of the empty chamber clicking sounded like someone hitting an anvil with a ten-pound sledge. The general pulled the trigger again, then once more, with the same heart stopping sound, and the same result.

"Surprise, Tinkerbell, no bullets." Smitty reached into his pocket and brought out Dad's .45. "You see, I figured you'd never expose yourself until you felt you had the upper hand. So, I only put two shells in the chamber. One was more than enough to attend to Stepdaddy. I fired the second through that hole in the roof, just to make sure the chamber was truly empty. I figured that you would not be a long time coming once I attended to your errand. Then you'd think you'd have something you could hold over me my entire life to get me to do your bidding. God knows how many other weak-minded fools you were able to set up and trap. But that's the way with you. It's a great technique, and you used it effectively on both my father and Dickless over there, his late brother, and God knows how many others, for thirty years. But, unfortunately for you, it won't work this time."

"So what happens now?" Chuck raised his hands, still holding the Magnum. "You going to kill me?"

"No, sir," Smitty said with certainty. "There's a few dozen people who can't wait to get you injected with truth serum. Probably solve most of the unknown espionage cases from the Cold War 'til now."

Smitty smiled and added roguishly, "Hell, we might even find out what really happened to JFK."

"You bastard." Chuck cocked his arm and threw Smitty's Magnum directly at him in rage and disgust.

Smitty ducked. The .357 sailed directly over his head, bounced off the roof of the '35 pickup, and went spinning off into the shadows of the first floor. Smitty heard it hit with a plopping sound that he was sure meant that his friend of twelve years was now resting comfortably in a big pile of cowshit.

Smitty cocked the .45 and shoved the general up against the wall. He frisked Chuck, relieving him of the .45 he wore in an inside shoulder holster. Smitty sent it spinning over the railing to join his own Magnum. He slowly backed away toward the door, keeping the general constantly in the crosshairs of the revolver.

"Now, General, we're going to take a little walk to the farmhouse so I can make a call. Let's go." Smitty motioned with the pistol.

The door opened quietly behind him.

"Hello, Irishman." Smitty felt his heart sink.

"Hello, Polack." Smitty lowered his weapon and, as he expected, saw his former Nam bud pointing his own .45 directly at Smitty's head.

"This one's loaded," Ron said pleasantly, but there was no mistaking the deadly intent behind his words.

Smitty dropped his gun.

Waving Smitty back with his weapon, Ron advanced into the barn and picked up the .45, handing it to the general. "Are you all right, Father?"

"I'm fine," Chuck said. "Now then, Godson, we were discussing how you wanted to talk. I think you'll do it; I think you'll do it now."

"Why should I?"

"Because, you annoying motherfucker, you know that the minute you stop you'll be dead. And minutes are a precious commodity to a condemned man," Ron said.

Smitty brought the tobacco pouch out his back pocket and leisurely began to fill the pipe. He purposely busied himself with this until the general became upset, which was his intent.

"Well?" General Chuck demanded angrily.

"What are we waiting for? Let's kill him and get out of here."

"Listen and learn," the general said. "This young man had defied, and survived, our very best efforts to disassociate and kill him. Aren't you at least curious as to how?"

"Yes, sir," Ron said in a sullen voice. Smitty was sure that if the decision was left to him, then he'd just shoot him and be done with it.

Seeing Chuck's enraged expression, Smitty asked, "Where would you like to start? With the pompous acts of treason of a U.S. senator or with his equally treasonous but psychotic son?" He glanced disdainfully at Ron. "Or grandson?"

"Don't you dare say that about my father!" Chuck slapped Smitty across the face with all the gentleness of a scorned ex-lover. "He was a patriot."

"Okay, let's start with Daddy's treason, and we'll work up to you," Smitty said.

Pausing to relight the pipe, Smitty began.

"Your father was a chairman of the committee in the Senate that oversees and sets the guidelines for intelligence gathering for the military and civilian government agencies. As such, and also because he was a confidant of President Roosevelt, he had access to all classified military and civilian documents.

"The Octagon mission was special. It was to be deep and dark, so it was classified with a Presidential Eyes and Dissemination Only security clearance—the highest classification possible.

"General Wilson told me about it in Vietnam, when we mutually laid our cards on the table and explained it in more detail when we discussed it while I was at Reed. That meant, outside of the team, there were only six people who had a high enough security clearance to entitle them to know the intimate details of the mission. The president, who approved it, the head of the OSS, the secretary of war, the chairman of the joint chiefs, the army chief of staff, and your father. Interestingly, the vice president, Henry Wallace, was left out of the circle after Donovan brought to Roosevelt's attention the fact that Wallace was unintentionally disclosing information. He was talking to his brother-in-law Charles Brudman, the Swiss ambassador to the United States, through a German intelligence plant in the Swiss Embassy in Bern. To ensure that the mission was airtight, Roosevelt, with his known mania for secrecy, did not allow any notes to be taken during any of the planning meetings. Only Donovan, his confidant, knew the complete plan.

"When the president asked who should lead it, the answer was obvious: the man who thought of it. That would have made then Captain Thompson the seventh man. But at the last minute, he was removed from the team. Why, I can only speculate, but I'll bet my next gold crown it had to do with your daddy lobbying the president hard that Captain Thompson was too valuable to risk on a single incursion mission.

"Anyway, whatever the reason, it worked. Captain Thompson was promoted to major, then assigned as the overall project coordinator for all incursion missions in the European Theater of Command and for Easy Does It. In spite of the promotion, since he'd thought up the original mission, Major Thompson did retain the responsibility for team makeup.

"Having the entire resources of the Easy Does It espionage unit to pick from, and the entire service for that matter, he picked my father, Sergeant Mike, Sergeant Stanley Baker, and then First Lieutenant Wilson.

"Seeing the team makeup and sensing a tremendous political opportunity for himself with the vice presidency—and perhaps the presidency itself—now up for grabs should Roosevelt fail to live out his upcoming fourth term, your father again lobbied the president hard for you and your brother to be added. You were an up-and-coming young first lieutenant and fighter pilot ace who was promoted to captain and assigned as the team commander.

"And, based on what my father told me in a bar two years ago, that makes your older brother the boy genius on loan. He was a graduate of MIT and was employed as a designer at the leading aircraft manufacturer in the country—the same one I work for now. With an IQ well into the lofty levels of genius and a photographic memory, he was perfect for the part.

"The team trained in secret. People were told that it was a court-martialable offense to even approach any team member or question them. There was one other thing. To make it seem real, they had to kiss off their current relations in such a way that, when they were checked up on by the German spies later, the path to treason was well-established. So, prior to the beginning of training, each man was encouraged to become entangled with a female who could be conveniently dumped at the right time."

"Pure speculation, son, pure speculation. But by all means go on, it's quite entertaining," General Chuck said contemptuously.

"The mission planning and the incursion worked perfectly also. The six of you 'escaped' in a stolen bomber from a little airfield south of London and flew to Sweden. There you asked for and received asylum in the German Embassy. It didn't take them long to check your stories and hustle you out of there on the first transport to Germany; you were a plum falling right into their laps. After another two weeks' delay, you were transported to the German rocket facility and with your brother's memory button on play, gained instant credibility by giving them the innermost secrets of all our newest aircraft designs.

"They checked your stories again, and again, they checked out. Why wouldn't they? Only six people knew the truth, and, thanks to neutralizing the vice president's loose lips, the Germans sure as hell didn't have spies who reached that high in the U.S. government.

"Intelligence missions, even suicidal ones such as this, were enthusiastically embraced by your father and OSS Director Donovan as being the most efficient use of limited assets early in the war. The president and Secretary of War Stimson were not nearly as enthusiastic, seeing these near-certain-death missions as only a necessary defensive evil until such time as America could carry the offensive war to Germany.

"From the time this idea was hatched in the securest corners of the White House until it was implemented was well over a year. Time marches on and so did the war effort. In November of 1942, when Easy Does It was conceived, the Allies were in dire straits, reacting mostly in a defensive mode as the American military war machine was gearing up in every town and factory across the United States.

"But by the time the bureaucratic hurdles were cleared, the team picked, the training completed, and the team inserted, it was the second week of January of 1944, and things had begun to change. Good from the overall allied perspective, but bad from the perspective of the team and more importantly, your father. The mission that had seemed so vitally important as to be classified a fundamental key to the war effort just fourteen months ago was now being second-guessed as overreactive.

"When it was finally disclosed to selected members of Congress and the president's staff in the spring of 1944—after the team had already been inserted, by the way—they were appalled and counseled the president that if the public ever found out that the United States government sponsored a mission whose sole purpose was to commit treasonable acts, there would be hell to pay—no matter what the reason—and he'd probably be impeached.

"Conveniently, as politicians do—mostly because they're concerned about their own legacy—the president followed the recommendation of his staff. The mission was canceled and the team was ordered withdrawn.

"Remembering your father's arduous campaign to have you and your brother placed on the team, and the recent disclosure of his illegal offspring to the press as you yourself told me a year or so back, the president had himself a built-in fall guy.

"He conveniently assigned the blame to your father and quietly dropped his plans to include him on the next ticket as vice president—opting, as we now know for 'the buck stops here' Harry. Your father, his reputation ruined, and his career, credibility, and patriotism now being openly questioned by the president, resigned from his Senate Intelligence Committee and went home in shame and into seclusion for the balance of his term.

"When the word reached you, through secret code, of the president's decision, and your father's subsequent political demise, you were bitter. Bitter against the president, bitter against your country, and most importantly, bitter against the individual, your father's key political rival in the Senate, who, at President Roosevelt's direct request, had championed assigning blame to your father.

"But a plot was hatching to get even, but to do it, you'd have to have a scapegoat. That was the painful lesson of your father's demise: make sure you have someone to take the blame. And that someone was close at hand, your own Boy Scout brother. The brother you hated because he was everything you weren't—and never could be—and so he became the object of your distorted, psychotic jealousy.

"The mission orders were specific. If team members were exposed, or threatened to expose other members, they were to be killed. So you set it up, much like a little boy having an 'I'll show you' tantrum. You ratted your own brother out by telling Lieutenant Wilson that your brother was a collaborator who was planning to sell them out—probably to Messerschmitt himself. You conned my father into pulling the trigger with the 'I can't kill my own brother' bit, and he fell for it and did your dirty work for you.

"Now, you had a marker to use on my father for the rest of his life. But before you could eliminate the rest, Major Thompson parachuted into Germany and canceled the mission.

"The team escaped when you were ordered to fly them out of there in a stolen, conventional German bomber. Stan the Man, acting as the team's demolition specialist, destroyed the entire underground manufacturing facility, but not before you stole the letter from Dad's knapsack and copied all the prints to the new German jet plane, the ME 262, that you'd planted on your brother.

"As we now know, the introduction of the ME 262 did not change the outcome of the war, but would have, if Hitler had listened to his staff and introduced it as a fighter rather than a bomber. It was years ahead of its American counterpart, the XP59A. Not only was it over one hundred miles an hour faster, but also Hitler was rushing to put it into service in mid-'44. And most importantly, the intel that the real plane existed in '41 had set off paranoia and panic inside the White House, particularly with Roosevelt, whose withered body was racked by polio and twelve years of the unique, debilitating kind of stress that only the weight of the presidency could bring—to say nothing of the added burdens of the Depression and the second World War.

"The complete set of prints, even without the actual plane, would have been worth a small fortune. They wound up in Russian hands in August of 1944. Coincidentally, that was the same month you accompanied a contingent of senior military advisers to Moscow to lend your expertise on fighter tactics.

"You intended to eliminate the entire team, but they were ordered home, and told under no circumstances would they be allowed to fight in the war—in Europe or Japan—again. Their identities had been compromised and the Axis would shoot them on the spot as spies. Now you were stuck.

"To divert attention away from yourself, you implicated all the other team members in guilt by association with your brother, tarnishing their reputations and retarding their future career advancements, leaving them all emotionally scarred and planting the seeds for a lifetime of unhappiness.

"Not understanding what was happening to them, most tried to put their lives back together as best they could and move on, never realizing that they'd been manipulated, used in a high-stakes game of government chess, and then abandoned.

"Others, like my dad, you kept under your wing to ensure that they did your day-to-day work by convincing them that you were the only thing standing in the way of their being dropped from the service.

"But you had even bigger problems. Prior to insertion, following orders, the rest of the team became entangled with Saturday night floozies. My father, without meaning to, screwed up. He became entangled with the love of his life, Sally, and was going to quit the team rather than go on.

"Dad had talked it over with Lieutenant Wilson, who after listening to his reasons agreed and even went out of channels and approached Major Thompson with a request that Dad be relieved.

"But surprise, surprise. After a talk with you, Dad reversed his stand and went along. You promised him something, General. What was it—maybe that you'd have your daddy see to it that he got a commission to second lieutenant when this mission was over, or was it something even better?

"Anyway, that wasn't the real reason, was it? Sally was a big-boned, big-breasted, ash blonde girl who caught your eye. You wanted her for yourself and knew that if Dad left the team, you'd never have a chance. So you talked him into staying with the mission, using the God, country, and patriotism spiel, knowing that Dad would be leaving the love of his life behind.

"And just to be sure they'd never be together again, you called your daddy and had him declare Sally a security risk to the team. He had her banished to the Philippines. You figured that you'd work out some way to eliminate my father during the mission, then you'd have Sally returned from exile and pick up your secret courtship where you left off when the mission was over.

"But Sally had gotten captured by the Japanese in the fall of the Philippines and was imprisoned for the next two years. You knew what happened to those women, didn't you? And Sally confirmed it to me. Sally was now damaged goods, and you didn't want her anymore. So you used your father's power to have her reassigned to the Asian command when she was released and told her that my father was dead. Then you told my father the same thing about Sally when he returned.

"And, based on the fact that a hussy had brought down your father, in your sick mind, that's what they all became to you: Tools to be used for your own twisted plans and momentary pleasure. In your twisted mind, that's all women were to you.

"You met my mother at a party just before you left on the Octagon mission. She was attractive and had a way of turning a man on with a seductive look and fit the role of floozy in your demented mind perfectly. But she wasn't ready for someone like you; she was just a seductive tease. You got her drunk, and when she passed out, you raped her. Why not? All women were just sluts to you, weren't they? Remember what you called that girl in the Washington gin mill? 'A dumb sperm repository.'

"When she found out she was pregnant, your daddy, who had considerable power, had her sent away to your aunt's house to deliver the baby. Only there was not one, but two—two boys. Your father secretly had them placed through private adoptions. But you made sure you knew where they were. You had plans for them.

"Eight weeks after my mother had delivered her illegitimate twosome and four weeks after the team returned to the States, you had her set up on a blind date with my dad. Just to make sure the cover-up was complete, you told my father that my mother had been engaged to a pilot, gotten pregnant, and that the baby was stillborn after the pilot was killed. You told him he should be very nice to her.

"Dad, reeling from what he thought was the loss of Sally, and my mother, with her self-esteem somewhere near zero, decided to get hitched the day before D-Day, several months later. In their tortured minds, they thought it was love, but in reality, it was just a marriage of mutual support, contrived by you to cover up your own cruelty.

"A week later, your father resigned from the Senate. Two weeks after that, he blew his brains out in the study of his home. Because of his confidant position to the president, Roosevelt ordered his home sealed. When it was searched by the FBI, they found a secret panel with copying equipment, and the entire plans for the pending invasion of Japan. On the threat that the invasion plans had been compromised, the invasion had to be delayed, prolonging the war almost six months at a cost of thousands of American lives. Your mother protested your father's innocence to the end of her life—with good reason.

"Lieutenant Wilson suspected that you had planted the information to deflect attention away from yourself; he was right. So you set him up on a fake affair, complete with lurid pictures, and left the package for his wife. Ingeniously, it killed two birds with one stone. It tied him up in a messy divorce, effectively neutralizing him from pursuing his suspicions, and, at the time, it ruined his career.

"But that didn't matter to you, did it? You'd found your modus operandi, and you stuck to it. You were going to get even with your country for what they did to your father—even if you had to use him to do it—and get even with the bitch that did your father in by fucking over, literally and figuratively, every 'sperm repository' you could get your hands on, then use your daddy's power base to cover up the damage path.

"First, it was the German ME 262 plans. Then it was the newest American designs, starting with selling the entire B-29 plans in 1945 to the Russians, which became the TU4 and made its maiden flight in May of 1947 at Vladivostok. After the war, as one of the first jet aces, you had the access and opportunity, and you made it count.

"On the outside, you continued to be the stalwart of democracy, the hero of heroes, the genial officer, the golden boy totally above reproach. While underneath, you were the night crawler slinking in and out of the sewers, selling your country's most treasured secrets for thirty pieces of silver, and raping women to satisfy your own psychotic urges.

"How does it feel knowing that, literally, thousands of American soldiers died in three wars because of your treachery?" Smitty asked, disgusted.

"Actually it feels pretty good, son. At least I don't have to worry about the same thing happening to me that happened to my father," the general said with a sadistic grin. "I won't have to worry about being tossed on the scrap heap at the whim of some bullshit politician who never even heard a shot fired in anger."

"General, you stole your country's most intimate secrets, arranged the death of countless people by setting them up for blackmail, and exposing them to be killed when they were no longer useful. You've raped innocent women and used the very Constitution you so adamantly claim to support to line your own pockets." Smitty spat at the general's feet. "If your father were alive, he'd be so proud."

"Enjoy that smoke, son, because it'll be your last," General Chuck said.

"Doesn't seem too wise having me killed here. Sergeant Mike won't like that."

"That old fool will be taken care of today, as well."

Then noting the look on Smitty's face, he said. "You don't seem surprised, Godson."

"I'm not. Where's your other bastard son, Gumdrops?" Smitty asked. "The one I'm going to kill after Ron."

"I imagine he's attending to your friend, Sergeant Mike, and his wife right now. I told him to kill the sergeant but not his old lady. She'll make a cute pass-around morsel for us to enjoy after we kill you."

Smitty's stomach churned at the thought of the three of them gangbanging Mike's wife. Twisted sadistic fucks that they were, they'd probably do it in the same bedroom where the old sarge lay dead on the floor.

But that was a later problem. Smitty had to deal with first things first, and the very first thing was his old Nam boss. His dad's wise words came rushing to the forefront of his brain: "It ain't being scared that matters; it's what you do when you're scared that counts." And he needed one more thing.

"General, I can't believe you're so cavalier about admitting to treason, murder, and rape," Smitty said.

"I killed only when it was necessary to accomplish my goals," the general said.

"Like my father, huh? I don't think you have the guts to admit to my face that you murdered the man who considered you a lifelong friend."

"Don't bet on it, sonny boy. I killed your father—murdered him in cold blood—before you could get to him and have him inform on me to that Eagle Scout General Thompson," the general said loudly. "He even talked to me about it, said he was having a fit of conscience."

"And what about Ron there? Was he the mysterious major who set up Big Walt in Saigon, then killed him later in Savannah when he was no longer useful?"

"You're goddamn right I did," Ron said. "It was a pleasure shooting that stuttering doofus through the back of the head. He was playing us to learn our methods and then was going to tell you everything. Besides, it was a clean shoot. The dumb-ass Savannah cops still think it was a drug deal gone south. And just to make sure, I capped his cellmate and butt-fucked his old lady before killing her and made sure that four-eyed idiot got framed for it."

"Well, Polack, you got away with it, but you won't for long," Smitty said.

"What the fuck are you talking about?" Ron brandished the weapon in Smitty's face.

"Ron, please believe me, I'm appealing to you as my former Nam commander and bro. I have no desire to see you hurt. Please put down your weapon or you will be killed," Smitty said.

"You think you can reach me and take this weapon from me before I kill you? Dream on, asshole." Ron snorted.

"Don't play games with him, son. Just shoot him and let's get out of this shithole and on to the pleasures of the middle-aged cutie waiting for us in the farmhouse," the general said.

"Last chance," Smitty said with a smile.

Both Ron and Chuck looked at Smitty with a disbelieving I-think-he's-nuts look as they both sighted their weapons and began to finger the triggers.

"Okay, Sergeant, fire!" Smitty yelled toward the door and executed a perfect dive behind Dad's Hillman.

Both the general and Ron turned their heads instinctively and cursed themselves at having fallen for the most obvious trap. But it was too late.

Shots rang out in rapid succession, jerking Ron with spastic contractions as one round after another riddled his body. He fell lifelessly to the floor, his body still contorting in agony even as he died. The general screamed and clutched his arm in pain as a round found his wrist, and Dad's .45 went spinning out of his hand.

The door to the barn was flung wide open, and Sergeant Mike entered with a CAR-15 in his hand, followed closely by General Wilson, armed with a .45 pistol. At a safer distance behind was Colonel Evans with medical bag in hand, followed by four soldiers in camouflaged uniforms wearing full facemasks and also carrying CARs.

Smitty dove for the pistol, got to it before General Chuck could reach it, rolled up on one knee, and zeroed the .45 directly at his forehead.

Smitty's eyes narrowed in all-consuming anger, the general's arrogant smirk only serving to increase his rage. In those psychotic eyes Smitty saw the smiles of Glenda, Linda, Frenchy, LZ, Whippoorwill, and Hogs. He imagined the pain and the suffering caused by this vile excuse for a human being to hundreds of others. But most of all, he saw faces. The faces of the nameless thousands, friend and foe, who had died through the decades as a result of his greed and treachery . . . The kaleidoscope of blurred images coming clearly into focus on the face of his father . . . The gentleness and calming reassurance of his smile that Smitty remembered from his boyhood, and the hollowness of his face as he lay lifeless in his casket at the funeral as a result of his murder . . .

He fingered the trigger of the .45, then he cocked it.

"Lunge at me, General!" Smitty growled. "It will give me the greatest pleasure to kill you for murdering my father."

"Captain, don't," General Wilson said. "He's not worth it."

"You call it, 1LT." Sergeant Mike pointed his CAR-15 directly at General Wilson's heart.

The four soldiers looked on in confusion, unsure of who was in charge or what they should do next. They looked first at the old sergeant with fear-filled eyes, then at the general in hopeful anticipation. Seeing no one moving, they waited silently for their next instruction, although they seemed to be unsure of who would give it.

General Wilson ignored Sergeant Mike's threat and stepped forward. He gently laid his right hand on Smitty's left arm. "Don't do it Smitty. You'll become what you hate."

General Chuck froze, his defiance fading as he realized that the battle was lost, and more importantly, that Smitty was just itching to shoot him. Dad always said the eyes were the keys to the soul, and the general's were no exception. His shoulders slumped in resignation and defeat.

"Why waste good ammunition on a turd?" Smitty asked tiredly, lowering the weapon.

"Smart move, son," General Wilson said. "A man who lives in anger, and solely for revenge, only keeps himself a prisoner."

Smitty handed the weapon to the general. He looked up at the loft, where Major Jim and Stan the Man each stood holding hunting rifles with scopes. "Butch, Sundance . . . nice shootin'."

Stan and Jim waved.

"Where's Officer Gumdrops?" Smitty turned to Sergeant Mike.

"He's joined his half-brothers in hell." Sergeant Mike made a throat-cutting motion with his left thumb.

"Then we've got them all," General Wilson said in a satisfied voice.

"Good," Sergeant Mike said. "Now would somebody please tell an old country bumpkin sergeant what the hell it's all about?"

"Captain, you want to do the honors? You're the one who's responsible for the U.S. government bringing to conclusion a thirty-year-old espionage case—the largest in the history of the United States."

"Yes, sir. But may I suggest first we let Colonel Evans treat Johnboy?"

"You mean he's not dead?" General Chuck asked.

"No, General. I just bounced one off the side of his skull. Made him bleed a lot. He'll have a hell of a headache, but he'll live to scam another day." Smitty paused. "To paraphrase my late daddy, if I meant to kill him . . . he'd be dead."

"Colonel Evans, if you please?" General Wilson waved his hand. He looked at Smitty curiously, "Why didn't you kill him?"

"For being a schmuck?"

"Explain it to them," General Wilson said. Stan the Man and Major Jim descended from a rope ladder and joined them.

"Well, the pattern that General Chuck used was repetitive but on different people. That was clever, but I finally figured it out," Smitty said simply. He patted General Wilson on the shoulder affectionately. "And I had a lot of help."

Smitty took a deep breath. "I guess it began on that cold winter day in Dearfield in '59 when I overheard Dad make reference to Mission Octagon through the pass-through window to the general's office.

"Then, when future Stepdad was air-freighted out of there that Christmas, it made me suspicious. Dad always said, when a sudden change occurred and someone was packaged for overnight shipment, there were always two reasons: the one stated and the real one.

"The stated reason from Dad was that he got a little out of line with my mother at the Christmas party, and the colonel had him shipped stateside. But Dad confirmed on the ride home from the airport that night, that Mom was going to stop in to see Johnboy in Washington, and I could tell by the hurt in his eyes that it was more than just a one-time thing.

"There was a history there, and even though I was only ten years old, I could tell that something was very wrong. If a man knew that his wife was headed to the States to get laid by another man, why wouldn't he stop her? Dad was the kind of man who faced things head-on. There had to be another reason, much more serious, and much bigger than simple adultery, for him to let it pass.

"It also meant that for Dad not to stop it, someone had a very big hold on him. At the time I didn't know who, but it showed me a pattern that I would come to recognize.

"The incident itself served only one purpose—it forever after made me suspicious of what I saw on the surface because there were always sharks swimming somewhere just below.

"Those suspicions were confirmed in Miami. LZ, Frenchy, and I did the right thing and paid a terrible price for it. But again, Dad wasn't surprised by what I was into. That meant that someone was keeping him well-informed. He knew, and yet he didn't try to stop it.

"Dad was a man who never ran from anything in his life, and yet here again he wasn't helping. It could only mean one thing: Dad knew that Johnboy there was in Miami. He knew because someone was keeping him informed, like maybe his former comrade from Mission Octagon, Stan the Man, the police captain. So again, there's the question: if he knew, why didn't he stop it?

"When we moved back to Savannah, trouble again seemed to be following me, and again Dad was not surprised. Someone was keeping the local authorities well-informed, to the point that when trouble started at the party that night, I was the first one blamed, even though I had long since left.

"But by now, I was old enough to start to think for myself. I knew that whatever the terrible secret that Dad was carrying, I had to find out what it was because Dad and I were close enough that whoever had a hold on him would assume that I knew and would be after me in the same way. Whoever was holding it over Dad had him by the balls, and if the secret was going to be found, I'd have to separate myself from him to find it. I had hoped to separate myself so completely that they'd stop chasing him and turn full force on me. So I dropped hints that I knew. That way, I could confirm that it was not only real, but that I was on the right path—sort of like being a moonshine blocker cutting in front of the cops so they'll chase him and forget about the hooch car.

"I was not surprised that Dad backed Mom that night when I ran away from home. He had to; she was part of the secret. In Miami, just before I killed him, Keith confirmed that I was on the right path, that he was only the flunky, and that there was a mastermind behind it.

"I passed on my thoughts to Stan the Man. Based on the way he and my father shook hands that night in the police station, I felt he was a man I could trust. I also knew that if my hunch was right, then Stan would pass the information on to the right person and reinforcements would soon be on the way.

"But killing that Neanderthal Keith was a revelation. Because it showed me that if others could be manipulated into killing for what's wrong, then I could be manipulated into killing for what's right. It also showed me that right and wrong are two sides of the same coin, separated only by point of view.

"It occurred to me that the same person could be manipulating both parties, playing one against the other in a real-life game of chess where he was a king of both colors, manipulating the pawns and the rooks and screwing the queens for his own sadistic pleasure and gain. It was a painful lesson, but, again, one I never forgot.

"From then on, I didn't bother to look for the master puppeteer. I knew he would look for me—he had to. I was playing out the good guy role. He needed me to keep chasing the bad guys to keep them from guessing the truth also.

"In order to survive the game, I would have to understand his methods of operation so I would know how to counter them. In order to win, I'd have to use those same methods against him. I figured all I had to do was stand still and he'd find me, and find me he did.

"And that's when I first got on to you, General," Smitty said, as the general winced in pain from Colonel Evans' less-than-gentle first aid on his damaged wing.

"I was suspicious when you suddenly reappeared in my life when I was assigned as your driver at that all-service conference. But thirty years of practicing espionage without getting caught had made you arrogant, and an arrogant man gets careless.

"You took me to dinner that night and read me the letter from my father that he closed with 'I ask it in the name of the favor you've owed me since Mission Octagon back in '44.'

"You had mentioned it in Dearfield in 1960 in confidential conference with my father. You then had him threaten me within an inch of my life if I discussed what I'd overheard with anyone. And now Dad had mentioned it in the letter seven years later in a plea for help. But you tried to shrug it off as being nothing. So now I knew that the source of the hold you had on my dad occurred during Mission Octagon.

"Next, you read me that letter from Stan the Man, in which Stan reported that I believed there was a mole either in the Miami police department or the Dade County Government—or both—who was pulling all the strings. But he also reported that he had been unsuccessful to date in determining who, or what, was behind it. Stan was the only one I'd shared my suspicions with, and the only one I could trust. He knew, or suspected, that you'd read me that letter, or at least the appropriate parts of it, and was really just confirming I was right, but he couldn't prove it.

"Finally, you read me a note from your brother in his report on our security mission. 'Sergeant Smith and his comrades are given highest marks for their performance under combat conditions. However, if their unique skill set is to be capitalized to its fullest potential, further training in mission planning and combat situational leadership is required.' Your brother was either with you or not. Whether he was or not, you needed his help to keep the scenario you'd set up viable.

"Lastly, you closed with a shot at Major Gates, subtly told me his brother, Johnboy there, was in Miami, and in so doing, set up the bad guys for me to chase.

"When I asked you where we go from here, you said, and I quote, 'That depends on you, kiddo.'

"You were even overconfident enough to warn me that not only were the brothers the bad guys, but that there were others who could be manipulated into killing for what's wrong—and they were not always wearing dog tags. You admitted you set up the fight in the bar and closed by saying 'Someone wants to keep you dead-center in the bull's-eye.' You felt so invincible that you were in effect telling me that you were the master puppeteer—although I didn't know it at the time—and daring me to do something about it. I got your warning, General. It was a warning that I took to heart."

"Why didn't the general just kill you?" Mike asked pointedly.

"He couldn't," General Wilson answered before Smitty could respond. "For two reasons. First, Smitty wasn't anywhere he could arrange an accident without there being an investigation, and second, he couldn't kill him until he found out what he knew and to whom he'd told it."

"So Smitty played it slow, which is the cornerstone of good espionage anyway. Isn't that right, General?" Sam asked deliberately. General Chuck scowled in reply.

"Anyway, from then on, I had a lot of help. Starting with that drummed-up intelligence mission into Savannah when I first met Ron, until now. I've had a series of guardian angels assigned to keep me out of your harm's way, while I blundered my way to the truth," Smitty said, smiling at his comrades. "Because I was the one person the general didn't have a direct hold on.

"Through your late son there, I was the bait, and I figured that someone—it turned out to be General Wilson—was the spotter, figuring whoever came near me was suspect.

"It started with the appearance of Major Jim in basic training, to counteract the introduction of your bungled attempts to bribe that MP sergeant to have me set up and killed. Then Lieutenant Colonel Wilson intervened directly on that special mission months later. He was there to check up on the report that was obviously sent to him by Stan the Man.

"Next, Colonel Wilson split up the four musketeers when we got to Nam, in a vain attempt to get Frenchy, LZ, and Big Walt out of harm's way, then arranged for me to be assigned to his group in Nam, and ultimately to SOG. It was there I got onto Ron.

"It was the incursion mission when Whippoorwill took my spot because, ironically, I was hung up at Big Walt's trial—Walt, whom Ron had set up.

"Ron was really upset when I got called to Saigon. Why? Because he'd already set a trap to have me killed by tipping off the VC to the team's landing zone. But he couldn't very well call them back, yell 'fins' when I wasn't part of the mission, and tell them that it was just a personal thing. That would have damaged his credibility and shut down the transportation pipeline of that attaché case with the secrets in it that the general there had set up Major Patsy to transport.

"So he let it happen. I was the first to reach Whippoorwill, where I found, although he'd been decapitated, there was no blood. The ghastly deed was done after he was dead, not before.

"But just before he died, he left me a message—a message that put me onto Ron from that point on. He closed his fist and raised a single digit. Then he made sure it would stay closed by wrapping his knuckles with a rubber band around the back of his wrist. The meaning was clear. The team had been fucked. And since Ron was the assignment officer, he was the only one who knew their final insertion point and, therefore, the only one who could have ratted them out.

"After the rescue mission to reclaim the bodies, when Ron conveniently pulled a fainting spell, I took a gamble and had a frank talk with Colonel Wilson. I told him not only my suspicions about Ron, but also my belief of the colonel's link to Major Jim by placing him there to masquerade as the MP corporal/captain. I also told him about the hit on the SEAL team to which LZ was assigned in the South. It was too convenient to be mere coincidence, as Ron tried to convince me.

"Unlike Ron, who told me I was nuts, the colonel didn't. He got me transferred to Okinawa and onto R&R so that Ron couldn't get at me again. But also to allow me to become the bait again and see if any other fish were hungry. Detective Wallace bit. He followed me to Hawaii and had a go at me on that road on the backside of the island.

"So now I had Ron connected to Detective Wallace, but I had no idea what the common denominator was. They were from different states from different parts of the country and apparently had a connection only through the mysterious string-puller.

"I needed a connection to the general then to see who else was involved. But to ensure that Ron would have a hard time getting at me, the colonel played it very coy. He recalled you, Sergeant Mike, from Germany where Ron had banished you after fucking you over on his first tour, and had you assigned to my Mike Force as the team sergeant."

"You did that, Sam?" Sergeant Mike asked.

"Yes, Mike, I did," General Wilson admitted. "I wasn't sure where the young sergeant was going with all of this, but given his father's status on Mission Octagon, and the fact that, as he predicted, they'd had a go at him in Hawaii, I thought he could use protection, and you were the best man I knew."

"Now I know why you told me to go to Captain Bartkowski and apologize for screwing up on my first tour in '66, and tell no one I did it. Even though, in reality, the little bastard was the one who fucked me over."

"I'm sorry, Mike. I had to have the sergeant protected at all costs. I hope you'll understand and can forgive me."

"No apology required, Sam." Sergeant Mike whistled to himself. "The little fuzz nuts kinda grew on me." He reached out and patted Smitty affectionately on the chin.

"Continue, Captain," General Wilson said.

"Several months later, Ron had one last go at me, when he became conveniently unavailable and abandoned Sergeant Mike, Hogsbreath, and me at that firebase. But we fucked up and survived. After that, Colonel Wilson had him banished to Saigon but had him under surveillance from then on. We—I should say General Wilson—had information on him individually, but nothing to tie it together. Ron's major job in Nam seemed to be to separate me from my friends to isolate me.

"I suspect that General Chuck now figured that I was getting help, so he ordered Ron to kill me in Da Nang. But again, it backfired when fate intervened. My dad had a heart attack and I cut out for home. Again, since Ron had arranged the attack on Da Nang, he couldn't stop it, and Linda and several others were killed.

"But two coincidental near-misses had you running scared, General. Sensing Major Gates's usefulness was nearing an end and afraid if we took him he might talk, you told Ron to inform the Vietnamese of the patrol he was leading. But what Ron didn't know was that I carried a letter relieving him of his command. I also gave Gates a verbal message from Colonel Wilson that detailed his treason and offered him immunity if he surrendered.

"When I presented him the letter, he realized too late, even though he slapped it away and didn't read it, that he was just the latest of the general's pawns to be blackmailed into doing his bidding, then tossed on the scrap heap. He couldn't surrender. The humiliation and loss would have been too much, so, in effect, he forced me to shoot him.

"Finally, with my deal already struck with the general's brother, and time running out, Ron had one last go at me. But he screwed up when I made sure he was on the last helicopter with us, the one Ron had told them to shoot down because it would create a tremendous political victory. Since the VC had never seen their mysterious informer, Ron had to try to save Mike and me; he was saving himself also because the VC would have shot him on sight.

"Again, surprise, surprise. When I was in the hospital at Reed, Claire, masquerading as Florence Nightingale, was planted by you, General, to watch me, and as quickly pulled out and dropped out of sight as conveniently when General Wilson appeared in the hospital room and spotted her.

"But General Wilson and I agreed that we now knew how your organization worked, General. The deal I made with the army was shot down. Somebody informed the president. That somebody was you, General. It provided us an unforeseen opportunity to use your own methods against you.

"I staged the fight in that bar with you and Dad, the same way you did for me three years earlier, not to get even, but to short-circuit your military career. According to General Wilson, you were in line for a fourth star, then air force chief of staff. He told me that in my room that day with the double talk about my favorite team, the Baltimore Orioles.

"God knows what you would have done to the country if you'd risen to the top spot in the military. Unfortunately, it took out your brother's career also, who was a hard-working, diligent three-star, who was deservedly headed along the same path with the army.

"The added benefit was that, by short-circuiting your political aims, General, it freed up General Wilson. You had been the main person to hold him back, based on your own negative reports about his mishandling of the security for Mission Octagon that resulted in your brother being killed—and then framing him after the war for a phony affair to assure he would pose you no problems in the future. General Thompson could now use his influence to convince the powers that be that they'd been wrong about their initial assessment of Sam, and as you noted, he made up for lost time.

"But since we still didn't have a direct link between you, Ron, and Detective Wallace, we established my call sign as a contact code, played it slow and waited. We agreed that, since I was injured, I would, in effect, drop off your personal radar screen for a while. I recovered, but went nuts in Savannah, partially because of all that happened to me in Vietnam, but specifically, through periodic updates from my unsuspecting father, to convince you, General, that I was now just some deranged Vietnam vet who was no longer a threat to you.

"It worked. It was convincing enough that Ron dutifully reported back to you that I was no longer a menace and moved out. So you put your organization back to work using Stepdad there as the latest conduit. But what you didn't know was that we were onto you, and we were waiting for you to do just that very thing.

"Since Mike could no longer be there, General Wilson assigned his son Fred, a real state policeman, to move in with me for two years and ensure that no harm would come to me. The stakes for industrial espionage were so high that he arranged to have Major Jim's younger sister assigned as Fred's girlfriend to check out Carla; fortuitously, they fell in love and married.

"It took two years, but your other bastard son, Detective Wallace, surfaced in Vietnam as a courier masquerading as an air force major. You approved his papers. General Wilson checked.

"Three months later, Stan tracked him to Miami. We trapped him in a hotel room and I killed him, hoping it would bring you out. But it didn't. We still had no direct link between you and your soldiers, so we couldn't pick you up. We had suspicions but nothing we could bring to court.

"Once again we had to stand and wait, but that's the way with espionage. Moments of intense activity followed by months, sometimes years, of nothingness as the paranoid go to ground, so to speak, until they think it's safe to start again.

"I purposely turned down your offer of greasing the skids for that position in the Defense Department, General, and instead accepted the job with the defense company.

Why? Because the general manager at the headquarters of the company I now work for was your half-brother, the one you failed to mention.

"That's another thing you forgot to tell me. You omitted your half-brother in the family review when I came to stay with you at Christmas the year before last. But what you didn't know was that Ron did not omit that fact that day at Fort Bragg. LZ and Frenchy may have missed it, but I thought it damn odd that an army first lieutenant, assigned to check us for security, would know how many brothers, sisters, and half-siblings a two-star air force general had.

"The half-brother was the last missing piece in the grand scheme. He not only designed equipment headed for military use, but he had friends and colleagues that he exchanged information with across the entire defense industry. Since you were an air force general, and, as Dad said, 'an ace blowtorch jockey who knows a lot about jets,' it was only natural for your half-brother to communicate with you on a regular basis. He told you what the next hot weapons systems were.

"If need be, Ron or Detective Wallace arranged to have the plans stolen or copied through intermediaries, killed them, then arranged for the Gates Brothers courier service to carry the information to contacts on the other side. You were very democratic. You sold to whoever would pay the highest dollar.

"From there, it was pretty easy to trap your half-brother's son into meeting me, then set both of them up for a political kill. Unfortunately, Major Jim's other sibling, his younger brother, my friend Cellmate, got the crap kicked out of him trying to delay them from leaving by propositioning them.

"You had Claire reappear once more to keep tabs on my movement, but by now, I was onto you. So onto you that I used her to set you up. I told her that I was going to see my father in November while I was down south doing business, and tell him everything. I was going to seek his help in trapping the kingpin, but I purposely didn't tell him who. Claire passed the information onto you, and you murdered my father before I could get there.

"At the wake, I purposely set up the disagreement with General Wilson because I knew that would cause you to try to win me over to your side. I started spending time with you, hoping you'd make a mistake, and you finally did when you invited me to spend Christmas with you that year. You talked just a little too much, enough to give me the link I was searching for. Then in your overconfidence, you went to bed and left me alone to search for it.

"You see, Sally told me about being raped by her boyfriend's commanding officer in Korea, just before I got out of college. I did a little checking; you were the commander. When I put it together with Mom's unwanted pregnancy, I struck gold. Once we knew that, figuring out how you, Detective Wallace, Ron, and Gumdrops were related was child's play. 'Related' in this case is a key word since they were all your children, three bastards. But your children all the same.

"Recruiting Ron and Detective Wallace was easy. You waited until they were in their late teens, shocked them with the news that you were their father, then told them you would have married their mother—my mother—except she dumped you because your father, the senator, was a traitor to his country. You also told them that my father wouldn't marry her unless she gave you two up for adoption.

"You used the same method to recruit Gumdrops, using his own half-brother Detective Wallace to carry the message. Only this time, you substituted Sally for my mom—same song, different verse, same villain.

"All we needed then was something to bring it all together, and Dad's dedication was it. Sally thought it up on her own as a completely separate gesture, but you, General, were all for it. You even called me trying to get me to ride down with you, but I declined. You wanted me along so you could find a convenient place on the way home to get me to tell you what I knew—with the aid of modern drugs. Then you would have disposed of me where there would not be witnesses.

"But General Thompson saved you the trouble. He provided the opportunity and the place, and you fell for it. You told me, just a few moments ago, that you called Sergeant Mike last night, and he told you I would be here this afternoon to reclaim the car. Don't know how you could have done that, General, since General Thompson waited until I had met with Ron at lunch today, and confirmed that Ron was having me tailed, before calling General Wilson and having him call Mike."

"And even then, General, all I said to him was the code word Anastasia and to clear out the civilians," General Wilson interrupted. "Isn't that right, Mike?"

"Yes, sir. Three minutes after your call, Freddie and Ginger arrived and took my lady and my kids to safety in a state police car."

"So what happens to me?" Johnboy got up from the floor with the help of Colonel Evans and shakily crossed over to join them.

"Well, that's up to Jim in the Justice Department and General Thompson," Smitty answered. "But I imagine that if you cooperate, they'll probably arrange to give you immunity for your testimony."

"Something like that," Jim said.

Smitty paused then added, "Especially since Jim, Cellmate, and Ginger are General Thompson's legitimate offspring. Isn't that right, Jim?"

"That's my pop," Jim answered.

"I'm glad it's over," Johnboy said in a relieved voice. "That bastard has been bleeding first my brother, then me, dry for as long as I can remember. Since you know everything, I assume you know why?"

"Two reasons," Smitty said. "First, your father was the general's father's—the senator's—main rival and the one who was instrumental in convincing President Roosevelt to drop him from consideration for the vice presidency."

"And the second?" Johnboy seemed certain that Smitty knew this one too.

"The general knew that you were the biological father of my brother, Billy. That's the real deadly hold he had on my father and mother. The general was able to use it to keep getting Dad to volunteer for one assignment after another whenever he needed Dad's help with outfits in trouble and keep you close at hand as a reminder to Mom to behave. But he miscalculated on one thing," Smitty said.

"What's that?" Johnboy asked.

"Well, Dad always said that when you meet your soul mate, the one that God meant you to be with, you'll sacrifice anything to be with that person. It will be a stronger addiction than any narcotic. Dad added that you'll know it's the right person because the two of you will be out of your clothes and whapping the bedpost against the wall so fast that you won't even remember undressing.

"Mom and Dad's marriage was a contrivance of the general's twisted manipulation. Dad was meant to be with Sally. You were meant to be with my mom. You met her when Dad was stationed in Kansas with the general there in the late '40s, and you were attending law school nearby.

"Being the brightest of the new breed of jet jockeys, the general was one of the first into Korea when the war started. Quite naturally, as we now understand, his favorite

Master Sergeant was right behind him.

"You met my mother at a bond drive two months before Dad left, and the attraction was instantaneous. You both tried to fight it, but the addiction of true love is the most powerful emotion on the planet; it overpowered you. And, as you soon learned, my mother was one of those women you only had to shake hands with to get pregnant.

"Billy was born eight and a half months after Dad shipped out for Korea. Since it fit within the magic nine-month window, you and Mom, in a way just like Dad and Sally years before in the last war, decided to do the noble thing, sacrifice your own happiness and break it off. That worked until Dearfield, where the flames were rekindled and soon became a wildfire out of control.

"The general had you assigned, hoping to use you as part of his organization to courier the secrets of the Titans to the Russians and to continue to wreak vengeance on his father's family enemies. The affair was an unexpected bonus that he used to major advantage."

"So, what are you going to tell Billy?" Johnboy asked.

"John, the question isn't what I'm going to tell him; it's what you and Mom are going to tell him. Because like Dad always said, if you don't sleep with someone, it ain't none of your fuckin' business," Smitty said earnestly, offering his hand.

"Thanks, son," John grabbed Smitty's right hand and took Smitty's paw in his.

"You're welcome."

"1LT, why didn't you just kill him?" Sergeant Mike asked.

Smitty smiled, then answered slowly in his best John Wayne imitation, "Wwwelll, I guess because I'm a Joe College graduate, now see." Smitty paused and said wryly, "I leave that sort of thing to uncouth sergeants like you."

Mike gave him the bird. Time may pass, and people grow older, but ol' sergeants are a constant and never change.

Soon to be ex-General Chuck said sarcastically, "Very clever, Captain, very, very, clever. But it really doesn't matter, because you'll never convict me. You have no hard evidence. Espionage is a hard thing to prove, especially now. And after Watergate, a public trial would tear this country apart."

Smitty reached in his pocket and pulled out the transistor radio. He pressed the on button, and asked quietly, "General Thompson, are you there?"

"Reading you, Captain," the general said.

"Sir, did you record the general's confession to killing my father?"

"Every word."

"There you are, General. A confession made and recorded, with witnesses, will guarantee you a one-way ticket to the hot seat."

"You may convict me, you may even kill me, but I'll always have the satisfaction of knowing some things that you'll never have."

"Like for instance?" Smitty asked evenly.

"You'll never recover any of the money they paid me; you'll never figure out how I murdered your father; and I may rot in hell, but like your father, I'll have the satisfaction of knowing that you'll never be with Claire, the one you were meant to be with."

Smitty smiled tolerantly at the general. "That's not exactly true."

With an amused look at Sergeant Mike, Smitty continued, "My friend the sergeant there, with a lot of help from his wife, who used to be a theatrical makeup artist during the war, makes a passable likeness of you, General.

"During his six-week trip to Europe, wearing that disguise he made a stop in Switzerland, specifically at a certain bank in Zurich.

"Using the identity codes that I found in the safe at your ranch that Christmas and, with Major Jim there acting as his aide, they made a withdrawal and wire-transferred all but a couple of hundred thousand dollars to a bank in Washington.

"The almost half a billion dollars that you've accrued over the last thirty years is, as we speak, being dispersed to different charities around the country, in secret, with enough held back to set up a widows' and orphans' fund for those who lost loved ones due to your cowardice and treachery." Smitty smiled sardonically. "Not to put to fine a point on it, but General, you're broke.

"And as to my father's murder, General Wilson has in his possession the nitroglycerin bottle that was setting on Dad's dresser the day he died. The bottle is filled with sugar pills, which you substituted. We know that because the outside of the bottle is covered with one set of your prints, while the top is covered with the other.

"Also, you requisitioned sixty sugar pills—for your wife—from the dispensary two days before your visit. I think Major Jim, with the help of Colonel Evans, will have no trouble establishing the link between those pills and Dad's last heart attack two days later.

"You can count on it," Colonel Evans said with certainty. "They showed up in the autopsy we did that night at the funeral home."

"By the way, Colonel Evans is part of this stew also. He's General Wilson's nephew. His aunt, the general's older sister, basically raised him after his other sister, doc's mother, died in a scaling accident when the doc was six. Knowing for sure that he was one of the good guys, the good general had him assigned to me at Reed so that I wouldn't accidentally slip on a bedpan, so to speak.

"But the joke's really on you, General. You'll be tried for murder, but if you'd just waited, Mother Nature would have taken care of the problem for you. And there wouldn't have been a single thing that I or Jim, or even General Thompson, could have done about it."

"What the fuck are you talking about?" the general snarled.

"I went to see Dad's doctor just before I left Savannah. Dad had inoperable cancer that had already spread to his stomach at the time you killed him. He had only months to live at best.

"And as to Claire—General Wilson, if you please?"

"My pleasure," General Wilson said. "General Martin, General Thompson and I have been onto you a long time; we just couldn't prove it. I knew about those pregnancies from the captain's mother, but you had no way to know I knew."

"Bullshit!" General Chuck said disbelievingly.

Ignoring him, General Wilson continued. "What you didn't know, was that, in violation of orders, your brother, the one you set up as a traitor, had secretly been married to my other sister who became pregnant soon after the Octagon team disappeared per the parameters of our mission.

"When word reached my sister of her husband's treason, she killed herself in shame. General Thompson secretly took the baby, a girl, and raised her as his own—fearing, and rightly so, that if you discovered her, she'd be killed. When you started approaching your sons, General Thompson was watching and waiting.

"Realizing we needed a deep cover agent, the general told 'his' daughter, Claire, the truth about her parents and also what he suspected about you. Claire volunteered to work for the general in exposing you, and he assigned her to me.

"She came to you, General, telling you she was your niece, and pretending to be angry with her adopted father. You recruited her. So in effect she became a double agent doing your bidding but then reporting your actions to me.

"Unfortunately, Smitty, like his father before him, sacrificed the thing he loved most for the county he loved best. And she did the same. Playing the role of the seductive vamp at Walter Reed and the role of liar at his father's funeral.

"You know it's ironic, General; you and I were doing the same thing. We both sent the same girl to watch our target, just for different reasons."

General Wilson laid a hand gently on Smitty's shoulder. "I'm sorry, son. You didn't know, and because of the risk of exposure to her I couldn't tell you."

"Water under the bridge now, General," Smitty said, while inside his heart was breaking.

"Well, General," Sergeant Mike said, "How does it feel to realize a three-star air force general and a national hero just got butt-fucked by a whaleshit 1LT?"

"It was a long wait, General, but I got you now. And there will be no escaping my vengeance," Smitty rubbed his hands together in satisfaction.

Emitting a guttural growl, the general charged Smitty, diving at his legs. Smitty stepped to the side and dropped him with a light tap from the Brooklyn special. He landed on the hard floor with all the grace of a four-year-old doing a belly-flop into the kiddy pool and made no further movement.

"Nicely done, Captain, very nicely done," General Wilson said. "I thought for a minute back there you were going to shoot him."

"Like I said sir, why waste good ammunition on a turd?"

"Then it's finally over," Sergeant Mike said.

"General Wilson's Handbook for Spies, rule number four: if you believe in something, you'd sure as hell better fight for it now, 'cause after you're dead, you can't hardly take aim."

"Not quite." General Wilson elbowed Smitty into silence and he reached in his pocket. "Son," the general said, turning to face Smitty, "on behalf of the President of the United States, it gives me great pleasure to award you the Distinguished Service Cross for your many meritorious actions during your combat time in Vietnam."

General Wilson stepped forward and pinned the decoration on Smitty's shirt, stepped back, came to attention, and saluted. The salute was matched by Colonel Evans, Major Jim, Stan the Man, Sergeant Mike, and even Johnboy.

"Thank you, sir." Smitty snapped to attention and returned the general's salute.

"Also, on behalf of the president, I extend his personal thanks and give you these." General Wilson handed Smitty a set of silver clusters.

"Lieutenant colonel?" Smitty asked, startled.

"Your new rank, son; SJS inactive reserve. We may need you again, sometime."

"Thank you, sir," Smitty said in a choked-up voice. Then he added, "And please thank the president."

"Thank him yourself, son," General Wilson said. "You, I, and all the surviving members of Mission Octagon and their families, are invited to the White House for dinner next week.

"Not only does the president wish to thank you personally, but I expect there will be a formal apology on behalf of the country for all the misery that came about as a result of that mission. And who knows, maybe even a CMH for a certain LTC who, despite overwhelming odds and hardship, persevered."

"Aw, shit, Sam," Sergeant Mike said sarcastically. "Now there'll be no living with the little asshole."

"That's Lieutenant Colonel Asshole to you, Sergeant," Smitty said.

"Yes, sir, 1LTC, sir!" Mike said with a very formal salute, punctuated by, as expected, his hand forming the bird.

EPILOGUE

It was now June 1977, and a year since General Chuck was led away in handcuffs, alternatively proclaiming his innocence and vowing revenge in extremely foul language.

A year ago, as Smitty hugged Sergeant Mike good-bye, Mike volunteered to retrieve his .357, clean it up, and send it to him.

Smitty had declined. "I don't remember the words exactly, Mike, but it has something to do with the sign of the United Nations building that says, 'they will beat their swords into plowshares, and men will study war no more.' You keep it."

"I'll keep it for you, 1LTC," Mike said with a final wave as Smitty drove away.

The year since had been a quiet one for Smitty. He'd settled into his new routine and job in Arizona and was enjoying, tremendously, the sense of normality it brought with it for the first time in his life.

About six weeks earlier, General Chuck, his brain now picked clean of secrets, had drowned, mysteriously, in his own swimming pool at the ranch.

Smitty attended the formal military funeral for the general, at General Thompson's request, and dutifully played out the charade to its conclusion. Delivering a stirring eulogy, in his uniform with the DSC and silver clusters on it, in remembrance of his father's lifelong friend, he even received the general's flag as his father's substitute and the general's godson.

Two days later, Chuck's surviving half-brother and his son—Cellmate's alley nemeses—were killed in a head-on collision with a government semi on a back road in Vermont on their way to a hunting lodge. As Professor Strickland would have said . . . how curious.

Today was a celebration of sorts. The general's last will and testament was probated in court, by Major Jim—who was named in the will as the executor, which might not seem so unusual to those in the know since Jim wrote it. Since the general had no living heirs, he left rather large donations to several unsuspecting recipients. LZ's mother, Glenda's mother, and Linda's parents each received $500,000 in after-tax cash, enough to keep them comfortable for the balance of their lives.

Frenchy's widow, Sondra, received an endowment fund that would cover the raising of her three children and their college costs, as well as a monthly income to ensure that she would be taken care of comfortably. At first she was left off the list, until a small-time crook picked up in New Orleans let slide, in return for a plea bargain, that he'd been paid $25,000 by a short squatty guy, who was the spitting image of Officer Gumdrops, to run Frenchy off the road.

Other endowments in varying degrees were made to the spouses, parents, sweethearts, and survivors of those left to live on, but who had been affected and would continue to be affected by this tragedy for the rest of their lives.

Despite an intensive search, no living relative of Big Walt was ever located. The place of birth listed on his army records turned out to be false. No such person was known to have existed in the little town of Winterville, West Virginia. Speculation was that his parents, or parent, brought him to this country illegally by entering via Canada and that they were killed or they simply abandoned him, and the big guy grew up eking out a living literally from the kindness of strangers.

Speculation was that he entered the army the same way as Smitty, LZ, and Frenchy—on falsified papers—making the enigma of his death as much a mystery as the way he lived his life.

Smitty's mother and Johnboy turned state's evidence. After spending six months at a federal detention camp to basically spill their guts about what they knew, they were discharged and living somewhere in the United States with new identities under the Federal Witness Protection Program.

Sally was still living in Macon and was the recipient of a rather generous seven-figure donation herself, which she passed straight through to a local charity to create a museum at the nearby air force base. The balance of the estate itself was left to the Commonwealth of Virginia to open a state park and petting zoo in the spring of 1978.

In the past year, more than 150 citizens of the United States had been quietly charged with various forms of espionage and treason. Forty-seven diplomats from sixteen foreign counties had been expelled from the United States or refused entry. The count was expected to go even higher as those charged confessed and implicated others.

Smitty had not expected any financial remuneration from General Chuck's will but was honestly not surprised when he sent in his first mortgage payment in Arizona and had the check returned with the mortgage documents marked paid in full. In what Smitty thought was a further fitting touch of poetic irony, he came home one day two months back to see construction starting on a swimming pool with a six-foot privacy fence right next to his patio in his back yard. Again, not surprisingly, he found he'd won this grand prize in a local radio giveaway. What made this even more ironic was, that for the life of him, Smitty couldn't remember entering. Smitty had celebrated its completion with a first ceremonial skinny dip.

At times, Smitty was still pinching himself; he'd not expected to be here. If General Chuck had used his own gun instead of picking up Smitty's, he'd have been joining his father at the pearly gates, instead of stopping at Mike's to call Sally to let her know he was coming home. He wished with all his heart that it was not alone.

He wondered about Claire, where she was now, and if she was okay. In this whole disgusting business, there had been no winners, only various kinds of losers and none more so than Claire. She was the real lynchpin. Without her willingness to sacrifice her body, and her very self, none of this would ever have come about. None of it would have ever been known.

The president had apologized in a carefully arranged private dinner, devoid of press coverage, but only after it was moved from the glare of the White House to the relative anonymity of Andrews Air Force Base. He even extended a few handshakes and thanks, but that wouldn't change the classification of that mission or the disastrous effects it had had on all those who were involved—not to mention the effect on their offspring, who had spent a lifetime caught in the endless cycle of jealousy, envy, hatred, and revenge.

The names and the faces began to dance across Smitty's mind like pixies. From Jimmy and Gena to Ron, they were caught on the endless treadmill of death and destruction. Either it was happening to them or they were dispensing it; it really didn't matter.

As he always did when he passed the photos, Smitty glanced up at the top of his stereo cabinet and gave a semiformal salute to those who were no longer here.

In the center was the picture of the four musketeers taken on that fateful night in Seattle so long ago. The faces mugging for the camera were reflective of the lost innocence of an entire generation. To the right, pictures of Glenda and Linda, to the left, Hogs and Smitty's father. All, in one form or another, had traded their lives in return for Smitty's dogged quest for the truth, and his obsession with doing the right thing.

Smitty had just slipped on a pair of jogging shorts after coming in from his first swim when he heard the sound of a car, glanced out the window, and started to walk toward the front entrance. A black Cadillac limousine pulled into the gravel driveway.

Smitty opened the front door as the limo stopped and the rear widow came down; an arm appeared and made definite "come here" motions with a crooked finger. The arm was encased in a blue coat sleeve. Smitty had seen that sleeve before and remembered the force of the right fist attached to it.

General Thompson—who, to no one's surprise, turned out to be the head of the SJS organization—obviously had something he wanted to say. And as Smitty had learned, it wasn't nice to fool with Father Nature.

"Afternoon, Colonel, how are things?" General Thompson began easily.

"Fine, sir, and you?"

"Excellent, thanks to you." He lit a Cuban cigar, passed it out to Smitty and lit one for himself. "Your pool about done?"

"Yes, sir. That was very generous of you. Thank you."

"Least I figured we could do, m'boy."

"Would you like to come in for a cold one, sir?" Smitty asked.

"No, son, I can't stay. I was just passing and thought I'd bring you a present from Sergeant Mike. He's the only retired sergeant major I know that has a four-star general as a delivery boy." General Thompson laughed as he handed Smitty a basket of Belles of Georgia through the window.

Smitty stuck the cigar between his teeth and laughed in spite of himself. "Peaches, ain't he sweet."

"I won't tell him you said that." The general reached out and touched Smitty firmly on the arm. "M'boy, there's just one thing I would like you to answer."

Knowing from experience that this was a vaguely disguised direct order to respond, Smitty waited quietly in anticipation.

"When you had that sadistic bastard in the sights of your ol' man's .45, why didn't you shoot him right between the eyes? I sure as hell would have, especially since he cold-bloodedly murdered the Ol' Sarge."

Smitty paused to collect his thoughts.

"Well, sir, if I had killed General Martin, I would have crossed over. When you feel no remorse at the death of another human being, you're living in anger and solely for vengeance. Anger turned outward is rage; anger turned inward is motivation. I lived a good portion of my life caught in the mind-numbing endless cycle of violence, revenge, and anger. Killing the general would only have perpetuated that cycle."

The general was quiet for a moment, smiled with understanding and stuck out his hand. "Look, m'boy, I've got to go. Take care."

"I will, sir." Smitty balanced the basket in his left hand and took the general's with his right.

"When you get it inside, look in the bottom." The general signaled the driver, who pulled away immediately with a spraying of gravel.

"Good luck, Joe College," the general said with a wave.

With a half-wave at the departing general, Smitty turned and walked back inside the house. He set the gift on the eat-in kitchen table, and began to remove the fuzzy fruit.

He'd only removed ten when he saw it. Smitty reached into the basket and removed his .357, now spotlessly cleaned and polished and encased in a plastic bag.

Smitty removed the weapon from the bag and hefted it in his hand, smiling in silent reminiscence as he read Mike's note toe-tagged to the barrel:

Fuzz Nuts,

Thought you'd like your keepsake back, even if you are one of those Joe College assholes now. Anytime, anywhere, 1LTC, for the rest of your life, you call and I'll be there. You can count on me.

Your Mike

Underneath the package was a tape recorder. Smitty removed it as he walked to the refrigerator, grabbed a beer, and walked out on the back patio with the pistol and recorder in hand.

He set the tape recorder on a table and dropped into a chair. He picked up his can, and with a brew in one hand, pistol in the other, and cigar in his mouth, turned on the tape.

As the first sounds of Dad's voice filled his ears, his eyes began to wet with tears.

Hello, son,

I know that your quest is ended, and I'm sorry I can't be there to shake your hand; wish I could. I recorded this tape in the summer of 1974 when I knew my time was running out. I am sending you this final tape in the hope that you'll hear this song, and the message within.

You've righted a terrible wrong, and for that, you have my personal thanks and everlasting gratitude.

Do you remember the arguments we had over the music you listened to? I do, too. So I'll leave you with a song from one of them. Listen to it, because in the words, expressed in three minutes, will be words to last a lifetime.

Go with God, my Son.

Smitty listened to the entire song without making a sound. It was the song Dad had personally destroyed many years ago as being nothing more than pinko-communist brainwashing. At the end, there was five seconds of silence followed by Dad's voice again.

Rewind the tape and play it again, my son. Play it over and over until you can feel it in your heart.

Smitty did as instructed; then did it again. It was on the fourth replay that he thought he heard voices.

Smitty looked up at the puffy white clouds against the clear blue Arizona sky.

"C'mon, baby, sing." He heard Linda's enchanting voice as the clouds began to fill with her beauty.

"Yeah, baby, sing," a voice that sounded distinctly like Glenda's called out as her vision began to form in the clouds next to Linda, and her soft voice joined Linda's in a duet.

Smitty rubbed his eyes in disbelief and was just about to check it off as an illusion when another voice said caustically, "Sing, my brother, sing." LZ's smiling image was now appearing beside Glenda.

"Mon ami, sing." Frenchy joined the group.

"Yeeessss, yooooou sshhoould," Big Walt squealed, making it a foursome.

"You be a singin' now, Lieutenant," Hogsbreath drawled, making it a fifth.

"Sing out, troop, that's an order." Dad's image completed the sextet.

Smitty reacted just as if the order were real and his dad still here to give it. He smiled and joined in immediately on the last line of the first verse.

While the music was playing, before the second verse started, Smitty hefted the .357 in his hands, and pointed it playfully at the images in the clouds.

"Don't shoot, Colonel, I'll cooperate," said a feminine voice.

Slowly, almost like out of a dream, a figure approached from the patio gate and walked toward him in three-inch-heels that made her hips sway like a grandma's porch swing. It couldn't possibly be, but it was—brunette hair and a sedate dress that could not even begin to hide the opulent breasts straining underneath to be released.

"Hi, soldier. If you promise not to shoot me, I'll do whatever you want." Claire stopped two feet away and posed for him, wiggling her hips enticingly.

"That depends," Smitty said, "on what you mean by whatever."

"Daddy asked me to give you something—personally." Claire extended her right hand.

Smitty took the package, a small, blue velvet box and opened it.

"I accept." Claire plucked the engagement ring out of the slot in the box, slipped it on her finger, and held it up to the late afternoon sun to admire it. "I've been after you for a long time, you know," Claire said.

"Oh?"

"You were my first crush, and the first boy I kissed at fifteen when I was in the Hunter Base Hospital recovering from surgery. I went by the name of Claire-Beth then. I hope our bedroom's soundproof."

"I'll work on it," Smitty answered agreeably, and as Claire plopped herself down on his lap, he took her in his arms and kissed her. When the second verse of the song began, Claire and Smitty began to sing together. When Smitty looked up at the clouds, all the images were gone, as if they'd never been there in the first place. Even if Claire didn't see them, the images were real to him. Maybe it was the final way for his friends to say good-bye and that they could now be at peace . . . and so could he.

And Smitty knew that for the rest of his days, he'd hear their voices, especially that one craggy voice, barking out that anti-war line from the Fifth Dimension song like it was a military order.

In my mind, I can't study war nooo mooore.

And if you listen . . . if you really listen . . . then maybe you will hear that voice, too . . .